KU-407-790

The Judas Kiss
The Captive

BY THE SAME AUTHOR

Mistress of Mellyn
Kirkland Revels
The Bride of Pendorric
The Legend of the Seventh Virgin
Menfreya
The King of the Castle
My Enemy the Queen
The Shivering Sands
The Secret Woman
The Shadow of the Lynx
On the Night of the Seventh Moon
The House of a Thousand Lanterns
The Curse of the Kings
The Demon Lover
The Devil on Horseback
The Spring of the Tiger
Lord of the Far Island
The Mask of Enchantress
The Pride of the Peacock
The Landower Legacy
The Queen's Confession
The Time of the Hunter's Moon
The Road to Paradise Island
The Silk Vendetta
Secret for a Nightingale
The India Fan
Snare of Serpents
Daughter of Deceit

The Judas Kiss
The Captive

Victoria Holt

Diamond Books
An Imprint of HarperCollins*Publishers*,
77–85 Fulham Palace Road
Hammersmith, London W6 8JB

This Diamond Books Omnibus edition first published 1994

ISBN 0 261 66293 7

Printed and bound in Great Britain by
BPC Hazell Books Ltd
A member of
The British Printing Company Ltd

The Judas Kiss

Greystone Manor

I was seventeen years old before I discovered that my sister had been murdered. It was then nearly five years since I had seen her, but every day I had thought of her, longed for her bright presence and mourned her departure from my life.

Before she went away, Francine and I had been as close as two people could be. I suppose I, being the younger by five years, had looked to her for protection, and after the death of our parents when we had come to make Greystone Manor our home, I had had great need of it.

That had happened six years before, and when I looked back on those very early days it seemed to me that we had lived in a paradise. Distance enchants the view, Francine used to say to comfort me and so imply that the island of Calypse had not been completely perfect, so perhaps Greystone Manor was not as gloomy as we, newly become its inmates, believed it to be. Although she was as fragile as a piece of Dresden china in looks, I never knew anyone who had a more practical grip on life. She was realistic, resourceful, irrepressible and always optimistic; indeed she seemed unable to visualize failure. I had always believed that whatever Francine decided she would do, she would do successfully. That was why I was so shattered, so overwhelmed with disbelief when I found that newspaper in Aunt Grace's trunk in the attic at Greystone. I knelt there holding the paper in my hand while the words danced before my eyes.

Baron von Gruton Fuchs was found murdered in his bed at his hunting lodge in the Grutonian province of Bruxenstein last Wednesday morning. With him was his mistress, a young Englishwoman whose identity is as yet unknown, but it is believed she had been his companion at the lodge for some weeks before the tragedy.

There was another cutting attached.

The identity of the woman in the Gruton Fuchs murder has been discovered. She is Francine Ewell, who had been a close friend of the Baron for some time.

That was all. It was incredible. The Baron was her husband. I remembered so well how she had told me she was going to be married and how I grappled with myself to cast out the desolation of losing her and trying to rejoice in her happiness

I just knelt there until I realized my limbs were cramped and that my knees were hurting. Then I took the newspaper cuttings and went back to my bedroom, sitting there, dazed, thinking back . . . to everything she had been to me, until she had gone away.

Those idyllic early years had been spent on the island of Calypse with our adored, adoring and quite unrealistic parents.

They were the beautiful years. They had ended when I was eleven and Francine sixteen, so I suppose I did not really understand a great deal of what was going on around me. I was unaware of the financial difficulties and the anxiety of living through those periods when no visitors came to my father's studio. Not that any of these fears were shown, for Francine was there to manage us all with the skill and energy which we took for granted.

Our father was an artist in stone. He sculpted the most beautiful figures of Cupid and Psyche, Venus rising from the waves, of little mermaids, dancing girls, urns and baskets of flowers; and visitors came and bought them. My mother was his favourite model and next to her, Francine. I posed for him too. They would never have thought of leaving me out, although I had never had that sylph-like quality of Francine and my mother which lent itself so perfectly to stone. They were the beautiful ones. I resembled my father, with hair which was rather nondescript in colour and could be called mid-brown, thick, straight and invariably untidy; I had greenish eyes which changed colour with their surroundings and what Francine called a 'pert' nose, and a mouth which was rather large. 'Generous', Francine called it. She was a great consoler. My mother had a fairylike beauty which she had passed on to Francine – blonde and curly hair, blue, dark-lashed eyes and that extra fraction of an inch on the nose which was sufficient to make it beautiful, and with all this went a shortish upper lip which revealed ever so slightly prominent pearly teeth. Above all, there was that air of helpless femininity which made men want to fetch and carry for them and protect them from the hardships of the world. My mother might have been in need of that protection; Francine never was.

There were long warm days – rowing the boat out to the blue lagoon and swimming there, taking desultory lessons with Antonio Farfalla who was repaid by a piece of sculpture from our father's studio. 'It will be worth a fortune one day,' Francine assured him. 'You only have to wait until my father is recognized.' Francine could convey great authority in spite of her fragile looks and Antonio believed her. He adored Francine. Until we came to Greystone it seemed that everyone adored Francine. She was charmingly protective even of him, and although she joked a great deal about his name, which in Italian meant Butterfly, and he was the most cumbersome man we ever knew, she was always sympathetic when he was distressed by his clumsiness.

It was some time before I began to be worried by my

mother's constant illnesses. She used to lie in her hammock, which we had fixed up outside the studio, and there was always someone there talking to her. At first, my father had told me, we had not been accepted very warmly on the island. We were foreigners and they were an insular people. They had lived there for hundreds of years cultivating the vines and the silkworms and working in the quarry from which came the alabaster and serpentine in which my father worked. But when the people of the island realized that we were just like them, and were ready to live as they did, they finally accepted us. 'It was your mother who won them over,' he used to say, and I could well imagine that. She looked so beautiful, ethereal, as though the wind would carry her off when the mistral blew. 'They gradually came round,' my father said. 'There would be little gifts on the doorstep, and when Francine was born we had a houseful of helpers. The same with you, Pippa. You were made just as welcome as your sister.'

They always reminded me of that. There came the time when I began to wonder why it should be necessary.

Francine discovered all she could about our family history. She was always eager to learn everything. Ignorance worried her. She wanted to know the smallest detail – why the silkworm yield was higher or lower; how much Vittoria Guizza's wedding feast cost, and who was the father of Elizabetta Caldori's baby. Everything that went on was of the greatest interest to Francine. She had to know the answer.

'They say,' said Antonio, 'that those who seek to know all may some day discover that which does not please.'

'In England they say "Curiosity killed the cat",' Francine told him. 'Well, I am not a cat but I intend to be curious . . . even if it kills me.'

We all laughed at the time, but looking back I remembered that.

Blissful island days they were – the warm sun on my skin,

the pungent smell of frangipani and hibiscus; the gentle swish of the blue Mediterranean sea against the shores of the island; long dreamy days lying in the boat after swimming; sitting round the hammock in which our mother gently rocked; watching Francine come into the studio when we had visitors. They came from America and England, but mainly from France and Germany, and over the years Francine and I acquired a fair understanding of these languages. Francine would bring out wine in glasses at the sides of which she had arranged hibiscus flowers. The visitors loved that and they paid high prices for my father's work when Francine talked to them. They were making an investment, she would assure them, for my father was a great artist. He was here on the island because of his wife's health. He should be in his salon in Paris or London. Never mind, it gave these good people an opportunity to acquire works of art at the best possible prices.

They would recognize the beauty of Francine in the statues and they would buy them, and I am sure preserved them, and remembered for a long time enchanted afternoons when they were waited on by a beautiful girl who served them wine in a flower-trimmed glass.

So we lived in those long-ago days – never thinking beyond the moment – rising in the morning to the sunshine and going to bed at night deliciously tired out after days of pleasant activities. It was fun, though, to sit in the studio and listen to the rain as it pelted down. 'This will bring out the snails,' Francine used to say; and when it was over we would go out with our baskets and gather them. Francine was an expert at picking out those which could be sold to Madame Descartes, the Frenchwoman who kept the inn on the waterfront. She would instruct me not to pick those whose shells were soft because they would be too young. 'Poor little things, they have had no life yet. Let them live a little longer.' It sounded humane, but of course Madame Descartes wanted only those which were edible. We would take them to the inn and receive a little money for them. A few weeks later when the snails had been taken out of the cage in which they had been kept, Francine and I would go along to the inn and Madame Descartes would give us a taste of them. Francine thought they were delicious cooked with garlic and parsley. I never really fancied them. It was a ritual, however – the end of the snail harvest – and therefore I went solemnly through it with my sister.

Then there was the vine harvest when we donned wooden shoes like sabots and helped in treading out the grapes. Francine joined in with verve – singing and dancing like a wild dervish, her curls flying, her eyes shining, so that everyone smiled at her and my father said: 'Francine is our ambassadress.'

Those were the happy days and it never occurred to me that they could change. My mother was growing weaker but somehow she managed to conceal the fact from me. Perhaps she did from my father too, but I wondered whether she did from Francine. But if it did occur to my sister, she would dismiss it as she always did anything she did not want to happen. I sometimes thought that life had bestowed so many gifts on Francine that she believed that the gods were working for her too, so that she only had to say 'I don't want that to happen' and it wouldn't.

I remember the day well. It was September – wine harvest time – and there was that excitement in the air which always heralded it. We would go, Francine and I, and join the young people on the island to begin our stamping on the grapes to the tunes from Verdi's operas which old Umberto would scrape out on his fiddle. We would all sing lustily and the old people would sit and watch, their gnarled hands clasped on their black laps and the light of reminiscence in their rheumy eyes, while we danced until our feet were weary and our voices grew more and more hoarse.

But there was another harvest. One of the poems I liked best was called 'The Reaper and the Flowers'.

There is a Reaper whose name is Death
And with his sickle keen
He reaps the bearded grain at a breath
And the flowers that grow between.

Francine explained it to me; she was good at explaining things. 'It means young people sometimes get in the way of the sickle,' she said, 'then they get cut down too.' It seems significant now that she should have been one of those flowers which grew between. But then it was our mother who died and she was like a flower. It was not time for her to die; she was too young.

It was terrible when we found her dead. Francine had taken in the glass of milk she had every morning. She was lying quite still and Francine said afterwards that she went on talking for quite a while before she realized my mother was not listening. 'Then I went to the bed,' said Francine, 'I just looked at her and then I knew.'

So it had happened. All Francine's magic could not hold it off. Death had come with his sickle and taken the fair flower which grew between.

Our father was as one demented. He was very much the artist and when he worked in his studio making those beautiful women who had a look of my mother or my sister, he had always seemed far away. We always laughed at his absent-mindedness. Francine bustled about the studio keeping us all in order. Our mother, for a long time, had been too ill to do very much; she was just there a benign presence and an inspiration to us all. She had talked to visitors and made them welcome and they all enjoyed that; and as long as Francine was there everything held together.

Now she was gone Francine took over completely. She talked to the visitors and made them feel they were getting bargains. I don't know how we should have got through that year without her. When our mother was laid to rest in the little cemetery close by the olive groves we should have been a desolate household but for Francine. She became in a sense the head of the household, although she was only fifteen years old. She shopped; she cooked; she kept us going. She refused to take any more lessons with the Butterfly, as she called Antonio, but she insisted that I should. Our father lived with his stone but his figures had lost a certain magic which they had had before. He didn't want Francine to pose for him. That brought back too many memories.

The gloomy months began to pass and I felt a change in myself. I was at that time ten years old but I ceased to be a child.

Our father talked to us during that time. It was in the evenings when we would sit on the green slope which ran down to the sea, and as the darkness fell we would watch the sheen of phosphorescence which came from the shoals of fish and were like will-o'-the-wisps on the water . . . eerie and yet comforting in a way.

He talked about his life before he came to the island. Francine had been curious about it for a long time and had gleaned a little information which she had extracted from him or our mother during their unwary moments. We often wondered why they were so reluctant to talk about the past. We were soon to discover. I suppose everyone who had lived in Greystone Manor would want to escape from it and even forget he or she had ever been there. For it was like a prison. That was how our father described it; and later I was to understand.

'It's a fine old house,' said my father, 'a mansion really. Ewells have lived in it for four hundred years. The first Ewell built it before the reign of Elizabeth. Think of that.'

'It must be strong to stand up to all that time,' I began, but Francine silenced me with a look, and I knew she meant that we must not remind our father that he was thinking aloud.

'They knew how to build in those days. Their houses might have been uncomfortable but they could stand up not only to the weather but to attackers.'

'Attackers,' I cried excitedly, only to be silenced again by Francine.

That was when he said: 'It was like a prison. To me it was a prison.'

There was a deep silence. Our father was looking back right over the years to when he was a boy, before he had met my mother, before Francine was born. It was hard to imagine a world without Francine.

Our father was frowning. 'You children have no idea,' he said. 'You have been surrounded by love. We have been poor, yes. It has not always been a comfortable life . . . but love there has been in abundance.'

I ran to him and threw myself at him. He held me very tightly in his arms. 'Little Pippa,' he said, 'you have been happy, yes? You must always remember Pippa's song. We named you for that, Pippa.

'God's in his Heaven,
All's right with the world.'

'Yes,' I cried. 'Yes, yes.'

Francine said: 'Go and sit down, Pippa. You're interrupting Father. He wants to tell us something.'

Our father was silent for a while and then he said: 'Your grandfather is a good man. Make no mistake about that. But sometimes good men are uncomfortable to live with . . . for sinners, that is.'

Silence again, this time broken by Francine who whispered: 'Tell us about our grandfather. Tell us about Greystone Manor.'

'He was always proud of the family. We had served our country well. We had been soldiers, politicians, squires, but never artists. Well, there was one . . . long ago. He was killed in a tavern near Whitehall. His name was never mentioned except with disgust. "Poetry-writing is no life for a man," said your grandfather. You can imagine what he said when he knew I wanted to be a sculptor.'

'Tell us,' whispered Francine.

Our father shook his head. 'It seemed just impossible. My future was planned for me. I was to follow in his footsteps. I was not to be a soldier, nor a politician. I was the only son of the squire so I should follow in my father's footsteps. I should learn how to manage the estate and spend the rest of my life trying to be exactly like my father.'

'And you couldn't do that,' said Francine.

'No . . .I hated it. I hated everything about Greystone. I hated the house and my father's rule, his attitude towards us all – my mother, my sister Grace and myself. He regarded himself as our master. He wanted obedience in all things. He was a tyrant. And . . . I met your mother.'

'Tell us about that time,' said Francine.

'She came to the house to make dresses for your Aunt Grace. She was so gentle, so fragile, so beautiful. It was meeting her that decided me.'

'So you ran away from Greystone Manor,' said Francine.

'Yes. I broke out of prison. We ran away to freedom – your mother from a life of drudgery with the dressmaking house for which she worked . . . I from Greystone Manor. We neither of us ever regretted it for a moment.'

'Romantic . . . beautiful,' murmured Francine.

'There were hard times at first. In London . . . in Paris . . . trying to make a living. Then we met a man in a café. He had the studio on this island and he offered it to us. So we came. Francine was born here . . . and so were you, Pippa.'

'Didn't he come back to claim the studio?' asked Francine.

'He came back. He stayed with us for a while. You were too young to remember that. Then he went to Paris where he became quite wealthy. He died some years ago and left me the studio. We have managed to make a living . . . a poor one, but we have been free.'

'We have been very happy, Father,' said Francine firmly 'No girls could have been happier.'

Then we all embraced each other – we were a demonstrative family – and Francine suddenly became very practical and said it was time we all went to bed.

It was only a few weeks after that conversation that our father was drowned. He had taken the boat out to the blue lagoon, as we so often did, when a sudden storm blew up and the boat capsized. I wondered afterwards how great an attempt he had made to save himself. Since our mother's death life had certainly lost its savour for him. He had his two girls, but I think he thought Francine was more capable of looking after herself and me than he was. Besides, he would have guessed the turn events would take, and perhaps he thought it was the best thing for us.

I felt fatalistic, almost as though I knew what was going to happen. I had already come to the conclusion that nothing could be the same after my mother's death. We had tried to regain our old cheerfulness and Francine had managed very well, but even she could not entirely pretend.

We faced each other in the studio on the day he had been laid beside my mother near the olive groves. 'It was where he wanted to be since she was put there,' said Francine.

'What are we going to do?' I said.

She was jaunty almost. 'We have each other. There are two of us.'

'You'd always be all right and see that I was,' I replied.

'That is so,' she answered.

Our friends on the island smothered us with kindness. We were fed, caressed and made to feel that we were well loved.

'It's nice for a beginning,' commented Francine, 'but it won't go on. We have to think.'

I was nearly eleven then, Francine sixteen. 'Of course,' she said, 'I could marry Antonio.'

'You couldn't. You wouldn't.'

'I am fond of the Butterfly, but you are right. I couldn't and I wouldn't.'

I looked at her questioningly. She was rarely short of ideas but on this occasion she was. There were dreams in her eyes. 'We might go away,' she suggested.

'Where to?'

'Somewhere.' Then she told me that she had always known that one day she would go away. She could not bear to be shut in, and that was what we were on the island. 'It was different when our parents were alive,' she said. 'It was our home then. It isn't any more really. Besides, what should we do here?'

Our problem was solved by a letter for Francine.

'Miss Ewell,' said the address on the envelope.

'I am that,' Francine explained. 'You are Miss Philippa Ewell.'

As she opened it I saw the excitement in her eyes. 'It's from a solicitor,' she said. 'He's acting for Sir Matthew Ewell. That's our grandfather. In view of the unfortunate circumstances, Sir Matthew wishes us to return at once to England. Our rightful home is Greystone Manor.'

I stared at her aghast, but her eyes were shining.

'Oh, Pippa,' she said. 'We are going to the prison.'

There was the excitement of preparing for departure, which was a good thing in a way because it stopped our brooding on our loss, and how great that was we had not yet begun to realize. There was the packing up and the disposal of the studio and its contents which Antonio sadly took over from us.

'But it is best for you,' he said. 'You will live like great ladies. We always knew that Signor Ewell was a grand gentleman.'

One of the men from the solicitor's office came to take us to our new home. He wore a black frock-coat and a shiny top hat; he looked quite out of place on the island where he was regarded with great respect. He was a little shy of us at first, but Francine soon put him at his ease. She had become very dignified since our father's death, very much Miss Ewell who was of higher rank than Miss Philippa Ewell. His name was

Mr Counsell and it was clear that he thought the conducting of two girls to England was a very strange task for a man in his position.

We said a sad farewell to our friends and promised to return. I was on the point of inviting them all to England, but Francine gave me one of her warning looks. 'Imagine them in the prison,' she said. 'They would never come,' I told her. 'They might,' she answered.

It was a long journey. We had made the trip to the mainland on several occasions, but it was the first time I had been in a train. I found it absorbingly interesting and I was a little ashamed of myself because I was enjoying it. I was sure Francine was too. People looked at Francine, as I realized they always would. Even Mr Counsell was a little fascinated by her charm and treated her as a beautiful young woman rather than a child. She was, I suppose, in between the two. In some ways she was a very innocent sixteen, in other ways quite mature. She had managed our household, dealt with the customers and taken on the role of guardian of us all. On the other hand, life on the island had been lived simply and I think that at first Francine was inclined to judge everyone by the people she had known all her life so far.

We crossed the English Channel, and to Mr Counsell's dismay we missed the train which was to take us to Preston Carstairs, the station for Greystone Manor, and were told we had several hours to wait for the next. He took us to an inn near the docks, where we had a meal of roast beef and potatoes in jackets, which seemed exotic and delicious, and while we were eating the innkeeper's wife came to talk to us. When she heard that we had to wait so long she said: 'Why don't you see a bit of the countryside while you're waiting? You could take the trap out a little way. Our Jim's got an hour or so to spare.

Mr Counsell seemed to think it was a good idea and that was how we came to see Birley Church. Francine had cried out in delight as we were about to pass it by. There was something very interesting about that church. It was Norman, grey stone, and, said Francine, exciting when you thought of all the years it had stood there. Mr Counsell said he did not see why we should not visit the church, so we did. He himself was quite an authority on architecture and he enjoyed passing on information of which he was clearly proud. While he pointed out the interesting features, Francine and I stood in wonder. We didn't care that the pillars and semi-circular arches held up the high walls of the clerestory; we were interested in the queer smell of damp and furniture polish and the stained-glass windows with the beautiful colours that threw blue and red shadows everywhere; we studied the list of vicars who had held office since the twelfth century.

'When I marry I should like to be married in this church,' said Francine.

We sat in the pews. We knelt on the prayer mats. We stood in awe before the altar.

'It's beautiful,' said Francine.

Mr Counsell reminded us of passing time and we went back to the inn and from there to the station, where the train took us to Preston Carstairs.

When we arrived there a carriage was waiting for us. It had an elaborate crest on it. Francine nudged me. 'The Ewell crest,' she murmured. 'Ours.'

Relief now sat on Mr Counsell's homely features. He had delivered his charges safely.

Francine was looking excited, but, just as in my case, the apprehension was beginning to take hold. It was all very well to joke about the prison when it was miles away. It was a different matter when you were within an hour of being incarcerated.

A stern-faced coachman was waiting for us.

'Mr Counsell, sir,' he said, 'is these the young ladies?'

'Yes,' answered Mr Counsell.

'The carriage is here, sir.'

He was studying us and as was to be expected his eyes rested on Francine. She was wearing a simple grey cloak, which had been our mother's, and on her head was a straw hat with a marguerite in the centre and ribbons under the chin. It was simple attire but Francine could never look anything but enchanting. His eyes scanned me and then he was back to Francine.

'Better get in, young ladies,' he said.

The horses' hoofs rang out on the road as we skimmed along past green hedges, through leafy lanes until we came to a wrought-iron gateway. The gates were opened immediately by a boy who touched his forelock to the carriage and then we were bowling up a drive. The carriage stopped before a lawn and we alighted.

We stood together, my sister and I, hand in hand, and I knew that even Francine was overawed. There it stood, the house which our father had spoken of so vehemently as the prison. It was huge and grey stone as its name implied, and there were embattled turrets at either end. I noticed the battlements and the lofty archway through which I could see a courtyard. It was very grand, awe-inspiring, and it filled me with apprehension.

Francine pressed my hand firmly, holding it very tightly as though she took courage from the contact, and together we walked across the grass towards a great door which had swung open. A woman in a starched cap was standing there. The coach had gone forward under the archway into the courtyard and the woman stood in the doorway watching us.

'The master is ready to see you as soon as you arrive, Mr Counsell,' she said.

'Come along.' Mr Counsell smiled reassuringly at us and we went forward towards the door.

I shall never forget stepping inside that house. I was quivering with excitement, which was really a mingling of apprehension and curiosity. The ancestral home! I thought. And then: The Prison.

Those thick stone walls, the coolness as we stepped inside, the awesomeness of the great hall with its vaulted roof, the stone floor and walls on which glittered weapons, presumably used by long-dead Ewells – they thrilled me and yet made me fearful in some way. Our footsteps sounded noisy so I tried to walk quietly. I saw that Francine had lifted her head and was putting on that bold look which meant that she was a little more apprehensive than she would like people to know.

'The master said you were to go straight to him,' the woman repeated. She was rather plump, with greying hair very tightly drawn back from her forehead and all but concealed by her white cap. Her eyes were small, her lips tightly shut, like a trap. She seemed to suit the house.

'If you'll step this way, sir,' she said to Mr Counsell.

She turned and we followed her to the grand staircase which we ascended. Francine was still holding my hand. We went along a gallery and paused before a door. The woman knocked and a voice said: 'Enter.'

We did so. The scene remained imprinted on my mind forever. I was vaguely aware of a darkish room with heavy draperies and large dark pieces of furniture, but it was my grandfather who dominated the room. He was seated there in a chair like a throne and he himself looked like a Biblical prophet. He was clearly a very big man; his arms were folded across his chest and what struck me immediately was his long luxuriant beard, which rippled over his chest and concealed the lower part of his face. Beside him sat a woman, middle-aged and colourless. I guessed she was our Aunt Grace. She looked small, ineffectual and modest, but perhaps that was in comparison with the imposing central figure.

'So you have brought my granddaughters, Mr Counsell,' said my grandfather. 'Come here.'

This last was addressed to us and Francine advanced, taking me with her.

'H'm,' said my grandfather, his eyes surveying us intently,

giving me the impression that he was trying to find fault with us. What astonished me was that he seemed unimpressed by Francine's charm.

I had thought he might have kissed us or at least taken our hands. Instead he just looked at us as though there was something rather distasteful about us.

'I am your grandfather,' he said, 'and this is now your home. I hope you will be worthy of it. I doubt not that you will have much to learn. You are now in a civilized community. It will be well for you to remember that.'

'We have always been in a civilized community,' said Francine.

There was silence. I saw the woman seated beside my grandfather flinch.

'I would disagree with that,' he said.

'Then you would be wrong,' went on Francine. She was very nervous, I could see, but she sensed in his remarks a slur on our father and she was not going to tolerate that. She had immediately transgressed against the first rule of the house, which was that our grandfather was never wrong, and he was so startled that for a moment he was lost for words.

Then he spoke coldly: 'Indeed you have much to learn. I had expected we might have to deal with uncouth manners. Well, we are prepared. Now the first thing to do is to give thanks to our Maker for your safe journey and we will express the hope that those of us in need of humility and gratitude will be granted these virtues, and will follow that course of righteousness which is the only one acceptable in this house.'

We were bewildered. Francine was still smarting with her indignation and I was growing more depressed and afraid every moment.

And there we were, tired, hungry, bewildered and desperately apprehensive, kneeling on the cold floor in that dark room, giving thanks to God for bringing us to this prison and praying for the humility and gratitude which our grandfather expected us to feel to him for the miserable home he was giving us.

It was Aunt Grace who took us to our room. Poor Aunt Grace! When we referred to her it was always *poor* Aunt Grace. She looked drained of life; she was extremely thin and the brown cotton of her dress accentuated the sallowness of her complexion. Her hair, which might have been beautiful, was drawn straight back from her brow and plaited into a rather unwieldy knob in the nape of her neck; her eyes were pleasant, nothing could alter that. They were brown with abundant dark lashes – rather like Francine's except for the colour – only where my sister's sparkled, hers were dull and hopeless. Hopeless! That was the term one immediately applied to Aunt Grace.

We followed her up another staircase and she walked ahead, not speaking. Francine grimaced at me. It was rather a nervous grimace. I guessed Francine was realizing she would not find it easy to charm such a household.

Aunt Grace opened a door and stepped into a room, standing aside so that we could enter. We did so. It was quite a pleasant room but the dark curtains which half obscured the windows made it gloomy.

'You are to be together,' said Aunt Grace. 'Your grandfather thought there was no point in using two rooms.'

I felt a sudden surge of pleasure. I should not have relished sleeping alone in that eerie mansion. I remembered Francine's once saying that nothing is all bad . . . or all good, for that matter; there had to be a little bit of the other, however slight. It was a comforting thought just now.

There were two beds in the room.

'You may choose how you will use them,' said Aunt Grace, as though, Francine afterwards remarked, she were offering us the kingdoms of the world.

She said: 'Thank you, Aunt Grace

'Now you will want to wash and perhaps change after the

journey. We dine in an hour's time. Your grandfather will not tolerate unpunctuality.'

'I am sure he will not,' said Francine, and there was a note of hysteria in her voice. 'It's so dark in here,' she went on. 'I can't see anything.' She went to the windows and pulled back the curtains. 'There! That's better. Oh, what a lovely view.'

I went to the window and Aunt Grace came and stood immediately behind us.

'That is Rantown Forest down there,' she said.

'It looks interesting. Forests always do. How far are we from the sea, Aunt Grace?'

'About ten miles.'

Francine had turned to her. 'I love the sea. We lived surrounded by it, you see. It makes you love it.'

'Yes,' said Aunt Grace, 'I suppose it must. Now I will have hot water sent up to you.'

'Aunt Grace,' went on Francine, 'you are our father's sister yet you don't mention him. Don't you want to hear about your brother?'

I saw her face clearly in the light Francine had let in. It twitched and she looked as though she were going to cry. 'Your grandfather has forbidden us to mention him,' she said.

'Your own brother . . .'

'He behaved . . . unforgivably. Your grandfather . . .'

'He makes the laws here, I see,' said Francine.

'I . . . I don't understand you.' Aunt Grace was trying to look severe. 'You are young,' she went on, 'and you have much to learn, and I will give you a piece of advice. Never . . . never again speak to your grandfather as you did today. You must never say he is wrong. He is – '

'Always right,' added Francine. 'Omnipotent, omniscient . . . like God, of course.'

Aunt Grace suddenly put out a hand and touched Francine's arm. '*You* will have to be careful,' she said almost pleadingly

'Aunt Grace,' I put in – for I thought I had glimpsed something which in her indignation Francine might have missed – and it was in that moment that my aunt became *poor* Aunt Grace for me, 'are *you* glad that we have come?'

Her face twitched again, and there was a clouded look in her eyes. She nodded, and said: 'I will send the hot water.'

Then she was gone.

Francine and I stood looking at each other.

'I hate him,' she said. 'And our aunt . . . what is she? A puppet.'

Oddly enough I was the one who could comfort Francine. Perhaps because she was older than I she could see more clearly what our lives would be like here. Perhaps I was clutching at straws for comfort.

'At least we are together,' I reminded her.

She nodded and looked round the room.

'It's better now you've let in the light,' I added.

'We'll make a vow. We'll never draw those hideous curtains again. I expect *he* ordered them to be put there to shut out the sun. He would hate the sun, wouldn't he? But, Pippa, they are all so dead. That woman who let us in . . . the coachman . . . It's like dying. Perhaps we are dead. Perhaps we had an accident on that train and this is Hades. We are waiting while it is decided whether we shall go to Heaven or Hell.'

I laughed. It was good to laugh and soon she was laughing with me.

'Puppets,' I said. 'They are like puppets, but puppets can be jerked, you know.'

'But look who is the puppet-master!'

'*We're* not his puppets, Francine.'

'Never!' she cried. 'Never!'

'I think Aunt Grace is rather nice really. *Poor* Aunt Grace.'

'Aunt Grace! She is nothing. "Never again speak to your grandfather as you did today . . ."' she mimicked. 'I will if I want to!'

'He might turn us away. Where should we go if he did?'

It was a sobering thought and she was at a loss for words.

I put my hand in hers and said: 'We have to wait, Francine. We have to wait . . . and plan.'

Plans always excited Francine.

She said slowly: 'You're right, Pippa. Yes, you are right. We have to bide our time . . . and plan.'

We lay in our beds without speaking for a long time. I was reliving that strange evening and I knew that Francine was doing the same.

We had washed and changed into the dresses of coloured cotton which we had always worn on the island. That they would seem incongruous here did not strike us until we joined our grandfather and aunt. Poor Aunt Grace's look of horror warned me. I saw our grandfather's cold eyes on us and I prayed that he would not provoke Francine beyond endurance. I had a vision of our being turned out, and although I was by no means enamoured of Greystone Manor and my relations, I realized that there could be worse fates than that which awaited us here.

We were taken into the dining-room, which was large and should have been bright and colourful. But all that was needed to make a room mournful was our grandfather's presence. One single candle lighted the long and intricately carved table, and I found myself wondering what my father had felt when he had sat at that table. Because of its size we seemed a long way from each other. Grandfather was at one end, Aunt Grace at the other and Francine and I opposite each other.

We made a mistake in the first moment by sitting down when it was the custom at Greystone Manor to stand and say grace.

'Are you not prepared to thank your Maker for your food?' demanded our grandfather in a voice of thunder.

Francine pointed out that we had not had it yet.

'Savages,' muttered my grandfather. 'On your feet at once.'

Francine looked at me and I thought she was going to refuse, but she didn't. Grace went on interminably. Our grandfather apologized to God for our ingratitude and promised this should not happen again. He gave thanks on our behalf and his voice went droning on until I felt frantic with hunger, for we had not eaten for some time.

At last it was over and we sat down. Our grandfather talked all the time about church affairs, about people on the estate and the difference our coming to the household would make, so that we felt we were going to be an encumbrance. Aunt Grace murmured yes or no at the appropriate moments and all through the monologue wore an expression of rapt attention.

'It would seem that you are without education. A governess should be found without delay. Grace, that will be your province.'

'Yes, Father.'

'I cannot have it said that my granddaughters are ignorant.'

'We had a tutor on the island,' said Francine. 'He was very good. We have fluent Italian, both of us. Some French and quite good German . . .'

'We speak English here,' interrupted my grandfather. 'You clearly need to be educated in deportment and general behaviour.'

'Our parents brought us up.'

Aunt Grace looked so frightened that I threw a beseeching look at Francine who interpreted it and hesitated.

'Grace,' went on our grandfather, 'you must take charge of your nieces until the governess arrives. Make them understand that in polite society such as ours, children speak only when they are spoken to. They are seen but not heard.'

Even Francine seemed subdued, although she said afterwards that she was too hungry to want to argue with that dreadful old man and all she could think of was the food. Besides she had an idea that he might have some notion that little children should be sent to bed without their supper if they were recalcitrant, so she was playing it carefully . . . just at first.

'Just at first!' That became our watchword in those early days. We would endure it until we discovered how we could escape from it. 'But first,' said Francine, 'we must discover the lie of the land.'

So on that first night we lay there silently for a while and then we went over the events of the day, recalling every detail of our encounter with our grandfather.

'He is the most horrible old man I ever met,' said Francine. 'I hated him from the moment I saw him. I'm not surprised Father said it was a prison and he escaped from it. We shall escape in time, Pippa.'

Then she talked about the house. 'What a place to explore! And just think . . . *our* ancestors lived there for hundreds of years. That's something to be proud of, Pippa. We've got to find a way of showing the old man that *we* don't think he is God and if he were I'd be an atheist. He is not the least interested in us. He is just doing his duty. If there is anything I could hate more than that old man it's being a duty to somebody.'

'Well,' I reminded her, 'you've got both your worst hates under one roof.'

That made us laugh. How thankful I was then for Francine . . . as never before. I went to sleep thinking that while we were together, nothing was so bad.

The next day we made our discoveries. Hot water was brought by a maid. We were both asleep when it arrived as we had lain awake until late talking. That was when we first saw Daisy.

She was standing between our beds and laughing. I sat up with a start at the same time that Francine did. The realization of where we were came flooding over us and what struck us forcibly was that we were looking at someone who was actually laughing.

'You are a couple of sleepy 'eads,' she said.

'Who are you?' asked Francine.

'I'm Daisy,' she answered. 'Under housemaid. I've been sent up with your wash water.'

'Thank you,' said Francine and she added in a tone of wonder: 'You sound very cheerful.'

'Bless you, Miss, ain't no sense in being aught else . . . even in this 'ouse where a smile is thought to be a step along the road to 'ell.'

'Daisy,' said Francine, sitting up and shaking her fair curls out of her eyes, 'how long have you been here?'

'Six months and it seems like twenty. I'll be moving on as soon as my luck turns. My, you're pretty.'

'Thank you,' said Francine.

'It won't be liked . . . not in this 'ouse. I'm said to be on the flighty side myself.'

'Are you?' asked Francine.

Daisy gave a very pronounced wink which made us laugh.

'I'll tell you one thing,' she said, 'here's one who's glad you've come. Liven this old place up a bit. I'll tell you something else, there's more fun to be had in the old boneyard than here.' She laughed as though something struck her as very funny. 'Yes, 'strue. There's a whole lot of fun to be had in the aforementioned place . . . that's if you haven't gone there to bury a loved one. Well, there's the living to think of, I always say. The dead has gone and none the worse they'll be thought of for having a bit of fun when they was alive.'

This was an extraordinary conversation and Daisy herself seemed to realize it, for she brought it to an abrupt conclusion by saying: 'Better look smart. The master don't like latecomers. And breakfast is at eight.'

She went out, turning at the door to give us the benefit of that amazing wink.

'I like her,' said Francine. 'Daisy! I must say I'm surprised to find there is someone in this house whom we can like.'

'It seems a good omen,' I commented.

Francine laughed. 'Come on, get dressed. We have to be at breakfast soon. Remember, our sainted grandfather does not like to be kept waiting. Moreover, he won't tolerate it. I wonder what today will bring forth.'

'Let's wait and see.'

'A very profound remark, dear sister, because there is simply nothing else we can possibly do.'

Francine was back to her old self and that was comforting.

Breakfast was like a repetition of the previous meal with different food. There was plenty of that, which must be because, in spite of his saintliness, Grandfather liked his food. When we arrived he gave us a nod and as there were no complaints, I gathered we were not even a fraction of a second late. Grace was said at some length and then we were allowed to help ourselves from the sideboard after Grandfather and Aunt Grace had done so. There was sizzling bacon, devilled kidneys and eggs in various forms. How different from the fruit and brioche we had had on the island, rising when the mood took us and helping ourselves to whatever there was to eat, sometimes alone, sometimes together, while our father had often worked through the night in the studio to finish some masterpiece and would sleep long into the next day because of it!

This was very different. Here everything ran to order.

As he tackled his food with appreciative gusto, our grandfather barked out orders. Aunt Grace should get into immediate touch with Jenny Brakes. She should be summoned to the Manor without delay to make some suitable garments for his granddaughters. It was clear that on that outlandish island they had run loose like natives. They could scarcely be presented to the neighbourhood until they were suitably accoutred. I caught Francine's eye and was alarmingly near to giggling. 'He made us sound like Roman soldiers going into battle,' she said afterwards.

Then Aunt Grace must find a suitable governess.

'Enquire of your friends at the rectory.' I thought he spoke rather sneeringly and as Aunt Grace flushed slightly there seemed to be some subtlety in that remark, which I would report to Francine later if she had not noticed.

When Grandfather had finished eating he wiped his hands rather ceremoniously on his table napkin, flung it aside and rose ponderously to his feet. This was the signal for us all to rise. No one lingered at the table after he had decided the meal was terminated. 'Like Queen Elizabeth,' commented Francine. 'Fortunately he appears to be a great trencherman so that gives us an opportunity to tuck a bit away too.'

'First,' he announced, as he rose to his feet, 'they should be taken to their grandmother.'

We were astonished. We had forgotten that we had a grandmother. As no mention had been made of her I had presumed she was dead.

Aunt Grace said: 'Come with me.'

We followed her. As we left we heard our grandfather say to the butler: 'The bacon was not crisp enough this morning.'

Following Aunt Grace, I thought how easy it would be to get lost in Greystone Manor. There were staircases in unexpected places and numerous long corridors, with smaller ones turning off from them. Aunt Grace went on with the practised air of one who was well acquainted with the twists and turns of the house and she brought us at length to a door. She knocked and it was opened by a woman in a white cap and a black bombazine dress.

'Mrs Warden, I have brought my nieces to see their grandmother.'

'Yes. She is ready waiting.'

The woman looked at us and nodded. She had a serene face. I noticed this particularly because I had been aware of the lack of that quality in the house.

Aunt Grace led us in and there, seated on a chair beside a four-poster bed, was a little old lady in a frilled cap and a gown in which ribbons were threaded. She looked fragile. Aunt Grace went to her and kissed her and I was immediately aware of a different atmosphere in the room from that which prevailed in the rest of the house.

'Are they here?' asked the old lady.

'Yes, Mama,' replied Aunt Grace. 'Francine is the elder. She is sixteen years old and Philippa is five years younger.'

'Bring them to me.'

First Francine was pushed forward. My grandmother lifted her hands and touched my sister's face. 'Bless you,' she said. 'I am glad you have come.'

'And this is Philippa.' I was brought forward and the fingers gently touched my face.

Francine and I were silent. So she was blind.

'Come, my dears,' she said, 'sit one on either side of me. Have you stools for them, Agnes?'

Mrs Warden brought two stools and we sat down. Our grandmother's fingers lingered on our hair. She was smiling. 'So you are Edward's girls. Tell me about him. It was a sad day when he left us, but I understand. I hope he always knew I understood.'

Francine had recovered from her surprise and began to talk about our father and how happy we had been on the island. I joined in now and then. That hour we spent with our grandmother was such a change from everything else we had found in this house.

Aunt Grace had left us to talk with her. She said she had many things to see to – the dressmaker and finding a governess, for instance. Her departure reminded us of the stern world outside this room. 'Like an oasis in a desert,' Francine was later to describe it.

Our grandmother was clearly delighted to have us with her, telling her everything she asked. She wanted to hear about our father most of all. The time flew past and once we had recovered from the initial shock her blindness had given us we were completely at home in that room.

'May we come to see you often?' I asked.

'As often as is possible,' replied our grandmother. 'I hope you will want to come.'

Francine said: 'Oh, we will. You are the first one who has made us feel that we are wanted here.'

'Oh, you *are* wanted here. Your grandfather would not for one moment have considered refusing you a home.'

'He would consider it right and our grandfather is always right,' said Francine with a hint of mockery. 'But we don't want to be taken in because it is right, but because we are wanted and this is our home.'

'You are wanted, child, and this is your home. *I* want you and my home is yours.'

Francine took the thin white hand and kissed it.

'You've made it all so different,' she said.

Mrs Warden then said that Lady Ewell was a little tired. 'She tires easily,' she whispered, 'and this has been an excitement to her. You must come again and see her often.'

'Oh, we will, we will,' cried Francine.

We kissed the soft cheek and were ushered out of the room by Agnes Warden.

We were standing in the corridor uncertain which way to turn, and Francine looked at me with sparkling eyes. 'Now is our chance to explore the house,' she said. 'We have lost our way and have to find it, don't we?'

We held hands and ran along the corridor.

'We are very high up,' said Francine, 'right at the top of the house.'

At the end of the corridor there was a window. We went to it and looked out

'It's beautiful,' commented Francine. 'Different from the island and the sea . . . beautiful in a different way. All those trees and the forest over there and the greenness of everything. If our grandfather were like our grandmother I could begin to like it here.'

I stood close to my sister feeling the comfort of her presence. Nothing could be really bad while we could share it.

'Oh, look,' she cried. 'There's a house over there. It looks interesting.'

'It's old, I think.'

'Tudor, I'd say,' said Francine knowledgeably. 'All that red brick . . . and it looks like leaded windows. I like it. We'll have to go and have a look at that.'

'I wonder what this governess will be like?'

'They have to find her first. Come on, let's go and explore.'

We descended a small spiral staircase and came to a landing. We walked through a door and were in a long room with a spinning-wheel at one end.

'This is a voyage of exploration,' said Francine. 'We are now going to discover all the nooks and crannies, the dark secrets of our ancestral home.'

'How do you know there are dark secrets?'

'There are always dark secrets. Besides, you can feel them here. Now this would be called the solarium, I believe, because it gets the sun for most of the day . . . hence the windows on either side. It's beautiful. There should be parties and balls and lots of people here. If ever I inherit, that is how it shall be.'

'*You* inherit? Francine, how could you?'

'I'm in the line of succession surely. Father was the only son. Aunt Grace is not likely to prove fruitful. Perhaps *she* is the crown princess . . . the heir apparent. I could be the heir presumptive. It depends how they work these things out.'

I was laughing aloud and so was she. She could be relied on to bring laughter to most situations.

We went through the solarium and along another corridor, up a staircase similar to that by which we had descended and found a passage full of bedrooms with the inevitable four-posters and the heavy drapes and dark furniture.

We descended once more and came to a gallery.

'Family portraits,' mused Francine, 'and look. I am sure that is one of King Charles the First. Charles the Martyr; and those gentlemen who all look rather like him. I bet we were loyal to the monarchy. I wonder if our father is here. Perhaps we shall be . . . you and I, Pippa.'

We heard footsteps and an agitated Aunt Grace burst in on us.

'Oh, there you are. I've been up to your grandmother's room to warn you. I couldn't find you. You'll be late for the service.'

'The service?' asked Francine.

'We have three minutes in which to get there. Your grandfather will be most displeased . . .'

Poor Grace. She would probably be blamed. Francine and I ran with her.

The chapel was reached by a flight of steps from the main hall. It was small, as chapels go, made to accommodate the family and servants, who were all assembled there when, breathless, we arrived.

I saw the curious eyes of the servants on us and was amazed by their number. Seated right at the back was the maid Daisy who had brought our hot water. Our eyes met and she gave me one of her winks. The rest of them looked very demure, eyes lowered as we were hustled to our seats in the front row.

Our grandfather, already seated, looked neither to the right nor to the left. Aunt Grace sidled in beside him, then Francine and next to her myself.

The service was conducted by a young man who must have been in his middle twenties. He was tall and very thin with restless dark eyes, and hair which looked almost black beside the pallor of his skin.

We sang hymns of praise and there was a good deal of praying when we stayed on our knees for what seemed an interminable length of time. Then the young man gave an address, during which he reminded everyone of the care of the

Almighty who had brought them to Greystone Manor where they found food and shelter and all that was necessary not only for their physical, but for their spiritual comfort.

Our grandfather sat through this with his arms folded and now and then would nod in agreement. Then there was a song of praise, more prayers and the service was over. It had lasted only half an hour but it had seemed endless. The servants all filed out, and we were left with our grandfather, Aunt Grace and the young man – some sort of parson, I imagined.

Our grandfather was not exactly smiling, but he was looking with approval at the young man.

'Arthur,' he said, 'I wish you to meet your cousins.'

'Cousins!' I sensed Francine's surprise. It could not have been greater than mine.

'The Reverend Arthur Ewell,' said our grandfather. 'Your cousin is in Holy Orders. You did not meet him last night as he was administering spiritual comfort to a sick neighbour. I am glad you arrived back in time for the service, Arthur.'

The Reverend Arthur bowed his head with a sort of smug humility and said that Mrs Glencorn had seemed to have profited from their prayers.

'Arthur, your cousin Francine.'

Arthur bowed rather curtly.

'How do you do, Cousin Arthur,' said Francine.

'And,' went on our grandfather, 'this is the younger of your cousins, Philippa.'

The dark eyes of Cousin Arthur surveyed me rather briefly, I thought, but I was used to people's greater interest in my sister.

'Your spiritual welfare will be in good hands,' went on our grandfather. 'And please remember that the meeting in the chapel takes place every morning at eleven. Everyone in the household attends.'

Francine could not suppress her comment: 'I can see that our spiritual welfare will receive a great deal of attention.'

'We shall make sure of that,' said our grandfather. 'Arthur, would you like to have a word in private with your cousins? You might wish to discover what religious education they have had. I fear you may receive rather a shock.'

Arthur said he thought that would be an excellent idea.

Our grandfather and Aunt Grace went out of the chapel, leaving us to the mercy of Cousin Arthur.

He suggested we sit down and began asking us questions. He was shocked to hear that we had not been to church on the island but perhaps that was as well, as the natives were probably of the Catholic Faith – natives often were and worshipped idols.

'Lots of people worship idols,' Francine reminded him. 'Not necessarily gods of stone but sets of rules and conventions which sometimes result in the suppression of loving-kindness.'

Arthur kept looking at her and although his expression was disapproving I saw a gleam in his eyes which I had noticed in people before when they looked at Francine.

We talked to him for a while – at least Francine did. He had little to say to me. I was sure during that time she thoroughly shocked him with what she told him of our upbringing and he would tell our grandfather that intensive instruction would be needed to bring us to grace.

When we escaped from him it was almost time for the midday meal. Afterwards we might like a little exercise, suggested Aunt Grace, and could take a walk in the gardens. It would not be wise for us to stray beyond them and would we remember to be in by four o'clock when tea was taken in the red drawing-room which led off from the hall. She herself was going to the vicarage. There was something of importance she had to see the vicar about. We should be able to go visiting when we had suitable clothes – and that would not be long, for Jenny Brakes would arrive tomorrow morning with materials and the dressmaking session would begin.

'Freedom,' cried Francine, when we were alone. 'And stay

in the garden! Never! We are going to look round, and our first mission shall be to take a closer look at that interesting old house we saw from the window.'

'Francine,' I said, 'I believe you are starting to enjoy this.'

It was true, she was. She was fascinated by Greystone Manor and each hour brought fresh revelations. She sensed some sort of battle ahead and it was just what she needed to recover from the shock of our parents' deaths. I knew this because I felt the same myself.

So in a spirit of adventure we set out that afternoon. We had two hours or so to ourselves. 'We must be back in time for tea,' said Francine. 'It would never do for them to discover that we have been adventuring on our own. They must believe that we have been meandering through the garden paths,' she went on, 'admiring the orderliness of everything, for I am sure it is orderly, and exclaiming every now and then on the excellence of our grandfather, who is so holy that I wonder he is not considered too good for this earth.'

We were careful until we came through the drive and slipped out by the lodge gate. Fortunately the occupants of the lodge were out of sight. Perhaps the hour of our grandfather's siesta was their only time for relaxation.

We were in a road bounded on either side by high hedges, and when we came to a gate Francine suggested we pass through it and cross the field, for she was sure that was the direction in which the house lay.

This we did and at the top of the field was a row of four cottages and outside one of these was a woman shaped rather like a cottage loaf, with hair which straggled out of a bun at the back of her head while the light breeze played with the straying strands.

She looked up as we approached. I supposed she did not see many people for she was obviously surprised.

'Good day to you,' she called, and as we came closer I saw the curiosity in her lively dark eyes, and there was a look of extreme interest and pleasure on her rather plump face. One noticed these things after even a short time at Greystone Manor, where the general rule was to look solemn and glum.

'Good day,' we answered.

She had been pegging wet clothes on a line, which was fixed to a post at one end and attached to the side of the cottage on the other. Removing a peg from her mouth, she said: 'You the new young ladies up at Greystone.' It was a statement rather than a question.

Francine said we were and how did she know?

'Why, God love you, there's not much I don't know about what goes on up at Greystone. My girl's up there.' Her eyes widened as she stared at Francine. 'My, you're pretty. Not what you expected up there, was it?'

'We didn't know what to expect,' said Francine.

'Well, we knew Mr Edward. He was a good man, he was... not like... Oh no, he was different, he was... and that lovely young girl he ran off with... Pretty as a picture, and you, Miss, you're the spitting image of her. I reckon I'd have known you anywhere... picked you out I could.'

'It's nice that you knew our father and mother,' said Francine.

'Dead... both of them. Well, that's life, ain't it? The best often goes... and the rest stays on.' She nodded her head, momentarily sad. Then she was smiling again. 'You'll know our Daise.'

'Daise,' we both said simultaneously. 'Oh... Daisy.'

'Got herself a job up there. Under housemaid. Mind you, I don't know if it will last. Our Daise is a bit of a caution.' The woman winked in a way which reminded me of Daisy herself. They must be a winking family, I commented afterwards to Francine.

'Always a bit of a wild one,' went on the woman. 'I didn't know what to do with her. I say to her: "You mark my words, Daise, you'll be in trouble one day." She laughs at that. I don't know. She always liked the boys and the boys liked her. It was the same even when she was in her cradle. I've got six of them. She's my eldest too. I said to Emms . . . he's their father, you know . . . I said, "Now, Emms, this is enough." But would you believe it, there's another on the way. What can you do with a man like Emms? But we got Daise to the big house. I thought if this can't make her respectable, nothing can.'

'We have met Daise,' said Francine. 'Just once. She brought us hot water. We liked her.'

'She's a good girl . . . at heart. It's just the boys. Can't seem to stay away from them. I was a bit like that myself at one time. Well, it makes the world go on.'

Francine said: 'What is the big Tudor house over there?'

'That's Granter's Grange.' She began to laugh. 'Regular old to-do that caused.'

'We thought it looked interesting and we should like to see it closer.'

'It was bought by foreigners . . . that's a year or two ago. Sir Matthew wanted it but he didn't get it. That's upset him. He thinks he owns these parts and he does in a way. But Granter's Grange . . . well, the foreigners got in before him.'

'Who are the foreigners?'

'Oo . . . now you're asking! Very high-up foreigners . . . Grand Dukes and things . . . but from some outlandish place. They don't count for much round here.'

'Grand Dukes,' whispered Francine.

'Oh, they're not there now. They're not often there. They come and go. The place is all covered up and left, and then servants come and there's a regular spring clean, then the Dukes come. It's all very grand . . . royal stuff. Your grandfather doesn't like it . . . he doesn't like it at all.'

'Is it really any concern of his?' asked Francine.

That made Mrs Emms roar with laughter and produce one of her winks. 'He reckons so. He's the lord of this place. Emms says the Queen herself couldn't be more of a sovereign over all England than Sir Matthew Ewell is over us all here . begging your pardon, he being your grandfather.'

'There's no need to ask pardon. I think we agree with you,' said Francine, 'although we have not seen much yet. Are the Grand Dukes in residence now?'

'Oh, bless you no, and haven't been these last two months. But they'll be here . . . oh yes, they'll be here. It makes a bit of excitement. You never know, you see. One day I'll look out of my back windows and I'll see them there. They're just at the back of me so I get the best view.'

'Well, we'll go and look at it,' said Francine. 'We haven't much time. We have to be back by four. So the house is just at the back of you.'

'Yes . . . look. There's a short cut round by the cottages, you can't miss it. Through the hedge and there you are.'

'Thank you, Mrs Emms. We hope we shall see more of you.'

She nodded and winked again. Francine said: 'Come on, Pippa.'

So we came to the house. There was a deep silence everywhere and a great excitement gripped me. I am sure Francine felt the same and I wondered afterwards whether it was a premonition because this house was going to play such an important part in our lives.

There was the gate supported by marble columns and an archway on which we could just make out the date: 1525. We unlatched the gate and went in. I reached for Francine's hand and she gripped mine tightly. We almost tiptoed across the stretch of lawn which was overgrown and spotted with daisies. We reached the house and I put out a hand to touch the red bricks. They were warm from the sun. Francine was looking in through the window. She gave a little gasp and turned pale.

'What is it?' I cried.

'There's someone . . . standing there . . . a ghost . . . in white.'

I began to tremble, but I pressed my face against the glass. I started to laugh. 'It's a piece of furniture,' I said. 'It's covered over with a dust sheet. It does look like someone standing there.'

She looked again and then we were rolling about in an excess of mirth – which perhaps had a touch of hysteria in it. There was something about the house which affected us deeply.

We walked round it; we looked in through all the lower windows. Everywhere the furniture was covered in dust sheets.

'It must be wonderful,' I said, 'when the Grand Dukes come.'

Francine tried the door. It was of course locked. There was a gargoyle on a sort of knocker which seemed to be jeering at us.

'I'm sure he moved,' said Francine.

'This is a place where you could fancy things,' I reminded her.

She agreed. 'Imagine coming here at night. I'd like to.'

I shivered, fearful that she might suggest it. 'Let's look at the gardens,' I said. We did. The lawns were mostly all in need of attention. There were groves, statues, colonnades and little pathways through shrubberies.

I said: 'We should go back. We're not quite sure of the way and if we're late and they find out we haven't been walking in the gardens . . .'

'Come on then,' she said. 'Let's go back past the cottages.'

We did with great speed for it was half past three. Daisy's mother was not there, but the line of flapping washing showed that she had completed her task.

We ran all the way back and were punctual at the tea-table and as we listened to the usual grace, we were both thinking of the afternoon's adventure.

We saw Daisy next morning when she came in with our hot water. We told her that we had met her mother and she laughed with pleasure.

'Good old Ma.' she said, 'was she pleased to get her eldest respectable!'

'Are you respectable then, Daisy?' asked Francine.

'Oh . . . as near as makes no difference. You've got the dressmaker coming today. Pity. I like your little frocks. They're pretty.'

'We don't see you during the day,' said Francine.

'Working in the kitchens, that's me.'

'It was nice seeing your mother. She told us about Granter's Grange.'

'Ah, that's a place I'd like to be at.'

'There's no one there.'

'When there is it will be a real sight, I can tell you. Balls and fêtes. They do themselves proud. A lot of people come over from abroad. They say it belongs to a King or something.'

'A Grand Duke, your mother said.'

'She'd know. Reckon she talks with the servants up there. Foreigners, most of them, but trust Ma.'

She winked and went out, and we hastily dressed to be in time for breakfast.

It was very much the same as the previous day. In fact, I was beginning to think that once we had settled into a routine every day was going to be like every other. We visited our grandmother again; Aunt Grace collected us in time to be at the service at the chapel and told us that the rest of the morning would be spent with Jenny Brakes, and we should have dresses which were suitable; we should have a governess who might well arrive within the week and there would be religious instruction from our Cousin Arthur. Our grandfather had said that we must be taught to ride as that was part of a gentlewoman's training. So it seemed our days would be well accounted for.

We got through the chapel service and Francine confided to me that she heartily disliked Cousin Arthur, largely because he looked so virtuous and Grandfather clearly had a high opinion of him. Poor little Jenny Brakes was so pale and over-eager to please that I felt sorry for her and stood as still as I could while she knelt beside me with a mouthful of pins and adjusted the dark blue serge which I disliked intensely.

So did Francine. 'We're going to look as dismal as Greystone Manor,' she commented. She was wrong, for she could never look dismal and the navy blue serge of our everyday dresses and the brown poplin of our best ones only accentuated her fair beauty and by its contrast, her charm. They were not so kind to me. I hated the colours, which did not suit my darkness; but I was glad that our new clothes had not spoilt Francine's looks.

That our coming had made a subtle change to the household was obvious to everyone, I think – except perhaps our grandfather. He was so immersed in his own importance and piety that I imagine he rarely thought anything or anyone else of any significance. He wouldn't have known that our grandmother grew quite excited at the prospect of our morning visits. I believe he paid daily visits – as was his duty – and I could imagine what they would be like.

Within a week our governess had arrived. Miss Elton was in her mid-thirties, with brown hair severely parted in the middle and worn in a little knot at the nape of her neck; she wore severe grey gowns on weekdays and a dark blue one on Sundays, which did honour to the Sabbath by sporting a lace collar. She tested us and found us abysmally ignorant, except in one respect – languages. She spoke fair French herself, but her German was excellent. She told us afterwards that her mother had been German and she had been brought up to speak that language as well as English. She was delighted with our proficiency and said we must aim to perfect it. It would certainly be one of the subjects we studied with enthusiasm. She was obsequious to our grandfather and gently polite to Aunt Grace.

'Subservient,' commented Francine slightingly.

'Don't you understand?' I replied warmly. 'She wants to

keep her post here. She's afraid of losing it. So be kind to her and see her point of view.'

Francine looked at me thoughtfully. 'Do you know, sister Philippa,' she said, 'you have a certain wisdom and you can put yourself in other people's places better than most. It's a rare gift.'

'Thank you,' I replied, gratified; and I noticed that she was beginning to respect my judgement more and more. I was quieter than she was, more observant perhaps. I sometimes thought it was because I was more on the edge of things, an observer rather than a main actor. Francine, with her outstanding looks and personality, would always be at the centre of events, and sometimes people like that did not see as clearly as those who were slightly removed from the scene.

However, she accepted my view of the governess and instead of teasing her as she might have done, she became quite a docile pupil and after the first days of strangeness we established a certain rapport with Miss Elton, and lessons went fairly well.

We were now having riding lessons which we both enjoyed. These were conducted under the supervision of the coachman who had met us at the station, and usually there was his son Tom who worked as a stable boy and must have been about eighteen or nineteen years of age. He had to prepare the horses and take them after the lessons. We spent hours riding round the first paddock on leading reins, then without. I was proud when he said: 'Miss Philippa, you're a natural. You're going to be a rider, you are.' 'And what of me?' Francine asked. 'Oh, you'll get by, Miss, I reckon,' was the answer. I couldn't help being thrilled. It was the first time I had ever excelled over Francine but almost immediately I felt apologetic and ashamed of my feelings. But I need not have done. Francine was delighted for me.

One day she took a toss as we were cantering round the paddock. I was horrified and when I saw her lying on the ground I realized how very much she meant to me. I was off my horse and running to her, but Tom was already there.

Francine grimaced at us and got up rather gingerly. She was moved by my emotion which I couldn't hide and she pretended to laugh at it. 'It's what happens to those who are not naturals,' she said.

'Francine, you are all right . . . you are sure . . .'

'I think so.'

'You're all right, Miss,' said Tom. 'You'll feel it tomorrow though. You'll want some liniment to put on the bruises. Reckon you'll have some beauties. Never mind, they'll be where they don't show. I'll send Daise up with the liniment. Just one application. No more. It's strong stuff and would have the skin off you in no time.'

'Ought I to get on the brute who threw me and show him I'm the one in command?'

Tom grinned. 'Oh, he knows who that is, Miss, and it ain't you – not yet, but it will be. I'd go and lie down if I was you. It's best. Then ride tomorrow.'

'Yes,' I said. 'I'll go up with you and Daisy can come down at once for the liniment.'

I took Francine to our room, still anxious about her.

'Don't look so worried, Pippa,' she said. 'It'll take more than that miserable old nag to kill me.'

I sent for Daisy and told her to get the liniment. 'Tom's expecting you,' I said. 'He'll be down in the stables.'

'I know where to find Tom,' she replied and went off. She was soon back with the liniment which we applied to the bruises which were already beginning to show.

I insisted that Francine should lie down although she declared that she felt all right. Daisy came in and said should she take the liniment back and I said she could as we had finished with it.

Francine lay down and I was standing at the window when I saw Daisy running towards the stables. Tom came out to meet her. They stood for a moment very close. She held out the liniment to him; he took it and with it her arm. He was dragging her towards the stables and she was pretending not to want to go, but I could see that she was laughing. I thought of her mother's remark: 'She's a one for the boys.'

'What are you looking at?' asked Francine.

I replied: 'Daisy and Tom. They seem to be having a game of some sort.'

Francine laughed and Aunt Grace came in then. She was all concern. We must expect the occasional mishap, she said, and hoped no harm was done.

Francine said faintly: 'Aunt Grace, I don't feel well enough to come down to dinner tonight. May I have something sent up?'

'Of course.'

'And Aunt Grace, could Philippa have hers up here too? In case I . . .'

'It shall be arranged,' said Aunt Grace. 'Now you rest. And Philippa, stay with your sister.'

'Oh, I will, Aunt Grace.'

She left us and when she had gone Francine started to laugh. 'Just think. We'll miss one of the appalling meals. Both of us. Out of evil cometh good.'

It was almost an hour later when I saw Daisy emerging from the stables. I was sitting in the window talking to Francine who was still lying down. Daisy's hair was rumpled and she was buttoning up her blouse. She ran swiftly into the house.

Francine was rather more affected than we had first thought and the next morning the bruises were violently marked. Daisy screamed at the sight of them and said she would go and see Tom at once because he might have something.

However, within a few days they started to subside and Francine was riding again. Cousin Arthur expressed a certain concern and warned Francine that she should pray before she took her lesson. It might be that God would give heed to her safety

'Oh, I expect He's too busy to bother about that,' said Francine flippantly. 'Just imagine! When He's contemplating some universal problem an angel runs in and says it's time for Francine Ewell's riding lesson and You let her fall off the other day. Shall we send out a guardian angel? She has said her prayers.'

She enjoyed shocking Cousin Arthur. In fact she disliked him as much as she did our grandfather, and there was a growing animosity between Francine and the old man. I think that, being quieter and less noticeable, I appeared to be more biddable. He recognized in Francine the rebel . . . like our father, and he was watchful of her. He probably thought I was more like Aunt Grace. I was determined not to be.

I looked forward to our visits to our grandmother. Her face used to light up when we came in and she would hold out her hands and let her fingers explore our faces. Agnes Warden would hover round while our grandmother talked about the past, and of course we wanted to hear. Although she was old – of a different world from our own – we could talk to her openly. Constantly she asked us questions about the island and I think within a week she had a clear picture of it. Francine, who was always frank and perhaps spoke before she had considered her words, asked her how she could ever have come to marry our grandfather.

'It was arranged,' she said. 'It always is with people like us, you know.'

'But our father didn't do what his father wanted,' Francine pointed out.

'There would always be the rebels, my dear, even in those days. Your father was one. Odd . . . he was a quiet boy. You remind me of him, Philippa. He was purposeful, as I think you would be . . . if the occasion arose. But I was very young when I married your grandfather. I was sixteen . . . your age now, Francine. But I seemed much younger. I knew nothing of life.'

Francine's face expressed her horror. Married to my grandfather at the same age as herself! I think it was hard for Francine to imagine a worse fate. Francine had not spoken, but it was amazing how sensitive my grandmother was to a mood. She said at once: 'Oh, he was different then. He has grown away from the young man he was.'

'Poor Grandmother,' said Francine, kissing her hand.

'Of course,' went on our grandmother, 'he ruled the household with his rod of iron . . . right from the first. He was content with the marriage because it joined up the lands, you see, and he had always cared passionately about the family's estate. It has been with the Ewells for so long. It is understandable. We Granters were considered to be something of upstarts by him. We had only been in the Grange for a hundred years or so.'

'That's the Tudor house.'

'Yes . . . yes. Oh, there was trouble about that. My brother refused to sell it to your grandfather. He wanted it very much. He could not bear that anything . . . just anything . . . in the neighbourhood did not belong to him. You see, he now owns the whole of the Granters' estate – except the Grange. Much of it came with me as my dowry, but there was a larger portion of it which went to my brother. He wasn't the clever businessman your grandfather was. He lost most of it. He said your grandfather cheated him. It wasn't true, of course, but there was a quarrel and although your grandfather acquired most of the estate my brother was determined not to let him have the Grange. He sold it to a foreigner . . . someone from an embassy in some faraway country. I think it was Bruxenstein . . . or something like that.'

'That house fascinated me,' said Francine.

'It means something to me, said our grandmother. 'It was my old home.'

She was silent for a while and I knew Francine was

remembering, as I was, how we had peered through the windows and thought we saw a ghost.

'It's not used a great deal,' said my grandmother. 'Agnes tells me they come here from time to time, and then they go away and it's neglected again. And when they come back . . . in a flash it's full of life again. A strange way to go on. I heard that when they originally bought it, it was for one of their exiled noblemen and that after he'd been in residence for a month or two there was some coup in the country and he went back again.'

'They could have sold the house to our grandfather then,' said Francine.

'No. They wanted to keep it. Perhaps they wanted it for another exile. There is always trouble, I believe, in those small German states. We heard from time to time that they change their rulers. Grand Dukes . . . or Margraves . . . whatever they call them. However, it is strange to think of those sort of people in my old home.'

'Romantic,' added Francine; and my grandmother gently ruffled her hair.

I could see that Francine was getting more and more interested in the Grange now that she knew that it had been our grandmother's home; she said she was pleased the romantic princes or whatever they were had secured it and that Grandfather had been outdone for once in his life.

On another occasion our grandmother told us about our father and Aunt Grace. She blossomed when she talked with us and her great pleasure in our company seemed to have made her younger. I could almost see her as a young girl coming to Greystone Manor as a bride, a young girl who did not know what marriage was about. We should be thankful that we were not ignorant on that score. They had been a passionate race on the island and we had often seen lovers lying on the beaches wrapped in an embrace; we knew that when some of the girls became pregnant it was due to those embraces and I was fully aware that they had forestalled their marriages. I knew too what Mrs Emms had meant when she had said Daisy was a one for the boys and I could guess what had happened when she had gone into the stables with Tom.

But our grandmother's coming to marriage must have been a great shock and I could not imagine our grandfather as a tender lover. 'He was a passionate man in those days,' said our grandmother. 'He longed for children and was overjoyed when your father was born. He began planning from that day. I was unfortunate in my efforts afterwards, and it was not until five years later that Grace was born. Your grandfather was disappointed because she was a girl. He never cared for her as he did for Edward. He thought Edward was going to be just such another as himself. These plans always go wrong. Then there was Charles Daventry.'

'Tell us about him,' prompted Francine.

Our grandmother needed no persuasion. 'Edward went to Oxford and from that time everything went wrong. Before that he was interested in the estate. Your grandfather was stern and strict, as you can imagine, but there was never any real friction between them until he went to Oxford. It was there that he met Charles. Charles was a sculptor and the two of them had a great deal in common. They became close friends. Edward brought him home during the vacation and your grandfather took an immediate dislike to him. He disliked artists of any sort. He used to say they were dreamers and no good to themselves or to anybody.'

'Our father was a great artist,' said Francine hotly. 'He should have been recognized. I think he will be one day . . . all those beautiful things he made . . . they're scattered all over the world. One day . . .'

It was the Francine of the studio days who was impressing the customers.

Our grandmother patted her hand. 'You loved him dearly,' she said. 'He was very lovable. Your grandfather said there was no money to be made from chipping stone, but while it was a hobby he was prepared to tolerate it. There was

Grace too. She was shy and retiring . . . but pretty in those days. She was like a young fawn – brown eyes, brown hair . . . very pretty hair she had in those days. I remember they used to go to the graveyard together . . . all three of them. They were all interested in the stone statues on the graves. Charles Daventry was a nephew of the present vicar and the two young men got into touch because of this connection. It was strange how they should both have this taste for sculpting, but I suppose that was why they became great friends.'

'I think people should be allowed to do what they want in this life,' said Francine hotly.

'Ah yes,' agreed our grandmother, 'and the strong-willed ones do! Your father made up his mind in the end. I have never seen your grandfather so shocked as he was when he knew that Edward had left. He just could not believe it. You know that your mother came here to sew.'

'Yes, we knew that,' Francine told her.

'She was exceptionally pretty – dainty as a fairy, and your father loved her from the moment he saw her.'

'Until the moment he died,' I added quietly.

I felt my grandmother's fingers caressing my hair and I knew that she understood I was near to tears.

'They went off together. Your father did not see your grandfather before he went. He told me though. He said, "You will understand, Mother, that I cannot talk to Father. That's his tragedy. No one can talk to him. If only he would listen sometimes . . . I think he would have been spared a lot of dissatisfaction." He did suffer when Edward went . . . though he wouldn't admit it. He raged and stormed and cut him out of his will, I think he was hoping Edward would have a son who would come back here to us.'

'And all he had was two daughters!' said Francine.

'Now that I know you I wouldn't have had it different. After your father had gone your grandfather turned to Grace. But she had grown fond of Charles Daventry and he was out of the question.'

'Why?' asked Francine.

'Well, your grandfather said he was no match for her. He came to live here . . . I think it was to be near Grace. He has a small place adjoining the vicarage . . . a sort of yard, I suppose you would call it, and there he makes his statues. People buy them for graves and our graveyard is noted for some of the fine figures and effigies he does. He is said to be very clever but it is a poor living. Fortunately for Charles he can live with his uncle at the vicarage. He does certain jobs in the parish too. He's a delightful man . . . a bit of a dreamer. He and Grace . . . well, it's hopeless really. He's not in a position to marry and your grandfather would never hear of it.'

'Poor Grace,' I said.

'Poor Grace . . . yes,' echoed our grandmother. 'She is a good woman. She never complains but I sense a sadness . . .'

'It's monstrous!' cried Francine. 'How dare people interfere with the lives of others!'

'It takes a strong will to go against your grandfather and Grace always avoided trouble. When she was a little girl she used to hide away until it was over. Your grandfather washed his hands of Grace. He then started to show an interest in his younger brother's boy – your Cousin Arthur.'

Francine grimaced with distaste.

'He's been Arthur's guardian since the boy was sixteen. That was when Arthur's father was killed in Africa. His mother had gone into a decline some years before. Your grandfather said Arthur was young enough to be moulded. Arthur's father had not left a great deal and your grandfather took over the boy's education. When he heard that he wanted to go into the Church he did not deter him. Your grandfather, as you know, is a very religious man. There was no reason why Arthur should not take Holy Orders even though he was intended to inherit the estate. One great point in his favour is his name. He's a Ewell and it is very important in your grandfather's eyes to keep the name alive. Francine . . how do you like your Cousin Arthur?'

'*How* do I like him?' cried Francine. 'I don't like him in any way. The answer is Not at all.'

Our grandmother was silent.

'Why are you disturbed?' I asked.

Our grandmother reached out for Francine's hand. 'I think I should warn you,' she said. 'Your grandfather has plans. Arthur is a sort of second cousin to you, it is true, but second cousins marry.'

'Marry!' cried Francine. 'Cousin Arthur!'

'You see, my dear, it would make a neat solution and your grandfather loves neat solutions. You are his granddaughter in direct line you might say. He would like you to continue that direct line and if you married Arthur your children would be doubly Ewell and the name would survive. I think he has been meaning to make Arthur his heir . . . unless your father had had a son. I am guessing a certain amount of this. It wouldn't come about for a year or so, but, Francine, my dear, I didn't want it to be a shock when it did come.'

We were silent with horror. I knew Francine wanted to get away to discuss this fearful possibility.

We had talked it over and over. We had discussed what we should do if it were ever suggested. We should have to get away, said Francine. Where to? We would lie in bed talking about it. Perhaps we could go back to the island. To do what? How could we live? We should have to go and work somewhere. Could she be a governess? Francine wondered. And what of me? What should I do? 'You would have to stay here until you were old enough to get away.'

But then we should be separated and that must never be.

For a few days the shadow hung over us while Francine's distaste for Cousin Arthur grew. During religious instruction she was curt with him. I was surprised how meekly he took it. Then it occurred to me that she might be having the same effect on him as she had had on many others. In his mild and very proper way he was rather attracted by her. But perhaps this was due to the fact that he knew our grandfather intended them to marry.

It was not like Francine to be depressed for long and after those first few days of gloom she began to recover her spirits. It wouldn't be for a long time. She was only sixteen. It was true our grandmother had been only sixteen when she had married, but there was time to start worrying when it was suggested to her. In the meantime she would indicate to Cousin Arthur that her feelings towards him were very cold indeed, and perhaps his pride would stop him pursuing the matter. Moreover, the older she grew the easier it would be to find a solution. So the matter was shelved.

After what we had heard of Aunt Grace's romance our curiosity led us to the yard close to the vicarage and there we made the acquaintance of Charles Daventry. We liked him at once because he reminded us of our father, and because of who we were he was interested in us.

He made tea on an old spirit lamp in his workshop and we sat on stools drinking it and telling him about the island and how we had lived there. He showed us some of his models. I fancied most of the women had a look of Aunt Grace.

He was a sad, quiet man, Francine said of him afterwards. 'He makes me impatient. They deserve their fate because they just let life flow over them . . . tossing them wherever it wants to. They make no effort. That's no way to live. We'll never be like that, Pippa. Our father wasn't, was he? We won't let that old Patriarch [her name for our grandfather] rule our lives.'

Summer had come. The countryside was beautiful – in a different way from that of the island. I realized that there had been a sameness about the blue sea which only changed when the rain came and the mistral blew. Here everything seemed different almost every day and it was wonderful to see the burgeoning of the trees . . . the forming of the buds and the bursting into flower, the blossoming of the fruit trees, wild roses and strawberries in the hedgerows and mayflies dancing over the water on the ponds, to listen to the cries of birds and try to recognize them, to see the bluebells under the trees and later the foxgloves, the honeysuckle filling the air with its sweet perfume – and the long twilight hour which made one feel that the daylight was reluctant to depart. I had a feeling that I had come home, which was strange when I had been born on the island and had lived most of my life there.

I liked to be alone and lie in the long grass listening to the sound of the grasshoppers and the buzzing of the bees who were marauding in the purple buddleia or the sweet-smelling lavender. I thought then: This is Peace. And I wanted to hold time still and stay like this for a long while. This was probably because I sensed a menace in the air. We were getting older. Soon our grandfather would be making his wishes known to Francine and she would never obey. What then? Should we be turned away?

I remembered how our father had talked to me when we had sat outside the studio and he had looked over the sea with a kind of nostalgia which all exiles must feel at some time. He often quoted to me what he called my song. 'Pippa's song,' he would say, 'written by a great poet who knew what it was like to long for home.'

'"The year's at the spring
And the day's at the morn,
Morning's at seven,
The hillside's dew-pearled;
The lark's on the wing
And the snail's on the thorn,
God's in his Heaven,
All's right with the world."'

I felt it lying there in the grass. 'All's right with the world.' And just for that moment I could forget the gathering clouds.

'The clouds pass,' my father used to say. 'Sometimes you get a drenching. But then the sun shines and afterwards all's right with the world.'

Later that day Francine and I took our walk and it led us past Granter's Grange. We hardly ever passed it without taking a look through the windows at the shrouded furniture and Francine wailed as she invariably did: 'Oh, Grand Duke, when are you coming to enliven the scene?' I always pointed out that it would make no difference to us whether they came or stayed away, to which she said that it would be nice to have a glimpse of grandeur.

We went to see Charles Daventry. We liked to watch him work. He was glad to see us and liked to tell us stories of the life he and our father had led at Oxford, and how they had had grand plans for sharing a studio in London or Paris and having a sort of salon where artists and the literati assembled.

'You see what tricks life plays,' said Charles. 'Your father ends up in an island studio and I am here . . . a sort of stonemason. What else?'

'It's what you want,' Francine pointed out. 'If you take what you want you must take the consequences with it.'

'Ah, we have a philosopher here,' said Charles.

'As I see it, you have to be bold in life,' Francine went on. In her heart she continued to be impatient with him because he was living here alone and Aunt Grace was at Greystone Manor, and neither of them had the courage to defy our grandfather.

Francine leaped up suddenly and said we must go, and as she did so she tripped over a block of stone. She picked herself up and tried to stand but found she could not do so. She would have fallen if I had not caught her.

'I can't put my foot to the ground,' she said.

'It's a sprain most like,' said Charles, kneeling and feeling her ankle.

'I'll have to get back. How?'

'There's only one way.'

Charles lifted her up and carried her. When we arrived at the house there was tremendous excitement. Daisy came dashing out, her mouth a round O of astonishment when she saw Francine was being carried and when she realized by whom her excitement increased. She went to get Aunt Grace, who turned red and then white. I learned afterwards that Charles had been forbidden to enter the house and Grace to have any communication with him. My grandfather would have liked to banish Charles from the neighbourhood, but the vicar stood out against him and was not going to turn his nephew away to please him, and they were on bad terms because of this.

Aunt Grace murmured: 'Charles!'

'Your niece has had an accident,' he said.

I was sure Francine was enjoying the drama even though she was in some pain. Charles said he would carry her to her bed and then go off and ask the doctor to call.

White-faced Aunt Grace, delighted and yet fearfully apprehensive, stammered: 'Oh yes . . . yes, please, Charles . . . and thank you. I am sure Francine is very grateful.'

Charles laid her on the bed and Grace was in a fever of impatience to get him out of the house while at the same time she longed to keep him there.

The doctor came. It was a bad sprain and she would have to keep to her bed for a few days, possibly a week, and we were to apply hot and cold poultices. I had instituted myself as my sister's nurse and Aunt Grace sent Daisy up to help.

The pain had subsided considerably within the next few hours and Francine only felt it when she put her weight on her ankle and, as the doctor's orders were that she was not to do this, she hopped everywhere with my help or that of Daisy. She was soon feeling comfortable and congratulating herself for once again escaping those interminable meals, prayers and the company of the odious Arthur.

There followed the most pleasant week we had known since coming to Greystone Manor. We were in our little oasis, as Francine called it, and Daisy was constantly with us. She entertained us with local gossip and showed us how to tighten our dresses so that we showed our figures to advantage.

'Not that you've got one yet, Miss Pip,' she said. She called me Miss Pip which amused Francine and me. 'But you will,' she added. 'As for you, Miss France,' she had a habit of shortening names, 'well, you've got a figure in a thousand, you have. Curves in the right places, shaped like an 'ourglass, and no spare flesh to speak of. It's a sin to put you in that blue serge. I once saw some of the grand ladies up at Granter's. Their dresses was all sparkling. It was a ball or something . . . and they was all out of doors as well. You could hear the music. I was rather friendly with one of the footmen there. Hans . . . or something like that . . . Funny name for a man, but he was Hans all right. Hands everywhere they shouldn't have been if you ask me -- but I shouldn't be talking like this in front of Miss Pip.'

'My sister is well aware of your meaning,' said Francine, and we were all laughing together.

'Well,' went on Daisy, 'this Hans got very friendly with me. He used to take me into the kitchens and show me round. Used to give me things to take home. It was before I got a place up at Greystone. We was hoping I'd get a place at Granter's and I would have done if they'd stayed. Let me comb your hair for you, Miss France. I've always wanted to get my hands on that hair. It's what I call real pretty hair.'

Francine laughed good-humouredly and let Daisy dress her hair for her. It was amazing what she did with it.

'I've got a real gift. One of these days I'll be a lady's maid, you see. Perhaps when you get married, eh, Miss France?'

The talk of Francine's marrying set a gloom over us.

'Oh, it's that Mr Arthur, is it?' said Daisy. 'He looks a cold fish, but you never know with men. Not your sort at all . . . no more than he would be mine. Not that he'd look at me . . . well, not with a view to marrying. Some of them has notions though . . . a quick bit of fun and no more said and the next day looking at you as though he can't remember who you are. I know that sort. But Mr Arthur is not one of them.'

Aunt Grace came up to see us. She had changed and

Charles Daventry's coming to the house had had its effect on her. There was an alert look in her eyes. Was it a hopeful look?

Francine said she was proud to have been the means of bringing them to each other's notice again.

'Now,' she said, 'we will watch for results.'

How we revelled in those days of freedom! To be in this ancient house was exciting, as it was to feel its mystery and lure; to laugh, to forget the menace of the future. What pleasure that was! And we lived in the present – Francine and myself – and I fancy Daisy did all the time.

Aunt Grace was the first one to break the spell. She paid daily visits at precisely the same time every afternoon and brought messages from Cousin Arthur. Daisy said he would consider it improper to enter a girl's bedroom unless he were married to her. That sobered us a little. Talk of marriage in the same context as Cousin Arthur always did.

There was a softness about Aunt Grace. I wondered whether she had visited Charles Daventry and came to the conclusion that she had. She looked at Francine with great sympathy in her doe's eyes. 'Your grandfather is pleased to hear that you are progressing well. He always asks how you are.'

'I am grateful,' said Francine with a touch of irony. 'It's very gracious of him.'

Aunt Grace hesitated. 'He will have something to say to you when you come down.'

She was looking speculatively at Francine and my heart sank. I knew what our grandfather would have to say. After all, Francine's seventeenth birthday was not far away. Seventeen was a mature age . . . mature enough for marriage.

What should we do?

Aunt Grace's efforts to make the prospect sound pleasant failed miserably. She knew what it meant to suffer from our grandfather's efforts to rule our lives.

'I won't do it,' said Francine emphatically when Aunt

Grace had gone. 'Nothing would induce me. Now we had better start thinking of a way out.'

The subject lay heavily upon us when next day Daisy came in to us in a twitter of excitement.

'I was leaning over the fence down at the cottage with Jenny Brakes when I saw them arriving . . .'

Jenny Brakes occupied the cottage next to the Emmses; the other cottages were occupied by gardeners who worked at the Manor.

'You can imagine I was all ears and eyes. They'd all come from the station . . . just like they did before. I called out to Ma and out she came and we stood there . . . watching. They all went into Granter's. Some of the servants, they was . . . and there'll be more coming now. It's all set for the transformation scene . . . that's what it is. We're in for a bit of fun. High jinks up at the Grange.'

We forgot what our grandfather was going to suggest to Francine when she appeared downstairs. We talked excitedly with Daisy and she told us what had happened on other occasions when the exotic inhabitants returned to Granter's Grange.

❧ Strangers at the Grange

From that time there was change.

Francine could no longer cling to the refuge of our room and must appear at meals. Our grandfather welcomed her with the faintest glow of warmth in his eyes. Cousin Arthur, though restrained, was clearly pleased to see her back. As for Aunt Grace, she still wore that bemused look which had settled on her since Charles Daventry had carried Francine into the hall and I noticed that she wore a rather pretty lace collar on her dress.

The tension was rising and it was most noticeable in our grandfather who had become almost benign. He was as near affectionate towards Francine as he could possibly be. He came upon her once in the gardens and said he would walk with her and she told me afterwards that he talked all the time about the estate, how vast it was, how profitable and how it had been Ewell land for centuries. One morning he said he wished her to ride with him to see some of the tenants and they went off in his carriage, Cousin Arthur accompanying them; they took wine at the house of Mr Anderson the agent, who, said Francine, was ominously polite to her. 'In fact,' she said, 'the situation is becoming more ominous every day. Soon I shall be presented with the royal command. What *am* I going to do, Pippa?'

I had no suggestion to offer, though we had discussed the matter endlessly. Francine was making up her mind that there was only one thing to do and that was run away. That was an easy answer but the great problem was: Where to?

Our grandmother sensed the growing tension, of which she seemed more aware than sighted people. 'Something will turn up, my dear,' she said. 'Be true to yourself.'

Daisy burst into our room one day. She no longer behaved as a servant with us. We were like conspirators. Daisy was no respecter of persons; she was impetuous, affectionate and good-natured. She was resourceful too. Continually in trouble with the housekeeper, Mrs Greaves, and threatened with dismissal, she was never downcast.

'What is to be, will be,' she said with feeling. 'And something will always turn up,' she added as our grandmother had. She was full of wise sayings and they were all optimistic. 'Wait and see. There's something round the corner. The Good Lord will take care of you.' I did point out to her once that the only time she mentioned the Good Lord was in his capacity to take care of wayward sinners. 'He won't mind,' she retorted. 'He'll say it's only that Daise.'

She was in a state of great excitement. 'Hans is back,' she told us.

'Hans of the straying hands?' asked Francine.

'Oh, he's all that . . . worse than he ever was, if you ask me. Is he glad to see me!'

'Tom won't be pleased,' I said.

'Oh, Tom's got nothing to complain of, I promise you.'

'Don't promise us, promise him,' laughed Francine. And we were all laughing together. We were glad to forget the shadow looming over us, if only temporarily.

'There'll be grand doings up there, Hans says. This Baron's coming. He's ever so important. He's of their branch of the family. The others, of course, are against it.'

'What are you talking about, Daisy?' demanded Francine.

'Well, Hans talks a bit about it, you know.'

'Don't become involved in Germanic politics, Daisy,' said Francine with mock seriousness. 'I hear they are very involved.'

'Hans says he'll show us over the house. I told him you'd

like to see it. That'll be before they arrive. It'll have to be soon. They're due any day.'

'It's nice to be able to send out our agents,' said Francine.

'You get away with you,' retorted Daisy.

A few days later she told us we could go that afternoon because the family was due to arrive the next day. An air of excitement prevailed throughout the morning. I don't know how we got through our lessons without Miss Elton's suspecting that something was afoot. It was necessary to slip out quietly and we met Daisy, as we had arranged, at her mother's cottage.

'We'll have to go round by the stables,' she told us. 'Hans says most of the servants will be taking a nap at this time. They do, you know.' Daisy clicked her tongue. 'Foreigners!' she added.

'Some people do here, you know,' said Francine, who could never resist stating a truth.

'Well, *they* do regular. And Hans says it's safe. He says even if some of them's about it don't matter. They know who you are, and they'll like to see you there. Hans says that Miss France is *schön* . . . or something like that. When I said you wanted to see the house he kissed his hand and threw it out . . . just as though he meant it for you. He's a one, he is. Are you ready?'

Daisy, like Francine, always liked to add a touch of drama to a situation, and I thought Daisy's attitude to life was just what Francine needed at this time and I was grateful to her.

When we reached the stables at Granter's Grange, Hans was waiting for us. He clicked his heels and bowed from the waist and it was obvious from the way he looked at Francine that he admired her. When she addressed him in German he was delighted. He was very fair – almost white-haired, and his eyes had a startled look because his eyebrows and lashes were so fair they were scarcely perceptible. His skin was fresh, his teeth good and his smile merry.

The Baron will be coming,' he said. 'It's a very important visit.'

Daisy insisted that this should be translated for her benefit and Francine asked how long the Baron would stay.

Hans lifted his shoulders. 'It is not known,' he answered. 'So much depends,' he said in English with a strong foreign accent. 'We are not sure. There has been . . .'

'Not another of them coops?' suggested Daisy.

'Oh . . . a coup . . . yes . . . You could say.'

'They're always having them,' said Daisy, who was enjoying her role.

'Come,' went on Hans. We followed and he led the way through a side door. We were in a dark passage and followed him into a large kitchen with tiled floor and benches round two sides, under which were arches in which stood baskets containing vegetables and food of various kinds – all strange to us. On a chair was a fat man fast asleep.

Hans held his hands to his lips and we tiptoed through.

We were in a lofty and beautifully panelled hall. There was an enormous fireplace at one end with seats on either side and I noticed very fine linenfold around it. In the centre of the hall was a massive oak table on which stood a candelabrum. There were several wooden seats against the wall and on these walls weapons which must have been used by our ancestors, since this was the home of our grandmother and it had obviously been sold furnished to the foreigners. 'The great hall,' announced Hans.

'It's a lovely old house,' remarked Francine. 'Very different from Greystone Manor. Do you feel it, Pippa? There isn't that air of gloom.'

'It's our dark furniture,' I said.

'It's our grandfather,' added Francine.

'There is the staircase,' Hans went on. 'There are steps down to the chapel. We do not use that. So we will go up. Here is the dining salon.'

It was a beautiful room with three large leaded windows

On the big table stood a candelabrum similar to that in the hall; there were tapestries on the walls in blues and cream colours and they matched the tapestry on the chairs.

'It's beautiful,' breathed Francine.

'I can understand our grandfather's wanting to buy it,' I murmured.

'I'm glad he didn't,' said Francine vehemently. 'He would have made it as gloomy as the Manor. Now it's a wonderful house. Do you sense it, Pippa? Something in the air?'

Dear Francine, she was really very worried. She was looking for some miracle and she was getting so depressed that she was looking in the most unlikely places.

We mounted some more stairs. 'It is here that they come to drink the wine.'

'It's where the ladies retire after dinner,' said Francine, 'when they leave the men at the table with their port.'

There were stairs leading out of an archway and we were in a corridor. We went along this, past several doors. Hans lifted a finger to warn us to be quiet. Daisy giggled softly and I wanted to do the same. The fact that we were trespassing could only add to the excitement. I was longing to tell my grandmother that we had seen her old home.

We mounted more steps to the solarium, which was not unlike the one at Greystone. There were windows on each side and my imagination peopled it with glamorous men and women in splendid clothes talking excitedly about what was happening in their country. In the solarium was a hole in the wall and so discreetly did it merge into the stone that I should not have known it was there if Hans had not pointed it out to us.

'From it you can look down into the hall,' he explained. 'On the other side is another. You can look down on to the chapel. Very good idea. You can see who comes . . .'

'How fascinating!' cried Francine. 'Do you remember our grandmother talked of the Peeps? That's what she called them. She said they sometimes did not go down to the chapel service but watched from the solarium.'

Hans was suddenly alert. He stood very still, his head on one side and the colour slowly drained away from his face.

'What's wrong?' asked Daisy.

'I can hear carriage wheels. Oh no . . . no. This must be . . .'

He ran swiftly to the window and putting his hands to his head looked as though he were about to tear out his hair.

'Oh, what shall we do! They have come. It is too soon. It should be tomorrow. What shall I do with you?'

'Don't worry about us,' said Daisy.

'I must go,' cried Hans in desperation. 'I must be there. The whole staff is assembling. I must not be missing . . .'

'What should we do?' asked Francine.

'You stay . . . You hide . . .' He looked about him. 'See those curtains . . . Hide behind them if anyone comes. I will get you out as soon as I can. I will free you. But now . . . I must go.'

'You go,' said Daisy soothingly. 'We'll be all right. Leave it to us.'

Hans nodded and stumbled out of the room.

Daisy was shaking with laughter. 'Well, here's a nice kettle of fish!' she said.

'What will they think of us,' said Francine. 'We've no right to be here. We shouldn't have come.'

'No use crying over spilt milk, Miss France. No good shutting the stable door when the horse is stolen. Hans will get us out. He's clever, Hans is.'

The house which had been quiet before was now alive with the sound of the bustle of important arrivals. Daisy tiptoed to the Peep and beckoned to us.

The hall was full of people. The fat cook whom we had seen slumbering in the kitchen now wore a splendid white coat and a tall white hat and gloves. He was standing at the head of a line and opposite him was a woman of very proud bearing whose bodice sparkled with black jet.

The door opened and a magnificently attired man came in and shouted something. Then the personages arrived. There were a man and a woman, and the servants who had formed into lines bowed so low that I thought they were going to knock their heads together. The recipients of all this homage were dressed in travelling clothes; with them was a tall, youngish man with very fair hair. Others were coming in – about twenty in all and among them were a girl and a boy.

The servants began to move away, scuttling in all directions while the arrivals were making their way to the staircase.

'We have to look out now,' said Daisy. 'We'd better hide behind these curtains. Hans will know where to look for us when he comes.'

'They won't come here,' I said. 'They'll go to their rooms to wash off the stains of travel.'

'They might,' said Francine. 'Come on, let's hide ourselves.'

There were sounds of running footsteps on the stairs and a babble of voices. We had hidden ourselves just in time when the door of the solarium was opened. I felt my heart beating wildly as I visualized the outcome of exposure. I imagined our being sent back to the Manor while complaints were made to our grandfather. That we should be in great trouble, I knew.

A girl came into the room. She appeared to be about my age. She stood for a moment looking round while we all held our breath asking ourselves if we were properly hidden. She tiptoed forward and stood still as though listening. Then she said in German: 'Who's there?'

I felt sick with shame and horror. Then she said in heavily accented English: 'Who is hiding? I know you are there. I see a foot under the curtain.'

It was Francine who stepped out. She knew exposure was imminent anyway.

'Who are you?' asked the girl.

'I am Francine Ewell of Greystone Manor,' said Francine.

'You are visiting us?'

'Yes,' answered Francine.

'And there are others?'

Daisy and I came out then. The girl's eyes rested on me, I supposed because we were of the same age.

'You visit?' she said, looking at me.

I decided that the best thing was to tell the truth. 'We were being shown over the house,' I said. 'We were interested because it was our grandmother's old home.'

'You know my father . . . my mother . . .'

'No,' I said.

Francine cut in then. 'I have no doubt we shall if they are staying long in the neighbourhood. We are from Greystone Manor. Perhaps we should go now.'

'Wait,' said the girl. She ran to the door. 'Mutti,' she called.

A woman had come into the room. She was stately and stood looking at us in astonishment. Now we knew we were truly caught.

Francine stepped forward and said in fair German and with dignity: 'You must forgive us. We have been guilty of an indiscretion. We were eager to see the house because it was once our grandmother's home and she often talks of it. We did not know that you would be returning and we thought it would be a good opportunity to look over it today . . .' She trailed off. It was a limp excuse and the woman continued to look at her very curiously.

'What is your name?' she asked.

'Francine Ewell. I live at Greystone Manor with my grandfather. This is my sister Philippa and Daisy our maid.'

The woman nodded. Then she smiled slowly. She kept her eyes on Francine who, I must say, looked particularly lovely with the flush in her cheeks and the sparkle in her eyes which the adventure had given her.

The woman said: 'We have just arrived. It was good of you to call. You must drink a glass of wine with me.'

Daisy had stepped back. I think she was quite speechless with admiration for Francine's skill in extricating us from a delicate situation.

'Come with me,' said the woman. 'And you . . . you are?'

'Daisy,' said Daisy, for once overawed.

'I shall send . . .'

At that moment Hans appeared. He was intensely nervous and when he saw who was there he looked as though he was uncertain whether to turn and run or break out into incoherent explanations.

'We have visitors, Hans,' said the woman in German which both Francine and I could understand perfectly. 'Take . . . Daisy to the kitchen and give her some wine. And send up more wine to the *Weinzimmer*.'

Hans certainly looked astonished. Daisy went over to him and I was sure she gave him one of her winks, though I couldn't see her. She went off with him, and Francine and I followed our hostess down the stairs to the smaller room through which we had recently passed.

'Please to sit,' commanded our hostess. 'Now tell me. You are from Greystone Manor. It is the Big House here. Bigger than this one. We are just the Grange, eh? It is good of you to call.'

Francine said it was hardly a call. It was a piece of impertinence.

'Impertinence?' she cried. 'What is this impertinence? An English custom?'

Francine laughed in her infectious way and our hostess was soon joining in.

'You see,' Francine explained, 'we were very curious.'

The woman listened intently as the wine came and with it the girl who had first discovered us.

'Tatiana, what is it you wish?' asked the woman.

The girl said in voluble German that she wished to see the visitors and the woman, whom we presumed to be her mother, chided her. 'It is not polite to speak in a language other than that of our guests. You have your lessons in English. Come . . . you must speak in that language.'

Francine said. 'We have some German. We learned to speak it when we were with our parents. And now we have a governess who is half German and speaks the language with us.'

'Ah, that is very good. Language can be a problem. Now they tell me this room was known as the Punch Room. I said, "What is this Punch?" and they tell me it is a drink . . . a kind of wine. Then I say "This shall be the *Weinzimmer*" . . . so here we drink our wine with our guests.'

Tatiana sat down and watched us intently. During the conversation our hostess told us that she had had a Russian mother and that her daughter had been named for her. She was the Gräfin von Bindorf and she and the Graf with their family would be staying here for a while.

It was an extraordinary half-hour. Here we were being entertained by the Gräfin von Bindorf, sipping the wine which had been brought to us and being treated like honoured guests instead of interlopers. She asked a great many questions about us and we told her how when our father had died we had come to Greystone Manor to be with our grandparents. Tatiana asked a few questions, mostly concerning me, and as Francine was talking freely with the Gräfin, I saw no reason why I should not do the same with Tatiana.

At length Francine said we should go, and the Gräfin replied that we must call again. I could see Francine wanted to invite her to Greystone Manor but restrained herself from that folly in time.

We were accompanied to the door where we were joined by Daisy. We were all excited and still marvelling, and talked incoherently all the way home. Daisy said that Hans was amazed at the way it had turned out and he was grateful to us for keeping him out of it.

Francine thought the Gräfin charming. She was dismayed at the prospect of her calling at the Manor.

'It makes you realize,' she said, 'what restricted lives we lead. Is it going to be like that forever?'

I saw by the light in her eyes that she was determined that it should not be.

We did not sleep that night but lay awake talking about the adventure, and Francine came to the conclusion that we might let a week pass and then call again.

Daisy was in a state of great excitement. She and Hans were very friendly again and Tom of the stables was green with jealousy. Daisy was delighted to be the object of so much desire.

Francine's seventeenth birthday was in a few weeks' time and as we sat at dinner the night after our adventure our grandfather commented on the fact, and added that he thought it was an occasion which we should celebrate. Aunt Grace nervously fingered her collar and tried to simulate excited interest. She knew all too well what the purpose of this entertainment would be and being herself a victim of our grandfather's despotic orders she feared for Francine.

Francine said afterwards: 'You know what he will do at the party. He will announce the engagement.'

I nodded gloomily and waited for some inspiration.

'I'm going to call on the Gräfin,' said Francine. 'We'll go this afternoon.'

'It will be fun,' I replied. 'But how is that going to help?'

'I don't know,' she replied, but there was speculation in her eyes as though she had some scheme in mind.

Boldly we went through the gates; we pulled the bell and heard it clanging through the house. A servant in colourful livery opened the door and we stepped into the hall.

'We have come to call on the Gräfin in response to her invitation,' said Francine importantly in German.

The man replied: 'The Gräfin is not at home.'

'Oh?'

'What about the Lady Tatiana?' I said with sudden inspiration. She had been interested in us so perhaps she would receive us.

The servant shook his head. It seemed that she was not at home either. So there was nothing to be done but retire crestfallen. The door shut on us and just as we were turning away a man on horseback rode up. He leaped down, looked at us and bowed. He called out and a groom came running to take his horse.

'You look . . . lost,' he said, his eyes on Francine. 'Perhaps I can help.'

He spoke good English with only the faintest trace of a foreign accent. Francine had brightened considerably. He was extremely handsome, tall, blond and in his early twenties I imagined, with grey eyes and a ready smile.

'We had come to see the Gräfin,' Francine explained. 'She did ask us to call . . . and now we find that she is not at home.'

'She will be here later today, I believe. I wonder if it would be acceptable for me to take her place? Come, let me offer you tea . . . is that not what you would take at this hour?'

Francine's cheeks were touched with the delicate rose colour which was so becoming and her blue eyes sparkled with excitement. 'That would be most kind,' she said.

'Come then.' He pulled the bell and the manservant opened the door. 'We have guests,' he added.

The servant showed no surprise to see us back again and the young man gave orders in German for tea to be served. Then he ushered us into the room in which we had taken wine on the previous occasion and bade us sit down.

'You must be related to the Gräfin,' said Francine.

'No . . . no. We are not related. Tell me about yourselves.'

Francine explained that we lived at Greystone Manor and how we had met the Gräfin. 'She did say we might call again,' she insisted again.

'She would hope for that. She will be desolate to have

missed you. That is unfortunate for her . . . but fortunate for me.'

'You are very gallant,' said Francine with a hint of coquetry.

'Who could be aught else in the presence of such beauty,' he answered.

Francine, as always, blossomed under admiration, even though she had always had a great deal of it, and she was soon chatting away telling him about our life on the island and at Greystone Manor, to which he listened very attentively.

'I am so happy that I came when I did,' he said. 'It has been a great pleasure meeting you and the silent one.'

'Oh, Pippa is not usually silent. She generally has plenty to say for herself.'

'I shall look forward to discovering what she has to say.'

Tea had arrived and with it the most appetizing little cakes I had ever seen. They were decorated with whorls of cream and were of various colours.

The young man was looking at Francine. 'You must do . . . what do they say? . . . the honours? It is the lady's place, is it not?'

Francine settled happily behind the teapot, her fair hair breaking free of the ribbon which tied it back and which she was expected to wear at the Manor, and falling about her face. I had rarely seen her look so lovely.

We discovered the young man's was Rudolph von Gruton Fuchs and that his home was in a place called Bruxenstein.

'It sounds very grand and far away,' said Francine.

'Far away . . . well, yes, perhaps. And grand? Maybe you will visit my country one day and see for yourself.'

'I should enjoy that.'

'It would be a great joy to welcome you. Just now . . .' He hesitated and looked at her ruefully. 'There are troubles,' he added. 'There often are.'

'It's a troublesome part of the world, I suppose,' she said.

'You could call it that But it is far away, eh, and we are here on this delightful afternoon.'

He turned his eyes on me but I had the impression that he found it hard to tear them away from Francine.

'You must have many adventures,' said Francine.

'None,' he assured her, 'as pleasant as this one is proving to be.'

Francine was talking a good deal. She seemed to be intoxicated with the pleasant afternoon. She was determined to enjoy herself in a fever of excitement because she was so dreading what her birthday party would bring forth. Although she swore she would never accept marriage with Cousin Arthur, she was practical enough to wonder what we would do when our grandfather became incensed by her refusal . . . or worse still would not accept it. So for this brief interlude she was determined to enjoy herself. She likes Rudolph, I thought. She likes him as much as he likes her. I could see that she was trying to prolong the afternoon but eventually and most reluctantly she rose and said we must go.

'So soon?' he asked.

But it was not soon. We had been talking for an hour and a half.

'There is a strict rule in our house,' she said. I thought it was rather indiscreet of her to talk about our home in the manner she did.

He said he would walk back with us but that threw Francine into such a panic that he desisted. But he did walk with us to the gate and there, bowing low, kissed our hands. I noticed that he held Francine's longer than he did mine.

We broke away and started to run across the field to the Manor.

'What an adventure!' said Francine. 'I don't think I ever had an adventure like that.'

The invitation came through Hans to Daisy who brought it to

Francine. It was from the Gräfin and she asked Francine to visit her that day at three o'clock as she had a request to make of her. I was not mentioned in the invitation so Francine went alone. I was all agog to hear what had happened and was waiting for her in the field near the cottages.

When she came away about an hour later she looked flushed and more excited than I had seen her for a long time.

'Did you see him?' I asked. 'This . . . er . . . Rudolph?'

She shook her head. She looked bemused. Had she found another admirer? I wondered.

'It's so exciting,' she said. 'I saw the Gräfin. What do you think? She has asked me to the ball.'

'To a ball! What do you mean?'

'That they are to have a ball and I am invited. It's as simple as that.'

'It doesn't sound in the least simple to me. Will Grandfather agree? And you'll need a ball dress.'

'I know. I thought of all that. But I said I'd go.'

'In blue serge or perhaps your best poplin?'

'Don't be defeatist. I'll have a new dress somehow.'

'Somehow is the word.'

'What's the matter with you, Pippa? Are you jealous?'

'Never!' I cried. 'I want you to go to the dance with Rudolph, but I can't see how you're going to manage it, that's all.'

'Pippa,' she said, and I have never seen a stronger purpose in anyone's face than I saw in Francine's at that moment, 'I *am* going.'

All the way back to the house and halfway through the night we discussed it. Rudolph had not been there. She had had tea with the Gräfin, who had told her that there was to be this ball and she would be delighted if Francine would attend. She was unsure what she should do about sending an invitation. We must have conveyed very clearly what it was like living at Greystone Manor and she no doubt guessed that to have sent an invitation through our grandfather would have meant an instant refusal Francine must come, she said. If she did not the ball would not be the same.

In an excess of euphoria and a certain unswerving belief in her powers to achieve the impossible, Francine had promised, sweeping the practical details airily aside. Something would turn up.

'A fairy godmother?' I suggested. 'Who'll that be? Perhaps they have them in Bruxenstein. I can't imagine one in the Manor. Shall we be able to find a pumpkin for the carriage? I believe there are a few rats around so we might be all right for the horses.'

'Pippa, stop joking about a serious matter.'

It was all rather hopeless but I was glad that temporarily her mind was taken off those impending birthday celebrations.

When we visited our grandmother the next day, with that acute sensibility of hers, she immediately realized that something had happened. She knew that Francine had been tense and uneasy because she feared she was about to be forced into marriage with Cousin Arthur, and it was not long before the whole story was drawn out of us. She listened entranced. 'So the old Punch Room has become the *Weinzimmer*. I like the sound of the Gräfin and the charming Rudolph.' Our grandmother was a very romantic lady and it must have been a terrible tragedy to be married to a man like our grandfather. Miraculously the experience had not soured her; it had made her more gentle and tolerant.

She said: 'Francine must go to the ball.' I listened in amazement. Our grandmother had an answer to everything. The dress? Wait a moment. She believed there was some material in one of her chests. Once she had dreamed she would celebrate the birth of her second child. No . . . not Grace . . . the one who had been stillborn. She had bought at the time some beautiful blue silk chiffon embroidered with stars in silver thread. 'It was the most beautiful material I ever saw,' she said. 'But when I lost the child I couldn't bear to look at it. I folded it up and put it away. If the silver stars haven't tarnished . . . We'll ask Agnes to find it.'

Agnes was delighted to see her mistress so happy. She once whispered to me that she had changed since we came. 'She was a little like your sister, I imagine, when she was young . . . but there's more freedom now.' Not much more, I thought. It was gratifying that Agnes was an ally, for we needed allies.

We found the material. Francine cried out in delight when she saw it. The stars were as bright as they had been on the day when our grandmother had bought it.

'Take it,' she said, smiling as though she could see it clearly, and I was sure she could in her mind. 'Go to Jenny and get her working at once. She'll do it well. She makes ball dresses for girls' coming out now and then.'

Excitedly we called on Jenny. Daisy came with us for she considered she was involved in the adventure as it had been through her that we had first come to the Grange and set everything in motion. She herself was deep in an emotional affair of her own. Tom of the stables had discovered her friendship with Hans and, as she said, he was 'hopping mad' and threatening all sorts of reprisals. Life was certainly exciting for these two heroines of romance – and I was content to be a looker-on.

Daisy had it from Hans that the Gräfin had been more or less commanded to invite Francine because of the Baron, who was very important. He was in fact the most important of them all. Hans knew why but he wasn't telling even Daisy. 'He will . . . given time,' said Daisy confidently. She clearly enjoyed being drawn into this vortex of intrigue.

Jenny Brakes was a little astonished when she saw the material and heard that she was to make it into a ball gown.

'For your birthday party, Miss Francine?' she asked. 'Miss Grace has already told me I was to go up to the house. She's got a nice piece of taffeta she tells me for your party dress. It's going to be a very special occasion.'

'No,' said Francine. 'This is to be a very special dress.'

'Made in secret,' added Daisy.

Jenny looked frightened.

'Come on,' said Daisy. 'Who's to know?'

'Really . . . I don't understand, Miss Francine . . .'

'It's simple,' Francine explained. 'I want a ball gown made quickly, and you just do not mention that you are making it for me.'

'But you're having the taffeta . . .'

'I'm having this too,' said Francine.

Poor Jenny Brakes! I knew how she was feeling. She greatly feared to offend my grandfather. She lived in one of his cottages and if he knew that she was making a ball gown for his granddaughter he would be very angry indeed; and when he was angry he was a man to show no mercy. It was I who came up with the solution. Jenny need not know at all that it was in secret. The gown was to be made for Francine and as it was needed in a hurry it was simpler for Jenny to make it in her own cottage, as she sometimes did. If we were discovered Jenny could be proved to be entirely innocent of any intrigue.

At last she agreed and sketched out a design right away. What fun we had making our suggestions. It must be daring; it must be simple; it must be cut to show Francine's swanlike neck. It must accentuate her tiny waist. It must have a billowing skirt.

The excitement was so intense that I thought Francine would betray it. I believe Aunt Grace knew something was in the air but she was too immersed in her own life at the moment, for since Charles Daventry had carried Francine into the house, I believed she was visiting him in secret.

We made a great plan of action. On the night of the ball Francine would slip out of the house and go to the Emmses' cottage. Daisy's mother was a willing conspirator, so there could be no blame attached to Jenny. Mrs Emms would keep the dress in her cottage for Francine to change into. Then she could slip across the lawn to the Grange. Like her daughter,

Mrs Emms was fond of adventure. If she were discovered and my grandfather's wrath was aroused she would take the consequences. 'He would never turn us out,' she said. 'Not the Emmses. We've been in this cottage too long and my Jim's too useful a man.'

So it was all settled.

Daisy reported that this was going to be the most magnificent of all the balls they had had at the Grange. It was in honour of a very important personage – presumably Francine's admirer. 'The preparations . . .' cried Daisy. 'All the food . . . all the flowers and things. It'll be royal . . . that's what it'll be. I reckon they couldn't do better at Buckingham Palace or that Sandringham where the Prince of Wales enjoys himself so much.'

The great day came and we could scarcely contain our excitement. Somehow the hours passed. We were very absent-minded at our lessons and Miss Elton remarked on our inattention. I think she knew something was afoot and as the whole household was aware that Francine was destined to marry Cousin Arthur, I was sure that if they knew what it was they would have done their best to shield her.

I went with Francine to the Emmses' cottage and there, with Daisy, I helped to dress her. Several little Emmses looked on in wonder and when she was ready she looked like a fairy princess. Excitement enhanced her beauty and there could not have been a colour which suited her better than the blue silver-spattered chiffon. Of course she needed silver shoes and had only her black satin ones, but they scarcely showed. She looked perfect, I told her.

The arrangement was that I should be watching at our window and when she came home I would creep down and let her in. She would have been to the Emmses' first and changed into her day clothes, leaving the gown at the Emmses' cottage to be brought back next day by Daisy.

'Such an operation needs careful planning,' I had pointed out. 'Every detail has to be thought of.'

'Philippa is our General,' cried Francine with a giggle. 'I must obey her commands.'

So as everything had been so precisely arranged I felt that only bad luck could upset our plans. After watching – from a safe distance – Francine enter the Grange with the other guests, I went back to the Manor. I sat at my window, looking out over the lawns. In the distance I could see the towers of the Grange and the lights; I could even hear the faint strains of music. I could see the church too and the grey tombstones and I thought of poor Aunt Grace and Charles Daventry who had lacked the courage to make their own lives. Francine would never lack that courage.

'God's in his Heaven,' I thought, looking up at that black velvet sky, at the glittering stars and the moon that was almost full. What a beautiful sight! I prayed then for Francine's happiness, for a miracle to save her from Cousin Arthur. I remembered the old Spanish proverb my father referred to once. It was something like, 'Take what you want,' says God. 'Take it and pay for it.'

One took and one paid. One must never grudge the price. My father had taken a certain way of life which had denied him his patrimony, an old house full of family tradition. My grandfather had taken his own way. He might make others dance to his tune but he was bereft of love. I would not have been my grandfather for all the power in the world.

It was about eleven o'clock when I heard the commotion below. My heart beat so violently that it shook my entire frame. There had been no sign of Francine. She was to have come below my window, and I was to be at my post – which I was. But there was no Francine and surely eleven o'clock was too early to leave a ball.

I went to my door and listened. I could hear my grandfather's voice. 'Disgraceful . . . Fornicating . . . Sinful . . . Go to your room. I shall deal with this as you deserve. I will see you in the morning. You are disgusting. I could not believe my eyes . . . Under my roof . . . caught . . . *in flagrante delicto.*'

Someone was moving towards the stairs. I hastily shut my door and leaned against it, waiting. I expected Francine to burst in at any moment.

Nothing happened. Where was she? He had said: 'Go to your room.' But she did not come and I could not understand what it meant.

I was back at the window. All was quiet down there. I went to my door and listened. There were steps on the stairs. That was my grandfather going to his room.

I was bewildered and dreadfully afraid.

It was about half an hour later when there was a gentle knock on my door. I ran to it and Daisy almost fell into the room. Her hair was tousled and her eyes wide.

'It's that Tom,' she said. 'That's who it was. He told on us.'

'Was it you whom my grandfather was talking to?'

She nodded.

'Oh, Daisy. What happened?'

'We was caught . . . Hans and me . . . in the old bone-yard. I always liked it there. It's soft on the grass and it's life, ain't it . . . life among death.'

'You're crazy. I thought it was Francine. Come and sit by the window. I must keep watch for her. She'll still be at the ball.'

'For a long time, I reckon.'

'Tell me what happened with you.'

'Hans said he could slip away at half past ten and I said I'd be near Richard Jones. He had three wives and buried them all with him. It's a lovely stone he had done for himself and the three of them. You can lean against it and there's a beautiful guardian angel over it. It makes you feel kind of safe and happy. Tom liked it there too.'

'What were you doing?'

'The usual.' She smiled at the recollection. 'There's something about Hans, you know. Of course, Tom was hopping mad. Hans wrote a note saying he'd be there by Richard Jones and I lost the note. Tom must have got his hands on it. I never thought he'd tell like that . . . but you know how it is with jealousy. But you wouldn't, of course, being so young. Sometimes I forget how young you are, Miss Pip. What with me and your sister . . . well, we're sort of bringing you up fast. So there we were. Your grandfather must have seen us meet. Must have been hiding there. I bet it was behind Thomas Ardley. I never liked that stone. It always gave me the creeps. Then he ups and catches us . . . right in the act . . . you might say. He called out to us and there was I with my bodice open and half out of my skirt. And Hans . . . well. Your grandfather kept saying, "And in such a place . . ." Then he took me by the arm and dragged me back. You must have heard him in the hall. "Up to your room," he says. "I'll deal with you in the morning." It'll be out for me. What'll Ma say? She was dead set on me getting this place and settling down respectable.'

'You'll never be respectable, Daisy.'

'I reckon you're right,' she admitted ruefully. 'But I'll be out tomorrow. It'll be the tin box on my shoulder and home to Ma. She'll miss the money. Still, perhaps I'll get a place at the Grange. Hans could speak for me.'

We sat on at the window. Midnight struck on the old church clock. I felt wide awake. Daisy would certainly be dismissed. I tried to imagine what it would be like without her, for she had played a big part in our lives.

It was nearly two o'clock when Francine came in. I sped down and drew back the heavy bolt. She was starry-eyed, still living in a wonderful dream as we tiptoed back to our room. Daisy was still there and we hastily told Francine what had happened.

'Daisy, you idiot!' she cried.

'I know,' replied Daisy. 'But I'll be all right. I'll go and see Hans.'

'What was the ball like?' I asked.

She clasped her hands and her ecstatic expression told us all. It had been wonderful. She had danced with the Baron all the evening. Everyone had been charmed by her. They had all been foreigners, of course. 'It might have been that the ball was given in my honour. That was how it felt. And the Baron Rudolph . . . he is perfection. Everything I ever dreamed a man should be.'

'Everything that Cousin Arthur is not,' I added, and immediately wished I hadn't mentioned him because I feared his name would break the spell.

But it didn't. She scarcely noticed. She was bemused. It was no use trying to talk to her that night.

I told Daisy she should go to her room and get a little sleep. She must remember the ordeal she would have to face the next day. Reluctantly she went and Francine undressed slowly.

'It is something I shall never forget,' she said. 'No . . . no matter what happens. He wanted to bring me home so I had to explain and he took me to the Emmses' cottage and waited outside while I changed, and when I came out in my old serge he was still there. He brought me right to the edge of the lawn. I told him everything . . . about Grandfather and Cousin Arthur. He was very understanding.'

'It's over now, Francine,' I said.

'No,' she answered. 'It's only just beginning.'

The next morning we were all assembled in the chapel for the solemn denunciation. Francine and I sat together in the front row with Aunt Grace. The glow was still on my sister. I could see that, in her thoughts, she was still at the ball. Our grandfather came in with Cousin Arthur and I noticed a look of suppressed excitement in the former's face as though this was not entirely distasteful to him.

He stood up in the pulpit after Cousin Arthur had taken nis seat beside Francine. She moved a little closer to me as he did so and I wondered whether he noticed.

Grandfather lifted his hand and said: 'This is an occasion of great sorrow to me. I am faced with a situation which fills me with disgust and humiliation. One of my servants – one whom I had harboured under my roof – has behaved in such a manner as to bring disgrace to this house. I cannot express my horror at my discovery.'

Yet you are relishing that horror, Grandfather, I thought.

'This wanton creature has behaved in such a manner as decency forbids me to describe. She has been caught in the very act. Feeling it my duty, I forced myself to witness her depravity. She was in my care and I could not believe that a servant of mine could be guilty of such an act. I had to see it with my own eyes. Now she will stand before us all in her sinfulness. Yet I am going to ask God to show mercy to her, to give her an opportunity to repent.'

'Magnanimous of him,' Francine whispered.

'Let her be brought in,' he called.

Mrs Greaves came in with Daisy, who was wearing a coat over her dark dress, which was not the uniform provided to all the Greystone servants.

'Come here, girl,' said my grandfather. 'Let all see you that they may learn the lesson of your folly.'

Daisy came forward. She was pale and less sure of herself than I had ever seen her before, slightly defiant, not the chirpy Daisy we knew so well.

'This creature,' went on our grandfather, 'is so deeply immersed in depravity that not only does she sin but she must do it in a holy place. It may well be that there will be a result of last night's work. The evil that we do lives on to the third and fourth generation. I am going to ask you all to get down on your knees and pray for the soul of this sinner. There is yet time for her to repent her evil ways. I pray God she will do so.'

Our grandfather's eyes were glistening as he looked at Daisy and I believe he was imagining her in that position in which he had caught her and revelling in the memory in some strange way. I wondered if he were pleased when people committed sins because it made him appear all the more virtuous. But this was a particular sort of sin which had this effect on him. It was different when someone was caught stealing. One of the men had been dismissed for that and there had not been this ceremony in the chapel. This was like the puritans I had read about. I wondered he didn't want Daisy to have a scarlet letter sewn on her bodice.

Cousin Arthur preached a short sermon about the wages of sin and then we prayed again; and all the time Daisy was standing there looking rather bewildered. I wanted to go to her and put my arms about her and tell her that whatever she had done in the churchyard wasn't half as bad as what my grandfather was doing to her now.

At length the ceremony was over. My grandfather then said: 'Take your box, girl, and go. Never let us see your face here again!'

Francine and I went into the schoolroom. Miss Elton was there, pale and silent.

Francine suddenly burst out: 'I hate him. He's a wicked old man. I will not stay here.'

She was close to tears and we gripped each other's hands tightly. I knew I would never forget that horrible scene in the chapel. Miss Elton did not reprove us. She too had been shaken by what she had seen.

Later that day Francine said to me: 'I'm going to see Daisy. Are you coming?'

'Of course,' I replied, and we made our way to the cottage. Mrs Emms was there and as usual there were several children running in and out. Daisy was not at home.

'She's up at the Grange,' Mrs Emms told us, 'seeing that Hans.' Mrs Emms nodded grimly. 'So she's out of the Manor. I thought at first it was all along of you and that ball dress.'

'Our grandfather doesn't know anything about that,' said Francine.

Mrs Emms winked. 'It would be a case of God 'elp us all if he ever did.'

'Somehow now . . . I don't care about him. I hated him this morning . . . and that smug Arthur. I hate Greystone. I want to get away from it.'

'My poor Daise. And all for having a bit of fun in the graveyard. She's not the first, I shouldn't wonder.'

'We're worried about Daisy. What will she do?'

'She'll find something. Always able to look after herself, our Daise.'

'Do you think she'll be back soon?'

'Who's to say? Her own mistress now, she is.'

'Will you tell her we called,' said Francine. 'Tell her we hated it all as much as she did. Tell her we thought it was horrible.'

'I'll tell her that, Miss. She thinks a powerful lot of you two young ladies.'

As we were about to go Daisy herself came in. She looked quite different from the dejected sinner of the chapel. We flew at her and hugged her. She looked very pleased and Mrs Emms said: 'Well, fancy that.'

'Daisy,' cried Francine, 'we were so worried about you.'

'No need,' cried Daisy triumphantly. 'I've already got myself a situation.'

'No!' we cried together.

'Oh yes, Miss. Well, I had half a promise of it before. Hans says, "Why don't you come up the Grange? I'll speak for you." Well, there I am. And I've seen the chef there. A very important gentleman . . . all twirling moustache and fat cheeks. He gave me a pat and said, "Start tomorrow." Kitchen maid! And what a kitchen.'

'It's wonderful!' I cried.

Mrs Emms sat down, legs apart, a hand on each plump knee. She was nodding her head sagely. 'What 'appens when they go?' she asked. 'They never stay more than a few months.'

'Hans says he reckons I could go with them.'

The gaiety of the last few moments had faded. We were all thinking of when they were going. Mrs Emms would not want to lose Daisy. Nor should we. But Francine quite clearly found the prospect of their leaving so depressing that she could not bear to think of it.

Events moved quickly after that. The date of our house party was announced. It was to be the first week in September. Guests would arrive on the Monday; Francine's seventeenth birthday was on the Tuesday; there would be another day of entertainment and the guests would leave on the Thursday.

Jenny Brakes came to the house and made up the taffeta for Francine. It was in a dark red colour; I was to have dark blue – a nice, serviceable colour, said Aunt Grace. Poor Jenny Brakes was a little embarrassed; her recent sin in making the blue chiffon sat heavily upon her and in view of what had happened to Daisy Emms she was very uneasy. Making up a dress illicitly could not be as great a sin as fornication in a churchyard, but my tyrannical grandfather was greatly feared. Francine pointed out that it would have been the same if Daisy had not had a family nearby to go to; she would have been turned out just the same. 'He has no pity,' she said. 'If that is being a good man, then God preserve me from them.'

Her spirits were high during those days of approaching doom because she was going to the Grange every day. Sometimes she would ride out alone. But I knew she did not continue alone and that she was going to some rendezvous with the romantic Baron.

The invitations were sent out to the guests. Great preparations were being made. Mrs Greaves was delighted and said this was how it should be in a big house. She reckoned that in future there would be a great deal of entertaining. There would be the newlyweds to bring a younger spirit into the house and then they would have to think of a match for Miss Philippa.

I was very apprehensive because Francine was not nearly so disturbed as she should have been and I wondered what that meant.

About two weeks before the party our grandfather sent for Francine. She went to the library with her head held high and I waited in our bedroom terrified of what might happen, for it was perfectly obvious that we were moving towards a crisis.

In half an hour she came to our bedroom, her cheeks slightly flushed, her eyes very bright.

'Francine,' I cried. 'What happened?'

'He told me I was going to marry Cousin Arthur and that that sainted nephew of his had asked his permission for my hand which he had graciously given. Knowing that it was his wish, he had no doubt that I would accept it with delight.'

'What did you say?'

'I have been very clever, Pippa. I have let him believe that I will.'

'You mean you've changed your mind?'

She shook her head. 'I can't tell you any more yet. I'm going out now.'

'Where?'

She shook her head. 'I promise I'll tell you. Before I do anything I'll let you know.'

It was the first time I had not been completely in her confidence, and I was apprehensive. I felt that everything was changing about me. Daisy had gone. And what had Francine meant? Was she going to do what our grandfather wished and marry Cousin Arthur? Or else what?

Miss Elton asked me where she was and when I said I did not know she did not pursue the matter. Miss Elton had always seemed a colourless person, but I think she understood a good deal of what was going on; everyone in the household must have realized that Francine and Cousin Arthur were just about as unsuited to each other as two people could be.

I went up to our grandmother. We had told her about the ball and she had sat there smiling and holding our hands, as she liked to. She had been alarmed for Francine and believed that if Francine married Cousin Arthur her life would be intolerable. 'I would die happy if I knew you two girls were all right,' she had said. 'And by all right, I mean leading worthwhile lives which might not always be lived in perfect bliss . . . that would be asking too much . . . but lives you have made for yourselves. Your grandfather made my life what it was . . . empty . . . not mine at all. He has done the same for Grace. He tried to with your father. You must strike out boldly to live your own life. Take it . . . live it . . . and do not regret the consequences because it is what you have chosen.' I knew she was right. I told her about Daisy.

She said: 'He would call himself just. He has set up a code of morals which do not always add up to morality. Daisy is a girl who will always have men. She may well find herself in trouble through it. But she will work her way out. And his unkindness, his harshness, his revelling in that so-called justice which brings hardship to others, is a greater sin than any Daisy could commit in the graveyard. Dear child, this seems strange coming from me. In the old days I would not have said it . . . would not have thought it. It was only when blindness descended on me and I knew my life was virtually finished that I looked back over everything more clearly than I ever had when I could see with my eyes.'

'What do you think is happening at the Grange?' I asked.

'We can only guess. Perhaps there is an avenue of escape. She must not marry where she does not love. She must not become your grandfather's victim.'

Soon after I left my grandmother Francine came back. I had never seen her so excited. 'I am leaving Greystone,' she said. She threw herself into my arms and we clung together.

'Going away . . .' I stammered. 'I shall be left . . .'

'I will send for you. I promise.'

'Francine, when . . . how?'

'Rudolph and I are going to be married. We are leaving at once. It is all very complicated.'

'You are leaving England?'

'Yes. I shall go to his country. Pippa, I am so happy . . . It's all very involved. I shall learn about it. Pippa, I am so happy . . . except for one thing . . . leaving you.'

I had known that it was inevitable. She would never have married Cousin Arthur. This was escape and she was in love at the same time. I tried to think of her happiness, but I could only think of myself and the terrible loneliness of being without her.

'Cheer up, Pippa,' she said. 'It won't be for long. Rudolph says you can come to us . . . but not yet. He has to leave rather quickly. He is very important in his country and there are all sorts of intrigues . . . and that sort of thing. We can't do without each other . . . we both know that. So I'm going with him. We're leaving tonight. Help me get a few things together. Not much. I shall have everything new. I shall take my starry ball dress. I'll get that from the Emmses' cottage. Daisy is helping. Oh, Pippa, don't look so frightened. Don't look so lost. I'll send for you.'

I helped her get a few things together. She was so excited she could hardly speak coherently. I said, 'You must see our grandmother before you go. You must tell her.'

'She'll understand,' said Francine.

It was a strange evening. We dined as usual. Grandfather was in a benign mood because he believed everything was going to be as he wished. Cousin Arthur looked smug so I presumed he had heard that Francine would favour his suit. Aunt Grace said very little, as usual, but I think she was rather sad. Perhaps she had hoped Francine would not submit as she had had to. Perhaps she was planning rebellion herself and wanted the support of another rebel.

Francine was unnaturally bright, but no one seemed to notice it. Our grandfather looked at her with something like affection – or as near to that emotion as he could get.

As soon as the meal was over we retired to our room. Francine was leaving at ten o'clock and at a quarter before the hour she slipped out of the house with my help. I carried her cloak so that if we were seen she would not be dressed for outdoors.

We stood there, facing each other for a few moments. The night was still – not the slightest breeze to ruffle the leaves. Francine laughed on a high note. Then she reached for me and held me tightly.

'Oh, little Pippa,' she said, 'I wish you could come with me. If only I could take you I'd be perfectly happy. But soon . . . soon. I promise you.'

'Goodbye, Francine, write to me. Let me know all that happens.'

'I promise. Goodbye.'

She was gone.

I stood there for some minutes listening. I visualized her at the Emmses' cottage. Daisy would be there.

I remained there . . . listening. There was no sound at all. Then I turned and crept back to the quiet house, a feeling of desolation creeping over me such as I had never before known in the whole of my life.

Visits to a Vestry

Four years had passed since that night when Francine ran away and I had not seen her since. She wrote to me by way of the Emmses, feeling that if her letters were sent to Greystone Manor they might have been kept from me.

I never want again to live through such a time as that which followed her departure. My sense of loss was heartbreaking, so much so that my grandfather's wrath passed over me without affecting me in the least. I could only know that my beloved sister had gone. I had even lost Daisy. A few weeks after Francine's flight, the Graf and Gräfin with their household left the Grange, and Daisy, as a member of the staff, went with them.

On the morning after Francine had left the storm broke Her absence at breakfast naturally meant that I was questioned. When I said I did not know where she was, it was presumed at first that she had taken an early morning walk and forgotten the time. I did not say that her bed had not been slept in, for I did not know how far she had gone by that time and I had visions of my grandfather's going after her. In his new mood of tolerance towards my sister – for he was convinced she was going to fall in readily with his plans he allowed her absence at breakfast to pass. Although Miss Elton knew when she did not appear at lessons and Aunt Grace was aware of her absence, the news did not reach my grandfather until midday

Then the storm broke. I was questioned and blamed for not

reporting that she had left the night before. I faced him defiantly, too wretched to care what happened to me.

'She has gone away to be married to a Baron,' I said.

I was shouted at and shaken. I had been wicked. I should be severely punished. I had known what was happening and had done nothing to prevent it. His granddaughter was disgraced and dishonoured.

I took refuge with my grandmother and she kept me with her all day. My grandfather came up to her room and started shouting. She lifted her hand and raised her sightless eyes and said: 'Not here in this room, Matthew. This is my refuge. The child shall not be blamed. Pray leave her to me.'

I was surprised that he obeyed. She comforted me, stroking my hair. 'Your sister will lead the life she has chosen,' she said. 'She had to go. She could not have stayed here under your grandfather's rule. She has chosen the right way. As for you, little Pippa, you are desolate because you have lost your dearest companion, but your time will come. You will see.'

But she could not comfort me because there was no comfort. Perhaps somewhere within my innermost thoughts I knew that I had lost Francine forever. In the meantime I was at Greystone Manor – at the mercy of my grandfather.

After the Graf and his household had left the Grange we seemed to settle down to normal . . . the household, that was. Nothing could be as it had been for me without Francine. My grandfather ceased to mention my sister's name. He had announced in the beginning that she would never cross his threshold again, but he implied that he would still do his duty by me.

There was even stricter supervision than there had been before. Miss Elton was to go with me when I went out so that I was never alone. My religious instruction was to be intensified. It was quite clear that my beginnings in that heathen island had had a bad effect if the behaviour of my sister was anything to go by.

Miss Elton was sympathetic and that was a great help. She

had been fond of Francine as almost everyone had been and she hoped that everything would go well with her. So when I was with Miss Elton I was allowed to call at the Emmses' cottage and Daisy would meet me there. 'I promised your sister I would keep an eye on you,' she told me. 'Poor little Miss Pip. Not much fun up there with that old ogre as Miss France used to call him.'

When the Grange was empty again and Daisy had gone I was at my lowest ebb. Once I persuaded Miss Elton to let me run and look through the windows. When I saw the dust-sheeted furniture and the tallboy which looked like a human figure I wanted to fling myself to the ground and weep. I never went to peer in again. It was too heartbreaking.

I disliked Cousin Arthur as much as Francine had done. I hated the lessons I took with him. He was very fond of praying and would keep me on my knees for a long time while he exhorted the Almighty to make me a good woman obedient to my guardian, and full to overflowing with gratitude towards him.

I would find my thoughts straying to Francine and wondering what it would have been like if she had married Cousin Arthur instead of her Baron.

At least, I thought, she would be here.

Poor Aunt Grace was sympathetic but too much in awe of my grandfather to let it be known. My only solace in those days was my grandmother. She was the only real friend I had. Agnes Warden encouraged me to visit her often. I think she loved my grandmother dearly.

They say time heals all and although that is not entirely true it certainly numbs the pain.

A whole year passed – the most melancholy of my life, and my only interest was the constant hope of news from Francine.

One day when I was in the garden I saw one of the Emms children staring at me.

'Miss Pippa,' he called.

I turned to him and he looked about him to see if we were being watched. 'My mum's got something for you.'

'Thank you,' I said.

'Says will you go along and get it.'

'Tell her I'll be there as soon as I can.'

I had to go carefully. The order was that I was not to go out alone, so when I walked out with Miss Elton I said I wished to call at the Emmses' cottage and she waited for me in the field while I went.

Mrs Emms took a letter out of a drawer.

'Reckon it's that sister of yours,' she said. 'It come here. And there's one from our Daise. Jenny Brakes read it to me. Doing well, our Daise is. Oh, talk about high society. You can read Daise's. She got Hans to help her. Not much with a pen, our Daise. But I reckon you'll want to see what your sister's writ.'

'I'll take it home and read it there and I'll come back and see Daisy's letter tomorrow.'

Mrs Emms nodded and I ran out to Miss Elton. She did not ask what it was I had but I think she guessed, for when I reached Greystone Manor I went straight up to my room. My fingers were trembling as I opened the letter.

It was written on thick white paper almost like parchment, and there was a heavy gold crest on it.

My dearest Pippa,

I am taking the first opportunity to write to you. So much is happening here and I am very happy. Rudolph is everything I ever wanted a husband to be. We were married in Birley Church. Do you remember that church we looked at and liked so much? It caused some delay but Rudolph had arranged it before we left because we had to get away as quickly as possible. Rudolph is very important in his own country. I can't tell you how important.

We are surrounded by intrigue and have our enemies who are trying to rob him of his inheritance. Oh, it is hard to understand when you think of the way we have lived . . . the island and then Greystone. We didn't know a thing about the outside world, did we? Certainly not a place like Bruxenstein. There are several dukedoms here. There are margraves and barons, and they all want to be the chief one. But I am digressing. It is no use my trying to explain their politics to you because I don't understand them myself. But it does mean that we live rather dangerously. You want to hear about my adventures, though.

Well, Rudolph said we should be married *before* we reached Bruxenstein. It must be a *fait accompli* because there would be people who would try to prevent it. So we were married and I became Baroness von Gruton Fuchs. Fancy me with such a grand name. I call myself Mrs Fox-Fuchs, you see. It's much easier and it amused Rudolph.

So we were married and crossed the Channel and then we travelled right through France to Germany, finally reaching Bruxenstein. I wish you could see it, but you will. You are coming as soon as everything is settled. Rudolph says that I must not bring you here yet. It would cause trouble. You see he is what is called a great *parti*, which means he is the most eligible man here. He's a sort of heir to the crown . . . only it is not a kingdom . . . and they wanted him to marry someone else . . . someone they had chosen for him. These people will interfere . . . just like our grandfather. So it is a little awkward. I know you'll understand. Rudolph has to go carefully.

Well, I have the most wonderful clothes. We stopped a few days in Paris where they were made for me. I kept the blue starry dress. Rudolph said he will always love that one because I wore it on that night you remember.

But my things are truly magnificent now. I have a kind of tiara which I wear sometimes.

It would be such fun if you were here. Rudolph says it won't be long. They're afraid of what Daisy always used to call a 'coop'. Remember? They're always having these upheavals . . . it's jealousy between the rival members of the family. Some seem to want what others have got.

Now I have a secret to tell you. It's going to make a lot of difference if it's a boy. Yes, Pippa, I'm pregnant. Isn't that wonderful? Just fancy, you'll be an aunt. I tell Rudolph that I can't do without you and he keeps saying soon. He indulges me. I'm so happy. I wish they would stop their stupid quarrels though. I have to keep away from the castle . . . particularly now I'm pregnant. Rudolph is afraid for me. You see, if I have a son . . . But I'm talking their silly old politics again.

Dear Pippa, be ready at any time. One day you're going to find there is a bustle of preparations at the Grange. Then the army of servants will arrive and I shall be there . . . and next time, Pippa, dearest little sister, you are coming with me.

I love you more than ever.

Francine.

I read and re-read the letter. I carried it inside my bodice so that I could feel it against my skin. It livened my days and when I was feeling particularly unhappy I read it once more.

The hope that one day when I went past the Grange I should see signs of activity there, sustained me through the difficult times.

The days went past more quickly after the first few months. It was the same routine every day; breakfast with my grandfather, Aunt Grace and Cousin Arthur, prayers, lessons and riding with Miss Elton, visits to my grandmother and religious instruction from Cousin Arthur. I hated it and it would have been unendurable but for those sessions with my grandmother when we talked about Francine and imagined what was happening to her.

A whole year elapsed before I heard from Francine again. Once more the letter came through Mrs Emms.

Dearest Pippa [she wrote],

Don't think for a moment that I have forgotten you. Everything has changed so much since I last wrote. Then I was making plans for you to come here. Alas, they have all foundered. We had to move about a great deal and now we are living in a sort of exile. If you wrote to me I never received your letter and it may be that you did not get mine either. I expect it is still that dreary routine. Poor Pippa. As soon as everything is all right again you are coming here. I have told Rudolph that I must have my little sister with me. He agrees. He thought you were a darling – although he always says he hadn't eyes for anyone but me. But he wants you to come. He really does.

Now I must tell you about the Great Event. Yes, I am a mother. I have a son, Pippa. Think of that. The most adorable being you could ever imagine. He is fair with blue eyes. I think he is like Rudolph but Rudolph says he is the image of me. He has a grand name: Rudolph (after his father) Otto Friedrich von Gruton Fuchs. I call him my little Cub. Fox-cub, you see. I have no need to tell you that Cubby is the most miraculous child that ever was born. From the moment he arrived he showed an amazing grasp of affairs. But what would you expect of my child? I'd love you to see him. Oh, you must. We will think of something.

I wish these wretched old troubles would stop. We have to be so careful. It's all quarrelling between the various branches of the family. This one should have the margravate . . . or that one should. It is very tiresome and disrupting. Rudolph is always deeply involved. There are secret meetings and comings and goings at the hunting lodge at which we are now staying. Don't imagine it is some poor broken-down place. Nothing of the sort. These margraves and counts and grafs and barons knew how to look after themselves very well. We live in magnificent style but we have to be careful. Rudolph chafes against it. He says that as soon as we are back in the castle I may send for you. I can't wait. I tell Cubby about you. He just stares at me but I swear he is taking it all in because he looks so wise.

My love to you, dear sister. I think of you a great deal. Never fear. I am going to rescue you from Greystone Manor.

Francine, the Baroness (Mrs Fox).

After receiving the letter I lived in a state of euphoria for some weeks. I was constantly going past the Grange looking for signs of activity. There was none. I called on Mrs Emms often.

'No letters?' I would ask, and she would shake her head dolefully.

'There's one from Daise. All chuffed up she is. She's married that Hans. She's not with your sister though. She has to be with Hans, you see. She says they're all afraid of some coop or other.'

Then I began to be alarmed. I felt so frustrated. This talk of coups and life in a world far removed from the quiet peace of our Victorian England was hard to imagine. Everything about the Grange and its inhabitants had seemed to belong to a highly coloured romantic world where the strangest adventures were possible. It was something I could have imagined and talked of with Francine but the unreality of it all had come too close and Francine was drawn into it.

I prayed for her safety every night. That was a new element now. Fear for her safety.

There was another letter. This time it was all about the child. It was more than three years since Francine had left and her little Cubby must be eighteen months old now. He was beginning to talk and she could hardly bear him out of her sight. She talked to him about his Aunty Pippa.

> He likes the word Pippa and keeps saying it. It's strange how they like some words, and Pippa is a word which certainly appeals. He has a funny little toy. They call it a troll here. This troll goes to bed with him and he sucks its ear. He won't go to sleep without it. He calls it Pippa. There you are, sister. There is a troll named after you.
>
> You would love my baby. He is perfect.
>
> Your sister Francine.

That was the last letter I had had for a long time and I was very anxious. Mrs Emms said there was no news from Daisy either.

I was getting older too and those clouds which had seemed merely shadows on the horizon were beginning to gather overhead.

I had been only twelve when Francine had gone and now I was approaching my sixteenth birthday. There were ominous signs. My grandfather was taking an interest in me. He invited me to ride round the estate with him and I remembered how he had taken Francine. He was more affable to me. When I went riding with him Cousin Arthur came with us. Gradually I began to grasp the significance of this.

He had washed his hands of Francine but he had another granddaughter and in a short time she would be of a marriageable age.

My sixteenth birthday was celebrated with a dinner-party to which several of the surrounding families were invited. Jenny Brakes made a taffeta dress for me in a rather grown-up style and Miss Elton told me that my grandfather had expressed the wish – no, command – that I put my hair up for the occasion.

This was done and I looked quite grown up. I had an inkling of what was planned for my seventeenth birthday.

When I sat side by side with Cousin Arthur he would place his hand on my knee and I would feel my whole being recoil from him. I tried not to show my repugnance and for the first time since Francine had left I became obsessed with my own problem. I hated Cousin Arthur's cold flabby hands for I could guess what he was thinking.

I was able to talk to my grandmother of my fears.

'Yes,' she agreed, 'it is coming and you might as well realize it. Your grandfather is going to insist that you marry your Cousin Arthur.'

'I will not,' I replied, as firmly as Francine had said it in the past.

'He will insist, I fear. I don't know what he will do, but it will be impossible for you to stay here if you do not agree.'

'What can I do?'

'We must think,' she said.

I talked it over with Miss Elton. She was rather anxious herself because she could see her post coming to an end. My grandmother said that the only way out, as far as she could see, was for me to take some post and she thought that I should be looking around for something, for such situations were not easy to find and my grandfather might try to force me into an engagement at any time now. The wedding would probably be planned for my seventeenth birthday but I would have to be prepared before that.

I had not felt so depressed since the first months after Francine's departure. I was worried about her because there were no more letters, but my personal problem was so acute and as far as I could see my only way out was to take some post and I gave a good deal of thought to that prospect.

Miss Elton told me that there were certain posts advertised in the papers and she would get those papers and we would look together, for she had made up her mind that she was not going to be caught either.

We looked through the advertisements. 'Your age is against you,' she said. 'Who would look at a girl of sixteen as a governess or a companion. You will have to pretend you are older.'

'I shall be seventeen next year.'

'Even seventeen is very young. I think you might just pass as eighteen if you draw your hair right back from your face. If you had a pair of spectacles . . . wait a moment.' She went to a drawer and brought out a pair of glasses. 'Try these on.' I did and she laughed. 'Yes, that would do the trick and with your hair back you look quite severe . . . all of twenty . . . perhaps twenty-one or two.'

'I can't see a thing through them.'

'They can be obtained with plain glass. One thing I am certain of. Your obvious youth would debar you from getting anything. You can't possibly hope to do that for two years at least.'

'Two years! But I am sure he is planning my wedding for my seventeenth birthday.'

I was able to laugh at my appearance in Miss Elton's cloak and scraped-back hair and glasses.

Miss Elton then said she would get the glasses for me. She would say someone at the house wanted them just as a shield against the winds which gave her a headache. She had become very sympathetic to me since Francine left and that had drawn us close together.

She did manage to acquire the glasses and when I put them on I thought how Francine would have laughed to see me.

Miss Elton looked for posts and found several that might suit her. She was, after all, an experienced governess of mature age. The more we talked, the more I began to see the hopelessness of my situation and laughed at myself derisively for thinking that a pair of spectacles would make up for a lack of experience.

It wasn't going to work, I knew, and even Miss Elton's will to proceed in her own search flagged a little.

'Perhaps it is early days yet,' she said. 'Perhaps something will turn up.'

While we were thinking of all this a major event took place in Greystone Manor. Aunt Grace eloped with Charles Daventry. Perhaps if I had not been so involved in my own affairs I should have seen it coming. There had been a marked change in Aunt Grace ever since Francine had gone. There had been rebellion in the air and although it had taken her some years to come to the decision, Aunt Grace had finally broken the shackles with which her father had bound her. I was delighted for her.

She just walked out one day and there was a note for my grandfather saying that she had at last decided to live her own life and would soon be Mrs Charles Daventry, which was what she should have been ten years before.

My grandmother had been in the secret, of course, and I wondered how strongly she had urged Grace to act as she did.

My grandfather was incensed. There was another meeting in the chapel at which he denounced Aunt Grace. She was an ungrateful child, such as the Lord abhorred. Had He not said 'Honour thy father and thy mother'? She had bitten the hand that had fed her and the Almighty would not turn a blind eye to such dishonouring of her obligations.

I said to Cousin Arthur afterwards: 'I think my grandfather sees God as a sort of ally. Why does he presume that God is always on his side? Who knows? He might be for Aunt Grace.'

'You must not talk like that, Philippa,' he replied sombrely.

'Why should I not say what I feel? What has God given me a tongue for?'

'To praise Him and honour your betters.'

'You mean my grandfather and perhaps . . . you, Cousin Arthur?'

'You should have a respect for your grandfather. He took

you in. He gave you shelter. You must never forget that.'

'Grandfather doesn't and he is certainly determined that I shall not either.'

'Philippa, I will not mention what you have said to your grandfather, but if you continue to talk in this vein you would compel me to.'

'Poor Cousin Arthur, you are indeed my grandfather's man. You are the Holy Trinity – you, my grandfather and God.'

'Philippa!'

I looked at him scornfully. Now you really have something to tell my grandfather.

He did not, in fact. Instead he became rather gentle towards me, and my distaste for him grew in proportion to the passing of time.

I went to see Aunt Grace in the shack near the graveyard. She was visibly happy and did not look like the same grey woman who had inhabited Greystone Manor.

I embraced her and she looked at me apologetically. 'I wanted to tell you, Philippa,' she said, 'but I was afraid to tell anybody . . . except Mama. Oh, my dear, I am sure if you and your sister hadn't come I should never have had the courage. But ever since Francine went I have been thinking of this. Charles has been urging me for years but somehow I could never quite make up my mind to . . . and then when Francine went I suddenly thought, Enough is enough . . . and then what seemed impossible gradually began to seem quite easy. I only had to do it.'

Charles kissed me and said: 'I have to be grateful to you and your sister. How do you think Grace is looking?'

'Like a new woman,' I answered.

Aunt Grace was full of plans. They had Charles's room in the vicarage and they must live in that for a while. It meant that my grandfather would be furious but he had no jurisdiction over the vicar. The living was a matter for the Bishop and the Bishop had never – 'only don't mention a word of this,' begged Aunt Grace – liked our grandfather.

They had been at school together and there had been a feud between them. As for the vicar, he had never been on very good terms with Greystone Manor, and with the Bishop's backing he didn't have to be.

Grace babbled on excitedly and I was so happy for her.

'I shan't be able to see my mother,' she said, 'because I have been forbidden the house and she can't come out, but you'll take messages for us, won't you, and you'll tell her how happy I am.'

I promised I would.

It was a pleasant afternoon sitting among the stone figures and drinking tea which Charles brewed for us. In Grace's happiness I forgot briefly my own difficulties and when I did remember them the realization that I could talk to Aunt Grace comforted me.

'Yes,' she agreed, 'he is going to try to marry you to Cousin Arthur.'

'I will never marry him,' I said. 'Francine was determined not to and so am I.'

Her face clouded when I mentioned Francine. I went on: 'I do worry about her. I haven't heard from her for so long. I can't understand why she doesn't write.'

Aunt Grace was silent.

'It is strange,' I went on. 'Of course I always knew it might be difficult to get the letters . . . she being so far away.'

'How long is it since you heard?' asked Aunt Grace.

'It's more than a year now.'

Aunt Grace was still silent but after a while she said: 'Philippa, I wonder if you would bring some of my things for me. You'll have to smuggle them out of the house. I expect you'll be forbidden to see me.'

'I will disobey those orders,' I promised.

'Be careful. Your grandfather can be a very harsh man. You cannot stand on your own yet, Philippa.'

'I'm going to have to, Aunt Grace. I may try and find some post where I can earn my living. Miss Elton is helping me.'

'Oh . . . has it gone as far as that?'

'It has to . . . because of Cousin Arthur.'

'It's the best thing. You have to start a new life. I used to think of taking a post myself . . . but I always lacked the courage. You want to put the past behind you, everything . . . just everything, Philippa. Then perhaps you will find some good man. That would be the best. Forget everything . . . and start again.'

'I would never forget Francine and our life together.'

'You will find the way. And Philippa, there is something I want you to bring to me. It is my commonplace book. It is in the brown trunk in the first of the attics. There are newspaper cuttings and all sorts of things in it. It's a red book. You'll see my name written on the fly leaf. I should like to have it. Do go and look for it. You cannot fail to find it.'

The earnestness in her eyes, the manner in which her hand shook and the sudden darkening of that glow which her newly found happiness had brought her . . . all that might have warned me that I would find something startling in the commonplace book.

As soon as I returned to the house I went up to the attic. I opened the trunk and there was the book for which she had asked. I opened it. Her name was written inside just as she had said, but it was the newspaper cutting which caught my eye. The words formed themselves into sentences and they made terrible pictures for me.

> Baron Rudolph von Gruton Fuchs was found murdered in his bed at his hunting lodge in the Grutonian province of Bruxenstein last Wednesday morning. With him was his mistress, a young Englishwoman whose identity is as yet unknown, but it is believed that she had been his companion at the lodge for some weeks before the tragedy.

I looked at the date of the paper. It was over a year old. There was another cutting.

The identity of the woman in the Gruton Fuchs murder has been discovered. She is Francine Ewell, who had been a close friend of the Baron for some time.

The paper slipped from my hands. I just rocked there on my knees while my mind conjured up pictures of a bedroom in a hunting lodge. Rather grand, she had described it. There would be many servants. I pictured her lying in a bed with the handsome lover beside her . . . and there would be blood everywhere . . . my beloved sister's blood.

So this was why I had not heard. They had not told me, and there had been no mourning for her; my dear, beautiful, incomparable sister might never have existed.

Dead! Murdered! Francine, the companion of my happy days. The months of anxiety had culminated in this. Always before there had been hope. No longer could I call at the Emmses' cottage to be bitterly disappointed because there was no news. How could there be news . . . ever again?

They had said she was his mistress. But she was his wife. They had been married at Birley Church before they had crossed the Channel. She had written to tell me that. They had a son. Cubby. Where was Cubby? There was no mention of him.

'Oh Francine,' I murmured, 'I shall never see you again. Why did you go? It would have been better to have stayed here . . . to have married Cousin Arthur . . . anything . . . anything rather than this. We could have gone away together. Where? How? Anywhere . . . anything rather than this.'

I tried not to believe it. It must be someone else. But it was his name . . . and hers. Had she told me the truth about the marriage? Had she thought that I would want it to be respectable and proper, conventional and right? Yes, I should nave done. But she need not have lied to me. She could have omitted to mention the ceremony. And then there was the child. What had become of the child? Why didn't the paper mention him? It was just such a brief cutting as it would be in the English papers. Just a little of the usual trouble that cropped up in those turbulent Germanic states remote from peaceful England. The only reason it was mentioned at all was because the woman involved was English.

Was that all I was to know? Where could I find out more?

Clutching the red commonplace book under my arm I ran to the vicarage. Aunt Grace was waiting for me among the statues. She must have known that I would come. I just held the book out, looking at her.

'I didn't tell you,' she stammered. 'I thought it would upset you too much. But now . . . I thought . . . she is older. She ought to know.'

'All this time I have been waiting to hear from her . . .

Aunt Grace's lips trembled. 'It's terrible,' she said. 'She should never have gone.'

'Is there anything else I should know, Aunt Grace? Are there more cuttings . . . more reports . . . ?'

She shook her head. 'Nothing. That was all. I read it and cut it out. I didn't show it to anyone. I was afraid someone would see it. Your grandfather perhaps. But people don't take much notice of foreign news.'

'She was married to him,' I said.

Aunt Grace looked at me piteously.

'She was,' I insisted. 'She wrote and told me so. Francine would not lie to me.'

'It must have been a mock marriage. Those sort of people do things like that.'

'But there was a child,' I cried. 'What of the child? There is no mention of a child.'

Aunt Grace murmured: 'I should never have let you know. I just thought it would be best.'

'I had to know,' I cried. 'I want to know all about her. And all this time I have been in the dark . . .'

I could think of nothing but Francine. I could not shut out the thought of her lying dead in that bed . . . murdered. Francine . . . so full of life. I could not imagine it. I would rather have believed she had forgotten me, that her life was so full and varied that she had no time to remember a drab little sister. But Francine would never have been like that. The bond between us was too strong and had been forever . . . until death parted us. Death. Irrevocable . . . violent shocking death!

Never to see her again! Francine and that handsome young man whom I had met briefly and who had been all that a romantic hero should be – a fitting husband for the most beautiful of girls. But they had lived dangerously, of course.

There was no one to whom I could talk but my grandmother. She had learned of Francine's death recently, for Aunt Grace had told her.

'I should have been told,' I cried passionately.

'We should have told you . . . in time,' she said. 'But we knew of your devotion to each other and we thought you were so young. We wanted to wait until your sister had become a remote memory. It would have softened the blow.'

'She would never have become a remote memory.'

'But it was better, my child, that you should have thought she had forgotten you in the excitement of her new life than that you should know that she was dead . . . just at first, that was.'

'It happened a year ago.'

'Yes, but it was better to wait until now. Grace acted on the spur of the moment. She is a changed woman now. All her life she hesitated . . .'

'They say Francine was not married. Grandmother, I *know* she was.'

'Well, my dear, look at it like this. He was someone of very high rank in his country. Marriages are arranged for people like that. If they marry outside the laws . . .'

'It says she was his mistress. Francine was his wife. She told me.'

'She would tell you that. Of course she would. She thought of herself as his wife

'She said they were married in church. I've been to the church. We saw it the very day we arrived in England. We went there because we had time to spare when we were waiting for the train at Dover. I remember it well. Francine said at the time it would be a nice church to be married in, and she was.'

My grandmother was silent and I went on: 'What of the child?' for I could not stop thinking about him.

'He will be taken good care of.'

'Where? How?'

'It would have been arranged.'

'She was so proud of him. She loved him so much.'

My grandmother nodded.

I cried out: 'I want to know what happened.'

'My dear child, you must forget about it.'

'Forget Francine! As if I ever would. I should like to go there . . . to find out everything.'

'My dear child, you have problems of your own.'

I was silent for a moment. The sudden discovery had wiped everything from my mind. My problem did remain though. Even as I sat there, my mind full of pictures of Francine . . . ones that I remembered and imaginary ones, chief of all that of a bedroom in a hunting lodge . . . I could almost feel Cousin Arthur's flabby hands on me; I could see the bridal suite at Greystone, a dismal room with heavy grey velvet curtains and a high four-poster bed; I could see myself lying there and Cousin Arthur coming to me; I could picture his kneeling by the bed praying to God to bless our union before he set about the practical means of bringing it into action. I could never, never endure that.

And yet I could not think of that for long. All I could see was Francine lying in that bloodstained bed with her lover dead beside her.

I went to the Grange and looked at it. Sadly I passed the Emmses' cottage. I often saw Mrs Emms hanging out the washing; she seemed to be washing clothes interminably. I supposed she would be with a large family and yet they did not give an impression of excessive cleanliness. I stopped and talked to her.

'Never hear from Daise these days,' she said. 'I often wonder what's happening to her with that there Hans. Well, they go to foreign parts and it seems you've lost them. No news from your sister either?'

I shook my head. I did not want to talk about the tragedy with Mrs Emms.

Yet I could not stop myself looking at the house. I felt so frustrated. I railed against my youth. Something could and must be done.

Miss Elton had heard from her cousin who was working somewhere in the Midlands as a children's nurse. She said they would shortly be needing a governess and she had spoken for Miss Elton. The position was hers if she could wait for three months when they would be ready to take her.

Miss Elton was settled. She had had an interview with my grandfather when she explained that she believed I would soon not be needing a governess and that she had this offer of a post in three months' time. He graciously commended her wisdom in looking ahead and said he would be very happy to retain her services for another three months when, as she rightly divined, I should no longer be in need of a governess.

There was something irrevocable about that. My grandfather looked complacent. I was sure he thought he would not have the same difficulty with me as he had had with my sister.

Then, to my great excitement, there was activity at the Grange. Young Tom Emms told me when he came to help his father in the garden. He sought me out and I was sure Mrs Emms had ordered him to tell me.

'There's people up at the house,' he whispered conspiratorially.

'The Grange!' I cried.

He nodded.

It was all I needed. As soon as the midday meal was over I was off.

Mrs Emms was waiting for me. When she wasn't hanging up clothes she was in her garden watching.

She was at her door as soon as I approached. 'Only the servants, so far,' she said.

'I'm going to call,' I told her.

She nodded. 'I went over to ask about our Daise. I thought she might be there.'

'And she's not?'

Mrs Emms shook her head. 'I got quite the cold shoulder. No, Daise wasn't there. Nor was Hans. They're not the same lot as before. Funny way of going on, I must say.'

I was not going to be put off and I left her and made for the Grange. My heart was beating wildly as I went up the drive. I lifted the gargoyle knocker and the sounds echoed through the house.

At length I heard footsteps coming and a man opened the door.

We stood for a moment looking at each other. He raised his eyes interrogatively and I said: 'I have come to call. I am from Greystone Manor.'

He said: 'Not at home. No one here.'

He was about to shut the door but I had stepped forward so that he could not do so without forcing me out.

'When will the Gräfin arrive?' I asked.

He lifted his shoulders.

'Please tell me. I met her some years ago. My name is Philippa Ewell.'

He looked at me oddly. 'I do not know when they will come. Perhaps not at all. We are here because the house has been left so long. Good day.'

I could only step back defeated.

But I was in a fever of impatience. The arrival of the

servants had in the past meant that the house would be occupied in due course and surely someone there would be able to give me some infotmation about Francine.

A strange thing happened soon after my call at the house. There was a man whom I seemed to meet constantly. He was of heavy build with a thick short neck, and there was a Teutonic look about him which stamped him as a foreigner. I fancied he must be a tourist who was staying at the Three Tuns Inn close to the river, where occasionally people came for the trout-fishing. What was strange was that I met him so often. He never spoke to me; in fact he never seemed aware of me. He just seemed to be frequently there.

Miss Elton, whose own future was now secure, was becoming very sympathetic towards me and genuinely anxious on my behalf. The time was passing. In six months I should be seventeen. She knew that I loathed the thought of marrying Cousin Arthur. Yet what alternative had I?

She said: 'You should have a plan of action.'

'Such as?' I asked.

'You're so listless about yourself. You're obsessed by what happened to your sister. She is dead. You are living and you have to go on living.'

'I wish I could go to that place Bruxenstein. I'm sure there is some mystery to be cleared up.'

'It is all simple really. She was bewitched by him. She went away with him. He promised marriage . . .'

'He *did* marry her. It was in the church we visited once.' I was hit by an idea. 'Don't they have registers and things in churches? Well, if she were married there . . . there would be an account of it, wouldn't there? And wouldn't it be in the church?'

Miss Elton was looking at me intently. 'You're right,' she said.

'Oh, Miss Elton. I must go to that church. I must see it for myself. If it were there, that record of their marriage . . . it would prove part of that report was wrong, wouldn't it?'

Miss Elton was nodding slowly.

'I'm going then . . . somehow. Will you come with me?'

She was silent for a while. 'Your grandfather would want to know.'

'Am I going to be his slave all my life?' I asked.

'Yes, if you don't take some action now.'

'I will take action, and my first will be to go to Birley Church to see if there is any record of my sister's marriage.'

'And if there is?'

'Then I must do something. It makes a difference, don't you see? I want to find out why my sister was murdered. And there is something else. I want to find her son. What of that little boy? He must be three years old now. Where is he? Who is looking after him? He is Francine's child. Don't you see? I can't just sit here and do nothing.'

'I can't see what you can do, apart from prove whether your sister was married or not. And how is that going to help?'

'I'm not sure. But it would ease my mind a little. It will show that she was telling the truth if that record is there. She said she was the Baroness. She called herself Mrs Fox. One of his names was Fuchs, you see.'

'She always was rather frivolous.'

'She was the loveliest person I have ever known and I can't bear it.'

'Now don't get upset again. If you're set on going to that place . . . near Dover, is it? We could go there and back in one day. That makes it easy.'

'You'll come with me, Miss Elton?'

'I will, of course. You can't tell your grandfather what we are going to do, can you? How would it be if I told him that our lessons have been touching on the ancient churches of England and there is a particularly interesting Norman one near Dover which I should very much like you to see.'

'Oh, Miss Elton. You are so good.'

'He is inclined to be a little less severe with us now. Perhaps because I shall soon be going and he thinks you are going to be a docile granddaughter and obey his wishes.'

'I don't care what he thinks. I want to go to that church and look at the records.'

She was right about my grandfather. He graciously agreed to the outing and we set out early in the morning from the station at Preston Carstairs. We could catch the three o'clock train back. It was strange that just as we were getting into the station the mysterious man from the Three Tuns came hurrying on to the train. He did not look at us at all but the thought crossed my mind that it was strange that he should be there once more – and travelling on the very same train that we were; but I was so excited by the prospect ahead that I had soon dismissed him from my mind. He was very likely on holiday and seeing something of the countryside, and as the town of Dover and its environs were of outstanding historical interest, it was natural that he should wish to visit it.

It was a fairly long journey and to my impatient mood we seemed to chuff along at a very leisurely pace. I looked out at green meadows, oast houses, the ripening hops and the fruit-laden trees of the orchards which were a feature of this part of the country. Everything was green and pleasant but I was so anxious to reach the church.

As we came into Dover I saw the castle at the top of the hill and the fantastic view of white cliffs and sea; but I could only think of what I was going to find – for I had no doubt that it would be there.

We alighted from the train and made our way out of the station.

'The church is not very far,' I said. 'Francine, Mr Counsell and I went there in a trap and the people from the inn drove us there.'

'Could you find the inn?'

'I am sure I could.'

'Then we'll go there and have what they have to offer us to

eat and then we can enquire about the trap to take us to Birley Church.'

'I never felt less like eating.'

'We need something. Besides, it will give us a chance to talk to the innkeeper.'

We found the inn easily, and we were offered hot bread straight from the oven with cheddar cheese, sweet pickle and cider. It would have been tasty if I had been in the mood for eating.

'I have been here before,' I told the innkeeper's wife.

'We get so many,' she answered, apologizing for not remembering me.

'When I was here before I visited Birley Church.'

'We should really like to see it again,' said Miss Elton. 'How far is it?'

'Oh . . . some three miles or so from the edge of the town.'

'Last time we drove there in a trap,' I explained. 'The trap was one of yours. Is it possible to take us again?'

She lifted her shoulders and looked faintly dubious. 'I'll ask,' she said.

'Oh, please arrange it,' I begged. 'It is so very important to me.'

'I'll see what I can do.'

'We shall have to pay her,' I said when she had gone.

'Your grandfather gave me some money for this educational jaunt,' said Miss Elton comfortingly. 'And it won't be so very much surely.'

The woman came back and said that the trap would be ready in half an hour. I was so impatient, it was hard to wait and as I sat there longing for the time to pass I saw a figure walk quickly past the window. I was sure it was the man I had seen getting on the train. So he had even arrived at this inn!

When the half-hour was up there was the trap waiting for us and I then saw the man again. He was examining one of the horses belonging to the inn and striking a bargain for it.

I immediately forgot him as we rattled along, for my mind

was taken back so poignantly to when Francine and I had sat so close together as we drove along this road, and were so apprehensive of what awaited us at our grandfather's house.

We came to the church – small, grey and ancient – and made our way across the graveyard where many of the tombstones were brown with age and the engraving on them almost illegible. I remembered how Francine had read some of them aloud and I could hear her high laughter at the sentiments expressed. We went into the porch and I smelt that odour indigenous to churches of this kind – damp, age and some sort of furniture polish used for the pews. I stood facing the altar; the light flickering through the stained-glass windows shone on the brass lectern and the gilded fringe of the altar cloth. There was silence everywhere.

Miss Elton at length broke it. 'I suppose we should go to the vicarage,' she said.

'Yes, of course. We must see the vicar.'

We turned to go and as we did so the door creaked and a man came into the church. He looked curiously at us and asked if he could help.

'I'm the churchwarden here,' he said. 'Are you interested in the church? It's Norman, you know, and a very fine example for its size. It's been restored recently and we have had to repair a great deal of the tower. People don't come to see it very often, but that's because it's a bit off the map.'

Miss Elton said: 'We have a purpose other than to see the architecture. We wanted to know if it is possible to see the records. We want to make sure that a wedding took place here.'

'Well, if you have the dates and the names of the parties that should not be an impossibility. Our vicar is away until the weekend. That's why I'm looking in, you see. If I can be of any help.'

'Could you show us the records?' I asked eagerly.

'I could do that. They're kept in the vestry. I'll have to get the keys. Was it very long ago . . . ?'

'No. Four years,' I said.

'Well, there should be no problem there. People usually want to see a hundred years back. They're chasing their ancestors. There's a lot of that done nowadays. I'll just pop into the vicarage. I'll be back with you shortly.'

When he had gone we looked at each other triumphantly. 'I do hope you find what you want,' said Miss Elton.

True to his promise the churchwarden soon returned with the keys, and, tingling with excitement, I followed him into the vestry.

'Now . . .' he said. 'What date did you say? Ah yes . . . Here it is.'

I looked. It was true. There it was. Their names as clear as I could wish.

I gave a cry of triumph and turned to Miss Elton. 'There!' I shouted. 'There is no doubt. It's proved.'

I was possessed by a great excitement for I knew that having proved Francine had been married, I was not going to leave it at that. I had to find out more of what happened. Moreover I had begun to be haunted by the thought of that little boy, the child who had liked to say my name and had called his troll after me.

As we came out of the church I thought I saw a figure lurking among the tombstones. It was a man. He was stooping over a grave and seemed to be reading the inscription on the stone.

I took no further notice. I was so elated by what I had seen that I could think of nothing else all the way home

I could not wait to see my grandmother. I sat on the stool at her feet and told her what I had seen in the church register.

She listened intently. 'I'm glad,' she said. 'So Francine was speaking the truth.'

'But why should they say that she was his mistress?'

'I suppose it was because he was a man who was in an important position. It may be that he already had a wife.'

'I don't believe it. Francine was so happy.'

'My dear Philippa, you must stop thinking about it. Whatever happened it's over and done with. You have your own life to think of. Soon you will be seventeen. What are you going to do?'

'I wish I could go to Bruxenstein. I wish I could find out what it was all about.'

'You could not do that. Now if I were younger . . . If I had my sight . . .'

'You would go with me, wouldn't you, Grandmother?'

'I should be tempted to do so . . . but just as it is impossible for me to do that, so is it for you. Dear child, what are you going to do about this matter nearer home? I have been thinking that if your grandfather insists that you marry your cousin you might go and stay with Grace.'

'How could I? They have only one room in the vicarage.'

'It would be difficult, I know. I am just trying to find a solution. You are clutching at straws, my dear child. You have immersed yourself in this mystery which you cannot solve, and even if you did, that would not bring your sister back. Meanwhile you yourself are in danger.'

She was right, of course. Perhaps I should try to find a post as Miss Elton and I had at first thought I should. But who would employ me? When I considered that, the whole scheme seemed ridiculous.

The next day there was a dinner-party. The guests were the Glencorns with their daughter Sophia. 'Just a small intimate dinner-party,' my grandfather had said, looking at me with the satisfaction he was beginning to show towards me. 'Six is a pleasant number,' he added.

I dressed disconsolately in the brown taffeta which Jenny Brakes had made for me. It didn't suit me. Brown was not my colour. I needed reds and emerald greens. Not that I was the least interested in clothes or how I looked now. My thoughts were far away with Francine's little boy. I felt I knew him. Fair-haired, blue-eyed, a miniature Francine holding a troll.

What did a troll look like? I imagined some sort of Scandinavian dwarf. A troll whom he had named Pippa after me.

He was somewhere far away . . . unless they had murdered him too. Perhaps they had, and being a child he did not rate a mention in the English papers.

I piled my hair on top of my head. It gave me height and took away that look of extreme youth. Now I looked like a person who might be able to defend herself.

I hated the thought of the dinner-party. I had met the Glencorns once or twice. They lived in a big house on the edge of my grandfather's estate. I gathered he had bought land from the Glencorns who had reluctantly sold it because, as my grandfather remarked gleefully, they had no help for it. Sir Edward Glencorn had never been able to manage the estate he had inherited. He was a fool, said my grandfather. He despised fools, but the Glencorns were neighbours and when their property came on the market, which he was sure it must within the next few years, he wanted to get the first chance of acquiring it. Acquisition was the aim of my grandfather's life, which was why he had been so angry when the Grange had passed out of his orbit. Land and people – he had a desire to possess them all, to make them work for him, to fulfil his plans. He was like an earthly God creating his own universe. So although he despised Sir Edward Glencorn he liked to be in his company, which naturally gave him an even greater sense of his superiority.

Dinner was an ordeal, as all meals were, and I found it hard to concentrate on the conversation. Being in the company of Cousin Arthur was making my flesh crawl more than it ever did. I knew the time was getting nearer when I should have to accept him or find myself alone and destitute.

At a gathering such as this it was hard to put all that behind me and as I was still in a state of shock over Francine's fate, I was to say the least absent-minded.

Sophia was a quiet girl although I had always had the

feeling that one could never really know her. Often I would find her watching me intently as though she were trying to read my innermost thoughts. If Francine had been with me and this terrible fear and uncertainty had not been hanging over me, I realized we should have been rather interested in Sophia Glencorn.

Sir Edward was complimenting me on my looks – quite conventionally, I was sure, for I knew that the brown taffeta suited neither my skin nor my colouring and I must surely show some sign of my anxieties. Moreover he had been talking to me for some time and I couldn't remember what I had answered, so he must be thinking me half-witted.

'No longer the little girl, eh? Quite the young lady.'

My grandfather was looking almost benign. 'Yes, it is surprising how quickly Philippa has seemed to grow up.'

Ominous words. I could see the plans in his eyes. The wedding . . . the birth . . . the heir, the little Ewell who would be moulded by my grandfather.

'Philippa is taking a great interest in the estate,' added Cousin Arthur.

Was I? I hadn't noticed it. I cared nothing for the estate. My thoughts were entirely occupied with my own affairs and my sister.

My grandfather nodded, looking down at his plate One has to consider all the time,' he said. 'One inherits lands, possessions and with them responsibilities.'

How amused Francine would have been.

'Philippa is taking an interest in architecture also,' went on Cousin Arthur.

How I wished they would not talk about me as though I wasn't there.

'Miss Elton has groomed her in the subject,' went on my grandfather. 'What was that church you visited recently?'

I said it was Birley Church . . . not far from Dover.

'Quite a way to go to see a bit of stone,' commented Lady Glencorn.

Grandfather gave her an indulgent but rather contemptuous smile.

'Norman, wasn't it,' he said. 'I believe the most interesting feature of Norman architecture is the way they built the roofs . . . timber boarding in the roof-trusses to make tunnel-shaped ceilings. Is that so, Philippa?'

I was only vaguely aware of what he was talking about for Miss Elton and I had not thought of architecture until I wanted to go to Birley Church.

'Oh yes, yes,' I said. 'Miss Elton is rather sad because she will be leaving us so soon.'

My grandfather could not hide his contentment. 'Philippa is getting too grown up for a governess now. She will have other matters with which to concern herself.'

It was strange really for I had never felt so important. But it only meant that I was now quite a significant piece on the chessboard to be moved this way and that at his pleasure.

I was glad when the meal was over and we went into the solarium where after dinner wines and liqueurs were served when we had guests. Sophia was invited to play for us on the piano. She had quite a strong voice and she sang some of the old songs like 'Cherry Ripe' and 'Drink to Me Only with Thine Eyes'. This last she sang very soulfully while Arthur stood beside her and turned the leaves of the music as she sang. I noticed that when he leaned over and turned the page his hand rested on her shoulder and lingered there for quite a while.

I had always watched Cousin Arthur's hands with a sort of repellent horror because I hated it when he touched me; and he was rather fond of physical contact, I noticed. I had thought this was reserved for myself, but it seemed it was a habit of his. I noticed him do it again and again with Sophia at the piano and it comforted me in an odd way. It did mean that it was not specially for me.

The evening was over at last and the Glencorns left in their carriage Grandfather, Cousin Arthur and I saw them off and when they had gone Grandfather sighed with satisfaction.

'It would not surprise me,' he said, 'if old Glencorn were not on the edge of bankruptcy.'

Each day seemed long in passing, yet looking back one week had gone and we were halfway through another. I knew I was fast approaching a precipice. Miss Elton had only one month to go, for we were now well into February. My grandfather's ultimatum was about to burst upon me and I was still dreaming impossible dreams about getting to that remote country which was only a name to me. I had looked at it many times on the atlas – a little pink spot very small and insignificant compared with the mass of America, Africa and Europe, with our little island flung out on the side. But then there were all those red pieces which were British – that Empire on which the sun never set. But the place that I longed to see and to know more about was that little pink spot in the midst of all those brown mountain ranges.

In despair I decided to call at the Grange once more. I started across the lawn, and as I did so a man came towards me.

I was startled for a moment because I thought he was Francine's lover. I caught my breath and must have turned pale.

'Is anything wrong?' he asked.

'No . . . I just came to call on . . . er . . .'

'To call on?' he repeated encouragingly.

'I met the Gräfin when she was here some years ago. She was kind enough to invite me to . . . call again.'

'She is not here, I'm afraid.' He spoke impeccable English with only the faintest trace of a foreign accent. 'Can I be of any help?'

'You are . . . ?'

'Oh, I am just here to see that things are well with the

house. It is some time since it was lived in. That is not good for houses. May I know your name?'

'It is Philippa Ewell.'

He was alert. A picture of those newspaper lines flashed into my mind. 'We know the identity of the Englishwoman. She is Francine Ewell . . .'

He would have recognized the surname, but all he said was: 'How do you do?' and added, 'Would you like to come into the house?'

'You say the family is not at home?'

He laughed. 'I am sure the Gräfin would not wish me to be inhospitable. I will welcome you on her behalf.'

'Are you a sort of . . . what do you call it? A major domo?'

'That is a good description.'

I had the position clearly. He was a servant but a very superior one. He had come to make sure that all was well with the house. That sounded very reasonable.

'I suppose you are getting the house ready for them?'

'That could well be,' he said. 'Come in and I will refresh you. You drink tea at this hour, do you not?'

'Yes, we do.'

'I believe we could have tea.'

'Is that in order, do you think?' I asked dubiously.

'I don't really see why not.'

I remembered how Hans had shown us round and how embarrassing that had been. Still, I was certainly not going to refuse such an offer. I was tremendously excited. I could feel my cheeks beginning to burn as they did on such occasions. Francine had said: 'Don't worry about it. It makes you quite pretty.'

He opened the door and we went in. I remembered it so well – the dining hall, the stairs, the small room where we had been entertained by the Gräfin.

Tea was brought by a serving maid who did not seem in the least surprised. He smiled at me. 'You would perhaps as I believe they say . . . do the honours, yes?'

I poured out the tea and said: 'I . . . I wonder if you ever met my sister.'

He raised his eyebrows. 'I have been very little in England lately. I spent some years here in my youth . . . for my education.'

'Oh,' I said, 'this was four or five years ago. She met someone in this house. She was married and then . . . she died.'

'I think I know to what you refer,' he said slowly. 'It was a big scandal at the time. Yes . . . I remember the name of the Baron's friend.'

'My sister was his wife.'

He lifted his shoulders slightly. Then he said: 'I knew there was a friendship . . . a liaison.'

I felt myself growing hot with indignation. 'That was not true,' I said shrilly. 'I know the account in the press mentioned her as his mistress. I tell you she was his wife.'

'You must not get angry,' he said. 'I know how you feel, of course. But the Baron could not have married your sister. His marriage was of the utmost importance to the country because he was heir to the ruling house.'

'Do you mean my sister would not have been considered good enough for him?'

'Not necessarily so, but he would have married someone of his own nationality . . . someone chosen for him. He would not have married outside that.'

'I must assure you that my sister was worthy to marry . . . anyone.'

'I am sure she was, but you see it is not a matter of worthiness. It is a matter of politics, you understand?'

'I know that my sister was married to him.'

He shook his head. 'She was his mistress,' he said. 'It is what will happen, you know. She would not have been the first or the last . . . had he lived.'

'I find these comments most offensive.'

'You must not find the truth offensive. You must be a realist.'

I stood up. 'I will not stay here to hear my sister being insulted.' I felt the tears in my eyes and I was enraged with him for making me show my emotion.

'Now come, please,' he said gently. 'Talk reasonably. You must look at this as a woman of the world. They met romantically, I suspect. They loved. Well, that is charming. But marriage for a man in his position with someone who . . . oh, I am sure she was beautiful and charming, I am sure she was worthy in every way . . . but it was simply not suitable. A man in his position must consider his liabilities . . . and he always did that.'

'I tell you they *were* married.'

He smiled at me and his calmness angered me more than anything else. That he could talk of this tragedy almost as though it were an everyday occurrence wounded me so deeply that I felt I should lose control of myself completely if I stayed any longer and had to look at that unruffled, smiling face.

'If you will excuse me . . .' I said.

He stood up and bowed.

'I must go,' I said. 'You are talking nonsense and telling lies . . . I think you are aware of it. Goodbye.'

With that I turned and ran out of the house. I was just in time, for the tears were now running down my cheeks and the last thing I should have wanted was for him to see them.

I hurried into the house and up to that room which I had once shared with Francine. I threw myself on my bed and for the first time since I had seen those horrible newspaper cuttings, I wept uncontrollably.

I didn't want to go to the Grange after that. I found it hard to understand why he had upset me so. Perhaps it was because he had reminded me a little of Francine's Baron. This man was a servant, I told myself, and wanted everyone to know that although he was a servant he was a very superior one. Rudolph had worn his royalty – or whatever it was these Grafs and Barons had – very lightly. Everyone had known he was the Baron and he did not have to remind them. Perhaps I was being rather unfair to the man, just because he had been so sure that Francine had not been married.

Anyway I did not want to see him again. But perhaps that was foolish for he might know something. He might be aware of what happened to the child.

Already I was beginning to regret my hasty departure. Why should I have cared if he saw my grief?

I saw him again next day. I think he was waiting to catch me for when I went out for my afternoon walk he must have seen me leave the house. I went towards the woods at a fast pace but he followed me.

Inside the wood I sat down under a tree and waited for him to come up.

'Good afternoon,' he said. 'So . . . we meet again.'

Since I was sure he had waited for me and knew he had followed me this seemed, to say the least, deceitful.

'How do you do?' I said coldly.

'May I?' he said and sat down beside me. He was smiling at me.

'I am glad you are no longer angry with me,' he said.

'I was rather foolish, I'm afraid.'

'No . . . no.' He leaned towards me and put his hand over mine for a moment. 'It was natural that you should be upset. It was a terrible thing that happened to your sister.'

'It was wicked. I wish I knew . . . I wish I could find her murderers.'

'It was not possible to find them,' he said. 'There was a search, of course. Nothing came to light and it therefore remains a mystery.'

'Will you please tell me all that you know about it? There was a child. What happened to the boy?'

'A child! There was no child.'

'My sister had a son. She wrote and told me so.

'That is impossible.'

'Why should it be impossible for two people to have a child?'

'It is not an impossibility in the way you suggest, but in view of Rudolph's position.'

'His position had nothing to do with it. He married my sister and it is the most natural thing in the world that they should have a child.'

'This is something you do not understand.'

'I should be pleased if you would not treat me as a child and a half-witted one at that.'

'Oh, I do not consider you a child and I am sure that you are in full possession of your wits. I know too that you are a very fiery young lady.'

'This is something which is very important to me. My sister is dead but I will not allow her memory to be desecrated.'

'You use strong words, my dear young lady.'

He had leaned towards me and tried to take my hand, which I firmly removed. 'I am not your dear young lady.'

'Well . . .' He put his head on one side and regarded me. 'You are young. You are a lady . . .'

'Of a family not worthy to marry with foreigners who honour our country by visiting it occasionally.'

He laughed aloud. I noticed the firm line of his jaw and the gleam of strong white teeth. I thought: He reminds me of Arthur . . . by the very contrast.

'Worthy . . . worthy indeed,' he said. 'But because of certain political commitments such marriages cannot take place.'

'Do you think that a girl like my sister would condescend to become the mistress of this high and mighty potentate?'

He looked at me solemnly and nodded.

'You are talking nonsense,' I said.

'Where I was wrong,' he went on, looking at me in an odd

intent sort of way, 'was to call you *my* dear young lady. You are not mine.'

'I find this an absurd conversation. We were talking about a very serious matter and you have introduced this light and frivolous note.'

'It is often wise when talking of serious matters to introduce a light-hearted note. It prevents tempers rising.'

'It does not prevent mine.'

'Ah, but you are a very hot-tempered lady.'

'Listen to me,' I said, 'if you are not prepared to talk seriously about this matter, there is no point in our talking at all.'

'Oh, do you feel like that? I'm sorry. I have been thinking that there is a great deal of point in talking on any subject. I should very much like to know you better and I hope you feel some curiosity about me.'

'I have to find out what happened to my sister and why . . . and I want to be assured that her child is being cared for.'

'You are asking a great deal. The police were not able to solve the mystery of what happened that night in the hunting lodge. As for the non-existent child . . .'

'I will not listen to any more.'

He did not speak, but sat still glancing sideways at me. My impulse was to get up and leave him and I should have done so if I had not wanted more than anything to learn the truth.

I did start to move away but he reached out and, taking my hand, looked at me appealingly. I felt myself flushing. There was something about him which stirred me. I disliked his arrogance and his assumption that Francine's Baron could never have stooped to marry her. In fact his implication that Francine and I were romancing about the whole matter infuriated me, and yet . . . I could not say what it was, because I had had too little experience of the world; and yet to be near him brought me such a feeling of excitement as I did not remember ever feeling before. I could tell myself that it was because I was on the verge of discovering something and was actually in the presence of someone who had known Baron Rudolph. Somehow this man gave me the impression that he was aware of more than he was letting me know, and I told myself that whatever effect he had on me I had to see him as much as possible.

I don't know how long we were like that – he holding my hand, myself making a half-hearted effort to break away from him while he watched me with a rather mischievous smile, as though he could read my thoughts and, moreover, knew my vulnerability.

'Please sit down,' he said. 'We obviously have a great deal to say to each other.'

I sat down. I said: 'In the first place, you know who I am. My sister and I lived at Greystone Manor until she went to this unfortunate ball.'

'Where she met her lover.'

'She had met him before and the Gräfin invited her. It wasn't easy. Do not imagine that we at Greystone Manor thought it such an honour. My sister had to go to all sorts of subterfuge in order to attend that ball.'

'Deceit?' he asked.

'You are determined to be offensive.'

'Certainly not. But I must insist that if we are to discover anything we must look facts straight in the face. Your sister slipped out of the house in her ball gown and went to the Grange. Her family – with the exception of her little sister who was in the secret – knew nothing about it. Is that right?'

'Yes . . . more or less.'

'And there she and the Baron fell in love. They eloped. She travelled as his wife . . . to placate conventions.'

'She *was* his wife.'

'Now we are right back at the beginning. The marriage could have not taken place.'

'But it did. I know it did.'

'Let me explain to you. Rudolph's country is a small one. It is always fighting to preserve its autonomy. That is why there must be no stepping aside from conventions. There are neighbouring states always casting greedy eyes on it, always seeking to aggrandize themselves, to make themselves more powerful. One day they will all band together into one state and that will doubtless be a good thing, but at the moment there are these petty states – dukedoms, margravates, principalities . . . and so on; Bruxenstein is one of them. Rudolph's father is an old man. Rudolph was his only son. He was to marry the daughter of a ruler of a neighbouring state. He would never have made this mésalliance. Too much was at stake.'

'Nevertheless he did.'

'Do you really believe that possible?'

'Yes. He was in love.'

'Very charming, but love is a different thing from politics and duty. The lives of thousands are involved . . . it is the difference between war and peace.'

'He must have loved my sister dearly. I can understand. She was the most attractive person I have ever met. Oh, I can see you are cynical. You don't believe me.'

'I believe she was all you say she was. I have seen her sister and that makes it easy to imagine.'

'You are laughing at me. I know that I am plain and quite unlike Francine.'

He took my hand and kissed it. 'You must not think that,' he said. 'I am sure you have as much charm as your sister but perhaps in a different way.'

Once again I firmly removed my hand. 'You must not tease me,' I said. 'You don't want to talk of this, do you?'

'There is nothing really to say. Your sister and Rudolph were murdered in the hunting lodge. It was a political murder in my view. It was someone who wanted the heir out of the way.'

'Well, who would inherit this dukedom . . . or principality . . . or whatever it is? Perhaps he is the murderer.'

'It's not as simple as that. The next in line was not in the country at the time.'

'Well, those sort of people have agents, don't they?'

'There was a thorough investigation.'

'It could not have been so very thorough. I expect they are not very efficient in that little place.'

He laughed. 'They are, you know. There was a detailed enquiry but nothing could be brought to light.'

'I suppose my sister was killed because she happened to be there.'

'It looks like it. I am so sorry. What a pity she ever left Greystone Manor.'

'If she hadn't she might have been married to Cousin Arthur . . . but she never would have done that.'

'So . . . there was another suitor.'

'My grandfather wanted the match. I suppose it is rather like your Bruxenstein. He hasn't a dukedom or a principality but he has a fine old house which has been in the family for generations and he is very rich, I believe.'

'So you have the same problems as we have in Bruxenstein.'

'Problems created by people's pride. There should be no problems at all. No one should attempt to choose people's husbands for them. If people love they should be allowed to marry.'

'Well spoken,' he cried. 'Do you know we have at last found agreement.'

I said: 'I shall have to go now. Miss Elton will be looking for me.'

'Who is Miss Elton?'

'My governess. She is leaving very shortly. I am considered to be no longer in need of one.'

'Almost a woman,' he commented.

He was beside me and he laid his hands on my shoulders. I wished he would not touch me; when he did so an incomprehensible desire to stay with him came to me. It was the opposite effect of that which Arthur's flabby hands had on me, but it did occur to me that they both had a habit of using them a good deal.

He drew me to him and kissed me very lightly on the forehead.

'Why did you do that?' I demanded, hastily drawing back and flushing scarlet.

'Because I wanted to.'

'People do not kiss strangers.'

'We are hardly that. We have met before. We have drunk tea together. I thought that was an English ceremony. If you take tea you are immediately friends.'

'You obviously know nothing of English ceremonies. One can take tea with one's bitterest enemies.'

'Then I misjudged the situation and you will forgive me.'

'I forgive you for that but not for your attitude towards my sister. I know she was married. I have evidence that she was, but it is no use trying to convince you so I will not attempt to do so.'

'Evidence?' he said sharply. 'What evidence?'

'Letters. Her letters, for one thing.'

'Letters to you? In which she insists she was married.'

'She doesn't insist. She didn't have to. She only had to tell me.'

'May I see . . . these letters?'

I hesitated.

'You have to convince me, you know.'

'All right then . . .'

'Shall we meet here . . . or would you care to come to the Grange?'

'Here,' I answered.

'Tomorrow I shall be here.'

I ran out of the wood. When I reached the edge of it I looked back and saw him standing among the trees. There was a strange smile on his lips.

I was in a bemused state for the rest of the day. Miss Elton, who was in the midst of packing, did not notice my abstraction. She would be leaving in a few days and I knew that she was anxious about me, but could really see no practical way out of my difficulties. I wondered whether to tell my grandmother about this man but for some reason I was reluctant to do so. I did not even know his name. He was over-familiar. How dared he kiss me! What did he think? That all girls here could be lightly kissed and engaged in intimate relationships without marriage?

I stayed up late that night reading the letters. It was all so clear; her ecstasy and her marriage. Hadn't I seen the entry in the register? I should have told that man about this piece of irrefutable evidence. Why hadn't I? Perhaps I had deliberately held it back so that when I did tell him and prove him to be wrong he would be made to feel very humble indeed. Of course Francine had been married. There was her talk of the baby – dear little Cubby. Even suppose she had told me of the marriage – because she thought she ought to be married – she would never have invented the child. Francine was not the most maternal of women, I was sure; but once she had a child she had loved him and that came over in the letters.

The next day I was early at our meeting place but he was already there.

My heart started to beat faster at the sight of him. I wished that he did not have this effect on me because it made me feel at a disadvantage. He came forward; he bowed, I thought with a certain mockery, and, clicking his heels, took my hand and kissed it.

'There is no need to stand on ceremony with me,' I said.

'Ceremony! This is no ceremony. An ordinary form of greeting in my country. Of course, with elderly ladies and children we often kiss the cheek instead of the hand.'

'As I am neither you can at least dispense with that.'

'Somewhat regretfully,' he said.

But I was determined that I would not allow this rather

offensive bantering to intrude on the seriousness of the occasion.

'I have brought the letters to show you,' I said. 'When you read them you will accept the truth. You will have to.'

'Shall we sit down? The ground is a little hard and this is not the most comfortable place for a consultation. You should have come to the house.'

'I hardly think that would be right while your employers are away.'

'Perhaps not,' he said. 'Now . . . may I see the letters?'

He took them and began to read them.

I watched him. I suppose it was that excessive masculinity which was affecting. It must have been something like that which happened to Francine. Oh no, that was absurd. She had fallen violently in love. My feelings were quite different. I felt antagonistic towards this man, although I was intensely excited in his presence. I had known few men. One could not count Antonio and the people on the island. I had been far too young then. But few people came to my grandfather's house and I supposed I judged everyone by Cousin Arthur, which meant that they all must seem devastatingly attractive.

I started suddenly. I had the feeling that we were being overlooked. I turned sharply. Did I see a movement among the trees? It must have been imagination. I was in a state of excitement, I realized that. I had been ever since I had met this man . . . solely because I thought I had fitted in a few more pieces in the jigsaw of mystery concerning the murder in the hunting lodge. A crackle of dry bracken . . . the sudden flutter of a bird as though it had been disturbed had given me this strange uncanny feeling of being overlooked.

'I fancy someone is nearby watching us,' I said.

'Watching us? Why?'

'People do . . .'

He put down the letters and sprang to his feet. 'Where?' he cried. 'In which direction?' I was sure then that I heard the sound of hastening footsteps.

'Over there,' I said, and he ran off in the direction I had indicated. After a few minutes he came back.

'No sign of anyone,' he said.

'Yet . . . I was sure . . .'

He smiled at me and sitting down picked up the letters. When he had read them he handed them back solemnly to me.

'Your sister thought she would set your mind at rest by telling you she was married.'

Now was the moment. 'There is something you don't know,' I told him triumphantly. 'I have definite proof. I have seen the church register.'

'What!' That moment had been worth waiting for. He was completely taken aback.

'Oh yes,' I went on. 'It is there as plain as it could be. So you see you have been absolutely wrong.'

'Where?' he asked tersely.

'In Birley Church. Miss Elton and I went to look for it and found it.'

'I cannot credit Rudolph for behaving so . . .'

'It is not for you to credit or discredit. The marriage took place. I can prove it.'

'Why did you not tell me before?'

'Because you were so pigheadedly cocksure.'

'I see,' he said slowly. 'Where is this place?'

'At Birley . . . not far from Dover. You should go there. See it with your own eyes . . . then perhaps you'll believe it.'

'Very well,' he said. 'I will.'

'You can take the train to Dover. It is quite simple. You can get a horse and trap to take you out to Birley. It's about three miles from Dover.'

'I will most certainly go.'

'And when you have seen it you will come back and apologize to me.'

'Abjectly.'

He folded up the letters and began, as though absent-mindedly, to put them in his pocket.

'They are mine, remember.'

'So they are.' He gave them back to me.

I said: 'I don't know your name.'

'Conrad,' he told me.

'Conrad . . . what?'

'Don't bother with the rest. You would find it unpronounceable.'

'I might be able to manage it.'

'Never mind now. I should like to be just Conrad to you.'

'When will you go to Birley, Conrad?'

'Tomorrow, I think.'

'And will you meet me here on the following day?'

'With the greatest pleasure.'

I tucked the letters into my bodice.

'I believe,' he said, 'that you suspect me of planning to steal them.'

'Why should I?'

'You are rather suspicious by nature and particularly of me.'

He moved towards me and put his hand on the neck of my bodice. I cried out in alarm and he dropped his hand.

'Only teasing,' he said. 'You have put them in a rather . . . shall I say tempting spot.'

'I think you are impertinent.'

'I fear you are right,' he said. 'Remember I come from that outlandish place of which you had never heard until your sister went there.'

My eyes clouded and I started to think of her as she had been on the night she left. He saw it at once and his hands were on my shoulders.

'Forgive me,' he said. 'I am clumsy as well as impertinent. I know your feelings for your sister. Believe me, I admire them tremendously. I will see you the day after tomorrow. I shall come prepared, I assure you, to eat humble pie . . . that is what you call it, is it not? . . . if you can prove me wrong.'

'Then you had better start preparing for that dish immediately. I warn you I shall want abject apologies.'

'If you can prove your case you can have them. That's better. You are smiling now . . . satisfied . . . complacent. You know you are right, don't you?'

'I do. Goodbye.'

'Au revoir. Auf wiedersehen. Not goodbye. I don't like that. It's too final. I should not be at all pleased if it were goodbye between us.'

I turned and ran off. I was already a little sad because a day must elapse before I saw him again. But the day after tomorrow I should have the satisfaction of seeing his dismay and that would be worth waiting for.

As soon as I entered the house I decided to go and see my grandmother. She would have awakened from her afternoon sleep and would probably be having a cup of tea. I must tell her about Conrad, but I would be careful not to betray to her the effect he had on me. I was being rather silly about that. It merely meant that he was the first man with whom I had ever been on such terms and as Miss Elton would probably have commented if she had noticed my abstracted state, it was going to my head. That was the case. I was lonely. No one had paid any attention to me except Cousin Arthur who was acting on my grandfather's instructions, and here was an attractive man attempting to carry on in a rather flirtatious manner with me. Sometimes I felt he was in earnest and really liked me; at others I thought he was laughing at me. Perhaps it was a little of each.

I knocked at my grandmother's door and Agnes Warden came out.

'Oh, it's Miss Philippa,' she said. 'Your grandmother is sleeping.'

'Still? Isn't she having her tea?'

'She had a bit of a turn this afternoon. She's sleeping it off.'

'A turn?'

'Well, her heart's not good, you know. She has these turns now and then. They leave her very tired and the only thing is rest after them.'

I was disappointed.

I went back to my room and met Miss Elton coming into the corridor.

'I want to leave tomorrow if possible,' she said, 'instead of waiting until the end of the week. My cousin can meet me and she says we could have a week's holiday before going to our employers. She has arranged for us to stay with a friend of hers. Do you think your grandfather would agree to my leaving tomorrow?'

'I'm sure he would. In any case you have really ceased to be employed by him.'

'But I wouldn't want to upset him. I have my reference to think of.'

'I should go to him at once. I am sure it will be all right.'

'I will.'

She came to my room about ten minutes later looking flushed and pleased.

'He has agreed that I shall go. Oh, Philippa, it is all so exciting and of course my cousin says it is an easy house and the children are delightful.'

'A little different from Greystone. My grandfather is not the best of employers.'

'But I had you two girls. I don't think I shall ever feel the same about other pupils.'

'About Francine, of course.' I felt the sadness overwhelming me again. Miss Elton put her arm about me.

'You too . . . just as much,' she said. 'I grew very fond of you both. That is why I am so concerned for you now.'

'I shall miss you.'

'Philippa, what have you decided? Very soon now . . .'

'I know. I know . . . I just cannot think for a moment. I will though. I'll think of something.'

'There's so little time.'

'Please, Miss Elton, don't worry about me. I have a dream sometimes that I go to that place and find out what's really happened. There's the child, you know.'

'You would best forget it. You need to get away from here . unless you are going to agree to your grandfather's wishes

'Neve' . never . . .' I said emphatically. Since I had met Conrad the thought of Cousin Arthur's flabby hands groping for me had become something of a nightmare.

Miss Elton shook her head. I could see she believed that in the end I would accept my fate. Normally I should have talked to her, but because my thoughts were full of Conrad I did not wish to. I did not understand myself but somewhere at the back of my mind was the thought that he would provide some sort of solution – just as his fellow countryman had for Francine.

'Well,' said Miss Elton, 'tomorrow I must say goodbye. It is always hard leaving one's pupils but this is the hardest wrench.'

When she had left me I looked at the bed which had been Francine's and a desolation swept over me. My grandmother was ill; Miss Elton would be gone; I should be alone.

I realized then how I depended on those two.

And yet I could not stop thinking of Conrad.

The next morning Miss Elton left. I clung to her for a last farewell and she was very emotional.

'May everything go right with you,' she said fervently.

'And with you,' I replied.

Then she was gone.

I went up to see my grandmother. Agnes met me at the door. 'You should not stay long,' she said. 'She is very weak.'

I sat by her bed and she smiled at me rather wanly. I longed to tell her about Conrad and the strange feelings he aroused in me. I wanted to discover for myself whether it was due to him or merely because he came from that place where

Francine had met her death. But I realized that my grandmother was not quite sure who it was who sat by her bed, and at moments was confusing me with Grace; and as I left her my desolation increased.

I could scarcely wait for Conrad's return. I was in the woods before the appointed time, waiting. He was on time and my heart leaped with excitement as he came striding towards me.

He took both my hands and bowed before he kissed first one and then the other.

'So?' I said.

'I went as we arranged I should,' he said. 'It's not a bad journey.'

'And you saw it?'

He looked at me steadily. 'I found the church. The vicar was helpful.'

'He was away when Miss Elton and I went. We saw the churchwarden.'

He looked at me intently. 'You mustn't mind this,' he said. 'I know you thought you saw this entry . . .'

'*Thought* I saw it. I did see it. What are you talking about?'

He shook his head. 'The vicar showed me the register. There was no entry.'

'This is the most absurd nonsense. I saw it. I tell you I saw it.'

'No,' he insisted. 'It was not there. I had the right date. There was no doubt of it. There was no entry.'

'You are provoking me.'

'I wish I were. I'm sorry to upset you in this way.'

'Sorry! You're glad. Besides, it's a lie. You can't say this. I tell you I saw it with my own eyes.'

'I'll tell you what I think,' he said soothingly. 'You wanted to see it. So you imagined it.'

'In other words I suffer from delusions and I'm mad. Are you suggesting that?'

He looked at me sadly. 'My dear, dear Philippa, I

am sorry. Believe me, I wanted to see it. I wanted you to be right.'

'I shall go there myself. I'll go again. I'll find it. You must have been looking in the wrong place.'

'No . . . I had the correct date . . . the date you gave me. If they had been married it would have been there. It is not there, Philippa. It is definitely not there.'

'I am going there. I shall lose no time.'

'When?' he asked.

'Tomorrow.'

'I will come with you. I will show you that you have made a mistake.'

'And I will show you that I have not,' I said vehemently.

He took my arm but I shook him off.

'Don't take this to heart,' he said. 'It's over and done with now. Whether she was married or not . . . what difference does it make?'

'It makes a difference to me . . . and the child.'

'There was no child,' he said. 'No marriage . . . no child.'

'How dare you suggest my sister was a liar or that I am mad! Go away . . . Go back to your own country.'

'I fear I shall have to . . . very soon. But first you and I will go there . . . tomorrow.'

'Yes,' I said determinedly, 'tomorrow.'

I had not thought how I was to get away. It had been different when I had gone before. But I was reckless. I could think of nothing but proving Conrad wrong. I told Mrs Greaves that I was going to look at an old church and was not sure how long I should be away.

'Your grandfather would not want you to go without someone with you,' she said.

'I shall have someone with me.'

'Who will that be? Miss Sophia Glencorn?'

I nodded. It was the only way. I did not want a hue and cry before I started.

Conrad was at the station as we had arranged.

As I sat opposite him I thought how pleasant it could have been if we were just taking a trip somewhere together. I studied his face as he sat, his arms folded, his eyes on me.

It was a strong face with firm features and deeply set, bluish-grey eyes. It was a Nordic face. The blond hair grew back strongly from a high forehead. I could imagine his coming to our shores in one of the tall ships; a Viking conqueror.

'Well,' he said, 'are you summing me up?'

'Just casually observing,' I replied.

'I hope I meet with your approval.'

'Does it matter?'

'Enormously.'

'You are bantering again. It is because you know what we are going to find when we get to the church. You're trying to make a joke of it. I think it's a very poor joke.'

He leaned forward and laid his hand on my knee. 'I would not dream of joking about a subject which is so near to your heart,' he said seriously. 'I don't want you to feel too badly when . . .'

'Shall we talk of something else?'

'The weather? It is quite a pleasant day for the time of the year. Now in my country it is not so warm in the winter . . . I believe it is because you are singularly blessed by the Gulf Stream . . . one of God's gifts to the English.'

'I think it would be better to be silent.'

'Just as you wish. My great desire is to please you now as always . . . and forever.'

I closed my eyes. His words touched a deep chord in me. Always and forever. It sounded as though our relationship was not the transient one that I had thought it to be and the idea lifted my spirits considerably.

As we chuffed along in silence his eyes remained on me. I looked out of the window but I scarcely noticed the passing scenery. At length I smelt the tang of the sea and there was the approach to the town . . . the white cliffs again, the view of the castle which medieval kings had called the gateway to England.

We made our way to the inn, for he insisted that we have some food.

'It's necessary if we take the trap,' he said. 'Besides, you need a little refreshment.'

'I could eat nothing,' I said.

'But I could,' he replied, 'and you will.'

We had the bread and cheese again with cider. I did manage to eat a little.

'There, you see,' he commented. 'I know what is good for you.'

'How soon can we start?' I asked.

'Patience,' he retorted. 'Do you know, in different circumstances I should be enjoying this thoroughly. Perhaps you and I can take some trips round the countryside. What do you say?'

'My grandfather would never allow it.'

'Has he allowed this?'

'There was a little . . . subterfuge.'

'Oh, you are capable of intrigue then?'

'I had to come,' I said. 'I would not have stayed away for anything.'

'You are so vehement. I like it. In fact, Miss Philippa, there is so much I like about you. I feel I know very little, though, and there is so much more to know. It would be a glorious voyage of discovery.'

'I am afraid you would find it rather dull.'

'What a woman for contradictions you are! One minute you are raging against me for not having a high opinion of your mental powers and then next you are telling me how unworthy you are for study. Now what am I to make of you?'

'I should give up the study if I were you.'

'But I am so intrigued.'

'Do you think we have finished now?'

'Such impatience!' he murmured.

We went out to the trap and I could scarcely contain my impatience as we approached Birley Church.

'We'll go first to the vicarage and find that charming vicar,' he said. 'He was so helpful to me. I shall have to give a large donation to the upkeep of the church.'

We went to the vicarage which was almost as old as the church. A woman who was obviously the vicar's wife came to the door and said we were lucky. The vicar had just come in.

We went into a drawing-room – shabby but cosy. The vicar greeted Conrad warmly.

'It is a pleasure to see you again,' he said.

'I have another request,' replied Conrad. 'We want to look at that register again.'

'That's no problem. Did you have the wrong date?'

My heart was beating fast. I knew there had been a mistake somewhere and I believed I was on the verge of discovering what it was.

'I'm not sure,' said Conrad. 'It might have been. This is Miss Ewell, who is particularly interested. She has been here before.'

'I didn't see you then,' I said to the vicar. 'You were away. I saw your churchwarden.'

'Oh yes, Thomas Borton. I was away for a while. That is not so long ago. Well, if you come into the church you can see what you want.'

We made our way to the church. There was the familiar smell of damp, old hymn books and that unusual furniture polish.

We went into the vestry and when the register was produced eagerly I turned the pages. I stared. It was not there. There had been no wedding on that date.

I stammered: 'There is a mistake . . .'

Conrad was beside me. He had slipped his arm through mine but I threw him off impatiently. I looked from him to the vicar.

'But I saw it,' I went on. 'It was here . . . It was in the book . . .'

'No,' said the vicar. 'That could not be. There is a mistake in the date, I think. Are you sure you have the right year?'

'I know I have. I know when it happened. The bride was my sister.'

The vicar looked shaken.

I went on: 'You must remember it. It would have been a rather hasty wedding . . .'

'I was not here at the time. I took over the living only two years ago.'

'It *was* here . . .' I could only insist. 'I saw it . . . It was there . . . plainly . . . for anyone to read.'

'There must be some mistake. You will find you have the wrong date.'

'Yes,' said Conrad, close to me. 'It's a mistake. I'm sorry. But you insisted on seeing for yourself.'

'The churchwarden brought us here,' I cried. 'He would remember. He showed us the book. He was here while we found it. Where is the churchwarden? I must see him. He will remember.'

'There's no need for that,' said Conrad. 'It's not here. It was a mistake. You thought you saw it . . .'

'One does not think one sees things! I saw it, I tell you. I want to see the churchwarden.'

'I am sure that is possible,' the vicar told us. 'He lives in the village. His house is number six, the Street. There is only one street worthy of the name in the village.'

'We will go and see him at once,' I said.

Conrad turned to the vicar. 'You have been most helpful,' he said.

'I am sorry there has been this upset.'

I turned back to the register and looked again. I was trying to conjure up what I had seen on that day with Miss Elton. It was no good. It was simply not there.

Conrad put two sovereigns into the offertory box in the porch as we went out and the vicar was most grateful.

'You'll find Tom Borton in his garden, I dare say. He's a great gardener.'

It was not difficult to find him. He came out to see us, looking mildly curious.

'The vicar gave us your address,' Conrad told him. 'Miss Ewell here is very anxious to see you.'

As he turned to me there was no recognition in his eyes.

I said: 'You remember I came to see you not long ago. There was a lady with me.'

He wrinkled his eyes and flicked a fly off the sleeve of his coat.

'You must remember,' I persisted. 'We looked at the records in the vestry. You showed us . . . and I found what I wanted.'

'We get people now and then to look at the records . . . Not often . . . but now and then.'

'So you do remember. The vicar was away . . . and we saw you in the church . . .'

He shook his head. 'I can't say as how I remember.'

'But you must. You were there. You *must* remember.'

'I'm afraid I can't remember anything about it.'

'I recognized you at once.'

He smiled. 'I can't say as I remember ever seeing you before, Miss . . . er . . . Ewell, did you say?'

'Well,' put in Conrad, 'we're sorry we troubled you.'

'Oh, that's all right, sir. Sorry I couldn't have been better help. I think the young lady's thinking of something else. I reckon I never saw her before in all my life.'

I was led away feeling bewildered. I felt that I was living in some sort of nightmare from which I must soon wake up.

'Come, we must get our train,' said Conrad.

We sat on the station with five minutes to spare. He had taken my arm and was holding it tightly. 'You mustn't be too upset,' he said.

'I am upset. How can I help it? I saw it clearly and that man was lying. Why? He must have remembered seeing me. He said himself that not many people come to look at the registers.'

'Listen, Philippa, strange things happen to us all at times. What happened to you was a sort of hallucination.'

'How dare you say that?'

'What other explanation is there?'

'I don't know. But I'm going to find out.'

The train came in and we got into it. We had a carriage to ourselves, for which I was grateful. I felt exhausted with emotion and a certain fear. I was almost beginning to believe that I had imagined the whole thing. Miss Elton had gone so I could not ask her. She had looked at the register with me. But had she actually seen the entry? I wasn't sure. All I remembered was seeing it myself and calling out in triumph. I tried to reconstruct the scene. I could not remember her actually standing beside me and looking at the book.

But the churchwarden had said he had never seen me before, yet he showed the register rarely. Surely he *must* have remembered.

Conrad came and sat beside me and put an arm about me. I was amazed that I could find some comfort from the action.

He said: 'Listen to me, Philippa. The entry is not there. It's all over now. Your sister is dead. If you had found that entry it would not have brought her back to life. It is a sad episode, but it is over now. You have your own life to live.'

I was not listening to him. I just felt the comfort of his being near me and I did not want to move away.

When we left the station he brought me as far as the woods. I would not let him come any nearer. There would be a great deal of explaining to do if I were seen with a man.

As I went into the Manor, Mrs Greaves was standing at the top of the staircase.

'Is that you, Miss Philippa?' she said. 'You are back. What a relief. Your grandmother was taken very ill this afternoon.'

She was looking at me steadily.

I said: 'She's dead, isn't she?'

And she nodded.

Suspected of Murder

I was in a bewildered state. I had schooled myself to offer some explanation for my absence, but it was not needed. My grandmother's death had meant that I had not been missed.

'She slipped away quietly in her sleep,' Mrs Greaves told me.

It must have been just at the time when I was coming face to face with the blank register.

'She didn't ask for me?' I said.

'Why, Miss, she has not been conscious at all through the day.'

I left her and went up to my bedroom. I stood in the middle of the room and let the desolation sweep over me. It was a feeling of utter loneliness. I was losing everyone. Francine, Daisy, Miss Elton and now my grandmother. It was as though a cruel fate was robbing me of everyone I cared for.

The thought of Conrad suddenly came to me. He had been kind. I was sure he had been really sorry that we could not find the entry.

We met at dinner that night – myself, my grandfather and Cousin Arthur.

My grandfather discussed funeral arrangements and said the family vault would be opened. Cousin Arthur should go to see the vicar. Our grandfather couldn't endure the man Besides, he might meet Grace or her husband.

Cousin Arthur said: 'I am only too happy to be of assistance to you, Uncle.'

'You are always that, Arthur,' replied my grandfather.

Arthur lowered his head and looked as pleased as the circumstances and his overwhelming humility would let him.

'It's a great blow to us all,' went on my grandfather, 'but life has to go on. The last thing she would have wished would be for us to upset the lives of those who have to go on living. We must think of what she would wish.'

I thought that it would be the first time he had ever done that. Did people have to be dead to get some consideration?

The coffin had been brought to the house – a magnificent affair of polished mahogany and lots of ornamental brass; it was placed in the room next to my grandfather's. She was closer to him there than she had been for many years. The funeral was to take place in five days' time. Meanwhile she lay there and all the servants went one by one to pay their last respects.

All through the night candles burned in that room. There were three at the head of the coffin and three at the foot.

I went in to see her. The smell of the wood and the memory of that room of death would remain with me forever. There was nothing eerie about it. She lay there – just her face visible and a starched cap hid her hair. She looked young and beautiful. She must have been something like that when she first came to Greystone Manor as a bride... One could not be afraid even though the room was full of shadows cast by the flickering candlelight. She had been so good and kind in her life, how could anyone fear her in death?

There was just a terrible desolation – a frightening sense of loss, and the understanding, as never before, how very much alone I was in the world.

Two days later I went to the woods. I sat under a tree hoping that Conrad would come. This was the hour when I took my walk. Would he think enough of me to come?

It seemed that he did and my spirits lifted when I saw him coming towards me.

He threw himself down beside me and, taking my hand, kissed it. 'How are you feeling?' he asked.

I said: 'When I reached home I learned that my grandmother had died.'

'Was it unexpected?'

'I suppose not. She was old and an invalid and she had been very unwell for some days. But it was a great shock, particularly as . . .'

'Tell me,' he said gently.

'Everyone has gone,' I said. 'There was my sister and Daisy the maid, who was a friend too. Then Miss Elton and now my grandmother. There is no one left.'

'My dear little girl . . .'

For once I did not mind being called a little girl. He went on softly: 'How old are you?'

'I shall soon be seventeen.'

'So young . . . and so troubled,' he murmured.

'If my parents had not died everything would have been different. We should have stayed on the island. We were happy there. Francine would never have died. I should not be here alone . . . without anyone.'

'What about your grandfather?'

I laughed bitterly. 'He will force me to marry Cousin Arthur.'

'Force you! You do not seem to me the sort of person who would be forced.'

'I have always said I wouldn't be, but I should have found some post. But who would employ someone of my age?'

'You are certainly young,' he agreed. 'And of course you are not exactly fond of Cousin Arthur.'

'I hate Cousin Arthur.'

'Why?'

'If you saw him you would understand. Francine hated him. She was to marry him. She was the elder, you see . . . but she married Rudolph. They *did* marry, I know they did.'

'Let us consider your problem. It really is of the greater importance.'

'When I am seventeen my grandfather wants me to marry

Cousin Arthur and I shall soon be seventeen. Then it will be a case of "Marry Arthur or get out". I'd like to get out, but where would I go to? I shall have to take a post. If only I were, say . . . two years older . . . You see what I mean?'

'I do indeed.'

'My grandmother was kind and good and understanding. I could talk to her. Now there is no one.'

'Well, I'm here,' he said.

'You!'

'Yes. My poor little girl, I don't like to see you unhappy. I like you full of fire raging against me . . . yes. Though I should prefer to see you tender perhaps. But I do not like to see you in despair.'

'I am in despair. I wanted to talk to my grandmother. I wanted to tell her about the register. There is no one to talk to now. I am all alone.'

He put his arms round me and held me tightly. He rocked me gently and kissed my forehead, the tip of my nose and then my lips. I was almost happy in those moments.

I drew back from him a little, afraid of my emotions. It was extraordinary that I could feel thus towards someone who had just proved me wrong on a matter so near my heart.

I was confused, not knowing which way to turn.

He said gently: 'You are not alone, you know. I am here. I am your friend.'

'My friend!' I cried. 'Why, you have tried to destroy my belief in my sanity.'

'You are not being fair. All I did was confront you with the truth. The truth must always be looked at . . . straight in the face . . . even when it is unpleasant.'

'That was not the truth. There's some explanation. I wish I knew what it was.'

'I can tell you this, my dear Philippa. You are so concerned with the past that you are letting the dangers of the present creep up on you. What are you going to do about Cousin Arthur?'

'I will never marry him '

'Then . . . when your grandfather turns you out . . . what then?'

'While I have been sitting here it has occurred to me that my grandmother's death will delay matters a little. There could not be a wedding following so close on a funeral, could there? My grandfather would always observe the conventions.'

'So you think the evil day is postponed.'

'It will give me time to find a way out. My Aunt Grace would help me. She escaped from Greystone Manor and is very happy now. Perhaps I could stay a while at the vicarage.'

'A ray of hope,' he said. 'And how do you think you will enjoy going into some strange household with the status of a servant after the way in which you have lived?'

'I have not lived so happily at Greystone Manor. I have always felt I have been something of a captive here. Francine felt it too. So I have not such a glorious past to look back on. Besides, I might be a governess. They are not servants . . . exactly.'

'Somewhere in between,' he said. 'Poor, poor Philippa. It's a grim prospect which lies before you.'

I shivered and he held me closer.

'I have to tell you,' he went on, 'that I am leaving England tomorrow.'

I was completely shattered and unable to speak. I just stared wretchedly ahead of me. Everyone was going. I should be left to the mercy of my grandfather and Cousin Arthur.

'Do I discern that you are a little sorry that I am going?'

'It has been comforting talking to you.'

'And I am forgiven for the part I played in that disastrous register affair?'

'It wasn't your fault. I don't blame you.'

'I thought you hated me for it.'

'I am not quite as foolish as that.'

'And you promise me that you are going to forget it? You are going to stop looking back?'

'I couldn't stop myself wanting to know. She is my sister.'

'I know. I understand perfectly. Dear Philippa, don't despair. Something will turn up for you. I'm sorry I have to go. It's vital that I should.'

'I suppose you have been called back by your employers?'

'That's the idea. But I have one more day. We'll meet tomorrow. I'm going to try to come up with a solution to your troubles.'

'How could you possibly do that?'

'I'm something of a magician,' he said. 'Didn't you guess that? I'm not quite what I seem.'

I gave a forced laugh. I was really miserable because he was going and I did not want him to know how deeply I felt about it.

'I'm going to save you from the arms of Cousin Arthur, Philippa . . . if you'll let me.'

'I don't think you have enough magic for that.'

'We'll see. Will you trust me?' He rose to his feet. 'I have to go now.'

He held out a hand and pulled me up. We stood close to each other. Then his arms were round me. His kisses had changed. They were bewildering, a little frightening and I wanted them to go on.

When he released me he was laughing. 'I think you are a little more kindly disposed towards me now,' he said.

'I don't know what I feel . . .'

'There is a little time left to us,' he replied. 'Will you trust me?'

'What a strange question. Should I?'

'No,' he answered. 'Never trust anyone. Particularly people you know nothing about.'

'You are warning me?'

He nodded. 'Preparing you, perhaps.'

'You do sound mysterious. At one moment you are going to help me and the next you are warning me against you.'

'Life is full of contradictions. Will you meet me here tomorrow? I may have a solution. It will of course depend on you.'

'I will be here tomorrow.'

He took my chin in his hands and said: '*Nil desperandum.*' Then he kissed me lightly and walked with me to the edge of the wood where we parted.

I went into the house past the chamber of death up to my bedroom and threw myself on Francine's bed, which seemed to bring her nearer to me.

There was no doubt about it. Conrad excited me, and I wanted to be with him. When I was, I could forget almost everything else.

I could not bear to be in that house of death and yet the sense of loneliness had lifted a little. Conrad would meet me tomorrow and he had said he would find a solution. I could not believe this was possible and yet it was a comforting thought. Being with him was a sort of opiate and I was in such a desperate state that I was ready to grasp at anything.

I could not endure to stay in the house so I went out into the garden, and while I was there one of the Emms boys came to me.

He said: 'I was told to give you this when no one was looking, Miss.'

I seized it.

'Who . . . ?' I began.

'From the Grange, Miss.'

'Thank you,' I said.

I slit the envelope and took out a thick white paper with a golden crest at the top. Grange paper, I thought; and then I was reading what had been written.

Philippa,

I have to leave early tomorrow morning. I must see you before I go. Please come this evening, can you, at ten o'clock. I'll be waiting for you in the Grange shrubbery.

C.

My hands were trembling. So he was going tomorrow. He had said he would find a solution for me. Could it be possible?

I should have to slip out of the house and leave the door unlocked. No. That might be discovered. There was a window in the courtyard which was low. If I left that unlatched I could easily get through it . . . just in case when I returned the door had been locked.

I must see him.

I don't know how I lived through the rest of that day. I pleaded a headache and did not join my grandfather and cousin for dinner. It seemed a reasonable enough excuse, for the normal routine of the household was naturally somewhat disrupted on account of my grandmother's death, and the preparations for the funeral.

I had tested the courtyard window. People rarely went past it, so it should be safe enough.

At a quarter to ten I was on my way. He was waiting for me in the shrubbery and when he saw me he caught me in his arms and held me against him.

'We'll go into the house,' he said.

'Should we?' I asked.

'Why not?'

'It isn't your house. You're only the equerry.'

'Shall we say I'm in charge? Come along.'

We walked into the Grange, and as we passed through the hall I looked up anxiously at the high holes in the wall which I knew could be peered through in the solarium.

'No one will see us,' he whispered. 'They are all asleep. They have had a busy day preparing for departure.'

'Are they all going tomorrow?'

'They'll be leaving in a day or so.'

We went up the stairs. 'Where are we going?' I asked. 'To the *Weinzimmer*?'

'You'll see.'

He threw open a door and we entered a room in which a fire was burning. It was a large room with heavy velvet curtains. I noticed the alcove in which was a four-poster bed.

'Whose room is this?' I asked quickly.

'Mine,' he answered. 'We're safe here.'

'I don't understand.'

'You will. Come and sit down. I have some excellent wine here. I want you to try it.'

'I know nothing of wine.'

'Surely you drink it at Greystone Manor?'

'My grandfather always decides what it shall be and everyone else has to drink it and like it.'

'A despot, your grandfather.'

'What is it you have to say to me?'

'I am going away. I thought I had to see you.'

'Yes,' I said, 'you told me.'

He took my hand and, sitting down in a large throne-like chair, he drew me down to him so that I was sitting on his knees.

'You should not be afraid,' he said quietly. 'There is nothing to fear. Your welfare will be my greatest concern from now on.'

'You say the most extraordinary things. I thought I had come here to say goodbye to you.'

'I am hoping you won't do that.'

'How could it be otherwise?'

'The difficulties are not insurmountable.'

His hands were on my neck caressing it gently. I was beginning to feel that I wanted to stay in this room forever.

'How do you feel about me?' he asked.

I tried to free myself from his searching hands.

'We hardly know each other,' I stammered. 'You're not... English.'

'Is that a great handicap?'

'Of course not, but it means . . .'

'What?'

'That we probably think differently about everything. I would rather sit on a chair and hear what it is you have to say to me.'

'But I would rather you stayed here . . . near me. Philippa, you must know that I am falling in love with you.'

I felt dizzy with sudden happiness, as though I were slipping into a deep pool of contentment, but I was conscious of warning voices within me. It was a dangerous pool.

'Philippa,' he went on. 'It's rather a dignified name.' He repeated it. 'Philippa.'

I said: 'My family always called me Pippa.'

'Pippa. Short for Philippa. I like it. It recalls a poem called Pippa's Song . . . or Pippa Passes. You see, I may not be English but I was educated here. I know my Browning. "God's in his Heaven, All's right with the world." That's Pippa's Song. Is it true for you?'

'You know very well that it is far from being so.'

'So perhaps I could make it so. I should be very happy if I could. "All's right with the world." I want you to tell me that that is the case.'

'Yes, you are going away and I shall not see you after tonight.'

'That is what I have to talk to you about because whether you continue to see me or not depends on you.'

'I don't understand you.'

'It's simple. I could take you with me.'

'Take me to . . .'

'That's right. Take you back with me.'

'How could that possibly be?'

'Quite easily. We meet tomorrow at the station. We do not go to Dover as we did before. We go to London and from there to Harwich. We take ship and after our journey across the sea we take another train and in due course we come to my home. What do you say?'

'You are teasing me.'

'I swear I'm not. I want you with me. Don't you understand I have fallen in love with you?'

'But . . . how could I possibly come with you?'

'How could you not?'

'My grandfather would never agree.'

'I thought we were going to outwit Grandfather and Cousin Arthur. So we don't need the agreement of either of them. Pippa . . . let me show you how I love you.'

'I . . . don't . . .'

'Then let me teach you,' he said.

He had unbuttoned my bodice. I put my hands up to stop him, but he took them and began to kiss them. I was afraid and yet overcome by an excitement such as I had never known before. Everything seemed to fade away . . . the past . . . the future . . . everything that frightened me. There was nothing but this moment. He was kissing me as he took off my bodice.

'What is happening?' I stammered. 'I must go . . .'

But I made no attempt to. I was overwhelmed by an irresistible longing.

He kept telling me that he loved me, that I had nothing to fear. We were going to be together forever and ever. I could forget my grandfather, forget Cousin Arthur. They were in the past. There was nothing else that mattered except this wonderful love of ours.

The contrast to all I had felt since Francine had gone was so great that I had to shut out everything but this moment. There was one part of me that was trying to reason. but I wouldn't listen.

'I must go now . . .' I began; and I heard him laugh softly and then I was in the four-poster bed and he was there with me. All the time he was murmuring endearments and I was shocked and shattered and overwhelmed with delight.

Afterwards he just lay still holding me. I was trembling and very happy and in an odd way defiant, telling myself that I wouldn't have it different if I had a chance to go back.

He stroked my hair and told me I was beautiful, adorable, and that he would love me forever.

'Nothing like this has ever happened to me before,' I said.

'I know,' he answered. 'Is it not wonderful to be together like this? Come, little Pippa, tell me the truth?'

I told him it was.

'And you have no regrets?'

'No,' I said firmly. 'No.'

Then he kissed me and made love to me again; and this time it was different; the shock was gone and there was a different kind of ecstasy. I realized that my cheeks were wet, so I must have wept, for he kissed my tears away and said he had never been so happy in his life.

He got up and put on a silk robe of blue with gold figures on it. The blue matched his eyes and he looked like one of the Norse gods.

'Are you mortal?' I asked, 'or are you Thor or Odin or one of the gods or perhaps heroes of the Norsemen?'

'You know something of our mythology, I see.'

'Francine and I used to read of it with Miss Elton.'

'Who would you like me to be? Sigurd? I always thought he was a bit foolish to drink the potion and marry Gudrun when his true love was Brunhild, didn't you?'

'Yes,' I answered. 'Very foolish.'

'Oh, little Pippa, we are going to be so very happy.' He went to the table and poured out more wine. 'Refreshment after our exertions,' he said. 'It will give us strength to renew them.'

I laughed. Something was happening to me. I drank the wine. He seemed to grow taller than ever and I felt a little dizzy.

I said: 'It's the wine.'

Then his arms were round me and we were caught up again in our love.

That was a night of awakening for me. I was no longer a child, no longer a virgin. I slept a little and when I awoke the effect of the wine was no longer with me.

I sat up hastily and looked at Conrad. He stirred and reached for me. As though to warn that the magic night was over I heard the church clock strike four. Four o'clock in the morning and I had been out since ten!

I touched my naked body in dismay. My clothes were lying on the floor.

I cried out: 'I must go.'

He was wide awake now. He put his arms round me.

'There's nothing to be afraid of. You are coming with me.'

I said: 'Where shall we be married . . . in a church like Francine?'

He was looking at me in silence. Then he smiled and drew me to him. 'Pippa,' he said, 'there can't be a marriage any more than there could be for Francine.'

'But we have . . .'

My eyes took in the disorder of the bed and the man naked beside me. There were memories of the night we had spent together, the empty wine bottle, the ashes in the fireplace.

He smiled gently.

'I love you,' he said. 'I will take you with me. I will care for you always. We will have children perhaps. Oh, you will have a wonderful life, Pippa. You will lack for nothing.'

'But we *must* marry,' I said foolishly. 'I thought that was what you meant when you said you loved me.'

He smiled, still tender but just faintly cynically, I thought. 'Love and marriage don't always go together.'

'But I cannot be . . . with you like this . . . if I am not your wife.'

'But you can and you have proved it, for you have.'

'But . . . it is impossible.'

'In the world of Greystone Manor perhaps. We are leaving that behind us and everything will be different now. I would to God I could marry you. That would make me very happy. But I am already as good as married.'

'You mean you have a wife?'

He nodded. 'You could say that. That is how it is in my country. Wives are chosen for us and we go through a ceremony which is tantamount to marriage.'

'Then you should never have deceived me into thinking that we should be married.'

'I did not deceive you. Marriage was not mentioned.'

'But I thought that we were going to be. I thought that was what it all *meant* . . . You said you would take me away with you.'

'Everything I have said I would do, I will do. The one thing I cannot do is marry you.'

'Then what are you proposing? That I should be your mistress?'

'Some would say this is what you already are.'

I covered my face with my hands. Then I was off the bed and searching for my clothes.

'Pippa,' he said, 'be sensible. I love you. I want you with me all the time. Please, dearest Pippa, you must understand.'

'Yes, I do understand. You do this sort of thing because it amuses you. You do not love me. I am just a light o' love. I believe that is what they call it.'

'A rather old-fashioned expression, I believe.'

'Please do not joke. I see I have been foolish again. You enjoy making me seem so. First the entry. It wasn't the right register, was it? You arranged that.'

'I assure you I did no such thing.'

'You planned this. You gave me that wine . . . and now . . . you have ruined me.'

'My dear child, you talk like a character in a cheap melodrama.'

'I am cheap perhaps . . . cheaply come by I succumbed

very readily, did I not? And you took advantage of that . . . and now you say you have a wife. I don't believe you.'

'Once again I assure you it is true. Pippa, you must believe that if this had not been so I should have asked you to marry me. I am sure you must see that what is between us will grow and grow . . . It will be the sort of love which is the most worthwhile thing in the whole world.'

I was so miserable. My puritanical upbringing at Greystone made me see myself as ruined, a fallen woman.

'Listen to me,' he said. 'Come away with me. I will show you a new life. There is more to relationships between two people than signing a name in a register. I love you. We can have a wonderful life together.'

'And your wife?'

'That is something apart.'

'You are cruel and cynical.'

'I am realistic. I was involved in this marriage for family reasons. It is a marriage of convenience. That is accepted. It is not meant to prevent my loving someone else . . . someone who could become dearer to me than anyone on earth. You don't believe me, do you?'

'No,' I replied. 'I have heard of men like you. I did not think of that in the beginning. I was carried away.'

His arms were round me once more. He said: 'You are adorable. You love me. You see. You wanted me. You did not say then, "When are you going to marry me?" That did not come into your head.'

'I realize I know very little about the ways of the world.'

'Then come with me and learn. Customs are made for men and women, not men and women for customs.'

'I could not take your view of life.'

I had started to dress. He said: 'What are you going to do? Will you be at the station this morning?'

'How could I? It would be wrong.'

'So you will let me go . . . alone?'

'What alternative have I?'

'"Come live with me and be my love and we will all the pleasures prove!" Another of your English poets. You see, I know them well. Oh, little Pippa, you are a child still . . . in spite of the fact that I have made a woman of you. You have so much to learn. If you do not come with me today you will regret it all your life.'

'I could regret it if I came.'

'That is a chance we must take in life. Pippa, take your chance. Do what you want to do.'

'But I know it would be wrong.'

'Throw away your conventions, Pippa. Throw them away and learn to live.'

'I must go back,' I said.

'I will take you back.'

'No . . .'

'But I will. Give me a moment.'

I stood there watching him and there were wild doubts in my heart. I was seeing myself setting out for the station. He would be there. We would board the train together . . . to love and adventure. It was like Francine's story repeating itself.

'Come.' He slipped his arm through mine and as he did so he kissed me tenderly. 'My darling,' he went on, 'I promise you, you will never regret.'

It seemed that Francine was very close to me then. And what of the entry in the register? Had I really seen it? Had Francine had to face the same dilemma? I felt lost and bewildered and very inexperienced.

We came out into the cool air of the early morning.

'You should go,' I said. 'You should not be seen with me.'

'Let us hope no one sees you returning at this hour of the morning.'

He was holding my hand firmly against him. 'This morning,' he said. 'Ten o'clock at the station. Be careful. We'll get on the train separately. I shall have your ticket.'

I drew myself away and ran. My heart was beating wildly as I came into the courtyard. By good fortune the window was as I had left it. I scrambled through and closed it, and hurrying through into the hall started up the stairs.

Suddenly I felt myself go cold with apprehension. Mrs Greaves was standing on the top stair watching me. She was in dressing-gown and slippers and her hair was in iron curlers.

She cried out: 'Oh, Miss Philippa. You gave me a shock, you did. I thought I heard someone. Wherever have you been?'

'I . . . I couldn't rest. I went for a little walk in the gardens.'

She looked disbelievingly at my tousled hair. I was sure I must have appeared rather strange.

I sped past her as she stood aside and once in my room I sank on to my bed. I felt bruised and bewildered and was trying not to look ahead to what the future held.

I think I must have slept at last, for I was physically and mentally exhausted. I awoke startled and saw that it was nine o'clock. I lay in bed thinking of the events of last night and I longed to be with him. I wanted to forget my scruples and go with him. I wouldn't care if it was wrong, if it was all against my upbringing. I just wanted to be with him.

It was all I could do to restrain myself from throwing a few things together and running to the station. What did it matter if we could not marry? I had already been a wife to him. If only Francine could have been with me! She would have said: 'You must go with him!' Francine would have gone. Hadn't she gone with Rudolph? Was it similar? Had her assertions that she had married been a fabrication, a sop to the conventions? Had I imagined I had seen that entry in the register? Life was becoming like a fantastic dream.

If Miss Elton had been here she would have brought a certain sanity to the situation. I could imagine her folding her hands together and saying: 'Of course you cannot go and live with a man who will not marry you.' And I know I should have felt that that was not only right but the only possible answer.

Oh, but I wanted to go. How desperately I wanted to!

It was nine-thirty. Too late now.

There was a knock on the door. It was one of the maids. 'Miss Philippa, are you not well?'

'I have such a headache,' I replied.

'I thought you had. I told Sir Matthew that you weren't feeling well. He looked quite concerned.'

'Thank you, Amy.'

'Would you like something brought up, Miss?'

'Nothing, thanks. I'll get up later.'

Twenty more minutes to ten o'clock. Yes, it was too late I could never get there in time. I pictured him at the station, waiting for me, hoping, longing perhaps. He was fond of me. I was sure of that.

And when the train left and I had not joined him? Perhaps he would shrug his shoulders. 'A pity,' he would say. 'I liked her. I could have enjoyed teaching her to be a woman. But she did not come. She lacked the courage. She's a conventional little mouse, that's all. It is a pity -- but that is how it is.'

All I would be to him was an episode in his life.

As equerry to the Grand Duke or the Margrave or something like that, he would live a romantic life among the mountains, attending ceremonial occasions in some old schloss.

I wanted to be with him so much.

Ten o'clock struck stridently, it seemed, triumphantly. Too late. Virtue had prevailed.

I went through the day in a bemused state. At dinner my grandfather was quite solicitous and I had never known him to be so gracious before. He enquired about my headache and said he was glad to see that I had obviously recovered. After dinner he would like a word with me in his study.

Oddly enough my thoughts were so very much with Conrad that it did not immediately occur to me that the moment I had been dreading for so long had come, and even when he received me in the study as graciously as he had at dinner, I did not think of it. He was smiling kindly, not dreaming for a moment that he would find any obstruction to his plans.

He stood up, his hands in his pockets rather as though he were addressing a public meeting.

'This house is sadly bereaved,' he said. 'Your poor grandmother lies in her coffin and there is a great sadness on us all. But she would be the last to expect life to stand still merely because she had left it. She would be the first to wish us to go on with our lives and perhaps bring a little lightness into the gloom which is so dark at this time.'

I was scarcely listening to him. My thoughts were still with Conrad.

'I had planned a great celebration for your seventeenth birthday, your passing into womanhood.'

I wanted to shout: I am already there, Grandfather. I spent a glorious night in the Grange with the most wonderful lover, and now he has gone and I never felt so desolate in my life . . . not even when Francine went.

'That will not be seemly in the circumstances,' my grandfather was going on. 'Your grandmother's death . . .' He sounded a little peevish as though it were most inconsiderate of her to die at such a time . . . 'Yes, your grandmother's death rather precludes that. Still, I thought on the occasion we would have a dinner-party with friends . . and the announcement could be made then.'

'The announcement!'

'You know what my wishes are for you and your Cousin Arthur. His coincide with mine and I am sure yours will. I see no reason for a delay just because we have a death in the family. Of course the ceremonies will have to be conducted more quietly than I had at first thought . . . but there is no reason why we should delay. We shall announce the engagement on your seventeenth birthday. I always believed long engagements were a mistake. You can be married within three months, say. That will give everyone the time they need for preparations.'

I heard myself speaking then and it was as though my voice was disembodied and didn't belong to me.

'You are making a mistake, Grandfather, if you think I am going to marry Cousin Arthur.'

'What?' he cried.

'I said I have no intention of marrying Cousin Arthur.'

'You have gone mad.'

'No. I never intended to marry him any more than my sister did.'

'Don't talk about your sister to me. She was a harlot and we are well rid of her. I should not have wished her to be the mother of my heirs.'

'She was no harlot,' I retorted vehemently. 'She was a woman who would not be forced into marriage . . . any more than I will.'

'I tell you,' he cried, and he was so incensed that he was shouting at me, 'you will do as I say or you will not continue to live under my roof.'

'Then if that is so,' I said wearily, 'I must leave here.'

'All this time I have nurtured a viper in my bosom.'

I could not stop myself laughing hysterically. The cliché hardly fitted the case and the idea of my grandfather nursing anything in his bosom seemed hilariously funny.

'You brazen girl,' he shouted. 'How dare you! I think you have taken leave of your senses. Let me tell you, you will regret this. I had made plans for you. I had left you well provided-for in my will when you married Arthur. I shall send for my lawyers tomorrow morning. Not a penny shall you have. You are throwing away everything . . . do you understand? This house . . . a fine husband . . .'

'Not everything, Grandfather,' I said. 'I shall have my freedom.'

'Freedom? Freedom to do what? Starve? Or take some menial post. For that is the choice you will have, my girl. You will not stay under my roof . . . living a life of luxury. I have brought you here from a savage place . . . I have educated you . . . fed you . . .'

'I *am* your granddaughter, remember.'

'It is something I wish to forget.' His voice was raised and I wondered who was listening. I was sure the servants could hear it all.

His mood changed suddenly. He was almost placating. 'Now perhaps you have not given enough thought to this prospect . . . a glorious one. Perhaps you have spoken rather hastily . . .'

'No,' I said firmly. 'That is not so. I have known what was in your mind and have given much thought to the matter. In no circumstances will I marry Cousin Arthur.'

'Get out!' he cried. 'Get out . . . before I do you an injury. You will leave here tomorrow. I shall see my lawyer at once to make sure that you never benefit from anything of mine . . . ever. You will be penniless, penniless, I tell you. I shall make sure of that.'

I turned to the door and went out, my head high, my eyes blazing. As I came into the corridor I heard a scuffle and a rustling so I knew that we had been overheard.

I went to the stairs and mounted them. So it had come. Everything was happening at once. I was alone and tomorrow I should be homeless. I had no notion of where I should go or what I should do.

I opened the door of the room next to my grandfather's bedroom and in which the body of my grandmother lay in her coffin. The candles had been freshly lighted. They would all be replenished before the household retired and would burn through the night.

I stood on the threshold and looked at that peaceful face and I murmured: 'Oh, Grandmother dear, why did you not live to talk to me, to advise me what to do? Why did you leave me alone and desolate? Help me. Please help me. Tell me what I should do.'

How still it was in that room, and yet somehow I did feel a certain peace. I could almost believe that the cold lips smiled at me reassuringly.

I awoke from my sleep. It was dark and I wondered what had awakened me. When I had retired for the night I had lain awake for a long time wondering what the next day would bring, and where I should go when I left Greystone Manor. Then, from very exhaustion, I must have fallen into a heavy sleep.

Now I sat up in bed. I could smell something strange and I heard a sound which I did not immediately recognize.

I listened intently – and then I was out of bed.

It was fire!

I thrust my feet into my slippers and ran.

My grandfather's room was at the end of the corridor and next to it was that one in which my grandmother had lain in her coffin. Then as I stood there I saw the tongue of flame creeping along the top of the door.

'Fire!' I shouted. 'Fire!'

I ran towards my grandfather's room and as I did so Cousin Arthur appeared.

'What is it?' he cried; and then, realizing: 'Oh . . . God help us.'

'There is a fire in my grandfather's room,' I called to him.

By this time several of the servants were on the scene. Cousin Arthur had opened the door of my grandfather's room and as he did so the flames burst out.

'Give the alarm!' shouted Cousin Arthur. 'Keep away from the room. It's ablaze. The room next to it too.'

One of the footmen was already making his way through the smoke and flames. He had disappeared into my grandfather's room and when he came out he was dragging my grandfather along the floor.

Cousin Arthur was calling out: 'Get water . . . quickly!

Douse the fire! The whole place will be ablaze . . . These timbers are as dry as straw.'

Everyone was rushing about. I went over to Cousin Arthur who was leaning over my grandfather.

'Send one of the servants for the doctor . . . quickly,' he said.

I ran downstairs and found one of the grooms who had heard the commotion and seen the fire from his rooms over the stables.

He was off without a word and I went back again. There was water everywhere and the smoke was choking me, but I could see that they were getting the fire under control.

It appeared to have started in the room in which my grandmother lay.

Cousin Arthur said: 'I never thought it safe to have those candles burning all night.'

It was a shock to see my grandfather lying in the corridor, a pillow under his head and blankets covering him. He looked quite unlike the man who a few hours before had thundered at me in his study; he looked forlorn, vulnerable, with his beard completely burned and burns on what I could see of his face and neck. He must be in terrible pain, I thought, but no sound came from him.

When the doctor arrived I was still standing there. The fire had been put out and the danger was past.

The doctor took one look at my grandfather and said: 'Sir Matthew is dead.'

A strange night . . . with the smell of the fumes still in my nostrils and my grandfather who but a short time before had been screaming abuse at me . . . dead.

I try to piece together the events of that night but it is not easy.

I remember Cousin Arthur in a long brown dressing-gown offering me something to drink. He seemed kinder than he ever had before, less self-righteous, more humane. He was clearly very shaken by what had happened. His benefactor was dead. He looked as if he couldn't believe it.

'You must not upset yourself, Philippa,' he said. 'I know you had a bit of trouble with him tonight.'

I was silent.

He patted my hand. 'Don't fret,' he said. 'I understand.'

The doctor was looking grave. He wanted to have a few words with Cousin Arthur. He was disconcerted and uneasy. He did not think my grandfather's death was due to suffocation. There was a cut on the back of his head.

'He must have fallen down,' said Cousin Arthur.

'It could have been so,' replied the doctor dubiously.

'This has been a terrible night for my cousin,' went on Cousin Arthur. 'I wonder if you could give her a sedative.' He looked at me with such compassion that I wondered if I had ever really known him before. Moreover he was acting with a new authority as though he were already master of the house. Summoning one of the maids, he told her to take me to my room.

I allowed her to lead me away and back in my bedroom I fell on to my bed. I could not believe this was really happening. My life had taken an unexpected turn. For so long it had gone along uneventfully and now one dramatic event was following on another.

I took the drink which the maid brought up to me and which she said had been given to her by the doctor. Soon I had fallen into a heavy sleep.

The next morning the nightmare continued. The house was in turmoil and there were strangers everywhere.

Cousin Arthur asked me to come to my grandfather's study and there he told me that they had taken my grandfather's body away because they were not satisfied about the way in which he had died. There would be an inquest. He said something about a blow on the back of his head.

'Do you mean he fell down and struck his head?'

'It could have been that he became aware that there was a fire and in rushing to get out of his room, he fell. It seems one of the candles round your grandmother's coffin must have fallen over and perhaps set the rug alight. The coffin was on that side of the room which was in immediate proximity to your grandfather's bedroom. As you know, there is a communicating door between the two rooms and there were cracks in the side of the door through which the flames could penetrate. I am not sure, of course. I am surmising . . . but the fact is . . . those two rooms are the only ones which are damaged – and your grandfather's bedroom is more so than the room in which the coffin lay. Fires start in all sorts of ways.'

I nodded.

'I know how you will be feeling, Philippa, because of that altercation last night.'

'I had to tell him how I felt,' I said.

'I know. And I am aware of the subject you discussed. I want you to understand that I am your friend, Philippa. Your grandfather's wish was that we should marry but you did not want that. It is a disappointment to me but I don't want you to think for one moment that I hold it against you.'

One of the most bewildering aspects of this situation was the change in Cousin Arthur. He had taken on a new stature with the passing of my grandfather. Gone was the humble, grateful relation, so eager to ingratiate himself. He was now behaving like the head of the house; he was even being kind and understanding to me.

He smiled ruefully. 'We cannot force our affections where they will not go,' he said. 'Your grandfather wanted to provide for you and use you to continue the direct line. Well, he is dead now, and I would not wish you to be forced into a marriage distasteful to you. On the other hand I want you to regard this house as your home . . . for as long as you wish.'

'Oh, Cousin Arthur, that is good of you, for now I suppose all this will belong to you.'

'Your grandfather always said I should inherit. Perhaps I am being a bit premature in talking thus. What I should say is that if it works out as we have been led to believe it will -- then this is your home for as long as you wish.'

'I couldn't stay here,' I said, 'knowing that he had turned me out. I shall make some plans but I am relieved by your kind offer to allow me to stay until I do so.'

He smiled at me affectionately. 'Then that little matter is settled. There will be anxious days ahead. I do not want to add to your anxieties. There may be some unpleasantness. That blow on the head . . . Well, obviously he fell, but you must not reproach yourself, Philippa.'

'I don't. I had to tell him the truth. I would do exactly the same again. I could not allow him to force me . . .'

'No, of course not. There is one other matter. Your grandmother's coffin has been scarred by the fire, but it is intact and I think the best thing we can do is to carry on as far as her funeral is concerned as though this had not happened. She will be buried tomorrow . . . and we will follow all the usual arrangements. Do you agree that is the best thing to do?'

I did agree.

'All right,' he said, patting my shoulder. 'That is how it will be.'

Of course he too had been under the dominating sway of my grandfather. He had no more wanted to be forced into marriage than I had. The difference in us was that he was prepared to go to great lengths to please my grandfather and get his inheritance, whereas I was not. I supposed that Arthur would have been turned out penniless into a harsh world if he had not obeyed my grandfather, and I have no doubt that being some low-paid curate did not appeal to him. I could understand that and I was even liking him a little now.

My grandmother's funeral took place the next day. Aunt Grace came to the house with Charles Daventry and we talked together. Aunt Grace was very upset at the death of her mother and that she had not been allowed to visit her at the end. She was shocked by the death of her father, but if we were absolutely honest we would have to admit that it was a relief to us all.

We stood round the grave and as the scarred coffin was lowered into the earth and we listened to the clods being thrown on to it, I was thinking of our talks and all that she had done for us during those first difficult days at the Manor. She had been a kind of anchor to two bewildered young people. I was going to miss her sadly.

But everything would be changed. I must begin to find a post. At least I should soon be seventeen, which was a landmark to maturity. If I explained that I had suddenly fallen into poverty after having lived at Greystone Manor with my grandfather, perhaps I could now get by.

We went back to the house and in my grandfather's study over biscuits and port wine, we assembled to hear the reading of the will.

We were astonished to learn that my grandmother had had a considerable estate, unknown to my grandfather. I was sure he would have wished to deal with it had he known how rich she was in her own right, and I have no doubt would have taken control of it so that it would no longer have been hers. I had always known that she was a strong-minded woman; her gentleness was misleading. She was kindly too, but once having been forced into marriage, she had been determined not to be completely dominated by her husband. So she had kept her secrets and this was one of them.

The disposal of the money was an even greater surprise to me. Agnes Warden must have been in the secret because she admitted afterwards that she had brought the lawyer to my grandmother. Agnes herself was left a legacy to provide an annuity; there were one or two other bequests, but the bulk of it was split between her daughter Grace and her granddaughter Philippa 'to enable them to live independent lives'.

I was stunned.

The great problem which had lain before me had been pushed aside by this gesture of my grandmother. I was to be comparatively rich. I need not worry about finding that post. I could go from this house as a rich woman of independent means.

'To lead independent lives!' I looked at Grace. She was crying quietly.

The following day the inquest on my grandfather took place. That day stands out in my memory as the strangest of my life. I sat there with Cousin Arthur and Grace and Charles and listened to the doctor's evidence. The heat of the room, the drone of the voices, the ritual of it all was awe-inspiring. I tried to grasp the significance of what the doctor was saying. Sir Matthew Ewell's death was not due to suffocation or the result of burns, and while it might have been caused when he fell and struck his head on the edge of a fender or some piece of furniture, on the other hand there was a possibility that it could have come through a blow administered by some person or persons unknown. It was likely that he had awakened from his sleep to become aware of the fire which had come through from the room next to his. He could have stumbled out of bed in a hurry and fallen. But this was conjecture and it was not possible to prove because the body had been dragged out of the room and it was not known what position it had been in at the time of death.

There was a great deal of discussion about this and at length the inquest was adjourned until the following week.

'What does it mean?' asked Aunt Grace of Charles.

Charles said it meant they were not entirely satisfied with the findings.

It was a strange week which followed. I went about the house in a kind of daze. I longed to get away . . . right away.

'You can't make plans until this wretched business is over,' said Cousin Arthur.

I noticed the servants were looking at me strangely. I read

suspicion in their looks. It could mean only one thing. They had heard my quarrel with my grandfather and they knew that he was threatening to turn me out. And now this talk about his having been struck by someone . . . I knew the implication. Someone had struck him, killed him, and then started the fire to cover up the deed.

I couldn't believe it. Did those dark looks implicate me? Could they possibly think that *I* had done this?

I began to be frightened.

I noticed Mrs Greaves particularly. She watched me closely. It was ridiculous. It was such nonsense. As if I would kill my own grandfather!

Agnes Warden was kind to me; so were Aunt Grace and Charles.

'I can't think what they want to make all this fuss about,' said Charles. 'It is quite obvious that Sir Matthew fell and killed himself.'

'There is always this sort of enquiry in cases of sudden death,' added Cousin Arthur.

My grandfather's will was read. Arthur had inherited the estate and the house. I was mentioned. There was to be a settlement on the occasion of my marriage to Arthur and there would be a small income for me for life, to be increased on the birth of every child I should have.

This was what he had planned to change when the lawyer would have been summoned. He had clearly wanted it to be definitely understood that in view of my ingratitude I should never have a penny of his money.

Arthur took charge of the household and I continued to be astonished by his consideration towards me.

'I think,' said Grace, 'he is hoping you will change your mind and it will all work out as my father wished.'

'That could never be,' I told her. 'I am grateful for Cousin Arthur's consideration, but I could never marry him.'

Grace nodded. Secure in her new life with Charles, she felt she knew a great deal about love and marriage.

Mrs Greaves's manner towards me became so cool that one day I asked her if anything was wrong.

She looked at me steadily. She had a hard, even a cruel face. I had always thought that long years of service in my grandfather's household had made her like that.

'I think that is a question you should ask yourself, Miss,' she said severely.

'What do you mean, Mrs Greaves?'

'I think you know well enough.'

'No,' I replied. 'I don't.'

'Well, there's a lot of speculation as to how that poor gentleman died . . . and it's thought that someone in this house might be able to throw a little light on that.'

'Do you mean *I* could?'

'Ask yourself, Miss. We heard the quarrel that went on on the last night of my master's life. I was not far off . . . accidentally . . . I couldn't help hearing.'

'It must have been a great distress to you to have been forced to listen, Mrs Greaves.'

'If you'll forgive my saying so, Miss, that's the sort of thing I'd expect to hear from you. I heard it because I was there and I saw you go into your grandmother's room after.'

'What did you think I did? Set the place on fire and let it burn slowly for hours before I guided it into my grandfather's room?'

'No. The fire was started later.'

'Was started, Mrs Greaves? You mean it began. Nobody started it.'

'Who's to say, and I fancy some of them people at the inquest has got their own opinions.'

'What are you trying to say? And why don't you say it outright?'

'Well, it seems to be a bit of a mystery, Miss. But mysteries get cleared up and all I can say is some people are not what they seem. I don't forget, Miss, that I saw you coming in in the early morning hours . . . and that not so long ago. I just wondered what you were up to. It only goes to show that you can never tell what people will do, can you?'

I was terribly shaken that she should refer to that night with Conrad. I felt angry and hurt. Why did I not run away with him? Why did I let my foolish puritanical conscience stand in my way? If I had gone I should not have been here when my grandfather died. There would never have been that scene in the study.

Mrs Greaves had seen how her words affected me. I heard her give a slight snigger as she turned and went silently away.

It occurred to me then that I was in a very dangerous situation.

I think I was too bemused by everything that had happened so suddenly to realize the extent of that danger, which was perhaps fortunate.

Arthur was so kind to me – almost tender; and I wondered vaguely whether Grace was right and he was trying to make me change my mind towards him.

'If they should ask you questions,' he said, 'all you have to do is tell the truth. If you do that no harm can come. One must never tell a lie in court for if one is discovered one is never believed on a single thing. You'll be all right, Philippa. We shall all be there.'

I had never visualized anything like this – the court with all its dignitaries. And it was only a coroner's court. No one was accused. This was only to decide whether my grandfather had died by accident or design. If the latter was decided then there would be accusations . . . and perhaps a trial.

I just could not believe that this was really happening to me. All I could tell myself was that if I had obeyed the instincts of my heart I would now be happy in some vaguely foreign land with the man whom I realized now I undoubtedly loved.

People gave evidence. The doctors who had examined my

grandfather's body confirmed that he had not died of asphyxiation but from the blow on the head, which could have occurred an hour or so before the fire was discovered. There could be an explanation of this. He could have smelt the smouldering rug, risen from his bed and fallen and killed himself. The fire was clearly slow burning, for the room in which my grandmother lay had not been so badly burned as had my grandfather's room. Experts agreed that it was possible for the rug to have smouldered for the best part of an hour before bursting into flames, and this would account for the lapse of time between my grandfather's receiving the blow and the presence of the fire being discovered by other members of the household.

People were put in the witness-box after the doctors. Cousin Arthur first. He told how he had heard the cry of Fire and had rushed to the spot. He had immediately gone to my grandfather's room where one of the servants was dragging out the body. He had thought my grandfather was alive and had sent for the doctor. Had there been a quarrel between Sir Matthew and a member of the household on the previous night? he was asked.

Cousin Arthur, obviously reluctant, said that there had been a disagreement between Sir Matthew and his granddaughter Philippa.

Did he know what it was about?

Cousin Arthur thought that Sir Matthew had expressed his wish that there should be a match between himself and Sir Matthew's granddaughter and that she had refused to agree to this.

'Did he threaten her at all to your knowledge?'

'I was not present,' said Cousin Arthur evasively. 'But Sir Matthew was a man who could lose his temper easily if crossed.' He believed he had shouted a little.

'To what effect? That he would cut her out of his will? That she would have to leave the house?'

'It may have been so.'

'Was Philippa Ewell upset by this?'

'I did not see her at the time.'

'When did you next see her after the argument?'

'On the landing outside the rooms which were on fire.'

'Did she sleep in the corridor?'

'Yes, several bedrooms were there.'

'Was yours?'

'Yes.'

'And the servants?'

'They were on the floors above.'

Arthur left the box and Mrs Greaves was called. She said she had overheard the quarrel between my grandfather and me.

'Did he threaten to turn her out of the house and cut her out of his will?'

'He did,' said Mrs Greaves readily.

'You have very good hearing, Mrs Greaves?'

'The best.'

'Very useful in your position. Did you see Miss Philippa Ewell after the interview?'

'Yes. I saw her go to the room where her grandmother lay in her coffin.'

'And did you see her later?'

'No, I didn't. But that did not mean that she stayed in her room all the night.'

'We are not asking for your opinions, Mrs Greaves, only for facts.'

'Yes, sir, but I think I ought to say that Miss Ewell did have strange habits. She did roam about at night.'

'That night?'

'I didn't see her that night. But I saw her one early morning. I had heard a noise . . .'

'Your excellent hearing again, Mrs Greaves?'

'I thought it my duty to go and see who was prowling about. I have to look after the maids and make sure they behave, sir.'

'Another excellent quality! And on this occasion . . .'

'I saw Miss Philippa coming into the house. It must have been five o'clock in the morning. She was fully dressed and her hair was loose.'

'And what conclusion did you come to?'

'That she had been out all night.'

'Did she tell you this?'

'She said she had been for a walk in the gardens.'

'I see no reason why Miss Ewell should not take an early morning walk if she wishes to, nor should I expect her to dress her hair before doing so.'

It was clear that Mrs Greaves was not making the impression she intended, but the reference to that morning shocked me deeply. I wondered what I could say if asked about it.

Should I tell them that I had spent the night with a lover? I should be condemned if I did so. There were many people who would think loose morals – for that was what I should be accused of – was as great a crime as murder. I had never felt so frightened in my life.

Then it was my turn.

'Miss Ewell, your grandfather wished you to marry your cousin and you refused to do this.'

'Yes.'

'And your refusal angered him?'

'Yes, it did.'

'He threatened to turn you out of the house and cut you out of his will.'

'He did.'

'What did you say to that?'

'I said: "I cannot marry someone I do not love and I will leave the house as soon as possible." '

'And you would have done that the following day? Where would you have gone to?'

'I had thought I might go to my Aunt Grace or to one of the cottages until I had found a suitable home.'

'And after this stormy interview what did you do?'

'I went into my grandmother's room to take a look at her in her coffin. We had been very fond of each other.'

There was a nod of sympathy. I had a feeling that the questioner liked me and believed me and I felt, also, that he had disliked Mrs Greaves and suspected her of malice. That gave me a certain courage.

'What happened in your grandmother's room?'

'I just looked at her and wished that she were alive to help me.'

'Were the candles burning when you went into her room?'

'Yes. There had been candles burning since her death.'

'Did you notice any insecurity about them?'

'No.'

'I believe your grandmother has left you money with the wish that you may live an independent life. Was she of the opinion that your grandfather made harsh demands upon you?'

'Yes.'

'You may step down, Miss Ewell.'

It had been easier than I had thought it possibly could be and I was so relieved because there had been no mention of that early morning encounter with Mrs Greaves.

After that it seemed that it went on for a long time. There was a great deal of discussion and I sat there limply waiting. Cousin Arthur reached for my hand and pressed, and for once I did not want to reject his hands.

Then the verdict: Accidental death. In the coroner's view there was insufficient evidence to say how the blow had been inflicted and he was of the opinion that Sir Matthew had fallen and struck his head against the sharp edge of a fender – for there was evidence of such a fender surrounding the fireplace in his bedroom.

So we were free. The fearful menace which I had only half understood was lifted.

As I left the court with Cousin Arthur, Aunt Grace and her

husband, I thought I saw someone I vaguely recognized. I couldn't think who it was for the moment, but it came to me later in a flash. It was the man whom I had seen when Miss Elton and I had gone to Dover to look at the register, the man whom I had assumed to be staying at the local inn and exploring the countryside.

I dismissed him from my thoughts. There was so much else to occupy me.

I was free now to make my plans.

I did not want to stay in Greystone Manor. There was a horrible atmosphere of suspicion there, instigated I was sure by Mrs Greaves. I noticed the servants watching me furtively, and if I looked up and caught them suddenly they would look embarrassed and turn away.

Cousin Arthur continued to be extremely kind. 'You must stay here as long as you like,' he said. 'In fact you can regard Greystone Manor as your home.'

'I certainly couldn't do that. My grandfather ordered me out and I shall go.'

'It belongs to me now, you know.'

'It's kind of you in view of everything, but I must go quickly.'

It was Aunt Grace who came to my immediate rescue. 'You must come and stay with Charles and me,' she said. 'Stay as long as you like, my dear. We have the money now to buy a house for ourselves and there is one not very far away from the vicarage, Wistaria Cottage. Do you remember it? Charles thinks it would suit us beautifully and there is a big garden which he can have as his workshop and display his statues. Come and help us make the move.'

It was good of her. She was delighted to have the money which had been left to her and to have the approval of her marriage which her mother had implied. In death my grandmother had given us both the help we needed.

So I left Greystone Manor and went with her. The vicarage

was a roomy house and the vicar kindly let me have a room until the move to Wistaria Cottage could be arranged.

Aunt Grace did a lot for me in those weeks. She and Charles talked to me a great deal and we planned what I should do. There was no need for me to take some uncongenial post now. I was a free woman and I needed time, said Aunt Grace, to decide how I should live.

Fate decided for me.

I was in Charles's shed sorting out some books for him when I heard footsteps outside. I went to the door and to my amazement and delight there stood Daisy.

She had changed since I last saw her; she had grown plumper but her cheeks were as rosy as ever and the mischief still sparkled in her eyes. As though to show her pleasure and that it was an extremely happy occasion, she favoured me with one of the winks I remembered so well.

'Miss Pip!' she said.

'Oh, Daisy!' I cried and we hugged each other fiercely. 'So you've come home . . . at last.'

'Only on a visit. The servants are up at the Grange . . . preparing it like they always do. I came with them. Hans isn't with me, but he let me come with them. He said I deserved to see my own folks and it was only right for me to. He's had to stay behind. He's got an important job now. I'm married, you know. Frau Schmidt, that's me. What do you think of that? Hans made an honest woman of me . . . when young Hans was born. I'm a mother now. Think of that, Miss Pip. You never saw a little man like my Hansie. He's a regular tartar, I can tell you.'

'Daisy, when are you going to stop for breath? Do you mean to say they're opening up the Grange?'

'Somebody will be coming over soon. Not sure when, but it has to be all ready and prepared.'

'And you . . .'

'Oh, I'm not one of the servants now. Frau Schmidt, that's me. I'll stay here till some of the servants go back . . . and I'll go back with them. But first tell me . . . what about you? And that old man . . . dead now. Well, I don't think he'll get quite the welcome he's expecting from the angels.'

'You heard about it, did you?'

'Haven't heard of anything else.'

'Daisy, they suspect me.'

'Not my Ma don't. Nor Pa. They said that old tartar got out of bed in a rage and got what he deserved. Mind you, you mustn't speak ill of the dead, they say, but in his case I reckon it's allowed. I won't ever forget standing in that chapel in what he called my shame . . . and all for having a bit of fun in the churchyard. But that's all done with. What about you, Miss Pip? How many years is it since I saw you?'

'Too many. It must be five. I was twelve when you and Francine went away . . . and I'm seventeen now.'

'I'd hardly have known you. Quite grown up, you are. Just a little shaver you was then.'

'Daisy, what do you know about Francine?'

'Oh.' Her face was solemn momentarily. 'That was a bit of a scandal, that was. I cried myself to sleep when I heard of it. I used to think she was the most beautiful girl I'd ever seen . . . or ever likely to . . . and to think of her getting murdered . . .'

'I want to know what happened, Daisy.'

'Well, it was in this shooting lodge. That's where they were at the time. It was never cleared up. Who killed them we don't know. It wasn't anything to do with Miss Francine. She was just there with him . . . when they came to kill him, and because she was with him they killed her too.'

'Who could have done it?'

'Now you're asking me. If *they* don't know, how could I?'

'Who's they?'

'All the army . . . and the reigning family and the police . . . all of them.'

'It's been such a mystery to me and I want you to tell me all you know. Come into the shed. There's no one here. My aunt and her husband are at Wistoria Cottage getting ready to move in.'

'Oh. I heard about that. What a change-about, eh? Miss Grace getting married and all. She ought to have done it years ago.'

'I'm glad she did before she got the money. She had to break away, as I did. But sit down, Daisy, and tell me all you know about my sister.'

'Well, she went off, didn't she?'

'Yes, yes,' I said impatiently.

'And the Gräfin and Graf and her household went off and I got my job with them . . . so off I goes. It's a wonderful place if you like that sort of thing. The trees and mountains . . . oh, it's beautiful. I get a bit homesick at times, though, for the fields and the hedges and the lanes and the buttercups and daisies. But Hans was there and me and Hans . . . well, we get on together a treat. It's funny. He laughs at me . . . the way I try to say their words . . . but I can laugh at him for saying ours. We like it.'

'So you are happily married. I am so pleased. And you have that adorable little Hans. But what do you know about my sister?'

'Only that she came over with the Baron. I didn't know who he was then. I knew he was important, of course, but not that important. Hans told me. He said this Baron Rudolph is the only son of this Grand Duke or something . . . and this Grand Duke is a sort of king. Not like our Queen, of course . . . but the ruler of this dukedom, or whatever it is. But it's different over there. It's like a lot of little countries, all with their own kings, and though they seem little to us, they're thought to be pretty big over there.'

'I understand, Daisy.'

'Well, I'm glad you do, Miss Pip, because it's more than I do. But what I'm telling you is that when Rudolph came back with your sister there was a regular to-do. You see, he's the heir and he's supposed to marry some sort of grand lady from one of those other places and there could be war if he didn't. There's always going to be war . . . and they're afraid of that. So Baron Rudolph is supposed to marry this lady. That means having Miss France there he had to keep her out of the way.'

'He was married to my sister so how could he possibly marry this grand lady?'

'Well, it seems he wasn't exactly *married* . . .'

'He was. They were married near Dover before they left the country.'

'Well, they said she was his mistress. That was all right with them. He'd had them before . . . and all Grand Dukes had. But with marriage it was different . . . if you understand me.'

'Listen, Daisy, my sister was married to him in Birley Church. I saw . . .'

I stopped. I *had* seen that entry, hadn't I? In view of everything that had happened I was beginning to doubt it.

'I reckon it had to be one of them mock marriages,' said Daisy. 'It would be the only way and Baron Rudolph would have known it. He had to keep her out of the way . . . or he should have done. But there was one part of the country where he was very popular . . . and I believe he was there with her.'

'You never saw her, Daisy?'

'Oh no. I was in the Graf's slosh.'

'Where?'

'The slosh. They have a lot of them over there. They're very pretty. Like castles.'

'Oh, I see, a *schloss*.'

'That's it. No, they didn't come to our slosh. The Graf was very loyal to the Grand Duke and he and the Gräfin thought that Rudolph ought to settle down and learn how to rule the country, which he would have to do when the Grand Duke dies, and they thought he ought to do all he could to stop this war they were all worried about, which would come if he didn't marry this one they'd got for him.'

'So all this time you never saw her. What about the child?'

'Child? What child is this you mean, Miss Pip?'

'My sister had a little boy. A son. She was very proud of him.'

'I never heard nothing of that.'

'Oh, Daisy, I wish I knew what happened.'

'You know she was killed in that shooting lodge.'

'Where exactly was the lodge?'

'It's not so far from the slosh. Right in the middle of the pine forest, it is. It was an awful shock when it happened. The town went into mourning for a whole month. They said it nearly broke the Grand Duke's heart . . . his only son, you see. They looked for the murderers . . . high and low they searched . . . but they couldn't find them. They said it was political. You see, there's a nephew. He's to be the next Grand Duke when the old man dies.'

'Do they think *he* killed them?'

'They don't dare go as far as to say that. But this Baron Sigmund . . . you see, he's a son of the old man's brother and next in line, which is because of Rudolph's death . . . if you get my meaning. So if anybody wanted Rudolph out of the way it could be Sigmund . . . though Hans thinks it could be someone who just wanted Rudolph out of the way . . . he being not what they considered right to be the next Grand Duke.'

'So someone who wanted Rudolph out of the way murdered him in the shooting lodge . . . and just because Francine was with him she was shot too . . .'

'That's about it. It's the general view. Nobody can be sure . . .'

'But what about the child? Where was he at the time?'

'Nobody's ever said nothing about a child, Miss Pip.'

'It's a great mystery to me. I am sure Francine was truly married and I am sure there was a child. I want to *know*, Daisy. It's the only thing I really care about now.'

'Oh, you wouldn't want to get muddled up in all that, Miss

Pip. You ought to settle down and marry some nice young man. You haven't got to worry about money now, have you? Get married and have babies. I can tell you this . . . there's nothing I can think of better than holding your own little baby in your arms . . .'

'Oh, Daisy, it's lovely to think of you as a mother.'

'You ought to see my little Hansie.'

'I wish I could.' I was looking straight at her. 'Daisy,' I went on, 'why shouldn't I?'

The idea had come and it would not be dismissed. It excited me as I had not been excited for a long time. It would give me a reason for living; it would get me away from the atmosphere of furtive suspicion from which I could not escape. At the back of my mind was the thought that I might see Conrad again.

During the last weeks the possibility that there might be results from my encounter with him had occurred to me. Somehow I had rather hoped there would be. It would add very much to the complications of my life, but I think the joy it would have brought me would have compensated for that. It would have put me in a desperate situation . . . but to have had a child, a living memory of the hours I had spent with Conrad, filled me with longing.

It was a strange mingling of relief and disappointment when I knew that I had definitely not become pregnant and I felt I had to give myself a reason for living; and now Daisy had appeared she had, in a way, opened a door for me.

'Daisy,' I said, 'how would it be if I came back with you?'

'You, Miss Pip! Back with me?'

'I have money now. I am free . . . thanks to my grandmother. I want to find that child of Francine's. He exists, I know. Sometimes I feel he is calling for me. He would be nearly four years old by now. If he's there I should like to see him. I want to make sure that he is well looked after.'

'Well, as I said, I never heard nothing about no child, and I reckon there'd have been plenty of people to find out if there was one. They're very fond of a bit of gossip over there . . . just as they are everywhere.'

'I am convinced that there *is* a child and that my sister was married. This is what I want to settle, Daisy.'

'All right then. When do you want to go?'

'When do you leave?'

'I was to stay till one or two of the others went back, but I don't really want to wait that long. I'm missing my two Hanses very much, I can tell you.'

'Could you come back with me? We could travel together. You'd be such a help to me as you've done it before. Could we go together?'

Daisy's eyes were sparkling. 'I reckon we could manage that. How long would you want to wait?'

'I want to leave as soon as I can.'

'I see no reason why we shouldn't go when you're ready.'

'I could go to the town and stay in an inn somewhere . . . while I look round.'

'There are inns all right. But I'll tell you what. Why couldn't you stay with me until you got sorted out? You see, I've got a cottage . . . a lovely little place in the valley just below the slosh. We had it when I was going to have the baby. That was when Hans didn't want me to work no more. The Gräfin is very good to her servants and she and Miss Tatiana gave me things to furnish it with. So you could stay with me . . . till you found what you wanted.'

'Oh, Daisy, that would be wonderful. That would help me a lot. I could then look round and find out what I ought to do. I want to do this. I want to do it so much. It needs thinking about, though. I am going there and I am going to find out who killed my sister. I'm going to find her baby.'

Daisy smiled at me indulgently. 'Well, if you can do better than the Grand Duke's police and guards you are a bit of a marvel. Don't you think they tried to find the murderer?'

'Oh yes. We are very quiet at the moment. I am not entertaining at all. Only the Glencorns have been once or twice, but they are such old friends. I do hope that when you come back you will visit me often. As you know, there would always be a home for you at Greystone Manor.'

'It is good of you, Cousin Arthur. I don't know what my plans will be. I want to get this . . . er . . . holiday over first and then see how I feel.'

'All very natural, dear Philippa. You have been through a trying time. Get right away and forget it, eh?'

'I will try.'

I helped Aunt Grace move into Wistoria Cottage while I was making my preparations. I saw a great deal of Daisy, for there were so many plans to be made. She described the country to me and something of the life she lived. She was very happy in her cottage in the valley close to what she persisted in calling the 'slosh', and she told me that Hans came home every evening so that it was all very cosy and life had turned out romantically and happily for her.

'Of course,' she commented, 'some would have said I was a bad and wicked girl to go off with Hans. I never thought I was. I reckon if you love it's all right. After all, it's better than marrying someone for money . . . or so it seems to me. Well, all's well that ends well, as they say, and Hans and me is very well, thank the Lord.'

She didn't know how close I had come to doing what she had done, and I often wondered how different my life might have been if I had obeyed my natural impulses on that night.

However, as Daisy herself would be the first to admit, what was done was done, and we had to go on from there. It was a favourite expression of hers.

The more I thought of my decision, the more it seemed like a miracle that I was able to do what in my heart I had always wanted to. I was going over there . . . to Conrad's country. Would I see him again? What if there should be another chance? I should have to wait and see what life had to offer

'Oh yes. We are very quiet at the moment. I am not entertaining at all. Only the Glencorns have been once or twice, but they are such old friends. I do hope that when you come back you will visit me often. As you know, there would always be a home for you at Greystone Manor.'

'It is good of you, Cousin Arthur. I don't know what my plans will be. I want to get this . . . er . . . holiday over first and then see how I feel.'

'All very natural, dear Philippa. You have been through a trying time. Get right away and forget it, eh?'

'I will try.'

I helped Aunt Grace move into Wistoria Cottage while I was making my preparations. I saw a great deal of Daisy, for there were so many plans to be made. She described the country to me and something of the life she lived. She was very happy in her cottage in the valley close to what she persisted in calling the 'slosh', and she told me that Hans came home every evening so that it was all very cosy and life had turned out romantically and happily for her.

'Of course,' she commented, 'some would have said I was a bad and wicked girl to go off with Hans. I never thought I was. I reckon if you love it's all right. After all, it's better than marrying someone for money . . . or so it seems to me. Well, all's well that ends well, as they say, and Hans and me is very well, thank the Lord.'

She didn't know how close I had come to doing what she had done, and I often wondered how different my life might have been if I had obeyed my natural impulses on that night.

However, as Daisy herself would be the first to admit, what was done was done, and we had to go on from there. It was a favourite expression of hers.

The more I thought of my decision, the more it seemed like a miracle that I was able to do what in my heart I had always wanted to. I was going over there . . . to Conrad's country. Would I see him again? What if there should be another chance? I should have to wait and see what life had to offer me. Perhaps he would not want to renew our acquaintance. That he was a man who must have had many love-affairs I could readily believe, but I did think that his sense of chivalry would have stopped his casually seducing a young virgin. I liked to think that it was only because he had been carried away by his passion that he had done so, and that he had really intended that we should be together. Oh yes, I really did believe that he had cared for me.

'I tell you what you're going to be,' said Daisy gleefully, 'some sort of detective . . . that's what. Now there's something that's struck me. You're the same name as your sister and there was quite a bit about her in the papers. They called her "the woman Ewell". You see what I mean. Some people might remember the name. It might stop them telling you things if they thought you was snooping around. Do you follow me?'

I did follow her.

'You could call yourself something else,' suggested Daisy. 'I reckon that would be best.'

'You're right. It is clever of you to have thought of this.'

'When they was over here you came to the Grange, didn't you? Some of them saw you. Well, if they was to see you again and heard you was Philippa Ewell, they'd remember right away. Twelve you was then. You're different now . . . five years older . . . and that makes a lot of difference. If you called yourself something else . . . they'd never guess who you were.'

'I tell you what I'll do. I'll call myself by my mother's name before she was married. That was Ayres. I'll be Philippa Ayres.'

'There's still the Philippa.'

'Well, what about Anne Ayres? Anne is my second name.'

'That sounds all right to me. Nobody's going to compare Anne Ayres with Philippa Ewell if you ask me.'

That day when I was preparing my clothes for departure I came across the spectacles with the blank glass in them which Miss Elton had procured for me when we were talking about my seeking a post. I put them on. They certainly were effective. Then I took my rather heavy hair and pulled it back from my forehead. I screwed it into a bun on the top of my head. The effect was startling. I really did look like another person.

When Daisy came to see me I received her wearing the glasses and my new hairstyle. She stared at me, not recognizing me for a few moments.

'Oh, Miss Pip,' she cried. 'You look so funny. Not like you at all.'

'It's my disguise, Daisy.'

'You're not going to travel like that, are you?'

'No, but I shall take the glasses with me for use if the need arises.'

The time was passing now. We were ready to leave – and so I set out for Conrad's country with Daisy as my guide.

The Hunting Lodge

Our journey was long but never tedious, for I was in a state of great excitement from the outset. It was the most wonderful piece of luck that Daisy had come to England at this time. She was a very resourceful young woman and liked to imagine herself the seasoned traveller.

I had insisted that we travel first class and that I should pay for Daisy as she was going to be my companion and guide. As we took the train to Harwich and I sat back in the first compartment looking at a very complacent Daisy, I knew that Cousin Arthur had been right when he had said this was the best thing I could do. I was starting a new life and I was glad to escape from the last weeks, which had become almost intolerable.

I was convinced that from now on my life would be adventurous. I had an important project in mind and I felt as though I were setting out to seek my fortune.

The crossing from Harwich to the Hook of Holland was uneventful and after staying the night at an inn we boarded a train and travelled for miles across the flattest country I have ever seen.

'Never mind,' said Daisy, 'you'll have mountains and forests enough when you get to Bruxenstein. Perhaps you'll be wishing for a bit of flat there.'

'I can't wait to arrive,' I said.

'You've got a long way to go yet, Miss Pip.'

How right she was! Once again I had reason to be grateful to Cousin Arthur, who had made the arrangements for us with a company in London who looked after such matters, so that we knew exactly which way we had to go. We were to spend a night at Utrecht before taking the train to Bavaria, and the journey was beginning to be so interesting that had I not been so eager to reach my destination I should have liked to linger longer over every detail of it.

The first class carriages had four seats in front and four behind and each carriage was subdivided into two sections by a central door, just as in our first class carriages at home. But there was a more formal atmosphere here. One was conscious of a display of discipline and the attendants wore cocked hats and carried swords so that they looked almost military.

'We're a bit like that in Bruxenstein,' Daisy explained. 'All that clicking heels and bowing from the waist... It sometimes makes me want to laugh.'

At Arnhem two men and a woman joined our carriage. They looked pleasant and smiled in our direction. I explained that we were English and they thereupon began to talk to us in our own tongue although they only had a fair command of it, and my German, thanks to Miss Elton and my early grounding, was better than their English.

Were we going beyond Utrecht, they wanted to know, and I told them we were travelling to Bruxenstein.

'Is that indeed so,' said the man. 'Interesting place, Bruxenstein . . . at the moment.'

'Why do you say at the moment?' I asked. 'Is there some reason why it is now so?'

'Things have been a little . . . what do you call it? . . . in the boiling pot since the death of the Baron Rudolph.'

My heart began to beat faster. Daisy sat demurely beside me, like the quiet little maid she had said everyone would think she was, because she looked the part and I looked like the mistress.

'Wasn't there some scandal . . . ?' I began.

'Scandal indeed. He was shot dead in his hunting lodge. There was a woman with him and she was killed too.'

'I heard of it.'

'So the news travelled to England.'

The woman said: 'That was probably because the lady in the case was English.'

'That may be,' said the man, 'but in any case the country has been a little uneasy since.'

'Mind you,' put in the other man, 'there is always something going on in these little states. It's time they were all joined up and became part of the Germanic Empire.'

'Being a Prussian you would say that, Otto,' said the other with a smile.

'Do you know what really happened about this shooting matter?' I asked.

'No one really knows but one can guess. There are theories . many of them. Perhaps the lady had another lover who was jealous. That's one of the theories. But I don't think that's the answer. No. Someone did not want Rudolph ruling over the province so that person – or persons – put a bullet through him. Probably someone from the other side.'

'You mean he has a rival?'

'There is always someone next in the line of succession. There's this nephew of the reigning Duke. What's his name, Otto?'

'Baron Sigmund.'

'Yes, son of a younger brother of the Grand Duke. Isn't that so?'

'Exactly. Some seem to think he'd suit the part better and that it is not such a bad thing that Rudolph is out of the way.'

'Murder is rather a drastic way of settling these matters!' I said.

'Still,' went on Otto, 'it is better that one – or two – should die than that thousands should be submitted to tyranny.'

'Was this Rudolph a tyrant then?'

'Far from it. I've heard that he was something of a sybarite, a young man too fond of pleasure to make a good ruler. That kind always get surrounded by the wrong people who rule for them. The present Grand Duke has been a good ruler. It's a pity he's so old. I gather he was old when Rudolph was born. He married twice . . . the first time being unfruitful. His brother was killed fighting in one of the rebellions or wars . . . and that left Sigmund heir after Rudolph.'

'You know a great deal about the family.'

'It's common knowledge. It's a small principality . . . or dukedom rather, and the royal family lives close to the people. Different from in your country, Miss . . . er . . .'

I hesitated and then said quickly: 'Ayres. Anne Ayres.'

'Very different, Miss Ayres, although I suppose your Queen's private life is not exactly a closed book to your people.'

'It is so exemplary,' I replied, 'that there is no need for it to be. If there are differences and family friction, I suppose there would be a tendency to keep that secret.'

'How right you are! And I dare say there is very much the people of Bruxenstein do not know about their ruling family. Do you intend to spend any time in Utrecht?'

'Only an hour or so . . . possibly a morning . . . as we have to wait for trains.'

'You'll enjoy it. It's one of the most interesting of the Dutch cities, I always thought. Tremendous history. The Romans built a fortress there to guard the river . . . one of the branches of the Rhine, you know, where it is joined by the Vecht. You must see the remains of the great cathedral . . .'

I was scarcely listening. My thoughts were with Francine lying dead on that bed in the hunting lodge.

We said goodbye to our travelling companions at Utrecht and continued our journey, and as we crossed the border into Germany, my excitement increased. Those fir-covered mountains, those little streams, the glorious river with its castles looking down almost scornfully, it seemed, on the scene below, the little villages which seemed to have come straight out of stories by the Brothers Grimm which Miss

Elton used to read to us in the original . . . all this seemed to me the stuff of legend. This was the land of goblins and elves, of trolls and giants, of mountain kings and snow queens and children lost in enchanted woods where wolves roamed and there were gingerbread houses. It was the land of the Norse Gods – Odin, Thor and Baldur the beautiful and mischievous Loki. It was in the air. I could sense it – in Höllenthal Gorge, called the Valley of Hell, in the glorious forests of the Schwarzwald, the Thuringian Wald, and the Odenwald . . . the vine-covered hill slopes. There were miles and miles of trees – oak, beeches, but mainly the firs and pines of the forest. It was the romantic land – Conrad's land – and the farther I penetrated the more I thought of him.

The journey had taken us several days as it had been the advice of those who planned it that we should take it comfortably. I realized that they were right and although I longed to be in Bruxenstein, where I was beginning to believe the answer to the mystery would be found, I did feel that I was getting an understanding of the country, and even the people, through those I met on the journey.

In due course we arrived at the town of Bruxburg which was, I gathered, the capital city of Bruxenstein, and we were able to take a trap out to the cottage which was the home of Daisy and Hans, and in this we rode through the town. It was quite large, but on that occasion I saw very little of it beyond the square with the town hall and a few impressive buildings. But I noticed immediately the castle on the incline, presiding, as it were, over the town, and looking very much like those I had seen throughout our journey through the country. It looked impressive and very beautiful, I thought, with its towers and grey stone walls.

'We're right below it,' said Daisy. 'It's easy to get up to the slosh. There's a road runs from our cottage right up to it.'

'Daisy,' I said, 'what are you going to tell Hans about me?'

'About you! What do you mean?'

'He'll know me.'

'I shouldn't think so.'

'But don't you think some of the servants . . . when they come back from the Grange . . .'

'They'll never recognize you now. You've changed a lot from that little twelve-year-old. I'll tell Hans all about it and we'll explain that as your name is Ewell and there was that scandal about your sister, you've decided to call yourself Anne Ayres. Hans will see the point. We'll let it be known that you came out with me. Miss Ayres is someone I knew in England and as she was coming out I said why didn't she stay. A sort of paying guest, you see.'

So she lulled my fears to rest.

The trap deposited us with our luggage – mostly mine – at the cottage and Hans came out to meet us. He and Daisy were immediately caught up in a delighted embrace; then he turned to greet me. I remembered him well. He clicked his heels and bowed while Daisy began explaining the situation to him in rather a breathless manner. I was going to be their paying guest until I decided what to do. I wanted to see something of the country. She knew it was all right. And how was her darling little Hans?

Little Hans was well. Frau Wurtzer had looked after him well and Hans had seen him almost every day while Daisy had been away.

'I'll be off first thing in the morning to get that young fellow,' said Daisy.

I went into the cottage which was spotlessly clean. I later discovered that there were two bedrooms and a sort of boxroom upstairs and two rooms downstairs with a kitchen. It was delightfully fresh and I could smell the pines of the nearby forest.

Hans welcomed me warmly and I wondered whether this was due to natural politeness or whether in fact he resented my presence in this rather small house.

As we went in a round-faced woman appeared from the

kitchen. She was in a large, very clean print apron and her sleeves were rolled up; she carried a ladle in her hands.

Daisy flew at her. 'Gisela!' she cried.

'Daisy . . .'

Daisy turned to me. 'This is my good friend, Gisela Wurtzer, who has been looking after Hansie for me.'

The woman smiled and looked conspiratorially at Hans.

'He's here!' cried Daisy. 'My little Hans is here.'

She flew up the stairs and Hans looked at me and smiled. 'She missed her baby,' he said, 'but I thought she should take the opportunity to see her mother and her father. There is a duty to the parents when they are getting old, eh?'

I agreed that this was so and Gisela nodded to imply that that was her opinion also. Daisy came down the stairs holding a sturdy boy who was rubbing his eyes and looking a little cross because he had obviously been wakened from his sleep.

'Look at him, Miss . . .' She had been going to say Pip and stopped herself in time. 'Now tell me, did you ever see a more beautiful boy?'

'Never!' I cried.

She kissed him fervently and now, fully awake, he regarded me from a pair of light blue eyes.

I took his fat little hand and kissed it.

'He likes you,' said Gisela.

'It's true,' agreed Daisy. 'He's a very sharp young fellow. How's he been, Gisela? Missing his Mum?'

Hans had to translate most of Daisy's words which were spoken in English and as Gisela had no English, conversation was a little difficult. But the rapport between the two women was obvious.

'Tell her how good it was of her to bring him so that I didn't have to wait,' commanded Daisy.

Gisela smiled when she heard. 'But of course I brought him,' she said.

I had to hear of all the wonderful qualities of young Hans

which I did in English from Daisy and in German from Gisela and Hans.

'Gisela knows,' said Hans, 'for she is especially good with children.'

'I should be,' replied Gisela. 'I have six of my own. Numbers help. The big ones look after the little ones.'

Young Hans showed signs of wanting to return to his bed, so Daisy took him upstairs and Gisela, who had set the table, said that food was ready. We partook of a soup of a rather mysterious but delicious flavour with rye bread, after which there was cold pork with vegetables, and to follow, a pie containing apples. It was a good meal and Gisela was clearly proud of it. She served it and ate with us while we talked of the journey and then she said she must get back because Arnulf did not like to be left too long to look after the children.

Hans walked home with her.

'Now you see, Miss Pip,' said Daisy when we were alone, 'what a nice little situation I've got myself into.'

'I do, Daisy,' I replied. 'But shouldn't you stop calling me Miss Pip?'

'I must. Miss Ayres sounds so funny. Not a bit like you. Miss Pip is just right. It won't matter much if I get a slip of the tongue. That's what is so good about this. You say something you shouldn't and you just blame the language. It helps the wheels go round.'

'Oh Daisy, how happy you must be. Hans is so good and the baby such a darling.'

'Well, as I say Miss P . . . I mean Miss Ayres, I reckon I've done pretty well for myself.'

'You deserve all the good luck in the world.'

'Well, come to think of it, you could use a bit yourself and by rights you ought to have it.'

She showed me my room. It was very small with chintz curtains, a bed, a chair and a cupboard . . . very little else, but I was grateful for it.

'We don't use it often,' she said apologetically. 'It's to be for young Hans when he gets a little older. In the meantime his bed's in the very small room next to ours and that'll be all right for a few months more.'

'I shall be gone by then.'

'Don't talk about going. You've only just come.' Daisy had turned to me, her eyes shining. 'It's ever so exciting, you coming here like this. I reckon we'll make a fine pair of detectives . . . you and me.' She paused. 'You know Gisela . . . well, she was caretaker at the lodge . . . Still keeps an eye on it, you know.'

'Daisy!' I cried. 'Well then, she might know . . .'

'Don't you think we've talked? She doesn't know any more than anyone else. I haven't found out anything from her . . . because she doesn't know.'

'No one – however friendly – must know why I am here.'

'Trust me,' said Daisy. 'Silent as the grave, that's me.'

Hans returned and Daisy reckoned it was time we had a good night's sleep.

'We can talk in the morning,' she added.

And we all agreed with her.

The next day I decided to explore the town. Daisy could not accompany me because she had her son to look after. When she went into the town one of the servants from the schloss would bring down a pony carriage which they used for short journeys and take her in. They did this twice a week so that she could shop. Hans, it seemed, now held quite an important position in the Graf's household which entitled him to such privileges.

It was a beautiful morning. The sun was shining on the green and red roofs of the houses and the grey walls of the schloss. Here and there the sharp flint edges twinkled like diamonds where the sun caught them.

I was in a mood of exultation. I had accomplished so much and I was certain that something tremendous would happen soon. I wondered what I should do if I came upon Conrad sauntering through the town. I knew so little of him. I did not even know his surname. He was simply Conrad to me. I must have been in a bemused state not to ask him more questions and to be so easily put off with evasions. Equerry to a nobleman! I wondered if that could be the Graf as he had been staying at the Grange, although the house was used by several families, I believed. But if the Graf were his employer he might at this very moment be within those grey stone walls.

How wonderful it would be to see him again. I tried to imagine our greeting. He would be surprised? Delighted? Had he perhaps dismissed me from his mind as the sort of woman a man meets, makes love to and rides away . . . forgotten in a few months . . . even weeks . . . just one of the women who amused him for a while.

I could see the bluish grey stream of the river winding its way through the town to where the slopes on either side were covered with pines and fir trees, and away in the distance the vines were growing in abundance. I was again transported to those days when Miss Elton read to us. There in the forest I knew I should hear the cowbells ringing through the mist. Miss Elton had told us of her visits to such places when she was taken to see her mother's people. There the gods roamed and the valkyrie rode. I could sense it all. In that square I could see the mayor and his corporation sitting in dismayed discussion; I could see the Pied Piper playing his magic pipes and luring first the rats into the river and the children into the mountainside. It moved me deeply. I was aware of much of the past. I pictured Francine coming here with Rudolph. I wondered how she had felt, whether she had been aware from the beginning that her liaison – I had ceased to call it a marriage in my thoughts – was to be kept a secret.

There were several large houses with oriel windows projecting from the façades and carved woodwork at these windows. It appeared to be a prosperous town. There was the Minster with its pointed spire and around it streets of small houses. I guessed that many of the people who were not employed in the big houses worked in the vineyards. I passed a forge and a mill . . . and then I was really in the town.

I wandered through the market where dairy produce and vegetables were for sale. Some people looked at me rather curiously. They would know at once that I was a stranger and I guessed that they did not get a great many tourists here.

At length I came to an inn over which a sign creaked in the wind. It proclaimed itself to be the Grand Duke's Tavern. I saw stables which contained several horses and at the back of the inn there was a garden in which tables and chairs had been set up. I sat down at one of these and a plump, smiling woman came out to ask what I should like.

I guessed it was one of the *Biergartens* of which I had heard and I asked her for a tankard of beer, wondering as I did so whether women did this sort of thing here or whether I was acting strangely.

She brought me a goblet of beer and seemed inclined to talk.

'You are travelling through our town, Fräulein?'

'I am staying for a visit,' I told her.

'That is very good. It is a beautiful town, eh?'

I agreed that it was. An idea had occurred to me. 'I see you have horses here. It is not always easy to go round on foot. Do you hire out your horses?'

'There is not much call for it. But I think my husband might.'

'I want to see something of the country. I ride a great deal at home in England. If I could hire a horse . . .'

'Where do you stay, if I may ask, Fräulein?'

'I am staying in a cottage. It belongs to Herr Schmidt. I am a friend of his wife.'

'Ah!' A smile broke out on her face. 'You speak of the good Hans. He is a very proud man. He has an English wife and a fine little boy.'

'Oh yes . . . young Hans.'

'His wife . . . she is very nice.'

'Very nice.'

'And you are from the same country . . . come to see your friend?'

'To see her and the baby and your beautiful country.'

'Oh, it is very beautiful. You could see much on horseback. You are an experienced rider, Fräulein?'

'Yes, indeed. I ride a great deal at home.'

'It will be arranged. There must be a charge.'

'But of course.'

'When you have drunk your beer you must see my husband.'

'I will.'

'He will be in the inn.'

She seemed reluctant to leave me and I think she may have been a little fascinated by my foreign appearance and perhaps by my speech, for although I was fluent enough I guessed that my accent might betray my country of origin.

'Such nice places to visit,' she went on. 'You can go to the old ruined schloss which was the home of the Grand Dukes years ago. You can go to the hunting lodge . . . oh, but perhaps not.'

'The hunting lodge?'

'Yes, it is the Grand Duke's lodge. You cannot see his schloss . . . No, it is not that one you see on the hill. That is the schloss of the Graf von Bindorf. The Grand Duke's can only be seen from the other side of the town. You cannot go in, of course, but there is a good view and that is worth seeing.'

I said: 'What about the hunting lodge?'

She lifted her shoulders. 'There was a tragedy there,' she said.

'You mean the one where the Baron was murdered?'

She nodded. 'It was a few years ago.'

'Is it near here?' I asked quickly.

'It is about a mile and a half from Herr Schmidt's cottage. You would not want to see it. It's dismal now. At one time . . . oh, but there it is. No, you would not want to visit it now.'

I did not reply. I was going to get that horse and see that hunting lodge just as soon as I possibly could.

I went to see the innkeeper before I left. Then I walked back to Daisy's cottage, having booked a horse for the next day. I was making progress. I was about to visit the scene of the crime.

I did not mention even to Daisy that I was about to visit the hunting lodge. I merely told her that I had been to the Grand Duke's Tavern and seen horses there and had decided to hire one to help me around to see the countryside. She was pleased because looking after the cottage and young Hans was really as much as she could find time for.

So accordingly, on the next day, I went into the town, and was soon riding back the way I had come, past Daisy's cottage, for the innkeeper's wife had said the lodge was a mile and a half from that spot.

I had known that Daisy's cottage was on the edge of the forest, so I was not surprised to find that after I had left it a little way behind the trees grew closer together. There was only one path through them, so I took it.

It was a beautiful morning. I made my way through the trees. There were the occasional oak and birch, but they were chiefly fir and pine and the resinous smell was strong in the air. I could not rid myself of the feeling that I had stepped into one of Miss Elton's fairy tales of the forest.

After I had ridden some way I came to a cottage and wondered if it were Gisela's. I was about to stop and ask but I was anxious that no one should guess that I was unduly interested in the lodge . . . even a friend of Daisy's.

The door of the cottage was shut, but it had a little garden and in this was a child's wheelbarrow. I passed it and went on up the path. I must have gone for about half a mile when I saw it. It was bigger than I had thought it would be. A hunting lodge suggests something rather small . . . a place where people stayed for a night or two when hunting in the forest. But of course this was a royal hunting lodge, so naturally it would be more grand.

My heart was beating fast. I pictured Francine coming here through the forest with her lover. How had it been with them? This would have been her home. She had stayed here because her lover was so important that he could not admit to marrying someone quite unsuitable. The idea of Francine's being considered unsuitable for anyone because of her unworthiness made me feel really angry. I told myself not to be foolish. If I were going to get foolishly emotional I should soon betray myself.

The hunting lodge was in grey stone and looked like a miniature schloss. It had two towers – one at either side – and an arched porch. There were several windows in the front. There could be no doubt that this was the place. I dismounted and tethered my horse to a post which I found and which was obviously meant for that purpose. There was an eeriness about the scene. Was it because I knew that a murder had taken place here or because the trees grew so close together, making it dark and full of shadows and because the faint breeze stirring the leaves sounded like whispering voices?

My heart was beating wildly as I went uneasily forward, picking my way through the long grass scattered with pine cones.

I approached the porch, tingling with excitement. I stood in the porch and listened. There was a bell on the side of it with a long chain. I pulled this and the sound which broke the silence was deafening.

I held my breath, listening. I noticed a shutter in the door which could be pulled back to allow someone on the inside to look out and see who was standing there. I stared at it. Nothing happened. And then I heard an almost imperceptible sound and it came from within. It was as though someone was creeping towards the door.

I stood very still and my heart seemed as though it would leap from my body. I was already forming in my mind what I would say if I were confronted by someone who demanded my business here. I was a stranger. I was lost in the forest. I wanted to know my way back to the Schmidts' cottage where I was staying during my visit to Bruxenstein.

I stood there waiting and then I began to wonder whether the sounds I heard were merely the wild beating of my own heart. No, surely not. There was the sound of something being dragged along the floor. I waited in trepidation, but nothing happened. Of one thing I was certain. There was someone inside the hunting lodge.

I stood there for some minutes. There was complete silence, but I knew that someone was on the other side of the door.

I rang the bell again and the sound burst out loud and clanging. I listened, keeping my eye on the shutter. But nothing happened.

I walked away and as I did so I heard a faint noise behind me. The shutter had moved. Oh yes, I was right. Someone was in the house, someone who would not answer my ringing. Why? I wondered.

It was all rather uncanny.

I walked along to one of the windows and looked in. Dust sheets covered the furniture. I walked round to the back.

'Oh Francine,' I murmured, 'what happened? Someone is in there. Is it some human? Or is it ghosts?'

I had come to the back of the lodge. I could hear a bird singing somewhere in the forest. A gentle breeze ruffled the pine trees and their scent seemed stronger than ever. There was a door at the back and I went to it and rapped loudly on it and while I stood there I heard a movement behind me. Turning sharply, my eyes went immediately to a clump of bushes, for I thought I detected the movement there.

'Who is there?' I called out. 'Come out and tell me the way. I'm lost.'

I heard a soft laugh, more like a giggle. I went towards the bushes.

They stood before me with wide blue eyes and tousled hair. They were both dressed in dark blue jerkins and blue skirts. One was slightly taller than the other, but I guessed them to be of the same age, which could not have been more than four or five years old.

'Who are you?' I asked in German.

'The twins,' they answered simultaneously.

'What are you doing in this place?'

'Playing.'

'Have you been watching me?'

They started to laugh and nodded.

'Where have you come from?'

One of them pointed vaguely.

'Are you a long way from home?'

The same one nodded.

'What are your names?'

One pointed to the blue jerkin and said 'Carl'. The other did likewise and said 'Gretchen'.

'So you're a little girl and you're a little boy.'

They nodded, laughing.

'Is anyone in there?' I asked, pointing to the lodge.

Again they giggled and nodded.

'Who?'

They hunched their shoulders and looked at each other.

'Won't you tell me?' I asked.

'No,' said the one named Carl. 'You've got a horse.'

'Yes. Would you like to come and see it?'

They both nodded with enthusiasm. As we walked round to the front of the lodge I looked towards the porch and so did they. I guessed they knew who was in the house and I promised myself that I would get it out of them.

The children were delighted with my horse. 'Don't go too near him,' I warned and obediently they stood back.

I turned my head sharply. The shutter was open and we were being observed.

'Can you take me into the lodge?' I asked the twins.

They looked at each other without answering.

'Come on,' I said. 'Let's go and look. How do you get in?'

Still they did not speak and as we stood there a boy appeared. He must have come round from the back of the lodge. He called out: 'Carl! Gretchen! What are you doing?' He looked rather flushed and defiant.

'Hello,' I said. 'Where have you come from?'

He didn't answer and I went on. 'I'm lost in the forest. I saw this place and thought you would tell me the way.'

I fancied he looked relieved.

'Was it you in the house?' I asked. 'Did you look at me through the shutter?'

He didn't answer. Instead he said: 'Where did you want to go? The town is in that direction.' He pointed to the way I had come.

'Thank you,' I said. 'What an interesting place this is.'

'There was a murder here once,' he told me.

'Was that really so?'

'Yes. It was the heir to the throne.'

'How did you get in?'

'I have a key,' he said rather importantly, and the twins looked at him with undisguised admiration.

'How did you get the key?'

He was silent, shutting his lips firmly.

'I wouldn't tell tales,' I promised him. 'I'm a stranger here . . . just someone who's lost her way in the forest. I'd love to look inside that place. I've never seen where a murder was committed.'

He looked at me pityingly. I guessed him to be about eleven years old.

I went on: 'What's your name?'

He said: 'What's yours?'

'I'm Anne Ayres.'

'You're a foreigner.'

'That's right. I'm here looking at the country. It's very beautiful but most of all I'd like to see a place where a murder was committed.'

'It was in the big bedroom,' he said. 'It's all covered up. Nobody comes now. People wouldn't want to sleep in a place where there had been a murder, would they?'

'I should think not. Are there ghosts here?'

'I don't know,' he said.

'Do you come often?'

'We have the key,' he said importantly again.

'Why do you have the key?'

'So that my mother can go in and clean it.'

Now I was sure who the children were.

'I see. Would you take me in?' He hesitated and I said: 'Take me in and I'll give you a ride on my horse.'

I saw the sparkle in his eyes and now it was my turn to receive the awed glances of the twins.

'All right,' he said.

'Come on then.'

We walked round to the porch, and I said to him: 'You heard me ring, didn't you?'

He nodded.

'And you looked through the shutter at me. And you had to pull something up to see through it.'

'Next year I'll be tall enough.'

'I am sure you will be.'

Proudly he opened the door. There was a creaking sound as he did so. We were in a hall with wooden floors and oak walls. There was a large table in the centre and on the walls were spears and lances. Everything was covered up with dust sheets. The door shut and the twins, hand in hand, walked behind us.

'By the way, what is your name?' I asked the boy. 'I know the twins are Carl and Gretchen.'

'Arnulf,' he said.

'Well, Arnulf, it is good of you to show me round.'

He seemed suddenly to lose his suspicion of me. He said: 'I'm not supposed to come here.'

'Oh, I see. That's why you didn't open the door.'

He nodded.

'Gisela was coming with me.'

'Who is Gisela?'

'My sister. She wouldn't come. She was afraid of ghosts. She said I wouldn't dare go alone.'

'And you wanted to show her that you would.'

He looked disparagingly at the twins. '*They* follow me everywhere.'

The twins looked at each other and smiled as though they had done something clever.

'I wouldn't let them come in, though. I made them wait outside. I thought that if there were ghosts they might not like the twins in here, giggling. They're always giggling.'

'You didn't think the ghosts would mind you?'

'Well, they're such babies. And they never go anywhere without each other.'

'Twins are often like that,' I said sympathetically.

He started up the stairs. 'I'll show you the bedroom,' he said. 'It's where it happened, you know.'

'The murder,' I whispered.

He threw open the door with the gesture of a showman who is about to reveal his masterpiece.

Now I was actually there . . . where Francine had been murdered.

The bed was partially covered in dust sheets but the four posts with their elaborate red hangings were visible. I was overcome by my emotion. Face to face with the scene of the crime I could picture it so clearly. My beautiful sister in that bed with her handsome, romantic but oh so dangerous lover. I wanted to throw myself on those dust sheets, to touch the soft velvet of the draperies and just release the bitter tears I had tried so hard to hold back . . . to weep for the sadness of it all.

'Are you all right?' asked Arnulf.

'Yes . . . yes. It's a big bed.'

'It had to be. There were two of them.'

My voice shook a little. I said: 'What do you know of them? Why were they killed?'

'Because they didn't want him to be Grand Duke and because she was there and saw it.' He dismissed the cause as though it were of little importance. 'My father is the caretaker,' he added proudly. 'And my mother comes in to clean.'

'I see. That explains everything. Do you come here often?'

He hunched his shoulders and did not answer. Then he said: 'We've got to go now.'

I was torn between my desire to stay in that room and a desperate need to get away if I were going to control my feelings. I said quickly: 'May I take a look at the rest of it?'

'Quick then,' he said.

'Then you show me.'

He enjoyed showing me. He liked best the kitchens where, he told me, venison was cooked on the great spits and in the cauldrons, relics of a previous age which had been used until recently. There were several bedrooms for servants and huntsmen, I guessed, and there was one room which was full of guns.

I looked out of a back room window and saw the stables, which were empty now.

'Come on,' said Arnulf. 'It's getting late.'

'Perhaps another time you'll show me some more,' I said. 'I want you to have this.' I gave him a coin which he looked at in amazement. 'Guides are always paid,' I told him.

'Am I a guide then?'

'You have been this morning.'

He looked at the coin almost disbelievingly and the twins

came closer to inspect it. It was clear that they had a very high opinion of their brother.

'Arnulf is a guide,' said Carl to Gretchen.

She nodded and they kept repeating the word: Guide.

'So,' I said, 'if I should wish to see it again . . .'

Arnulf smiled at me.

'Tell me where you live,' I said. 'Is it far from here?'

He shook his head.

'I'll take you home,' I said. 'I tell you what, you can all ride on my horse and I'll walk beside you. How's that?'

They all nodded gleefully. Arnulf carefully put back the bench he had drawn to the door in order that he might look through the shutter, and we went out and he locked the door.

The three children sat on my horse and we were on our way. I was not surprised when Gisela came to the door of the cottage, but she was.

'Why,' she said, 'it's Fräulein Ayres!'

Arnulf suffered a moment's apprehension when he realized I knew his mother.

I said quickly: 'Well, fancy the children's mother being you. We met in the forest. We talked and I offered them a ride home.'

Her plump face was creased in smiles.

'Well, you have had a good morning,' she said. 'And the twins too.'

I lifted them down. Arnulf showed his superiority by needing no help.

'I think,' said Gisela, 'that we must ask Fräulein Ayres if she would care to have some refreshment.'

'Oh yes please, Mutti,' cried Arnulf, and the twins nodded vigorously. It was pleasant to know that they had taken a fancy to me as I had to them.

I tethered the horse and we went into the cottage, which was small but exceptionally clean. We sat at a table and Gisela poured some soup into platters. It was rather like that which I had sampled on my arrival at Daisy's house and we ate rye bread with it.

I said: 'This is very good of you. I was wondering whether I should return to the town and go to the inn for something to eat.'

'Did you see the hunting lodge?' she asked. 'This is the road to it, you know.'

There was a moment's silence at the table while three pairs of eyes watched me anxiously to see if their owners would be betrayed.

'It's the rather palatial place about half a mile from here, is it not?'

'That's it. This is in the nature of being the lodge cottage. Part of the royal estate. Arnulf and I had to look after the place. Those duties go with the cottage.'

'Arnulf is my father,' the young Arnulf explained. 'It's not me. I'm named after him.'

'I see,' I said.

Gisela smiled at Arnulf and at me. She was a very motherly woman and I liked her more than ever.

'You took the twins with you,' she said to Arnulf. 'Where are the others?'

'Gisela wouldn't come with us.'

'And the others are with her, I suppose.' She smiled at me. 'They love playing in the forest and Gisela won't let them go too far. Arnulf, go and call in the others.'

Arnulf went out and the twins followed him rather reluctantly, I thought. They were torn between the habit of following their elder brother and staying to study the stranger.

Gisela said: 'They keep me busy, but when the elder ones look after the small ones it makes life easier.'

'You must have a great deal to do . . . your own house . . . your children . . . and the hunting lodge.'

'I only go there two or three times a week now. In the old days it was different. There were people there then. They would have parties too. It was one of the Baron's favourite places.'

'The one who was murdered?'

'That's right.'

'He was there with . . .'

'Yes, his lady friend. She was a very beautiful young woman.'

'Did you know her?'

'Why yes, I was up there . . . looking after the place and when there was all that trouble she was living there. He used to come when he could. They were very much in love. It was such a shame.'

'Was she there very long?'

'Quite a long time. You see, he couldn't very well set her up in the town. The Grand Duke would not have allowed that.'

'But if they were married . . .'

'Oh, there was nothing of that. Rudolph had had his ladies before . . . but this one seemed . . .'

'Seemed what?'

'Well, rather different. She was a lovely lady . . . kind to the servants . . . always laughing. We all liked her and it was a blow to us when it happened. There's a lot of rivalry here among the various noble houses, you know.'

I was growing tremendously excited. This had been a rewarding morning. Not only had I visited the scene of the crime but I was actually talking to someone who had known Francine well.

'I did hear there was a child,' I began tentatively.

She stared at me in amazed horror. 'Where on earth could you have heard such a tale!'

'I . . . er . . . heard it,' I replied lamely.

'Since you have been here?'

'N – No. There was something about the murder in the English papers.'

'Did they mention a child then?'

'It was some time ago . . .'

'Yes, a few years. But a child! I'm surprised about that.'

'Well, you would know . . . living here.'

'Oh yes, I should have known. I must say I'd rather we didn't have to look after the place now. It always seems a bit ghostly nowadays. Of course it was always dark and rather damp in the heart of the forest as it is, and now being shut up.'

'Do you think it will be used again?'

'In time, I dare say. In a while all this will be forgotten. I reckon when the Grand Duke dies and Sigmund takes his place, there will be changes.'

'Do you think that will be a good thing?'

'We should all be sorry to see the old Grand Duke go. He's been good for the country. Sigmund . . . ? Well, he's a bit of a puzzle at the moment. He has a certain fascination . . . well, Rudolph had that. They've got good looks and charm, the whole family. There's no doubt about that. When Sigmund marries the young Countess I should think he will probably settle down.'

I wasn't interested in the future. It was the past which obsessed me. I took my leave with many thanks and Gisela requested that I would call again and meet the rest of her family very soon.

I said I would.

Eventually I took the horse back to the inn with the promise that I would hire it again.

I was extremely satisfied. It had been a rewarding day.

After having made such a good start and got, as I thought, so far within a few days of my arrival, I was due for a disappointment.

I told Daisy about my encounter in the forest and how I had found the lodge and Gisela's cottage.

I said: 'Daisy, you must have seen my sister when you visited Gisela.'

'No, I didn't visit her when your sister was here. It was only when young Hans was born that we got the cottage and became neighbours. Before that I was up at the slosh and that's a good way from the forest.'

'Two or three miles, I suppose.'

'That would be about it and there wasn't much call for me to go her way or her to come mine. It's only since I've lived here.'

'It was strange that I should meet the children like that.'

'A bit of luck, though. I dare say Gisela would have shown you round if she'd been there. I can see it's upset you, seeing all that. What good does it do? Come to think of it, what good is it going to do if you find out who murdered her?'

'There are two things I want to discover, Daisy. And those are: Was she really married and the whereabouts of her child.'

Daisy shook her head. 'These barons don't marry like that. It's all arranged and there was no mention of a child.'

'But Daisy, Francine *told* me in her letters. She told me she was married and where the ceremony had taken place. I went to the church and saw the entry in the register . . . and then when I went again it wasn't there. She told me she had a little boy, Rudolph. She wouldn't have made that up.'

Daisy was thoughtful: 'She might,' she said. 'Think of the shock it would be to her, for I reckon she *thought* he was going to marry her and then when she found he couldn't she started to dream up what might have been. You know Miss France. She was one to look on the bright side of things and if it didn't work out right she'd want to believe it did.'

'But I tell you I saw the entry.'

'But when you went again you didn't see it.'

I realized she thought I was a little like Francine. If things were not what I wanted, I imagined they were so strongly that I believed what I wanted to.

A week passed, and I had got no further. I had hired the horse on several days and ridden into the forest. It was no use just looking at the hunting lodge. That would not get me very far. I explored the town; I sat in the *Biergarten*. People talked to me now and then because I was a stranger, I supposed. They gave me directions how to see the best of the country. There was one subject I wanted to discuss but I dared not do that too frequently. The information I gleaned was always the same. Rudolph had been murdered by some political enemy and his mistress with him because she happened to be on the spot. There was never a mention of a child.

I visited the hunting cottage and gave the children rides on the horse. I talked to Gisela over hot soup and rye bread, for there always seemed to be a cauldron of it bubbling on the open fire in the living-room. I met the other children: Gisela, Jacob and Max. Max was the baby and about two years old. Jacob was older than the twins and came somewhere in between Arnulf and Gisela. It was interesting and enjoyable, but I had a sole purpose and I was getting restive.

Daisy noticed it.

'Well, I don't know what you think you're going to find out,' she said. 'I reckon the secret's in higher circles than you'll find here. It's not in the forest, that's for sure. It's up there somewhere, I reckon. The answer will be with them up at the slosh.'

'I do wish I could find out.'

'Well, you won't get an invitation to the slosh by telling them you're Miss Philippa Ewell, sister of the dead lady, who's come to sort out the mystery. That's for sure.'

She was right and the thought depressed me.

Then, just as I was beginning to despair and to feel that I had been foolish to hope just because of my initial success, I had an amazing stroke of luck.

It came through Hans.

I was sitting in the little garden with Daisy and young Hans was running round on the small patch of lawn, taking water from a bucket and attempting to water the flowers which grew round the border. Daisy and I were laughing at his antics, for Hans himself got more water than the flowers, but he was so delighted with his work that we couldn't help joining in the merriment. Hans the elder was suddenly coming towards us.

'I thought I'd come home to tell you,' he said, and he was looking directly at me. 'It's like this. It's the Countess Freya . . .'

'Who is she?' I asked.

'She is betrothed to Sigmund, the heir, and she is at the Grand Schloss, being brought up in the Grand Duke's household. She has been there ever since she was betrothed. It is the custom that these brides are brought up with their future husband's family. It is supposed to get them used to the ways and habits of their future homes.'

'Yes, Hans, we know she's there,' said Daisy impatiently.

'Miss Philippa didn't.'

'No, that's true, and she's Miss Ayres while she's here, remember.'

'Yes,' said Hans. 'I'm sorry. Well, what I've heard is that the Countess Freya has to improve her English. Her present governess has taught her something of the language but they reckon her accent is wrong, and they want an Englishwoman to put her right.'

I was staring wildly at Hans as a hundred possibilities crossed my mind.

He nodded, smiling at me. 'That's what I thought,' he said. 'If you got inside the schloss you'd be able to find out if there is anything in all this talk . . .'

'Teaching English to the Countess,' I murmured.

'What's this?' cried Daisy, and when it was translated for her she was as wildly excited as I was. 'It's the very thing. You're getting tired of being here with nothing happening . . . You'll be going away soon unless something does pretty quick. But to go there . . . to the slosh, wouldn't that be a lark!'

'Oh, Daisy, it would be so exciting.'

'Now listen to me,' said Hans, 'if you thought you'd like to do it I'll go along to the Comptroller of the Grand Duke's household. He's a friend of mine and a recommendation from me would go a long way. But you see, if they knew you were Miss Francine's sister . . .'

'Why should they?' demanded Daisy. 'Oh, how right you were to come here as Miss Ayres.'

'If you were found out I should say I knew nothing about it,' said Hans quickly. 'I'd say you were someone my wife knew and she'd heard you wanted to stay for a little, and as we could do with a little extra, you became a paying guest.'

'That's right,' said Daisy. 'That fits the book.'

'But, Daisy, *you* couldn't very well say you didn't know who I was.'

'Let's cross that stile if ever we get to it. When I'm asked awkward questions I always say I don't speak the language.'

'It's the great opportunity,' I cried. 'It's manna from Heaven. I was just beginning to think how hopeless everything was and that I should never get anywhere . . . and now this.'

'So you're going to do it,' said Daisy.

'Yes. Please, Hans, will you speak for me?'

Hans was a cautious man, and I could see that he did not wish to be involved in anything that could bring him trouble.

'Why should you know who I am?' I persisted. 'You had hardly ever seen me in England. I am here as Anne Ayres. Even Daisy hadn't seen me for five years. If I'm found out I'll say I knew Daisy was here and I came as Anne Ayres. But I really don't see why my true identity should be discovered.'

'Of course it won't be.' Daisy supported me. I could see she was as excited as I was.

Finally we agreed that I should try for the post and Hans went off to speak to the Comptroller of the Grand Duke's household, and within a few days I was making my way to what was known as the Grand Schloss to be interviewed by the Comptroller and the Mistress of the Household for the important task of instructing the august young lady in English.

A carriage had been sent to convey me to the schloss and

when it arrived at the cottage Daisy and I regarded it with something like awe. Engraved on the side were the royal arms of Bruxenstein – crossed swords under a crown and the words which, translated, were 'Advance to Victory'.

I had debated with Daisy for a long time how I should dress, and we had decided that I should wear my plainest clothes and that my hair – which was rather unmanageable, yet at the same time was my only real claim to beauty because it was fine and very abundant – should be taken right off my face and gathered into a knot at the nape of my neck, which enabled my dark blue straw hat to sit on top of my head in a demure fashion.

I wore a dark blue skirt and coat with a white blouse, and I thought I looked capable and as though I had never even heard there was such a thing in the world as frivolity.

Daisy clapped her hands when she saw me and I felt I had left Philippa Ewell behind me and taken on a new personality: Miss Anne Ayres.

A liveried footman helped me into the carriage and jumped up at the back of it, while the driver of the two fine bays whipped them up and we were off. I knew that Daisy would be watching us from the top window of the cottage, as excited as I was, for Daisy had often said: 'I can't bear nothing to happen. I'd almost as soon have *any*thing . . . rather than nothing.'

As we gambolled through the town a few people stopped to stare at the royal carriage which they immediately recognized, and I fancied one or two of them who were able to catch a glimpse of its occupant were wondering who this plainly dressed and rather prim young woman could be.

We went past the guards at the gate of the schloss, who looked very splendid in their light blue uniforms and splendid helmets with the pale red feathers in them and their swords clanked at their sides as they saluted the royal coach.

We came into a courtyard where we alighted and I was conducted into a hall a good deal larger than the one in the hunting lodge, but built on the same lines with the vaulted roof and the thick stone walls into which stone benches had been cut.

A liveried servant appeared and told me to follow him. I did so into a small room which led from the hall.

'You will please to wait for a moment,' he said.

I nodded and sat down.

Some five minutes elapsed before I heard footsteps in the hall and the door was opened. A man and woman came in.

I rose and inclined my head. They inclined theirs.

'You are Fräulein Ayres?' the man asked. 'I am Herr Frutschen and this is Frau Strelitz.'

I wished them good day, which greeting they returned in a most courteous manner.

I knew that Herr Frutschen was the Comptroller of the Household and the friend of Hans and I gathered that Frau Strelitz was the Mistress of the Household, and that she was the one I should have to impress if I were to get the post.

'You are from England?' she asked.

I agreed that I was.

'And you are seeking a post here?'

'I was not looking for a post, but I heard of this through Herr Schmidt and I thought I should like to do it.'

'You are not a governess.'

'No, I have never worked in such a post.'

'You are very young.'

My heart sank. Could it be that my demure hairstyle had not done for me what I had hoped it would?

'I am nearly eighteen years old.'

'And you came to visit this country?'

'My grandmother left me money and I thought it would be a good idea to realize a long-standing ambition to see the world.'

'So you intended to go on and your stay here was temporary?'

'I had no definite plans. I thought this would be interesting.'

The Comptroller looked at Frau Strelitz. She nodded almost imperceptibly.

'Your task would be to teach a young lady to speak English fluently. She has learned the language but has difficulty with the accent.'

'I understand exactly.'

The woman hesitated. 'It would only be for a year . . . no more. Until the Countess marries.'

'I understand that.'

'That will be in about a year's time. She is fifteen years old at the moment. The ceremony will very likely take place when she is sixteen.'

I nodded.

'You have been well educated, I believe.'

'I was educated by a governess who was half German, which I think accounts for my own command of the language.'

'It is good, good,' put in the Comptroller, who clearly wanted me to be given the post because of his friendship with Hans.

'Yes,' agreed Frau Strelitz, 'it is good.'

'Fräulein Ayres is a very well-educated lady,' said the Comptroller. 'That is important for the right accent.'

'This is a very important post,' went on the woman. 'You must understand, Fräulein Ayres, that your pupil will one day be the first lady in the land. She is to marry the Grand Duke's heir. That is why we have to be so careful.'

'Of course,' I said. 'I understand perfectly.'

'Your references from a previous employer . . .'

'I have no previous employer.'

'Is there anyone who could vouch for you?'

I hesitated. I thought of Charles Daventry and the vicar. But they had never heard of Anne Ayres. There was Cousin Arthur. I wondered if I could explain to them.

I said: 'At home, yes. I have friends . . . and the vicar . . . if you wished . . .'

'We shall leave you for a moment,' said Frau Strelitz. 'Please excuse us.'

'Certainly.'

They went out, shutting the door behind them. I was in a fever of impatience. Something told me that I must get this post, that if I did not there could be nothing to do but admit defeat and go home.

Good luck was with me. In ten minutes they came back. The Comptroller was beaming.

The woman said: 'We have decided to give you a trial, Fräulein Ayres. I hope you do not think we are being impolite. It is such an important post because of the young lady involved. She herself must be happy in our choice. We will give you a week's trial . . . and then three weeks after that. If at the end of that time we find you suitable, then . . .'

'Of course,' I cried. 'I understand.'

'We have decided not to write to England for references,' said the Comptroller. 'My friend, Herr Schmidt, tells us that you are a lady from a good family. That is what we want . . . in view of the rank of our young lady. Nor do we want someone who is looking for a more permanent post. So if you would care to start at the beginning of next week, that would be good. Now, shall we discuss remuneration?'

I knew there would be no difficulty about that. All I wanted was to get into the royal schloss.

I was driven back in the royal carriage. I rushed into the kitchen where Daisy was bending over the stove.

'I've got it!' I shouted. 'Behold the English governess of the most important lady in the land!'

We danced round the kitchen and young Hans toddled out and, seeing our gaiety, joined in. We were breathless with laughter.

'This is the beginning,' I said.

The English Governess

On the following Monday the carriage came to collect me and my travelling bag. I was leaving some of my things at Daisy's and was in a fever of excitement when I presented myself at the schloss and was taken to the same small room in which I had been interviewed. It was not long before I was joined by Frau Strelitz.

'Ah, Fräulein Ayres,' she said, 'the Countess is very eager to meet you. Her apartments are on the third floor. There is a schoolroom there and you will have a room in her apartments. She has a governess. You will work out with her the time of her studies, but the Grand Duke has stressed that her English must be improved. That is the most important of her studies at this time. The Baron, her future husband, who will be our ruler in due course when the Grand Duke dies . . . but that, God willing, will not be for some time yet . . . I was saying that the Baron speaks good English and she must do the same. When he visits her he will expect improvements.'

'You may rest assured that I will do my best to see that that is brought about.'

'I am sure you will. You may have some difficulty with Countess Freya. She is a high-spirited girl and naturally her awareness of her position has made her somewhat . . . well, expecting to have her own way. It is a great responsibility which is yours, Fräulein Ayres, and you do not seem a great deal older than the Countess.'

She was looking at me dubiously. Perhaps my hair was not

quite so severely controlled. I could feel it beginning to work out of its confinement.

'I have travelled, Frau Strelitz, and I am sure that a lady of the world such as yourself will understand that the acquisition of knowledge is not necessarily a matter of age.'

'You are right in that, Fräulein. Well, I wish you good fortune. I must tell you that if the Countess does not take to you she would make it very difficult for you to continue here.'

'I suppose that situation arises with any governess.'

'And it is not as though you are dependent on this post for your livelihood.'

'I shall pursue it with all the more zeal,' I said. 'With me it will be a labour of love rather than necessity.'

I think I impressed her a little, for her manner warmed towards me.

'Very well,' she said. 'If you will follow me I will show you your room and introduce you to your pupil.'

The Grand Schloss was worthy of its name. It was built on a hill overlooking the town, of which it commanded a good view from all its windows. There were liveried servants everywhere, it seemed to me, and I was taken through galleries past rooms at which the guards were stationed and finally to the apartments of the Countess.

'The Countess has occupied these since she came from Kollenitz. That was, of course, after the death of Baron Rudolph when she became affianced to Baron Sigmund.'

I nodded. 'It was then, of course, that she became so important,' went on Frau Strelitz, 'for both the Margrave of Kollenitz and the Grand Duke are eager to unite the margravate and the duchy by this marriage.'

Frau Strelitz paused and knocked at a door. A voice called: 'Enter!' and we went in. A middle-aged woman rose and came towards us.

'Fräulein Kratz,' said Frau Strelitz, 'this is Fräulein Ayres.'

Fräulein Kratz had a pale lined face and a rather harassed

look. I felt sorry for her at once and could see that she was surprised by my youth.

A young girl had risen from the table and she came towards me somewhat imperiously.

'Your Highness,' said Frau Strelitz, 'may I present Fräulein Ayres, your English governess?'

I bowed and said in English: 'I am delighted to make your acquaintance, Countess.'

She replied in German: 'So you have come to teach me to speak English as the English do.'

'Which is, of course, the best way to speak it,' I continued in English.

She was very fair – so fair in fact that her eyelashes and eyebrows were scarcely perceptible. Her eyes were light blue, not large enough for beauty, particularly as she lacked the darker lashes which would have enhanced them; the very lightness of these gave her a look of perpetual surprise which I found rather endearing. She had a long, somewhat aquiline nose and very firm mouth. Her thick fair hair was worn in braids and she looked rather like a petulant schoolgirl. I was wondering what effect I had on her.

'I hope you will be a good pupil,' I went on.

She laughed, for she understood my English very well. 'I expect I shall be a bad one. I am often . . . am I not, Kratzkin?'

'The Countess is really very bright,' said Fräulein Kratz.

The Countess laughed. 'You spoilt it with the "really", didn't she, Fräulein Ayres? That gives it all away.'

'Well, Fräulein Ayres,' put in Frau Strelitz, 'you and Fräulein Kratz will make your arrangements about lessons. Shall I take you to your room and later you can settle things between you?'

'*I* shall take Fräulein Ayres to her room,' announced the Countess.

'Your Highness . . .'

'My Highness,' mimicked the Countess, 'will have it so.

Come, Fräulein, we have to get to know each other, do we not, if we are to converse in your abominable language.'

'You mean my beautiful language, of course, Countess,' I said.

She laughed. 'I am going to take her. Class is dismissed. Kratzkin and Frau Strelitz, you may leave us.'

I was somewhat appalled by the imperious manner of my pupil, but I felt my spirits rising. I could see that we were going to have some interesting encounters.

'Have her bags sent up at once,' ordered the Countess. 'I want to see what she has brought.' She laughed at me. 'I come from Kollenitz where they are rough and ready in their manners. We are not as cultivated as they are here in Bruxenstein. Have you gathered that, Fräulein Ayres?'

'I am beginning to.'

That made her laugh.

'Come on,' she said. 'I have to talk to you, don't I?'

'In English,' I said, 'and I see no reason why we should not begin right away.'

'Well, I do. You are merely a governess. I am the Countess, the Grand Duchess Elect. So you had better take care.'

'On the contrary, it is you who have to take care,'

'What do you mean by that?'

'I am a lady of independent means. I do not need to stay here. I am doing it because the idea appeals to me. It is not a case of earning my living. I think I should make that clear from the start.'

She stared at me. Then she began to laugh again.

The two women were still hovering in the doorway and she cried out: 'You heard me tell you to go. Leave at once. I will look after the English governess.'

I smiled apologetically at Frau Strelitz. 'It is good that we should talk together,' I said. 'I shall refuse to speak to the Countess except in English, as I have decided that that is a rule of paramount importance.'

The young girl was too surprised to argue with me and I

felt I had won the first round. I had also won the admiration of poor harassed Kratzkin and the approval of Frau Strelitz. But it was the Countess with whom I had to deal.

'This is your room,' she said, flinging open a door. 'I am at the end of this corridor. I have finer apartments, of course, but this is not bad for a governess.'

'I dare say I shall find it adequate.'

'Far better than you are accustomed to, no doubt,' she said.

'In fact no. I was brought up in a large manor house which I think on the whole was every bit as luxurious as your schloss.'

'And you really are doing all this . . . for fun?'

'You could call it that.'

'You are not very old, are you?'

'I am experienced in the ways of the world.'

'Are you? I wish I were. I'm not nearly as experienced as I should like to be.'

'It comes with the years.'

'How old are you?'

'I shall be eighteen in April.'

'I am fifteen. There is not much difference.'

'Actually there is a great deal. The next four years will be some of the most important of your life.'

'Why?'

'Because one grows out of girlhood into womanhood.'

'I shall be married next year.'

'So I gathered.'

'People talk about us a lot, don't they?'

'They know certain facts.'

'I wish you wouldn't keep talking in English.'

'It is what I am here for.'

'It restricts the conversation. I want to know so much about you and I can't always understand as I want to if you will speak in English.'

'It will be an incentive for you to master the language.'

'You talk just like a governess. I have had quite a number

but they never stay very long. I'm a difficult person. I've never had one like you.'

'It will be a change for you.'

'I don't suppose you'll stay long.'

'Only while you need me, of course.'

'I dare say you'll leave before that. I am not easy, you know.'

'I have gathered that.'

'Poor Kratzkin is terrified of me. Frau Strelitz is a bit, too.'

'I don't think you should look so smug about that.'

'Why not?'

'The fact that you make things uncomfortable for them should not make you glow with satisfaction. It is easy, is it not, to score over those who cannot reply?'

'Why don't they reply then?'

'Because they are employed here.'

'Shall I score over you?'

'Most definitely not.'

'Why not?'

'Because I am not dependent on pleasing you. If you don't like me you can tell me to get out, and if I don't like you I can go with equal ease.'

She looked at me in astonishment. Then she smiled slowly.

'What's your name?'

'Fräulein Ayres.'

'I mean your first name.'

'Anne.'

'I shall call you that.'

'What is yours?'

'You know. Everybody know. I'm the Countess Freya of Kollenitz.'

'Freya. That's one of the goddesses.'

'The goddess of beauty,' she said complacently. 'Did you know that when Thor lost his hammer the giant, Thrym, would only give it back if Freya came to Giantland as his bride?'

'I did. And Thor dressed as Freya and went to Giantland and got his hammer back. Those legends used to be told to me by my governess. She went often to the Black Forest for her holidays. She had a German mother.'

'So you had a governess too. Was she nice? Did you like her?'

'She was very nice and I liked her.'

'You were a good girl, I expect.'

'Not always. But we were always well mannered.'

'Who were *we*?'

'My sister and I.' I felt myself flush a little and she was quick to notice.

'Where is your sister now?'

'She died.'

'That makes you sad, doesn't it?'

'Very sad.'

'Tell me about your governess.'

I told her all I could remember of Miss Elton and her family.

She was very interested but I noticed that her mind flitted from one thing to another very quickly. She had seen my bags. 'Are you going to unpack?' she asked.

'Yes,' I said.

'I'll watch you.'

And she did, as I took my clothes out and hung them up. She made comments on them as I did so. 'That's ugly. That's not so bad.

I said: 'I see what you mean about Kollenitz manners!' which sent her into peals of laughter. There was a book lying on the top of my case and she seized it. She read slowly with a strong German accent: 'The poems of Robert Browning.'

I said: 'I can see that we shall have to work hard on your accent.'

The book opened naturally at a certain page and there was a reason for it, for I had often turned to that particular poem.

'Pippa's Song,' she read out slowly.

'"The year's at the spring
And the day's at the morn . . ."

Oh, I can't read this. Poetry's very difficult.'

I took the book from her and read the poem aloud. There was a slight tremor in my voice when I reached the last lines.

'"God's in his Heaven,
All's right with the world."'

I shut the book. She was looking at me intently. Then I smiled slowly and she returned the smile.

I thought: It's going to be all right. I'm going to like my little Countess.

The next few days were crowded with new impressions. To the surprise of the servants, the Countess and I got on remarkably well. I think this may have been due to a certain aloofness which I was able to display and which was the result of my independence and the fact that I could, at any moment, leave if I wished without any financial considerations, which affected my manner and hers. I interested her as she interested me. She liked to be with me and wanted to neglect her other studies for the sake, as she rather unctuously said, of 'improving my English'. It was not difficult for me because there were no lessons to prepare. She had been grounded in the language and it was only conversation that she needed, so we were able to talk on various subjects, and when she made a mistake I would point it out to her.

Sometimes I would say to her: 'Shouldn't you be with Fräulein Kratz?'

She would grimace. 'Oh, I want to get on with my English. That is the most important. Who cares about mathematics . . . silly stuff anyway. Who cares about history? What does it matter what kings and queens did years ago? I can't change that, can I? I really do feel that I need to get on with my English.'

I replied to that: 'You forget that I must have my free times. You are encroaching on them.'

I think it was rare for her to consider anyone but herself, but she did become thoughtful and went back to the schoolroom rather subdued.

I was flattered. When I visited Daisy I heard that Hans had been told by the Comptroller of the Household that they were amazed by my success with the Countess. It was very gratifying.

So we were together a great deal and I think, in a way, becoming friends. Life in the royal household was not exactly what I had expected. We were very much segregated and although two weeks had passed since my arrival, I had never once had a glimpse of the Grand Duke. The turret in which we had our apartments was quite separate from the royal apartments, and although there was much arriving and departing of emissaries and such like, they affected us not at all. It was like living in the wing of a country house – part of the main residence and yet completely cut off from it.

Freya and I walked in the grounds of the schloss; we rode together; she was a good horsewoman but I could compare favourably with her.

Once she said with a grudging admiration: 'You can do everything.'

She was always soberly dressed when she rode out and we always had to take two grooms with us, which irked her. I remarked that they were very discreet and kept their distance. 'They had better,' she said, her eyes flashing.

We rode through the forest together and she told me stories which had been passed down through the ages. She showed me an old ruined schloss where some Baroness was said to have walled up her husband's mistress. 'She said she wanted a new room added, and when the workmen were making it, she brought this beautiful girl to them and made them wall her in. They say you can still hear the girl's screams on certain nights.'

She showed me the Klingen Rock with the ravine far below. 'They used to take people out there and invite them to throw themselves over . . . to avoid a worse fate.'

'You have some very pleasant customs in Bruxenstein.'

'All people have them,' retorted Freya. 'They don't talk about them though and this was long ago.

'Klingen Schloss once belonged to a robber baron who used to waylay travellers, capture them and hold them to ransom. He used to chop off their fingers one by one and send them to their relatives, and with each finger the ransom was increased, and if the ransom wasn't paid they would be thrown from the rock . . . to get rid of them.'

'It's horrible.'

'The gods are nicer,' admitted Freya, and her eyes glowed when she talked of Thor. 'He was strong . . . the God of Thunder.' He was her favourite among the gods. 'He had red hair and a red beard. He was the strongest of them all and very gentle, but when he was angry sparks flew out of his eyes.'

'I hope he did not get angry often. Getting angry is foolish. It never helps.'

'Don't you ever get angry, Fräulein Anne?'

'Oh yes . . . now and then. Fortunately I am not Thor so you have no need to fear the sparks.'

She laughed. She was constantly laughing in my company. I noticed how the servants would look at us when they heard her, and there was no doubt that I was getting a reputation for knowing how to handle the Countess.

I did understand that she had lived in a rarefied atmosphere and that her position had set her apart; she had known few other children and she had never had a playmate. All she had was her royalty which manifested itself in her power over others. She had exerted it because it was all she had.

I was beginning to feel rather sorry for my arrogant little Countess. I encouraged her to talk. She had little to tell of her daily life; she lived in a world of her own, populated by gods and heroes. She talked constantly of Freya which was natural enough, as she had been called after that goddess.

'She was golden-haired and blue-eyed,' she told me on one occasion, looking complacently at her reflection in the glass as she spoke, 'and she was considered to be the personification of Earth because she was so beautiful. She married Odur who was a symbol of the summer sun and she had two daughters who were as beautiful as herself... well, not quite, but almost. She loved them dearly, but she loved her husband more. He was a wanderer though and could not be content at home. I wonder whether Sigmund will be a wanderer. I think he will be. He is hardly ever here. He is travelling now. Perhaps he doesn't want to be where I am.'

I said: 'You must not think that life is going to be for you just as it was for this goddess. We live in modern times.'

She looked at me intently and said with a flash of wisdom: 'But people don't change much, do they? Whenever they lived they are much the same. They marry . . . and are unfaithful and they go wandering.'

'It will be your task to see that Sigmund does not go wandering.'

'Now you are talking like Kratzkin. Oh, please don't be like her. Be like yourself. I couldn't bear it if you became like someone else.'

'I hope I shall always be myself, and I should imagine that this Freya who was so beautiful should have let her husband go wandering and not have bothered about him.'

'She was so unhappy. She wept and when her tears fell into the sea they turned into amber.'

'I hardly think that is the scientific explanation of that substance.'

She laughed again and I was glad to see her merriment because I sensed beneath these conversations her preoccupation with her coming marriage to this Sigmund and I realized she was apprehensive. I hoped that some time she would confide her feelings to me.

'She went in search of him and she wept so much that where she wept gold was found later.'

'Many people must be very grateful to the lachrymose lady,' I said.

'Well, it all seems hard to believe now, but I'm glad they called me Freya. Though Freya did not marry Sigmund. He married Borghild . . . but she was wicked and he put her from him. Then he took a new wife in her place. She was Hiordis. You see, she wasn't Freya either.'

'You have lived too much with these old legends,' I told her. 'They are not always meant to be taken so seriously. In any case your Sigmund was one of the heroes, wasn't he? I know you regard yourself as a goddess, but I should remember that Sigmund is a man. And you are a woman and if you want to live together happily you must not forget this.'

'You make it all sound so easy, Fräulein Anne. Is it always so easy for you?'

'No,' I said firmly, 'it is not.'

'I want to tell you something.'

'Yes?'

'I'm glad you came here.'

It was remarkable progress, and that after two weeks!

She told me about life in Kollenitz. 'It was much less formal than here,' she said. 'Of course my father, the Margrave, governs only a little place . . . but it is important. That is the point. It is where Kollenitz is situated . . . not our power or our wealth or anything like that. Bruxenstein needs to be friends with Kollenitz so that Kollenitz can be what they call a buffer state. Do you understand?'

'Yes.'

'Well, how would you like to be a buffer?'

She looked at me questioningly and I replied on impulse: 'I think it would depend on Sigmund.'

That made her laugh yet again. 'Sigmund is tall and

handsome. I think the Hero Sigmund must have been rather like him. But perhaps he is more like Sigurd. I always liked him better really. He was my favourite among all the Heroes.'

'You must get away from all those myths. Tell me about Kollenitz.'

'I was the only child. It's a great blow when they don't have sons. They seem to blame it on you.'

'I'm sure they don't.'

'I am sure they do and please don't talk like Kratzkin.'

'All right. Shall we say then that they feel a little resentful towards a female child?'

'That's better,' she said.

'But as it was no fault of yours you should not allow it to upset you.'

'It didn't much. But . . . perhaps it did a little. It made it difficult for them . . . nurses . . . governesses . . . I wanted them to know that even if I was a girl I was also important . . . the heiress. Well, then I was betrothed to Sigmund and that was after Rudolph was murdered.'

'What do you know about that?' I asked eagerly.

'About Rudolph? He was with his mistress in the hunting lodge and someone came in and killed them with one of the guns from the gun room there. I didn't hear about it until after, though if he had lived I should have married Rudolph.'

'*You* would?'

'Yes, because of Kollenitz being the buffer. They want Kollenitz allied with Bruxenstein.'

'What happened then?'

'It was a long time ago and I was very young at the time. I used to hear them whispering together, but they always shut up when they saw me. Then I heard I was going to be betrothed to Sigmund. I couldn't understand it at first because they had always told me before that Rudolph was going to be my husband.'

'When did you learn that he had died?'

'When I was betrothed to Sigmund. They had to tell me

then that it was not going to be Rudolph and why. I didn't go through any ceremony with Rudolph. It was all in treaties, but there was a betrothal ceremony in the *Schlosskapelle* here and Sigmund and I made our vows. It wasn't a marriage . . . it was just a betrothal; but it does mean that we are promised to each other. We couldn't marry anyone else now without a dispensation and that would never be given because my father and the Grand Duke would never allow it.'

'I see what an important person you are.'

'A buffer,' she answered.

I laid my hands on her shoulders. 'Countess,' I said, 'I see that you are going to be very happy.'

'Where do you see it?'

'In your stars.'

'Can you tell?'

'I can tell you that this will be so.'

'I wonder why Sigmund stays away so long. Do you think it is because he doesn't like me?'

'Certainly not. It is because he is arranging treaties and suchlike with foreign powers.'

She laughed. Then she was serious. 'Perhaps it is,' she said. 'You see, it was only when Rudolph died that he became important. Before that, he was only the son of the Grand Duke's younger brother.'

'It must have made a lot of difference to his life.'

'Of course. He'll be a Grand Duke when this one dies. Oh, I do hope he's not going wandering like Freya's husband.'

'He won't, and you won't go crying after him, even if it does add to the world's supply of amber and gold.'

'Oh, Fräulein Anne, I do like you. It's because you are funny, I think. I am going to call you just Anne . . . not Fräulein any more, because that makes you seem like any old governess.'

'I can see we are making rapid strides. Your manners are improving with your English accent. You ask my permission. Dear Countess, I should like you to call me . . . just Anne.'

'And will you call me Freya?'

'When we are alone,' I said. 'But before others it might be wise to stand on a little ceremony.'

She kissed me then and I was deeply moved. We were indeed becoming friends.

I had been with Freya for nearly a month when she said she wished to go to the mausoleum because this was the anniversary of her great-grandmother's death and she was buried there. I wanted to know how this came about and she told me that her great-grandmother had made a second marriage into Bruxenstein and had lived the last years of her life there, though the children of her first marriage had remained in Kollenitz.

I was very eager to see anything connected with the family and I greatly looked forward to the visit.

It was necessary to get the key to the mausoleum from the Comptroller of the Household and he greeted me with smiles. Like everyone else, he knew of the success I was having with the young Countess, and he regarded himself as responsible for this happy appointment. He had even been congratulated by the Grand Duke himself, he told me, for he had had an account from Frau Strelitz and others.

I told him that I was enjoying the work and that the Countess was making excellent progress.

'It is said that she is so interested in her English studies that she is inclined to neglect others,' he said complacently.

'Fräulein Kratz and I try to keep an even balance.'

The Comptroller beamed and gave me the key to the mausoleum, asking that when the visit was over I should return it to him.

This I promised to do and Freya and I set out on foot, for the church was adjoining the schloss. It was beautifully situated high up with magnificent views of the town below. Some of the graves had been made quite recently and fresh flowers and wreaths lay on them.

The mausoleum was imposing and quite grand. Freya whispered to me that it had been there for many years and had been designed by one of the greatest architects.

She opened the door and descended a few steps. The floor was of marble, as was the chapel; and there were side galleries in which the sarcophagi had been placed.

'How quiet it is!' I said.

'Quiet as the grave,' agreed Freya. 'Anne, are you just a little bit frightened?'

'What is there to be afraid of?'

'Ghosts?' suggested Freya.

'The dead cannot harm the living.'

'Some people think so. What if they have been murdered? They say that if people have died violently they can't rest.'

'Who says?'

'*They*.'

'I never believe *them*. They are always so vague and it is as though they are afraid to say their names.'

'This is the coffin of my great-grandmother. I always wonder about her when I come here. She came from Kollenitz to Bruxenstein . . . just as I did. But she was older than I and had been married before . . . so she knew something about it. I say a little prayer and hope that she is happy in heaven. I saw a picture of her once. They say she was like me.'

'*They* again. They seem to be everywhere?'

She laughed out loud and then put her fingers to her lips. 'Perhaps we shouldn't laugh in here.'

'Why not?'

'They might not like it.'

'Here *they* come again.'

She was serious. 'I mean the ghosts this time,' she whispered.

'Well,' I said loudly, 'we have nothing to fear from them or they from us.'

'Come and look at this,' she said, and she led me to the coffin which lay on one of the ledges. 'Can you read it?'

I leaned forward. 'Rudolph Wilhelm Otto, Baron von Gruton Fuchs. Aged twenty-three years . . .'

'Yes,' she interrupted. 'It's the one who was murdered. I wonder if he rests in peace?'

I stared in shocked silence, stunned, although I should have realized that he would be buried here. My mind had gone back over the years to the day when I had first seen him coming to the Grange and taking Francine away.

Then suddenly I realized that I was alone. I turned sharply and heard the key turning in the lock. I was startled and then deeply shocked. Freya had locked me in.

I stared at the door. Then I went to it and said sternly: 'Open this immediately.'

There was no response. I banged with my fists but that made little impression.

I did not know what to do. This was not serious. I should soon be missed and they would know where I was because the Comptroller had given me the key to the mausoleum, and if Freya returned without me they would come immediately and release me. But my first feelings were disappointment that Freya could have done this. I knew she was trying to break through my calm and frighten me, to show that I possessed the same weaknesses that she did; but to be locked in a mausoleum with no company but the dead was a terrifying experience and of this she would be very much aware, and yet in spite of our friendship she had subjected me to it.

It was indeed eerie in this place. I looked at the sarcophagi on the side galleries and thought of the dead – Rudolph among them. If he could but come alive and tell me the truth of what happened, I would be ready to face anything for that.

I sat on the steps and stared ahead of me. 'Oh, Rudolph . . . Rudolph . . .' I murmured to myself, 'come to me now, I won't be afraid. I want so much to know . . .'

And then suddenly . . . I was aware of a presence . . . close to me. I fancied I heard the sound of suppressed laughter.

I turned sharply and the silence was broken by Freya's merriment. She had quietly opened the door and was standing behind me.

'Were you frightened?' she asked.

'When you foolishly locked me in, shall we say I was very surprised.'

'Why?'

'That you could do something so . . .'

'Childish?'

'No. That would have been forgivable.'

'Are you angry then? Aren't you going to forgive me? Will you go away?'

I turned to her and said: 'Freya, some people might have been very frightened indeed to be locked in such a place.'

'You wouldn't.'

'How did you know?'

'You are not frightened of anything.'

'Good heavens! Have I given you that impression?'

She nodded.

'It was cruel of you,' I continued. 'You should never do a thing like that to anybody.'

'I know. I got frightened as soon as I'd done it. I thought your hair would turn white in a minute. Some people's do when they're frightened. I thought you might die of shock. Then I told myself you'd be all right. Then I got frightened that you would be so angry that you would go away. So I opened the door . . . and there you were just sitting there talking to yourself.'

'Give me the key,' I said. 'Did you take it out of my pocket?'

She nodded.

'It was all rather silly,' I commented.

'It wasn't in a way,' she argued, 'because it shows me that you really are very brave and just as I thought you were. You didn't scream or shout. You just sat there and waited because you knew I would be sorry almost at once.'

I led her firmly out of the mausoleum and locked the door. As we made our way back to the schloss she said: 'I know another grave. I'll show you if you like?'

'What grave?'

'It's rather a special one. It's a secret. I'll take you tomorrow. I do like you, Anne. I'm sorry I took the key and locked you in. But you were not frightened, were you? I don't think you ever would be. I think you've got special powers.'

'Now please don't confuse me with your gods and heroes. I'm not one of them.'

'What are you, Anne?'

'The long-suffering English governess.'

It was a pleasant trait in Freya's character that she was really penitent about locking me into the mausoleum and tried very hard to make up for her conduct.

I dismissed it all as of little importance and pointed out that as she had so quickly repented we could forget it.

She was determined to please me though, and only the next day suggested that we take a ride into the forest. We set out with two grooms riding behind us at a safe distance, and I was amazed to find that we were making our way towards the hunting lodge. We passed the cottage. None of the children was visible.

I said: 'I have friends in that cottage.'

'The lodge people?' she asked.

'Yes, I met them once. They have some charming children.'

'Oh, they're the people who looked after the hunting lodge when it happened.'

'Yes.'

We fell into silence for a while, then she said: 'We shall come to it in a minute.'

And there it was, looking more imposing than ever. Freya had pulled up and to my astonishment dismounted.

'We are going in there?' I asked, and I hoped she did not notice the excitement in my voice.

She shook her head. 'There's nothing in there,' she told me. 'Nobody goes there now. Well, would you want to? Where a murder had been committed?'

I shivered.

'You looked really scared, Anne.' She was regarding me intently. 'You look more frightened than you did in the mausoleum. Well, not exactly frightened . . . but odd somehow.'

'I assure you I'm not frightened.'

'All right then. Come on.'

'Where are we going?'

'I told you. I promised to show you something.'

My excitement was increasing. I felt that I was on the verge of a discovery and that it should come through the Countess was amazing.

She called to the grooms who were following at a discreet distance: 'We are going to walk round the lodge. Stay there with the horses. Come on,' she went on to me. 'This way.'

I followed her, wondering whether Arnulf, the twins or one of the other children were close by. But there was no sign of life anywhere.

She led me round to the back of the house, not pausing but going straight on until we came to a gate which opened out into a part of the forest which had been shut in with green palings. There was a gate made of the same palings and Freya went to this.

'Can you guess what's in here?' she asked.

'No.'

'It's a grave.' She opened the gate and we went through. There was a mound in the centre of the patch and on it someone had planted a rose-bush; the surrounding grass had been neatly cut.

I knelt and read the inscription on the plate which was almost hidden by the rose-bush.

'Francine Ewell,' I read. And there was the date of her death.

I was overcome with emotion. This was the last thing I had expected. I wanted to throw myself on that earth and weep for her, my dear, beautiful and beloved sister. Now she lay there under this earth. At least I had found her grave.

I was aware of Freya beside me. 'That is . . . the woman,' she whispered.

I did not answer. I could not have spoken then.

'They must have buried her here . . . near the lodge where she died,' went on Freya.

I stood up and she continued: 'That's what I wanted to show you. I thought you'd be interested . . . because you are, aren't you? You like hearing about the murder.' She was studying me intently. 'Are you all right, Anne?'

'Yes, thank you. I'm quite all right.'

'You look a bit odd.'

'It's the light here . . . all these trees. They make you look pale too.'

'Well, that's what I wanted to show you. It's interesting, isn't it?'

I agreed that it was.

I tried to appear normal but I kept thinking of Francine's body being taken out of the lodge and buried close by.

As we rode home the thought struck me. Somebody tends her grave. Who would that be?

I longed to return there . . . alone. That seemed impossible, for I could not absent myself long enough. Then I told Frau Strelitz that I should like half a day's freedom as I wished to visit Frau Schmidt with whom I had lodged before I came to the schloss.

'But of course, Fräulein,' she said. 'We don't want you to think of yourself as a prisoner. You must take free time often.

You and the Countess have become almost like friends and it did not occur to me that you wished to go off alone.'

It was not so easy with Freya. She could not understand why she could not come with me.

'It would be embarrassing for my friends. They are not accustomed to entertaining personages in their tiny cottage.'

'*I* should not mind.'

'That is not the point. *They* would.'

'It's Herr Schmidt's wife, isn't it? He works for the Graf von Bindorf.'

'So you know that.'

'I like to know *all* about you, Anne.' She laughed aloud. 'Why, you looked scared for a moment. I believe you have a secret. Oh, have you . . . ? Have you?'

'Now you are going off into your wild imaginings.'

I turned the matter off as lightly as I could and I wondered if I deceived her. She was very astute.

However, I did have my free afternoon and rode over to Daisy who was delighted to see me, and told me she had heard from Hans that I was making a great success of the post and that the Countess was spending a great deal of time with me.

'Well,' she said, 'it's natural. You was brought up at the Manor and I reckon a real English lady is as good as any foreign Countess.'

'Don't let anyone hear you say that. I am sure they wouldn't agree.'

'We'll keep it to ourselves,' said Daisy with a wink. 'Now let me get you a glass of wine. I've got some good wine cakes too. I keep them for Hans's friends when they drop in.'

I sipped the wine and told her that I had seen Francine's grave.

She was startled.

'The strange thing is,' I said, 'that someone is looking after it.'

'I wonder who that could be?'

'Daisy, it must be someone who knew her.'

'It might not be. People do look after graves. It's a sort of respect for the dead.'

'I want to go and look at it again.'

'Why now?'

'It's an opportunity and they are not easy to get.'

'I've heard what a fancy the Countess has taken to you. Poor little thing. Rushed into marriage. Rudolph was for her. All right. He's murdered so it's Sigmund instead.'

'Rudolph could never have married her,' I said firmly, 'because he was married to Francine.'

Daisy said nothing. She did not want to contradict me over a matter on which I felt so strongly. 'I'll see you on the way back,' she said.

I think she was rather disappointed that I did not stay with her, but she did understand my burning desire to have another look at the grave.

I rode off with all speed and in a short time had passed Gisela's cottage. I glimpsed the twins playing in the garden. They noticed me and called after me. I turned and waved and went on.

I came to the lodge, dismounted, tethered my horse to the mounting block and made my way round to the back of the house. I found the grave and went through the green paling gate. I knelt beside it and thought of Francine.

I wished that I had brought some flowers to put on her grave. Would that be foolish? Would someone notice? Would they say, why does this strange Englishwoman visit the grave?

I shouldn't have come perhaps. I might already have betrayed my emotion to Freya. What if someone found me here?

I stood up. I felt as though eyes watched me, that someone was peering through the forest trees. I fancied I could hear whispering voices but it was only the wind murmuring through the pine trees.

I must not be found here. I had been discovered at the hunting lodge by the children. If it were known that I had returned, what would they think? Surely they would begin to wonder at my apparent morbid interest in a crime which had been committed some time ago.

I hurried to my horse and rode away. When I came to the cottage Gisela was at the door, a young child in her arms. I gathered this was Max.

She called good-day to me. 'How are you? Frau Schmidt was telling me about your post up at the Grand Schloss.'

'Yes, I am enjoying it. The Countess is charming.'

'And she is a good pupil?'

'Very good . . . with her English.'

'Have you been to the lodge?'

'I passed it.' I hesitated, then I rushed on: 'By the way, what is that little enclosure with the palings round it . . . at the back of the lodge?'

She looked puzzled for a moment and then she said: 'Oh . . . I think what you mean is a grave.'

'It's a strange place for a grave.'

'I suppose there were reasons.'

'It looks as though someone looks after it . . . a friend, I suppose, of the person buried there.'

'Oh . . . did you go and look?'

'I had dismounted so I went through the little gate. It seems to be well tended. I wonder who does it?'

'I tidy it up a bit now and then. It's so near the lodge and as I was seeing to that . . .'

'Who is buried there? Do you know?'

She hesitated and said: 'It was the young woman in the shooting case.'

'Strange that they should bury her there. Why not in an ordinary cemetery?'

'I heard it said they buried her quickly. They didn't want to make a ceremony of it. So few people come out here . . . But I don't know. I'm guessing.'

'Well,' I said, 'it was a long time ago.'

'Yes, a long, long time ago.'

I took my leave and rode thoughtfully back to Daisy's. I was disappointed. I had hoped to find someone who had tended her grave lovingly, someone who had known her in life. If there had been such a person he or she could have told me a good deal.

I stayed talking with Daisy, mainly about my life at the Grand Schloss, which interested her very much.

'You've not found out anything yet?' she asked anxiously.

I shook my head and told her that I had seen Gisela who had said she tidied up my sister's grave.

'She would, Gisela would. She'd want to tidy up the place. She's got the German passion for tidiness.'

'It looked more than just tidying up,' I said. 'It looked as if someone tended it with care.'

I said goodbye to Daisy and rode back through the town to the Grand Schloss. As soon as I came near the gates I was aware that something had happened. A man on horseback was riding out as I came up to it, and he passed me as though he were in a great hurry.

The guards were about to challenge me and then, recognizing me, they let me pass. As I entered the hall one of the servants hurried to me.

'Frau Strelitz would like to see you in her room without delay.'

I went there in some trepidation wondering what could have happened.

She was waiting for me.

'Ah, Fräulein Ayres, I am glad you are back. The Grand Duke has had a seizure.'

'Is he . . .'

'No, no, but dangerously ill. He has had this sort of thing before. But if he should die Baron Sigmund would become Grand Duke immediately. As you can imagine, this could cause trouble. Because of this unfortunate death of Rudolph, who was the undoubted son of the Grand Duke thus assuring the accepted succession, it is not quite so straightforward.

There are some who feel that another has prior claim. He is called Otto the Bastard because he claims to be the illegitimate son of the Grand Duke. Our great desire is to keep the Grand Duke alive . . . but we must make sure that he does not die before Sigmund arrives.'

'Where is the elusive Sigmund? I hear so much about him.'

'He is travelling abroad. It is his duty to meet the heads of state in various countries. We have sent couriers to him at once. He'll have to come back now. The only thing is he must do so because if the Grand Duke dies . . . You understand. We don't want to be plunged into war.'

'So that is why there is this change. I sensed it as soon as I passed the gate.'

'It may be necessary for you to take the Countess away from the Grand Schloss for a while. We are not quite sure what is going to happen yet. But I wanted you to be prepared. We must pray for the recovery of the Grand Duke.'

I went to find Freya. She was waiting for me.

'You see what happens when you go away,' she said. 'Now the Grand Duke is ill.'

'That has nothing to do with my going out for the afternoon.'

She narrowed her eyes and looked at me steadily. 'I think it might be,' she said. 'Fräulein Anne, you are not what you seem.'

'What do you mean?' I asked sharply.

She pointed her finger at me. 'You're not a witch, are you? You're one of the goddesses returned to earth. You can assume which shape you like . . .'

'Stop this nonsense,' I said. 'You know this is very serious. The Grand Duke is very ill.'

'I know. He is going to die and I can only think of one thing, Anne, Sigmund is coming home.'

Frau Strelitz sent for me the next day.

She told me at once that the Grand Duke was a little better.

The doctors were with him and they had made an announcement. He had had a seizure like this before and had recovered. There was every hope that he would do so again.

His ministers had been talking through the night, she told me. 'They eagerly await the return of the heir. In the meantime they consider that the Countess Freya should not be in the Grand Schloss . . . in case of trouble. So we have decided that she should leave with you and Fräulein Kratz and a few of her servants.'

'I understand. When do we leave?'

'Tomorrow. The Grand Duke's ministers think the sooner the better . . . just in case, of course. We have every hope of the Grand Duke's recovery. It is thought that she should not be too far away. The Margrave of Kollenitz would be very suspicious if we moved her away from the capital, so we have arranged that she shall go to the schloss on the other side of the river, and the Graf von Bindorf has offered you all hospitality until the situation is clarified.'

I felt as though the room were spinning round me. I was to go into the household of the Graf and Gräfin von Bindorf. Some members of that household had seen me before, including the Gräfin and her daughter Tatiana. Would they recognize me? And if so, what would happen? I was sure that my coming here under an assumed name in order to attempt to uncover a mystery involving my sister would not be regarded with any great pleasure.

I was in my bedroom getting my things together when Freya came in and sat on my bed. I was holding the glasses which Miss Elton had procured for me and considering whether I should wear them on entering the von Bindorf schloss.

'What have you got there?' demanded Freya. 'Oh . . . spectacles. You don't wear them, do you?'

'Sometimes . . .'

'Have you got weak eyes? Oh, you poor Anne! All that

reading you have to do. Do your eyes get tired? Do they make your head ache?'

'I suppose I should wear them more,' I said.

'Put them on and let's have a look at you.'

I did so and she laughed. 'You look different,' she said.

I was glad to hear that.

'You look severe,' she went on. 'Just like a governess. You look quite alarming.'

'Then I should certainly wear them more.'

'You're prettier without them.'

'There are things more important than looks.'

'I think you're just wearing them for a reason.'

She alarmed me. Sometimes she seemed to see right into my mind. She was now looking at me slyly, teasing me as she loved to do.

'What reason?' I said sharply.

'What reason could there be but to try to make me afraid of you?'

I laughed with relief. But sometimes her comments shook me.

As we prepared to leave for the von Bindorf schloss, I kept remembering fragments from that long-ago meeting. Could the Gräfin remember anything about me? I had been young then, a schoolgirl, nondescript, like so many other girls of my age. I had grown several inches taller because I had shot up rather suddenly, and from being a small girl had become a fairly tall young woman. I supposed that anyone who had known me would have recognized me, but the Gräfin had seen me for only a short time and then she had obviously been so much more interested in Francine.

The spectacles might well be useful. I would wear them when there could be a need to do so, and I did not believe that Freya had any real suspicions about them. I was over nervous. I had nothing to fear. It was hardly likely that the Gräfin would take much notice of her important guest's English governess.

The next day the carriage drove us over to the schloss. There were little knots of people in the streets and quite a crowd outside the Grand Schloss. The Comptroller of the Household had attached a bulletin of the Grand Duke's condition on the gate and there was a crowd reading it. I noticed the faces of the people as we passed through. They gave a little cheer for the Countess, who acknowledged it with the grace and solemnity which the occasion demanded.

I thought: She will make a good duchess when the time arises.

Fräulein Kratz and I sat well back in the carriage as we went through the town and across the bridge to that other schloss. I thought: I shall be nearer Daisy, and Hans will be under the same roof. It was a comforting thought.

We went under a kind of portcullis and into a courtyard where the Gräfin and the Graf were waiting to greet the Countess. On either side of them stood a young man and a young woman. The young woman looked vaguely familiar and I immediately thought: Oh, yes, Tatiana. And again I was touched by a shiver of apprehension. I had to escape detection not only by the Gräfin but by her daughter, and casting my mind back it occurred to me that Tatiana would have been interested in one of her own age. I should have put on the glasses.

Freya was helped out of the carriage by one of the footmen and she went straight to the Graf and Gräfin who bowed and then embraced her.

Fräulein Kratz stepped out of the carriage and moved to one side. I followed her, head lowered. She had taken up her stand on the edge of the group; I kept close to her; and I was relieved that everyone seemed intent on watching Freya and that I did not receive more than a cursory glance.

I watched Tatiana greet Freya and the young man clicked his heels and bowed. Freya smiled graciously and the Gräfin took her by the hand and led her into the schloss.

I mingled with a group of people. Those, I thought, who are of little importance; and I thanked Heaven for them.

I saw Hans suddenly. He was looking for me, I guessed, and he came over and spoke to me.

'I will take you to the apartments which have been assigned to you and Fräulein Kratz,' he said. 'They are next to those of the Countess.'

I smiled my appreciation and with Fräulein Kratz slipped away from those surrounding the main party. We were conducted through a narrow passage and up a stone staircase – the spiral kind, each step being built into the wall at one end and consequently very narrow, and much wider at the other end. There was a thick rope handrail.

'Your apartments can be reached by the main staircase,' Hans told me, 'but on this occasion it is better to use this one.'

I was grateful to him. He must have guessed that I would be apprehensive.

He showed us a suite of rooms. Fräulein Kratz and I were next to each other and there was a large room which could be used for a schoolroom On the other side of this were those apartments allotted to the Countess.

Fräulein Kratz nervously said that she hoped the Grand Duke would soon recover.

'They say it is almost certain that he will,' Hans told her.

'I feel quite exhausted,' she said.

'Have a little rest,' I suggested.

'I must settle in first,' she said, and went into her room, which left me alone with Hans.

I looked at him questioningly.

'They'll never recognize you,' he said. 'You look quite different. I didn't know you again when I saw you after all that time. They hardly ever look at people unless they are grand dukes or counts. It will be all right.'

'Hans, if I am discovered, I hope it doesn't make trouble for you.'

'I shall disclaim all knowledge. Daisy will come up with something. You can trust Daisy.'

He tried to restore my spirits by giving me an imitation of one of Daisy's winks, which looked so grotesque on him that it made me smile.

'I reckon you won't be here long,' he said. 'As soon as the Duke's better you'll be going back. And he will recover. He has before.'

I was in my room when I heard the Countess being brought up to hers. There was a great deal of conversation and I could detect Freya's high-pitched voice.

Then I heard her say: 'Gräfin, you must meet my very good friend, Fräulein Ayres. She's an English lady and teaches me English . . . just for fun.'

I felt suddenly sick with fear. I put on the glasses and pretended to be looking at the view as the door opened and Freya came in with the Gräfin. I stood with my back to the light.

When I turned I saw that Tatiana and the young man were with them.

'Fräulein Ayres,' said Freya, very much on her dignity, 'I want to present you to the Gräfin von Bindorf and to Count Günther and the Countess Tatiana.'

I bowed low.

The Gräfin's eyes momentarily swept over me and I thought dismissed me. As for Tatiana, she appeared to have become a very haughty young woman who would not deign to give the English governess more than a passing glance. It was different with Günther.

'Welcome,' he said. 'I hope you will be happy here.'

'Oh, we shall be,' said Freya. 'Fräulein Ayres and I are always happy. We love our English chatter, do we not?'

I tried to look governess-like. I said: 'The Countess is making excellent progress.'

The Gräfin turned away with the air of one who has humoured the whim of a child. She laid her hand on Freya's arm and said: 'Come, dear Countess, we have much to talk of.'

As they went out Tatiana threw a backward glance at me I had lowered my eyes and turned away.

They had no idea who I was, I was sure.

During the next few days I saw less of Freya. She deplored this. She said they were always making demands on her. The Gräfin was determined to honour her. 'She is looking to the future when I shall be Grand Duchess,' said Freya. 'I don't know what it is . . . but she looks down her nose at me when she thinks I don't see her and is always flattering me to my face. I don't think she likes me one little bit, although she pretends to admire me. I wish we were back at the Grand Schloss. Günther's nice, though. He's different from the others and I think he is really pleased that I am here.'

The bulletins of the Grand Duke continued favourably and it now seemed certain that he was going to recover after all.

My fears were lulled. It was quite clear that I was going to see very little of the Gräfin and her daughter and if ever I was summoned to their presence, I would make sure that I was wearing my glasses and that my hair was more severely dressed than usual.

There seemed little fear that I should be and I felt immensely relieved. Our stay here would be short, since the Grand Duke was improving every day and as long as I could remain in obscurity no one would think of connecting me with Francine. It occurred to me once again how wise I was to have come as Anne Ayres. My own name would have betrayed me immediately.

It was three days after our arrival when Freya burst into my room.

'Hello, Anne,' she cried. 'We see so little of each other, I don't like it. I'll be glad when we go back. But you know that, don't you? Now I'll tell you something you don't know.'

'Well?'

'Sigmund is coming tomorrow.'

'Oh, it's about time, isn't it?'

'They had to let him know and then he had to travel back. He will go to the Grand Schloss first to see the Grand Duke and then he will come here. It will be evening when he arrives and the Gräfin would like to make a grand occasion of it, but of course it can't be all that grand because of the Grand Duke's illness.'

'Just an intimate dinner-party, I suppose.'

'More than that. You see, the Duke is so much better. He has actually been sitting up in bed taking nourishment.'

'That is good news. Sigmund need not have interrupted his pleasure.'

'He should be here. State duties and all that. He'll be a sort of Regent. Besides he has to woo me.'

'Poor man! What a task!'

'Anne, it is good to be with you. The others are all so serious. They never laugh and what I like best is laughing.'

'It shows a happy temperament,' I said.

'Anne, listen. There's to be a sort of minor ball.'

'What on earth is that?'

'A ball . . . but not a grand ball, of course. Less people . . . less fuss . . . less ceremony . . . but a ball all the same.'

'And I can see the sparkle in your eyes. Is that for the ball or the laggard Sigmund?'

'Why do you call him a laggard?'

'Because he has delayed so long. He's a laggard in love. I hope not a dastard in war.'

'Are you quoting poetry again?'

'I admit it.'

'You do love it, don't you? I am to have a new dress for this ball and I am going to Madame Chabris who has set up in the town as the court dressmaker She is from Paris and you know all the best fashions come from there.'

'I have heard it,' I replied. 'When do we go to Madame Chabris?'

'Immediately.'

'Will there be time to make this dress by tomorrow?'

'Madame Chabris is a marvel. She knows my size. She has made dresses for me before. She knew that Sigmund would be coming home and that I should be needing an exquisite gown. It would not surprise me if Madame Chabris had the very thing waiting for me.'

'She sounds as though she is very clever.'

'But the good news is this. You are coming too, Anne.'

'I!'

'I insisted. I don't deny it was hard. The Gräfin said: "A governess!" I explained that you were a very special sort of governess. You have been brought up almost as nobly as we have. You are only doing this because you are seeing the world and doing the grand tour and finding it all rather boring travelling aimlessly. You could leave us at any minute, which *I* should not like at all, and *I* should never forgive anyone who made you feel like a servant in *any* way. Tatiana didn't like it either, but *I* don't like Tatiana in any case. Günther thought it was all right. He said: "What harm will it do, Mama? Let the English lady come. She will be swallowed up among the guests." How do you like the thought of being swallowed up?'

'Wait a moment. Do you really mean that *I* am to come to the ball?'

'Cinderella, yes. I am your fairy godmother. I shall wave my magic wand.'

'It's impossible. I have no dress.'

'Isn't that just what dear Cindy said? I will arrange that with Madame Chabris, of course.'

'There is no time.'

'We are going to Madame Chabris this morning and I'll wager . . .'

'Please do not talk of laying wagers. It is unseemly and as the Gräfin quite clearly does not approve of my going I shall most certainly not . . .'

'Wait a minute. You *are* coming, Anne Ayres. To please me you are coming. I want you to come. I am the Countess – Grand Duchess to be – and unless you want to offend me, which will be at your peril, you will come.'

'You forget I shall not be one of your subjects. I can leave here and go home when I wish.'

'Oh dear, dear Anne, you would not disappoint me. I have worked so hard to make them agree and the reason is I am really frightened. I have to meet this Sigmund . . . and I need to know you are there.'

'What nonsense,' I said. 'He is not a stranger to you.'

'No. But I need your support. You must come. Oh, promise . *promise* . . .'

I hesitated. I felt a tremendous excitement creeping over me. I was making very slow progress. Who knew what I might discover if I mingled with people who in all probability actually had known Rudolph?

'Get on your cloak,' she urged. 'I have ordered the carriage. We are leaving at once for the salon of Madame Chabris.'

It was a revelation to see myself gowned by Madame Chabris. Her salon was beautiful. I said: 'It's almost as grand as I imagine the Hall of Mirrors at Versailles to be.'

'Well, she is French,' Freya reminded me.

We were given a very warm welcome. Madame Chabris herself, elegant in the extreme, perfectly coiffured and shod as well as exquisitely gowned, greeted us.

She had the very dress which Freya needed. She admitted that she sometimes designed dresses to suit people whom she admired, so it was not to be marvelled at that she had just the right thing for the Countess Freya. As for myself, I had a good figure, she commented, and naturally she had the very dress which would suit me.

Freya tried on her dress and pirouetted in front of the mirrors, seeing herself reflected all round the room.

'It's beautiful,' she cried. 'Oh, Madame Chabris, you are a marvel.'

Madame Chabris looked quietly pleased, as though such hyperbole was commonplace to one of her genius.

Then it was my turn. The dress was deep blue and there was a vein of gold running through it.

'I call it my lapis lazuli,' said Madame Chabris. 'It is beautiful . . . a little expensive, alas.'

'Fräulein Ayres is a lady of independent means,' said Freya quickly. 'She works only because she wishes to. We are good friends, so I know.'

'Then I am sure she will consider the price a minor matter when she sees how the lapis will bring out the glow of her skin.'

I tried it on. Madame Chabris was right. That dress did a great deal for me.

'The alterations are infinitesimal,' said Madame Chabris airily. 'My work girls will do them in two hours. You are very slender, Fräulein. You have the beautiful figure . . . but if I may say, you have not yet realized it. The lapis will show you. Step in here, please, and I will send a fitter.'

I went into a small cubicle and was soon joined by a middle-aged woman with a pocketful of pins.

I had to admit the transformation was miraculous.

When I had been pinned the dress fitted me perfectly. There was a gold-coloured girdle to match the veins in the material and the effect was startling.

Freya clapped her hands and danced round in an ecstasy of joy when she saw me.

'The Fräulein's hair will need attention,' said Madame Chabris warningly.

'It will receive it,' promised Freya.

She had suddenly remembered that she was the future Grand Duchess and became somewhat imperious.

'You will have the dress, Fräulein. Madame Chabris, you will make the alterations and deliver tomorrow morning early. That will give Fräulein Ayres time to try it on and make sure all is well.'

'It shall be done, Countess,' said Madame Chabris.

Freya laughed all the way back to the schloss.

She kept saying: 'Oh, Fräulein Anne, I do like being with you. We laugh a lot, don't we?'

So I was to go to the ball. I was greatly excited and knew instinctively that I was walking into danger, but I did not care. I had to do this, I reminded myself, if I were to discover anything.

My dress arrived and I tried it on. Fräulein Kratz, who saw me in it, stared in astonishment.

'The Countess insisted,' I said.

'And the Gräfin has agreed?'

I nodded.

'The Countess is very wayward.'

'She is charming,' I insisted. 'She has a strong character and will make a very good Grand Duchess.'

'I wish she were a little more . . . orthodox.'

'Oh come, she is an individualist. That is far more interesting than following the crowd.'

'When one is in her position it is often better to follow the crowd,' retorted Fräulein Kratz. 'As for you, Fräulein Ayres, aren't you terrified? I should be.'

'Terrified? Why should I be?' I spoke sharply. Sometimes, I thought I must give away the fact that I have something to hide.

'Well, I should be,' she said lightly. 'The last thing I should want is to go to one of their balls.'

'I am looking forward to it,' I said firmly and she turned away, shrugging her shoulders.

I was living in the clouds for the rest of that day. I had never been to a ball before. Grandfather had never entertained in that style at Greystone Manor. The most he had had was a dinner-party. But I supposed I should be very much in the background.

Freya gave me an indication of what was likely to happen. Sigmund would arrive and be greeted by herself and the Graf, the Gräfin, Tatiana and Günther. Then they would come into the great hall where people would be assembled. Everyone there would form into two lines. 'You'll be somewhere at the end, I'm afraid, Anne.'

'But of course,' I replied.

'Then Sigmund will take my hand and we shall walk between the two lines. Sigmund will say something to the important ones. Not you, Anne.'

'Indeed not.'

'You have to curtsy as we come through.'

'I think I can manage that very well.'

'That's all there is to it. Then we shall dance . . . rather discreetly, and then we shall all go to supper and it will end at midnight out of respect for the Grand Duke.'

So I dressed in the most beautiful and becoming gown I had ever possessed. I was amazed at the transformation. While I was struggling with my hair Freya came in with a small dark woman who carried combs and pins on her head.

'This is the Gräfin's lady's maid,' she announced. 'She has done my hair. Is she not clever? Now she is going to do yours.'

'Oh but . . .' I began.

'It needs it,' retorted Freya. 'And *I* have said she shall.'

'You are good to me,' I said suddenly.

Freya's lips twitched slightly, and I was deeply touched as always by these signs of her unselfishness. She really was a very charming girl.

So my hair was dressed and I went to the ball in some trepidation. I joined some men and women who were gathered at one end of the hall. They smiled at me rather nervously, I thought, and I guessed they were the poor relations of some noble house and were slightly overawed in the assembled company. I had a feeling that my place was with them. It occurred to me that it might be from such people that I could discover something which would help me unravel the mystery.

Freya was not present. I knew she was with the Graf and Gräfin, Tatiana and Günther, and from the sounds without it appeared that the great Sigmund had arrived. The company began forming into two lines as, with the sound of trumpets, a group of men in uniforms of blue with plumes in their helmets and swords at their sides, came into the room.

In their midst was a man slightly taller than the rest. I could not see him clearly for my view was obscured by people in the line.

Now the party was moving towards us. I noticed that everyone was standing very still, their eyes cast down; so I did the same.

They were moving along the Graf on one side of this illustrious personage and Freya on the other.

I began to feel a little dizzy. There was something very unreal about this. I thought: I must be dreaming. This is not really happening.

For there he was standing before me. Conrad . . . my lover. Conrad whom I had never forgotten although I had tried to deceive myself into thinking that I had.

'This is Fräulein Ayres who teaches me such good English.' Freya was beaming, proud of me . . . proud of him . . . her face alight with joy.

I curtsied as I had seen the others do.

'Fräulein Ayres,' he murmured. It was all there, the voice, the look, all that I remembered. His bewilderment was as great . . . perhaps even greater . . . than my own.

'You are English,' he said. He had taken my hand. Mine was trembling. He was staring at me. 'I understand that you are a very good teacher.'

Then he passed on. I felt as though I was going to faint. I must recover myself. Vaguely I heard him speaking to someone else along tne line

I wanted to get away. I wanted to escape from this room and think over what I had just discovered.

When he had reached the end of the line, he took Freya's hand and they went into the centre of the hall to lead the dance. People started to fall in behind them.

Someone was at my elbow. It was Günther.

I stammered: 'Count Günther . . .'

'Countess Freya asked me to keep an eye on you.'

'She is such a dear girl,' I replied. 'But perhaps I should not speak so of the Countess.'

'It is true,' he said. 'She speaks highly of you too, and she is anxious about you. She told me that she insisted that you came to the ball. May I have the pleasure of this dance?'

'I don't really know your dances, but thank you.'

'This is easy. Come . . . just a few steps and then twirl.'

'Did the Countess tell you you must ask me to dance?'

He admitted it.

'Well, then you have done your duty.'

'Not duty,' he replied with a charming smile, 'a pleasure.'

'I think I should retire after this. It was so good of the Countess Freya to insist on my coming . . . but I really feel I should not be here.'

He had drawn me on to the floor and I found I was dancing easily.

'You are doing splendidly,' he said. 'Look at Countess Freya. She will make a charming Grand Duchess, do you not think so?'

'I do. When will the marriage celebrations take place?'

'Not for a year . . . now the Duke is recovering. At least, I hope so.' He looked a little wistful and it occurred to me that he was quite taken with my young Countess.

I wondered whether Conrad was too.

Why had he given me a false name? He must have decided that he did not want to betray his identity. Why had he pretended to be the Graf's equerry? Had he? Had I assumed that? He had not contradicted it. I felt very uneasy and suddenly terribly sad.

I wanted to get away from this ball now. I could not bear to see him there. People surrounded him. Of course they did. He was the heir to the dukedom, the most important man here. This gathering was in his honour, although it was only a small ball because of the Grand Duke's illness, but there must be a celebration of some sort because the Duke's heir was coming.

He would ignore me, of course. I hoped he would. How could I face him in this room?

I must get away quickly.

I chose my opportunity. It was not difficult. I slipped away, but as I did so I saw him glance my way. He was smiling and talking and went on doing so.

I felt heartsick. What a fool I had been to fall in love with the first man who crossed my path! I should have had more sense. And how easily I had fallen into the trap he had laid for me! Easily come by and therefore not valued overmuch.

But what a man he was! He was like the hero of a legend. I remembered I had thought of him as Sigurd when I had first met him. A Norseman. A Viking commander. That was what he had looked like then. Now in his uniform he looked more than ever like a hero of legend. He was outstanding among all the people there. He was everything that I had tried to shut out of my mind.

I should never have come here. It was a foolish thing to have done. What could I do now? I must go away – that was clear. I must forget why I had come here. I must go back to England. I could stay with Aunt Grace. I must live quietly and unadventurously. It was the only way not to get hurt more desperately than I had already been.

I sat down by my open window. I could see the lights of the town, the bridge and the river winding like a black snake through the town. I had grown to love the place: I had grown to love Freya. I would never forget it and there would always be an ache in my heart when I thought of it.

And him? Would I ever forget him? I had told myself that I had forgotten him. I would not allow myself to think of him; I had tried to forget that interlude, to tell myself it had never really happened; I had refused to admit even to myself that he was constantly in my mind and that I could not rid myself of those flashes of memory when I saw so vividly scenes from that time we had spent together. Secretly I had always known that I should never forget him. Conrad the deceiver, Sigmund the heir to a troubled dukedom, betrothed to my little Freya.

They would marry in due course. That was irrevocable. They were bound together. That was what he had meant when he had said he could not marry me.

There was a footstep in the corridor. Someone was at the door. The handle was slowly turning.

And there he was, looking at me.

'Pippa,' he said. 'Pippa!'

I tried not to look at him. I said: 'I am Anne Ayres.'

'What *is* this? What does it mean?'

I retorted: 'What are you doing in my room, er . . . What do I call you, Baron?'

'You call me Conrad.'

'What of the great lord Sigmund?'

'My ceremonial name. Sigmund Conrad Wilhelm Otto. They gave me a large supply. But, Pippa, names are unimportant. What of you?'

He had come across the room and taken my hands. He had pulled me to my feet and held me against him. I felt my resistance slipping.

I could only say: 'Go away. Go away, please. This is no place for you.'

He had taken my chin in his hands and was looking into my face. 'I searched for you,' he said. 'I have been in England. I came back for you. I was going to take you away with me . . . by force if necessary. I couldn't find you . . . and then in desperation I came back here . . . and here you are. You came to find me, did you not? While I was searching for you, you were searching for me.'

'No . . . no. I did not come here for you.'

'You are lying, Pippa. You came for me, and now we have found each other we shall never part again.'

'You are wrong. I shall not see you again. I shall go back to England. I know who you are now and that you are betrothed to the Countess Freya and that your betrothal is tantamount to marriage. You cannot escape it. I have learned something of your problems here. There is Kollenitz, the buffer state. You need its help and you have to marry Freya because you could never deny the marriage . . . but you know all this and you know now that I shall have to go home.'

'This will be home to you now. Listen, Pippa, you are here. We have found each other . . . never to part again. We'll be together. I'll find some place where we can make our home.'

'There is an unoccupied lodge in the forest nearby,' I said with a touch of bitterness.

'Don't speak of it. It won't be like that. I love you, Pippa. Nothing can change that. As soon as I had gone I knew how much. I should not have left when you did not come to the station. I should have come back for you and made you come with me. It is the only way for us. But you came to me. It was clever of you to change your name . . . better for no one to know that you are Francine's sister. But you came here . . . My dear, clever Pippa. This is different from anything that has ever happened to either of us. You know that as well as I do. We are going to be together now . . . no matter what happens.'

'You have taken me by surprise.'

'As you have taken me, my love,' he answered and he was kissing me fiercely, and in my thoughts I was at once transported back to that firelit room in the Grange. I wished I was there at that moment. I wished I could forget his involvement with Freya. I wanted so much to be with him.

'The most wonderful surprise of my life,' he said. 'You here . . . my own Pippa . and never, never going to leave me again.'

I was aware of the intensity of his passion and how ready I was to meet it. I remembered so much from that other occasion. Instinctively I knew that he was a man who had never learned to deny himself. There was so much I knew about him. And I loved him. It was no use trying to convince myself otherwise now that he was here . . . close to me . . . holding me in his arms . . . I could never forget him. I was a fool, for I realized the hopelessness of our situation. I was terrified that here . . . now . . . my resistance would melt away as it had on that other occasion. I had to try to think of Freya. Suppose she came in and found him here. She might not notice my absence but she would notice his. Everyone would notice it. What if she came to look for him? She would never look for him in *my* room, of course . . . But what if she came to me . . . what if she found me in the arms of her future husband?

The situation was dangerous and impossible.

I drew away from him and said as coolly as I could: 'You will be missed in the ballroom.'

'I care nothing for that.'

'Do you not? The heir to all this . . . Of course you care. It is your duty to care. You must go back and we must not see each other again.'

'You suggest the impossible.'

'What use can it be?'

'I have plans.'

'I can guess the nature of those plans.'

'Pippa, if I go now will you promise me something?'

'What is it?'

'We meet tomorrow. In the forest, shall we say? Please, Pippa, I must talk to you. Where? Where?'

'There is only one spot I know in the forest.'

'Then we shall meet there.'

'The hunting lodge,' I said.

'We'll meet there and we'll talk and we'll talk.'

'There is no more to be said. I was misled. Perhaps it was my fault. I did not ask enough questions. I accepted you as some equerry . . . some servant of the Graf and you did not attempt to enlighten me . . . and you must have known that I had no idea who you really were.'

'It seemed of no consequence.'

I laughed rather bitterly. 'No, I suppose not. You proposed to amuse yourself during your brief stay in England. I understand that perfectly.'

'You do not understand. You do not understand at all.'

I was alert, listening. 'The music has stopped,' I said. 'They will have noticed the absence of the guest of honour. Please go now.'

He had taken my hands and was kissing them with passion. 'Tomorrow . . .' he said, 'at the hunting lodge. At ten o'clock.'

'I cannot be sure. It is not easy for me to leave. You must remember I am employed here.'

'The Countess said that you came as a sort of favour and that she had to please you or you would leave.'

'She exaggerated. Remember, I may not be able to come.'

'You will,' he said. 'And I shall be there . . . waiting.'

I drew myself away from him, but he caught me again and held me fast. He kissed my lips and throat. It was so like that other time that I feared for myself.

Then he had gone.

I turned to the window and looked over the town.

I remained at my window for a long time without noticing the passing of time. I was back at the Grange living through those hours I had spent with him, and which I had deceived myself into thinking I had erased from my mind. Then suddenly I heard the town clock strike midnight. That would be the end of the ball because it was to finish at that hour on account of the Grand Duke's illness. I could hear the commotion below which signified that the guests were leaving. Ceremony would accompany him wherever he went, except of course when he was away from home living incognito

I must change my plans. I must abandon all hope of staying here and unravelling the mystery surrounding my sister's death and at the back of my mind was the thought that somewhere – probably near here – her child was living. I could never be at peace until I knew what had become of that little boy – and yet, how could I stay here. My position with Freya had become untenable.

I was still sitting there in my lapis lazuli dress when there was a knock on my door and it was abruptly opened before I had time to give permission for whoever was there to enter.

As I expected, it was Freya. Her face was flushed, her eyes dancing, and she looked very pretty in her Chabris dress.

'Anne,' she cried. 'You ran away. I looked for you. I sent Günther to look for you and we couldn't find you anywhere.'

I shivered inwardly, wondering what would have happened if she had come upon her betrothed in my bedroom.

'I should never have been at the ball,' I said quietly.

'What happened?'

'Well . . . I came away.'

'I mean *something* happened. You look . . .' She was eyeing me suspiciously.

I said quickly – too quickly: 'What do you mean? How do I look?'

'Strange . . . exalted . . . shining in a way. Did you meet Prince Charming?'

'Really, Freya,' I said rather primly.

'Well, we did say you were like Cinderella. She did, didn't she, and she ran away and dropped her slipper.'

She looked down at my feet and in spite of everything I could not help smiling at her childishness.

'I can assure you I retained *both* my slippers. I did not have to leave on the stroke of twelve, and there was no Prince Charming for me. He . . . was for you.'

'What did you think of Sigmund? He spoke to you, didn't he?'

'Yes,' I answered.

'I hope you liked him. Did you? Did you? Why don't you answer?'

'It is difficult for me to answer that.'

She threw back her head and laughed. 'Oh, Anne, you are funny. You are going to say that you don't make decisions about people on a slight acquaintance. I am not asking for an assessment of your conclusions on his character.'

'That is wise of you, for you won't get it.'

'I just meant did he make a favourable impression?'

'Why, yes, of course.'

'And you think he'll be a good husband?'

'That is for you to discover in due course.'

'Oh, cautious, cautious! He is handsome, is he not?'

'Yes, I think he would be called that.'

'He has such an air. He is a man of the world. That is what you would call him, wouldn't you?'

'I have told you that I . . .'

'I know you only spoke to him once in line. Günther danced with you, didn't he? I saw him. I told him to, you know.'

'I know you did. It was sweet of you, but you need not have done so. I didn't expect it. However, he did his duty nobly.'

'He is rather nice, Günther . . . don't you think?'

'Yes, I do.'

'Oh, you can be definite enough about him. Of course, he's not really so devastatingly attractive as Sigmund is. I'm a bit in awe of Sigmund. He seems well . . . too worldly. Is that the right word?'

'I think it may well be exactly the right word.'

'I am sure he has had a host of mistresses. He's the sort of man who would. They all do . . . particularly the Fuchses. They are very much like that, you know . . . lusty and amorous.'

'Freya,' I said solemnly, 'do you want to marry this man?'

She was thoughtful for a moment. Then she said: 'I want to be the Grand Duchess.'

I said then that it was time we went to bed and I was ready if she were not.

'Good night then, Anne . . . dear Anne. When I'm married I shan't want you to go. You can stay and comfort me when Sigmund is unfaithful with all his mistresses.'

'If you feel so sure of his future infidelities you should not marry him.'

She jumped up and gave a mock salute. 'Bruxenstein,' she cried. 'For Kollenitz! Good night, Anne,' she went on. 'At least it is all rather exciting, isn't it?'

I admitted that, at least, it was.

I rose early next morning. I looked in on Freya who was fast asleep. I was glad. It would give me a chance to get out. I drank a cup of coffee and managed to eat one of the bread rolls spattered with caraway seeds which I had enjoyed since I had arrived in Bruxenstein. I did not taste it on this morning. Then I went into the stables and saddled a horse.

In less than half an hour I was at the hunting lodge. He was already there, impatiently waiting. He had tethered his horse by the mounting block and helped me to dismount. He held out his arms as I did so and I slid into them. He held me tightly, kissing me.

I said: 'It is no use.'

'You're wrong,' he contradicted. 'Let's walk and talk. I have lots to say to you.'

He put an arm about me and we walked into the forest, away from the lodge.

'I have been thinking about us all night,' he said. 'You're here and you are going to stay. I am in this position . . . thrust into it . . . an accident of birth, but I am not one to accept a fate which is thrust on me and give up what I could never live without. I have to go through with this marriage. I have to do my duty to my country and my family . . . but at the same time I am determined to live my own life. It is not an unusual situation. It has happened to so many of us. It is the only way in which we can do what we have to. My family life . . . the life I want and am determined to have . . . and the path of duty. I can manage them both.'

'As Rudolph did?'

'He and your sister could have been happy. Rudolph was careless. He always was. He was killed because someone – some members of a party – were determined that he should not rule. It was purely a political murder. Unfortunately for your sister, she was with him.'

'It could happen to you,' I said, and I wondered whether he noticed the tremor of fear in my voice.

'How do any of us know what will happen to us from one moment to another? Death can come unexpectedly to the most lowly peasant. I know that Rudolph would not have been a popular successor to his father. He was too weak, too pleasure-loving. There were factions working against him.'

'And you?'

'I was not concerned in it. The last thing I wanted was to be where I am today.'

'You could refuse to accept your position, could you not?'

'There is no one to take my place. There would be chaos in the country, our enemies would step in. They need a ruler. My uncle has been a strong one. I hope to God he will go on living, for while he does we have security. I have to preserve that security.'

'And you can?'

'I know I can . . . providing our allies support us.'

'Such as Kollenitz?'

He nodded. He went on: 'I was betrothed to the child, Freya, as soon as Rudolph died. This special betrothal commitment is tantamount to marriage in all but the consummation. On her sixteenth birthday there will be an official marriage ceremony. Then we must produce an heir.

Therein lies my duty, my inescapable duty. But I have my own life to lead. This is my public life; but I shall have my private one.'

'Which you plan to share with me?'

'Which I am going to share with you. I could not live without it. One cannot be a puppet all one's life . . . moving in the way which is ordained. No! I will not do that. I wish I could give it all up and go off quietly with you . . . and live in peace somewhere. But what would happen if I did? Chaos. War. I don't know where it would end.'

'You must do your duty,' I said.

'And you and I . . .'

'I shall go back to England. I can see that it is impossible to live the life you suggest.'

'Why?'

'Because it would not work. I should be an encumbrance.'

'The most adored and loved encumbrance that ever was.'

'An encumbrance nevertheless. I sometimes think that Rudolph's involvement with my sister may have been the cause of his death. It might be that I should be the cause of yours.'

'I'd be prepared to risk that.'

'And children?' I said. 'What of children?'

'They should have everything a child could desire.'

'My sister had a child. I wonder where that child is now? Imagine it. A little boy. I know it was a boy because she told me. What happened to him? Where did he go when they killed his father and his mother? You talk of our being together, having children. In secret, I suppose. And Freya, what about her part in this?'

'Freya would understand. She knows ours is an arranged marriage. I should make her understand.'

'I know her very well. I doubt she would understand . . . and that *I* should be the one . . . that would be insupportable. I can see the impossibility of it all and that I must get awav quickly.'

'No,' he cried. 'No! Promise me this: You will not run away and hide yourself. You will tell me before you do anything.'

He had stopped and put his hands on my shoulders. I wished that he would not look at me in that way, because it was harder when I faced him and I felt all my resolutions melting away.

'Of course I will tell you when I am going,' I said.

He smiled confidently. 'In time I will make you see. Tell me . . . what did you feel when you saw me?'

'I thought I was dreaming.'

'I too. I have dreamed of it often . . . coming face to face with you . . . finding you suddenly. I always knew I should find you. I intended to. And to think that I might still be in England . . . searching . . .'

'What did you do? Whom did you ask?'

'I went to the stonemason's place. I knew that you were friendly. He was no longer there. The vicar was away. There was someone doing his duties in his absence. He told me that your aunt and her husband had moved away, but he did not know where. There was no one at Greystone Manor except servants.'

'Surely my cousin was there.'

'They said he was away on his honeymoon.'

'Honeymoon! Oh no. That could not be.'

'That's what I was told. It was like a conspiracy against me. I did hear of your grandfather's death.'

'What did you hear about that?'

'That he had died in a fire.'

'Did you hear anything about . . . my connection with that?'

He frowned. 'There was some innuendo. I didn't understand what it meant. It was oblique comments. I stayed at the inn. They didn't seem to want to talk very much.'

I said: 'On the night my grandfather died I quarrelled with him. People in the house heard it because he was shouting at me. He was insisting that I marry my Cousin Arthur and he threatened to turn me out if I didn't.'

'How I wish I had been there!'

'That night he died. His room and the one next to it were burned out. The fire was confined to those two rooms. My grandfather was dead when they brought him out . . . but it was not asphyxiation. He had had a blow on the head. They thought he might have fallen . . . but on the other hand he might not.'

'You mean they thought it was foul play.'

'They were unsure. The verdict at the inquest was "Accidental Death". But several people had heard the quarrel between us.'

'Good God! My poor Pippa. If I had been there . . .'

'If only you had! I had my Aunt Grace. She was good to me and Cousin Arthur was kind . . . and my grandmother left me money which enabled me to get away . . . to come here.'

He held me tightly against him. 'My dearest Pippa,' he said. 'I shall look after you from now on.'

For a moment I lay against him, letting him believe it could be possible – and perhaps deluding myself.

He said: 'That's all over now. It must have been a nightmare. I should have been there. I hesitated on that platform. I was coming back to get you and then I thought, "How can I if she does not want to come?"'

'I did want to come. I did. I did.'

'Dear, dear Pippa, if only you had!'

'Where to? To this hideaway you are planning? A hunting lodge in the forest? It is like a pattern repeating itself. Francine and myself. We were always close . . . like one person. Sometimes I think I am reliving her life. We were always together until she loved so unwisely . . . and now it seems I have done the same.'

He was looking at me earnestly. 'It is going to be the wisest thing you ever did – to love me.'

I shook my head. 'I wish you were an ordinary person – an

equerry perhaps, as I first thought you to be . . . whatever that is. I have never been sure . . . I wish you were anything but what you are . . . with those commitments . . . and particularly Freya.'

'We are going to rise above all that. I am going to show you the place I will find for you. Our home. I want to give you everything I have.'

'But you can't. You can't ever give me your name.'

'I can give you my devoted love . . . all of it, Pippa.'

'You must think of your marriage. I have grown fond of Freya. She is a child yet . . . and charming. She will lure you to love her.'

'I am not to be lured away from my Pippa. Oh, Pippa, dearest Pippa, listen to the birds singing. "The lark's on the wing . . . All's right with the world . . ." Remember that? It is Pippa's song. All must be right with the world while you and I are together.'

'I must go back. I shall be missed. You too, I dare say.'

'We shall meet again . . . tomorrow. I will find somewhere where we can be together. It has to be. It is no use fighting against it. From the moment we met, it was clear to me. I said, "This is the one out of the whole world and no one else will do."'

I shook my head. I was hovering between ecstasy and despair. I knew I was going to weaken. I knew that I had to take what I could get.

He was aware of it, too. I had betrayed my emotions too readily.

'Tomorrow. Tomorrow, Pippa. Promise. Here.'

So I promised, and we went back to our horses. When he had helped me to mount he took my hand and looked at me beseechingly and I loved him so much that I knew in my heart that I would do anything he asked of me.

I withdrew my hand, for I was very much afraid of my emotions and I said as coolly as I could: 'We must not ride away together. We might be seen. Please go ahead.'

'We'll go together.'

'No. I prefer it this way. It might be difficult for me to get away freely if we were seen together.'

He bowed his head and accepted the wisdom of that. 'Perhaps for a while we should be careful,' he said. He kissed my hand fervently and rode away.

I remained there for some moments looking at the lodge. I was in no mood to go back to the schloss immediately. I was forming excuses for my absence. Freya would want to know where I had been, and I decided to tell her that I had felt the need for fresh air and exercise after the previous night, and had decided to take it in the forest.

Suddenly I had the desire to dismount and go and look at Francine's grave. I felt as close to her as I ever had. I tethered the horse and walked round the lodge.

As I approached the grave I had the uncanny feeling that I was not alone. At first I thought that I was being followed by someone who had seen my meeting with Conrad. I felt cold with terror. Why is it that one can sense the presence of another person? Was it due to some sound I had heard? Was it instinct?

I had reached the enclosure. I saw a movement . . . a flash of colour. Then I realized that there was someone at the graveside.

I drew back, not wishing to make my presence known, for I guessed it must be Gisela. I stood very still holding my breath. Then a figure rose. She had a trowel in her hand and had been planting something.

It was not Gisela. This was a young woman, taller, fairer than Gisela. She stood still for a moment, looking down at her handiwork. Then suddenly she spoke. 'Rudi,' she called. 'Come here, Rudi.'

Then I saw the child. He must have been about four or five years old. His hair was like sunshine, fair and curly.

'Come here, Rudi. Look at the pretty flowers.'

I watched, while the child went and stood beside her.

'Now, we must go,' she went on. 'But first . . .'

I was amazed because they knelt down together. I saw the child, his eyes closed, the palms of his hands pressed closely together, his lips murmuring. I could not hear what was said.

They stood up. The woman was holding a basket in which was the trowel in one hand, with the other she took that of the child.

I drew back in the shadow of the bushes which grew in clumps in this spot, and I watched them come through the gate and walk away into the forest.

My heart was beating fast, my mind racing.

Who was she? Who was the child? And I stood there, numb, watching them. I should have spoken to her, discovered why she was tending my sister's grave.

But I had not lost her. I could at least follow her and see where she went.

I kept them in sight. It was not difficult for me to remain hidden because of the trees which provided me with good cover. And after all, if I were seen why should I not be someone who was taking a walk in the forest?

We had come to a house – small but pleasant. She released the child's hand and he ran on ahead of her up the path to the door. He danced up and down on the porch waiting for her. She came along and let herself and him in, while I stood there watching.

I felt amazed by what I had seen. Why had she tended Francine's grave? Who was she? More important still, who was the child?

I was not sure how to act. Could I knock on the door, ask the way and engage her in conversation?

It was already late. I should find it difficult to explain my absence. Another day, I thought. I'll come back. I shall have time to think how is the best way to tackle this.

With my mind whirling through what I had seen and my meeting with Conrad, I was bemused and uncertain, wondering what would happen next, and telling myself that I must be prepared for anything.

When I returned to the schloss I had to face Freya, who had missed me.

'Where have you been? Nobody knew what had happened to you.'

'I felt the need for fresh air.'

'You could have got that in the garden.'

'I wanted to ride.'

'You've been in the forest, haven't you?'

'How did you know?'

'I have my spies.' She narrowed her eyes and for a few seconds I thought she knew about my meeting with Conrad. 'Besides,' she went on, 'here is a clue.' She picked a pine needle from my jacket. 'You look really frightened. You are not what you say you are. You are planning a coup. That is why you are of independent means. Whoever heard of a governess who was not terrified of losing her post and being turned out on the streets?'

'You have,' I said, recovering my equilibrium. 'And here she is.'

'Why did you go off without telling me?'

'You were fast asleep after your experiences as the belle of the ball, and I thought you needed your rest.'

'I was worried. I thought perhaps you had left me.'

'Foolish child!'

She threw herself at me suddenly. 'Don't leave me, Anne. You mustn't.'

'What are you afraid of?' I asked.

She looked at me steadily. 'Everything,' she said. 'Marriage . . . change . . . growing up. I don't want to grow up, Anne. I want to stay as I am.'

I kissed her tenderly. 'You'll manage it all right when the time comes,' I reassured her.

'Will I?' she asked. 'I am very rebellious and I would never tolerate mistresses.'

'Perhaps there won't be any.'

'That,' she said firmly, 'is how it will have to be.'

'There is a saying in English that one should cross one's bridges when one comes to them.'

'A very good one,' she replied. 'That is what I shall do. But I shall cross them in my own way.'

'Knowing you, I am sure you will put up a good fight to get what you want.'

'The trouble is that Sigmund seems the sort of person to get *his* own way. Does he seem like that to you, Anne?'

'Yes,' I said slowly. 'He does.'

'Then it will be a question of which is the stronger.'

'There may not be a contest. It is just possible that you will both want the same things.'

'Clever Anne. You will be there with me. I shall insist. I shall make you my Grand Vizor.'

'That is something you put on your head. I think you mean Vizier, and I am sure I should be most unsuitable for the post.'

'We'll cross that bridge when we come to it,' quoted Freya, almost smugly.

I laughed but I was thinking: What am I going to do? I must go. Yet he will never allow it. I shall stay. We shall live out our lives together . . . in the shadows perhaps, but together . . as Francine and Rudolph did.

And I must discover who was the woman who planted flowers on Francine's grave. And perhaps more important than all, who was the child?

The King of the Forest

Fortune favoured me.

In the early afternoon Freya came to me. She was pouting. The Graf and Gräfin wanted her, Tatiana and Günther to visit the Grand Duke.

'Well, what is so unpleasant about that?' I asked.

'I wanted to go for a ride with you.'

'You can do that another time.'

'I doubt whether we shall see him and we always have to stand on such ceremony. Oh, I wish I didn't have to go.'

'It will be all over soon.'

'I expect Sigmund will be there.'

'Well, you will like to see him, I expect.'

She grimaced.

I watched the party leave and immediately went to the stables. I had a free afternoon and within a short time was riding into the forest towards the lodge, and then on to the house I had discovered.

The woman was in the garden. I recognized her at once and called a good afternoon, asking her the way back to the town, which I knew very well.

She came to the palings and, leaning over, directed me.

I said, trying to hold her in conversation: 'The forest is very beautiful.'

She agreed.

'Is it lonely living here?' I asked.

'I don't notice it. I have plenty to do. I keep house for my brother.'

'Just the two of you . . .' I murmured and wondered if I sounded both inquisitive and impertinent.

'Just the two of us and our maid and my little son.'

No mention of a husband, I noticed, and my mind was beset by possibilities.

'I came past the lodge,' I continued. 'It seemed deserted.'

'Oh yes, it is nowadays.'

She had a frank open face and she was friendly. Perhaps she relished a chat as no doubt she saw few people.

'Are you visiting here?' she asked.

'Not exactly. I am employed at the schloss.'

'Oh?' She expressed interest. 'My brother works there . . . for the Graf.'

'I am there . . . as an English governess to the Countess Freya.'

She was not particularly interested. 'Oh yes, I had heard that there was an English lady there. And you rode out and lost your way?'

'One can do that easily in the forest.'

'Nowhere more easily. But you are not far away. If you go back by the lodge and keep to the bridle path you'll come to the lodge cottage, and there is a road. You'll see the town from there.'

'I shall know where I am then. The lodge looks interesting but rather dismal.'

'Yes, it is never used now.'

'It seems a waste of what must have been a very fine old place.'

'Oh yes . . . They used it frequently in the past for hunting, you know. You should be careful walking in the forest. Although it is mostly deer there is the occasional wild boar.'

'I thought I saw a grave . . . somewhere at the back of the lodge.'

'Yes, there is a grave there.'

'It seemed a strange place to find a grave. Why should someone be buried there and not in a churchyard?'

'Well, there was a reason, I think.'

I waited but she did not seem as though she was going to continue, so I went on: 'It seems well tended.'

'Yes. I look after it. I don't like to see it overgrown. I don't think graves should be. If they are, it looks as though no one cares about the person buried there.'

'It was a friend of yours then?'

'Yes,' she said. 'You must excuse me. I can hear my little boy. He's awakened from his nap. You'll have no difficulty in finding your way. Good day to you.'

I felt I had mishandled the situation. I had discovered nothing except that she had known Francine and had been a friend of hers.

I would call again though. I had at least opened up a path where there had appeared to be nothing.

As I came back through the town I passed the inn where I had once hired a horse, and I decided to sit a while in the *Biergarten*, so I left my horse in the stable and did so. I think I wanted to talk to someone and the innkeeper's wife had been very friendly.

She remembered me and when she brought my goblet of *Bier* – a speciality of Bruxenstein – she told me so. She paused and it was not difficult to detain her.

I told her I was now working at the schloss.

'I heard the Countess had an English lady to help her speak the language,' she said.

'I am she,' I answered.

'Well, do you enjoy it?'

'Very much,' I replied. 'The Countess is charming.'

'She is popular and so is the Baron. It wouldn't surprise me if they put forward the marriage. It depends, I suppose, on the Grand Duke. If he recovers his health things will go on just as before, no doubt.'

I agreed and said I found the forest enchanting.

'Our forests are famous in legend and song,' she answered.

'They say all sorts of things can happen there. Trolls, goblins, giants and the gods of old . . . some reckon they're still there . . . and some people have the power to see them.'

'It must be rather eerie living in the heart of it. I passed a place today.'

'Was it the lodge?'

'Yes, I did see the lodge, but I was thinking of a house . . . a small one in the forest . . . near the lodge. I wondered who lives there.'

'Oh, I know where you mean. That would be the Schwartzes' place.'

'I did see someone there. I asked her the way.'

'That must have been Katia.'

'Has she a little boy?'

'Yes. Rudolph.'

'Does her husband work for one of the schloss families?'

'There isn't a husband.'

'Oh . . . I see.'

'Poor Katia. She had rather a bad time.'

'That's sad. She seemed so very pleasant. I thought her charming, in fact.'

'Yes, she is. Life was cruel to her, though. But she has the boy and she dotes on him. He's a nice little fellow.'

'I did notice a child. Would he be about four or five?'

'Yes, I suppose it must have been all those years ago. Rather a mystery really.'

'Oh?'

'Well, who can say what happens in these cases. It seems a bit unlucky . . . that part of the forest . . . considering what happened at the lodge.'

'You mean the murder?'

'Yes. That was terrible that was. Some say it was jealousy but I never believed that. It was someone who wanted Rudolph out of the way, so that Sigmund could step into his shoes.'

'You don't mean that Sigmund . . .'

'Oh . . . hush! I'd say it's all a mystery . . . and long ago now. Best forgotten. They tell me Sigmund has the makings of a fine Duke. He's strong and that's what we want. Listen.' She cocked her head on one side. 'I expect they're coming this way.'

'Who?'

'The Graf and the Gräfin with Sigmund and the Countess. I heard they'd been visiting the Grand Duke this afternoon. Sigmund will be escorting them back to the schloss. I'll pop out and watch.'

'May I come with you?'

'But of course.'

I stood with her and others crowded in the inn doorway, and my heart leaped with pride and fear as I watched him. He looked magnificent on his white horse, acknowledging the cheers of the people as he rode. And beside him was Freya, looking pink-cheeked, bright-eyed and very pretty. It was clear that the people liked her.

'Little duck,' I heard someone say. 'She's a charmer, isn't she?'

Then came the Graf and Gräfin with Günther and Tatiana. There were a few guards riding with them, colourful in blue and brown uniform with blue feathers in their silver helmets.

As I stood and watched, the hopelessness of my situation was borne home to me afresh, and I could see that there would be no real place for me in Sigmund's life. I would be his mistress, to be hidden away . . . to wait for those days which he could spare for me. And if there were children . . . what of them?

How could I do this? I must go away.

Oh Francine, I thought, was it like this with you?

When I arrived in my room one of the footmen was standing at my door.

He said: 'I have a note for you, Fräulein. I was told to deliver it into no other hands but yours.'

'Thank you,' I said, taking it.

He bowed and departed.

I knew before I opened it who had sent it. It was written on blue tinted paper with the crest of the lions and crossed swords which I had seen before.

My dearest [he had written in English],
I must see you. I want to talk to you. It is unendurable that you should be so near and yet away from me. I cannot wait for tomorrow. I want to see you tonight. There is an inn just below the schloss. It is called the King of the Forest. Come there. I shall be waiting. Please. I shall expect you at nine. You will have dined then and can slip away. C.

The King of the Forest. I had seen it. It was very close to the schloss gates. Could I do it? I supposed so. I could plead a headache, retire early and slip out. It would be unwise. It would be as it had been at the Grange. I must not go. Yet I thought of his waiting there. He would be so wretched. People like Conrad and Freya were used to having everything their way. They would have to learn that it could not always be so. And yet . . . I wanted to go.

But I must not, I admonished myself. Yet it was not possible to get a message to him. How could *I* ask someone to take a note to Baron Sigmund!

No. I decided I must go, and I must make him realize that I could not see him any more. I must leave the schloss. Suppose I went back to Daisy. That was not far enough. He would seek me out there. No. I would go and see him and explain that we must not meet again.

I managed to get away quite easily. Freya was a little absent-minded. She had enjoyed riding through the streets with Sigmund and she had obviously been gratified by the cheering crowds. When I said I should like to retire early because of a headache she just said: 'Have a good night's sleep then, Anne. Perhaps I'll go early, too.'

So I was able to slip out without much trouble.

He was looking out for me and before I reached the inn he had joined me. He was in a dark cloak and black hat like any travelling business man, but although I had seen many men dressed exactly like that, nothing could prevent his looking distinguished.

He held my arm tightly and said: 'I have engaged a room where we shall not be disturbed.'

'I have come to tell you that I must go away,' I said.

He did not answer, but pressed my arm more tightly to his side.

We went into the inn and up a back staircase. I thought: This is the way it will always be – always in the shadows. And suddenly I did not care. I loved him and I knew I should never be happy away from him. What was the old Spanish proverb? 'Take what you want,' says God. 'Take it and pay for it.'

It was a small room but the candlelight threw a pleasant glow over it, touching it with a romantic aura; but perhaps I felt that because I was here with him alone.

He pushed back the hood of my cloak and pulled the pins out of my hair and, unruly as ever, it easily escaped.

'Pippa,' he murmured, 'at last. I have been thinking of you . . . dreaming of you and now you are here.'

'I must not stay,' I began. 'I just came to tell you . . .'

He smiled at me and took off my cloak.

'No,' I said, trying to sound firm.

'But yes,' he answered. 'This is meant, you know. You can't escape it. Oh, Pippa, you have come back to me . . . never to be parted again.'

'I have to go,' I insisted. 'I should never have come. I thought you wanted to talk to me.'

'I want everything,' he replied.

'Listen,' I went on. 'We have to be sensible. It is different now. That other time I did not know who you were. I was carried away. I was quite innocent . . . inexperienced. I had never had a lover. I thought we should be married and live . . . as married people do. I was as guileless as that. It is all different now. This is wrong and I know it is.'

'My darling, these conventions are made for the convenience of society . . .'

I interrupted: 'That is not all. There is Freya. I have grown fond of her. What would she think if she saw us now? It is wrong . . . dreadfully wrong . . . and I must go.'

'I shall not allow it.'

'It is for me to decide.'

'You can never be so cruel.'

'I understand that I am still naive and that you must have been in many similar situations . . .'

'I have never loved until now,' he said. 'Isn't that good enough?'

'Is it really true?'

'I swear it. Now and forever I love you . . . and you only.'

'How can you know what you will feel in the future?'

'As soon as I saw you I knew. Didn't you?'

I hesitated and then I said: 'Perhaps for me I knew it would be so, but for you it would be different. If I went away you would forget me.'

'Never.'

'There would be so many in your life to compensate for any loss you might feel because one woman rejected you.'

'You won't understand. If it were just for myself I would be ready to throw everything aside.'

'All the shouting and the cheering. It means something to you. I watched you. I was in the porch of an inn when you rode by with Freya. I saw you. How you smiled. How you pleased the people, both of you, and I know how they pleased you. It is something you do very well because it means so much to you.'

'I have been brought up to it in a way,' he admitted. 'But I never thought all this would come to me because of Rudolph. I was just a branch from the tree. If Rudolph had lived . . .

But, my dearest, what of that? Let us make what we can of life.'

'No. I must go. I shall return to England. I think it is the best way. I shall go to my Aunt Grace and try . . .'

He had thrown my cloak aside and his arms were about me.

'Pippa,' he said, 'I love you and the time is short . . . for now. But we are going to be together through the years.'

'And your life . . . and Freya's . . . ?'

'I will work something out. Please, my darling . . . let us be happy . . . now.'

My lips said no, but the rest of my body cried: Yes, yes. He was irresistible to me and he knew it and I knew it.

There is no excuse. I make none. We were just carried away by the force of our passion. Neither of us could think beyond the fact that we were alone together in this room.

And it was as it had been at the Grange. There was nothing else but our love and our need of each other. I could hold out no longer and I lay in his arms half tearful, half laughing, ecstatically happy and pushing away the cloud of guilt and apprehension which would eventually settle on me.

Then I was lying quietly with his arms about me and he was tracing his fingers over my face as a blind man does.

'I want to know every part of you so intimately that it is part of myself,' he murmured. 'I must carry the memory of you when I am not with you. I have already found a home for us. Not far from the town . . . in the forest . . . a delightful little house which we shall make our own.'

I was brought to earth suddenly from the Olympian heights by a vision of the hunting lodge – dark, gloomy, haunted by ghosts.

'It is on the west side of the town,' he went on.

He meant that the town would be between us and the hunting lodge. 'I will show it to you and we shall make it our home. I shall be there every possible moment. Pippa, I would to God it could be different.'

'I will never do it,' I said. 'I cannot. I am filled with shame. Can you imagine what it is like being with that child . . . that dear innocent child? I have grown to love her . . .'

'I am the one you love, remember?' he reminded me. 'No one must stand in the way of that.'

'But I cannot stay with Freya . . . after this.'

'Then come to our home in the forest.'

'I must think about it. I cannot decide. I cannot imagine what I could say to her. What would her feelings be? She will be your wife. I shall be your mistress.'

'It is not like that,' he said.

'How else can it be described? I don't think I can do it. Not with Freya. Even now I feel despicable. The other day when she was feeling particularly affectionate she kissed me . . . and I returned her kiss. Then the horror swept over me. I was posing as her friend when all the time I was betraying her. I thought, That is the Kiss of Judas. No. No, it would be better if I went home. I could go to my Aunt Grace, I could look round and make a new life – perhaps somewhere well away from Greystone Manor.'

'You are staying here. I shall not allow you to go.'

'I am free. Remember that.'

'No one is free when he or she loves. You are shackled too, my darling. For the rest of our lives we belong together . . . accept that . . . and you will see that it is the only way.'

'The only way is for me to leave.'

'That is unacceptable to me . . . and to you. If I were but free to marry you I should be the happiest man alive.'

'There is no way.'

'Unless we discover a new heir. If only Rudolph had married . . .'

'He did marry.'

'Oh, the entry in the register. It wasn't there, was it? We searched. If only there had been proof of his marriage and there had been an heir. If we could bring forward that heir and say: "Here is the new ruler of Bruxenstein" should the Grand Duke die.'

'He would be only a child.'

'Children grow up.'

'What would happen? There would be a Regency, I suppose.'

'Something like that.'

'And you would be the Regent?'

'I expect that is how it would happen. But I should be free. Kollenitz would not want an alliance with a Regent. I dare say they would want Freya to marry the heir.'

'The difference in their ages would make that out of the question.'

'They would not be greatly concerned with such matters. There have been more incongruous marriages for the sake of the state. Suppose she were some ten years older, that would not be considered a deterrent. After all, I am eight years older than Freya. But we are wasting time on suppositions which are wide of the mark. We have to accept what is. I shall have to go through with this ceremony with Freya. I shall have to get an heir. When that is done . . . so is my duty. But I am not letting you go, Pippa . . . never, never, never. If you ran away I should come after you. I would scour the whole of England . . . the whole of the world and bring you back.'

'Against my will?'

'Dear, dear Pippa, it would never be against your will. All your resolutions would crumble away when we were together. Haven't we proved that twice?'

'I am weak . . . foolish . . . immoral . . . I see that.'

'You are gentle, loving and adorable.'

'You have no right to tempt me.'

'I have the right of true love.'

'What a fool I am! I almost believe you.'

'You are foolish not to believe me entirely.'

'Is it really so then?'

'You know.'

'I believe I do. We are two people caught up in an unusual situation. I wonder if it has ever happened before.'

'It happened to your own sister,' he said. 'Not exactly the same . . . but Rudolph could not have married her.'

'Why not?'

'Because he was destined for Freya.'

'But he had never gone through that betrothal ceremony which was tantamount to marriage.'

'It is true. But he knew he must not marry without the approval of the Grand Duke's ministers. Darling . . . forget it. Make the best of what we have. I promise you it will be a great deal.'

'I must go now. It is late.'

'Only if you promise that we will meet again soon. I want to show you the house we shall have. I want you to come here tomorrow night. Will you do that?'

'I cannot. How can I get away like this? It will be noticed. Freya will suspect.'

'I shall be here tomorrow at the same time. Dearest Pippa, please come.'

I put on my things and he came out with me almost to the castle gates. The guards looked at me oddly, and I wished I could still the wild exultant happiness which enveloped me, swamping my fears.

I did not know how I was going to face Freya. If she talked about Sigmund I should be very much afraid that I would betray myself. She was observant and she knew me so well. She would surely guess something had happened.

Strangely enough, there was a change in Freya since we had come to the schloss. She seemed to have become older, more withdrawn, obsessed with herself. Before, I believed she would have immediately noticed that my behaviour was a little unusual.

Fräulein Kratz had recognized the change in her.

'She is quite inattentive at her lessons,' she complained. 'I think coming here and seeing the Baron again and realizing what the future holds has turned her head.'

'It is enough to turn anyone's head.'

'She will not concentrate on anything for long and she is continually cancelling her lessons. It is very hard to exert one's authority. What do you think, Fräulein Ayres?'

'It is different in my case. It is not like a set lesson. We just talk English. We don't have to sit and study books, although I do like her to read in English.'

'I suppose one must accept it.'

'I should, Fräulein Kratz, and in any case it does give you a little free time.'

She admitted this was so. The same thing applied to me – which, to my relief, I found that very afternoon.

I saw her briefly for the midday meal. She was dressed for riding and looked very pretty in a light navy habit which set off her fairness to perfection.

'I am going riding this afternoon, Anne,' she said. 'I dare say you will want to do the same or go into the town.'

'Whatever you wish, of course.'

'Oh no . . . not that. I can't go with you. I have to go with Tatiana and Günther.'

My heart leaped with pleasure, for this would give me a little time to carry out a plan of my own.

'I hope you enjoy it,' I said.

'I'm sorry you can't come with us.'

'Of course I understand. Enjoy your ride.'

She threw her arms round my neck. 'Have a pleasant afternoon, dear Anne.'

'I will amuse myself.'

'And we'll talk a lot in English . . . tomorrow or the next day.'

I went to my room and put on my riding habit. It was early afternoon when I set out for the forest.

The plan had come to me when I had awakened that morning. I was going to see the woman who had tidied

Francine's grave. I had the strong conviction that she knew something and if she did I must find out what it was. I had been very interested in the child. Why not? It was a wild supposition but at least his name was Rudolph. Why should a boy of four be made to kneel at a stranger's grave? What if that little Rudolph were the child of whom Francine had written to me? If I could prove that Francine had been truly married, if I could find her child, then that little boy would be heir to the Duchy. He would come before Conrad. I saw now that when I had come to Bruxenstein to solve the riddle of my sister's life and death here, I might also be finding a solution to my own problem.

Perhaps my imagination was working too strongly; perhaps I was looking for too much simplification. I could but try; and I was going to with all the ingenuity I possessed.

As I rode through the forest past Gisela's house to the hunting lodge I was thinking of the previous evening, of Conrad, the wild demanding passion that consumed us both and robbed us of all awareness of everything else. How could I, who had always considered myself to be a fairly honourable sort of person, allow myself to be carrying on this passionate affair with the affianced husband of my pupil? I could not understand myself. I seemed different from the Philippa Ewell I had known all my life. I only knew that I must be with him; I must give way; I wanted above everything else to please him, to be with him forever.

I tethered the horse in the usual spot and walked round the lodge, past the grave and towards Katia's house.

As I came into the thicker part of the forest just past the lodge I heard the sound of a horse's hoofs. I stepped back from the rather narrow path and waited for the horse and rider to pass me.

It was a man and strangely enough he looked familiar to me.

He stared at me as he passed. He was walking the horse as he must along this bridle path. He inclined his head in a form of greeting and I responded. Then I passed on, wondering where I could possibly have seen him before. People came in and out of the schloss. Perhaps he was employed there.

In any case my mind was too full of other matters for me to waste my thoughts on a mere stranger. I came to the house. It looked quiet. Deliberately I opened the gate. I was in a porch in which potted plants grew. There was a knocker, so I knocked.

Silence and then the sound of footsteps. The door opened and Katia stood there. She stared at me in surprise, not immediately recognizing me as the woman who had asked the way.

I had rehearsed what I was going to say and I said it.

'I wonder if I can speak with you. There is something very important I have to ask you. Will you allow me to?' She looked bewildered and I went on: 'Please . . . it is very important to me.'

She stepped back and opened the door wider. 'I have seen you before,' she said.

'Yes. The other day. I asked for directions.'

She smiled. 'Ah . . . I remember now. Please come in.'

I stepped inside the hall, noticing how clean and polished everything was. She opened a door and we entered a pleasant room, simply but comfortably furnished.

'Please sit down,' she said.

I did so. 'I realize this may seem very strange,' I said. 'But I am very interested in the grave of the lady who was murdered with Baron Rudolph.'

'Oh?' She was faintly alarmed. 'Why . . . why do you ask me?'

'Because you knew her well. You were fond of her. You look after the grave. You take the little boy there and you clearly respected her.'

'I take my little boy with me because I could not leave him behind. He is sleeping now. It is the only time I have to do anything in the house.'

'Please tell me about your friendship with the lady who was murdered.'

'May I ask why you are interested?'

It was my turn to hesitate. Then I made a sudden decision, because I saw it was the only way in which I could hope to get the information I wanted so badly. I said: 'I am her sister.'

She was quite taken aback. She just stared at me in astonishment. I waited for her to speak, then she said: 'Yes, I knew she had a sister . . . Pippa, she spoke of her so . . . lovingly.'

Those simple words touched me deeply and I felt my lips trembling and the words began to rush out: 'You understand then. You know why I must . . .'

I saw at once that I should have discovered nothing of importance but for the fact that I had told her who I was, for the relationship between us had changed suddenly.

I went on: 'I saw you tending the grave. I saw you and the little boy kneel together. I knew then that you had loved my sister. That was why I decided to talk to you.'

'I did not really believe you had lost your way,' she said. 'I knew there was something.'

'I believe my sister was truly married to Rudolph.'

She lowered her eyes. 'They said she was not. They said she was his mistress.'

'Nevertheless there is proof somewhere . . .'

She was silent.

I went on: 'Tell me about her. She lived here in the lodge, didn't she? You must have been a near neighbour.'

'It was her home. You see, she could not be received at the schloss. The Baron had his duties. He came when he could. He came often. They were very much in love and she was such a happy person. She laughed all the time. I never saw her sad. She accepted the position. I am sure the Baron Rudolph escaped to her whenever he could.'

'Tell me how you knew her.'

'My father was alive then. He and my brother were in the employment of the Graf von Bindorf, as most people are hereabouts . . . either with the Graf or in the household of the Grand Duke. My brother Herzog is still with the Graf. He goes on missions for him. He is not here very often.'

'Yes,' I prompted.

'A terrible thing happened to me. It was in the forest. I was young and innocent, you understand. It was terrible. Nobody could know unless it happened to them. There was a man. I think he had watched me for some time . . . because I had sometimes fancied I was being followed. And then one day . . . it was dusk . . .' She paused and looked straight ahead, reliving the horror I imagined. 'He was one of the guards at the Grand Schloss. He caught me and dragged me through the trees and then . . .'

'He raped you.'

She nodded. 'I was so frightened. I knew he was one of the guards . . . I thought they would not believe me . . . so I said nothing. It was like a nightmare and I thought it was over and I must forget . . . But then . . . I found I was to have a child.'

'I am so sorry for you.'

'It is over now. These things fade. I do not think of it so much now. It is talking of it brings it back. My father was a very religious man, you understand? When he knew, he was horrified, and – ' her face puckered and I could see in her the poor defenceless girl she must have been at that time ' – they didn't believe me,' she went on. 'They said I was a harlot, that I had brought shame on the family. They turned me out.'

'And where did you go?'

'I did not know which way to turn and I went to her . . . your sister. She took me in. It was not just that . . . It was everything she did for me. *She* believed me. Not only that, she said, that even if it were true that I had agreed it was not such a sin after all. But she *believed* me. She said she would have helped me in any case. So . . . she did and my child was born in the hunting lodge.'

My heart was beating wildly. 'Did she have a child too . . . at about the same time?'

'I don't know of a child,' she said. 'I never saw one there.'

'It would be dangerous if she had had a child, wouldn't it?' I asked. 'He would be the heir to the duchy.'

She shook her head. 'There would have had to be a marriage.'

'I believe there was a marriage.'

'Everyone says there was not.'

'Did my sister ever talk of marriage?'

'No.'

'Did she say she was pregnant?'

'No.'

'And your baby was born at the hunting lodge, you say.'

'Yes. I was well looked after there. She saw to that. And when the baby came I stopped having nightmares. I couldn't be sorry for anything that brought him to me.'

'And you loved my sister, did you?'

'Who would not love someone who had done everything . . . who had saved me from such a terrible fate as that which could have overtaken me. I was half crazy with grief and fear. I thought I was damned as my father said I was. She laughed at all that. She made me see that I was not wicked. She helped me to bring a healthy child into the world. She saved us both. It is something I shall never forget.'

'And . . . because of all this . . . you tend her grave.'

She nodded. 'I shall do so for as long as I live and I am at hand. I never forget, and I don't want Rudolph to either. I shall tell him the story when he is old enough.'

'Thank you for telling me.'

'What are you looking for here?'

'I want to find her child, because I believe there was a child.'

She shook her head.

'There is something I have to tell *you*,' I went on. 'The Countess and those for whom I work do not know my true identity. I am here as Fräulein Ayres. You won't betray me?'

'I never would,' she said, with a rush of feeling.

'I guessed you wouldn't, and I had to tell you because unless I did I knew that you would not tell me your secret.'

She agreed this was so.

I told her that because I had inherited money I was able to come here. I said again that I believed fervently that there had been a marriage between my sister and Rudolph and that there was a child.

'You have your son,' I said. 'You will understand how my sister felt about hers. I want to find him. I want to be able to take care of him. It will be compensation for losing her. Besides, if he does exist, how can I know what sort of life he is having? I owe it to her.'

'I understand how you feel. If there were a child . . . but . . .'

'I had letters from her telling me about him.'

'She longed for a child, perhaps. I know she did. I remember her with my Rudi. Sometimes when people long for something they dream . . .'

It was the old explanation. Not Francine, I thought. Francine always had her mind firmly in reality. She had not been a dreamer. I had been that and yet I could not believe that in any circumstances I could have deluded myself into thinking I had a child . . . let alone writing letters about him.

I said: 'I am very grateful to you and thank you for looking after my sister's grave. If you should want to talk to me . . . if you have anything to tell me . . . remember I am here as Fräulein Ayres.'

She nodded.

I left the house then, not much wiser than when I had come, except that I had discovered the reason for her tending Francine's grave.

As I entered the schloss and was about to go up to my room I came face to face with Tatiana. She looked at me in the rather haughty way which was habitual with her and said. 'Good day, Fräulein.'

I responded and was about to pass on my way when she went on: 'The Countess is progressing well with her English, I believe.'

'Very well indeed,' I answered. 'She is a good pupil.' Tatiana regarded me with a certain interest and I grew uncomfortable under it and wished I was wearing my glasses. I knew my hair was escaping from under my riding hat.

'I think she is afraid that you are going to leave her. She has mentioned that you are a person of independent means.'

'It is true I am not obliged to work for a living, but I very much enjoy my work with the Countess.'

'So her fears are groundless and you will stay until her marriage?'

'That is looking rather far ahead.'

'A year . . . perhaps less. You know all the circumstances, of course. I believe you are very much in her confidence.'

'We are as good friends as we can be, considering our positions.'

She bowed her head, letting me know that she considered there was a big gap between our social positions.

Then she looked at me sharply and said: 'It is strange, Fräulein Ayres, but I fancy I have met you before.'

'Could that be possible, Countess?' I asked.

'Just, I think. I have been to England. I stayed in a house in the county of Kent.'

'I know Kent well. It is in the south-east corner of England. I was there at some time. But it would be rather unusual if we had met and I am sure such an occasion would stand out in my mind.'

I was alarmed that she might pursue the subject, but to my great relief she turned away to indicate that the conversation was at an end.

I went up to my room with a wildly beating heart. For a moment I thought she might have recognized me, but I was sure that if she had she would have questioned me more closely.

It must have been about an hour later when Freya returned. I was surprised because I had understood she had been with Tatiana and Günther. She came into my room; she was flushed and smiling.

'We've been miles and miles,' she said. 'Günther and I and two of the grooms lost the rest of the party.'

'You weren't lost in the forest?'

'Not exactly. But we did go a long way.'

'The Countess Tatiana was back a long time ago.'

Freya smiled at me conspiratorially. 'I don't much like Tatiana. I have an idea that she is always criticizing me. She is very much aware of her position and thinks I'm a bit of a hoyden.'

'Perhaps you are.'

'Am I? Am I? Do you know, I don't mind in the least if I am. You rather like hoydens, don't you?'

'I like you, Freya,' I said rather emotionally. 'I like you very much.'

Then she threw her arms round me and, remembering Conrad and all that had happened, I felt wretchedly ashamed.

Later that night I thought of his waiting at the King of the Forest. He would be frustrated and bitterly disappointed, I knew; but he would have to realize that he could not lightly continue with this deception, and even if it were easy for me to get away – and it was far from that – I must hesitate to do so.

It was very different considering all this in the quiet of my room – yes, very different from being swept off my feet by an overpowering passion which assailed my senses while it numbed my impulses of decency, while I fought in vain to resist. He must understand that when I could calmly assess the situation I deplored it. I was ashamed to face Freya; ashamed to face myself.

I awoke suddenly that night and sat up in bed wondering why I was suddenly so wide awake. Then I knew. I had had a revelation. It must have come to me in my dreams.

The man whom I had met in the forest when I was visiting Katia Schwartz was the same one whom I had seen near Greystone Manor on several occasions. He was the man who had been staying at the inn and who, I thought, had been exploring our countryside. I had seen him on the way to the church near Dover, when Miss Elton and I had gone there to look at the register.

That he should be here in Bruxenstein was a very odd coincidence.

I could not sleep. I lay there thinking of everything – my love passages with Conrad, my conversation with Katia Schwartz, the germ of suspicion I had seen in Tatiana's eyes – and now the man in the forest.

The next morning a note was brought to me from Conrad. I thought it was very reckless of him to write to me in this way, for it was not inconceivable that the notes would be intercepted, but I had already learned that when he wanted something he would not let minor considerations stand in the way of forging ahead to get it.

> My dearest [he wrote],
> You will be able to get away in the mid-morning. I am sending an envoy from the Grand Schloss with messages to the Graf and instructing that he must be entertained by them, including the Countess Freya. This will leave you free and the envoy will remain with them until the late afternoon.
>
> Meanwhile I shall be waiting for you at our inn and from there we shall go into the forest, for I have something I wish to show you.
>
> My love now and forever.
>
> C.

I was both elated and alarmed, for I could see myself slipping farther and farther into an intrigue from which I should be unable to extricate myself and which could have the most dire consequences. So I was free because Conrad had the power to arrange it.

In due course I arrived at the inn. I wondered how many his disguise deceived. I should have known him at once; but then perhaps that was because I loved him.

We had some food in a private room and I had rarely felt so happy as I did sitting there with him, while every now and then his hand would touch mine across the table. There was a gentleness in him that day. He was protective. He was planning not just a hasty encounter but our future.

He was all eagerness for me to see the house which he planned should be our home, although I was protesting all the time that I could never agree to deceive Freya.

'Come and see it for yourself,' he said. 'It's rather delightful.'

'However delightful, it could not influence my convictions that this is wrong and I should never be a party to it.'

He smiled at me appealingly. 'Let's pretend then . . . for a while.'

We rode together out of the inn yard across the town. The sun was high in the sky and shone warmly down on us and I thought for a moment: I will pretend. I will have this day and carry the memory of it through the years to come.

As we rode through the town we had to pass through a square where some ceremony was in progress. It was delightful. The girls and women were in the national costume with full red skirts and white blouses, with red flowers in their hair; and the men had white knee breeches with yellow stockings and white shirts; their caps were tightly fitting with long tassels which hung halfway down their backs.

They were dancing to the sound of a violin and we paused to watch it for a moment.

I thought how lovely it was there on that perfect summer's day with the people's faces shining with pleasure and contentment while the young people burst into song.

Then suddenly a young girl approached us. She was

carrying a little bunch of flowers which she presented to me. I took it and thanked her and then suddenly the people were crowding round us and singing what I recognized as the National Anthem.

'Sigmund!' they shouted. 'Sigmund and Freya!'

Conrad did not seem in the least perturbed. He smiled and spoke to them, telling them that he hoped they would enjoy the day and what pleasure it gave him to ride among them unceremoniously.

He had taken off his hat and was waving it to them. I wanted to turn and ride off as fast as I could. But Conrad was enjoying it. I knew that the approval of the people meant a great deal to him and seeing him thus I realized how fitted he was for his destiny . . . and how ill I fitted into it.

They crowded round us, and from one of the houses someone brought out several sheets which they knotted together and held across our path. They were laughing and cheering.

'Come,' said Conrad, and he caught my horse and led me along with him. We rode up to the sheets and with a great sigh they were allowed to fall to the ground. We passed through the cheering crowds and rode on towards the forest.

'They liked you,' said Conrad.

'They thought I was Freya.'

'They were pleased to see us.'

'They will know in time that I am not. In fact I am surprised that they mistook me for her. They see her now and then.'

'I think some of them knew. It couldn't be otherwise. Their first thought was Freya . . . and then when they realized you were not Freya they pretended that you were.'

'Surely not. What would they think?'

'They will smile on us. They do not expect me to give up the society of all other ladies.'

'Ah yes,' I said slowly. 'They will smile and shrug their shoulders . . . as they did with Rudolph.'

'Cheer up. It was an amusing incident.'

'It seemed significant in a way. I can see clearly how well you fit your role.'

'I have to accept it. I have to live with it. I have to see the country peaceful. There is no way out of that. The life you and I have together will have its drawbacks. I would not try to pretend otherwise, but we *must* be together. I refuse to consider anything else. We must take what the gods give us, Pippa . . . and enjoy it. Because it will be wonderful. I can promise you that. Just to be together . . . that is all I ask.'

When he spoke like that I felt limp with pleasure. I was aware of my principles slipping farther and farther away and myself growing closer to my sensual desires which were, in fact, becoming a need. I loved him. Every time I saw him I loved him more. I tried to imagine life without him and I could not bear to look into a future so dismal that it sent me into the depths of depression; and to contemplate the life he was planning for us filled me with a wild exhilaration . . . albeit apprehension.

I knew I was going to fall heavily into temptation. If it were not for Freya . . . I kept thinking; and then the enormity of what I had done overwhelmed me and I then thought: I shall have to go away. I dare not continue with this.

How beautiful the forest was! When the trees thinned a little I could see the mountains in the distance; they were covered with spruce fir and in the valleys I could see little houses huddled together; I could smell the smoke rising from those places where the charcoal burners were, and I took deep breaths of the pure mountain air.

'You like this countryside,' said Conrad.

'I find it delightful.'

'Here will be our home. Oh Pippa, I am so happy to have you here. You cannot imagine how I suffered when I thought I had lost you. I cursed myself for all sorts of a fool for letting you go. Never again, Pippa. Never again.'

I shook my head, but he laughed at me. He was sure of

himself, so confident that life would work out the way he wanted it to.

We rode on and were going uphill.

'Listen,' he said, 'to the sound of the cowbells. You will hear them through the mist. You will love the mist. There is something romantically mysterious about it. I used to call it the blue mist when I was a boy. It seemed always blue to me. You climb high through the forests and you walk into the blue mist . . . and then after a while suddenly you are in bright sunshine. I used to come here a great deal. This was one of our houses. Sometimes when it was hot in the town below we would ride up here and spend the day. Perhaps we would stay. We slept out of doors often. It's full of happy memories for me, but they will be nothing compared with what lies in store for us.'

'Conrad . . .' I began. 'I can never call you Sigmund.'

'Please don't. Sigmund suggests duty. Conrad is for those I love and who love me.'

'Conrad,' I went on, 'have you always had what you wanted?'

He laughed. 'Shall we say I've always made a good attempt to get it . . . and if you really make up your mind, what you want often comes to you. Dearest Pippa, cast off your fears. Be happy. We are here together. We are going to our home. It is a happy house and we'll make it entirely ours.'

The house was enchanting. It was built like a miniature schloss with pepperpot towers at the four corners and it was the size of an English manor house.

'Come,' he said. 'There is no one here. I arranged that we should be quite alone.'

'Who would otherwise be here?' I asked.

'The family who look after it. They have a house close by. Father, mother, two sons and two daughters. It's an excellent arrangement. They provide the entire domestic needs. If we used it for a large party we sent on our servants to help.'

'It's beautiful,' I said.

'I knew you would like it. It's a favourite place of mine. That's why I thought of it. It is known as Marmorsaal – Marble Hall. You'll see why. It has a rather exquisite floor in the hall which is the centre of the house really.'

There was a gateway leading to the house which was surrounded by low bushes. 'We keep them low so that it is not too dark,' said Conrad. 'I don't like darkness, do you? Well, who does? There's something menacing about it. This is always a happy house – so we cut down the trees and planted those small flowering shrubs to look pretty and not shut out the light.'

'There is an inscription on the gate,' I pointed out.

'Yes, that was put there by one of my ancestors who lived here for a while. He was a ne'er-do-well . . . the bad boy of the family so they sent him off here to live in the forest. His great hobby was hunting the wild boar. He wanted to be alone and resisted all the efforts of the family to bring him back into the fold. He had this inscription put on the gate. Can you read it?'

'"*Sie thun mir nichts, ich thue Ihnen nichts.*" Don't interfere with me and I won't interfere with you.'

'An excellent sentiment, don't you agree? No one will interfere with us, I assure you. This is our home, Pippa.'

He unlocked the door and picked me up in his arms.

'Is it the custom in England, too, to carry the bride over the threshold?'

'It is,' I answered.

'Then here we are, my dear one. The two of us . . . in our new home.'

It was beautiful, I had to admit. The hall floor was covered in marble slabs of the most delicate shades of blue. I could not help exclaiming at their exquisite beauty.

Pictures hung on the walls; there was a large table in the centre on which stood a bowl of flowers.

He stood there holding me tightly.

'You like it?' he asked.

It's quite magnificent.'

'We are going to be happy here – that is the most important.' And when he was there beside me I could believe it.

We explored the house. Everything was in perfect order. That would be on his instructions. I wondered what the people in the forest thought. They would guess that he was bringing a woman here . . . his mistress . . . and they would know that this was to be her home. They would smile and shrug their shoulders, as Conrad would say.

Should we go through life with people smiling and shrugging their shoulders? What of our children? What would happen to them? Perhaps already I was pregnant.

Oh yes, I had fallen a long way down the slippery slope and I was going to find it hard to climb back to the right way, the honourable way. And it was that. I only had to think of Freya's innocent face to know it.

Nevertheless I found myself exclaiming at the perfections of the house; the dining-room with its long narrow windows and its beautifully embroidered chairs; that room which was meant to catch the sun like our solarium at home; the bedrooms which were not large by schloss standards but which were light and prettily furnished. From the windows there were views of the forest and the distant mountains. It was a beautiful house in a perfect setting.

'You like it?' he asked eagerly.

I could only say that it was quite lovely.

'And you'll be happy here?'

I could not answer that. I knew in my heart that I could not be completely happy – neither with him nor away from him; and I could not pretend.

'I will banish all your scruples. I will make you see this as the only way to live.'

'One which has been followed by the barons and counts, grafs and margraves before you.'

'It is the only way. We are fettered for life if we do not break free. You must understand that, Pippa.'

'I wish . . . but what is the use of wishing, though.'

'Though what?'

'Here, I could imagine anything happening. It is the land of legend, of Grimm and the Pied Piper. There is magic in the air. I feel that in this forest . . . anything could happen.'

'We'll make our own magic. Come, be happy. Take what is given you. You love me, don't you?'

'With all my heart.'

'What else matters?'

'So much, alas.'

'Nothing that cannot be overcome.'

'I could never overcome my shame at my disloyalty to Freya.'

'But she is just a child. When she grows up she'll understand.'

I shook my head. 'I think that because I am the one she might not.'

'Forget her.'

'Can you?'

'I think of nothing but you.'

'You are such a practised lover. You say what I most want to hear.'

'It will be the aim of my life to please you.'

'Please . . . please, don't . . .' I begged.

He held me tightly against him. He was in an unusual mood. It was almost as though he thought that our being in the house like this was sacred in some way. It was almost like a ceremony.

I said: 'Is it just possible that you and I could be two ordinary people, that you could be relieved of your responsibilities, so that we could marry and bring up children . . . and live normal lives?'

'If Rudolph had not died it could have been like that. But he died too young . . . without an heir . . .'

I told him about my visit to Katia Schwartz and that I had

let her know who I was. That did not alarm him in the least. He brushed aside possible danger.

'If only there had been a child and your sister and Rudolph had married . . . well, then we could start thinking on different lines.'

'Would you want to marry me?'

'I want it more than anything in the world. If I could marry you instead of Freya I would ask nothing else.'

'I have always believed that my sister had a child.'

'Even if she had it would be of no consequence, as far as the succession is concerned.'

'If she and Rudolph had been married it would.'

'But they were not.'

I was about to say that I had seen the entry . . . but he had seen with his own eyes that it was not there.

'That would make all the difference,' I went on, 'if they had married and we found there had been a child?'

'But of course. However much the marriage would have been disapproved of, it would still be a marriage.'

A sudden wild hope was surging through me. It was the magic of the forest. It was the blue mist, the fir-clad mountains and the feeling that I was in an enchanted land where strange events took place.

So I gave myself up to the joy of being with Conrad in our new home. I had the strange conviction there that I was going to find what I needed.

When I arrived back at the schloss the envoy was still there. I was relieved. It gave me the chance to slip up to my room unnoticed. I was always afraid of seeing Freya immediately after my meeting with Conrad for I felt it might be obvious to her that something had happened to me.

I threw off my riding coat and sat on the bed thinking over the past few hours and my eyes strayed to my dressing-table. It struck me suddenly that the little pot in which I kept my hairpins was not in its usual position. I looked at it without much interest and wondered when I had moved it. It was a trivial matter but it did look a little strange as I had never before seen it out of place. I was lost in thought about Conrad – the mood I was usually in after having been with him, alternating between joy and fear. There were times when I gave myself up to dreams. I let myself imagine that Conrad and I were together and everything had turned out right for us. I found Francine's child and he was acclaimed the heir. Conrad was free and we married and lived happily ever after. Fancies . . . wild dreams . . . how could they ever come true?

I must change from my riding clothes. The envoy must surely be leaving soon and then Freya would come and tell me what sort of day she had had. She seemed to have grown up lately; I supposed that now she was getting closer to marriage she was becoming interested in the politics of the country in which as Grand Duchess she would have a part to play.

I sometimes fancied that life excited her. Was she perhaps falling in love with Conrad? That would be the easiest thing imaginable for a romantic young girl.

I hung up my coat and took a dress from the cupboard. I took off the scarf I had been wearing and opened a drawer to put it away. I had several scarves which I always kept in the drawer with my gloves and handkerchiefs. It was strange, but the gloves which were usually kept below the handkerchiefs were on top.

Then I had no doubt that someone had been looking through the drawer. Why?

A cold horror had begun to creep over me. There was one drawer which had been locked and in which I kept the papers which Cousin Arthur had helped me to get before I left England. They would reveal my true identity.

If someone had seen them I should be betrayed, for whoever found them would know that I was not Anne Ayres but Philippa Ewell – and they would remember that the young woman who had been murdered was Francine Ewell.

I searched frantically for the keys of the drawer. I had left them at the back of one of the other drawers behind some underclothes. They were not in their usual place. I unlocked the drawer and hastily searched. I found the papers but was sure they were not quite as I had left them.

Now I was almost certain that someone had been in my room, had looked for the papers and found them; and then had put the key back in the wrong place. In which case I was betrayed. Who would have done it?

My first thoughts were: Freya. I often felt she was suspicious of me. She had a mischievous way of regarding me. On more than one occasion she had said: 'You are not what you seem!' and there had been a calculating look in her eyes.

Could it be that she had determined to find out and had gone through my drawers while she knew I was away?

I would soon find out.

If she had seen the papers I should have to confess to her. I would tell her the whole story and I knew she would understand.

The thought that it was Freya was comforting in a way.

But of course it could be someone else.

The Discovery

There was to be a thanksgiving service in the Cathedral in the centre of the town to celebrate the recovery of the Grand Duke.

Conrad was naturally very much involved with the arrangements and the Graf, Gräfin, Günther and Tatiana stayed at the Grand Schloss for two days and nights to assist.

Freya and I were together during that time more than we had been lately and I was very wary of her, wondering all the time if she had seen the papers in my drawer. She gave no sign of having done so, which would have been strange with Freya. I should have thought she would have burst out the news of her discovery immediately.

She was a little quiet, it was true. However, I thought that was probably because her marriage was coming nearer.

We rode together into the forest. I avoided both the hunting lodge and the Marmorsaal; and she was in such a reflective mood that she allowed me to lead the way.

When we had ridden for a while we tied up our horses and stretched ourselves on the grass and talked.

'The forest is beautiful,' I said. 'Listen. Can you hear the cowbells a long way off?'

'No,' said Freya firmly. 'I am so glad the Grand Duke is better.'

'Everyone is. In fact it is going to be a matter for national rejoicing.'

'If he hadn't lived I should have been married by now.'

'Does that alarm you?' I asked cautiously.

'I'd rather wait,' she said.

'Of course.'

'Why didn't *you* get married?'

'For one very good reason, that nobody asked me.'

'I wonder why. You're quite attractive.'

'Thank you.'

'And you're not very old . . . yet.'

'Every day I get a little nearer to senility.'

So do I. So does everybody. Even Tatiana . . .'

'Why select Tatiana especially?'

'Because she thinks she is different from everyone else – like one of the goddesses.'

'I know someone else who had similar ideas about herself.'

'Oh, it was just the name with me. What's in a name?'

'"That which we call a rose, by any other name would smell as sweet."'

'Poetry again! Really, Anne, you can be the most irritating person. Talking poetry when I want to talk about marriage.'

I picked a blade of grass and stared at it. I was afraid she would see the rising colour in my cheeks.

I said slowly: 'Are you in love with . . . Sigmund?'

She was silent. Then she said: 'I think I *am* in love.'

'Well, then you must be happy.'

'I am. Yes I am. Do you think I am too young to marry?'

'Well, it won't be for some time yet, will it? In a year's time you'll be of a reasonable age.'

'I was thinking about *now*. How do you know you're in love? Oh . . . I forgot . . . you wouldn't know. You've never been in love and no one's ever been in love with you.'

I was silent.

Then I said: 'I think one would know.'

'Yes, I think so too.'

'So . . . are you?' I asked, and felt as though the entire forest was waiting with me for her answer.

'Yes,' she said firmly. 'I know I am.'

Then she threw her arms about me and hugged me. She

kissed me lightly. I put my lips against her forehead, and even as I did so I thought: the Judas Kiss.

I felt utterly depressed and wretched.

The thanksgiving service was to be held on the following Saturday. They were decorating the streets of the town and they had arranged pageants to halt the Grand Duke's progress through the streets, to assure him of their loyalty. There was no doubt that the people very much appreciated their Grand Duke.

Conrad, as the heir, would ride with the Duke in the grand coach, and they would be followed by other members of the royal household and nobility in their own carriages. The army would be out in full force and it would be very impressive.

'I am riding with the Graf and the Gräfin,' Freya told me. 'Tatiana is furious because she will be several carriages behind. Günther doesn't mind. He doesn't care so much about such things. I don't think Tatiana likes me.'

'Why shouldn't she?'

'Oh, she has her reasons.'

'Well, do you know them?'

'The main one is she wants to be *me*. She would like to marry Sigmund and be the Grand Duchess.'

'What makes you think so?'

'I just know. I keep my eyes open, you know, dear Anne.'

She looked at me quizzically and for a moment I felt sure she had seen those papers.

'Tatiana is ambitious,' she went on. 'She hates being just the daughter of the Graf. She'll make a very grand marriage, you see. But Tatiana wants the most important one. That, of course, is Sigmund . . . for she couldn't very well marry the Grand Duke, could she?'

'Hardly.'

'So she wants Sigmund, but he is betrothed to me, so she hasn't a chance. Poor Tatiana.'

'Do you think she is in love with . . . Sigmund?'

I wished I could stop myself always pausing before I said his name.

'Tatiana is in love with one person . . . herself. It's not such a bad thing to be in love with yourself. You never get disappointed, do you? And you always make excuses for the loved one. It's the way to have a perfect love-affair.'

'Freya, you are quite absurd.'

'I know. And you like me that way, don't you? Do you think my husband will?'

'I expect so.'

'Anne . . . has something happened to you?'

'What do you mean?' I asked in alarm.

'You seem different.'

'In what way?'

'Well, in one way you seem to be looking over your shoulder as though you are expecting something awful to happen . . . and another time you look as if something rather wonderful *has* happened. It's very disconcerting, you know. It must be one thing or the other. You should make up your mind.'

'You're imagining it.'

'Am I, Anne? Am I?'

'Of course,' I said brusquely.

'Perhaps I am fanciful. I must be in love myself. That makes people a bit odd, I think.'

'I dare say it does.'

And again I was wondering whether she had seen those papers.

There was another letter from Conrad.

> Dearest [he wrote],
> When this thanksgiving business is over, I want you to leave the schloss and come to our home. Make some excuse to Freya, but come. When you are there we will

make all sorts of plans. I'm so longing to be with you. All my love now and always.

C.

As usual his letters filled me with delight and apprehension, but as I looked at the seal on this one I had a fancy that it had been broken and resealed before it had reached me.

I wondered if that were possible. Conrad was reckless, I knew that. He had become so accustomed to having his own way and expecting immediate obedience that it might not have occurred to him that he could have a disloyal servant.

If someone had read that letter before it reached me, they would understand at once the relationship between us. Could it be Freya?

No. She could never keep such a matter to herself. But her recent conversations had set me wondering. Why had she talked as she had about love and marriage? It was almost as though her observations were full of innuendoes, that there was some meaning behind her words. Yet her affection for me did not seem to have abated. She had said she was in love. Then if she had read that letter she must be jealous of me. But she showed no sign of it.

It was disturbing to contemplate that the letter might have been intercepted. I tried to tell myself that I had imagined it had been because of my guilty conscience; but there was also the indication that my room had been searched.

One of the servants knocked on my door and when I told her to come in she took a letter from her pocket.

'This was given to me to hand to you,' she said, 'and I was told to give it to no one else.'

I immediately thought of Conrad, but surely he would not have given it to a serving girl. When I looked at the writing on the envelope I did not recognize it.

'A young woman gave it to me. She said you would understand.'

'Thank you,' I said.

I could scarcely wait for the maid to go before I opened the envelope.

> If you will come to the house [I read], I will show you something which I think you will want to see. Katia Schwartz.

I was tremendously excited, and I determined to go to the house in the forest as soon as I could.

It was not easy. Freya would demand to know where I was going and want to come with me. I could see nothing for it but to wait for the day of thanksgiving. I should be expected to be there, of course, but I could make some excuse to get away.

Freya told me that I was to ride in the carriage with Fräulein Kratz and perhaps two others.

'Dear Anne,' she said, 'I am sorry you have to ride with the governess.'

'Why be sorry? It's my place.'

'But you know you are . . . different.'

'On the contrary, I am here as the English governess and it is only right and proper that I should be treated as such.'

'I spoke to the Gräfin about it.'

'You shouldn't have done that.'

'I shall speak how and when I like.'

'I know that, but it was unwise.'

'Tatiana was quite angry. She said you were a governess and your place was in the carriage with Fräulein Kratz.'

'She was quite right.'

'She was not. You are my friend. I keep telling them that.'

'Freya, you must remember your position.'

'I do. That is why I let them know when I don't approve of something.'

'I shall be perfectly all right in the governesses' carriage. It's very kind of them to let us *have* a carriage in any case.'

'Now you are being humble. I always suspect you when you are like that.'

'Suspect me of what?'

She narrowed her eyes. 'All sorts of things,' she said.

'What shall you wear for the service?' I asked.

'Something bright and beautiful. After all, it is a time for rejoicing, isn't it?'

'It certainly is.'

The day came. It was warm and the air seemed filled with the scent of pines. It was always like that when the wind blew in a certain direction. I had grown to love it.

What a great occasion it was – and one of those when I realized more poignantly than ever the great gulf between myself and Conrad. What if I succumbed to his wishes? There would be many occasions when he would be attending some ceremony. And I? Where should I be? One of the crowd, I supposed. Or perhaps not present at all. That was not important really. I loved him enough to want to make his life as comfortable as possible, and if that meant taking an obscure role I did not mind that. And yet I found it sordid in a way, unacceptable . . . I was still hovering between my need of him and something within me which was warning me to get away while there was still time, before I became inextricably enmeshed.

The Grand Duke looked remarkably well considering the danger he had passed through. He acknowledged the cheers of the crowd with a kind of benign tolerance. Conrad was beside him in the carriage looking magnificent in the uniform of a general of the army – two shades of blue with touches of silver and a silver helmet in which waved a blue feather.

Freya rode immediately behind with the Graf and Gräfin and the ambassadors of Kollenitz. She looked very young and appealing, I thought. The people cheered her and I was touched by her obvious delight in their displays of affection.

Children in national costume presented her with flowers and sang hymns of patriotic fervour while banners waved across the streets which were crowded with spectators.

Then we entered the Cathedral and the service of thanksgiving began.

I was seated at the back with Fräulein Kratz and as I listened to the singing and the prayers and the sermon of thanksgiving delivered by one of the highest dignitaries of the Church, the incongruity of my situation was borne home to me. Thus it must have been with Francine. When had she realized that it would be impossible for her to lead a normal happy married life with Rudolph? Had she ever attended ceremonies like this?

Fräulein Kratz was singing fervently beside me. '*Ein feste Burg ist unser Gott.*' I noticed there were tears in her eyes.

As for myself, I felt a great desire to get away. Here I believed I could survey the future clearly and it seemed to me that I could only be an encumbrance to Conrad. Our meetings would be surreptitious – 'hole and corner' as Daisy would describe it. I must go back to England. I must slip away and hide myself. I could go to Aunt Grace and stay with her for a while. From there I could make plans, start a new life.

I wanted to get away, to be alone, to strengthen my resolve. If I were going to do what I saw now as my real duty I must not see Conrad again, for he unnerved me, he robbed me of my willpower; he refused to look the truth in the face and tried to make life fit in with his desires.

The service was over. Freya and the royal party would now go back to the Grand Schloss where there would be more celebrations; and Fräulein Kratz and I could go back to the Graf's schloss.

It occurred to me then that now that the Grand Duke was well Freya would not much longer be the Graf's guest. She would go back to the Grand Schloss to await her marriage and naturally I should go with her. I tried to imagine what it would be like, living under the same roof as Conrad, and I could see that we were, with every passing day, heading towards a climax.

It was four o'clock when we arrived at the schloss. I

changed into my riding habit and without delay set out for the forest.

Katia was expecting me. She said: 'My brother is at the celebrations. He has a high position in the Graf's employ. I thought you would come as soon as you could conveniently do so.'

'Thank you. I have been all eagerness since I received your note.'

'Come in. I will not keep you long in suspense.'

I was taken into the room where I had been before. She left me for a few moments and when she came back she was holding what looked like a sheet of paper in her hands.

She stood looking at me with a strange expression on her face and she seemed reluctant to hand it to me, although I knew this was that which she had to show me.

She said, almost hesitantly: 'You are her sister. You were frank with me. You could be in a very dangerous position . . . yet you told me the truth. I felt, therefore, that I could not withhold this from you.'

'What is it?' I asked; and she put it into my hand.

As I looked at it I felt the blood rush into my face. My hands were shaking. It was there . . . as plainly as I had seen it before . . . the signature, the proof of the marriage.

'But . . .' I stammered.

'The sheet had been removed . . . very carefully. My brother arranged it and brought it back here.'

'I knew I had seen it. I . . . I can't think clearly just now. This . . . this makes a lot of difference . . . It proves . . .'

She nodded. 'It proves there was a marriage. I did not think there had been . . . until I saw that. She always called him her husband . . . but I thought that was just because she regarded him as such. But he was . . . you see. And I thought I owed it to her. That's why I am showing this to you.'

I said slowly: 'It explains so much. I had seen it . . . and then it disappeared. Sometimes I thought I was not quite sane. What do you know about it?'

'I know that my brother brought it back from England.'

'Your brother . . . of course! He was the man I had seen. He had been following me . . . and after I had seen the entry he removed it. I . . . I don't know how to thank you. You can't realize what you have done for me. For so long I have wondered about myself, even. Why . . . why should he have removed this entry?'

'Because someone was anxious to deny there was a marriage.'

'You mean . . . the Graf?'

'Not necessarily. My brother is a spy. He could be working for several people.'

I was silent. Someone who was eager to deny the marriage. Who? If they were dead, could it matter? There was only one reason why it could. That was because there must be a child.

I said firmly: 'There is a child somewhere. He is the heir to the dukedom, because this proves without doubt that Rudolph and my sister were married.'

Dazzling possibilities had come into my mind. I would find that child . . . love him as Francine would have wished me to. I could go to Conrad and say: 'What we have longed for has come to pass. You are free. If we can find this child . . . if he still lives, you are no longer the heir. You can disentangle yourself from your commitment with Freya.' This was like a dream come true.

I could not stop staring at the paper in my hand. It was like a talisman – the key to my future.

But the child. I must find the child.

She was looking at me intently. Then she shook her head. 'I just thought you should know she was actually married. We can go no farther than that.'

There was a slightly fanatical look in her eyes and I had the impression that she did not want me to look for the child.

She said: 'I took a great risk in giving you that paper. My brother . . . and others . . . would kill me if it were known.'

'He will know it is gone.'

'No. He thinks it was stolen when he brought it back.'

'How was that?'

'He came back from England to this house. It was in a case of his . . . a flat leather case which he carried around with him when he went abroad. He arrived home exhausted after a difficult journey. I admit I was inquisitive. I wanted to know the nature of his business because I guessed it was not just an ordinary mission for the Graf, who sent him all over the world quite frequently. I looked at his case and saw the paper. I knew what it was and that it concerned the friend who had been so good to me.'

'Did you take it?'

'Oh no . . . not then. He had to go into the town to the schloss the next day, but before he did so it was necessary to take his horse to the blacksmith to be shod. While he was away I staged a robbery. I took the paper and a few other things as well, so that he should not think that someone had broken in to get just that. I damaged the lock on the door and disturbed the place. Then I buried the leather case under the inscription on your sister's grave. I gave him time to get back before I returned, so that he should be the one to find the place in disorder. He was almost demented. He said he would be ruined. He raged against me and said I should not have left the house unattended, to which I replied, how should I know how important the documents were. He never told me. He did not speak to me for days after that . . . but it passed, and I still keep house for him. Some of the things I took are still buried round the grave. I took out the paper though after I had met you and you told me who you were. I thought I should give it to you.'

'You have been very clever. It is one of the two things I came to prove.'

'There is no child,' she said firmly. 'But there is the proof of the marriage.'

'My search has brought me so far,' I said. 'It will carry me on.'

'Well, you know now. I feel a great relief. I owed it to her. That was how I saw it. She had been so good to me. No one was ever kinder . . . and in my time of need. I had to do that for her.'

'I am so grateful to you. Listen! Is that your little boy calling?'

She nodded and smiled. 'Yes. He has awakened.'

'Go and get him,' I said. 'I love children and he is such a bonny little fellow.'

She looked pleased and went out; in a short time she returned with the child. He was sleepy, rubbing his eyes with one hand and in the other carrying a toy.

I said: 'Hello, Rudi.'

'Hello,' he answered.

'I have come to see your mother . . . and now you too.'

He looked at me steadily.

'What's this you're carrying?' I asked, touching the limp-looking toy in his hand.

'It's my troll,' he said.

'Oh, is that what it is?'

I noticed that one ear was soggy. I touched it gently, and Katia laughed. 'Oh, he's a baby sometimes, aren't you, Rudi? He's had that troll ever since he was a baby. He won't go to bed without it.'

'My troll,' said Rudi with a kind of contemptuous affection.

'He still sucks his right ear. It was his comforter as a baby and I suppose it still is.'

I felt as if the room was spinning round me. Words danced before my eyes. What had Francine said? 'He has a troll which he takes to bed with him.' Didn't he find great comfort in sucking its ear?

I reached out and touched the child. I said: 'My sister's son was called Rudolph . . . like this little one. She wrote to me about him . . . so lovingly. He, too, had a troll which he took to bed and found great comfort in sucking its ear.'

She had moved a step away from me.

'So many children have them,' she said sharply. 'They always have something to suck . . . a toy . . . or a piece of blanket. It's natural. It's what they all do.'

She was holding the boy tightly and regarding me with something like suspicion. I thought then: I believe he is the child. He is about the age. He has the name and the troll.

There was nothing I could do about it . . . now. So I said: 'I suppose I should be riding back,' and the atmosphere relaxed immediately.

I must find out, I was thinking. I must ask Conrad what we should do. We will work together in this . . . and if it really is so . . . could everything come right for us?

I touched her arm gently and smiled at her gratefully. 'You cannot know what you have done for me,' I said.

I had folded the paper and tucked it into the neck of my dress. It was not going to leave that spot until I had shown it to Conrad.

Then I took my farewells and with many thanks rode off into the forest. Katia stood at the door until I was out of sight, the sleepy boy held tightly in her arms.

I spent the rest of the night in a fever of impatience. I studied the sheet from the register again and again. I went over it in my mind – that first time I had seen it when Miss Elton and I had stood in the vestry together. I pieced all the evidence together and a clear picture began to emerge. The man who had followed me and watched from the graveyard had been Katia's brother, and he was there to destroy the proof of that marriage. I wondered a great deal about the churchwarden who had denied ever seeing me before. Of course he had been bribed. Katia's brother would have been able to offer him a sum of money which would have seemed enormous to him . . . just to deny he had shown me the register. I could imagine how he must have been tempted, and looking back I realized now that he had been a little too glib, a little too certain. I should have pursued the matter, tried to trap him, but I had been so shocked that I had been easily brushed aside.

And now here was the evidence in my hand.

I wondered how I could get to see Conrad immediately. I even thought of riding over to the Grand Schloss but I dismissed that idea almost as soon as it came, for I could not possibly do that without arousing the curiosity of many people. No, I must be patient and await my opportunity.

The next day passed. I guessed he was busy with the foreign visitors who had come for the thanksgiving ceremony, but I did receive a note in the afternoon. He wanted me to meet him at the inn.

I slipped away, not caring very much if I was missed. I had seen little of Freya all day. I believed she had been with Tatiana and Günther, but as I rode out of the inn I saw Tatiana near the stables, so I presumed they had returned.

Conrad was waiting for me in the dark clothes he wore for these clandestine occasions. He caught me and held me in an embrace even more passionate than before.

'I had to see you,' he said. 'We'll go to the room here.'

'I have something to show you,' I told him.

We went up the back stairs and when we were alone he kissed me in the familiar demanding way.

'I have made a great discovery,' I said. 'It can change everything for us.' I drew the paper from my bodice. He stared at it, then at me.

'This is it,' I cried triumphantly. 'The missing sheet from the register. I did see it after all. Then, before I could show it to you, someone removed it.'

He was amazed. He said: 'But the churchwarden . . .'

'He was lying. Obviously he had been bribed to lie by the man who took it. It is all so very clear to me now.'

'Who?'

'I can even tell you that. It was Katia's brother.'

'Katia . . . ?'

'Katia Schwartz. She lives in the forest near the hunting lodge. She knew my sister. I discovered her when I saw that my sister's grave had been looked after. I trusted her and told her who I was, and she gave me this.'

'It's incredible,' he said.

'No, perfectly credible. Herzog Schwartz was spying for someone whose interest it was to remove that sheet.'

He was looking at me oddly. 'Who?' he said.

'I don't know.'

'Pippa, you don't think *I* ordered it to be done?'

'You!'

'Well, if you are looking for a motive, who stands to gain most?'

'Conrad . . . you didn't . . .'

'Of course not.'

'Then who could?'

'That is what we must find out.'

'There is only one reason why it should be necessary to do it,' I said.

He nodded. 'If there was a child . . .'

I cried: 'There *must* be a child. Why otherwise should Francine have told me that there was? Why otherwise should it have been necessary to remove that sheet from the register?'

He was silent. I could see that he was stunned.

I went on: 'If we could find the child . . .'

'He would be the heir to the dukedom,' he murmured very quietly.

'And you would be free, Conrad, to make your own life.'

'If that child exists . . .'

'He *does* exist. He must. Someone wants to hide the evidence of the marriage. He must be here . . . somewhere near, perhaps. I am sure he is Francine's son and the true heir to the dukedom.'

'We'll find him.'

'And then?'

He took my face in his hands and kissed me. 'You and I will have the freedom we want.'

'And Freya?'

'She will probably have to wait until the boy grows up. How old would he be?'

'About four years old.'

'A long time for Freya to wait.'

'And you would be free, Conrad. But . . . Freya would be hurt.'

'It would be no slight to her. It is merely that the positions of power would be changed. If we can find that boy I shall be free to act as I wish.'

'I think I have found the boy.'

'What!'

'His foster mother will not want to give him up and I am sure she will lie about his origins. But I feel certain of it.'

'What have you discovered?'

'It is Katia Schwartz. Poor woman. She gave me the paper out of gratitude to Francine. It will be hard if through doing so she will lose the child.'

'You have seen the child?'

'Yes. He is the right age, fair haired, blue eyed, and his name is Rudolph, which I know my sister's baby was called. She wrote to me about him and this is rather vital, I think. He had a toy, a troll, she told me in her letter, and he sucked one of its ears for comfort. When I was at the Schwartz home I saw the child; he had a troll and it came out that he sucked one of its ears for comfort and had been doing so since he was one year old.'

'I will have everything checked concerning the woman. I will find out every detail concerning the child.'

'If this could be proved true . . .' I whispered.

He said with a little laugh: 'I believe you are a witch. You come here in disguise . . . you discover secrets which have baffled everyone else. You enchant me. What are you, Pippa?'

'I hope I am the one you love. That is all I want to be.'

Then we talked of how we would proceed and what we would do if we could prove that the child in the forest was indeed the heir to the dukedom.

'I should have to be here until he was of age,' said Conrad. 'It would be my duty to hold the dukedom for him and to help teach him how to govern. We should have to spend long periods in the Grand Schloss but our home could be Marmorsaal. Oh, Pippa . . . Pippa . . . can you imagine that!'

I could and I did.

He said: 'I will set everything in motion tomorrow. It should not take long. Katia Schwartz will have to prove that the child she has with her is her own. If we get the answers we want, then we shall let it be known that Rudolph was lawfully married and had a son. That will be the best possible news.'

It was about two hours later when I left the inn. As we were about to go Conrad said to me: 'I didn't want to tell you before. I thought it would spoil our time together, but in two or three days I have to go away. It will only be for a week or so. I have to return with our guests from Sholstein. There are certain treaties I have to work out with them. When I come back, whatever happens, I want you to come to the Marmorsaal. No more dallying. Unless of course we find our heir, then we shall have a wedding. Instead of living together in respectable sin we shall be together in openly virtuous convention . . . all that every subject in this dukedom could wish.'

I could see that he took the matter more light-heartedly than I did and I was faintly disturbed. Would he regret just a little giving up that supreme power? Did it mean more to him than a regular union with me?

I think he was the sort of man who could have been completely happy as long as I was there. My uneasiness increased. If an outsider had come in and been asked whose interest would be best served by hiding the marriage of Francine and Rudolph and the existence of their child, his answer would surely be Conrad.

I shook myself free of such feelings, and reminded myself that he had been as eager as I was to find the child. He had kept the sheet from the register and said he would put it under lock and key, for it was unsafe for me to carry it around.

That had seemed the right thing to do when he had said it. But I wished I could throw off my doubts.

It was two days before I saw him again and he would be leaving the day after that. He came to the Graf's schloss unexpectedly when neither the Graf nor the Gräfin were at home. Freya was riding with Günther and a party. I think Tatiana was with them.

When I saw Conrad arriving my heart leaped. There was a great fluttering below because there was no one to receive him. I heard him in the hall, putting them all at their ease with that affable manner of his which earned him so much popularity.

'Leave me,' I heard him say. 'I will amuse myself until the Graf returns.' I had started to come down the stairs and he saw me. 'Ah,' he cried, 'here is the English governess. Perhaps she will entertain me for half an hour. It will be good practice for my English.'

I approached him and bowed. He took my hand and kissed it, after the custom.

'Let us go somewhere where we can chat, Fräulein . . .'

'Ayres, my lord Baron,' I said.

'Oh yes, Fräulein Ayres.'

I led the way into the small room which opened from the hall. He shut the door and laughed at me.

'For the life of me I couldn't remember your name. Darling Pippa I know well . . . but Fräulein Ayres . . . she is a stranger to me.'

Then I was in his arms.

'It is unsafe here,' I said.

'Soon we shall be free of such restrictions.'

'Have you found anything about the child?'

He shook his head dolefully. 'There is no doubt that the boy you saw was the son of Katia Schwartz. She was raped in the forest, so we do not know the father's name. The midwife who attended her has been questioned. She attended the birth of the child and looked after Katia afterwards. The boy was healthy, named Rudolph, and several people will testify that he has been living with his mother ever since.'

'But the fact that she knew my sister . . . that I found the troll . . .'

'She knew your sister, yes. That has never been denied. The troll is a common child's toy. Children all over the country have them . . . and I am told it is a custom for them to keep them and even suck their ears and toes. No, it is clear that Katia Schwartz's boy is her own.'

'He must be somewhere else then.'

'If he exists, we'll find him.'

'How?'

'I can have discreet enquiries made. Depend upon it, if that boy exists we shall find him, for without him the sheet from the register is of no consequence.'

'It is to me . . . even if we cannot find the boy for it proves that my sister was telling the truth. It proves that she was not Rudolph's mistress but his wife. And if when she wrote of the marriage she was telling the truth it follows that she was when she wrote of the boy.'

'We'll find him.'

We sprang apart suddenly, for the door had opened. Tatiana was standing there.

'I heard that you were here, Baron,' she said. She was in her riding habit and had clearly just come in. 'You must forgive us. It was most remiss of us not to be here when you called. What are you thinking of us?'

Conrad had stepped forward, taken her hand and kissed it as a short while ago he had kissed mine.

'My dear Countess,' he said, 'I beg of you do not ask *my* pardon. It is I who should ask yours for calling at such an inopportune time.'

'The schloss is always at your disposal,' she said. She was flushed and looking rather pretty. 'It is unforgivable that there should be no one here to receive you.'

'Fräulein Ayres has been doing the honours of the household.' He turned to smile at me and I wondered whether Tatiana would notice the somewhat mischievous twinkle in his eyes.

'It was good of you, Fräulein,' said Tatiana. 'I dare say you have a great deal to do.'

I knew what she meant. Dismissal. I bowed and went to the door.

'I sought the opportunity to improve my English,' said Conrad.

'It is always so useful,' murmured Tatiana.

As I went out I caught a glimpse of Conrad smiling at her.

I felt angry – ridiculously so. I seemed to forget that I was, after all, only the English governess.

I went up to my room. My euphoria of the last days had evaporated. The enquiries had come to nothing and Tatiana had made me realize how invidious was my position here.

It must have been an hour later when I saw him leave. I looked out of my window. Tatiana was with him. They walked together to the stables and seemed to be engaged in very amusing conversation.

I did not have an opportunity of seeing him again before he left for his week's trip. There was obviously no news or he would have found a way of telling me.

There was, however, a letter delivered to me on the day of his departure. It was the usual tender note, telling me that he was longing to be back with me and when he did return I must be with him. The Marmorsaal was waiting and there must be no further delay. He was having enquiries pursued in what he called Our Little Matter, and if anything came to light he would let me know at once.

A day passed and then another. Freya was absent-minded. She was extremely lively at one moment and the next seemed to be plunged in perplexity. I wondered how I could ever tell her about myself and Conrad. The more I tried to reason with myself, the more despicable my situation seemed. How could I say, 'I am in love with your future husband. We are already lovers and plan to continue so, even after your marriage.'

I should never have believed that I could have fallen into such a situation. I wished that there was someone in whom I could confide. I had been to see Daisy now and then and I was always made welcome and enjoyed playing with little Hans.

The day after Conrad left I did confide in her to a certain extent, because I felt that Daisy was the sort of person who had a natural gift for picking up information and for fitting it together to make the picture complete. She liked to hear snippets of gossip about the reigning family and although she was not on the spot, she did know what the people in the streets were saying, and it seemed a fact that all sorts of information seeped out to them and that they sometimes had a clearer picture than those of us who lived more closely to events.

So I found comfort in talking to Daisy. I had not told her about the recovery of the sheet from the register. I felt it was too dangerous even to tell her, but I did mention that I had met Katia, who looked after Francine's grave.

'That was a tragedy what turned out to have a happy ending,' commented Daisy. 'Poor girl . . . raped in the woods . . . and then blamed by that old father of hers. Really, some of these men want teaching a lesson or two.'

'Did you know her, Daisy?'

'I've seen her once or twice at Gisela's. But people did hear about her.'

'One would have thought she might have lost the child after such an experience.'

'Well, the child saved her sanity, they say. When she got him, she changed. It was like it was all worthwhile . . . to get him. She's been a devoted mother ever since.'

Hans showed me his toys, among them a troll similar to the one I had seen with Rudi.

I asked him about it.

'My trolly,' he said.

'Do you take him to bed with you every night?' I asked.

He shook his head. He was a bad troll, he told me. He had to sleep by himself in a dark cupboard. He took his dog to bed . . . if he were good.

Daisy surveyed him with wonder. Her little Hansie! She could understand how Katia felt about her Rudi.

'Little 'uns,' she said, 'I dunno. They plague you a bit, mind you. Into everything, that's our Hansie. But we wouldn't be without him for the world. Hans says so too. Well, after all, Hansie was the reason he made an honest woman of me. Talking of weddings, I reckon before the year's out we'll be having the wedding of the year. Things 'ull change for you then, Miss Pip.'

'Yes, they will. I shall have to have made my decision by then.'

'That's a fact you will. I hope you don't leave us. We've got used to having you around. I like to think of you up at the slosh. Hans says they think such a lot of you there. Well, Miss Freya does. I reckon she'll stay with the Graf and the Gräfin until the wedding. It don't seem right she should be under the same roof with her husband to be . . . even such a roof. Goodness knows there's enough of it! I wonder when that marriage will take place. There's talk, you know. They say Sigmund's got his eyes on someone else.'

I felt myself flushing and I looked down and picked up one of Hansie's toys. 'Oh . . . ?' I said faintly.

'Well, Freya's not much more than a child, is she? What can you expect?'

'Did you . . . say . . . there was talk in the town?'

'Oh yes. Quite a bit of it. Well, he sees a lot of her and human nature being what it is . . .'

'Tell me what they are saying, Daisy?'

'Well, it's the Countess Tatiana. It seems he sees a good deal of her. People have seen them together. Very friendly. If it wasn't for this contract he's got with Countess Freya . . . You see what I mean.'

'Yes,' I said quietly. 'I do.'

'Whether there's anything in it is another matter. I reckon the wedding will go through all right. It has to. Politics and all that. We don't want no trouble about a thing like that. Sigmund would be the first to see it. I reckon whatever he feels about Tatiana it will be Freya he marries. You seem very absorbed in that rabbit of Hansie's.'

'It's pretty,' I said.

'I think it's an ugly little beast. No accounting for tastes, as the saying goes. Hansie likes it though.'

I took my leave soon after that. I felt bewildered and deeply disturbed.

When I returned to the schloss Freya was not there. It occurred to me that during the last few days I had been so concerned with my own affairs that I had thought very little of her. Fräulein Kratz, however, felt the same. I told her that we must remember that Freya was now growing away from the schoolroom and we must expect her to evade her lessons now and then.

'It is certainly since the Baron returned and we moved to this schloss that she has changed.'

'It is all very natural,' I insisted.

My conscience worried me. Perhaps I should attempt to talk to Freya. Sometimes I wondered how much she knew concerning the gossip about Tatiana.

I saw her in the early morning when she greeted me somewhat absent-mindedly.

I said to her: 'Freya, is anything troubling you?'

'Troubling me?' she asked sharply. 'What could be troubling me?'

'I just wondered. You seemed a little . . .'

'A little what?' She spoke sharply again.

'Preoccupied?' I suggested.

'I have a great deal with which to be preoccupied.'

'We have spoken very little English lately.'

'My English is really quite good, I believe.'

'It is certainly better since I came here.'

'Which was, of course, the whole purpose of the enterprise,' she said pertly. Then she put her arms round me. 'Dear Anne,' she went on, 'don't fidget about me. I'm all right. What do you think of Tatiana?'

The question was so unexpected as that lady was very much in my mind that I was startled and showed it.

She laughed at me. 'Oh, I know what you're going to say. What you think of Tatiana is of no consequence. It is not your obligation . . . your duty . . . to have opinions of Tatiana. But that doesn't prevent your having one – and I'll swear you have.'

'I know very little of the lady.'

'You have seen her. You have drawn your conclusions. I think Sigmund likes her. In fact I think he likes her a great deal.'

'What do you mean by that?' I asked, and I hoped she did not notice the tremor in my voice.

'Exactly what I say. I'll tell you this. I am sure he would much rather be affianced to Tatiana than to me.'

'What rubbish!'

'Not rubbish at all. There she is – mature . . . nubile . . . Is that the right word? Beautiful . . . I suppose she is beautiful. Do *you* think she is beautiful?'

'I suppose she would be considered so.'

'Well then. Isn't it perfectly reasonable of him to prefer her?'

'It would be very wrong of him to,' I said with an air of shocked propriety which shamed me and made me feel a despicable hypocrite. 'And,' I added weakly, 'I am sure he would be too . . . too . . .'

'Too what?'

'Too . . . er . . . honourable, I suppose, to consider such a thing.'

'Anne Ayres, there are times when I think you are nothing but a babe in arms. What do you know of men of the world?'

'Perhaps very little.'

'Nothing,' she declared. 'Just nothing. Sigmund is a man . . . and men are like that . . . all of them except priests and those who are too old to bother.'

'Freya, I really think you are allowing your imagination to run away with you.'

'I observe. And I am sure that I am not the one he really wants to marry.'

'So you have settled on Tatiana.'

'I have my reasons,' she said darkly.

I could not help feeling that she did not seem greatly upset about the possibility, and yet at the same time there was a strangeness about her.

Klingen Rock

When I try to remember the events of that night even now they remain jumbled in my mind, but from the first it seemed to me that some hideous pattern was repeating itself in my life.

I think I awoke with a feeling of dread. Something strange was going on. I was aware of it as I came out of what was like a nightmare. Voices, running footsteps . . . strange unfamiliar sounds . . . and yet that horrible realization that I had heard it all before. And there it was. Unmistakable. The acrid smell of burning, the smoke-laden atmosphere.

I was out of my bed in an instant and rushing into the corridor.

Then I knew.

The schloss was on fire.

I was stunned. Freya . . . dead! And in this most horrible manner. The fire had started in her room and there had been no hope of rescuing her, even though the conflagration had been checked.

That night seemed endless. Even after the town's fire brigade had departed and we were huddled together in the hall talking in spasmodic whispers . . . it seemed to go on and on.

What had happened? No one was quite sure – except that the fire had started in the young Countess's room and she must have been overcome by the smoke almost immediately.

There had been repeated attempts to save her, but it was too late, no one had been able to penetrate that blazing room.

I sat shivering with the rest . . . waiting for the morning . . . thinking only of my bright pupil whom I had grown to love.

With the coming of the dawn it was realized that three or four rooms – including that one in which Freya slept – had been gutted, but because of the strong stone structure the rest of the building was undamaged and only lightly scarred round the scene of the fire.

Fräulein Kratz was beside me in the hall. She kept murmuring: 'Who would have believed this . . . She was so young . . .'

I couldn't bear to talk of her. I should never forget her, never forgive myself for having deceived her. Dear, innocent Freya who had never harmed anyone . . . to die like that!

I was desperately unhappy and at the back of my mind was the thought of how strange it was that something similar should have happened in my life before. I was taken vividly back to that occasion when there had been a fire at Greystone Manor and of the accusations which had been thrown at me.

I was shivering because there seemed to be some evil portent here.

I lived through the next day in a nightmarish daze. There was much coming and going at the schloss, and people talked together in whispers. I shut myself away. I could not accept the fact that Freya was dead. I had not realized until this moment how deeply I had cared for her.

In the evening of that day Tatiana came to me. She opened the door of my bedroom and walked in unannounced. She looked haggard, as I was sure I did. For a moment she did not speak, but just stood looking at me.

Then she said: 'So . . . this is your work.'

I stared at her questioningly.

'I know everything,' she said. 'You were too complacent. You thought you were so clever. I knew you were masquerading as someone else. I know you are Philippa Ewell, sister of Francine Ewell, Baron Rudolph's mistress. I suspected you almost as soon as I saw you. I had seen you before. You broke into the Grange, remember?'

'I came to look round. I did not break in.'

'This is no time to consider the niceties of words. You are an adventuress . . . like your sister. I have seen your papers.'

'So it was you . . .'

'I owed it to the Countess to find out what sort of woman you are.' Her voice faltered. 'That dear innocent child . . . now . . . murdered.'

'Murdered!' I cried.

'Do give me credit for some intelligence, Fräulein Ewell. I know who you are. I know a great deal about you. I know you tried the same trick on your grandfather. We have friends in all parts of the world watching our interests. Your sister had attempted to make a place for herself here, so we were watchful of her connections. You thought the trick worked with your grandfather so you tried it again here.'

'I don't . . .'

'You are going to say you don't understand. But you do understand – perfectly. That poor old man died, didn't he? So why not the young girl? They were both in your way. You have the strongest possible motive now – as you had then – but it is not easy to get away with murder the second time . . . even for one as clever as you think you are.'

'You are talking nonsense . . . wild nonsense.'

'I do not think so, and nor will others. It fits perfectly. You are looking for position and wealth as your sister did. She ended up dead in a hunting lodge. Where do you think you will end up, Fräulein Ewell?'

'I have no intention of being spoken to in this manner,' I said. 'I am not employed by you. My services, alas, are no longer required. I shall immediately resign from the household.'

'Murderesses must pay the penalty,' she replied.

'What is your accusation?'

'That you deliberately murdered Countess Freya in a manner which you had tried out before and which worked successfully then in the case of your grandfather. You are not going to deny that that gentleman died in a burning room?'

'I am not denying it, but it has nothing to do with this.'

'Allow me to contradict you. It has everything to do with this. Your grandfather displeased you. He was going to turn you out . . . so that was the end of him, and I believe you came very nicely out of the matter.'

'This is monstrous. My money did not come from my grandfather but from my grandmother. I had nothing to do with his death.'

'I have my friends there. I know exactly what happened. He threatened to turn you out and that very night he died . . . mysteriously. Oh, I know nothing was proved against you, but suspicion was strong, wasn't it? He was in a burning room which did not burn quite long enough to destroy the evidence. You were not going to make that mistake twice. You made sure that the evidence in the case of our poor Countess was completely destroyed.'

'You are talking wild nonsense. I loved the Countess. She and I were the best of friends.'

'Do you think I don't know how much you wanted to get rid of her? You are an ambitious woman, Fräulein. You thought if she were not there, if Baron Sigmund were free from his contract with her, you would reign as Grand Duchess of Bruxenstein.'

I stared at her aghast and she laughed bitterly.

'I know of those meetings,' she went on. 'I know of that tender little romance . . .'

I was afraid now. I could see it all fitting neatly together. I was reminded of the horror of those weeks at Greystone Manor when I had been under suspicion. I looked into Tatiana's malicious face and I felt the net closing round me.

It was true that if Freya were no more I had a chance of

marrying Conrad. While she lived I had none. But how monstrous that Tatiana could make such a suggestion, and yet when I looked at the evidence against me I saw that I was in acute peril.

Conrad would believe in me, I was sure. I must see him. He would surely come now that this terrible thing had happened to Freya.

I could not think clearly. I could only try to fight off this terrible numbness, this sense of impending doom which had possessed me.

'You have been clever up to a point,' Tatiana was saying. 'But not clever enough. You were too trusting in some quarters. You came here because your sister came. You thought you would follow in her footsteps but more successfully. You were going to try to prove that she was actually married to Baron Rudolph. I suppose you thought that would give you some standing.'

'She *was* married to Rudolph,' I said.

She snapped her fingers at me. 'You fool!' she cried. 'Whom do you think wanted Rudolph out of the way if it was not Sigmund and his friends? Sigmund has been too clever for you. He has told me of your cloying sentiment. I know of your affair with him, of course. He found it so amusing and he had to know exactly what you were doing. "So easy," he said, "to lead the Fräulein to great expectations and to discover what she was doing at the same time. She is shrewd enough . . . but she has her weaknesses and I found them." '

'I don't believe you.'

'No. That was your weakness. Easily gullible. But we are not here to talk about your amorous adventure with Sigmund. That is of no importance to him or to this case. You thought he would marry you when Freya was disposed of. Unfortunately for you, Sigmund was not what you thought . . . and in any case we knew too much about you. You cannot play the same trick twice.'

'This is a nightmare.'

'Think what it must have been like for poor Countess Freya.'

I covered my face with my hands. The loss of my dear little friend, the knowledge that I was discovered to be Francine's sister, the hints about Conrad which I did not believe, the terrible danger in which I stood – it was all becoming unbearable.

'You are under arrest,' said Tatiana. 'Accused of the murder of Countess Freya.'

'I want to see – '

'Yes?' she mocked. 'Whom do you want to see? Baron Sigmund is not here. Nor would he wish to see you if he were. Is there anyone else you would like to see . . . if you were permitted to do so?'

I thought of Hans, but I did not want to implicate him. The Graf was his employer. I thought of Daisy. But she was too close to Hans. Who else was there?

She was smiling at me contemptuously. 'Do not search your mind,' she said. 'Save yourself the trouble, for it would not be permitted. Put a few things together. I am removing you from here for your own safety. When it is generally known that the Countess Freya has been murdered and by whom and for what reason, the people will not leave you to the justice of the land. They will take the law into their own hands. It could be that Kollenitz will demand that you be delivered to them. I would not be in your shoes then, Fräulein Ewell.'

I cried out: 'I am innocent of what you accuse me, I loved her, I tell you. I would not have harmed her for anything on earth.'

'Get a few things together. My parents agree that we should get you away to a place of safety until you stand trial. Hurry. There is little time.'

She went to the door and turned to look back at me maliciously.

'Be ready in ten minutes,' she said.

The door shut and I sank back into a chair. This was indeed a nightmare. I must be dreaming. Not only was Freya dead, but I was accused of her murder.

Within half an hour I was riding out of the town with a company of guards. People stood about in little groups near the schloss, talking in whispers. There was a hushed atmosphere in the streets. I could smell the smoke in the air. I looked back at the schloss. The scarred wall stood out strongly in the sunlight.

We left the town behind us and came to the forest. We passed near the Marmorsaal and went on. We crossed the river and started to climb. It was about mid-morning when we came to the Klingen Rock. I remembered it from one of my rides with Freya, when she had told me the story of the Rock and the small schloss which stood near the mountain top.

Prisoners had been kept here in the old days and when they were condemned to death they were often given the choice of throwing themselves down from the Rock into the gorge below instead of facing execution.

I think I must have been in a state of shock because I could not quite grasp what was happening to me. Yesterday I had been free to ride through the forest, to go to my lover. Now, here I was, a prisoner . . . falsely accused of murdering one I had loved.

I had lost my dear Freya – a tragedy in any circumstances but in this way . . . I could not grasp the magnitude of what had happened. The loss of a dear one, the terrible suspicion that had come to me and my vulnerability to the dangers which surrounded me . . .

We were climbing a rough road cut into the mountainside and at length came to a gate, which was opened by a rough-looking man who regarded me steadily from under shaggy brows.

'So this is the prisoner,' he said. And then to me: 'Get down then. We've not got all night.'

I dismounted and he took my horse from me, examining it, I noticed, with a keen eye. A woman appeared.

'Here she is, Marta,' he said.

The woman took my arm roughly and peered into my face. I was dismayed by her hard, even cruel expression.

'Zigeuner!' she called, and a cowed-looking boy in ragged garments came running out.

'Take her up,' said the woman. 'Show her where she's lodged.'

I followed the boy into the stone-floored hall and he pointed to a spiral staircase at one end of it. The stone steps were steep and the banister was a rough rope.

'This way,' he said.

'Thank you,' I answered and he looked surprised.

We went up for a long way, round and round until we reached the top of a tower. He threw open the door and I saw a small room which contained a pallet bed, a jug and basin on a rickety table, and a stool.

He looked at me helplessly.

'Is this . . . all I have?' I asked.

He nodded. He had taken the key out of the door on the inside. 'I've got to lock you in,' he said with a wan smile. 'Sorry.'

'It's not your fault. Do you work here?'

He nodded again.

'What's your name?'

'They call me Zig because I'm from the gipsies. I was lost and came here. It was more than a year ago. I've been here ever since.'

'It's not very pleasant, is it?'

'There's something to eat.'

'Will they keep me here?' I asked.

'They'll try to persuade you.'

'To what?'

He nodded towards the window. 'Mustn't stay,' he said. 'They'll dock me supper.' He went out, shutting the door, and I heard him turn the heavy key in the lock.

What had he meant when he had said they would try to persuade me? I went to the window and looked out. I could see the overhanging Rock and the drop down to the gorge.

I sat down on the bed. I was still too shocked and bewildered to think clearly. This was becoming more and more like a fantastic nightmare. I was accused and condemned without a chance to speak for myself. I felt lost and desperately lonely.

Then from somewhere at the back of my mind came the thought: Conrad will come for me. He will discover what has happened and come to save me.

The boy brought up some stew for me. I could not eat it. He looked at me pityingly as I shook my head and turned away from it.

'Better eat,' he said.

'I don't want it,' I said. 'Do you have many people here like me?'

He shook his head.

'What have you done, Fräulein?' he asked.

'I have done nothing to warrant this treatment.'

He looked at me closely and whispered: 'Did you offend in high places, Fräulein? That's what they come here for.'

He left the plate with me and the sight of the congealing fat on the top of the stew sickened me. I turned away and looked out of the window. Mountains . . . pines everywhere . . . the great craggy Rock, and below . . . far below . . . the ravine.

This is madness, I thought. This is a bad dream. It was the sort of thing that happened when one strayed from the conventional path. Was that why people laid down rigid rules for society? Who would have believed that I, Philippa Ewell, rather quiet, not particularly attractive, could become the mistress of a person of great importance in a faraway country, and then be accused of murder and brought to this mountain castle to await trial . . . execution for murder.

What had happened at Greystone Manor when I had been suspected of causing the death of my grandfather was not to be compared with this.

I had strayed from the narrow conventional path. I might have married Cousin Arthur and then I could never have been in the position in which I now found myself. But I should never have known the ecstasy I had experienced with Conrad. I had chosen to live dangerously and now the moment had come to pay for it. Once again I thought of that old Spanish proverb. 'Take what you want,' says God. 'Take it . . . and pay for it.'

Both Francine and I had taken. Francine had paid with her life. Was I to do the same?

The day wore on. Darkness came. The boy arrived with a candle in an iron stick. When it was lighted it threw eerie shadows round the room which looked more and more like a cell. He threw a blanket on the bed. 'It gets cold at night,' he said. 'We're right up in the mountains and the thick stone walls keep out the warmth of the sun in the daytime. Don't say I gave you that. Say it was here . . . if they ask.'

'Zig,' I said, 'tell me who is here?'

'The old 'uns,' he said. 'And the Big 'Un and 'er and me.'

'The old ones are the man and woman I saw.'

'They're the keepers of the Klingen Schloss. Then there's the Big 'Un, he's a giant and he'll be there if he's wanted. Not for you, I reckon you're just a woman and then there's 'er and she's his wife.'

'So there are four of them.'

'And me – Zig. I do the work and get my food for it.'

'And who has been here before?'

'Some others.'

'What happened to them?'

His eyes strayed to the window.

'Do you mean they were thrown from the Rock?'

'It's what they're brought here for.'

'Is that what they intend to do with me?'

'Wouldn't have brought you here . . . else.'

'Who is they? Whom do you work for? Whom do *they* work for?'

'People in high places.'

'I see. It's a sort of politics.'

'They bring them here so they can have the choice. Taking the leap or facing what they have to face. It's when they like to keep it secret and they don't want there to be a big trial and all that. It's when they want to keep things dark.'

'What chance have I of getting away?'

He shook his head. 'There's the Big 'Un. If you tried he'd throw you over right away . . . and nobody would hear of you no more.'

'Zig, I am innocent of what they accuse me.'

'That don't make no difference sometimes,' he said gloomily, picking up the plate of uneaten food and going out. I heard him put it down and lock the door behind him.

That night in the Klingen Schloss seemed an eternity. Lying on the hard pallet, I tried to bring some order into the thoughts which chased each other round in my mind.

Was it possible to get away from here? What I wanted most was to explain to Conrad. Would he believe me guilty? That was something I could not bear. It seemed the worst aspect of the whole terrible business. He knew how very much I wanted to marry him and that I could not happily accept the situation he was offering me and that dear, innocent Freya stood in the way.

Could he really believe that I would kill her?

I could imagine how lucidly Tatiana would put her case to him. It fitted neatly enough. 'She did it before,' I could hear her telling him. 'She murdered her own grandfather. She got away with that and she thought she would get away with this Thank God I discovered her foul treachery. I sent her to

Klingen. I thought it would save so much trouble if she took the leap. And she did, of course, when she realized there was no other way out.'

But I would not take the leap. I would find some means of escape. I should be thinking of that now. No matter how impossible it seemed, there must be a way. I must get back to Conrad.

But what if . . . I must fight off these doubts. They were more than I could endure. But they would persist. There had been rumours concerning him and Tatiana. What if they were true? Tatiana said he had amused himself at my expense. I remembered how light-hearted he had been, how he had tried to persuade me to go to the Marmorsaal. How much did I know Conrad? I knew that he was shaped like the gods and heroes of his northern land; I knew that the looks of an ancient hero were combined with the suave and charming manners of a modern prince. He was the sort of man who would be any woman's ideal lover. Was he too attractive? Was he such a delightful lover because he was such a practised one?

I was wasting time with these suppositions. I should be thinking of a plan of escape. If I could get away from here, take the horse which had brought me, ride away . . . Where to? To Daisy? Ask her to hide me? To Gisela? To Katia? I dared not involve any of them. I was in the hands of my enemies and held on the serious charge of murder.

And the evidence against me could be made to appear irrefutable. I had been in the schloss when the fire started; I had been conducting a love-affair with Freya's affianced husband and it was feasible to think that but for her I might marry him and in time become the Grand Duchess. What a maze of intrigue I was caught up in and I could not find my way out of it. I had even come out here with a false name. I should be labelled *intrigante* and judged guilty.

Oh Freya, dear sweet child, how could anyone think that I could harm you! And Conrad . . . where are you? He would surely have heard what had happened by now. He would be the first to hear of Freya's death. He would come . . . He would surely come.

I could not forget Tatiana's words. Could it possibly be that *she* was the one he wanted? Had he really found the episode with me 'amusing'?

Another thought struck me. He knew why I had come, that I was determined to prove Francine's marriage and that there was a child. If there was he would no longer be heir to the kingdom. He had said that was what he had wanted. But could it be true?

So the thoughts went round and round in my head during that long and terrifying night and with the streak of dawn in the sky I was at the window looking at the Klingen Rock.

It was afternoon of the second day. The minutes seemed like hours. I was faint with lack of food, I suppose, for I had not eaten since the night of the fire. I was so exhausted that I even dozed for a moment.

No one came to me but the boy Zig. His presence did offer some small comfort because he was clearly sorry for me. He said the descent was swift and you'd be dead before you reached the jagged rocks at the foot of the ravine.

I went back over the past. I could smell the sea and the beautiful flowers on the island. I could clearly remember just how the bougainvillaea grew about the studio. I could see Francine assuring the customers of my father's genius, and my mother's bedside when we had all known such sorrow; I could hear my father's voice: 'It's Pippa's song. "God's in his Heaven, all's right with the world."'

So I brooded, waiting, living, it seemed, in a world of unreality, longing for that time to pass and yet fearing that the end of my life was very close.

Zig came in with another plate of stew and I turned from it shuddering. 'Ought to keep your strength up,' he said.

I believed that when he was outside the door he ate it

himself. Poor Zig, I suspected they gave him very little to eat.

Who were these people? Servants of the Graf? Did he always send his enemies to them for disposal?

It was so quiet in the mountains that one heard sounds from a long way off. That was why I was aware of the approach of riders before I saw them.

I was at the window. They were coming to the schloss. It was a party of six. Conrad, I thought. But no! He was not among them. I could not have failed to recognize him. He would have stood out wherever he was. Now they were close I could see that it was Tatiana who rode at their head and her companions looked like schloss guards.

I knew then that my doom had come upon me, for I was certain that Tatiana was determined to destroy me. She had judged me guilty and was going to make me pay the price.

I watched their approach. Their horses were taken and they entered the schloss. I waited, tense, knowing that before long Tatiana would come to me.

I was right. I heard the key turn in the lock and she was standing before me.

'I hope you found your quarters comfortable,' she said with a twist of her lips.

'You don't need an answer to that, surely,' I replied.

I felt reckless. I was going to die, but I would try to do it bravely.

'We have pieced the evidence together,' she said, 'and have found you guilty.'

'How could you without me there to defend myself?'

'There was no need for you to be there. The facts are evident. You had been meeting the Baron at the inn. He confirms this. You had made it clear that you hoped to marry him and that this would have been possible but for his contract with Freya. There could not be a stronger motive. And you tried it before with your grandfather. People are in your way and you eliminate them. Death is the penalty for murder.'

'Everyone should have a fair trial. That is the law.'

'Whose law? The law of your country perhaps. You are not there now. When you live in a country you obey that country's laws. You have been judged guilty and the sentence is death. Now, because of the people concerned this is an unusual case and it would be dangerous for you to return to be tried. It would create a situation of great uneasiness, possible war between Freya's country and mine. Freya was important and Kollenitz will want revenge for her death. They will want her murderess to be delivered to them. So I am offering you the choice.'

'You are offering me the Klingen Rock,' I said.

She nodded. 'It will save a great deal of trouble . . . perhaps war. You will throw yourself down and we will send your remains to Kollenitz. They will be satisfied to know that their Countess's murderess is dead. Justice will have been seen to have been carried out. We shall leave in ten minutes for the Rock and you will do what has to be done.'

'I shall not do it,' I said.

She smiled. 'You will be persuaded to change your mind.'

'I know what is meant by that. Is it on your orders?'

'Mine and others.'

'And who are the others?'

'The Grand Duke, the Baron Sigmund, my parents. We are all agreed that it is the best way and the most humane for you . . . though murderesses do not deserve to be let off so lightly, perhaps.'

'I don't believe this. I believe it is your judgement and yours alone.' She raised her eyebrows questioningly and I went on: 'Because you want me out of the way as you wanted Freya . . .'

'I should prepare yourself. It will not be long now.'

Then she had gone.

I stood at the window. Death, I thought. The quick plunge and then . . . darkness. And Conrad? If I could see him once . . if I could only hear him say that he had truly loved me . . that he had no part in this . . .

But I should never see him again. I should never really *know* . . .

They were at the door. It was the Big One this time. There was a woman with him. They had pale shut-in faces displaying no emotion, just cold, aloof, as though death was commonplace in their lives. Perhaps it was. I wondered how many they had thrown from the Klingen Rock.

I put on my cloak and the man went first down the stairs; I followed and the woman came after. In the hall the company was assembled. This was my funeral. How many people are present at their own funerals? And all those who were present were my enemies – except the boy Zig who stood there with his mouth slightly open and real compassion in his eyes.

Out into the cool mountain air. It was breathtaking after the confinement of my prison. I noticed the little white edelweiss and the sheen on the tiny rivulets which fell down the mountainside. There was an intensity about everything, a clarity. Did I see it more clearly because I was about to leave it?

Tatiana's eyes were glittering. She hated me. She was longing for the moment when I should go over the edge of the Rock . . . down to oblivion . . . out of her life forever.

We rode for a short way, then we left the horses and took the walk to the top of the ridge. The grass grew sparsely up here and our footsteps crunched on the brown earth.

Then suddenly silhouetted against the sky, right at the top of the ridge at that spot where I should have to stand to take my leap, stood a figure. It did not move. It remained stationary, facing us as we came along.

I thought: I am having hallucinations. Is this what happens when one approaches death? Then I heard the cry break from me: 'Freya!'

The figure did not move. It just stood there. It was unreal. It had grown out of my fevered imagination. Freya was dead. I was imagining I saw her there.

I turned to Tatiana. She was staring ahead, her face white, her body shivering with fear.

Then suddenly the apparition – if apparition it was – started to move towards us.

Tatiana started to cry out: 'No . . . no . . . You're dead.'

Then she started to run and I saw her struggling in the arms of the Big One.

Freya was saying: 'Anne . . . Anne . . . She was going to have you thrown over. Anne, what's the matter? Do *you* think I'm a ghost?'

Then she put her arms round me and held me to her. Shuddering sobs were shaking my body. I felt unable to speak, unable to control my feelings, unable to think of anything but that she was here . . . in some form . . . and that she had saved my life.

'Now, Anne,' she said, 'calm yourself. I'm not a ghost. I was only playing at being one. If you'll stop shaking I'll tell you what all this means.'

She gave a shout and several horsemen came out from behind a ridge of boulders where they had remained hidden, and among them was Günther.

He said to the Big One: 'Take my sister back to the schloss. We will follow.'

'She looks terrible,' said Freya. 'Who wouldn't? I knew that was what Tatiana would do. Have Anne thrown over the Rock. But let's get her back now.'

She would tell me nothing until we had returned to the schloss. Then she took me into the small room which led from the hall and made me sit in one of the chairs while she took a stool and sat at my feet. We were alone as she had insisted we should be.

'I didn't want anyone else here just at first,' she said. 'I wanted to tell you . . . all by ourselves. Günther will come in when I call him.'

'Oh Freya,' I cried. 'I can't think of anything but that you are here – alive – when we thought . . .'

'Now you mustn't get too emotional. Where is my nice calm English governess? Nobody was going to make me marry someone I didn't want to.'

'You mean Sigmund?'

'I didn't want Sigmund any more than he wanted me. Why should we be forced into marriage? It's ridiculous. I refused to accept it. So did Günther. You see, Günther and I decided that *we* were going to get married. They would never have allowed it, so the only way to do it was to marry and then say, "It's done!" Nobody could stop it then . . . pre-contract or not. We're married and have consummated the marriage, so there! Who knows? I might already be *enceinte.* I should think it very likely. So how could I marry someone else?'

'Oh Freya . . . Freya . . . you go too fast.'

'Well, we decided to run away. I am sure Providence was on our side that night. What I did was make up a roll of clothes and put them in the bed before I left. I arranged the bedclothes so that it looked as though the Countess Freya was sleeping there. That was just in case anyone looked in and raised the alarm before we had a chance to get far enough away. Tatiana planned to come in, hit me unconscious, and then start the fire. I knew it as soon as I came back and heard what had happened . . . because she came in before I had gone. I was sitting in my window with my dressing-gown over my outdoor clothes waiting for the moment to slip out when my door opened stealthily. I kept behind the curtains so I was able to hide to a certain extent and I saw her creep to my bedside. She was holding a fire-iron in her hand.

'I was sitting in the dark because I didn't want to attract attention . . . sitting in the window waiting for Günther to give the call from below that the coast was clear. I called out, "What do you want, Tatiana?" She was terribly startled. She said she thought she had heard me call out. I told her I had not and asked what she had in her hand. She said, "Oh, I just didn't wait to put it down. I was dealing with the fire in my room when I thought I heard you call . . ." Of course it was all very odd but I had other things on my mind and I forgot about it. Soon Günther and I were on our way. We went to the priest and got married, and being married is rather wonderful, Anne dear, when you are married to the Right One.'

'Oh Freya . . . dearest Freya . . .'

'No tears. I'm here. You're safe. This ridiculous case against you is over. You can't accuse someone of murder when there was no murder, can you? But Tatiana tried to kill me and would have done so if I hadn't run away that night to get married. You see how favoured I am. I am so happy, Anne. Günther is the most wonderful husband . . . far, far better than Sigmund would ever have been. Who wants to be the old Grand Duchess? I'd rather be Günther's wife . . . and think of the dear little babies we'll have . . . looking just like him . . . and some like me perhaps . . . for I am not bad-looking, am I? Günther thinks I'm beautiful.'

'Oh Freya, stop,' I cried. 'Talk seriously. Did Sigmund come?'

'They were trying to reach him to tell him what has happened. Of course, when I appeared with Günther everything was thrown into confusion. They had all decided that you were the murderess and I learned that you had been taken away for your safety. You can imagine the consternation when I arrived. You can't have a murder without a victim. The Graf and Gräfin were horrified. You know why, don't you? They thought if I were out of the way Tatiana would get Sigmund. Then I appear. There has been no murder . . . and someone has been hustled away for her own safety. My dear Anne, who wouldn't harm a hair of my head, and only chastises me by making me learn those horrible old English words. Why the English couldn't have made German their language I could never understand. It's so much easier, so much more reasonable.'

'Freya, Freya, *please* . . .'

'I know. I run on. It's because I'm happy. I've got Günther

and that's wonderful. And I saved you. Oh, Anne, I was terrified. I thought I would be too late. I knew she was the one. I understood why. You see, I had caught her before I went off. I knew she had come back. She had hit that bundle of clothes in the darkness . . . She wouldn't bring a light, would she? And when she thought I was unconscious she set fire to the bed. Then she blamed you for it. I heard you'd gone to Klingen and I knew then what she was going to do. So I pretended to be a ghost. She's very superstitious and I knew that would frighten her out of her wits. Well, it would, wouldn't it, to see the ghost of someone you thought you'd murdered. I did rather well, I think. And now she's confessed her guilt . . . or she will . . . and you and I will be together . . .'

I could not speak. I was so overcome with emotion.

We had been in the schloss less than an hour when Conrad arrived. He came galloping in at the greatest speed and when I was swept up in his arms I thought I should die of happiness. The transition from utter despair to the heights of bliss was too sudden. And when he held me at arm's length and looked at me as though he must take in every detail of my face to make sure I was really there, I wondered how I could ever have doubted him.

Freya regarded us with satisfaction.

'All is well,' she said. 'What a wonderful ending! Now I know what they mean when they say "And they all lived happily ever after." And to think that it is all due to *my* cleverness. Though I do admit Günther had a hand in it. Günther!' she called.

And there were the four of us, smiling, clinging together.

It was a wonderful reunion. I knew there would be difficulties ahead – and none knew that more than Conrad – but for the moment we gave ourselves up to the complete joy of being together, to a happiness which was the greater because of the fearful ordeal through which we had passed.

Conrad told me he had been terrified when he arrived at the Grand Schloss and heard that Freya was dead and I was accused of her murder and had been taken to Klingen.

He then learned that Freya had married Günther. He had raced to the Rock and until he had actually seen me, he had been in terror that he might arrive too late.

And he would have done, but for Freya.

'Oh Freya,' he cried, 'how can I ever be grateful enough!'

Freya beamed on us, looking like the beneficent goddess she had so delighted in imagining herself to be.

'I don't know why I should be so good to you when you preferred someone else,' she said severely.

'As for me,' he retorted, 'you jilted me. You just ran off and left me.'

'Nothing to what you did to me. Falling in love with my English governess. Never mind. I'll forgive you because I happen to like her quite a lot myself. And now I shall have to call her Philippa, which is very strange. I don't know how I shall manage that.'

Dear Freya! She could not look beyond the moment, and as it was a very happy moment, perhaps she was wise not to.

Later Conrad said to me: 'We must imitate Freya. We'll get a priest to marry us.'

'You are still the Grand Duke's heir,' I reminded him.

'I am no longer affianced to Freya. There will have to be dispensations and so on, but she has broken that contract irrevocably. I shall now marry to please myself.'

'It may be the people will not like it.'

'They must accept it or banish me.'

'You are risking a great deal.'

'I risk unhappiness for the rest of my life if I don't seize my opportunities.'

We rode to the Marmorsaal with Freya and Günther and there we found a priest who married us.

'The deed is done,' said Conrad with a laugh. 'There can be no turning back now.'

'I hope you will never regret it.'

Günther and Freya rode back to the town with us, and we were able to slip quietly into the Grand Schloss. There I was presented to the Grand Duke and Conrad told him that we were married. Freya and Günther were present and the four of us stood before the old man.

He gave us his blessing although it was clear that he found the situation very disquieting. It was a most unorthodox way in which to behave.

He said with a smile, as he looked at Conrad with real affection: 'I can see I shall have to live a little longer until they've all grown accustomed to the idea.'

He looked at me gravely: 'I know,' he said, 'that you have been wrongfully accused and I know there has been a long-standing friendship between you and the Baron. You have come into a way of life which will have many difficulties. I hope your affection for your husband will carry you through them.'

I kissed his hand and thanked him. I thought he was gracious and charming.

Later I talked with Conrad.

He said that his uncle understood the situation because he had explained it to him. Tatiana's ambition had been to be Grand Duchess in due course, and she had sought to achieve this ambition through marriage. Two people stood in her way: Freya and myself. So therefore she planned to be rid of us both at the same time. What had happened in England had been known to her family because they had been at the centre of that faction which had wanted to get rid of Rudolph and set up Sigmund in his place.

'There are always such intrigues going on in these small states and principalities,' said Conrad. 'I have always thought it would be a good thing if we could be joined up as one great country . . . a great empire. We should be more prosperous, a world power. As it is, we fight among ourselves. There are secret societies and continual intrigues. No one can accuse a single person of Rudolph's murder. It would doubtless have been carried out by a hired assassin.'

'Perhaps Katia's brother.'

'Very likely. He was close by and it would have been reasonable to choose him. But who can say? And in any case he could not be accused of murder for he would be acting on instructions as a soldier does. Your sister died solely because she happened to be there. There was no intrigue against her . . . unless there was a child, of course, whom she might bring forward. That's how it would have happened. It could happen to us, you know. Pippa, have you thought of the sort of life you are marrying into? You live dangerously here. It is a long way from your English village where the main cause for concern is the death watch beetle in the church roof and who will be elected to the parish council.'

'I know exactly what I am doing,' I said, 'and so did Francine. I wouldn't change it. It is what I want.'

He said: 'There is another thing. The people may not like our marriage. Kollenitz can't object because it was Freya who broke the contract. But the people here . . .'

'They would have preferred you to marry Tatiana.'

'Not now . . . because Tatiana will not come out of her convent, I imagine. She will be nursed back to health there, for they will say that she needs it. And very likely she will take the veil. It is what happens in such cases. She was always unbalanced. Now I believe her reason has deserted her. It may come back . . . and then she will not wish for any other but the convent life. And for us . . . we have to wait, Pippa. We shall have another marriage ceremony . . . one with celebrations in the streets. I'm sorry, but you did marry me, remember. You have to face them. I think they'll like you . . . in time. How can they help it? They might even think it is romantic . . . charming. They are like that, you know. Freya has been forgiven. There were flowers and cheers for her when she rode through the streets. They have always liked Freya.'

'I can well understand that,' I said. 'Freya is charming and young and fresh and natural . . .'

'They like Günther too. The fact is they like romance and the story of her running away with the one she loved has caught their imagination . . . as our story must do.'

'Conrad,' I said earnestly, 'you *don't* wish that you could give it up, do you? It means a great deal to you, this country . . .'

I saw the dreamy, faraway look in his eyes.

He had been brought up here. He belonged here. I had to learn to accept that.

❧ 'God's in his Heaven'

It was two months later when our ceremonial wedding took place, and I was almost certain at the time that I was going to have a child. The thought gave me confidence. My life was here and the child I carried would be heir to the dukedom.

Conrad looked splendid. I was dressed in a white gown which was covered in pearls. I had never worn anything so grand. Freya assured me that I looked magnificent, every bit the future Grand Duchess. The Grand Duke's presence at the wedding gave it the seal of official approval, and to my astonishment I came through the ordeal well enough.

I rode through the streets afterwards in the carriage with the ducal arms emblazoned on it. I stood on the schloss balcony with Conrad on one side of me and the Grand Duke on the other, while the people cheered us.

Conrad was delighted. I had come through with honours; and that night I told him about the child.

My child was due in six months and I was living, as they said, quietly, at the Marmorsaal in the forest. I would take rides out in a small carriage which had been selected for my use and because it was small and insignificant I could go out unceremoniously.

I had brought the young boy Zig into the household. I could not forget his kindness to me when I most needed it. His gratitude was moving and I knew I had a faithful servant for life.

I often visited Daisy who was delighted with the way

everything had turned out, and whenever I visited her she would be overcome with awe for at least five minutes before she forgot my new status and I became just Miss Pip to her.

And then . . . it happened suddenly and when I had no longer hoped that it ever could.

Gisela was visiting Daisy when I called unexpectedly. Daisy was in her usual temporary respectful flutter when she saw who it was and ushered me into her little sitting-room where Gisela's twins, Carl and Gretchen, were playing with Hansie.

'Now then . . . where can you sit yourself . . .' Daisy was fluttering round pink-cheeked and flustered; and Gisela was almost as bad.

'Oh, for Heaven's sake, Daisy,' I said, 'stop it. I'm just the same.'

Daisy winked at Gisela. 'Now listen to her, and her the Grand-Duchess-to-be. And how are you today, my lady? How's the little 'un?'

'Exceptionally lively, Daisy.'

'That's a good sign.'

'Good but uncomfortable. And how is Hansie?'

'Hansie's a good boy . . . sometimes.'

'And the twins?'

They stood up and regarded me solemnly and not without suspicion, for as children will they had caught the uneasy respect which their elders were feeling towards me.

'You know me,' I said to Carl.

He nodded.

'So show me your new toys.'

Gretchen picked up a furry lamb from the floor and held it out to me.

'He's very nice,' I said. 'What's his name?'

'Franz,' said Gretchen.

'He's a lovely lamb.'

The children nodded

'They play well together – the twins and Hansie,' said Daisy. 'It's nice for Gisela to come up here and for me to go visiting her. It makes company.'

I agreed that it was nice and it did.

'You wait till yours arrives,' went on Daisy.

'We shall have all the bells ringing then,' added Gisela.

'I've got a bell,' Gretchen announced.

'I've got a fox . . . a little fox,' added Carl.

'And what's his name?'

'*Fuchs*,' said Gretchen.

Carl sidled up to me. 'I call him Cubby,' he said confidentially.

Everything seemed to stand still suddenly. He had spoken the word with a perfect English accent. I was immediately back in the past reading the letter I had had from Francine and which I could remember word for word because I had read it so many times.

'What do you call him?' I asked, and my voice seemed to be shrill with my sudden excitement.

'Cubby!' he cried. 'Cubby, Cubby.'

'Why?' I asked.

'It's what my mummy used to call me,' he said. 'Long long ago . . . when I had a different mummy . . .'

There was silence in the room. Gisela had turned very pale. Carl had picked up his fox and was saying: 'Cubby . . . There's a good Cubby.'

I heard myself say: 'This is the child then. Carl is the child.'

She did not deny it. She stood staring at me, her eyes wide and frightened in her pale face.

Gisela realized that there was nothing to be done but tell the whole story. She assured me that she had never done so before, because Francine had made her swear that she never would until it was safe to do so.

Francine had lived a rather lonely life in the hunting lodge waiting for Rudolph's visits. She had formed friendships with

Gisela and Katia and through Katia she had gleaned some inkling of the intrigues which were building up. She must have been aware that Rudolph's life was in danger and when she discovered she was to have a child her fears had been doubled. Living obscurely as she was obliged to do, it was not impossible to keep her pregnancy a secret, but she had faithful friends in the two women, a priest and a midwife, all of whom lived not far from the hunting lodge. She and Rudolph determined to conceal the fact that she was to give birth to the heir to the dukedom until such a time as it would be safe to reveal it, and with the help of these friends she was able to do so.

The Grand Duke had been in ignorance of Rudolph's marriage, for he had been afraid to confess to his father in view of the political situation and the need for the help of Kollenitz in dealing with it. There would have been trouble on more than one front if it had been known that Rudolph had spurned the alliance with Freya.

Thus the great wall of secrecy had been built up. Rudolph had been a charming man, but he was weak and as far as I could gather had always taken the line of least resistance to any situation. So he had kept his marriage and the birth of his child secret.

Once the child was born and christened Rudolph the task was easier. At this time Gisela was giving birth to Gretchen and it seemed a great stroke of ingenuity to credit her with twins.

Thus Francine had her own child close to her. She could see him every day; and the two children, Gretchen and the little boy, whom they called Carl for safety, were with her constantly.

Francine had hoped that Rudolph would confess to his father, but he put off doing so and finally, when the child was about a year old, there came that night when Rudolph and Francine were murdered in their bed.

Now Gisela went in great fear. She loved her adopted child

and she knew that if it were realized who he really was, his life would be in great danger. Moreover, she had sworn to Francine that she would not betray his true identity until she was sure he would be accepted for who he was.

It was strange that the child himself had made the revelation.

The Grand Duke listened gravely to the story. He then put it in secret to his ministers.

The verdict was unanimous. The law of heredity must prevail. The child in the lodge cottage was heir to the duchy and must be educated and brought up with a realization of the duties which would one day be his.

It was decided that there should be no covering up. The whole story should be known. The marriage of Rudolph and Francine could be proved. There was the sheet from the church register and the priest who had married them could be found.

The midwife and everyone who had played even the smallest part in the conspiracy of silence should be brought forward and the truth established.

It was a wild, violent and romantic story – but such stories were not unusual. The truth was plain and the people should know it.

Those days stand out in my memory as some of the strangest in my life. I can remember riding through the streets with Conrad in the ducal carriage with the Grand Duke and little Carl - now Rudolph.

The boy took everything for granted, as though it were the most natural thing in the world for little boys who had been brought up in lodge cottages to ride in a carriage while the people cheered him.

There was one thing that did upset him, however, and that was being parted from Gretchen; so it was decided that Gretchen should be brought to the schloss and that the two of them should continue to be together.

Gisela was beside herself with pride. She was also greatly relieved, because she said it was as though a weight she had been carrying was lifted from her shoulders. She had always been afraid for Carl, and to think of her little Gretchen living in a schloss and becoming something of a scholar and being with Carl – for she would always think of him as Carl – was something she had never dreamed possible.

It was a good day for her when Francine, the beautiful lady from England, had become her friend.

It is amazing how quickly nine days' wonders are forgotten. Within six months the story seemed to have become distant history, and a year later when the Grand Duke died Bruxenstein had a Regent – Conrad – and a wife who, although she was English and had once been governess to the Countess Freya, was accepted as the Baroness, wife of the Regent. I had a son of my own by this time, whom I called Conrad after his father, and Freya, herself soon to be a mother, had been one of the sponsors at the grand christening.

I had come to accept ceremony as a way of life and as long as I was with my family I was happy. I was relieved to be accepted, for after all I was not only the wife of the Regent, but the aunt of the heir to the dukedom. To my surprise, during the last months of his life I had formed a friendship with the Grand Duke who, after the first shock, was not at all displeased by the turn of events, since the country continued in peace and prosperity.

Freya was happy; Günther was happy; the Graf and Gräfin whom I had never known very well nor understood had slipped into a quiet acceptance of the state of affairs. That they had been involved in that faction responsible for the assassination of Rudolph seemed very likely. Whether they had even then plans for marrying Sigmund to Tatiana or whether they felt, as so many people seemed to have done, that Rudolph's rule would have been disastrous for

Bruxenstein, I did not know. I had discovered that there were many stern patriots who believed that the death of Rudolph was preferable to a war into which weak rule might have plunged the country. It may well have been that the Graf and Gräfin had been among these. I did know that Sigmund had had no hand in Rudolph's death; in fact he had preferred the life of freedom he had had before the responsibilities of state were thrust upon him.

'It is in the past,' was his comment, 'and there is nothing to be gained by trying to unravel it . . . even if we ever could get to the whole truth.'

And he was right, of course.

Tatiana remained in her convent. Whether she was indeed of unsound mind or whether she found it expedient to appear so, was something else of which I was not sure. She had attempted to murder both Freya and myself, but as long as she remained shut away we were both prepared to forget what she had planned for us.

Thus the months slipped by.

When my son was two years old Conrad and I took a trip to England. The Grange was made ready for our arrival and it seemed so strange to go back there and see the row of cottages where Daisy's mother still sat outside on summer's evenings and could be seen pegging her clothes on the line.

Daisy accompanied us, which gave me a lot of pleasure, but we did not plan to stay long, for we hated leaving our children.

I stood and looked at the grey walls of the Manor. It seemed different now, for there were children playing on the lawn. There were four of them – two girls and two boys.

These must be Cousin Arthur's children.

Sophia made me feel very welcome. She was clearly happy and I thought how extraordinary it was that Cousin Arthur, who had seemed quite impossible as a husband to Francine and me, should have turned out so satisfactorily for Sophia.

I was even more astonished when I saw Cousin Arthur. He had grown plump and he looked amazingly contented. He clearly enjoyed family life and I was astonished to see that his children were not in the least in awe of him. I wondered what he was like when he gave them religious instruction.

When I was alone with him he became a little embarrassed, as though he were trying to tell me something and didn't know how to begin.

I said to him: 'Marriage has changed you, Cousin Arthur.'

He admitted that it had. 'I must have seemed insufferable to you and Francine,' he muttered.

'You did,' I agreed. 'But you are like a different person now.'

'I was a hypocrite, Philippa,' he confessed. 'When I look back I just despise myself. And that's not all. I have been really criminal . . .'

I laughed. 'Surely not. What do you call criminal? Forgetting to say your prayers one night?'

He leaned towards me and took my hand. 'I was afraid of poverty,' he said. 'I didn't want to have to eke out some poor living as a miserable curate . . . which is what I should have done but for your grandfather. I wanted Greystone Manor . . . I wanted it desperately. It came to me . . . but I didn't deserve it.'

'Oh, nonsense. You have made it a happy place. The children are adorable.'

'That's true,' he said, 'but I don't deserve my good fortune. I'm glad to have an opportunity of talking to you. I wronged you, Philippa. I was ready . . . But let me explain. I wanted Greystone Manor badly, so I made myself exactly what your grandfather wanted so that he made up his mind that I should marry either you or Francine. We know what happened about that. Well, I didn't want to marry either of you. It was always Sophia for me.'

'Oh, Cousin Arthur, if only we had known!'

'I dared not let it be known. Sophia and I had been in love for some time . . . Then she became pregnant. I had to do something. There came that night when your grandfather died. You had quarrelled with him and everyone heard. He was in an excitable mood. I thought that now he had lost all hope of getting you to fall in with his wishes he wouldn't want to lose us all, and while he was in this mood was the time to tell him what I had done. So I went to his bedroom. I had confessed that Sophia and I must marry now. I shall never forget his face. He was in his nightcap and his fingers trembled as he grasped the sheet. He stared at me unbelievingly and then got out of bed. I think he was going to strike me. He came towards me and I put out my hands to ward him off. I don't know whether I pushed him or not. It all happened so quickly. He fell backwards and struck his head. I was panic-stricken for I realized that he was dead. I didn't kill him. He fell. I saw that there would be a great deal of trouble. Everything would come out . . . I had to think of Sophia . . . I had to act quickly . . .'

'So,' I said, 'you set fire to the place.'

He nodded.

'I should never have allowed you to suffer for it, Philippa,' he said quickly. 'If it had gone further . . . I should have had to tell the truth. But there was Sophia and the child she was carrying . . . You understand. If we could keep it quiet . . . if it could all blow over . . .'

'Even though suspicion rested on me?'

'They never brought a charge. It was accidental death. It *was* accidental death and, Philippa, you were young . . . you went away. I felt no guilt . . . except where you were concerned.'

My thoughts slipped back to those strange days. I remembered how kind, how unexpectedly sympathetic he had been to me. I could hear the shouts of the children on the lawn, and I gripped his hand.

I was suddenly very happy. I looked up and saw a blackbird flying high.

I said:

'"The lark's on the wing,
The snail's on the thorn,
God's in his Heaven,
All's right with the world."'

The Captive

The House in Bloomsbury

I was seventeen when I experienced one of the most extraordinary adventures which could ever have befallen a young woman, and which gave me a glimpse into a world which was alien to all that I had been brought up to expect; and from then on the whole course of my life was changed.

I always had the impression that I must have been conceived in a moment of absent-mindedness on the part of my parents. I could picture their amazement, consternation and acute dismay when signs of my impending arrival must have become apparent. I remember when I was very young, having temporarily escaped from the supervision of my nurse, encountering my father on the stairs. We met so rarely that on this occasion we regarded each other as strangers. His spectacles were pushed up on to his forehead and he pulled them down to look more closely at this strange creature who had strayed into his world, as though trying to remember what it was. Then my mother appeared; she apparently recognized me immediately for she said: 'Oh, it's the child. Where is the nurse?'

I was quickly snatched up into a pair of familiar arms and hustled away, and when we were out of earshot I heard mutterings. 'Unnatural lot. Never mind. You've got your dear old Nanny who loves you.'

Indeed I had and I was content, for besides my dear old Nanny I had Mr Dolland the butler, Mrs Harlow the cook, the parlourmaid Dot and the housemaid Meg, and Emily the tweeny. And later Miss Felicity Wills.

There were two distinct zones in our house and I knew to which one I belonged.

It was a tall house in a London square in a district known as Bloomsbury. The reason it had been chosen as our residence was because of its proximity to the British Museum which was always referred to below stairs with such reverence that when I was first considered old enough to enter its sacred portals I expected to hear a voice from Heaven commanding me to take the shoes from off my feet for the place whereon I was standing was holy ground.

My father was Professor Cranleigh, and he was attached to the Egyptian section of the Museum. He was an authority on Ancient Egypt and in particular Hieroglyphics. Nor did my mother live in his shadow. She shared in his work, accompanied him on his frequent lecture tours, and was the author of a sizeable tome entitled *The Significance of the Rosetta Stone*, which stood in a prominent place of honour, side by side with the half-dozen works by my father in the room next to his study which was called the library.

They had named me Rosetta, which was a great honour. It linked me with their work which made me feel that at one time they must have had some regard for me. The first thing I wanted to see when Miss Felicity Wills took me to the Museum was this ancient stone. I gazed at it in wonder and listened enraptured while she told me that the strange characters supplied the key to deciphering the writings of ancient Egypt. I could not take my eyes from that basalt tablet which had been so important to my parents but what gave it real significance in my eyes was that it bore the same name as myself.

When I was about five years old my parents became concerned about me. I must be educated and there was some trepidation in our zone at the prospect of a governess.

'Governesses,' pronounced Mrs Harlow, when we were all seated at the kitchen table, 'is funny things. Neither fish nor fowl.'

'No,' I put in, 'they are ladies.'

'That's as may be,' went on Mrs Harlow. 'Too grand for us, not good enough for them.' She pointed to the ceiling, indicating the upper regions of the house. 'They throw their weight about something shocking . . . and upstairs, well, they're as mild as milk. Yes, funny things, governesses.'

'I've heard,' said Mr Dolland, 'that it's to be the niece of some professor or other.'

Mr Dolland picked up all the news. He was 'sharp as a wagonload of monkeys', according to Mrs Harlow. Dot had her own sources, gathered when waiting at table.

'It's this Professor Wills,' she said. 'They was at the University . . . only he went on to something else . . . science or something. Well, he's got this niece and they want a place for her. It looks certain we're going to have this Professor Wills's niece in our house.'

'Will she be clever?' I asked in trepidation.

'Too clever by half, if you ask me,' said Mrs Harlow.

'I'm not having her interfering in the nursery,' announced Nanny Pollock.

'She'll be too grand for that. It'll be meals on trays. Up them stairs for you, Dot . . . or you, Meg. I can tell you we're going to get a real madam.'

'I don't want her here,' I announced. 'I can learn from you.'

That made them laugh.

'Say what you will, lovey,' said Mrs Harlow. 'We're not what you'd call eddicated . . . except perhaps Mr Dolland.'

We all gazed fondly at Mr Dolland. Not only did he uphold the dignity of our region, but he kept us amused and at times he could be persuaded to do one of his little 'turns'. He was a man of many parts, which was not surprising because at one time he had been an actor. I had seen him preparing to go upstairs, formally dressed, the dignified butler, and at other times with his green baize apron round his rather ample waist, cleaning the silver and breaking into song. I would sit there listening and the others would creep up to share in the pleasure and enjoy this one of Mr Dolland's many talents.

'Mind you,' he told us modestly, 'singing's not my line. I was never one for the halls. It was always the straight theatre for me. In the blood . . . from the moment I was born.'

Some of my happiest memories of those days are of sitting at that big kitchen table. I remember evenings – it must have been winter because it was dark and Mrs Harlow would light the paraffin-filled lamp and set it in the centre of the table. The kitchen fire would be roaring away and, with my parents absent on some lecture tour, a wonderful sense of peace and security would settle upon us.

Mr Dolland would talk of the days of his youth when he was on the way to becoming a great actor. It hadn't worked out as he had planned, otherwise we should not have had him with us, for which we must be grateful although it was a pity for Mr Dolland. He had had several walk-on parts and had once played the ghost in *Hamlet*; he had actually worked in the same company as Henry Irving. He followed the progress of the great actor and some years before he had seen his hero's much-acclaimed Mathias in *The Bells*.

Sometimes he would beguile us with scenes from the play. A hushed silence would prevail. Seated beside Nanny Pollock, I would grip her hand to assure myself that she was close. It was most effective when the wind howled and we could hear the rain beating against the windows.

'It was such a night as this that the Polish Jew was murdered . . .' Mr Dolland would proclaim in hollow tones, recalling how Mathias had brought about the Jew's death and been haunted ever after by the sound of the bells. We would sit there shivering, and I used to lie in bed afterwards, gazing fearfully at the shadows in the room and wondering whether they were going to form themselves into the murderer.

Mr Dolland was greatly respected throughout the household, which he would have been in any case, but his talent to amuse had made us love him and if the theatrical world had failed to appreciate him, that was not the case in the house in Bloomsbury.

Happy memories they were. These were my family and I felt safe and happy with them.

In those days the only times I ventured into the dining-room were under the sheltering wing of Dot when she laid the table. I used to hold the cutlery for her while she placed it round the table. I would watch with admiration while she dexterously flicked the table napkins into fancy shapes and set them out.

'Don't it look lovely?' she would say, surveying her handiwork. 'Not that they'll notice. It's just talk, talk, talk with them and you don't have a blooming notion of what they're talking about. Get quite aerated, some of them do. You'd think they was all going up in smoke . . . all about things that happened long ago . . . places and people you've never heard of. They get so wild about them, too.'

Then I would go round with Meg. We would make the beds together. When she stripped them I would take off my shoes and jump on the feather mattresses because I loved the way my feet sank into them.

I used to help with the making of the beds.

'First the heel and then the head.

That's the way to make a bed,' we would sing.

'Here,' said Meg. 'Tuck in a bit more. Don't want their feet falling out, do you? They'd be as cold as that there stone what you was named after.'

Yes, it was a good life and I felt in no sense deprived by a lack of parental interest. I was only grateful to my namesake and all those Egyptian Kings and Queens who took up so much of their attention so that they had none to spare for me. Happy days spent making beds, laying tables, watching Mrs Harlow chop meat and stir puddings, getting the occasional titbit thrust into my mouth, listening to the dramatic scenes from Mr Dolland's frustrated past; and always there were the loving arms of Nanny Pollock, for those moments when comfort was needed.

It was a happy childhood in which I could safely dispense with the attention of my parents.

Then came the day when Miss Felicity Wills, niece of Professor Wills, was to come to the household to be governess to me and concern herself with the rudiments of my education until further plans were made for my future.

I heard the cab draw up at the door. We were at the nursery window, myself, Nanny Pollock, Mrs Harlow, Dot, Meg and Emily.

I saw her alight and the cabby brought her bags to the door. She looked young and helpless and certainly not in the least terrifying.

'Just a slip of a thing,' commented Nanny.

'You wait,' said Mrs Harlow, determined to be pessimistic. 'As I've told you often, looks ain't everything to go by.'

The summons to the drawing-room which we were expecting came at length. Nanny had put me into a clean dress and combed my hair.

'Remember to answer up sharp,' she told me. 'And don't be afraid of them. You're all right, you are, and Nanny loves you.'

I kissed her fervently and went to the drawing-room, where my parents were waiting for me with Miss Felicity Wills.

'Ah, Rosetta,' said my mother, recognizing me, I supposed, because she was expecting me. 'This is your governess, Miss Felicity Wills. Our daughter, Rosetta, Miss Wills.'

She came towards me and I think I loved her from that moment. She was so dainty and pretty, like a picture I had seen somewhere. She took both my hands and smiled at me. I returned the smile.

'I am afraid you will have to begin on virgin soil, Miss Wills,' said my mother. 'Rosetta has had no tuition as yet.'

'I am sure she has already learned quite a good deal,' said Miss Wills.

My mother lifted her shoulders.

'Rosetta could show you the schoolroom,' said my father.

'That would be an excellent idea,' said Miss Wills. She turned to me, still smiling.

The worst was over. We left the drawing-room together.

'It's right at the top of the house,' I said.

'Yes. Schoolrooms often are. To leave us undisturbed, I suppose. I hope we shall get along together. So I am your first governess.'

I nodded.

'I'll tell you something,' she went on. 'You're my first pupil. So we are beginners . . . both of us.'

It made an immediate bond between us. I felt a great deal happier than I had when I had awakened that morning and the first thing I had thought of was her arrival. I had imagined a fierce old woman and here was a pretty young girl. She could not have been more than seventeen; and she had already confessed that she had never taught before.

It was a lovely surprise. I knew I was going to be all right.

* * *

Life had taken on a new dimension. It was a great joy to me to discover that I was not as ignorant as I had feared.

Somehow I had taught myself to read with the help of Mr Dolland. I had studied the pictures in the Bible and had loved the stories told by him with dramatic emphasis. They had fascinated me, those pictures: Rachel at the Well; Adam and Eve being turned out of the Garden of Eden, looking back over their shoulders at the angel with a flaming sword; John the Baptist standing in the water and preaching. Then of course I had listened to Mr Dolland's rendering of Henry V's speech before Harfleur and I could recite it, as well as some of 'To be or not to be'. Mr Dolland had greatly fancied himself as Hamlet.

Miss Wills was delighted with me and we were friends from the start.

It was true there was a certain amount of hostility to be overcome with my friends in the kitchen. But Felicity – I was soon calling her Felicity when we were alone – was so gracious and by no means as arrogant as Mrs Harlow had feared, that she soon broke through the barrier between the kitchen and those who, Mrs Harlow said, thought themselves to be 'a cut above'. Soon the meals on trays were no more and Felicity joined us at the kitchen table.

Of course it was a state of affairs which would never have been accepted in a well ordered household, but one of the advantages of having parents who lived in a remote atmosphere of scholarship, apart from the mundane menage of a household, was that it gave us freedom. And how we revelled in it! When I look back on what many would call my neglected childhood, I can only rejoice in it, because it was one of the most wonderful and loving any child could have. But, of course, when one is living it, one does not realize how good it is. It is only when it is over that that becomes clear.

Learning was fun with Felicity. We did our lessons every morning. She made it all so interesting. In fact, she gave the impression that we were finding out things together. She never pretended to know. If I asked a question she would say frankly: 'I'll have to look that up.' She told me about herself. Her father had died some years ago and they were very poor. She had two sisters of whom she was the eldest. She was fortunate to have her uncle, Professor Wills, her father's brother, who had helped the family and found this post for her.

She admitted that she had been terrified, expecting a very clever child who would know more than she did.

We laughed about that. 'Well,' she said, 'the daughter of Professor Cranleigh. He's a great authority, you know, and very highly respected in the academic world.'

I wasn't sure what the academic world was but I felt a glow of pride. After all, he was my father, and it was pleasant to know that he was highly thought of.

'He and your mother have many demands made on them,' she explained. That was further good news. It would keep them out of our way.

'I thought there would be a great deal of supervision and guidance and that sort of thing. So it has all turned out much better than I expected.'

'I thought you'd be terrible . . . neither fish nor fowl.'

That seemed very funny and we laughed. We were always laughing. So I was learning fast. History was about people – some very odd, not just names and a string of dates. Geography was like an exciting tour round the world. We had a big globe which we turned round and round; we picked out places and imagined we were there.

I was sure that my parents would not have approved of this method of teaching, but it worked well. They would never have engaged anyone who looked like Felicity and who admitted that she had no qualifications and had never taught before – if she had not been the niece of Professor Wills.

So we had a great deal to be thankful for and we knew it.

Then there were our walks. We learned what an interesting place Bloomsbury was. It became a game to us to find out how it had become as it was. It was exciting to discover that a century before it had been an isolated village called Lomesbury and between St Pancras Church and the British Museum were fields and open country. We found the house where the painter Sir Godfrey Kneller had lived; then there were the rookeries, that area into which we could not venture – a maze of streets in which the very poor lived side by side with the criminal classes, where the latter could rest in safety because no one would dare enter the place.

Mr Dolland, who had been born and bred in Bloomsbury, loved to talk about the old days and, as was to be expected, he knew a good deal about it. There were many interesting conversations on the subject during meals.

We would sit there on winter evenings, the lamp shedding its light on the remains of Mrs Harlow's pies or puddings and empty vegetable dishes while Mr Dolland talked of his early life in Bloomsbury.

He had been born in Gray's Inn Road and in his boyhood he had explored his surroundings and had many stories to tell of it.

I remember details from those days so well. He really had dramatic powers and like most actors liked to enthral an audience. He certainly could not have had a more appreciative one – even though it was smaller than he might have wished.

'Shut your eyes,' he would say, 'and think of it. Buildings make a difference. Think of this place . . . like a bit of the country. I was never one for the country myself.'

'You're like me, Mr Dolland,' said Mrs Harlow. 'You like a bit of life.'

'Don't we all?' asked Dot.

'I don't know,' put in Nanny Pollock. 'There's some as swears by the country.'

'I was born and bred in the country,' piped up the tweeny.

'I like it here,' I said, 'with all of us.'

Nanny nodded her approval of that sentiment.

I could see Mr Dolland was in the mood to entertain us and I was wondering whether to ask for 'Once more unto the breach' or *The Bells*.

'Ah,' he said. 'There's been a lot going on round here. If you could only see back to years ago.'

'It's a pity we have to rely on hearsay,' said Felicity. 'I think it's fascinating to hear people talk of the past.'

'Mind you,' said Mr Dolland, 'I can't go back all that way, but I've had stories from my granny. She was here before they put up all these buildings. She used to talk about a farm that used to be just about where the top of Russell Street is now. She remembered the Miss Cappers who lived there.'

I settled happily in my chair, hoping for a story about the Miss Cappers. Mr Dolland saw this. He smiled at me and said: 'You want to hear what she told me about them, don't you, Miss Rosetta?'

I nodded and he began: 'They were two old maids, the Misses Capper. One was crossed in love and the other never had a chance to be. It made them sort of bitter against all men. Well-to-do, they were. They had the farm left to them by their father. Ran it themselves, they did. Wouldn't have a man about the place. They managed with a dairymaid or two. It was this dislike of the opposite sex.'

'Because one was crossed in love,' said Emily.

'And the other never had a chance to be,' I added.

'Shh,' admonished Nanny. 'Let Mr Dolland go on.'

'A queer pair they were. Used to ride out on old grey mares. They didn't like the male sex but they dressed just as though they belonged to it . . . in top hats and riding breeches. They looked like a couple of old witches. They were known all round as the Mad Cappers.'

I thought that was a good joke and laughed heartily, only to receive another reproving shake of the head from Nanny. I should know better. One should never interrupt Mr Dolland when he was in full flow.

'It was not that they did anything that was really wicked. It was just that they liked to do a bit of harm here and there. It was a place where boys used to like to fly their kites . . . it being all open to the sky. One of the Miss Cappers used to ride round with a pair of shears. She'd gallop after the boys with the kites and cut the strings so that the little boys were standing there . . . the string in their hands, watching their kites flying off to Kingdom Come.'

'Oh, poor little boys. What a shame,' said Felicity.

'That was the Miss Cappers for you. There was a little stream nearby where the boys used to bathe. There was nothing they liked more on a hot summer's day than a dip in the water. They'd leave their clothes behind a bush while they went in. This other Miss Capper used to watch them. Then she'd swoop down and steal their clothes.'

'What a nasty old woman,' said Dot.

'She said the boys were trespassing on her land and trespassers should be punished.'

'Surely a little warning would have done?' said Felicity.

'That wasn't the Miss Cappers' way. They caused a bit of gossip, those two. I wish I'd been around when they were alive. I'd like to have seen them.'

'You would never have let them cut your kite and send it to Kingdom Come, Mr Dolland,' I said.

'They were pretty sharp, those two. Then, of course, there were the forty steps.'

We all settled back in our seats to hear the story of the forty steps.

'Is it a ghost story?' I asked eagerly.

'Well, sort of.'

'Perhaps we'd better have it in the morning,' said Nanny, her eyes on me. 'Miss gets a bit excited about ghost stories at the end of the day. I don't want her awake half the night fancying she hears things.'

'Oh, Mr Dolland,' I begged. 'Please tell us now. I can't wait. I want to hear about the forty steps.'

Felicity was smiling at me. 'She'll be all right,' she said, wanting to hear as much as I did, and, having whetted our appetites, Mr Dolland saw that he must go on.

Nanny looked a little displeased. She was not as fond of Felicity as the rest of us were. I believed it was because she knew of my affection for her and was afraid it detracted from what I had for her. She need have had no qualms. I was able to love them both.

Mr Dolland cleared his throat and put on the expression which he must have worn when he was waiting in the wings to go on the stage and do his part.

He began dramatically: 'There were two brothers. This was a long time ago when King Charles was on the throne. Well, the King died and his son, the Duke of Monmouth, thought he would make a better king than Charles's brother James, and there was a battle between them. One of the brothers was for Monmouth and the other for James, so they were enemies fighting on different sides. But what was more important to them was their admiration for a certain young lady. Yes, the two brothers loved the same woman and it got to such a state that they made up their minds to fight it out between them, for this young lady was the Beauty of Bloomsbury and she thought quite a lot of herself, as such young ladies do. She was proud because they were going to fight over her. They were to fight with swords, which was how they did it in those days. It was what they called a duel. There was a patch of ground close to Cappers' farm. It was waste land and it always had had a bad reputation. It was the haunt of highwaymen and no one with any sense walked there after dark. It seemed a good place for a duel.'

Mr Dolland picked up the large carving knife from the table and brandished it deftly, stepping back and forth as he battled with an invisible opponent. Gracefully he held the knife but with such realism that I could almost see the two men fighting together.

He paused for a moment and, pointing to the kitchen stove, said: 'There on a bank . . . enjoying every minute, seeing each brother prepared to kill the other for her sake, sat the cause of the trouble.'

The kitchen stove became a bank. I could see the girl, looking a little like Felicity, only Felicity was too good and kind to want anyone to die for her. It was all so vivid; and that was how it always was with Mr Dolland's turns.

He made a dramatic thrust and went on in hollow tones: 'Just as one brother caught the other in the neck, severing a vein, the other struck his brother through the heart. So . . . both brothers died on Long Fields as it was called then, though afterwards the name was changed to Southampton Fields.'

'Well, I never,' said Mrs Harlow. 'The things people do for love.'

'Which one haunted her?' I asked.

'You and your ghosts,' said Nanny disapprovingly. 'There always has to be a ghost for this one.'

'Listen to this,' said Mr Dolland. 'While they were going back and forth –' he did a little more swordplay to illustrate his meaning '– they made forty steps on that blood-stained patch and where those brothers had trod nothing would ever grow again. People used to go out and look at them. According to my granny, they could see the footsteps clearly and the earth was red as though stained with blood. Nobody ever went there after dark.'

'They didn't before,' I reminded him.

'But the highwaymen didn't go there either . . . and still nobody went.'

'Did they *see* anything?' asked Dot.

'No. There was just this brooding feeling of something not quite natural. They said that when it rained and the ground was soggy you could still see the footsteps and they were tinged with red. Things were planted but nothing would grow. The footsteps remained.'

'What happened to the girl for whom they fought?' asked Felicity.

'She fades out of the story.'

'I hope they haunted her,' I said.

'They shouldn't have been such fools,' said Nanny. 'I've no patience with fools. Never have had, never will have.'

'It's rather sad, I think, that they both died,' I commented. 'It would have been better if one of them had remained to suffer remorse . . . and the girl wasn't worth all that trouble anyway.'

'You have to accept what is,' Felicity told me. 'You can't change life to make a neat ending.'

Mr Dolland went on: 'There was a play written about it. It was called *The Field of the Forty Steps*.'

'Were you in it, Mr Dolland?' asked Dot.

'No. A bit before my day. I heard of it though, and it made me interested in the story of the brothers. Somebody called Mayhew wrote it with his brother, which was a nice touch . . . brothers writing about brothers, so to speak. They played it at the theatre in Tottenham Street. It ran for quite a while.'

'Fancy all that happening round here,' said Emily.

'Well, we never know what's going to happen to any of us at any time,' commented Felicity seriously.

* * *

So the time passed, weeks merging into months and months into years. Happy, unruffled days with little to disturb our serenity. I was approaching my twelfth birthday. I suppose Felicity would have been about twenty-four then. Mr Dolland was greying at the temples which we declared made him look very distinguished and that added a certain grandeur to his turns. Nanny complained more of her rheumatics and Dot left to get married. We missed her, but Meg took her place and Emily Meg's and it was thought unnecessary to engage a new tweeny. In time Dot produced a beautiful fat baby whom she proudly brought round for us all to see.

There were many happy memories in those days; but I should have realized that they could not go on for ever.

I was growing out of childhood and Felicity had become a beautiful young woman.

Change comes about in the most insidious way.

There had been the odd occasion since Felicity had come to us when she had been invited to join one of the dinner parties given by my parents. Of course, Felicity explained to me, it was because they needed another female to balance the sexes, and as she was the niece of Professor Wills she was a suitable guest, although only the governess. She did not look forward to these occasions. I remember the one dinner dress she had. It was made of black lace and she looked very pretty in it, but it hung in her wardrobe – a depressing reminder of the dinner parties which were the only occasions when she wore it. She was always thankful when my parents went away for the reason that there could be no invitations to dinner parties. She was never sure when they would be forced on her, for to invite her was generally a last-minute decision. She was, as she said, a most reluctant makeshift.

As I grew older I saw a little more of my parents. I would take tea with them at certain times. I believe they felt even more embarrassed in my presence than I did in theirs. They were never unkind. They asked a great many questions about what I was learning and, as I had an aptitude for gathering facts and a fondness for literature, I was able to give a fair account of myself. So although they were not particularly elated by my progress, nor were they as displeased as they might have been.

Then the first signs of the change began, although I did not recognize them as such at the time.

There was to be a dinner party and Felicity was summoned to attend.

'My dress is getting that tired and dusty look which black gets,' she told me.

'You look very nice in it, Felicity,' I assured her.

'I feel so . . . apart . . . the outsider. Everyone knows I'm the governess called in to make up the numbers.'

'Well, you look nicer than any of them and you're more interesting, too.'

That made her laugh. 'All those deedy old professors think I'm a frivolous empty-headed idiot.'

'They are the empty-headed idiots,' I said.

I was with her when she dressed. Her lovely hair was piled high on her head and her nervousness had put a becoming touch of pink into her cheeks.

'You look lovely,' I told her. 'They'll all be envious.'

That made her laugh again and I was pleased to have lightened her mood a little.

The awesome thought struck me: soon I shall have to go to those boring dinner parties.

She came to my room at eleven that night. I had never seen her look so beautiful. I sat up in bed. She was laughing. 'Oh, Rosetta, I had to tell you.'

'Shh,' I said. 'Nanny Pollock will hear. She'll say you ought not to disturb my slumbers.'

We giggled and she sat on the edge of my bed.

'It was such . . . fun.'

'What?' I cried. 'Dinner with the old professors . . . fun!'

'They weren't all old. There was one . . .'

'Yes?'

'He was quite interesting. After dinner . . .'

'I know,' I broke in. 'The ladies leave the gentlemen to sit over the port to discuss matters which are too weighty or too indelicate for female ears.'

We were laughing again.

'Tell me more about this not-so-old professor,' I said. 'I didn't know there were such things. I thought they were all born old.'

'Learning can sit lightly on some.'

There was a radiance about her, I noticed then.

'I never thought to see you enjoy a dinner party,' I said. 'You give me hope. It has occurred to me that one day I shall be expected to attend them.'

'It depends on who is there,' she said, smiling to herself.

'You haven't told me about the young man.'

'Well, he was about thirty, I should say.'

'Oh, not so young.'

'Young for a professor.'

'What's his subject?'

'Egypt.'

'That seems a popular one.'

'Your parents tend to move in that particular circle.'

'Did you tell him I was named after the Rosetta Stone?'

'As a matter of fact I did.'

'I hope he was suitably impressed.'

And so we went on with our frivolous conversation and just because Felicity had enjoyed one of the dinner parties it did not occur to me that this might be the beginning of change.

The very next day I made the acquaintance of James Grafton. We had taken our morning walk – Felicity and I – and since we had heard the story of the forty steps and located them, we often went that way. There was indeed a patch of ground where the grass grew sparsely and it really did look desolate enough to confirm one's belief in the story.

There was a seat close by. I liked to sit on it, and so vivid had been Mr Dolland's reconstruction of the affair that I could imagine the brothers in their fatal battle.

Almost by force of habit we made our way to the seat and sat down. We had not been there very long when a man approached. He took off his hat and bowed. He stood smiling at us while Felicity blushed becomingly.

'Why,' he said, 'it really is Miss Wills.'

She laughed. 'Oh, good morning, Mr Grafton. This is Miss Rosetta Cranleigh.'

He bowed in my direction.

'How do you do?' he said. 'May I sit for a moment?'

'Please do,' said Felicity.

Instinctively I knew he was the young man whom she

had met at the dinner party on the previous night and that this meeting had been arranged.

There was a little conversation about the weather.

'This is a favourite spot of yours,' he said, and I had a feeling he was telling himself that he must include me in the conversation.

'We come here often,' I told him.

'The story of the forty steps intrigued us,' said Felicity.

'Do you know it?' I asked.

He did not, so I told him.

'When I sit here I can imagine it all,' I said.

'Rosetta's a romantic,' Felicity told him.

'Most of us are at heart,' he said, smiling at me warmly.

He told us that he was on his way to the Museum. Some papyri had come to light and Professor Cranleigh was going to allow him to have a look at them.

'It is very exciting when something turns up which might increase our knowledge,' he added. 'Professor Cranleigh was telling us last night about some of the wonderful discoveries which have been made recently.'

He went on talking about them and Felicity listened enraptured.

I was suddenly aware that something momentous was happening. She was slipping away from me. It seemed ridiculous to think such a thing. She was as sweet and caring as ever, but she did seem a little absent-minded, as though when she was talking to me she was thinking of something else.

But it did not immediately strike me on that first encounter with the attractive Professor Grafton that Felicity was in love.

We met him several times after that and I knew that none of these meetings was by chance. He dined at the house once or twice and on each occasion Felicity joined the party. It occurred to me that my parents were in the secret.

Felicity bought a new dinner dress. We went together to

the shop. It was not really what she would have liked but it was the best she could afford, and since she had met James Grafton she had become even prettier and she looked lovely in it. It was blue – the colour of her eyes and she was radiant.

Mr Dolland and Mrs Harlow soon became aware of what was going on.

'A good thing for her,' said Mrs Harlow. 'Governesses have a poor time of it. They get attached, like . . . and then when they're no longer wanted it's off to the next one until they get too old . . . and then what's to become of them? She's a pretty young thing and it's time she had a man to look after her.'

I had to admit I was dismayed. If Felicity married Mr Grafton she would not be with me. I tried to imagine life without her.

She was taking a great interest in ancient Egypt and we paid many visits to the British Museum. I no longer felt the awe of my childhood and was quite fascinated, and, spurred on by Felicity, I was almost as enthralled by the Egyptian Room as she was.

The mummies in particular attracted me . . . in a rather morbid way. I felt that if I were alone in that room with them they would come to life.

James Grafton used to meet us in the room sometimes. I would wander off and leave him to whisper with Felicity while I studied the faces of Osiris and Isis just as those who thought they were divine must have seen them all those years ago.

One day my father came into the room and saw us there. There was a moment of puzzlement until it dawned on him that here in this holy of holies was his own daughter.

I was standing by the mummy-shaped coffin of King Menkara – one of the oldest in the collection – when he came upon me. His eyes lit up with sudden pleasure.

'Well, Rosetta, I am pleased to find you here.'

'I have come with Miss Wills,' I said.

He turned slowly to where Felicity and James were standing.

'I see . . .' There was a look on his face which in others might have seemed quite puckish but with him it was just rather indulgently knowledgeable.

'You are attracted by the mummies, I see.'

'Yes,' I replied. 'It's incredible . . . the remains of these people being here after all those years.'

'I am delighted to see your interest. Come with me.'

I followed him to where Felicity and James were standing.

'I am taking Rosetta to my room,' he said. 'Perhaps you would join us in . . . say, an hour?'

'Oh, thank you, sir,' said James.

I knew what my father was doing. He was giving them a little time alone. It was amusing to think of my father playing Cupid.

I was taken to his room which I had never seen before. It was lined with books from floor to high ceiling, and there were several glass-doored cabinets which contained all sorts of objects such as stones covered in hieroglyphics and there were some carved images.

'This is the first time you have seen where I work,' he said.

'Yes, Father.'

'I am pleased that you are displaying some interest. We do wonderful work here. If you had been a boy I should have wanted you to follow me.'

I felt I ought to apologize for and defend my sex. 'Like my mother . . .' I began.

'She is an exceptional woman.'

Yes, of course. I could hardly aspire to that. Exceptional I was not. I had spent my happy childhood with people below stairs who had entertained me, loved me, and made me contented with my lot.

As the embarrassment which our encounters never failed

to engender seemed to be building up, he plunged into a description of embalming processes to which I listened entranced, all the time marvelling that I was in the British Museum talking to my father.

Felicity and James Grafton eventually joined us. It was an unusual morning, but by this time I had realized that change was on the way.

* * *

Very soon after that Felicity became engaged to James Grafton. I was both excited and apprehensive. It was good to see Felicity so happy and to know something which had never occurred to me until Mrs Harlow pointed it out, that she was secure.

But there was, of course, the question of what would become of me.

My parents were taking more interest in me, which was in itself disconcerting. I had been discovered by my father showing interest in the exhibits in the Egyptian Room of the British Museum. We had had a little talk in his room there. I was not exactly the ignoramus they had previously thought me. I had a brain which had lain dormant for all these years but I might possibly grow up to be one of them.

Felicity was to be married in March of the following year. I had passed my thirteenth birthday. Felicity was to stay with us until a week before the marriage; then she would go to the house of Professor Wills, who had been responsible for her admission into our household, and from there be married; and in due course she and James would set up house in Oxford to whose university he was attached. The big question was what course should my education now take?

Having received a gift of money from her uncle, Felicity was now able to indulge in replenishing her scanty wardrobe, a task in which I joined with great enthusiasm, though never quite able to escape from the big question of my future and the prospect of facing the emptiness which her departure must inevitably mean.

I tried to imagine what it would be like without her. She had become part of my life, and closer even than the others. Would there be a new governess of the more traditional sort – at cross purposes with Mrs Harlow and the rest? There was only one Felicity in the world and I had been lucky to have her with me all those years. But there is little comfort in recalling past luck which is about to be snatched away so that the future looks uncertain.

It was about three weeks before the date fixed for the wedding when my parents sent for me.

Since my meeting with my father in the British Museum there had been a subtle change in our relationship. They had certainly become more interested in me and in spite of the fact that I had always told myself I was happy to be without their attention, I was now faintly pleased to have it.

'Rosetta,' said my mother. 'Your father and I have decided that it is time you went away to school.'

This was not unexpected, of course. Felicity had talked to me about it.

'It's a distinct possibility,' she had said, 'and really it's the best thing. Governesses are all very well but you'll meet people of your own age, and you will enjoy that.'

I could not believe I would enjoy anything as much as being with her and I told her so.

She hugged me tightly. 'There'll be holidays and you can come and stay with us.'

I remembered that now, so I was prepared.

'Gresham's is a very good school,' said my father. 'It has been highly recommended. I think it will be most suitable.'

'You will be going there in September,' went on my mother. 'It's the start of the term. There will be certain preparations. Then there is Nanny Pollock, of course.'

Nanny Pollock! So I was to lose her, too. I felt a great sadness. I remembered those loving arms . . . those whispered endearments, the comfort I had received.

'We shall give her a good reference,' said my mother.

'She has been excellent,' added my father.

Changes . . . changes all around. And the only one who was moving to a happier state was Felicity. There was always some good in everything, Mr Dolland had said.

But how I hated change.

* * *

The weeks passed too quickly. Every morning I awoke with an uneasy feeling in the pit of my stomach. The future loomed before me, unfamiliar and therefore alarming. I had lived too long in unruffled serenity.

Nanny Pollock was very sad.

'It always comes,' she said. 'Little chicks don't stay that way forever. You've cared for them like they was your own . . . and then comes the day. They've grown up. They're not your babies any more.'

'Oh Nanny, Nanny. I'll never forget you.'

'Nor I you, lovey. I've had my pets, but them upstairs being as they are made you more my little baby . . . if you know what I mean.'

'I do, Nanny.'

'It's not that they was cruel . . . or hard-hearted . . . no, none of that. They was just absent-minded, like . . . so deep in all that unnatural writing and what it means and all those kings and queens kept in their coffins all them years. It was unhealthy as well as unnatural and I never did think much of it. Little babies is more important than a lot of dead kings and queens and all the signs they made because they didn't know how to write properly.'

I laughed and she was glad to see me smile.

She cheered up a little. 'I'm all right,' she said. 'I've got a cousin in Somerset. Keeps her own chickens. I always like a real fresh egg for breakfast . . . laid that morning. I might go to her. I don't feel like taking on another . . . but I might. Anyway, there's no worry on that score. Your mother says not to hurry. I can stay here if I want till I find something I like.'

At length Felicity was married from the house of Professor Wills in Oxford. I went down with my parents for the wedding. We drank the health of the newly married pair and I saw Felicity in her strawberry-coloured going away costume which I had seen before and in fact helped her to choose. She looked radiant and I told myself I must be glad for her while feeling sorry for myself.

When I returned to London they wanted to know all about the wedding.

'She must have made a lovely bride,' said Mrs Harlow. 'I hope she's happy. God bless her. She deserves to be. You never know with them professors. They're funny things.'

'Like governesses, you used to say,' I reminded her.

'Well, I reckon she wasn't a real governess. She was one on her own.'

Mr Dolland said we should all drink to the health and happiness of the happy pair. So we did.

The conversation was doleful. Nanny Pollock had almost decided to go to her cousin in Somerset for a spell. She had drunk a little too much wine and had become maudlin.

'Governesses . . . nannies . . . it's their fate. They should know better. They shouldn't get attached to other people's children.'

'But we're not going to lose each other, Nanny,' I reminded her.

'No. You'll come and see me, won't you?'

'Of course.'

'But it won't be the same. You'll be a grown-up young lady. Them schools . . . they do something to you.'

'They're supposed to educate you.'

'It won't be the same,' insisted Nanny Pollock, shaking her head dolefully.

'I know how Nanny is feeling,' said Mr Dolland. 'Felicity has gone. That was the start. And that's how it always is with change. A little bit here, a little bit there, and you realize everything is becoming different.'

'And before you can say Jack Robinson,' added Mrs Harlow, 'it's another kettle of fish.'

'Well, you can't stand still in life,' said Mr Dolland philosophically.

'I don't want change,' I cried out. 'I want us all to go on as we always did. I didn't want Felicity to get married. I wanted it to stay like it always has been.'

Mr Dolland cleared his throat and solemnly quoted:

'"The Moving Finger writes; and, having writ,
Moves on: nor all thy Piety nor Wit
Shall lure it back to cancel half a Line,
Nor all thy Tears wash out a Word of it."'

Mr Dolland sat back and folded his arms and there was silence. He had pointed out with his usual dramatic emphasis that this was life and we must all accept what we could not alter.

Storm at Sea

In due course I went away to school. I was wretched for a time but I soon settled in. I found community life to my liking. I had always been interested in other people and I was soon making friends and joining in school activities.

Felicity had done quite well with my education, and I was neither outstandingly brilliant nor dull. I was like so many others, which is perhaps the best thing to be for it makes life easier. No one envied me my scholarship and no one despised me for my lack of it. I soon mingled with the rest and became a very average schoolgirl.

The days passed quickly. School joys, dramas and triumphs became part of my life, although I often thought nostalgically of the kitchen at meal times and particularly of Mr Dolland's 'turns'. We had drama classes and plays were put on in the gymnasium for the entertainment of the school. I was Bassanio in *The Merchant of Venice* and scored a modest success which I was sure was due to what I had learned from Mr Dolland's technique.

Then there were the holidays. Nanny Pollock had decided to go to Somerset after all and I spent a week with her and her cousin; she had become reconciled to life in the country and, a year or so after she left Bloomsbury, the death of a distant relative brought complete contentment back to her life.

The deceased was a young woman who had left a two-year-old child and there was consternation in the family as to who would take care of the orphan. It was a heaven-sent opportunity for Nanny Pollock. A child to care for, one whom she could make her own and who would not be snatched from her as those of other people were.

When I went home I was expected now to dine with my parents and although my relationship with them had changed considerably I longed for the old kitchen meals. However, when they went away from London researching or lecturing, I was able to revert to the old customs.

We missed Felicity and Nanny Pollock, of course, but Mr Dolland was in as sparkling a form as ever and Mrs Harlow's comments retained the flavour of the old days.

Then of course there was Felicity. She was always delighted to see me.

She was very happy and had a baby named James and she had thrown herself whole-heartedly into the task of being a good wife and mother. She was a good hostess, too. It was necessary, she told me, for a man in James's position to entertain now and then, so that was something she had had to learn. Growing up as I was, I could attend her dinner parties and I found that I enjoyed them.

It was at one of them that I made the acquaintance of Lucas Lorimer. Felicity told me something of him before I met him.

'By the way,' she said, 'Lucas Lorimer is coming tonight. You'll like him. Most people do. He is charming, good-looking . . . well, good-looking enough . . . and he has the trick of making everyone feel they're enormously interesting. You know what I mean. Don't be deceived. He's like that with everyone. He's rather a restless sort of person, I imagine. He was in the Army for a spell. But he retired from that. He's the younger son. His elder brother Carleton has just inherited the estate in Cornwall, which is quite considerable, I think. The father died only a few months ago, and Lucas is rather at a loose end. There is plenty to do on the estate but I imagine he's the sort who would want to be in command. He's a little unsure of what he wants to do at the moment. A few years ago he found a charm . . .

a relic of some sort, in the gardens of Trecorn Manor . . . that's the name of this place in Cornwall. There was a certain excitement about this find. It was Egyptian and there's some speculation as to how it came to be there. Your father is connected with it.'

'I expect it was covered in hieroglyphics.'

'That must have been how they recognized its source.' She laughed. 'At the time he wrote a book about it. He became interested, you see, and did a bit of research. He found out that it was a medal awarded for some military service and that led him on to the ancient customs of Egypt and he came upon some which had never been heard of before. This book has interested one or two people like your father. Anyway you'll meet him and judge for yourself.'

I did meet him that night.

He was tall, slim and lithe; one was immediately aware of his vitality.

'This is Rosetta Cranleigh,' said Felicity.

'How delightful to meet you,' he said, taking both my hands and gazing at me.

She was right. He did make one feel important and as though his words were not merely a formality. I felt myself believing him in spite of Felicity's warning.

Felicity went on: 'Professor Cranleigh's daughter and my one-time pupil. In fact the only one I ever had.'

'This is so exciting,' he said. 'I have met your father . . . a brilliant man.'

Felicity left us to talk together. He did most of the talking. He told me how helpful my father had been and how grateful he was to have had so much of the important gentleman's time.

Then he wanted to know about me. I confessed that I was still at school, that this was my holiday and I had another two or three terms to come.

'And then what shall you do?'

I lifted my shoulders.

'You'll be married before long, I dare say,' he said, implying that my charms were such that husbands would be vying with each other to win me.

'One never knows what will happen to us.'

'How very true,' he remarked as though my trite remark made a sage of me.

Felicity was right. He set out to please. It was rather transparent when one had been warned, but pleasant, I had to admit.

I found myself seated beside him at dinner. He was very easy to talk to. He told me about the find in the garden, and how to a certain extent it had changed his life.

'The family have always been connected with the Army and I have broken the tradition. My uncle was a colonel of the regiment, hardly ever in England, always doing his duty at some outpost of Empire. I discovered it wasn't the life for me so I got out.'

'It must have been very exciting, finding this relic.'

'It was. When I was in the Army I spent some time in Egypt. That made it rather specially interesting. I just saw it lying there. The soil was damp and one of the gardeners was doing some planting. It was covered in hieroglyphics.'

'You needed the Rosetta Stone.'

He laughed. 'Oh, not quite so obscure as that. Your father translated it.'

'I'm glad of that. I was named after the stone, you know.'

'Yes, I did know. Felicity told me. How proud you must be.'

'I used to be. When I first went to the Museum I gazed at it in wonder.'

He laughed. 'Names are important. You would never guess what my first name is.'

'Tell me.'

'Hadrian. Just imagine being burdened with such a name. People would constantly be asking how you were getting on with the wall. Hadrian Edward Lucas Lorimer. Hadrian was out for reasons I've mentioned. Edward . . . well, there are a great number of Edwards in the world. Lucas is less used . . . so I became Lucas. But you realize what my initials make? It's rather extraordinary. H.E.L.L.'

'I am sure it is most inappropriate,' I said with a laugh.

'Ah, but you do not know me. Have you another name?'

'No, just Rosetta Cranleigh.'

'R.C.'

'Not nearly so amusing as yours.'

'Yours suggests someone very devout, whereas I could be an imp of Satan. It's significant, don't you think . . . the suggestion of people in opposite spheres? I am sure it means something concerning our friendship to come. You are going to turn me from my evil ways and be a good influence on my life. I'd like to think it meant that.'

I laughed and we were silent for a while, then he said: 'You are interested in the mysteries of Egypt, I dare say. As your parents' daughter you must be.'

'Well, in a mild way. At school one doesn't have much time to be interested in what isn't going on there.'

'I'd like to know what the words on my stone really meant.'

'I thought you said they had been translated.'

'Yes . . . in a way. All these things are so cryptic. The meaning is couched in words which are not quite clear.'

'Why do people have to be so obscure?'

'To bring in an element of mystery, don't you think? It adds to the interest. It's the same with people. When you discover subtleties in their characters you become more interested.'

He smiled at me, his eyes saying something which I did not understand.

'You will eventually discover that I am right,' he said.

'You mean when I'm older?'

'I believe you resent people referring to your youth.'

'Well, I suppose it implies that one is not yet capable of understanding much.'

'You should revel in your youth. The poets have said it passes too quickly. "Gather ye rosebuds while ye may."' He smiled at me with a benignity which was almost tender.

I was a little thoughtful after that and I guessed that he was aware of it.

After dinner I went out with the ladies and when the men joined us I did not talk to him again.

Later Felicity asked me how I had liked him.

She said: 'I saw you were getting on very well with him.'

'I think he is the sort who would get on well with anyone . . . superficially.'

She hesitated for a second, then she said: 'Yes . . . you are right.'

It seemed significant afterwards that what I remembered most clearly about that visit was my meeting with Hadrian Edward Lucas Lorimer.

* * *

When I came home for the Christmas holiday my parents seemed more animated than usual . . . even excited. The only thing I imagine which could make them feel so would be some new knowledge they had acquired. A breakthrough in their understanding of their work? A new stone to replace the Rosetta?

It was nothing of the sort.

As soon as I arrived they wanted to talk to me.

'Something rather interesting has occurred,' said my mother.

My father smiled at me indulgently, I thought. 'And,' he added, 'it concerns you.'

I was startled.

'Let us explain,' said my mother. 'We have been invited to do a most interesting lecture tour. This takes us to Cape Town and on the way back to Baltimore and New York.'

'Oh? You will be away for a long time.'

'Your mother thinks it would be interesting to combine a holiday with work,' said my father.

'He has been working far too hard recently. Of course we will not leave it altogether. He can be working on his new book . . .'

'Of course,' I murmured.

'We plan to go by ship to Cape Town . . . a long sea voyage. We shall stay a few days there while your father does one of his lectures. Meanwhile the ship goes on to Durban and we shall pick it up again when it returns to Cape Town. It is calling at Baltimore where we shall leave it again – another lecture – then we shall travel up to New York by land where your father will give the last of his lectures and then we shall take another ship for home.'

'It sounds very interesting.'

There was a slight pause.

My father looked at my mother and said: 'We have decided that you shall accompany us.'

I was too astonished to speak. Then I stammered: 'You . . . er . . . you really mean that?'

'It will be good for you to see a little of the world,' said my father benignly.

'When . . . when?' I asked.

'We are setting forth at the end of April. There will be a great many preparations to make.'

'I shall be at school.'

'You would be leaving at the end of the summer term in any case. We thought that little could be lost by cutting it short. After all, you will be nearly eighteen years of age. That is quite mature.'

'I hope you are pleased,' said my father.

'I am just . . . so surprised.'

They smiled at me.

'You will need to make your own preparations. You could consult Felicity Wills . . . or rather Grafton. She has become quite worldly since her marriage. She would know what you needed. Perhaps two or three evening dresses for functions . . . and some . . . er . . . suitable garments.'

'Oh yes . . . yes,' I said.

After brooding on the matter I was not sure whether I was pleased or not. The idea of travelling and seeing new places enthralled me. On the other hand I would be in the company of my parents and, I presumed, people so weighed down by their own scholarship that they would naturally reduce me to the status of an ignorant girl.

The prospect of new clothes was pleasant. I could not wait to consult Felicity.

I wrote to her and told her of the project.

She replied at once. 'How thrilling. James has to go up North for a few days in March. I have a wonderful nanny who adores Jamie and he her. So I could come to London for a few days and we'll have an orgy of shopping.'

As the weeks passed the prospect of travelling abroad so enchanted me that I forgot the disadvantages that would go with it.

In due course Felicity came to London and as I had expected she threw herself whole-heartedly into the business of finding the right clothes. I was aware that she regarded me in a different light now that I was no longer a schoolgirl.

'Your hair is most striking,' she said. 'Your greatest asset. We'll have to plan with that in mind.'

'My hair?' I had not thought about it before, except that it was unusually fair. It was long, straight and thick.

'It's the colour of corn,' said Felicity. 'It's what they call golden. It really is very attractive. You'll be able to do all sorts of things with it. You can wear it piled high on your head when you want to be dignified or tied back with a ribbon or even plaited when you want to look demure. You can have a lot of fun with it. And we'll concentrate on blue to bring out the colour of your eyes.'

My parents had gone to Oxford so we reverted to old

customs and had our meals in the kitchen. It was just like old times and we prevailed on Mr Dolland to do his Hamlet or Henry V and the eerie excerpts from *The Bells* for the sake of the old days.

We missed Nanny Pollock but I wrote and told her what was happening and she was now very happy, completely absorbed by little Evelyn who was a 'pickle' and reminded her of what I had been at her age.

I paraded round the kitchen in my new garments which resulted in oohs and ahs from Meg and Emily and a few caustic comments from Mrs Harlow who muttered something about fashions nowadays.

It was a very happy time and it did occur to me now and then that the preliminaries of travel might be more pleasant than the actuality.

It was with regret that I said goodbye to Felicity and she returned to Oxford. The day was fast approaching when we would set out for Tilbury to board the *Atlantic Star*.

There was constant talk of the coming trip in the kitchen. None of them had been abroad, not even Mr Dolland, although he had almost gone to Ireland once; but that, as Mrs Harlow pointed out, was another kettle of fish. I was going to see real foreign parts and that could be hazardous.

You never knew where you were with foreigners, commented Mrs Harlow and I'd be seeing a lot of them. She wouldn't have wanted to go, not even if she was offered a hundred pounds to do so.

Meg said: 'Well, nobody's going to offer you a hundred pounds to go abroad, Mrs H. So you're safe.'

Mrs Harlow looked sourly at Meg who, according to her, was always getting above herself.

However, the constant talk of abroad – its attractions and its drawbacks – was suddenly overshadowed by the murder.

We first heard of it from the newsboys shouting in the

streets. ''Orrible murder. Man found shot through the head in empty farmhouse.'

Emily was sent out to buy a paper and Mr Dolland sat at the table, wearing his spectacles and reading to the assembled company.

The murder was the main news at this time, there being nothing else of importance going on. It was called the Bindon Boys Murder and the Press dealt with it in lurid fashion so that people everywhere were reading of the case and wondering what was going to happen next.

Mr Dolland had his own theories and Mrs Harlow reckoned that Mr Dolland had as good a notion of such things as any of the police. It was because of the plays he knew so much about and many of them were concerned with murder.

'They ought to call him in, I reckon,' she pronounced. 'He'd soon put them to rights.'

Meanwhile, basking in the glory of such admiration, Mr Dolland would sit at the table and expound his views.

'It must be this young man,' he said. 'It all points to him, living with the family and not being one of them. That can be tricky, that can.'

'One wonders why he was brought in,' I said.

'Adopted son, it seems. I reckon he was jealous of this young man. Jealousy can drive people to great lengths.'

'I could never abide empty houses,' said Mrs Harlow. 'They give me the creeps.'

'Of course, the story is that he went into this empty farmhouse, this Bindon Boys as they call it, and shot him there,' went on Mr Dolland. 'You see this Cosmo was the eldest son and that would have made the young man a bit jealous on its own, he being the outsider as it were. Then there was this widow . . . Mirabel . . . they call her. He wanted her for himself and Cosmo takes her. Well, there's your motive. He lures Cosmo to this empty farmhouse and shoots him.'

'He might have got away with it,' I said, 'if the younger brother, Tristan . . . wasn't that his name? . . . if he hadn't come in and caught him red-handed.'

I pieced the story together. There were two sons of Sir Edward Perrivale – Cosmo and Tristan – and also in the household was the adopted son, Simon, who had been brought there when he was five years old. Simon had been educated as a member of the family but, according to the evidence, he had always been aware that he was not quite one of them.

Sir Edward was a sick man and in fact had died at the time of the murder so he would probably have been quite unaware of it. Bindon Boys – originally Bindon Bois, the Press told us, because of a copse nearby – was a farmhouse on the Perrivale estate. It was in need of renovation and all three young men were concerned in the management of the estate which was a large one on the coast of Cornwall. The implication was that Simon had lured Cosmo to the derelict farmhouse and calmly shot him. He probably had plans for disposing of the body but Tristan had come in and caught him with the gun in his hand. There seemed to be ample motive. The adopted son must have been jealous of the other two; and it seemed he was in love with the widow to whom Cosmo was engaged to be married.

It was a source of great interest to the servants, and I must admit that I too began to be caught up in it.

Perhaps I was getting a little apprehensive about the coming trip with my parents and seized on something to take my thoughts away from it. I would become as animated as any of them when we sat round the kitchen table listening to Mr Dolland pitting his wits against Scotland Yard.

'It's what they call an open and shut case,' he pronounced.

'It would make a good play,' said Mrs Harlow.

'Well, I am not sure of that,' replied Mr Dolland. 'You know from the start who the murderer is. In a play there has to be a good deal of questioning and clues and things and then you come up with the surprise ending.'

'Perhaps it is not as simple as it appears,' I suggested. 'It might *seem* as if this Simon did it . . . but he says he didn't.'

'Well, he would, wouldn't he?' put in Mrs Harlow. 'They all say that to save themselves and put the blame on someone else.'

Mr Dolland pressed the palms of his hands together and looked up at the ceiling. 'Take the facts,' he said. 'A man brings a stranger into the house and treats him as his son. The others don't want him . . . and the boy resents not being treated like one of the family. It builds up over the years. There'd be hatred in that house. Then there's this widow. Cosmo's going to marry her. There's always been this feeling between them . . . so he killed Cosmo and Tristan comes in and finds him.'

'What fancy names,' said Meg with a little giggle. 'I've always been partial to fancy names.'

Everyone ignored the interruption and waited for Mr Dolland to go on. 'Then there's the widow woman. That would be the last straw. Cosmo gets everything. And what's Simon? Just a bit better than a servant. Resentment flares up. There you have the planned murder. Ah . . . but before he could dispose of the body Tristan comes in and foils his plan. Murders always go wrong in plays. They always have to or there wouldn't have been a play . . . and plays are based on real life.'

We all hung on his words.

Emily said: 'I can't help feeling sorry for that Simon.'

'Sorry for a murderer!' cried Mrs Harlow. 'You're out of your mind, girl. How would you like him to come along and put a bullet through your head?'

'He wouldn't, would he? I'm not Cosmo.'

'You thank your lucky stars you're not,'. said Mrs Harlow. 'And don't interrupt Mr Dolland.'

'All we can do,' went on the sage, 'is wait and see.'

We did not have to wait long. The newsboys were shouting in the streets: 'Dramatic turn in Bindon Boys case. Read all about it.'

We did . . . avidly. It seemed that the police had been on the point of arresting Simon Perrivale. Why they had delayed was a mystery to Mr Dolland – and now Simon had disappeared.

'Where is Simon Perrivale?' demanded the headlines. 'Have you seen this man?' Then 'Police on trail. Arrest expected hourly.'

'So,' pronounced Mr Dolland. 'He has run away. He could not have said more clearly, I'm guilty. They'll find him, never fear.'

'It's to be hoped so,' added Mrs Harlow. 'A body don't feel safe in bed of nights with murderers running around.'

'He wouldn't have reason to murder you, Mrs Harlow,' said Meg.

'I wouldn't trust him,' retorted Mrs Harlow.

'They'll soon find him,' said Mr Dolland reassuringly. 'They'll have their men searching everywhere.'

But the days passed and there was no news of a capture.

Then the case ceased to be headline news. The Queen's Golden Jubilee was taking up the space and there was no room for a sordid murder with the chief suspect having left the scene. No doubt when he was captured there would be a fresh surge of interest; but in the meantime the news of Bindon Boys was banished to the back pages.

It was three days before we were due to depart when we had a caller.

I was in my room when my parents sent for me. I was to go to the drawing-room immediately. A surprise awaited me there. As I entered, Lucas Lorimer came forward to greet me.

'Mr Lorimer tells me that you met at Mr and Mrs Grafton's house,' said my mother.

'Why, yes,' I said, naïvely betraying my pleasure.

He took my hand, smiling into my eyes.

'It was such a pleasure to meet Professor Cranleigh's daughter,' he said, complimenting both my father and me at the same time.

My parents were smiling on me indulgently.

'We have some good news,' said my father.

The three of them were watching me as though they were about to inform a child of a treat in store.

'Mr Lorimer is sailing on the *Atlantic Star*,' said my mother.

'Really!' I cried in amazement.

Lucas Lorimer nodded. 'A great surprise for me and a great honour. I have been asked to give a talk on my discovery at the same time as Professor Cranleigh gives his lecture.'

I felt laughter bubbling up within me. I was amused by the fine distinction implied between a talk and a lecture. I could not really believe he was as modest as he sounded. The look in his eyes did not somehow fit his words.

'So,' went on my father, 'Mr Lorimer will be sailing with us on the *Atlantic Star*.'

'That,' I replied with truth, 'will be very pleasant.'

'I can't tell you how delighted I am to be going,' he said. 'I have often thought what a lucky day it was for me when I made that find in the garden.'

My father smiled and remarked that the message on the stone was a little difficult to decipher . . . not the hieroglyphics, of course, but the meaning . . . the accurate meaning. It was typical, he went on to say, of the Arabic mind. Always fraught with obscurity.

'But that is what makes it all so interesting,' put in Lucas Lorimer.

'It was good of you to come and tell us of your invitation,' my father went on, 'and your decision to accept.'

'My dear Professor, how could I refuse the honour of sharing a platform with you . . . well, not exactly sharing, but being allowed to follow in your footsteps, shall I say?'

My parents were clearly delighted, which showed they could emerge from the rarified atmosphere in which they usually lived to bask in a little flattery.

He was asked to luncheon, when we discussed the journey and my father, encouraged by my mother, went on to talk of the subject of the lectures he would be giving in South Africa and North America.

I could only think: he will be on the ship with us. He will be in foreign places with us. And a considerable excitement had been injected into the prospect.

In a way it took the edge off my apprehension.

Lucas Lorimer's presence would certainly add a spice to the adventure.

* * *

Boarding a ship for the first time was an exhilarating experience. I had driven to Tilbury with my parents and had sat demurely listening to their conversation on the way down, which was mainly about the lectures my father would give. I was rather pleased about this because it relieved me of the strain of talking. He did refer to Lucas Lorimer and wondered how his talk would be received.

'He will have only a superficial knowledge of the subject, of course, but I have heard he has a light-hearted way of representing it. Not the right approach, but a little lightness seems to be acceptable now and then.'

'He will be talking to people of knowledge, I hope,' said my mother.

'Oh yes.' My father turned to smile at me. 'If there are any questions you wish to ask, you must not hesitate to do so, Rosetta.'

'Yes,' added my mother, 'if you know a little it will enhance your enjoyment of the lectures.'

I thanked them and fancied they were not entirely dissatisfied with me.

I had a cabin next to my parents which I was to share

with a girl who was going to South Africa to join her parents who were farming there. She had left school, and was a little older than I. Her name was Mary Kelpin and she was pleasant enough. She had travelled this way several times and was more knowledgeable than I.

She chose the lower of the two bunks, which I did not mind in the least. I imagined I should have felt a little stifled sleeping below. She meticulously divided the wardrobe we had to share; and I thought that, for the time we were at sea, we should get on well.

It was early evening when we set sail and almost immediately Lucas Lorimer discovered us. I heard his voice in my parents' cabin. I did not join them but decided to explore the ship. I went up the companionway to the public rooms and then out to the deck to take the last glimpse of the dock before we sailed. I was leaning on the rail studying the activity below when he came upon me.

'I guessed you'd be here,' he said. 'You'd want to see the ship sail.'

'Yes, I did,' I replied.

'Isn't it amusing that we are taking the trip together?'

'Amusing?'

'I am sure it will be. A delightful coincidence.'

'It has all come about very naturally. Can you call that a coincidence?'

'I can see you are a stickler for the niceties of the English language. You must help me compile my speech.'

'Haven't you done it yet? My father has been working on his for ages.'

'He's a professional. Mine will be very different. I shall go on about the mysticism of the East. A sort of *Arabian Nights* flavour.'

'Don't forget you will be talking to experts.'

'Oh, I hope to appeal to a wider audience – the imaginative, romantic sort.'

'I am sure you will.'

'I'm so glad we're sailing together,' he said. 'And now you are no longer a schoolgirl . . . that is exciting in itself, is it not?'

'Yes, I suppose so.'

'On the threshold of life . . . and adventure.'

The sound of a hooter rent the air.

'I think that means we are about to sail. Yes, it does. Adieu, England. Welcome new lands . . . new sights . . . new adventures.'

He was laughing. I felt exhilarated and glad because he was with us.

I continued to be so. My parents were made much of by the Captain and certain other travellers. The information that they were going to lecture in Cape Town and Northern America quickly spread and they were regarded with some awe. Lucas was very popular and in great demand. I knew why. He was one of those people who are without inhibitions; when he arrived at a gathering there was immediate laughter and general animation. He had the ability to make everything seem amusing.

He was charming to me, but then he was to everybody. He went through life smoothly and easily, and I imagine getting his own way because of this rare gift of his.

My cabin mate was greatly impressed.

'What a charming man!' she said. 'And you knew him before you came on board. Lucky you!'

'Well, I met him briefly at a dinner party, and then he called to tell us he would be on board.'

'It's because of your father, I suppose.'

'What do you mean?'

'That he is so friendly.'

'He's friendly with everyone.'

'He's very attractive . . . too attractive,' she added ominously and regarding me speculatively. She was inclined to regard me as a simpleton because I had foolishly told her that I had cut school short to come on this trip. She had left the previous year, so must have been a year or so older than I.

I had an idea she was warning me against Lucas. There was no need, I wanted to tell her fiercely; and then I feared I might be too fierce. She was right in one thing; I was ignorant of the ways of the world.

But the time I spent with Lucas was certainly enjoyable.

During the first days we found a sheltered spot on the deck, for at that time the sea was a little rough and the wind strong. My parents spent a good deal of time in their cabin and I was left free to explore.

This I did with great interest and soon learned my way about the ship. I found the small cabin restricting, especially as it had to be shared with the rather loquacious and faintly patronizing Mary. I was glad to get out of it as much as possible. I found my top bunk a little stifling. I would wake early and lie there waiting for it to be time to get up.

Then I discovered that I could descend the ladder without waking Mary. I could slip on a few things and go out on deck. The early morning was exhilarating. I would sit in our sheltered spot and look out over the sea, watching the sunrise. I loved to see the morning sky, sometimes delicately pearl, at others blood red. I would picture figures in the formation of the clouds as they drifted across the sky and listen to the waves swishing against the sides of the ship. It was never quite the same at any other time as it was in the morning.

There was a man in blue overalls who used to swab that part of the deck where I sat each morning. I had struck up an acquaintance with him . . . if it could be called that. He would come along with his mop and pail, tip out the water and swab away.

At such an hour the deck was almost deserted.

As he approached I said: 'Good morning. I came out for a breath of fresh air. It was stifling in the cabin.'

'Oh yes,' he said, and went on swabbing.

‘Am I in your way? I’d better move.’

‘Oh no. It’s all right. I’ll go round and do that bit later.’

It was a cultured voice devoid of accent. I studied him – fairly tall, light brown hair and rather sad eyes.

‘You don’t get many people sitting out at this hour,’ I said.

‘No.’

‘I expect you think I’m crazy.’

‘No . . . no. I understand you want to get the air. And this is the best time of the day.’

‘Oh, I do agree.’

I insisted on getting up and he moved my chair and went on swabbing.

That was the first morning I saw him and on the next one I met him again. By the third morning I imagined he looked for me. It was not exactly an assignation, but it seemed to have become part of the day’s ritual. We exchanged a few words. ‘Good morning . . . it’s a nice day . . .’ and so on. He always kept his head down when he was swabbing, as though completely absorbed by what he was doing.

‘You like the sea, don’t you?’ he said on the fourth morning.

I said I believed I did. I was not sure yet as it was the first time I’d been on it.

‘It takes a grip on you. It’s fascinating. It can change so quickly.’

‘Like life,’ I said, thinking of the changes in mine.

He did not answer and I went on: ‘I suppose you’ve had great experience of the sea?’

He shook his head and moved away.

Mealtimes on board were interesting. Lucas Lorimer, as a friend, sat at our table and Captain Graysom had made a pleasant custom of taking his seat at each table in turn during the voyage so that he could get to know most of his passengers. He had many stories to tell of his adventures at sea and that happy custom made it possible for all to hear of them.

'It is easy for him,' said Lucas. 'He has his repertoire and all he has to do is give a repeat performance at each table. You notice he knows just where to pause for the laugh and get the best dramatic effects.'

'You are a little like that,' I told him. 'Oh, I wasn't suggesting repetition, but you know where the pauses should come, too.'

'I see that you know me too well for my comfort.'

'Well then, let me comfort you. I think one of the greatest gifts one can have is the ability to make people laugh.'

He took my hand and kissed it.

My parents, who were at the table when this dialogue took place, were a little startled. I think it might have brought home to them that I was growing up.

Lucas and I were taking a walk round the deck when we encountered Captain Graysom. He used to walk round the ship every day to assure himself, I supposed, that everything was in order.

'All well?' he asked as he approached.

'Very well indeed,' answered Lucas.

'Getting your sea legs now? They don't always come at once. But we've been moderately lucky in the weather . . . so far.'

'Isn't it going to continue?' I asked.

'You need a wiser man than I am to tell you that, Miss Cranleigh. We can only forecast . . . and never with absolute certainty. The weather is unpredictable. All the signs look good and then something quite unforeseen appears on the horizon and our forecasts go awry.'

'Predictability can be a little dull,' said Lucas. 'There is always a certain attraction in the unexpected.'

'I'm not sure that applies to the weather,' said the Captain. 'We'll shortly be putting into Madeira. You'll go ashore?'

'Oh, yes,' I cried. 'I'm looking forward to that.'

'It's a pity we only have one day there,' said Lucas.

'Just long enough to pick up stores. You'll like the island. You must sample the wine. It's good.'

Then he left us.

'What plans have you for Madeira?' asked Lucas.

'My parents haven't said anything yet.'

'I should like to escort you round the place.'

'Oh, thank you. Have you been there before?'

'Yes,' he replied. 'So you will be safe with me.'

* * *

It was exhilarating to wake up in the morning and see land. I was on deck early to watch our approach. I could see the green lush island rising out of a pellucid aquamarine-coloured sea. The sun was warm and there was no wind to disturb the water.

My father had a slight cold and was staying on board; he had plenty to occupy him; and my mother would be with him. They thought it would be an excellent idea if I went ashore with Mr Lorimer who had kindly offered to take me.

I was content, feeling somewhat guiltily, how much more enjoyable it would be without them. Lucas did not say so, but I felt sure he shared my view.

'Having been here before I shall know something about it,' he said. 'And if there is anything of which I am ignorant –'

'Which is most unlikely.'

'We shall discover it together,' he finished.

And on that note we set out.

I drew deep breaths of air which seemed scented with flowers. Indeed, there were flowers everywhere. Stalls were overflowing with brilliantly coloured blossoms, as well as baskets, embroidered bags, shawls and tablecloths and mats.

The sunshine, the chatter of people in a foreign language – Portuguese, I presumed – as they proffered their goods, the excitement of being in a foreign land and the company of Lucas Lorimer, all these things made me realize that I was enjoying myself as I had not for a long time.

It was indeed a day to remember. Lucas was the perfect companion. His smiles charmed people wherever we went, and I thought he was one of the nicest people I had ever met.

It was true that he did know a good deal about the place.

'It's quite small,' he said. 'I was here for a week and in that time I was able to go almost everywhere.'

He engaged one of the bullock-drawn carts and we drove through the town . . . past the cathedral where we called a halt that we might explore, past the market with more flowers, baskets and wickerwork tables and chairs.

From the town we caught glimpses of the *Atlantic Star* lying a little way out to sea and the launches which were ferrying the passengers between the shore and the ship.

Lucas said we must try the wine and we went into one of the wine cellars and there sat at one of the little tub-like tables while glasses were brought to us containing a little sample of Madeira wine in the hope, I supposed, that we should be so delighted that we would buy some.

It was dark in the cellar – a contrast to the bright light outside. We sat on stools and surveyed each other. Lucas lifted his glass.

'To you . . . to us . . . and many more days like this.'

'The next stop is Cape Town, I believe.'

'Well, you and I may have a chance to repeat the pleasure while we are there.'

'You will be busy with your lecture.'

'Please don't call it a lecture. That's for sterner stuff. It makes it sound so severe. There are connotations in that word. It can mean a severe talking-to . . . a reprimand. When they asked me to come it was as a light contrast to the Professor. I was honoured . . . and look, it has led to this. So . . . call it a talk. That's much more cosy. As a matter of fact, I have a feeling it will shock your parents. It's about gruesome things like curses and tomb robbers.'

'People might enjoy hearing about that sort of thing rather than . . .'

'I'm not letting it bother me. If they don't like it that will be that. So . . . I refuse to allow preparations to overshadow my pleasure. It's the greatest good luck that we are travelling together.'

'It's certainly pleasant for me.'

'We're getting maudlin. It's the wine perhaps. It's good, isn't it? We must buy a bottle to show our appreciation of the free sample.'

'I hope all the free samples make it worthwhile.'

'Must do, or they wouldn't continue with the old custom, would they? In the meantime it is very pleasant sitting here in this darkish room, on these uncomfortable stools, sipping their excellent Madeira wine.'

Several of our fellow passengers came into the cellar. We called greetings to each other. They all looked as though they were enjoying the day.

Then a young man walked past our table.

'Oh hello,' said Lucas.

The young man paused.

'Oh,' said Lucas, 'I thought I knew you.'

The young man stared at Lucas stonily and then I recognized him, which I had not done previously because he was not on this occasion wearing the overalls in which I had always seen him before. He was the young man who swabbed the decks in the morning.

'No,' he said. 'I don't think . . .'

'Sorry. I just thought for the moment I'd met you somewhere.'

I smiled and said: 'You must have seen each other on board.'

The deck hand had drawn himself up rather tensely and was studying Lucas, I thought, with a hint of uneasiness.

'That must be it,' said Lucas.

The young man passed on and sat at a table in a dark corner of the cellar.

I whispered to Lucas: 'He is one of the deck hands.'

'You seem to be acquainted with him.'

'I have met him on several mornings. I go up there to watch the sunrise and he comes round at that time swabbing the decks.'

'He doesn't look like a deck-swabber.'

'That's because he's not in overalls.'

'Well, thanks for enlightening me. The poor chap seemed a bit embarrassed. I hope he enjoys the wine as much as I have done. Come on. Let's buy a bottle to take back to the ship. Perhaps we'd better get two. We'll drink it at dinner tonight.'

We bought the wine and came out into the sunshine.

Slowly we made our way back to the launch which would take us to the ship. On the quay we stopped at a stall and Lucas bought one of the bags for me. It was heavily embroidered with scarlet and blue flowers.

'A memento of a happy day,' he said. 'To say thank you for letting me share it with you.'

I thought how gracious and charming he was; he had certainly given *me* a happy day.

'I shall always remember it when I see this bag,' I told him. 'The flowers . . . the bullock carts and the wine . . .'

'And even the swabber of decks.'

'I shall remember every minute of it,' I assured him.

* * *

Friendship grows quickly at sea.

After Madeira we were in balmy weather with smooth seas. Lucas and I seemed to have become even firmer friends since our day ashore. Without making arrangements we met regularly on deck. He would seat himself beside me and we would talk desultorily as we watched the calm sea glide past.

He told me a great deal about himself, how he had broken the tradition in the family that one of the sons should have a career in the Army. But it was not for him. He was not really sure what was for him. He was restless and travelled a good deal, usually in the company of Dick Duvane, his ex-batman and friend. Dick had left the Army when he had and they had been together ever since. Dick was in Cornwall now, making himself useful on the estate, which Lucas supposed was something he would have to come to eventually.

'Just at the moment I'm uncertain,' he said. 'There is enough to do on the estate to keep both my brother and me occupied. I suppose it would have been different if I had inherited. My brother Carleton is in charge and he's the perfect squire . . . such as I should never be. He's the best fellow in the world, but I don't like playing second fiddle. It's against my arrogant nature. So . . . since leaving the Army, I've drifted a bit . . . I've travelled a great deal. Egypt has always fascinated me and when I found the stone in the garden it seemed like fate. And so it was, because here am I at the moment, travelling with the élite such as your parents . . . and of course their charming daughter. And all because I found a stone in the garden. But I am talking all this time about myself. What of you? What are your plans?'

'I haven't made any. I've cut school, you know, to come here. Who knows what the future holds?'

'No one can be sure, of course, but sometimes one has the opportunity to mould it.'

'Have you moulded yours?'

'I am in the process of doing so.'

'And your brother's estate is in Cornwall.'

'Yes. As a matter of fact, it's not far from that place which has been in the papers recently.'

'Oh . . . what's that?'

'Did you read about the young man who was on the point of being arrested and disappeared?'

'Oh yes. I remember. Wasn't it Simon somebody? Perrivale, was it?'

'That's it. He took his name from the man who adopted him, Sir Edward Perrivale. Their place is some six or eight miles from ours. Perrivale Court. It's a wonderful old mansion. I went there once . . . long ago. It was about something my father was involved in to do with the neighbourhood and Sir Edward was interested. I rode over with my father. When I read about the case in the papers it all came back. There were two brothers and the adopted one. We were all shocked when we read about it. One doesn't expect that sort of thing to happen to people one knows . . . however slightly.'

'How very interesting. There was a lot of talk about it in our house . . . among the servants . . . not my parents.'

While we were talking, the deck-swabber came by, trundling a trolley on which were bottles of beer.

'Good morning,' I called.

He nodded his head in acknowledgement and went on wheeling.

'A friend of yours?' said Lucas.

'He's the one who swabs the deck. Remember, he was in the wine cellar.'

'Oh yes . . . I remember. Seems a bit surly, doesn't he?'

'He's a little reserved, perhaps. It may be that they are not supposed to talk to passengers.'

'He seems different from the others.'

'Yes, I thought so. He never says much more than good-morning and perhaps a comment on the weather.'

We dismissed the man from our minds and talked of other things. He told me about the estate in Cornwall and some of the eccentric people who lived there. I told him about my home life and Mr Dolland's 'turns'; and I had him laughing at my descriptions of kitchen life.

'You seem to have enjoyed it very much.'

'Oh, I was fortunate.'

'Do your parents know?'

'They are not really interested in anything that happened after the birth of Christ.'

And so we talked.

The next morning when I took my seat on deck in the early morning, I saw the deck-swabber, but he did not come near me.

* * *

We were heading for Cape Town and the wind had been rising all day. I had seen little of my parents. They spent a lot of time in their cabin. My father was perfecting his lecture and working on his book and my mother was helping him. I saw them at meals when they regarded me with that benign absent-mindedness to which I had become accustomed. My father asked if I had plenty to do. I might come to his cabin where he would give me something to read. I assured him I was enjoying shipboard life, I had something to read and Mr Lorimer and I had become good friends. This seemed to bring them some relief and they went back to their work.

The Captain, who dined with us occasionally, told us that some of the worst storms he had encountered had been round the Cape. It was known to ancient mariners as the Cape of Storms. In any case we could not expect the calm weather we had enjoyed so far to be always with us. We must take the rough with the smooth. We were certainly about to take the rough.

My parents stayed in their cabin but I felt the need for fresh air and went out on to the open deck.

I was unprepared for the fury which met me. The ship was being roughly buffeted and felt as though she were made of cork. She pitched and tossed to such an extent that I thought she was about to turn over. The tall waves rose like menacing mountains as they fell and drenched the deck. The wind tore at my hair and clothes. I felt as though the angry sea was attempting to lift me up and take me overboard.

It was alarming and yet at the same time exhilarating.

I was wet through with sea-water and found it almost impossible to stand up. Breathlessly I clung to the rail.

As I stood there debating whether it was wise to cross the slippery deck and at least get away from the direct fury of the gale, I saw the deck hand. He swayed towards me, his clothes damp. The spray had darkened his hair so that it looked like a black cap and sea-water glistened on his face.

'Are you all right?' he shouted at me.

'Yes,' I shouted back.

'Shouldn't be up here. Ought to get down.'

'Yes,' I cried.

'Come on. I'll help you.'

He staggered to me and fell against me.

'Is it often as rough as this?' I panted.

'Haven't seen it. My first voyage.'

He had taken my arm and we rolled drunkenly across the deck. He opened a door and pushed me inside.

'There,' he said. 'Don't venture out in a sea like this again.'

Before I could thank him, he was gone.

Staggering, I made my way to my cabin. Mary Kelpin was lying on the lower bunk. She was feeling decidedly unwell.

I said I would look in on my parents. They were both prostrate.

I came back to my cabin, took a book, climbed to the top bunk and tried to read. It was not very easy.

All through the afternoon we were waiting for the storm

to abate. The ship went on her rocky way, creaking and groaning as though in agony.

By evening the wind had dropped a little. I managed to get down to the dining-room. The fiddles were up on the tables to prevent the crockery sliding off and there were very few people there. I soon saw Lucas.

'Ah,' he said, 'not many of us brave enough to face the dining-room.'

'Have you ever seen such a storm?'

'Yes, once when I was coming home from Egypt. We passed Gibraltar and were coming up to the Bay. I thought my last hour had come.'

'That is what I thought this afternoon.'

'She'll weather the storm. Perhaps tomorrow the sea will be as calm as a lake, and we shall wonder what all the fuss was about. Where are your parents?'

'In their cabin. They did not feel like coming down.'

'In common with many others obviously.'

I told him I had been on deck and had been rather severely reprimanded by the deck hand.

'He was quite right,' said Lucas. 'It must have been highly dangerous. You could easily have been washed overboard. I reckon we were on the edge of a hurricane.'

'It makes you realize how hazardous the sea can be.'

'Indeed it does. One should never take the elements lightly. The sea . . . like fire . . . is a good friend but a bad enemy.'

'I wonder what it is like to be shipwrecked.'

'Horrendous.'

'Adrift in an open boat,' I murmured.

'Much more disagreeable than it sounds.'

'Yes, I imagine so. But it seems the storm is dying down now.'

'I'd never trust it. We have to be prepared for all weather. This has been a salutary lesson to us, perhaps.'

'People don't always learn their lessons.'

'I don't know why when they have a good example of how treacherous the sea can be. Smiling one moment . . . angry . . . venomous . . . the next.'

'I hope we shall encounter no more hurricanes.'

It was past ten o'clock when I reached my cabin. Mary Kelpin was in her bed. I went to the next cabin to say good-night to my parents. My father was lying down and my mother was reading some papers.

I told them I had dined with Lucas Lorimer and was now going to bed.

'Let's hope the ship is a little steadier by morning,' said my mother. 'This perpetual motion disturbs your father's train of thought, and there is still some work to do on the lecture.'

I slept fitfully and woke in the early hours of the morning. The wind was rising and the ship was moving even more erratically than it had during the day. I was in danger of being thrown out of my bunk and sleep was impossible. I lay still, listening to the wailing and shrieking of the gale and the sound of the heavy waves as they lashed the sides of the ship.

And then . . . suddenly I heard a violent clanging of bells. I knew at once what this meant for on our first day at sea we had taken part in a drill which would make us prepared, in some small way, for an emergency. We were told then that we were to put on warm clothing, together with our lifejackets which were kept in the cupboard in our cabins, and make for the assembly point which had been chosen for us.

I leaped down from my bunk. Mary Kelpin was already dressing.

'This is it,' she said. 'That ghastly wind . . . and now . . . this.'

Her teeth were chattering and space was limited. It was not easy for us both to dress at the same time.

She was ready before I was, and when I had fumbled

with buttons and donned my lifejacket I hurried from the cabin to that of my parents.

The bells continued to sound their alarming note. My parents were looking bewildered, my father agitatedly gathering papers together.

I said: 'There is no time for that now. Come along. Get these warm things on and where are your lifejackets?'

I then had the unique experience of realizing that a little quiet common sense has its advantages over erudition. They were pathetically meek and put themselves in my hands; at last we were ready to leave the cabin.

The alleyway was deserted. My father stopped short and some papers he was carrying fell from his hands. I hurriedly picked them up.

'Oh,' he said in horror. 'I've left behind the notes I made yesterday.'

'Never mind. Our lives are more important than your notes,' I said.

He stood still. 'I can't . . . I couldn't . . . I must go and get them.'

My mother said: 'Your father must have his notes, Rosetta.'

I saw the stubborn look on their faces and I said hurriedly: 'I'll go and get them. You go up to the lounge where we are supposed to assemble. I'll get the notes. Where are they?'

'In the top drawer,' said my mother.

I gave them a little push towards the companionway which led to the lounge and I turned back. The notes were not in the top drawer. I searched and found them in a lower one. My lifejacket rendered movement rather difficult. I grabbed the notes and hurried out.

The bells had stopped ringing. It was difficult to stand upright. The ship lurched and I almost fell as I mounted the companionway. There was no sign of my parents. I guessed they must have joined others at the assembly point and been hustled on deck to where the lifeboats would be waiting for them.

The violence of the storm had increased. I stumbled and slid until I came to rest at the bulkhead. Picking myself up, feeling dazed, I looked about for my parents. I wondered where they could have gone in the short time I had taken to retrieve the notes. I was clutching them in my hands now as I managed to make my way to the deck. There was pandemonium. People were surging towards the rail. In vain I looked among them for my parents. I suddenly felt terrifyingly alone among that pushing screaming crowd.

It was horrific. The wind seemed to take a malicious delight in tormenting us. My hair was loose and flying wildly about my head, being tossed over my eyes so that I could not see. The notes were pulled from my hands. For a few seconds I watched them doing a frivolous dance above my head before they were snatched up by the violent wind, fluttered and fell into that seething mass of water.

We should have stayed together, I thought. And then: Why? We have never been together. But this was different. This was danger. It was Death staring us in the face. Surely a few notes were not worth parting for at such a time?

Some people were getting into boats. I realized that my turn would not come for a long time . . . and when I saw the frail boats descending into that malignant sea, I was not sure that I wanted to trust myself to one of them.

The ship gave a sudden shivering groan as though it could endure no more. We seemed to keel over and I was standing in water. Then I saw one of the boats turn over as it was lowered. I heard the shrieks of its occupants as the sea hungrily caught them and drew them down.

I felt dazed and somewhat aloof from the scene. Death seemed almost certain. I was going to lose my life almost before it had begun. I started thinking of the past, which people say you do when you are drowning. But I was not drowning . . . yet. Here I was on this leaky frail vessel, facing the unprecedented fury of the elements, and I knew that at any moment I could be flung from the comparative safety of the deck into that grey sea in which no one could have a hope of survival. The noise was deafening; the shrieks and prayers of the people calling to God to save them from the fury of the sea . . . the sound of the raging tempest . . . the violent howling of the wind and the mountainous seas . . . they were like something out of Dante's *Inferno*.

There was nothing to be done. I suppose the first thought of people faced with death is to save themselves. Perhaps when one is young death seems so remote that one cannot take it seriously. It is something which happens to other people, old people at that; one cannot imagine a world without oneself; one feels oneself to be immortal. I knew that many this night would lie in a watery grave but I could not really believe that I should be one of them.

I stood there . . . dazed . . . waiting . . . striving to catch a glimpse of my parents. I thought of Lucas Lorimer. Where was he? I wished I could see him. I thought fleetingly that he would probably still be calm and a little cynical. Would he talk of death as nonchalantly as he did of life?

Then I saw the overturned boat. It was being tossed about in the water. It came close to the spot where I was standing. Then it had righted itself and was bobbing about below me.

Someone had roughly caught my arm.

'You'll be washed overboard in a minute if you stay here.'

I turned. It was the deck hand.

'She's finished. She'll turn over . . . it's certain.'

His face was wet with spray. He was staring at the boat which the violent wind had brought close to the ship's side. A giant wave brought it almost level with us.

He shouted: 'It's a chance. Come on. Jump.'

I was surprised to find that I obeyed. He had my arm still

in a grip. It seemed unreal. I was sailing through the air and then plunging right down into that seething sea.

We were beside the boat.

'Grip!' he shouted above the tumult.

Instinctively I obeyed. He was very close to me. It seemed minutes but it could only have been seconds before he was in the boat. I was still clinging to the sides. Then his hands were on me. He was hauling me in beside him.

It was just in time. The boat was lifted up on the crest of an enormous wave. His arms were about me and he was holding me tightly.

'Hang on . . . hang on . . . for your life,' he cried.

It was a miracle. We were still in the boat.

We were breathless.

'Hang on. Hang on,' he kept shouting.

I am not sure what happened in the minutes that followed. I just knew that I was roughly buffeted and that the velocity of the wind took my breath away. I was aware of a violent crash as the *Atlantic Star* seemed to rise in the air and then keel over. I was blinded by the sea; my mouth was full of it. We were on the crest of the waves one moment, down in the depths of the ocean the next.

I had escaped from the sinking ship to a small boat which it seemed certain could not survive in such a sea.

This must be the end.

Time had ceased to register. I had no idea how long I was clinging to the sides of the boat, while only one thing seemed important: to stay on.

I was aware of the man close to me.

He shouted against the wind. 'We're still afloat. How long . . .'

His voice was lost in the turmoil.

I could just make out the *Atlantic Star*. She was still in the water but at an unusual angle. Her prow seemed to have disappeared. I knew that there could be little chance of anyone's surviving on her.

We continued to rock uncertainly, waiting for each wave which might end our lives. All about us the sea roared and raged . . . such a flimsy craft to defy that monster sea. I found myself wondering what would have happened to me if this man had not come along when he did and made me jump with him. What a miracle! I could scarcely believe it had happened. I thought of my parents. Where were they? Could they have escaped?

Then it seemed as though the storm was a little less fierce. Was it my fancy? Perhaps it was a temporary lull. But it was a small respite. One of the lifeboats was coming close to us. I scanned it anxiously in the hope that my parents might be in it. I saw the strained white faces . . . unrecognizable . . . unfamiliar. Then suddenly a wave caught the boat. For a second or so it hung suspended in the air and then it was completely enveloped by another giant wave. I heard the screams. The boat was still there. It was lifted high again. It seemed to stand perpendicular. I saw bodies tipped into the sea. Then the boat fell back and was overturned. It was upside down in the water before it rose again as the sea tossed it aside as a child might have done when a toy it had been playing with suddenly bored it.

I saw heads bobbing in the water for what seemed interminable minutes and then disappearing.

I heard my rescuer shouting: 'Look. Someone's drifting towards us.' It was a man. His head suddenly appeared close to us.

'Let's get him on board . . . quick . . . or he'll go under and take us with him.'

I stretched out my arms. I was overcome with the emotion which assailed me then for the man we were attempting to haul into the boat was Lucas Lorimer. It was a long time before we succeeded. He collapsed and lay face downwards. He was very still. I wanted to shout at him: You're safe, Lucas. And I thought: As safe as any of us can be.

We turned him over onto his back. Recognizing him, my

companion caught his breath. He shouted to me: 'He's in a bad way.'

'What can we do?'

'He's half drowned.'

He bent over Lucas and started to pump the water out of his lungs. He was trying to save Lucas's life and I wondered then how long he would be able to keep at it.

It was helpful to have something to do. He was succeeding. Lucas looked a little more alive.

I noticed there was something odd about his left leg. Every now and then one of his hands would move to it and touch it. He was only half-conscious but he was aware that something there was wrong.

'Can't do any more,' murmured my rescuer.

'Will he be all right?'

He lifted his shoulders.

* * *

It must have been two hours or so before the wind started to subside. The gusts were less frequent at first and we were still afloat.

Lucas had not opened his eyes; he lay at the bottom of the boat, inert. My other companion was tinkering with the boat. I did not know what he was doing but it seemed important and the fact that we had kept afloat told me that he must have some knowledge of how the thing worked.

He looked up and caught me watching him. He said: 'Get some sleep. You're exhausted.'

'You too . . .'

'Oh . . . there's enough to keep me awake.'

'It's better now, isn't it? Have we a chance?'

'Of being picked up? Perhaps. We're in luck. There's a can of water and a tin of biscuits here . . . shut away under the seat. Put there as emergency rations. That will help us to keep going for a bit. Water's most important. We can survive on that . . . for a while.'

'And him . . .' I pointed to Lucas.

'In a bad way. He's breathing though. He was half drowned . . . and it looks as though his leg's broken.'

'Can we do anything?'

He shook his head. 'Nothing. No supplies. He'll have to wait. We've got to look for a sail. Nothing you can do so try to sleep. You'll feel better.'

'What about you?'

'Later, perhaps. Nothing more we can do for him. Have to go the way the wind takes us. Can't steer. If we're lucky we'll hit the trade routes. If not . . .' He shrugged his shoulders. Then he said almost gently: 'Best thing for you is to get some sleep. That will work wonders.'

I closed my eyes and, to my later amazement, I obeyed.

* * *

When I awoke the sun had risen. So a new day had broken. I looked about me. The sky was stained red which threw a pink reflection over the sea. There was still a strong breeze which set white crests on the waves. It meant that we were moving along at a fair pace. Where to, was anyone's guess. We were at the mercy of the wind.

Lucas lay still at the bottom of the boat. The other man was watching me intently.

'You sleep?' he asked.

'Yes, for a long time, it seems.'

'You needed it. Feel better?'

I nodded. 'What's happened?'

'You can see we are in calmer waters.'

'The storm has gone.'

'Keep your fingers crossed. It's abated for the time being. Of course, it can spring up in a matter of minutes . . . but at the same time we've got a second chance.'

'Do you think there is a hope of our being picked up?'

'Fifty-fifty chance.'

'And if not?'

'The water won't last long.'

'You said something about biscuits.'

'H'm. But water is most important. We'll have to ration it.'

'What about him?' I asked, indicating Lucas.

'You know him.' It was a statement, not a question.

'Yes. We were friends on board.'

'I've seen you talking to him.'

'Is he badly hurt?'

'I don't know. We can't do anything about it.'

'What of his leg?'

'Needs setting, I expect. We've nothing here . . .'

'I wish . . .'

'Don't wish for too much. Fate might think you were greedy. We've just had what must be one of the most miraculous escapes possible.'

'I know. Thanks to you.'

He smiled at me rather shyly. 'We've still got to go on hoping for miracles,' he said.

'I wish we could do something for him.'

He shook his head. 'We have to be careful. We could overturn in half a second. He's got to take a chance just as we have.'

I nodded.

'My parents . . .' I began.

'It could be that they got into one of the boats.'

'I saw one of the boats go off . . . and go under.'

'Not much hope for any of them.'

'I'm amazed that this little craft survived. If we get out of this it will be entirely due to you.'

We fell into silence and after a while he took out the water can. We each took a mouthful.

He screwed it up carefully. 'We'll have to eke it out,' he said. 'It's lifeblood to us . . . remember.'

I nodded.

* * *

The hours slipped by. Lucas opened his eyes and they alighted on me. 'Rosetta?' he murmured.

'Yes, Lucas?'

'Where . . .' His lips formed the word but hardly any sound came.

'We're in a lifeboat. The ship has sunk, I think. You're all right. You're with me and . . .'

It was absurd not to know his name. He might have once been a deck hand but now he was our saviour, the man in charge of our brilliant rescue.

Lucas could not hear properly in any case. He showed no surprise but shut his eyes. He said something. I had to lean over him to catch it. 'My leg . . .'

We ought to do something about it. But what? We had no medical supplies, and we had to be careful how we moved about the boat. Even on this mild sea it could bob about in an alarming fashion and I knew it would be easy for one of us to be thrown overboard.

The sun came up and the heat was intense. Fortunately the breeze – now a light one – persisted. It was now blowing us gently along but neither of us had any notion in what direction.

'It will be easier when the stars come out,' said our rescuer.

I had learned his name which was John Player. I fancied he had admitted to it with a certain reluctance. 'Do you mind if I call you John?' I asked, and he had replied: 'Then I shall call you Rosetta. We are on equal terms now . . . no longer passenger and deck hand. The fear of death is a good leveller.' I replied: 'I do not need such fear to call you by your Christian name. It would be absurd to shout, "Mr Player, I am drowning. Please rescue me."' 'Quite absurd,' he had agreed. 'But I hope you will never have to do that.'

I asked him: 'Shall you be able to steer by the stars, John?'

He shrugged his shoulders. 'I am no trained navigator,

but one picks up a bit at sea. At least if we get a clear night we might have some idea of where we are heading for. It was too cloudy last night to see anything.'

'The direction could change. After all, you said it depended on the wind.'

'Yes, we have to go where we are taken. That gives one a great sense of helplessness.'

'Like depending on others for the essential things in life. Do you think Mr Lorimer is going to die?'

'He looks strong enough. I think the main trouble is his leg. He must have got a battering when the lifeboat overturned.'

'I wish we could do something.'

'The best thing is to keep our eyes open. If we see the smallest sign on the horizon we must do something to attract attention. Put up a flag . . .'

'Where could we find a flag?'

'One of your petticoats on a stick . . . something like that.'

'I think you are very resourceful.'

'Maybe, but what I am looking for now is another piece of luck.'

'It may be that we had our share when we got away from the wreck.'

'Well, we need a little bit more. In the meantime, let's do our best to find it. Keep your eyes open. The least speck on the horizon and we'll send up a signal of some sort.'

The morning passed slowly. It was afternoon. We drifted slowly along. Lucas opened his eyes now and then and spoke, although it was clear that he was not fully aware of the situation.

The sun was fortunately obscured by a few clouds which made it more bearable. I did not know what would be worse – rain which might mean a storm or this burning heat. John Player had suddenly dropped into a sleep of exhaustion. He looked very young thus. I wondered about him. It took my mind off the present desperate situation. How had he come to be a deck hand? I was sure there was some hidden past. There was an air of mystery about him. He was secretive . . . almost furtively watchful. At least during the last hours I had not noticed these qualities because he was intent on one thing . . . saving our lives. That had brought about a certain relationship between us. I suppose it was natural that it should.

I could not keep my mind from my parents. I tried to imagine them coming out on to that deck in that childlike, bewildered way in which they faced life which did not centre round the British Museum. They were quite unaware of the practicalities of life. They had never had to bother about them. Others had done that, leaving them free to pursue their studies.

Where were they now? I thought of them with a kind of tender exasperation.

I imagined their being hustled into a lifeboat . . . my father still mourning the loss of his notes rather than his daughter.

Perhaps I was wrong. Perhaps they had cared for me more than I realized. Hadn't they called me Rosetta, after the precious stone?

I scanned the horizon. I must not forget that I was on watch. I must be ready if a ship came into sight. I had removed my petticoat and it was attached to a piece of wood. If I saw anything like another craft, I would wake John and lose no time in waving my improvised flag madly.

The day wore on and there was nothing – only that wide expanse of water all around us . . . everywhere . . . to the horizon . . . wherever I looked there was emptiness.

Darkness had fallen. John Player had awakened. He was ashamed to have slept so long.

'You needed it,' I told him. 'You were absolutely worn out.'

'And you kept watch?'

'I swear to you there has been no sign of a ship anywhere.'

'There must be some time.'

We had more water and a biscuit.

'What of Mr Lorimer?' I asked.

'If he wakes up we'll give him something.'

'Should he be unconscious so long?'

'He shouldn't be, but it seems he is. Perhaps it's as well. That leg could be rather painful.'

'I wish we could do something about it.'

He shook his head. 'We can't do anything. We hauled him aboard. That was all we could do.'

'And you gave him artificial respiration.'

'As best I could. I think it worked though. Well, that was all we could do.'

'How I wish a ship would come.'

'I am heartily in agreement with you.'

The night descended on us . . . our second night. I dozed a little and dreamed I was in the kitchen of the house in Bloomsbury. 'It was such a night as this that the Polish Jew was murdered . . .'

Such a night as this! And then I was awake. The boat was scarcely moving. I could just make out John Player staring ahead.

I closed my eyes. I wanted to get back into the past.

* * *

We were into our second day. The sea was calm and I was struck afresh by the loneliness of that expanse of water. Only us and our boat in the whole world, it seemed.

Lucas became conscious during the morning. He said: 'What's the matter with my leg?'

'I think the bone may be broken,' I told him. 'We can't do anything about it. We'll be picked up by a ship soon, John thinks.'

'John?' he asked.

'John Player. He's been wonderful. He saved our lives.'

Lucas nodded. 'Who else is there?'

'Only the three of us. We're in the lifeboat. We've had amazing luck.'

'I can't help being glad you're here, Rosetta.'

I smiled at him.

We gave him some water.

'That was good,' he said. 'I feel so helpless.'

'We all are,' I replied. 'So much depends on that ship.'

During the afternoon John sighted what he thought was land. He called to me excitedly and pointed to the horizon. I could just make out a dark hump. I stared at it. Was it a mirage? Did we long so much for it that our tortured imaginations had conjured it up? We had been adrift for only two days and nights but it seemed like an eternity. I kept my eyes fixed on the horizon.

The boat seemed not to be moving. There we were on a tranquil sea and if there really was land close by we might not be able to reach it.

The afternoon wore on. The land had disappeared and our spirits sank.

'Our only hope is a ship,' said John. 'Goodness knows if that is possible. How far we are from the trade routes, I do not know.'

A slight breeze arose. It carried us along for a while. I was on the look-out and I saw land again. It was close now.

I called to John.

'It looks like an island,' he said. 'If only the wind is in the right direction . . .'

Several hours passed. The land came nearer and then receded. The wind rose and there were dark clouds on the horizon. I could see that John was anxious.

Quite suddenly he gave a shout of joy. 'We're getting nearer. Oh God . . . please help. The wind . . . the blessed wind . . . it's going to take us there.'

A tense excitement gripped me. Lucas opened his eyes and said: 'What is it?'

'I think we're near land,' I told him. 'If only . . .'

John was right beside me. 'It's an island,' he said. 'Look, we're going in . . .'

'Oh, John,' I murmured, 'can it be that our prayers are answered?'

He turned to me suddenly and kissed my cheek. I smiled and he gripped my hand hard. We were too full of emotion in that moment for more words.

We were in shallow water and the boat scraped land. John leaped out and I joined him. I felt an immense triumph, standing there with the water washing above my ankles.

It took a long time for us to drag the boat onto dry land.

The island on which we had landed was very small, little more than a rock jutting out of the sea. We saw a few stunted palm trees and sparse foliage. It rose steeply from the beach which I supposed was the reason why it was not completely submerged. The first thing John wanted to do was examine fully the contents of the boat and to his delight in one compartment under the seat he found more biscuits and another can of water, a first aid box containing bandages with some rope which enabled us to tether the boat to a tree and this gave us a wonderful sense of security.

Finding the water particularly delighted John. 'It will keep us alive for another few days.'

My first thought was for Lucas's leg. I remembered that Dot had once broken an arm and Mr Dolland had set it before the doctor had arrived and commended him for his prompt action. It had been related to me in some detail and I now tried to recall what Mr Dolland had done.

With John's help I did what I could. We discovered the broken bone and tried to piece it together. We found a piece of wood which served as a splint and the bandages were useful. Lucas said it felt more comfortable as a result but I feared our efforts were not very successful and they had in any case come far too late.

It was strange to see this hitherto self-sufficient man of the world so helpless and dependent upon us.

John had taken charge of us. He was a natural leader. He told us that he had attended drills on board the *Atlantic Star*, which every crewman was expected to do, and he had learned something about how to act in an emergency. That stood him in good stead now. He wished he had paid more attention but at least he remembered something of what he had been taught.

We were impatient to explore the island. We found a few coconuts. He shook them and listened for the rattle of milk.

He turned his eyes to the sky.

'Someone up there is looking after us,' he said.

* * *

Those days I spent on the island stand out in my memory – never to be forgotten. John turned out to be quite ingenious; he was practical and resourceful and was constantly trying to find ways to help us survive.

We must keep an account of the time, he said. He was going to make a notch in a stick for this purpose. He knew we had been at sea three nights and so we had a start. Lucas was now fully aware of what was happening. It was maddening for him to be unable to move but I think his main concern was that he might be a hindrance.

We tried to assure him that this was not so and we needed someone to be on watch all the time. He could stay in the boat and keep a look-out while John and I explored the island searching for food, or doing any jobs that needed to be done. We had been provided with whistles with our lifejackets and if he spotted a sail or anything unusual happened he could summon us immediately.

It is amazing how very close one can become to another human being in such circumstances. Thus it was with John and me. Lucas had been my friend before this shipwreck. John had been almost a stranger. Now we seemed like close friends.

He would talk to me more frankly when we were alone than he did when Lucas was present. There was something very kind about him. He understood Lucas's feelings, realizing how he would feel in his position, and he never mentioned before him his fears about the water supply running out. He did to me, though. He had installed a system of rationing. We took water at sunrise, midday and sunset.

'Water is the most precious thing we have,' he said. 'Without it we're finished. We could very shortly become dehydrated. A healthy young person can do without food for perhaps a month, but that person must have water. It is only a little we're getting. Drink it slowly. Hold it in your mouth, roll it round to get the utmost from it. As long as we have water we can survive. We'll preserve some if it rains. We'll manage.'

I felt comforted to be with him. I had an immense confidence in him. He knew it and I believe my faith in him gave him courage and the power to do what might have seemed impossible.

He and I explored the island, looking for likely food, while Lucas kept watch. Sometimes we walked in silence, sometimes we talked.

We had gone a mile or so from the shore and climbed to the top of a slope. From there we would see the island clearly and gaze right out to the horizon all around us.

A feeling of utter aloneness swept over me and I think he felt it too.

'Sit down a while, Rosetta,' he said. 'I think I work you too hard.'

I laughed. 'You, John, are the one who works hard. We should never have survived if it had not been for you.'

'Sometimes I think we shall never get off this island.'

'Of course we shall. We have been here only a few days. Of course we'll get off. Look how we found land. Who would have believed that? A ship will come by . . . you'll see.'

'And if it does . . .' he said and stopped, frowning into the distance.

I waited for him to go on. Instead he said: 'I think this can't be the route that ships take.'

'Why shouldn't it be? You wait and see . . .'

'Let's face it. We're going to run out of water.'

'It'll rain. We'll collect it.'

'We've got to find food. The biscuits are running out.'

'Why do you talk like this? It is not like you.'

'How do you know? You don't know me very well, do you?'

'I know you as well as you know me. At times like this people get to know each other quickly. There is not all the fuss of conventions and great gaps in acquaintanceship which you get at home. We are together all the time . . . night and day. We've shared incredible dangers together. You get to know people quickly when it is like that.'

'Tell me about yourself,' he said.

'Well, what do you want to know? You saw my parents on board, perhaps. I keep wondering what has happened to them. Could they have got into one of the boats? They are so vague. I don't think they realized what was happening. Their minds were in the past. They often seemed to forget about me, except when they saw me. They would have been more interested in me if I had been a tablet covered in hieroglyphics. At least they named me after the Rosetta Stone.'

He was smiling and I told him of my happy childhood, mostly spent below stairs, of the maids who were my companions, kitchen meals, Mrs Harlow, Nanny Pollock and Mr Dolland's 'turns'.

'I can see I do not have to feel sorry for you.'

'By no means. I often wonder what Mr Dolland and the rest are doing now. They will have heard of the shipwreck. Oh dear . . . they'll be dreadfully upset. And what will happen to the house? And to them? I do hope my parents were saved . . . if not, I don't know what will happen to them all.'

'Perhaps you will never know.'

'There you go again. And it's your turn. What about you?'

He was silent for a while. Then he said: 'Rosetta, I'm sorry.'

'It's all right, if you don't want to tell me.'

'I do. I feel a compulsion to tell you. I think you ought to know. Rosetta . . . my name is not John Player.'

'No? I thought it might not be.'

'It's Simon Perrivale.'

I was silent. Memories came rushing back. Sitting at the kitchen table . . . Mr Dolland putting on his glasses and reading from the newspaper.

I stammered: 'Not the . . .'

He nodded.

'Oh . . .' I began.

He interrupted. 'You're startled. Of course you are. I'm sorry. Perhaps I shouldn't have told you. I am innocent. I wanted you to know. You may not believe . . .'

'I do believe you,' I said sincerely.

'Thank you, Rosetta. You know now I am, as they say, "on the run".'

'So you worked on a ship as . . .'

'Deck hand,' he said. 'I was lucky. I knew that my arrest was imminent. I was sure they would find me guilty. I wouldn't have a chance. There was so much against me. But I am innocent, Rosetta. I swear it. I had to get right away, and perhaps later on . . . if it were possible . . . find some way of proving my innocence.'

'Perhaps it would have been better to have remained and faced it.'

'Perhaps. Perhaps not. He was already dead when I got there. The gun was there beside him. I picked it up . . . it looked as though I were guilty.'

'You might have proved your innocence.'

'Not then. Everything was against me. The Press had made up its mind that I was a murderer . . . so had everyone else. I felt then that I didn't stand a chance against them all. I wanted to get out of the country in some way so I made my way to Tilbury. I had what I thought was an amazing stroke of luck there. I talked to a sailor in a tavern. He was drinking heavily because he didn't want to go back to sea. His wife was going to have a baby and he couldn't bear to leave her. He was heartbroken. I took advantage of the fact that he was drunk. I shouldn't have done so but I was desperate. I felt I had to get out of the country . . . give myself a chance. It occurred to me that I might take his place . . . and this is what I did. He was a deck hand on the *Atlantic Star*, John Player. The ship was sailing that day . . . it was going to South Africa. I thought if I could get there, I could start a new life and perhaps some day the truth would come out and I could get home. I was desperate, Rosetta. It was a crazy plan but it worked. I was constantly in fear that something might be found out . . . but nothing was. And then this happened.'

'I guessed at once that there was something different about you, that you didn't fit somehow.'

'On our morning meetings, of course.'

'Yes.'

'Was it so obvious?'

'A little.'

'I was afraid of Lorimer.'

'Oh, I understand. He did say something about his home being not far from the Perrivale house.'

'Yes. He actually came there once. I was about seventeen,

I imagine then. I was in the stables when he rode in. It was a very brief meeting and one changes a lot in the years. He couldn't have recognized me, but I was afraid.'

'And now?' I said. 'What now?'

'It looks as though this could be the end of the story.'

'What happened on that day? Can you bear to talk of it?'

'I think I could tell you. One wants to talk to someone and you and I . . . well, we've become friends . . . real friends. We trust each other, and even if I felt you might betray me, you couldn't do much harm here, could you? To whom could you betray me here?'

'I would not dream of betraying you anywhere! You've told me you were innocent anyway.'

'I never felt that I belonged at Perrivale. That's rather sad for a child, you know. I have vague memories of what I used to think of as Before. Life was comfortable and easy then. I was five years old before it changed into what I called Now. There was someone I called Angel. She was plump, cosy and smelt of lavender; she was always there to comfort me. There was another one, too. She was Aunt Ada. She did not live in the cottage with us but she came there often. On the days when she came I used to hide under a table which was covered with a red cloth, velvety and smooth. I can feel that cloth now and the faint odour of mothballs, and I can hear the strident voice saying, "Why don't you, Alice?" in tones of reproach. Alice was the cosy lavender-smelling Angel.

'I remember once going in a train with Angel. We were going to Aunt Ada, to Witch's Home. I believed then that Aunt Ada was a witch. She must be if she lived in Witch's Home. I clung to Angel's hand as we entered. It was a little house with leaded windows which made it dark but everything in it shone brightly. All the time Aunt Ada was telling Angel what she ought to do. I was sent out to the garden. There was water at the bottom of it. I was afraid because I was separated from Angel and I thought Aunt Ada might tell her that she ought to leave me there. I can remember now my great joy when I was in the train once more with Angel beside me. I said, "Angel, don't let's go to the Witch's Home any more."

'We did not go again but Aunt Ada came to us. I would hear her saying, you should do this, you should not do that, and Angel would say, "Well, you see, Ada, it's like this . . ." And they would talk about the Boy which I knew referred to me. Aunt Ada was sure I would grow into a criminal if a little more discipline was not shown. Some would say she was right. But it wasn't so, Rosetta. I am innocent.'

'I do believe you,' I told him.

He was silent for a while and his eyes looked dreamily back into the past.

He went on: 'There was a man who used to come and visit us. I found out in due course that he was Sir Edward Perrivale. He brought presents for Angel and for me. She always looked pleased when he came, so I was, too. I used to be put on his knee and he would look at me and every now and then give a little chuckle. Then he would say: "Good boy. Fine boy." And that was all. But I thought it was rather nice and a change from Aunt Ada.

'One day I had been playing in the garden and came into the cottage to find Angel seated in a chair by the table. She had her hand to her breast; she looked pale and was gasping. I cried, "Angel, Angel, *I'm* here." I was frightened and bewildered because she didn't look at me. And then suddenly she shut her eyes and she wasn't like Angel at all. I was frightened and went on calling her name, but she fell forward with her head down. I started to scream. People came in. They took me away then and I knew something dreadful had happened. Aunt Ada came and it was no use hiding under the tablecloth. She soon found me and told me I was a wicked boy. I didn't care what she called me, I just wanted Angel to be there.

'She was dead. It was a strange, bewildering time. I can't remember much of it . . . except that there was a constant stream of people coming to the cottage and it wasn't the same place any more. She lay in a coffin in the parlour with the blinds drawn down. Aunt Ada took me to have "a last look at her". She made me kiss her cold face. I screamed and tried to run away. It wasn't the Angel I had known lying there . . . indifferent to me and my need of her. Why am I telling you all this . . . and telling it as a child? Why don't I just say she died, and that's that?'

'You are telling it as it should be told,' I said. 'You make me see it as it was . . . as you lived it . . . and that is how I want to see it.'

He went on: 'I can hear the tolling of the funeral bell. I can see these black-clad figures and Aunt Ada like some grisly prophet of disaster . . . watching me all the time, menacing me.

'Sir Edward came down for the funeral. There was a great deal of talk and it concerned "the Boy". I knew my future was in the balance and I was very frightened.

'I asked Mrs Stubbs who used to come to the cottage to scrub the floors where Angel was and she said, "Don't you worry your little head about her. She's safe enough. She's in Heaven with the angels." Then I heard someone say, "Of course he'll go to Ada."

'I could not imagine a worse fate. I had half suspected it. Ada was Angel's sister and since Angel was in Heaven, someone had to look after the boy. I knew there was one thing I had to do. I had to find Angel, so I set out to go to Heaven where I should see her and tell her that she must come back or I would stay with her there.

'I did not get very far before I met one of the farmworkers driving a cartload of hay. He stopped and called down to me, "Where you off to, young fellow-me-lad?" And I replied, "I'm going to Heaven." "That's a long way," he said. "You going on your own?" "Yes," I told him. "Angel is there. I'm going to her." He said, "You're little Simon, ain't you? I've heard about you. Here. Hop in and I'll give you a lift." "Are you going to Heaven, then?" I said. "Not yet, I hope," he said. "But I know the way you ought to go." He lifted me up beside him. And what he did was take me back to the cottage. Sir Edward was the first to see me. Touching his forehead, the man who had betrayed me said, "Begging your pardon, sir, but the little lad belongs here. I picked him up on the road. On his way to Heaven, he tells me. Thought I'd best bring him back, sir."

'Sir Edward had a strange look on his face. He gave the man money and thanked him and then he said to me, "We'll have a talk, shall we?" He took me into the cottage and we went into the parlour which still smelt of lilies, but the coffin wasn't there and I knew with a terrible sense of loneliness that she would not be there any more.

'Sir Edward put me on his knee. I thought he was going to say "Fine boy", but he didn't. What he said was, "So you were trying to find your way to Heaven, were you, boy?" I nodded. "It's a place you can't reach." I watched his mouth moving as he spoke. He had a line of hair above the top lip and a pointed beard – a Vandyke actually. "Why did you go?" he asked. I was not able to express myself with lucidity. I said, "Aunt Ada." He seemed to understand. "You don't want to go with her. She *is* your aunt." I shook my head. "No, no, no," I said. "You don't like her?" I nodded. "Well, well," he said. "Let's see what we can do." He was very thoughtful. I think he must have made up his mind then, for a day or so later I heard that I was going away to a big house. Sir Edward was going to take me into his family.'

He smiled at me. 'You have drawn your own conclusions. I am sure they are correct. I was his son . . . his illegitimate son, though it was hard to believe that, he being the man I came to know later. I was sure he loved my mother, Angel. Anybody must. I sensed it when they were together, but of course he couldn't marry her. She was not the right sort for him. He must have fallen in love with her and set her up in the cottage and he came to visit her from time to time. I was never told this by Sir Edward or anyone. It was an assumption, but so plausible that it was accepted by all. Why else should he have taken me into his household and educated me with his sons?'

'So,' I said. 'That is how you came to Perrivale Court.'

'Yes. I was two years older than Cosmo and three than Tristan. That was fortunate for me; otherwise I should have had a bad time, I think. Those two years gave me an advantage. I needed it, for, having installed me in his nursery, Sir Edward seemed to lose interest in me, though sometimes I saw him watching me furtively. The servants resented me. If it hadn't been for the nanny I should probably have been as badly off as I would with Aunt Ada. But the nanny took pity on me. She loved me and protected me. I always remember how much I owe to that good woman.

'Then we had a tutor when I was about seven years old, a Mr Welling, I remember, and I got on well with him. He must have heard the gossip but it did not affect him. I was more serious than Cosmo and Tristan and I had those two years as an advantage.

'There was, of course, Lady Perrivale. She was a terrifying person and I was glad that she seemed quite unaware of my existence. She very rarely spoke to me and I had the impression that she did not see me. She was a large woman and everyone – apart from Sir Edward – was afraid of her. It was well known in the house that her money had saved Perrivale Court and that she was the daughter of a millionaire coal-owner or iron-master. There seemed to be a divergence of opinion as to which. She had been an only daughter and he had wanted a title for her. He was ready to pay a price for it and much of the money made from iron or coal had gone into bolstering up the roof and walls of Perrivale

Court. It must have seemed a good arrangement to Sir Edward for, as well as keeping the roof over his head, she provided him with two sons as well. I had one desire – to keep out of her way. So now you have a picture of the sort of household I was in.'

'Yes, and then you went away to school?'

'Which was decidedly better for me. There I was equal with the others. I was good at lessons, fair at sports and I did well. I lost a little of that aggressiveness which I had built up in the early years. I was ready to defend myself before there was any need to do so. I looked for slights and insults where there were none. School was good for me.

'Too soon it was over. We had ceased to be boys. There was enough work on the estate to keep us all busy and we worked comparatively well together. We were reasonable adults now . . . all of us.

'I was about twenty-four when Major Durrell came to the neighbourhood. His daughter came with him. She was a widow with a small child, a girl. The widow was startlingly beautiful – red-haired and green-eyed. Very unusual. We were all rather fascinated by her. Both Cosmo and Tristan in particular, but she chose Cosmo and their engagement was announced.'

I looked at him steadily. Had he cared for the widow, as had been suggested? Did the prospect of her marriage to someone else arouse his anger, despair, jealousy? Had he planned to have the widow for himself? No. I did believe him. He had spoken with such sincerity. He had made me see the nursery presided over by the kindly nanny and the arrival in their midst of the fascinating widow – Mirabel was what the papers had called her.

'Yes,' he went on. 'She had chosen Cosmo. Lady Perrivale was very pleased. She was very eager for her sons to marry and give her grandchildren and she was delighted that Cosmo's bride was to be Mirabel. Mirabel's mother, it seemed, had been an old schoolfriend of hers – her best friend, we heard. She had married the Major and, although she was now dead, Lady Perrivale gave a warm welcome to the widower and his daughter. She had known the Major when her friend had married him, and he had written telling her that he had retired from the Army and was thinking of settling somewhere. What about Cornwall? Lady Perrivale was delighted and found Seashell Cottage for them. That was how they came to be there. And then, of course, there was the engagement to Cosmo which followed very soon. You see how the stage was set.'

'I am beginning to see it very clearly,' I said.

'We were all working on the estate and there was this farmhouse, Bindon Boys. The farmer who had lived there and worked the farm had died some three years before and the land had been let out to a farmer on a temporary basis but no one had taken on the house. It was in a bad state and needed a bit of restoration as well as decorating.'

'Yes, there was a good deal in the papers about Bindon Boys.'

'Yes . . . it was originally Bindon Bois. There is a copse nearby. It was called Bindon Boys by the natives and that had become its official name. We had all inspected the house and were deciding what should be done.'

I nodded. I visualized the heavy black headlines. 'Bindon Boys Case. Police expect an arrest shortly.' I was seeing it all so differently now from the manner which I had when Mr Dolland had sat at the kitchen table and we had tried to piece the story together.

'We had been over there several times. There was a great deal of work to be done. I remember the day clearly. I was meeting Cosmo at the farmhouse so that we could discuss some plan on the spot. I went to the house and found him there . . . dead . . . the gun by his side. I could not believe it. I knelt beside him. There was blood on my coat. His blood. I picked up the gun . . . and it was then that Tristan came in and found me. I remember his words. "Good God,

Simon! You've killed him!" I told him I had just come in . . . that I had found him like this. He stared at the gun in my hand . . . and I could see what he was thinking.'

He stopped short and closed his eyes as though he were trying to shut out the memory. I laid my hand on his shoulder.

I said: 'You know you're innocent, Simon. You'll prove it one day.'

'If we never get away from this island, no one will ever know the truth.'

'We are going to get away,' I said. 'I feel it.'

'It's just hope.'

'Hope is a good thing.'

'It's heart-breaking when it is proved unfounded.'

'But it isn't in this case. A ship *will* come. I know it. And then . . .'

'Yes, what then? I must hide myself away. I must never go back. I dare not. If I did they would capture me and, having run away, they would say I had proved my guilt.'

'What really happened? Have you any idea?'

'I think there is a possibility that it might have been old Harry Tench. He hated Cosmo. He had rented one of the farms some years before. He drank too much and the place went to ruin. Cosmo turned him out and put in another man. Tench went away but he came back. He was tramping the road. He'd become a sort of tinker. People said he had sworn vengeance on the Perrivales and Cosmo in particular. He hadn't been seen in the neighbourhood for some weeks, but of course, if he'd planned to kill Cosmo, he would naturally be careful about being seen nearby. His name was mentioned during the investigation, but he was dismissed and no longer a suspect. I was a more likely one. They made a great play about the emnity between Cosmo and me. People all around seemed to remember signs of it which I was unaware of. They made much of Mirabel and Cosmo's engagement to her.'

'I know. The *crime passionnel*. Were you . . . in love with her?'

'Oh no. We were all a little dazzled by her . . . but no.'

'And when her engagement to Cosmo was announced . . . did you show that you were disappointed?'

'Tristan and I probably said how lucky Cosmo was and that we envied him or something like that. I didn't think we meant it very seriously.'

There was silence between us.

Then he said: 'Now you know. I'm glad. It is like a weight being lifted from my shoulders. Tell me . . . are you shocked to find you have a suspected murderer with you?'

'I can only think that he saved my life . . . Lucas's too.'

'With my own, of course.'

'Well, if you hadn't saved your own, none of us would be here. I am glad you told me. I wish something could be done . . . to make things right . . . so that you could go back. Perhaps one day you will.'

'You are an optimist. You think we are going to get off this godforsaken island. You believe in miracles.'

'I think I have seen a few in the last days.'

Again he took my hand and pressed it.

'You are right and I am ungrateful. We shall be picked up in time . . . and some day perhaps, I shall go back to Perrivale Court and they will know the truth.'

'I am sure of it,' I said. I stood up. 'We have talked for a long time. Lucas will be wondering where we are.'

* * *

Two more days passed. The water stock was very low and we were running out of coconuts. Simon had found a stout stick which Lucas used as a crutch. His leg was slightly less painful, he said, but I had little confidence in our attempts to set it. Still, he could hobble a few steps and that cheered him considerably.

When we were alone, Simon told me further incidents from his life and I began to get a clearer picture of what it had been like. I was fascinated by it all. I longed to be of help in uncovering the truth and helping to establish his innocence. I wanted to hear more of Harry Tench. I had decided that he was the murderer. Simon said Cosmo should not have been so hard on the man. True, Harry Tench was a poor farmer and if the estate was to prosper it must be maintained in a proper manner, but he could have kept Harry Tench on in some capacity perhaps. Cosmo had insisted that he was useless as a worker; moreover, he had been insolent, which was something Cosmo would not accept.

We used to discuss how it would have been possible for Harry Tench to have killed Cosmo. He had no fixed home; he often slept in barns; he had admitted sleeping in Bindon Boys. Perhaps he had been there when Cosmo arrived at the house a short time before Simon came in. Perhaps he had seized his opportunity. But there was the gun. That needed a little explanation. It had been discovered that it came from the gunroom at Perrivale Court. How could Harry Tench have got his hands on it?

And so on . . . but I am sure it was a great relief to Simon to be able to talk.

It was our fifth day on the island and late in the afternoon. Simon and I had been wandering round all the morning. We had found some berries which we thought might be edible and were considering the risk of trying them when we heard a shout . . . followed by a whistle.

It was Lucas. We hurried back to him. He was pointing excitedly to the horizon. It was just a speck. Were we imagining this or were we conjuring up in our minds something we so desperately wanted to see?

In breathless silence we watched. It had begun to take shape.

'It is. It *is*!' cried Simon.

In the Seraglio

Having been close to death for so long, I had thought that anything would have been preferable; but the fears of the next weeks were beyond anything I could ever have imagined.

How often did I tell myself that it would have been better to go down with the ship or that our little boat had been destroyed in a hurricane?

I recall now our joy when we first saw that ship on the horizon and then so soon after we had been rescued, I became sure that it would have been better if we had remained on the island, still vainly looking for a rescue. Who knew, we might have found some means of surviving; and we were together, enjoying a certain peace and security.

From the moment those dark, swarthy men waded ashore, red caps on their heads, cutlasses at their sides, our euphoria at being rescued had been replaced by a fearful apprehension. It was immediately clear that we could not understand their language. I guessed they must be of Arabic origin. Their ship was no *Atlantic Star*. It looked like an ancient galley. It had not occurred to me that there could still be pirates on the high seas, but I remembered the captain of the *Atlantic Star* one night at dinner when he told us that there were ships which still roamed about in certain waters, following some nefarious trade or other. And it instantly occurred to me that we had fallen into the hands of such men.

I did not like the ship; I did not like these men; and it

was clear to me that my suspicions were shared by both Simon and Lucas.

We stood close as though to shield each other. There were about ten of them. They gabbled together and stared searchingly at us. One of them approached and took a lock of my hair in his hands. They were crowding round and chattering excitedly. My hair was fairer now that it was bleached by the sun and I could only believe that they were astonished by my colouring which was so different from theirs.

I sensed the uneasiness of Simon and Lucas. They had edged closer to me. I knew they would both fight to the death for me, which brought a modicum of comfort.

Their attention had turned to Lucas who was standing there, leaning on the stick we had found for him. He looked pale and ill.

The men were chattering and shaking their heads. They gazed at me and then at Simon. They laughed and nodded to each other. I had a terrible fear that they were going to take us and leave Lucas.

I said: 'We'll all stand together.'

'Yes,' muttered Simon. 'I don't like the look of them.'

'Bad luck they found us,' murmured Lucas. 'Better . . .'

'What do you think they are?'

Simon shook his head, and I felt numb with fear. I was afraid of these men, their chattering voices, their sly sidelong glances, their implication as to what they would do with us.

Suddenly they made a decision. One, whom I took to be the leader, signed to them and four of them went to our boat, examined it and turned to nod at the others. They were taking our boat out to the galley.

Simon took a step forward but he was barred by a man with a cutlass.

'Let them take it,' I hissed.

It was our turn. The leader nodded and two men, their cutlasses drawn, came and stood behind us. They gave us all a little push and we saw what was indicated. We were to go out to the galley. Lucas hobbled between us . . . but the three of us were at least together.

Simon murmured: 'We wouldn't have lasted long on that island, anyway.'

It was difficult getting Lucas on board. None of them helped us. We had to mount a rope-ladder which was almost an impossibility for Lucas. I think Simon half carried him up.

Then we were all three standing on the deck surrounded by curious men. They all seemed to be staring at me. Several of them touched my hair. They laughed together, twisting it round their fingers and pulling it.

There was a sudden silence. A man had appeared. I guessed he was the captain of the vessel. He was taller than the others and his dark lively eyes held a hint of humour. Moreover, there was a certain refinement in his well-defined features which gave me a brief glow of hope.

He shouted something and the men fell back.

He looked at the three of us and bowed his head in a form of greeting.

He said: 'English?'

'Yes . . . yes,' we cried.

He nodded. That seemed to be the extent of his knowledge of our language, but his courtesy was comforting. He turned to the men and talked in a way which seemed threatening. They were clearly subdued.

He turned to us and said: 'Come.'

We followed him and were put into a small cabin. There was a bunk there and we sat down thankfully.

The captain lifted his hand. 'Eat,' he said.

He then went out and locked the door behind him.

'What does it mean?' I asked.

Lucas thought that the object would be to hold us for

ransom. 'It's a thriving business,' he said. 'I feel sure that that is what they have in mind.'

'Do you mean to say they roam the seas looking for shipwrecked mariners?'

'Oh no. They'll have another trade. Smuggling, perhaps . . . or even seizing ships where possible . . . like the pirates of old. They'd turn their hands to anything if there's a profit in it. They would presume we must have a home somewhere and we're English. They are inclined to regard all the English abroad as millionaires.'

'How glad I am we remained together.'

'Yes,' said Lucas. 'I think they were wondering whether I should be worth the effort.'

'What are we going to do?' asked Simon.

He looked at me steadily. 'We must do everything in our power to stay together.'

'I pray that we do.'

Food was brought to us. It was hot and spicy. In the ordinary way I should have declined it but we were near starvation and any food seemed palatable. Lucas advised us to eat sparingly.

I felt a little better afterwards. I wondered how they would send home for ransoms. To whom would they send? My father had a sister whom we had scarcely seen for the last ten years or so. Would she be ready to pay a ransom for her niece? Perhaps my parents had reached home, but they had never been rich.

And Simon? The last thing he would want was for his identity to be known. As for Lucas . . . regarding a ransom, he was probably in the best position of all of us, for he came from a wealthy family.

'I wish I knew where we were,' said Simon. 'That would be a help.'

I wondered if he had plans for escaping. He was very resourceful, as he had shown himself to be by escaping from England.

If he had done that, it was possible that he might be able to escape again.

So we brooded and all three of us, I am sure, were wishing we were back on the island. Food might have been scarce, hopes of survival slim, but at least we had been free.

* * *

I had an unpleasant experience on the first night. It was dark and we were trying to sleep when I heard stealthy footsteps outside the door and then the sound of a key being turned in the lock.

I started up as the door quietly opened.

Two men came in. I believed they were two of those who had come ashore to take us in but I could not be certain at this stage as one looked very like another to me.

They had come to take me. They seized me. I screamed. Lucas and Simon were immediately awake.

The two men were trying to drag me out of the cabin, and I could guess by their grunts and expressions what their intentions were.

I cried: 'Let me go!'

Simon struck one of the men. He was knocked across the cabin by the other. Lucas brandished his stick and hit out at them.

There was a great deal of shouting and others appeared at the door. They were all laughing and chattering. Simon got up; he came to me, seized me and thrust me behind him. I saw that his hand was bleeding.

A terrible fear swept over me. I knew I was in great danger.

I dared not imagine what would have happened to me if the captain had not appeared. He shouted an order. The men looked sheepish. He saw me cowering behind Simon and Lucas beside me.

Simon seemed somehow to indicate that if any one of them attempted to harm me he would have to face him, and he was formidable. Lucas was equally protective but of course he was crippled.

The captain had clearly summed up the whole situation. He knew what the motive of these men had been. I was different; I had long yellow hair such as they had not seen before. Moreover, I was a woman, and that was enough for them.

The captain bowed to me and his gesture suggested an apology for the crude behaviour of his men.

He indicated that I must follow him.

Simon stepped forward.

The captain shook his head. 'I see . . . safe,' he said. 'I . . . only . . . I . . . captain.'

Oddly enough, I trusted him. I knew he was the captain of a ship engaged in some nefarious trade, but for some reason I believed he would help me. In any case he was the captain. If we had attempted to disobey him, we should not have done so for long. We were at his mercy. For all their gestures, neither Simon nor Lucas could save me for long. I had to trust the captain.

I walked behind him through those men. Some of them put out their hands to touch my hair but none of them did. I could see that they were greatly in awe of the captain and his orders obviously were that none was to touch me.

I was taken to a small cabin which I think adjoined his. He stood aside for me to enter. It was more comfortable than the one I had left. There were covers and cushions on a bunk which was like a divan. I could rest more comfortably here. Behind a curtain was a basin and ewer. I could wash!

The captain spread his hands, indicating the cabin. He said: 'Safe here . . . I see safe.'

'Thank you,' I said.

I don't know whether he understood but my tone must have expressed my gratitude.

He bowed, went out and locked the door behind him.

I sank on to the bed. I started to tremble violently as I contemplated the ordeal from which the captain had saved me.

It was a long time before I could regain my composure.

I wondered what *his* intentions were. Perhaps Lucas was right. I felt sure he must be. It was a ransom they were thinking of; and if this were the case, they would want us to be returned unharmed.

I pulled aside the curtain and indulged in the luxury of washing myself.

I returned to the divan. I lay down. I was exhausted – physically, mentally and emotionally, and for a brief spell forgot the hazards about me.

I slept.

* * *

I think perhaps I tried to forget those days when I lived in a state of perpetual terror. Every time I heard a footstep, every time my door opened, I would be seized by an overwhelming apprehension. One's imagination in such situations can be one's greatest enemy.

Food was brought to me regularly and because of this I felt a respite from being constantly on the alert for danger; yet I knew it was all around me. I was not sure what their purpose was, but it was obvious that they were planning something for me. The captain certainly stood between me and a certain fate and at least I had to be thankful for that. I trusted the man . . . not because I believed in his chivalry but his attitude meant that I must be treated with a certain respect because of what he had in mind for me.

I found I could eat a little. My creature comforts were attended to. It was a great blessing to be able to wash frequently. I wished I knew where the ship was going and what fate was planned for me. I wished I knew where Simon and Lucas were.

The captain came to my cabin once. I had washed my

hair and it was just drying when the knock came. He kept staring at my hair, but he was very polite. I knew that he wanted to talk to me but his knowledge of English was exasperatingly limited.

'You . . . come in . . . ship . . . England?'

'Yes,' I said. 'But we were wrecked.'

'From England . . . alone? No?' He shook his head.

'With my parents . . . my father and mother.'

It was hopeless. I imagined he was trying to find out what kind of family I came from. Was there money? How much would it be worth to have me back?

He gave it up as hopeless, but I knew by the way in which he kept looking at my hair and smiling to himself that he was pleased with what he saw.

Then one morning when I awoke the ship was no longer moving. The sun had risen and when I looked out through the small porthole I caught a glimpse of white buildings.

I became aware of noise and bustle. People were shouting to each other in excited voices. One thing was certain. We had reached our destination and I must soon learn my fate.

During that morning it gradually dawned on me what it was to be and I was filled with the utmost horror. I began to ask myself if it would not have been better if I had never experienced my miraculous escape from the sea.

The captain came to my cabin. He brought with him a black cloak, a yashmak and a snood. He made it clear that these were for me to wear. My hair had to be piled into the snood and when I was fully clad I looked like any Arab woman who might be met within the souks of an eastern town.

I was taken ashore and to my great delight I caught a glimpse of Simon. But I was immediately anxious because there was no sign of Lucas.

Simon recognized me in spite of my covering and I was aware of his fear as he did so. We tried to reach each other but we were roughly held back.

The sun was dazzling and I was very hot in my robes. A man walked on either side of Simon, and with the captain beside me we waded ashore.

I shall never forget that walk. We were in what I took to be the Kasbah. The streets were narrow, cobbled and winding and crowded with men in robes and women dressed as I was now. Goats ran among us; there were a few hungry-looking dogs who sniffed at us hopefully. I caught a glimpse of a rat feeding in the refuse on the cobbles. There were small shops – little more than caves – open to the streets, with stalls on which lay trinkets, brass ornaments, small leather goods, and food – exotic, spicy and unappetizing in my eyes. The smell was sickening.

Some of the traders called a greeting to the captain and his men and I was becoming more and more apprehensive about my eventual fate, for they seemed to know the purpose of his visit and I wondered how many other young women had walked along these streets with him. If only I could get to Simon. And what had they done with Lucas?

At length we moved into a wider street. Some trees grew here – dusty palms, mostly. The houses were bigger; we turned in at a gate and we were in a courtyard where a fountain played. Around this squatted several men – servants, I presumed, for they jumped up as we entered and started to talk excitedly.

One of them came up and bowed very low to the captain, who nodded an acknowledgement and waved his hands. We were led through a door into a large hall. The windows were heavily draped and set in alcoves designed, I was sure, to let in the minimum of heat.

A man in splendid robes bowed to the captain and seemed eager to show him the utmost respect. He was obviously telling him to follow, for he led us through another door and there, seated on a dais on a very ornate chair, was a little old man.

He was flamboyantly dressed, but so small and wizened that his clothes only seemed to accentuate his age. He was very ancient except for his eyes, which were dark and very lively; they reminded me of a monkey's.

The captain went to the chair and bowed and the old man waved in greeting. Then the captain obviously told his men to leave him with Simon and me.

The captain pushed me forward. He let the cloak fall to the ground and pulled off my yashmak and snood so that my hair fell about my shoulders. The lively dark eyes opened wide. He muttered something which seemed to please the captain. The old man's eyes were fixed on my hair, and he and the captain began to talk excitedly. How I wished I knew what they were saying.

Then Simon was brought forward. The old man's shrewd eyes ranged over him, weighing him up and down. He looked very tall and strong, and it seemed to me that his physical strength made as good an impression as my hair.

The old man nodded and I guessed that was a sign of approval.

The captain moved closer to the old man and they were in deep conversation. That gave Simon and me a chance to get close together.

'Where is Lucas?' I whispered.

'I don't know. I was taken away and brought here. He wasn't with me.'

'I do hope he's all right. Where are we?'

'Somewhere along the north coast of Africa, I imagine.'

'What are they going to do with us? What are they talking about?'

'Probably bargaining.'

'Bargaining?'

'It looks as if we are being sold.'

'Like slaves!'

'It would seem so.'

'What shall we *do*?'

'I don't know. Wait for our opportunity. We are helpless just now. We'll have to wait for the right moment and then . . . get away . . . if we can.'

'Shall we be together?'

'I don't know.'

'Oh Simon . . . I do hope we don't lose each other.'

'Let's pray for it.'

'I'm very frightened, Simon.'

'I feel very much the same myself.'

'This old man . . . what is he?'

'A trader, I imagine.'

'A trader . . . in people?'

'That amongst other things . . . anything that comes to hand, I imagine, if it's worth while. And that would include people.'

'We must get away somehow.'

'How?'

'Run . . . anywhere.'

'How far do you think we'd get? No, wait. If we can keep together, we will. Who knows, the opportunity may come. We'll manage it.'

'Oh Simon, I believe we shall.'

I remember now the look which passed between us. I treasured it to remember in my darkest and most frightened moments. I was to think of it often during the weeks to come.

* * *

There are some things one does not wish to remember. One wants to shut them out and make believe they did not happen. Sometimes the mind helps so that they become a blurred memory. And that is what seemed to have happened to me.

I remember being in the trader's house. It must have been for just one night. I recall my terrible apprehension, the pictures supplied by a cruel imagination which continually taunted me as to what my fate would be. The old man seemed like a horrible ogre. There was only one comfort to me. Simon was in the house. The transaction with the captain concerned us both.

Later on the day of our arrival the captain left the house and I never saw him again.

The next day I was enveloped in the robes in which I had arrived and my hair was completely hidden as before. Then Simon and I were taken through the streets of the Kasbah to the harbour where a ship was waiting. The old man was clearly in charge of us but he took no notice of us and I had the impression that he was only there to protect his property, which we now were.

We could not imagine where he was taking us.

Simon and I found one or two opportunities on board to talk to each other. Our main topic was Lucas.

Simon told me that there had been one or two meetings with the captain. They had not been ill-treated. He said they had been very interested in Lucas. Simon thought he had been taken away somewhere. They had been separated and not able to talk but he fancied Lucas was hopeful – at least not unduly alarmed.

'I think he thought at one time that they might throw him overboard because he would be no use for work. I imagine that is what they want of me.'

I was silent, dreading to think what my fate might be.

Simon thought the place we had left was very probably Algeria.

'It used to be a refuge for pirates in the old days. They had the protection of the Turkish government. Perhaps it still remains a haven for them. The Kasbah must be an ideal spot for underhand business of any sort. I imagine few would want to venture there at certain times.'

He was probably right.

We pursued our journey along the Syrian coast to the

Dardenelles – and then to our destination which we learned in due course was Constantinople.

* * *

As we were approaching the Bosphorus, a woman came to my cabin. She had a girl with her and the girl was carrying what looked like an armful of diaphanous material. It turned out to be garments and these were laid out on the bunk. Then they turned their attention to me. I had seen these women about the ship and had wondered what their duties were. I soon realized they had come to the cabin to help me dress in these splendid garments.

There were long trousers made of flimsy silky material, baggy and caught in at the ankles. Over them went a gown of beautiful transparent material. It was sparkling with sequins which looked like stars. They unpinned my hair and spread it round my shoulders. They combed it and looked at one another, nudging and giggling.

When I was dressed they stood back and clapped their hands.

I said: 'I want my other clothes.'

They could not understand me. They just went on giggling and nudging each other. They stroked my hair and smiled at me.

The old man came into the cabin. He looked at me and rubbed his hands together.

My fear was greater than ever. I knew that Simon's surmise was correct. We were going to be sold into slavery – he as a strong man to work as directed while I was destined for a more sinister purpose.

I sensed that Simon was more worried about my fate than his own.

The cloak, yashmak and snood were brought in and my splendour was hidden from view. With Simon beside me, I was taken off the ship where a carriage was waiting for us and, with the old man and a younger one who, I imagined, was some sort of clerk or assistant, we were driven through the streets of Constantinople.

I was too concerned with my impending fate to take much note of my surroundings, but I learned later that there are two distinct parts of the city – the Christian and the Turkish – and these are connected by two bridges, rather clumsily constructed but adequate and very necessary. I was vaguely aware of mosques and minarets, and I felt, with great desolation, that we were very far from home.

It was to the Turkish section that we were taken.

I felt lost and very frightened. I kept looking at Simon to reassure myself that he was still there.

It seemed that we drove for a long time. It was like another world – narrow streets, incredibly dirty, fine buildings, dazzlingly white spires reaching to the bluest of skies; mosques, bazaars, wooden houses little more than hovels, noise, people everywhere. They scattered before the oncoming carriage, and again and again I thought we should run someone down but they always managed to escape from under the horses' feet.

At length we turned into a quiet avenue. The trees and bushes were bright with colourful flowers. We slowed down before a tall white building which stood back from the road.

When we alighted from the carriage a man in white robes came out to greet us. The old man bowed to him rather obsequiously and the greeting was returned in a somewhat condescending manner. We were taken inside, into a room which seemed dark after the brilliance of the sun. The windows were similar to those which I had seen before, recessed and heavily draped.

A tall man came forward. He wore a turban with a jewel in it and long white robes. He sat in a chair like a throne and I noticed that the old man had become more deferential than ever.

I thought in trepidation: Is this to be my new owner?

My cloak was removed and my hair displayed. The man in the chair was clearly impressed by it. I had never felt so humiliated in my life. He looked at Simon and nodded.

There had been two men standing at the door – guards, I supposed. One of them clapped his hands and a woman came in. She was somewhat plump, middle-aged and elaborately dressed in the same style as I was.

She came to me, studied me, took a strand of my hair in her hands and smiled faintly. Then she rolled up the sleeves of my gown and prodded me. She frowned and, shaking her head, made little sounds which I was sure indicated disapproval.

The old man started to talk very quickly; the other was reasoning. The woman said a word or two and nodded judiciously. It was maddening not to know what they were saying. All I could gather was that it was something about me and they were not as pleased with me as the old man had hoped they would be.

However, they appeared to come to some agreement. The old man was clasping his hands and the other was nodding. The woman nodded too. She was explaining something to them. The man was listening intently to her and she seemed to be reassuring him.

She signed to me to follow her.

Simon was left behind. I gave him an agonized look and he started after me. One of the guards stepped forward and barred his way, his hand on the hilt of his sword.

I saw the helplessness in Simon's face; then my arm was firmly taken by the plump woman and I was led away.

* * *

I was to learn that I was destined for the seraglio of one of the most important Pashas in Constantinople. All the men I had seen so far were merely his minions.

The harem is a community of women into which no

man is allowed to appear except the eunuchs, such as this important gentleman I had seen bargaining with the old man. He, I discovered, was the Chief Eunuch, and I was to see him frequently.

It took me some time to realize that I had reason to be thankful for the hardship I had suffered, because my physical state was the reason why, during those weeks, I was left unmolested. My yellow hair had made me outstanding. I was a prize object because I was so different from the women around me. They were all dark-haired and dark-eyed. My eyes were a definite blue and they and my yellow hair set me apart.

It seemed to those whose duty it was to relieve the Pasha's jaded senses that my very difference might make me especially acceptable. There was something else which I discovered later they had noticed about me. These women were subservient by nature. They had been brought up in the certain knowledge that they were the inferior sex and their mission on Earth was to pander to men's desires. Whereas there was a spirit of independence about me. I came of a different culture and it set me apart almost as much as did my blue eyes and yellow hair.

However, when I was stripped and subjected to one of the scented baths which had been prepared for me, it was seen by the watchful lady who was in charge of us all that my skin, where it had not been exposed to the sun, was very white and soft. Before I was offered up to the Pasha the whiteness of my skin must be restored to every part of my body. Moreover, I had become very ill-nourished and the Pasha did not like women to be too thin. The potential was there but it had to be recovered; and this process would take a little time.

How grateful I was! I had time to adjust myself, to learn the ways of the harem and perhaps to find out what had happened to Simon. Who knew? I had been remarkably fortunate as yet; what if there might still be hope of escape before I had reached that state which would render me worthy of submission to the man who had bought me?

As soon as I learned that I was safe – if only for a short time – my spirits revived. Hope came flooding back. I wanted to learn all I could about my surroundings and naturally I wondered a great deal about my companions.

The most important person in the harem was Rani, the middle-aged woman who had inspected me and decided that as yet I was unworthy to be submitted to the Pasha. If only we had had a common language I could have learned a great deal from her. The other women were very much in awe of her. They all flattered her and were most obsequious to her, for she was the one who selected those who were to be presented to the Pasha. When the order came she would give great thought to the matter and, during that time, it was amusing to see how they all tried to call attention to themselves. I was amazed to realize that that which I so much dreaded was greatly sought after by the rest.

There were some young girls in the harem who could not have been more than ten years old and women who must have been close on thirty. It was a strange life these girls lived, and I discovered later that some of them had been there since childhood . . . trained to give pleasure to some rich man.

There was little for them to do all day. I had to have my daily baths and to be massaged with ointments. It was a world remote from reality. The air was heavy with the scent of musk, sandalwood, patchouli and attar of roses. The girls would sit by the fountains, talking idly; sometimes I would hear the tinkle of a musical instrument. They picked the flowers; they entwined them in their hair; they studied their faces in little hand mirrors; they gazed at their reflections in the pools; sometimes they played games; they would chatter together, giggle, tell fortunes.

They slept in a large and airy room on divans; there were

beautiful clothes for them to wear. It was an extraordinary life to while away the days, thinking of nothing but how to beautify themselves, how to idle through the day hoping that that evening they might be selected to share the Pasha's bed.

There was a great deal of rivalry for this honour. I soon sensed that. I attracted a great deal of attention. I was so different from them and I supposed it was almost a certainty that, when I was considered worthy, I should be chosen for my very strangeness, if for nothing else.

Meanwhile the attempts to wipe out the results of the hardships I had suffered went on. I felt like a goose being fattened up for Christmas. I found it difficult to eat the highly spiced food. It was a little game, trying to dispose of it without Rani's knowing what I was doing.

It was an exciting day when I found out that one of the more mature women – and I think one of the most beautiful – was French. Her name was Nicole and I noticed from the first that she was different from the others. She also seemed to be the most important, under Rani, of course.

One day I was sitting by the fountain when she came up and sat beside me.

She asked me in French if I spoke the language.

Communication at last! It was wonderful. My French was not very adequate but at least it existed and we were able to talk.

'You are English?' she asked.

I told her I was.

'And how did you come here?'

In halting French I told her of the shipwreck and how we had been picked up.

She replied that she had been in the harem for seven years. She was Creole and had come from Martinique to go to school in France. On the way she, too, had been shipwrecked and taken by corsairs, brought here and sold, just as I had been.

'You have been here all those years?' I said. 'How have you endured it?'

She shrugged her shoulders. 'At first,' she said, 'there is great fear. I was only sixteen years old. I hated the convent. It was easy here. I liked the clothes . . . the idle life, I suppose. And . . . I was different . . . as you are. The Pasha liked me.'

'You were the favourite of the harem, I believe,' I said.

She nodded. 'Because,' she said, 'I have Samir.'

I had seen Samir—a beautiful child of about four years old. He was made much of by the women. He was the eldest of the harem children. There was one other – Feisal, who was about a year younger and also a very attractive boy. I had seen him with a woman, a few years younger, I imagined, than Nicole. Her name was Fatima.

Fatima was a voluptuous beauty with masses of black hair and languid dark eyes. She was self-indulgent in the extreme, indolent and vain. She would sit by the pool for hours, eating sweetmeats and feeding them to one of the little King Charles spaniels who were her constant companions. Fatima cared passionately for four beings – herself, Feisal and her two little dogs.

Both the boys were taken away at times and there was a great deal of preparation then. They went to see the Pasha. There were two other little boys in the harem but they were as yet only babies. There were no girls. At first I wondered why it was that all the Pasha's children were boys.

Nicole was very informative. She told me that if a woman gave birth to a girl child she went away, to her family perhaps. The Pasha was not interested in daughters, only sons; and if a woman gave birth to a son who was beautiful and intelligent such as Samir she was in high favour.

Samir, being the eldest, would be the Pasha's heir. That was why the other women were jealous of her. She had first been set above them by the Pasha's preference – but that could be fleeting – whereas Samir was always there, a reminder to the Pasha that he could beget fine boys; and he favoured the women who helped him prove this.

She told me that she had secretly taught Samir French and when the Pasha had discovered this she had been terrified of what he would do. But she had heard through the Chief Eunuch that he was pleased that the boy should learn as much as he could and she might continue teaching him.

It surprised me that a woman of the Western world could so adjust herself to this way of life and that she could be proud of her position and intensely hate anyone who tried to snatch it from her.

But how pleased I was to be able to talk to her and discover something of those around me.

I learned of the tremendous rivalry between her and Fatima who had great ambitions for her son Feisal.

'You see,' said Nicole, 'but for Samir, Feisal would be the Pasha's heir and she would be First Lady. She wants very much to take my place.'

'She will never do that. You are more beautiful and much cleverer. Moreover, Samir is a wonderful boy.'

'Feisal is not bad,' she admitted. 'And if I were to die . . .'

'Why should you die?'

She shrugged her shoulders. 'Fatima is a very jealous woman. Once, long ago, one of the women poisoned another. It would not be difficult.'

'She would not dare.'

'One woman dared.'

'But she was discovered.'

'It was long ago. Before the Pasha's day, but they still talk about it. They took her out. They buried her up to her neck in the grounds out there. They left her in the sun . . . to die. It was her punishment.'

I shivered.

'I would wish the same for Fatima if she harmed my son.'

'You must make sure that she does not.'

'It is what I intend to do.'

Life was easier now that I had made contact with Nicole. There were our beautiful clothes, our scents, our unguents, our sweetmeats, our lazy days; we were like birds of paradise in cages. After the hardships I had suffered this was a strange life to come to.

I wondered how long it would go on.

* * *

The Pasha was away – news which delighted me.

A lethargy fell upon the harem. They lay about, dreamily admiring themselves in hand mirrors which they carried in the pockets of their capacious trousers, nibbling their sweetmeats, singing or playing their little musical instruments, quarrelling together.

Two of them quarrelled very fiercely, rolling on the mosaic floor, tugging at each other's hair and kicking wildly until Rani came and beat them both, sent them off in disgrace and said they would not have a chance with the Pasha for three months. That soon sobered them.

Then he returned and there was great excitement. They all became docile and eager to please, displaying their charms, although there were only their companions and the occasional eunuch to see them.

Rani selected her six. I saw her eyes rest on me, and horror was replaced by relief when I realized that she considered me still not ripe for the great honour.

The six girls were selected – two who had been before and found special favour, and four novices.

We all watched them being prepared. They were bathed first, their skins anointed, and scent rubbed into their hair. Henna was applied to the soles of their feet and the palms of their hands. Their lips were reddened with beeswax and their eyes made large with kohl. Flowers were set in their hair, bracelets on their wrists and ankles before they were dressed in sequinned garments.

We all waited to see who would be sent back.

It was one of the youngest who was chosen on that occasion.

'She will give herself airs when she returns,' Nicole said to me. 'They always do . . . particularly the young ones. I thought it might be your turn.'

I must have betrayed my revulsion, for she said: 'You do not want?'

'I wish with all my heart that I could get away.'

'If he saw you . . . you would be the one.'

'I . . . no . . . no . . .'

'It will come. Perhaps soon . . .'

'I would do anything . . . anything to escape.'

She was thoughtful.

* * *

Nicole told me that if one was to receive those little privileges which were such a part of harem life, one must be on good terms with two people. One was Rani, of course; the other was the Chief Eunuch.

'He is the important one. He is the Pasha of the Harem. I have made him a very good friend of mine.'

'I can see you are very wise.'

'So long I have been here. It is the only home I know.'

'And you are reconciled to all this . . . to being one of many?'

'It is the way of life here,' she replied. 'Samir is my son. He will be Pasha one day. I shall be the Pasha's mother and that is a very honourable state, I can tell you.'

'Would you not like a normal marriage . . . a husband and children . . . not all the time wondering if someone will replace you?'

'I have always known this.' She waved her arms, indicating the harem. 'It is so with all of them here. They know nothing else. They want to be the Pasha's favourite. They want to have a son who surpasses all others . . . and makes for his mother the grand position from which none can shake her.'

'Can that be?'

'It can be.'

'And that is your ambition?'

'My ambition is in Samir. Tell me of your ambition.'

'To get away from here. To get back to my home . . . to my own people. To find those who were with me when I was shipwrecked.'

'It is almost certain that you will be the chosen of the Pasha. When Rani thinks you are ready, she will send you to him. He will like you because you are different. He must be tired of these dark-skinned beauties. You are something quite new. If you have a son . . . your future is made.'

'I would do anything to escape it. Nicole, I am frightened. I do not want this. It is not what I have been brought up to understand. I feel unclean . . . cheapened . . . just a slave . . . a woman without a personality . . . and no life of her own.'

'You talk strangely and yet I understand. I did not begin as one of them either.'

'But you have accepted this way of life.'

'I was too young for anything else and now there is Samir. I want this . . . for him. He will be Pasha one day. That is what I want more than anything.'

'You will get your wish. He is the eldest.'

'Sometimes I am afraid of Fatima. When she goes to the Pasha she takes with her a powerful draught. I know she brews it. There is a way of rousing a man's desire. I have heard it talked of. It is made of crushed rubies, peacock's bones and the testicles of a ram. They are mixed and slipped into the wine. I think when she goes to the Pasha she tries this.'

'Where . . . where would she find these things?'

'Rani has a secret cupboard in which are many strange things. Herbs . . . potions . . . all sorts of mixtures. Rani knows much of these things. She may have this draught among her scents and unguents.'

'But you say it is a secret cupboard.'

'She keeps it locked, but there may be means of finding the key. Fatima would be wise in this matter. I know her. She would do anything . . . just anything. That is why I am afraid.'

'But when does she see the Pasha?'

'We are the mothers of his favourite sons . . . she and I. He sends for us now and then . . . a sort of courtesy visit . . . to talk of our sons and to spend the night. Oh, I fear that woman. She is determined. She would do anything . . . anything. Her hopes are in Feisal. The Pasha is fond of him. The Chief Eunuch tells me this. Chief Eunuch does not like Fatima. That is not good for her. She is very foolish sometimes . . . and foolish women do rash things. When she was favoured she gave herself such airs. She thought she was First Lady already. She was disrespectful to Chief Eunuch . . . so they are now enemies. Silly Fatima. If she could, she would harm Samir and me in some way.'

'But Samir is the eldest and so bright and clever.'

'That I know, but it is in the hands of the Pasha. Now he likes Samir. He is proud of Samir. He is the eldest and the favourite. While he is so, all is well. But it is the Pasha who decides and he will have many sons. If Fatima could do me or Samir some harm it would be done.'

'I cannot believe she would attempt it.'

'It happened once . . . in the harem.'

'But it will not again. Everyone knows what happened last time. That would be enough to deter them.'

'I do not know. Fatima is a determined woman. She would risk much for Feisal and her own advantage. I must be watchful.'

'I will be watchful, too.'

'And now there will be you. You will have a son. That son would be different. He would be like you. In Samir and

Feisal, well, there is a likeness. But your son would be quite different.'

I was filled with horror at the thought of it and recoiled from her.

'It's true,' she said. 'And do you really mean that you would not want this?'

'I could almost wish I had not been saved from the ship. I wish we had stayed on the island. If only I could get away . . . Oh, Nicole, if only that were possible. I would do anything . . . anything.'

She was staring ahead of her, deep in thought.

* * *

A few days later I was sitting by the fountain when she approached and sat down beside me.

'I have something for you,' she said.

'For me?' I asked in surprise.

'I think you will be pleased. Chief Eunuch gave it to me for you. It is from the man who came with you.'

'Do you mean . . . Nicole, where is it?'

'Be careful. We may be watched. Fatima watches everything. Rest your hand on the seat. In a moment I will slip a paper into it.'

'No one is looking.'

'How can you be sure? There are watchful eyes everywhere. These women seem idle. They are idle . . . but because they have nothing to do, they invent intrigue . . . even when it is not there. They are bored . . . looking for excitement . . . and when it does not come they try to make it. They have nothing to do but watch and gossip. Do as I say if you want this note.'

'Oh, I do. I do.'

'You must be careful then. Chief Eunuch says it is very important. He could lose his life for doing this. He does it for me . . . because I ask.'

My hand was lying on the seat. She laid hers beside it

and after a few moments a crumpled paper was slipped under mine.

'Do not look at it now. Hide it . . .'

I slipped it into my trouser pocket. I could scarcely sit still. But she said it would be unwise of me to get up and hurry away. Someone might suspect something and that could mean dire consequences for us all.

I knew that for a man to communicate with the women of the harem could result in a cruel and lingering death, not only for the man but for the woman concerned. This had been the rule for centuries and I could believe that it still prevailed in this place which seemed to have slipped back – or never emerged from – another era.

I had to suppress my impatience until at length I felt I could wander off without arousing any undue curiosity. They were used to my being alone when I was not with Nicole, for she was the only one to whom I could talk. I went into the room where we slept. It was deserted, so I sat on my divan and brought out the piece of paper.

> Rosetta [I read],
>
> I am nearby. I was brought here with you and I am working in the gardens just outside the harem. I was able to do a service for an important person and his pride demands he repay me. This is how he is doing it, by bringing this note to you. We are close. I am thinking hard. I will do something. Never fear. Don't give up hope.
>
> S.

I felt limp with relief. I screwed up the paper. I wanted to keep it, to hide it away under my clothes, to feel it against my skin, to remind me that he had written it and that he was nearby and thinking of me.

But I must destroy it. It was dangerous and if it were discovered it could destroy us. It was dangerous. I tore it into as many pieces as I could. I would scatter them . . . a few pieces at a time so that it would never be discovered.

Later I talked to Nicole.

'You are happier,' she said. 'What I brought you pleased you.'

'Oh yes, but it is difficult to see how there can be change. Does anyone ever escape from here?'

'Husbands are sometimes found if the Pasha is no longer interested and knows he never will be again. A few have been returned to their families.'

'But does anyone ever run away?'

She shook her head. 'I do not think that would be possible.'

'Nicole,' I said, 'I must. I must.'

'Yes,' she said slowly, 'you must. If you do not, soon you will be sent to the Pasha. Your skin is becoming very white. You have put on flesh and no longer look like a skeleton. You are different from when you came. Rani is pleased with you. It will be soon . . . perhaps next time he sends.'

'He is away now.'

'Yes, but he will come back. When he comes back he always sends . . . Rani will say, "Yes, the fair one, she is ready now. How pleased he will be with me for giving him such a prize . . . something he has not had before." He will like you, I dare say. He may keep you with him. You will surely have a child. The Pasha will like you very much because you are different. He may like your child more than Feisal . . . more than Samir. Chief Eunuch says that Pasha is very interested in the West . . . in England particularly. He wants to know more of it. He wants to hear about the great Queen.'

'No . . . no,' I cried. 'I hate it. I won't stay here. I'll get away somehow. I don't care what they do to me . . . but I won't stay for that. I'll do anything . . . anything. Nicole, can you help me?'

She looked steadily at me and a smile played about her lips.

She said slowly: 'The Chief Eunuch is a friend of mine. He would not want me to be replaced as Chief Lady. He wants me to stay the mother of the next Pasha. Then we work together. We are friends, you see. I learn from him of outside and he learns from me of here . . . inside. I know what goes on here. I can tell him. He pays me back with information from outside. Perhaps . . .'

'Perhaps?'

'Well, just perhaps . . . I might discover something.'

I took her arm and shook her. 'If you can help me, Nicole, if you know something . . .'

'I will help,' she said. 'No one must replace Samir. Besides, we are good friends.'

Hope. It was the last thing left to me and I was learning that it can mean everything to those in desperate straits.

The note and what I had heard from Nicole gave me that much-needed hope now.

I thought of all the dangers through which I had passed since that night when disaster had overtaken the *Atlantic Star*. I had had amazing good luck. Could it continue? Nicole would help if she could, I knew. It was not only that we were friends but she thought I might be a threat to her position. Nicole was a realist. But the Chief Eunuch favoured her. No doubt he had his reasons. But did it matter what they were, as long as they worked in my favour?

I was desperate. I needed all the help I could get.

I had reason to hope. Two of the most important people in the seraglio were on my side. And Simon was not far off.

Indeed there was hope. For the first time since I had entered this place, escape did not seem a complete impossibility.

* * *

Rani was indicating pleasure in my appearance. She grunted with satisfaction when she massaged my person.

My heart sank. In the cold light of reason, escape seemed

remote. I had allowed myself to be carried away on a wave of euphoria. How could I escape?

That afternoon I went into the dormitory and lay on my divan. The blinds were drawn and the heavy drapes made the room cool and dark. Someone crept into the room. Through half-closed eyes I saw Nicole.

'You are sick?' she whispered.

'Sick with fear,' I replied.

She sat down on the divan.

'I am afraid that nothing is going to save me,' I went on.

She said: 'Rani plans . . . next time . . . she will send you.'

'I . . . I won't go.'

She shrugged her shoulders, a habitual gesture with her.

'Chief Eunuch says that he will be away for a week. When he comes back he will send . . .'

'A week. Oh Nicole, what can I do?'

'We have a week,' she said.

'What can we do?'

She regarded me steadily. 'Chief Eunuch likes your man. He wants to help him. They have talked. Rani wants very much to show you to the Pasha. She wants him to know that when you came here you were not very good . . . apart from your hair and that was without lustre. Now it shines. She has made you fit for the Pasha and now that you are as you are, you should be sent to him. He will be thankful to the man who brought you, who was the Chief Eunuch, but it is Rani who has nursed you back to health. But . . . as I say . . . we have a week.'

'What could we do? Please tell me.'

'Your friend will have to take care.'

'What would they do to him if they knew he had written to me?'

'Most certainly make a eunuch of him. They may do that in any case. That is the fate of a number of young men who are sold to the pashas. They are put into the gardens and there for a while they are normal young men, but if they are needed to work in the harem . . . well, how could he trust a normal young man among so many women? Hence the eunuchs. It would very likely be the fate of your friend. He will not be in the gardens for ever. Eunuchs make good servants. They can go among the harem women without temptation.'

'I cannot see what can be done.'

'You will do what you are told to do. You must remember that if you start this . . . you may be discovered and if you are . . . anything would be better.'

'I wonder if Simon will be ready to take such risks. When I think what might happen to him . . .'

'If you are going to escape,' she said, 'you must not dwell on failure. Soon Rani will send you to the Pasha. Remember that.'

I was silent, wondering how I could endure such a fate. Moreover, Nicole was talking in riddles. What plans could there be?

She was vague. Sometimes I thought she was talking so to comfort me.

* * *

As the days passed, my apprehension naturally grew greater. I told myself that I must in due course face the inevitable.

The Pasha was back. I noticed Rani's eyes on me, speculatively. She rubbed her hands together with a certain satisfaction and I knew the time had come; and when the Chief Eunuch visited Rani that evening I knew my fate had been decided.

As was the custom, five others were selected with me, for it would not do for Rani to choose for the Pasha; he must make his own decision as to which one he would honour.

Among the five was a very pretty young girl whose name

I discovered was Aida. She must have been about twelve years old . . . slender but just budding into womanhood; she had long dark hair and big eyes which managed to combine an impression of virginal innocence and dawning knowledge which I imagined would be very attractive to a man whose senses might well be jaded by excess.

I was interested in Aida because I was pinning my hopes on her. I felt certain that she had a good chance of being selected. The girl was so excited; she danced round the gardens, making no secret of her glee. Fatima grumbled that she was already giving herself airs.

I said to Nicole: 'She is very pretty. Surely he will prefer her?'

Nicole shook her head. 'Pretty, yes . . . but so are hundreds of others . . . and very like her. All the same hair . . . eyes . . . delight . . . eagerness. You will stand out among them. And the Chief Eunuch says the Pasha is very interested in England. He admires the English Queen.'

All of which depressed me and I felt sick with fear. What was the Pasha like? He must be fairly young. He had only recently become his father's heir. He spoke a little English, so Nicole had learned from the Chief Eunuch. Perhaps I could talk to him . . . interest him in England, become a sort of Scheherazade, holding him off with my interesting tales of English life.

That day seemed endless. There were moments when I almost convinced myself that I was dreaming. How could this be happening to me? How many girls living quietly conventional lives in England had suddenly found themselves transported to a Turkish harem?

Then I told myself I must prepare for my fate. The Pasha would notice the difference in me. First I must pray that he did not choose me. If he did not, it might be decided that I was unfit for the harem. What then? Perhaps I could persuade them to let me go. Aida was so pretty. She was so suitable to this way of life, and moreover she enjoyed it.

Rani came to me. It was time for the preparations to begin.

She smoothed my hair with her hands, almost crowing over it. She seized it and pulled it slightly; she stroked it. Then she clapped her hands and two of her girls appeared.

She stood up and beckoned.

I was taken to the bath and submerged under jets of perfumed water. When I was dry I must lie down while the unguents, smelling of musk and patchouli, were rubbed into my skin. My hair was scented. The smell of it made me feel sick and I knew that I should never smell it again without recalling that numbing fear I felt at that time.

I was dressed in lavender silk garments with the wide trousers caught in at the ankles with jewelled bands. Over the trousers I wore a tunic which fell to the waist. It was in silk with a layer of fine gauze over it. Sequins had been sewn in profusion over the silk and shone mysteriously through the gauzy material, giving a subtle sheen. I had to admit that the costume had great charm.

On my feet were sandals with curled points at the toes. They were in satin and bejewelled.

Then my hair was combed so that it fell about my shoulders and a garland of mauve flowers was put on my head and others about my ankles. My lips were reddened, my eyes carefully lined with kohl so that they looked enormous and a deeper blue.

I was ready for submission.

Wild thoughts came into my mind. What would happen if I refused to go, or if I tried to escape from the harem? How? The gates were locked and guarded by the Pasha's eunuchs . . . big men, all chosen for their size. How could I escape?

I had to face the truth. There was no escape.

Rani took my hand and shook her head at me. She was admonishing me for some reason. It must be because I looked so miserable. She was telling me to smile, to show happiness and appreciation of the great honour which might well be mine this night.

That was something I could not do.

Nicole was standing by. She was one of those who had helped to dress me. She said something to Rani, who appeared to consider.

Then Rani nodded and gave Nicole a key. Nicole left us.

I sat on the divan. I felt quite helpless. I had been brought so far for this. I had a vision of myself . . . chosen by the Pasha . . . bearing a child who would be the rival of Samir and Feisal. I had a father who was an important man, a professor attached to the British Museum. I wanted to tell them that, if the Pasha attempted to treat my father's daughter as though she were a slave girl, there would be trouble. I was English. The great Queen did not allow her subjects to be treated in this way.

I was trying to give myself courage. I knew I was talking a great deal of nonsense to myself. What did these people care who I was? They were the rulers here. I was nothing.

Perhaps I could tell him how eager the other girls were to share his bed. Why not take one of those who were so willing, and let this one go? Would it be possible to explain to him? Would he listen? And if he did, would he understand?

Nicole came back. She was carrying a goblet in her hand.

'Drink this,' she said. 'You will feel better.'

'No. I won't.'

'I tell you it will do you good.'

'What is it?'

One of the other girls added her persuasion. She wrapped her arms about herself and swayed to and fro.

'She is telling you that it will make you want love. It will make things easier for you. In any case, it was Rani who ordered it. She thinks you are not eager and the Pasha likes women to be eager.'

A sort of aphrodisiac, I thought.

'I will not,' I said.

Nicole came close to me. 'Don't be a fool,' she hissed. She was looking into my eyes, trying to tell me something. 'Take,' she went on. 'You will find it . . . good . . . just what you need now. Drink . . . drink . . . I am your friend.'

There was some hidden meaning in her words. I took the goblet and drank the contents. It was revolting.

'Soon . . .' said Nicole. 'Soon . . .'

After a few moments I began to feel very ill. Nicole had disappeared with the goblet. I tried to stand but I could not. I felt giddy.

One of the girls called for Rani, who came in great consternation. I could feel the sweat running down my face and I caught a glimpse of myself in one of the mirrors. I was very pale.

Rani was shouting to everyone. I was put on to a divan. I felt very ill indeed.

Nicole had appeared. I fancied she was smiling secretively.

* * *

I was *not* presented to the Pasha. I lay on my divan feeling sick unto death. I really believed my last moment had come.

I thought of Nicole smiling her secret smile. She had done this. She had feared that I would please the Pasha and bear a child who would oust Samir. Could this be so . . . or was she truly my friend? Whatever the answer, she had saved me from the Pasha that night.

In a day or so I began to recover and with my recovery came the belief that Nicole had done this to save me from what I had dreaded. True, at the same time she was helping herself. Why not? Nicole was French and took a realistic view of life. The fact that she could serve herself and me at the same time would make the idea doubly attractive to her.

As I began to feel better, I realized I had not been so ill

as I had believed. If I had, I could not have regained my health so quickly.

Nicole told me that when Rani had sent her to the cupboard to bring the aphrodisiac which was given to some girls before they went to the Pasha for the first time, she had substituted it for a draught which she knew would make me too sick to be sent.

'Was it not what you wanted?' she demanded. 'Did you not say that anything . . . anything . . .'

'I did. I did. And I thank you, Nicole.'

'I told you I was your friend. Aida was the chosen one. She has not yet returned. She must be in high favour. She would never have been if you had been there.'

'I am so glad. She longed to be chosen.'

'The little horror will be unbearable when she comes back. It is a great honour to be kept there in the Pasha's apartments. She will be too important to speak to us . . . insufferable. You will see.'

I was slowly recovering from my sickness and Rani from her disappointment. But she was a little reconciled because Aida had found such favour.

After three days, Aida returned. She had become a very important personage. She swept into the harem, her manner completely changed; she was languid and regarded us all with contempt. She had a pair of beautiful ruby earrings and a magnificent ruby necklace about her throat. Rani's attitude towards her had changed. Little Aida had become one of the important ladies of the harem.

She was certain she was pregnant.

'Silly creature,' said Nicole. 'How could she know yet?'

All the same, Nicole was worried.

'It may be you are safe for a little while,' she comforted me. 'For if he liked her so much as to keep her for three days and nights he might send for her again. That was what happened to me in my day. The most grateful woman in the harem must be Aida and that gratitude should be for you.'

'Perhaps he wouldn't have chosen me. He might have liked her better.'

Nicole looked at me disbelievingly.

It was with great relief that I heard, through Nicole, who had it from the Chief Eunuch, that the Pasha had gone away for three weeks.

Three weeks! A great deal could happen in that time. Perhaps I should hear something from Simon. If it were possible to devise some means of getting out of this place . . . and if anyone could do it, surely he could.

* * *

A few days passed. Aida was making herself very unpopular. She wore her rubies all the time and would sit by the pool taking them in her hands and admiring them, reminding everyone of the favour she had found and how she pitied them all for not having the beauty and charm necessary to enslave the Pasha.

She appeared languid and assumed the ailments of pregnancy.

Nicole laughed at her. So did the others. One of them had quarrelled with her so violently that they fought and Aida's face was maliciously scratched by the other.

That sent Aida into floods of tears. When the Pasha returned she could not go to him with a wound on her face.

Rani was angry and the two girls were shut away for three days. Rani would have liked to beat them, Nicole told me, but she was afraid of bruising their bodies, particularly Aida's. One thing about a harem was that its inmates were not submitted to physical violence while they were part of it.

However, it was a relief, said Nicole, to be free of the arrogant little creature if only for three days.

Aida emerged not in the least repentant. She was as

languid as ever, even more sure that she was pregnant and carried a male child. She slept in the ruby necklace and kept the earrings in a jewelled case beside her bed. As soon as morning came she put them on.

In spite of myself, I was caught up in the intrigues of the harem. My friendship with Nicole had done that. She told me that violent quarrels blew up now and then, and that there was great jealousy between the girls. Aida, like Fatima, was one who created trouble. They had been chosen and they could not forget it. If Aida were pregnant and bore a male child, that would add greatly to the rivalries.

'But Samir is the eldest,' said Nicole. 'He must remain first favourite son.'

I said I was sure he would.

I sensed that Nicole was less confident. She was going to work all the time on Samir's behalf, but she knew the matter was one which she must constantly bear in mind.

At this time Nicole's thoughts seemed to be fixed entirely on Aida. She was not the only one. Fatima's were too. They had been the main rivals, both possessing sons with a claim on the Pasha's wealth. Now they both watched Aida.

It was unusual for one girl to satisfy the Pasha for three nights in succession – also for her to be kept in his apartments. So there could be no doubt that Aida had made a certain impression on him.

Moreover, she had been long enough with him to become pregnant and there was a good possibility that she might have achieved this happy state. Therefore she was an object of concern to all, but especially to Nicole and Fatima.

It was in the early hours of the morning and I was half asleep. I was just aware of a sliver of a waning moon shining into the dormitory. Through half-closed eyes, I thought I saw a movement in the room. An outline of a figure bending over one of the divans in the corner. Sleep claimed me and I thought no more of the incident at the time.

The next day there was consternation. Aida's ruby earrings had disappeared. She wore the necklace all the time, she reminded us, but the earrings had been kept in the jewelled box beside her divan.

Rani came into the dormitory, demanding to know what all the fuss was about. Aida was shrieking in her fury, accusing everyone. Someone had stolen her earrings. She would tell the Pasha. He would not have thieves in his harem. We should all be whipped and sent away. Her beautiful earrings must be restored to her. If they were not returned this day she would ask the Pasha to punish us all.

Rani was angry.

'Little fool,' said Nicole. 'Doesn't she know yet that she must not anger important people? I suppose she thinks she is so important she can do without their support.'

The dormitory was searched, but the earrings were not found.

Fatima said it was a terrible thing and even the children should be searched. There were some children who were born thieves and if her Feisal were proved to be such, she would see that he was severely punished.

Rani said the earrings would no doubt soon be found. They could not be far off. There would be no point in anyone stealing someone else's jewellery. When would the thief be able to wear it?

I was with Nicole in the gardens.

She said: 'Serve her right. The arrogant little idiot. She will not get very far.'

'Someone must have taken the earrings.'

'As a joke perhaps?'

I said slowly: 'I remember something now. I was only half awake. It was someone standing in the room . . . yes . . . and it was by Aida's divan.'

'When?'

'Last night. I thought I was dreaming. I was in that state when I was not sure whether I was awake or asleep. I have had strange dreams . . . since I've been here . . . and particularly after taking that stuff you gave me to drink. Half sleeping . . . half waking . . . hallucinations almost. I am not really sure whether I dreamed this.'

'Well, if you saw someone at Aida's bedside and in the morning her earrings have gone . . . the chances are that you were not dreaming.'

Just at that moment Samir came up. He was holding something bright in his hands. 'Look,' he said. 'Maman, pretty things . . .'

She took the jewelled box from his hands and opened it. There lay the ruby earrings.

Nicole exchanged a glance with me, fearful and full of meaning.

'Where did you find this, Samir?' she asked in a voice which trembled.

'In my boat.'

His toy boat, the pride of his life. He was hardly ever without it. He used to sail it in the pools.

Nicole looked at me and said: 'I must take it to Rani immediately.'

I put out a hand to stop her. I looked at Samir hesitantly. She knew what I meant.

She said to him: 'Go away and play. Don't tell anyone what you found. It's not important. But don't say a word. Promise, Samir.'

He nodded his head and darted off.

I said: 'It's coming back. It could have been Fatima whom I saw last night. What if she stole the earrings? The more I think of it, the more I believe that this is what it is all about. Didn't she say we should all be searched . . . and she mentioned the children. Fatima is foolish sometimes. She has no subtlety. It is easy to read her mind. She wants to damage you . . . and Samir. So she stole the earrings, put them in the boat and wants it to be believed that Samir stole them.'

'Why?'

'To make a thief of him.'

'But he is a child.'

'Then perhaps I am wrong. What would have happened if the earrings had been found in his boat? He would have said he did not know how they got there, but would he have been believed? It might be reported to the Pasha. Aida would have reported it, if she went back to him . . . as she well might. Perhaps the boy would be punished. The Pasha would be displeased with him. Do you see what I mean? But perhaps I am wrong.'

'No . . . no. I do not believe that you are wrong.'

'I think she may say that Samir stole them and when the theft was discovered, he was afraid and gave them up.'

'Then what . . . ?'

'Let's get rid of them . . . at once. Drop them . . . anywhere. It would not do for them to be found with you. What explanation could you give? How did they come to be in Samir's boat? they would ask. Samir must have put them there, they would say. It would be an unpleasant business. Leave them . . . near the pool. The case will be conspicuous and soon found, then Samir will not come into it. I feel sure it is better that he does not.'

'You are right,' she said.

'Then the sooner it is out of your possession the better.'

She nodded. Cautiously she put the case down by the pool and we walked away.

I said: 'I feel sure it was Fatima. I am trying to remember what I saw in the night. It would have been so easy for her to slip off her divan when everyone was asleep . . . and take the case.'

'It was Fatima. I know it. She was the one. Oh, how I hate that woman. One day I will kill her.'

* * *

The case was found. Aida said she could not understand it. She had left it beside her divan. Someone must have taken it, and then become frightened and thrown it away.

Rani said the earrings were found and that was an end of the matter.

But it was not really so. The enmity between Fatima and Nicole grew alarmingly. It was almost certain that Aida was not pregnant and that deepened the rivalry between the mothers of Samir and Feisal. Aida was sullen. Someone said she had pretended her earrings were stolen to call attention to the fact that the Pasha had once liked her enough to present them to her. There was a great deal of wrangling and petty spite in the harem. Perhaps because there was so little for them to do.

Nicole was undoubtedly grateful to me. She could clearly see the danger through which she and Samir had passed, for if the boy could have been branded as a thief, his favour might have been tarnished with the Pasha, if not lost forever. It was a mean act and worthy of Fatima, Nicole was sure.

She became more open with me. I had always known that there was a special friendship between her and the Chief Eunuch, but now she told me that they had been on the ship together and there had been a friendship between them then. She did not say that they had been in love, but the seeds of it might have been sown. When she had been taken into the harem he had been sold to the Pasha at the same time. They had then been in urgent need of eunuchs and that had been his fate. He was tall, handsome and clever – so he had risen quickly to his present rank. Nicole passed on information to him from the harem and he gave her news of what was happening outside. They had both made the most of the life into which they had been thrust.

Now I knew how close they had been before they had been taken into captivity, I understood their relationship much better. It had taken some time for them to become resigned to this life; but he had become Chief Eunuch and she planned to be First Lady of the Harem in due course.

The relationship between myself and Nicole had deepened.

It was I who had saved her son from a situation which could have been damning to their chances. It was clear to me that I was accepted as her friend, and she wanted to repay me for what I had done for her.

I tried to make her understand that there should be no thought of payment between friends. She replied that she realized that, but if she could do anything for me, she would; and she knew that what I wanted more than anything was to escape from my present position. Once, long ago, she had felt exactly the same, and that gave her a special understanding of my case.

The first thing she did was to bring me a note. I think she had told her friend the Chief Eunuch the story of the earrings and enlisted his help; and for her sake he helped to bring this about.

The note was smuggled to me as before, and when I was quite alone I read it.

> Don't give up hope. Through a friend of mine I have heard what is happening on the other side of the wall. If an opportunity comes, I'll be ready. So must you be. Don't despair. We have friends. I do not forget you. We shall succeed.

What a comfort it was to read that.

Sometimes in a pessimistic mood, I asked myself what he could do. Then I assured myself that he would do something. I must go on hoping.

Nicole was watchful of Samir. I found myself watching him, too. He and I had become friends. He knew that I was with his mother a good deal and that there was a special understanding between us; it seemed to me that he wanted a share in it.

He was an enchanting child, and good-looking, healthy; and loving all people, he believed they loved him, too.

When I was sitting by the pool alone he came up to me and showed me his boat. We floated it on the pool and he watched its progress with dreamy eyes.

'It's come from a long, long way,' he said.

'From where?' I asked.

'From Mar . . . Mart . . .'

I said on sudden inspiration: 'Martinique.'

He nodded happily.

'It's going to a place in France,' he said. 'It's Lyons. There's a school there.'

I guessed his mother had told him her story, for he went on: 'Pirates.' He began to shout. 'They are trying to take us but we won't let them, will we? Bang, bang. Go away, you horrid pirate. We don't like you.' He waved his hand at imaginary vessels. He turned to smile at me. 'All right now. Don't be frightened. They've all gone now.'

He pointed to a tree and said, 'Figs.'

'Do you like figs?' I asked.

He nodded vigorously.

His mother came up. She had heard the last remark.

'He is greedy where figs are concerned, aren't you, Samir?' she said.

He hunched his shoulders and nodded.

I remembered that later.

* * *

I was sitting by the pool, thinking that the days were passing quickly and wondering when the Pasha would be coming back. Could I hope to escape again? There could not be another draught like the last. Rani would surely suspect if there were. And if I did take it, what effect would it have on me: how much did Nicole know about such potions? Moreover, I imagined that Rani would prepare the aphrodisiac this time. She was no fool. It might well be that she had a suspicion of what happened. Was there any hope? I wondered. Could Simon offer me anything but words of comfort?

Samir came up to me. He was holding a fig.

'Oh,' I said. 'What a nice fig, Samir.'

'Yes,' he answered. 'Fatima gave it to me.'

'Fatima!' A shiver of alarm ran through me. 'Give it to me, Samir,' I said.

He held it behind his back. 'It's not yours. It's mine.'

'Just show it to me.'

He stepped back a pace and, bringing out his hand, held up the fig.

I went to take it from him, but he ran and I went after him.

He ran full tilt into his mother, who caught him laughingly and looked at me.

'Fatima gave him a fig,' I said.

She turned pale.

'He's holding it now. He wouldn't give it to me.'

She snatched it from him. His face puckered. 'It's all right,' she said. 'I'll find you another.'

'But that's mine. Fatima gave it to me.'

'Never mind.' Her voice shook a little. 'You shall have a bigger and better one. This one's not very nice. It has worms in it.'

'Show me?' cried Samir excitedly.

'First of all, I'll get you a nice one.'

She put the fig into my hands. 'I'll be back,' she said.

She took Samir off and a few minutes later returned without him.

'What do you think?' I asked.

'She's capable of anything.'

'So think I.'

'Rosetta, I am going to test this.'

She sat on the stones holding the fig in her hand and

staring moodily before her. One of Fatima's little dogs came into sight.

She laughed suddenly and called to him. He came up and looked. She held out the fig to the dog who swallowed it at one gulp, and looked at us hopefully for more.

'Why should she give him a fig?' she asked.

'She might have been sorry about the earrings and wanted to please him.'

She looked at me scornfully. Then her eyes went to the dog. He had crept into a corner and was being sick.

She was triumphant.

'She is wicked . . . wicked . . . she would have killed Samir.'

'We can't be sure.'

'It's proof enough. Look at the dog.'

'It might have been something else.'

'He was well enough before he took the fig.'

'Do you think she would go so far? What would happen to her if she were discovered?'

'Death for murder.'

'She would think of that.'

'Fatima never thinks ahead. She would think only of getting rid of Samir so that Feisal could be the Pasha's favourite.'

'Nicole, do you seriously believe she would go to such lengths?'

The dog was now writhing on the ground. We stared at it in horror. Suddenly its legs stiffened and it lay on its side.

'It could have been Samir,' whispered Nicole. 'If you hadn't seen him with the fig . . . I will kill her for this.'

Aida came up. 'What's the matter with the dog?' she said.

'He's dead,' said Nicole.

'He ate a fig.'

'A what?'

'A fig.'

'How could he die of that? It's Fatima's dog.'

'Yes,' said Nicole. 'Go and tell her that her dog has died through eating a fig.'

I was really alarmed. I had been apt to feel somewhat contemptuous of their rivalries, but when they led to attempted murder, that was another matter.

* * *

It was not to be expected that that would be the end of the affair. Nicole was not the sort to let such a thing pass.

Her remarks about the fig and the death of the dog would be enough to show Fatima that she suspected her. And she had been the one who had given the fig to Samir – the fig which afterwards had poisoned the dog.

There was open warfare between Nicole and Fatima. Everyone was talking about the death of Fatima's little dog who had died after eating a fig.

Rani was worried. She hated trouble in the harem and liked to believe that she could keep everything in order.

Smouldering looks passed between Nicole and Fatima and we were all waiting for the trouble to start.

I begged Nicole to be careful. It would be best for her to tell Rani or the Chief Eunuch what she suspected; and they could deal with the matter.

She said: '*I* want to deal with Fatima. They might not believe she did what she did. They will say it was some other thing which caused the dog's death. They wouldn't want the Pasha to know that there had been attempted murder in the harem.'

I said fearfully: 'He will be back soon. Surely he will hear something about it then?'

'No. He would not hear such a thing. Besides, they will try to make it all die down before he gets back. But I am not going to let it. She tried to prove my son a thief and when that failed she tried to poison him.'

'At neither time did she succeed.'

'No. Thank God. And it was due to you. You have been my good friend and when I can I will repay you. Yes, I will repay you for the good you have done me and her for the evil. But repayment there shall be.'

It could not go on.

Fatima approached Nicole in the gardens.

She said: 'You are spreading evil tales about me.'

I had picked up enough of the language to understand a little now and then, so I could make out roughly what was being said.

'Nothing could be more evil than the truth,' cried Nicole. 'You tried to kill my son.'

'I did not.'

'You liar! You poisoned a fig and tried to kill him. Instead your dog died. It was proved.'

'I did not give the fig to him. The child is a liar as well as a thief.'

With that Nicole brought up her hand and dealt Fatima a stinging blow on the side of her face.

With a cry Fatima leaped upon her. I was terrified, for in her hand I saw a knife. Fatima had come prepared for battle.

Several women screamed.

'Fetch Rani,' someone said. 'Fetch the Eunuch. Call them.'

Fatima had plunged the knife into Nicole's thigh and her trousers were drenched with blood. It seemed to be spurting all around.

Rani had come and was shrieking to them to stop. With her was the Chief Eunuch. He was a big strong man, and was soon dragging a kicking, screaming Fatima away from Nicole, who lay on the ground bleeding profusely.

Two other eunuchs who were tending the gardens appeared. Rani ordered them to take Fatima away. The Chief Eunuch knelt beside Nicole. He said something to Rani.

Then he lifted Nicole tenderly in his arms and carried her into the building.

I was horrified. I had known that there would be trouble sooner or later between them, but I had not thought of fighting with knives. There had of course only been one and that had given Fatima the advantage. Now I was worried about Nicole. I had grown fond of her. She was the only one with whom I could communicate. She it was who had made life tolerable for me.

Then I thought of Samir. Poor child, what would become of him?

He was bewildered and came to me to be comforted.

'Where is my Maman?' he asked plaintively.

'She is ill.'

'When will she be better?'

'We must wait and see,' I told him – one of the most unsatisfactory answers possible, as I remembered from my own childhood.

Fatima was under restraint. I wondered what would happen to her. The incident would not be lightly passed over, of that I was sure. To do so would be to undermine law and order in the harem and that was something neither Rani nor the Chief Eunuch would allow.

From what little I could understand, the women were discussing the poisoned fig and Fatima's attack on Nicole; Aida and her pretensions were no longer the main topic of conversation.

Rani was seething with anger because Fatima obviously had access to her closet where the drugs were kept. I wondered how often these had been used with discretion to remove some unwanted person from the harem. I imagined orders coming from the Pasha, through the Chief Eunuch, of course, that someone was to be quietly removed. It must have happened now and then. The secrets of the closet should be closely guarded and the fact that Fatima had succeeded in getting access to it must give cause for alarm.

The Chief Eunuch was in constant communication with Rani. I saw him frequently in the harem.

Nicole was kept in a room by herself. I was allowed to visit her, presumably because she asked that I should. They were very anxious that she should recover and were ready to do anything to help her to that end.

I was shocked at the sight of her. Her thigh was encased in bandages and she was very pale; there were dark bruises on her forehead.

'That snake would have finished me . . . if she could . . . and she nearly did,' she said. 'How is Samir?'

'He asks for you.'

A smile illuminated her face. 'I did not want him to see me . . . like this.'

'I think he would like to see you anyway.'

'Perhaps then . . .'

'I'll tell him. He will be overjoyed.'

'You are looking after him for me?'

'As well as I can, but it is you he wants.'

'That wicked witch is shut away, I know. That is a great relief to me.'

'Yes. She is not with us any more.'

'Thank God for that. I could not lie here knowing she was there . . . and I powerless. How much does Samir know of the danger he was in?'

'He is too young,' I said.

'Children are sharper than you think. They listen. There is little they miss. Sometimes they put the wrong construction on things . . . but Samir will know something is wrong. He will sense danger.'

'I will look after him. You must not worry about him . . . and when you think he should come to see you, I am sure they will allow it.'

'Oh yes. They do not want me to die. The Pasha would ask questions. He would wonder how well Rani was looking after us. She might be replaced. That is always in her mind. He would remember me because I am the mother of his boy.'

'And what of Fatima? She also is the mother of his boy.'

'He never really liked Fatima. She is a fool. She always was. She is the mother of Feisal, true. But that is all. Feisal is a good-looking boy, but that does not mean Fatima will be kept in favour because of that if she is a menace in the harem. I did not have a knife. She was the one who produced it. She might have killed me. It was what she intended to do. As it is . . . I have lost a lot of blood. The wound is deep. It is going to take a long time to heal.'

The next day I took Samir to her.

He leaped on to the divan and they hugged each other. I felt the tears in my eyes as I watched them. The child's joy was great. She was there. She was still ill, he knew, but she was there.

He sat beside her and she asked what he was doing? How was the boat going?

'The pirates nearly took her,' he said.

'Really?'

'Yes, but I saved her in time.'

'That is good news.'

'When are you getting up?'

'Very soon.'

'Today?'

'Well, not today.'

'Tomorrow?'

'We'll have to see.' There it was again. Samir sighed, recognizing the vagueness of the reply.

'You've got Rosetta,' she told him.

He turned and smiled at me and held out his hand. Nicole was biting her lip and lowering her eyes. She was as touched as I was and in that moment I was sure she felt as great an affection for me as I did for her.

* * *

The next day when I was with her, Rani brought in the Chief Eunuch.

Nicole spoke to him in French. She told him what I had done and that it was my prompt action which had saved Samir. 'I owe Samir's life to her,' she said. 'I must repay her for what she has done for me.'

He nodded and I believe the look which passed between them was one of love.

The tragedy of their lives was brought home to me more vividly than ever. But for that one incident which had befallen them, everything could have been so different for them. In my imagination I saw the ship. I could picture the meetings . . . the friendship which sprang up as it can on board ship where people see each other every day if they wish. Relationships blossom in such an atmosphere. And that was how it would have been with those two young people. What would have happened if they had been allowed to stay together? I pictured them at sea . . . warm evenings, sitting on deck, the starlit sky, the gentle swishing of the calm sea as they drifted along. Romance in the air. And then . . . shipwreck . . . sold into slavery and the end of a love-story which had only just begun.

Could I not understand better than anyone? Had it not happened to me?

And poor Nicole! Cruelly separated, yet to live not far apart. Actually to see each other often: she the member of a harem to bear a child to an imperious master; he to lose his manhood because he was tall and strong and could be of use to that ruthless man. How dared some people inflict such horror on others! How dared they take us from a civilized world and submit us to their barbarous way of life! But they did dare. They had the opportunity and for the moment the upper hand – and with it they tampered with our lives.

Nicole was getting better. She was exceptionally healthy and Rani was a skilled nurse. She knew exactly how to treat the wounds. I wondered how much practice she had had in a community where very idleness bred violence?

I took Samir to see Nicole every day. He was happier now. He was no longer afraid. His mother was ill for a while but she was there, he could see her, and I was a fair substitute.

One day she said to me: 'The Chief Eunuch has just been to see me. He tells me much. They are eager to get this matter settled before the Pasha returns. Then he need not be told.'

'What of Fatima?'

'Rani will let it be known that she had to be sent away . . . back to her family. For some time she has been complaining of her conduct. It might even be said that she threatened me with a knife. If there are scars there would need to be an explanation. So much depends. There will be time to decide. But Fatima will be sent away.'

'What of Feisal?'

'He will remain. He is the Pasha's son. He cannot leave.'

'Oh . . . poor child.'

'He will be better off here than with his foolish mother.'

'Who will care for him?'

'The other women will. No one has any quarrel with Feisal. He cannot help having such a mother. Fatima will remain locked up for the time being. Quite right, too. She is a wild animal.'

'But what a terrible punishment for the child.'

'Fatima deserves to lose her life. She would have taken Samir's. Every time I think of that, I remember how much I owe you. I do not care to owe. I have spoken to Jean . . . to the Chief Eunuch. He understands . . . it may be that he can help. Yes . . . I think he will help.'

My heart started to beat so fast that I could scarcely speak.

'How . . .' I stammered.

'The Pasha has been delayed. He will not be back for two more weeks. It must be done before then.'

'Yes?'

'I told you, Fatima will be sent away. A carriage will come to take her. The Chief Eunuch will unlock the gates. The carriage will be waiting outside. It is to take her back to her family. Her presence is no longer required in the harem.'

'Does that happen often?'

Nicole shook her head. 'It is the ultimate disgrace. If she had killed me it would have been death. It may be that she will decide to kill herself,' she added with relish.

'Oh no!' I cried.

She laughed at me. 'She must not, for if she did it would spoil our plans. Listen.'

She paused for a few seconds. I could not hide my eagerness to hear more. Hope was suddenly surging up within me.

'All women are heavily veiled when they go out. It is only the lower classes who are not. One woman, therefore, looks very like another. Oh, I shall miss you . . . for we are good friends, are we not? But it is what you want. You would never have been a true harem woman. You have too much *esprit*. You cannot forget your pride . . . your dignity . . . no, not for all the rubies in the world.'

'Nicole, tell me what you mean. Don't keep me in suspense. You have been such a good friend to me. I don't forget that you saved me once with that potion you gave me.'

'And made you most uncomfortable for a while.'

'It didn't matter. It saved me. It gave me a respite.'

'A bagatelle. Did you not save Samir for me?'

'We have helped each other. Now . . . please . . . please, tell me what you have to say.'

'The Chief Eunuch will help . . . if it can be done.'

'How? What?'

'He will come to take Fatima away. She would be heavily cloaked and wearing a yashmak . . . and if behind those concealing garments it was not Fatima but Rosetta . . . why? What of that?'

'Is it . . . possible?' I breathed.

'It might be. He would take you through the gates. Nobody would have any idea that it was not Fatima but you. Everyone will have heard she is going back to her family.'

'And where is Fatima to be at this time?'

'In her room. She is to be ready at a certain time, but the carriage will come half an hour early. It makes no difference, the Chief Eunuch will say, and he is the one who makes the arrangement. He will come to see me. You will be here in this room . . . ready waiting. He will walk out with you and if anyone sees you . . . a few might dare to but they will be warned to stay in and not pry on Fatima's shame . . . they will think you are Fatima. The Chief Eunuch will unlock the gates and you will walk through with him. He will then lock the gates and you will get into the carriage which is waiting outside. It will all go according to plan, except that you will be the one who leaves instead of Fatima.'

'Where would he take me?'

'To the British Embassy. You will tell your story. They will send you home. You cannot give the name of the Pasha because you do not know it. Besides, a foreign country cannot interfere in the affairs of another. The duty of the Embassy would be solely to get you home.'

'I can't believe it. It sounds too easy.'

'It is not easy. It is clever and well planned. The Chief Eunuch is a very clever man.'

'And when it is found out what he has done . . . what will happen then?'

'It was a natural mistake. Everyone knew of your reluctance. You managed to pose as Fatima. He came to get a woman from the harem. The only one who could make trouble would be Rani and she will not be so foolish as to quarrel with the Chief Eunuch. She may suspect what she will, but she can do nothing. It is not as though the Pasha knows of your existence. You were to be a surprise for him. So there is no difficulty on that score. He will probably be told that there was trouble in the harem, and that Fatima attacked me with a knife. In the circumstances it seemed wise in the eyes of the Chief Eunuch and Rani to send her to her home. Depend upon it, very soon after you have gone, Fatima will be sent off.'

'Oh, Nicole, I can't believe this. For so long I have hoped and tried to think of possibilities. And now . . . you and the Chief Eunuch are planning to do this for me. I'm not dreaming, am I?'

'As far as I know you are wide awake.'

'The Chief Eunuch is risking such a lot for me.'

'No,' she said softly. 'For me.'

'Nicole, what can I say to you? That you should do this for me . . .'

'I like to pay my debts. This has to work . . . or I shall not have done so.'

'You owe me nothing. Anything I did . . .'

'I know what you mean. But you have done so much for me and it is my joy to give you what you most want.'

'Your escape could have been arranged.'

'There are times in life when it is too late and that time for me is now. It is too late for . . . us . . . but not for you. Now . . . be prepared. Betray nothing. If it is going to work, the utmost caution is necessary.

'I know. I just want to think of what I have to do. You have surprised me. Just now I feel bemused.'

'Think about it,' she said. 'You will have to go very carefully. It is very important that this should work.'

* * *

I could not sleep. I could not eat. I went over and over the plan in my mind. To be free once more! Not to have this terrible fear hanging over me . . . it was a relief too great to be realized at first. To be mistress of my own destiny once more, an individual who made her own decisions, no longer a minion depending on the whim of a master who could command my presence and submission at any time he thought fit.

I thought of Simon. How was he faring? When I was free I must let it be known what had happened to him. He must be rescued. People could not be sold into slavery. That had been abolished. There should be no slaves in the civilized world. Oh . . . but I had forgotten. Simon did not want to be found. He was in hiding. He might be working as a slave in the Pasha's garden, but at least he was not on trial for a crime he had not committed.

And what of Lucas? What had happened to him?

But I must not think beyond escape. I must remember that this was for what I had longed and prayed and that it was now about to happen. Miraculously, I had acquired powerful friends and they were in a position to help me and would do so.

It would be hazardous, I knew, but I must not allow my mind to be sidetracked. I must hold myself in complete readiness for when the moment came.

* * *

A few days passed. Then Nicole said to me: 'Tomorrow is the day. Fatima is now in a room alone, waiting to be taken away. She will be angry and very frightened. She will be sent home in disgrace. She will lose Feisal. Rani says she is lucky. She might have been punished by death. If Samir had died . . . if I had died . . . then it would have been murder. You saved her from that. She has been in the harem for several years. It is a terrible disgrace. She would kill herself if she could, I know. But enough of her. The Chief

Eunuch will come as if to take her but he will take you instead.'

'But she will be left here.'

'Naturally. He cannot take you both. But the trick will not be detected until you are well away. It is the Chief Eunuch's job to find the women and Rani's to look after them and prepare them for him. What the Pasha does not know he cannot miss.'

'But what of Rani? She has taken such pains.'

'Oh, she will be angry, but she knows she must not make trouble with the Chief Eunuch. It may be that Fatima will stay after all. On the other hand they might decide to send her away. So, who knows? You may be doing her another good turn. I do not know how it will work out, but that is not your affair. There will be a lot of chatter . . . much gossip . . . but these women are too interested in themselves to think long of others. It will pass.'

'And if Fatima stays after all, what of you and Samir?'

'Even Fatima learns lessons sometimes. If she stays, she will be meek, never fear. She has come too near to disaster to court it again.'

'I hope she stays. I hope for Feisal's sake.'

'You forget she would have murdered my son . . . me too, if she had had the chance.'

'I know. But she did it for love of her son.'

'And for herself. She so much wants to be First Lady.'

'You will be that, Nicole.'

'I intend to be. My Samir will one day be Pasha – of that I am determined. But the important thing now is to make our plan work. It will, of course. The Chief Eunuch will see to that.'

'Oh, Nicole, I wish you could come with me.'

She shook her head. 'I would not . . . if I could. My life is now here. Years ago, before Samir came, it would have been different. I have felt all you feel now . . . but fate was too much for me. There was nothing I could do – and now this is my life. Samir is to be the Pasha. That is what I want now . . . more than anything. That is what I pray for.'

'And I pray that you will succeed.'

She nodded fiercely. 'I intend to,' she said. 'You may think I have impossible ambitions. But it did happen once . . . some time ago. There was a girl like myself. Her name was Aimée Dubucq de Rivery. She came from Martinique, as I did, and was on her way home from her school in France. She was shipwrecked and sold into a Sultan's harem. I read of her long ago and it has often seemed to me that I am reliving her story. I knew how she felt . . . how desperate at first until she became reconciled, how she sublimated everything to her son's future. She succeeded and he became Sultan. You see, her fate is so like mine. She succeeded and so will I.'

'You will, Nicole,' I said. 'I know you will.'

* * *

The day had come.

Ever since her injury, Nicole had had a small room to herself, apart from the dormitory. The clothes I was to wear had been smuggled into this room on those occasions when the Chief Eunuch had come to see how she was progressing.

I dressed in them and then I looked like any other woman who might be encountered in the streets. I was a little tall, it was true, but I suppose some could be found who were my height.

The Chief Eunuch arrived. He saw that I was ready.

He said: 'We must be careful. Follow me.'

I went with him out of the room, taking one last farewell of Nicole. No one was about. He had given orders that everyone must stay in the dormitory and there must be no prying. No one was to see the departure of the disgraced member of the community.

It was simpler than I had dared hope. We went towards

the gates together. I lowered my head, as though in humiliated sorrow.

A guard unlocked the gates and we passed through, the Chief Eunuch ahead, I a pace or two behind. The carriage was waiting. The Chief Eunuch pushed me in and hurriedly got in beside me. The driver immediately whipped up the horse and we drove away.

We came to the road and drove on for some minutes. Then the carriage pulled up.

I wondered what was happening. Surely I was not going to be put out here, so close to the Pasha's domain? I was too bewildered at this stage to think clearly, but I was filled with apprehension at the notion.

The Chief Eunuch got out of the carriage and at the same time the driver leaped down from his seat. The Chief Eunuch immediately took his place and the driver got into the carriage beside me.

I thought I was dreaming.

'Simon!' I whispered.

He just put his arms round me and we clung together.

In those moments I felt I had awakened from a long nightmare. Not only was I free of all the fears which had beset me since my capture, but Simon was here.

I heard myself say: 'You . . . too!'

'Oh, Rosetta,' he whispered. 'There is so much to be thankful for.'

'When . . . ? How . . . ?' I began.

He replied: 'We'll talk later. For the time . . . this is enough.'

'Where is he taking us?'

'We'll see. He is giving us a chance.'

We did not speak further. We just clasped hands tightly as though we feared we might be separated.

It was not yet dark and through the carriage window I recognized some of the landmarks I had noticed on my journey to the Pasha's domain. I glimpsed the Castle of the Seven Towers, the mosques, the tumbledown wooden houses.

I felt a great relief when we crossed the bridge which I knew separated the Turkish from the Christian part of the city. We were then on the north side of the Golden Horn.

We went on for some little while before the carriage stopped abruptly and the Chief Eunuch descended from the driver's seat. He signed for us to get out. He lifted his hand in a gesture which somehow signified that this was the end of his obligation.

'We don't know how to thank you,' said Simon in French.

He nodded. 'Embassy over there. Tall building. You see.'

'Yes, but . . .'

'Go . . . go now. They may look for you.'

Almost abruptly he climbed up into the driver's seat.

'Good luck,' he cried; and the carriage started back.

Simon and I were alone in Constantinople.

* * *

I felt a great elation. We were free . . . both of us. We only had to walk into the Embassy and tell our story and we should be kept in safety, our families informed of our whereabouts and then we should be sent home.

I turned to Simon. 'Can you . . . believe it!' I cried.

'It's hard to. I'll take you to the Embassy. You'll have to explain that you have escaped from a harem.'

'It seems so incredible.'

'They will believe you. They will know what goes on . . . particularly in the Turkish section.'

'Let's go, Simon. Let's tell them. Soon . . . we'll be on our way home.'

He stood still and looked at me steadily. 'I can't go to the Embassy.'

'What . . . ?'

'Have you forgotten that I am escaping from English

justice? They would send me back to . . . you can guess what.'

I stared at him in dismay. 'Do you mean you are going to stay here?'

'Why not? For a while, perhaps, till I make plans. It's as good a place as any for a fugitive from justice. But I think I shall try to make my way to Australia. I've had experience on a ship. I think that is the most likely place.'

'Simon. I can't go without you.'

'Of course you can. You'll be sensible . . . when you have thought about it.'

'Oh no . . .'

'Rosetta, I am going to take you to the Embassy right away. You'll go in. You'll explain. They'll do everything possible to help you. They'll get you home . . . soon. We were brought here to the Embassy for that purpose.'

'For both of us,' I said.

'Well, how were they to know that I could not take advantage of it? But you can. And you will be foolish beyond all reason not to . . . and without delay. In fact, I shall insist that you do.'

'I could stay here with you. We'd find a way . . .'

'Listen, Rosetta. We've had great good luck . . . the greatest in the world. You can't turn your back on this chance now. It would be utter folly. We found valuable friends. Nicole for you, the Chief Eunuch for me. You were of service to her and I was lucky enough to strike up a friendship with him. Our cases were similar. It gave us something in common. He had been taken . . . the same as I was. We could talk in his language. When he knew that you and I were together, it seemed significant. He with the French girl . . . you with me. It gave us a fellow feeling. Don't you see, it's stupendous good fortune. We might have spent our lives in that place. You a slave girl at the Pasha's command . . . me guarding the harem with the eunuchs . . . perhaps becoming one of them. It could have been like that,

Rosetta. And we have escaped. Let us thank our guardian angels for taking such care of us. Now we have to make sure that it was not done for us in vain.'

'I know. I know. But I can't go without you, Simon.'

He looked about us. We were close to a church, which, on closer inspection, proved to be an English one.

There was a tablet on the wall. Simon drew me to it and we read that the church had been built as a dedication to those men who had fallen in the Crimean War.

'Let's go in,' said Simon. 'There we can think and perhaps talk.'

It was quiet in the church. Fortunately there was no one there. I should have looked incongruous in my Turkish garb. We sat in a pew near the door, ready to escape if necessary.

'Now,' said Simon, 'we have to be sensible.'

'You keep saying that, but . . .'

'It is so necessary to be.'

'You can't ask me to leave you, Simon.'

'I shan't forget you said that.'

'It has been so long. I have wondered and wondered what was happening to you . . . and now that we are at last together . . .'

'I know,' he said. There were a few moments of silence, then he went on: 'The Chief Eunuch kept me informed. I knew the French girl had saved you from the Pasha by giving you a dose of a certain medicine. He supplied the medicine for her to give to you.'

'He told you that!'

'Yes. I had spoken of you. I had told him of our shipwreck . . . how we had been together that time on the island. He said it reminded him of his own experience. And . . . the French girl had been taken into the harem. I think because it was so similar and there was a chance for us, he wanted us to have it. He used to say, "It will be the same story for you unless you get out of here." There seemed no hope.

Then this chance came. What fantastic good fortune we have had, Rosetta.'

'I can't believe that we're here together now. It seems from the start we have been looked after. First the ship . . . then the island, and now this.'

'We have had our opportunities and taken them. And now we must not turn away from them when they are offered to us.'

'I cannot leave you here.'

'Remember it was my original plan to get away from England. What would happen if I returned now?'

'You cannot stay here. They may look for you. What if they found you? The penalty for escaping is . . .'

'They won't find me.'

'We could prove you were innocent. Together we could do it.'

'No. It is not the time.'

'Will it ever be?'

'Perhaps not. But if I went back with you I should be arrested at once. I should be in the same position that I was in before I got out.'

'Perhaps you should never have gone.'

'Just think: if I hadn't we should never have met. We should never have been on that island together. Looking back, it seems like a sort of paradise to me.'

'An uncomfortable paradise. Do you forget how hungry we were . . . how we longed for the sight of a ship?'

'And then we found we were in the hands of corsairs. No, I am not likely to forget.'

'The island was no paradise.'

'But we were together.'

'Yes,' I said. 'Together, and that is how we should stay.'

He shook his head. 'This is your chance, Rosetta. You have to take it. I am going to make you take it.'

'But I want so much to stay with you, Simon. More than anything I want that.'

'And I want you to be safe. It will be so easy for you.'

'No, it will be the hardest thing I ever did.'

'You are letting your emotions of the moment get the better of your good sense. Tomorrow you would regret it. There will be a bed for you at the Embassy. There will be sympathetic listening to your story and all the help necessary to get you comfortably home.'

'And leave you behind!'

'Yes,' he said shortly. 'Now I will take you to the Embassy. Oh, Rosetta, don't look like that. It's the best for you. That is what I want. It's a great opportunity . . . such as comes once in a lifetime. You must not fail to take it. You are emotionally overwrought. You do not understand your true feelings. Later you will be able to assess them. Now you must go. I ask it. I have to fend for myself. That will be difficult enough. But I shall manage . . . alone.'

'You mean I would be a burden.'

He hesitated and then looked at me steadily. 'Yes,' he said.

I knew then that I had to go.

'It is best for you, Rosetta,' he went on gently. 'I shall never forget you. One day perhaps . . .'

I did not speak. I thought: I shall never be happy again. We have been through too much . . . together.

He took both my hands in his and held me against him for a few moments.

Then, together, we left the Memorial Church and made our way to the gates of the Embassy.

Trecorn Manor

In a few days I had passed out of the fantastic unreal world into normality. I was amazed by the manner in which I had been received by the Embassy. It almost made me feel that for a girl to be shipwrecked and sold into a harem was not such an unusual occurrence as I had imagined it to be.

Piracy must have been abolished almost a century ago, but there were still some who continued to ply their evil trade on the high seas, and potentates still maintained their seraglios behind high walls guarded by eunuchs, as they had in days gone by. Certain acts might not be performed openly, but they still existed.

The Embassy was a small enclave – a little bit of England in a foreign land, and from the moment I entered its portals I felt that I had come home.

I was soon divested of my foreign garments and conventional clothes were found for me. I was questioned and I gave my account of what had happened. It was well known that the *Atlantic Star* had foundered and there had been few survivors. Immediate contact would be made with London. I told my story of our escape with the help of one of the crew hands, how we had reached the island, where we had been picked up by corsairs who had sold us into slavery. I knew that I must say nothing about Simon's having escaped with me. My story was immediately accepted.

I was to stay in the Embassy for a while. I must try to relax, I was told, and to remember that I was now safe. I saw a doctor, an elderly Englishman, who was very kind and gentle. He asked me a few questions. I told him how I had been befriended and had been unmolested all the time I had been there. That seemed to give him great relief. He said I appeared to be in good health but I must take care. Such an ordeal as I had suffered could have had an effect on me which might not at first be discernible. If I wished to talk of it I was to do so; but if not, my wishes would be respected.

I was thinking a great deal about Simon, for naturally I could not get him out of my mind. This made me preoccupied and those about me probably thought I was brooding on the horror from which I had escaped.

Moreover, I could not help wondering what was happening at the seraglio and what Rani's reaction had been when she had discovered that I had gone instead of Fatima. And what would have happened when Simon's departure had been discovered? Fortunately the Chief Eunuch had been involved and he would doubtless see that there was as little fuss as possible. Rani would be very angry, I was sure. But even she had to bow to the Chief Eunuch.

I wondered about Nicole. Her debt was handsomely paid and I fervently hoped that she would be rewarded for all she had done for me and keep herself and Samir in high favour with the Pasha.

But I should never know. They had passed out of my life as suddenly as they had come into it.

Then I would be overcome by the wonder of freedom. I should soon be home. I should live the life of a normal English girl. I must never cease to be thankful that I had come safely through that ordeal – except that, on achieving freedom, I had lost Simon.

* * *

Those days I spent in the Embassy seem vague to me now. I would wake in the morning for a few seconds believing I was on my divan. The terrible apprehension would come flooding back. Will it be today that the summons will come? I had not realized until this time what a strain I had lived through.

Then I would remember where I was and a feeling of relief would sweep over me . . . until I thought of Simon. How was he faring in that strange city? Had he been able to find a ship on which he could work his way to Australia? I supposed it was one of the best places he could go to in the circumstances. How could he survive? He was young and strong as well as resourceful. He would find a way. And one day when he was able to prove his innocence he would come home. Perhaps I should see him again and we could resume our friendship from where it had been cut off. He had hinted that he loved me. Did he mean in a special way or was it just that affection which naturally grows up between two people who had endured what we had together?

Free to go home, back to the house in Bloomsbury. Or was the house still ours? What had happened to my parents? Were Mr Dolland, Mrs Harlow, Meg and Emily still in the kitchen? How could they be if my parents were not there? I had often pictured the scene, Mr Dolland at the end of the table, his spectacles pushed up on to his forehead, telling them about the shipwreck. But if my parents had not returned, what would have happened to my friends in the kitchen?

Sometimes life here seemed as uncertain as it had within the walls of the seraglio.

The Ambassador asked me to go and see him one day, which I did. He was tall, dignified with a ceremonial manner. He was very kind and gentle to me, as was everyone at the Embassy.

He said: 'I have news. Some good . . . some bad. The good news is that your father survived the shipwreck. He is at his home now in Bloomsbury. The bad news is that your mother was lost at sea. Your father has been informed of your safety and looks forward to your homecoming. Mr and Mrs Deardon are going home in a few days when their leave falls due. It seems a good idea – and would be most convenient – if you travelled with them.'

I was only half listening. My mother dead! I tried hard to remember her but could only think of her absent-minded smile when her eyes alighted on me. 'Ah . . . the child . . .' and 'This is our daughter, Rosetta. You will find her somewhat untutored, I fear.' I could remember Felicity on that occasion far more distinctly. And now my mother was dead. That cruel ocean had claimed her. I had always thought of her and my father together and I wondered what he was like without her.

Mrs Deardon came to me. She was a plump, comfortably cosy woman who talked continually, which I often found a relief as I had no wish to say much myself.

'My dear,' she cried. 'What an ordeal you have suffered. All you have been through! Never mind. Jack and I will look after you. We shall take ship from Constantinople to Marseilles and then travel through France to Calais. What a journey! I always dread it. But there it is. Needs must. But you do know that every minute you are getting nearer home.'

She was the sort of woman who gives you a summary of her life in five minutes or so. I learned that Jack had always been in the Service, that he and she had gone to school together, married when they were both twenty, had two children, Jack Junior who was now in the Foreign Office, and Martin who was still at university. He would assuredly go into one of the Services. It was a family tradition.

I could see that she was going to relieve me of making conversation and perhaps saying something I might regret. My great fear at this time was that I might be led into being indiscreet which would involve Simon. I must at all costs respect his desire for secrecy. I must remember that if his whereabouts were betrayed he would be brought back to face a death sentence.

In Mrs Deardon's company I went out to buy some clothes. We sat side by side in the carriage while she chattered all the time. She and Jack had been in Constantinople for three years.

'What a place! I was thrilled when Jack first heard of the posting . . . now I'd do anything to get out. I'd like a nice *cosy* place . . . Paris . . . Rome . . . somewhere like that. Not too far from home. This place is *miles* away and so *foreign*. My dear, the customs! And what goes on on the Turkish side! Heaven alone knows, you'd have experience of that. I'm sorry, I shouldn't have mentioned it. My dear, I know how you feel. *Do* forgive me. Look! You can see across the water to Scutari. That was very much in evidence during the Crimean War when wonderful, *wonderful* Florence Nightingale took out her nurses. I do believe *they* played a bigger part in the eventual victory than people know. We're on the north side of the Golden Horn, dear. The other side is quite sinister. Oh, there I go again . . . we're not far from Galata, that's the merchants' quarter . . . founded by the Genoese centuries ago. Jack will tell you all about that. He's interested in that sort of thing. Mind you, the streets are incredibly noisy and dirty. Our people wouldn't risk going there. We're in the best neighbourhood. Pera, you know. Most of the embassies are there . . . the legations and the consulates. There are some fine houses too.'

While she was talking, I would go into a kind of dream. Pictures of the island would flash in and out of my mind . . . of going off with Simon, leaving Lucas to watch for a sail . . . and then the arrival of the galley. On and on . . . and I would come back to the question: Where is he now? What will become of him? Shall I ever know?

'Now here is a very good tailor. Let's see what he can do. We have to get you presentable for home.'

Her discourse went on. The great charm about it was that she did not expect replies.

It seemed a long time before we sailed from Constantinople. To board the ship – much smaller than the *Atlantic Star* – to gaze across the Bosphorus at historic Scutari, where our men had suffered so much in that hospital which from a distance looked like a Moorish Palace, to look back at the towers and minarets of Constantinople, was an emotional experience.

Mr Deardon was a tall man with greying hair and a somewhat dignified manner. He was the archetypal English diplomat – rather aloof, giving the impression that nothing could ruffle his composure or break through his reserve.

The journey to Marseilles was, as Mrs Deardon had predicted, uncomfortable. The *Apollo*, being many times smaller than the *Atlantic Star*, took a battering from the rough seas as severe as I had previously suffered, and there were times when it seemed like a dream and that it was going to start again. If the *Atlantic Star* had succumbed to the fury of the storm, I wondered how the frail *Apollo* could survive.

Mrs Deardon took to her bunk and did not emerge. I missed her discourse. Mr Deardon accepted the fury of the storm with the equilibrium I expected of him. I was sure he would remain serene and dignified, no matter what the disaster.

I could now go on deck and I recalled vividly that occasion when Simon had found me there during the great storm and had chided me and sent me down. I thought: All my life there will be memories of him.

At length the ordeal was over. Mrs Deardon quickly recovered and was her old garrulous self. Mr Deardon listened to her perpetual chatter with composed resignation; but I was glad of it. I could listen to it vaguely while inwardly following my own thoughts, secure in the knowledge that if I betrayed inattention I should be immediately forgiven on account of the ordeal through which I had passed.

There followed the long journey through France and finally the arrival at Calais and the Channel crossing.

The sight of the white cliffs of Dover affected us all. Tears came to Mrs Deardon's eyes and even her husband, for the first time, showed a certain emotion by the twitching of his lips.

'It's home, dear,' said Mrs Deardon. 'It's always the same. You just think of Easter and the daffodils . . . and the green grass. There's no green like our green. It's what you think of when you're away. And the rain, dear, the *blessed* rain. Do you know, in Egypt they go for a year or even two without seeing a drop . . . just those horrible sandstorms. We were in Ismailia . . . how many years, Jack, was it? Surely it wasn't that . . . and . . . and hardly ever saw rain. That's what it is, dear. It's the white cliffs. Home. It's good to see them.'

And after that, London.

The Deardons insisted on delivering me.

'You must come in and meet my father,' I said. 'He will want to thank you.'

Mrs Deardon was eager to do so, but Mr Deardon was firm, and in this he showed his talent for diplomacy.

'Miss Cranleigh will want to meet her family alone,' he said.

I looked at him gratefully and said: 'My father will most certainly wish to thank you personally. Perhaps you could come and dine with us soon.'

'That,' said Mr Deardon, 'would be a great pleasure.'

So I said goodbye to them in the cab which waited until I had rung the doorbell and the door was opened. Then immediately and discreetly, Mr Deardon ordered the cabby to drive on.

* * *

The door was opened by Mr Dolland.

I gave a cry of joy and threw myself into his arms. He coughed a little. I did not realize at that moment that our household had changed. And there was Mrs Harlow. I rushed at her. There were tears in her eyes.

'Oh, Miss Rosetta, Miss Rosetta,' she cried, embracing me. 'You're really here. Oh . . . it's been terrible.'

And there were Meg and Emily.

'It is wonderful to see you all,' I cried.

And then . . . Felicity. We flew to each other and clung.

'I had to come,' she said. 'I'm here for two days. I said to James, "I've got to go."'

'Felicity! Felicity! How wonderful to see you.'

There was a little cough. Over Felicity's head I saw my father. He looked awkward and embarrassed.

I went to him. 'Oh, Father,' I said.

He took me into his arms and held me rather stiffly. It must have been the first time he had ever done so.

'Welcome . . . welcome home, Rosetta,' he began. 'I cannot express . . .'

I thought then: He does care for me. He does. It is just that . . . he cannot express.

A tall thin woman was standing a pace or two behind him. For half a second I thought my mother had been saved after all. But it was someone else.

'Your Aunt Maud is here,' said my father. 'She came to look after me and the household when . . .'

Aunt Maud! My father's sister. I had seen her only once or twice during my childhood. She was tall and rather gaunt. She had a look of my father, but she entirely lacked his obvious helplessness.

'We are all tremendously relieved that you are now safely home, Rosetta,' she was saying. 'It has been an anxious time for your father . . . for us all.'

'Yes,' I said, 'for all of us.'

'Well, now you are back. Your room is ready. Oh, it is such a relief that you are home!'

I felt numb with surprise.

Aunt Maud here . . . in my mother's place. Nothing would be the same again.

* * *

How right I was. The house had changed. Aunt Maud had proved to be a strict disciplinarian. The kitchen was now orderly. There was no question of my having meals there. I should have them with my father and Aunt Maud in the proper manner. Fortunately, for those first few days Felicity was with us.

I could not wait to hear the verdict of the kitchen. Mr Dolland discreetly said that Miss Cranleigh was a good manager and no one could help but respect her. Mrs Harlow agreed. 'Things were not really run right in the old days,' she said. 'Mind you, Mr Dolland worked wonders but there ought to be either a master or a mistress in a house – and a mistress is better because she knows what's what.'

So Aunt Maud apparently knew what was what; but the old unconventional house had disappeared and I desperately longed to catch the old flavour.

Mr Dolland still did the occasional 'turn', but *The Bells* had lost their horror for me. Having passed through some horrific adventures myself, I could no longer get a thrill out of the murder of the Polish Jew. Meg and Emily regretted the old days; but one thing I could rejoice in was the fact that some of those who had shared them were still here.

Meals were naturally different. Everything had to be served in the correct manner. The conversation was no longer dominated by ancient finds and the translation from some piece of papyrus. Aunt Maud discussed politics and the weather; and she told me that when my father had got over mourning for my mother, she proposed to give a few dinner parties . . . for his colleagues from the Museum . . . professors and such-like.

I was glad Felicity was with us for these first days, apart from my joy in seeing her. I knew that if she had not been there I should have wanted to shut myself away in my bedroom and avoid those interminable meals. But Felicity did lighten the conversation with amusing stories about life in Oxford and the exploits of her son Jamie, now aged three, and little Flora who was not yet one.

'You must come and see them, Rosetta,' she said. 'I am sure your father will spare you after a while. Now, of course, you have just come home . . .'

'Of course, of course,' said my father.

I could talk more freely to Felicity and I needed to talk. But I must do so guardedly – even to her. It was very difficult to speak of my adventures because Simon had played such an important part in them and the fact that I must not betray him made me very reticent, lest by some odd remark I might do so.

But Felicity and I had been so close and she guessed something was on my mind.

On the day after my arrival she came to my room. It was clear to me that, sensing some problem, she wanted to help me with it. If only someone could do that!

She burst out suddenly: 'Tell me frankly, Rosetta. Do you want to talk? I know how difficult it must be to discuss what has happened. Do say if it is. But I think it might help . . .'

I hesitated. 'I'm not sure . . .'

'I understand. It must have been very frightening. Your father told us how you were lost when you went back for his notes.'

'Oh yes. It's strange how little things like that can change one's life.'

'He blames himself, Rosetta. I know he doesn't betray his emotions . . . but that does not mean they are not there.'

'Everything is so different now,' I said. 'The house . . . everything. I know it can never again be as it used to.'

'It really is a very good thing that your Aunt Maud is here, Rosetta.'

'We never saw much of her when I was young. I scarcely recognized her. It seems so strange that she should be here now.'

'I gathered she and your mother did not get on. That's easy to understand. They were so different. Your parents were so immersed in their work and . . . your aunt is so efficient in running a house.'

I gave her a wry smile. 'I liked ours as it was . . . inefficient.'

'Your father misses your mother . . . terribly. They were so close in everything they did . . . always together. It is a sad blow for him. He cannot . . .'

'Cannot express,' I said.

She nodded. 'And you, Rosetta, when you feel more settled you must come and stay with us. James would be delighted and you would love the children. Jamie is a very independent young gentleman and Flora is just beginning to toddle. They are adorable.'

'It would be lovely to come.'

'You have only to say. I shall have to go back the day after tomorrow. But I had to be here for your return.'

'How glad I am that you were!'

'By the way, did you hear about Lucas Lorimer?'

'Lucas . . . no!'

'Oh . . . didn't you? I suppose you wouldn't. He came back, you know.'

'He came back . . .' I repeated.

'Obviously you haven't heard. He told us the story. We thought you had been drowned and it was a great relief to hear that you had escaped the wreck. But we were terribly worried to hear you had fallen into the hands of those wicked people. I've had nightmares wondering what had happened.'

'Tell me about Lucas.'

'It's a very sad story. That it should happen to him! I've only seen him once since he came back. James and I went down to Cornwall. James was lecturing at a college in Truro . . . and we called at Trecorn Manor. I don't think he is very pleased to see anyone. Trecorn Manor is a lovely old place. It's been in the family for years. Lucas's brother Carleton inherited. That was another sore point. It's always a bit of a strain for a man like that to be a second son. He used to be such a vital person.'

'What happened to him?'

'As you know, he was captured with you, but he somehow made a bargain with those people. He persuaded them to free him in exchange for some family jewels. How it was done I don't quite know. He obviously didn't want to talk about it, and one can't ask questions . . . not too many in any case. However, they let him go. It was a sort of ransom. Poor Lucas, he'll never be the same again. He so loved to travel. James always said he was something of a dilettante. It's his leg, you see. It was terribly hurt in the wreck. Of course, if it had had attention at the time. He's been to various bone people getting advice . . . all over the country and abroad . . . Switzerland and Germany . . . but it is always the same story. It was neglected at the vital time. He limps badly and has to walk with a stick and he's in considerable pain. He is a little better, I believe, but the leg will never be right. It's changed him. He used to be so witty and amusing . . . now he is quite morose. He is the last person this should have happened to.'

I was back in the past. I saw him clinging to the lifeboat, our clumsy efforts to set his leg . . . lying on the island, keeping watch for a sail while Simon and I went off to forage and talk secrets.

'So you don't see him often . . .'

'No. It's not really all that far away. I've asked him to come and stay, but he declines my invitations. I think he doesn't want to go anywhere . . . or to see anyone. You see, it is a complete change. He used to live such a busy social life, and he seemed to enjoy it.'

'I should like to see him again.'

'Why, yes. He might be interested in that. Or perhaps he wouldn't want to be reminded. It may be that he is trying to forget. I tell you what I will do. Come and stay and I'll invite him too. He might make the effort to see you. After all, you were together on that island.'

'Oh, please arrange it, Felicity.'

'I certainly shall . . . and soon.'

I felt excited at the prospect, but even to Lucas I could not talk of Simon. That was our secret . . . shared only by us two. Simon had told me because he trusted me. I must respect that trust. If he were hunted down and brought back through me, I should never forgive myself. To Lucas, Simon must remain the deck hand who saved our lives.

* * *

Felicity had to go home and the house seemed dull. There was an air of such normality about it that I was forced to look facts in the face and make a logical conclusion.

I had deluded myself into thinking that when I was home I should be able to prove Simon's innocence. How? I asked myself now. How did I set about it? Go to his home? Get to know people who had played a part in the drama which had led up to the shooting? I could not go to Perrivale Court and say: 'I know Simon is innocent and I have come to uncover the truth and solve the mystery.' How could I behave as though I were an investigator from Scotland Yard!

I needed time to think. I was obsessed by the need to prove his innocence so that he could come back and lead a normal life. But suppose I did achieve this seemingly impossible task, where should I find *him*? The whole scheme was wildly fantastic. It had no place in this logical world.

Aunt Maud's influence on the house was very marked. Its furniture was highly polished. Floors shone, brass gleamed and everything, however small, was in the place designed for it. Daily she went to the kitchen to consult Mrs Harlow on meals and both Mrs Harlow and Mr Dolland had assumed a new dignity; and even Meg and Emily did their work in a more orderly fashion – not cutting it short to sit over meals and listen to Mr Dolland's discourse on the old days of the drama; and I was sure that if they did indulge in this diversion, they would be interrupted by an imperious ringing, and Mr Dolland would have to leave his performance to don his black coat to make his ceremonial appearance above stairs.

I think I minded it more than they did. We had all been so happy-go-lucky in the past, but I came to realize that good servants prefer a well-run house to a happy one.

I often found Aunt Maud watching me speculatively. I knew that in due course I should be dragooned into her scheme of things, and in Aunt Maud's eyes there would be only one course to pursue since I was a young and nubile woman: marriage. These dinner parties she had hinted at would have a definite purpose: the search for a suitable husband for me. I pictured him: earnest, slightly balding, learned, erudite, perhaps a professor who had already made his mark in the academic world. Someone rather like James Grafton only not so attractive. Perhaps he would be attached to the British Museum or Oxford or Cambridge. It would keep me in the circle in which my family moved. Aunt Maud might think my father was absent-minded – and I gathered that she had had little respect for my mother as a housewife, which was the reason why we had seen so little of her during my mother's lifetime – but he was well respected in his profession and therefore it would be wise for me to marry into it. I was sure she felt that, schooled by her, unlike my mother, I might make a professor's wife *and* a good housewife at the same time.

She would preside over the affair and therefore it would be conducted in the most orthodox manner. Aunt Maud hated to waste anything – including time. I believed that, but for my strange adventure, operations would have been commenced long ago. As it was, I was allowed a little respite.

The doctor had evidently warned Aunt Maud that I must be treated with a certain care. The ordeal through which I had passed must not be forgotten and I needed time to rehabilitate myself to a civilized way of life in my own way. Aunt Maud followed his instructions with brisk efficiency, and my father did the same, remaining aloof. Mrs Harlow did so by making sure that I was comfortably seated and speaking to me rather as she used to when I was five years old. Even Mr Dolland lowered his voice and I would find Meg and Emily regarding me with awestruck wonder.

Only once did my father refer to the shipwreck. He told me how they had been caught up in a crowd going for the boats. They had wanted to wait for me, to go back and find me . . . but one of the officers had taken their arms and more or less forced them to go with the crowd.

'We thought you would join us at any minute,' he said piteously.

'It was such chaos,' I said. 'It couldn't have been otherwise.'

'I lost your mother while they were pushing us into the boats . . .'

'We mustn't brood on it,' I said.

'If you hadn't gone back for those notes we should all have been together . . .'

'No . . . no. You and my mother were parted . . . so should we have been.'

He was so distressed that I knew we must not speak of it. He must try to forget, I told him.

All this affected me deeply, and I felt a great desire to escape, to go down to Cornwall, to find Perrivale Court and to begin the impossibe task of finding out what really happened. I needed time. I needed a plan. I wanted desperately to take some action, but I was not sure how to begin.

I went down to the kitchen to try to recapture the spirit of the old days. I asked Mr Dolland for 'To be or not to be' and the speech before Harfleur. He obliged, but I fancied he lacked his previous flair and they were all watching me rather than Mr Dolland.

I said to him: 'Do you remember . . . just before I went away . . . there was a murder case?'

'What was that, Miss Rosetta? Let me see. There was that man who married women for their money.'

'And then done 'em in,' added Mrs Harlow.

'I wasn't thinking of that. I mean the case of those brothers . . . one of them was shot in an empty farmhouse. Didn't someone run away?'

'Oh, I know the one you mean. It was the Bindon Boys case.'

'Yes, that's the one. Did you ever hear what happened?'

'Oh . . . the murderer got away. I don't think they ever caught him.'

'He was smarter than the police,' added Mrs Harlow.

'I remember now,' said Mr Dolland. 'It all comes back to me. It was Simon Perrivale . . . adopted when he was a child. He shot the brother. There was a woman, I believe. Jealousy and all that.'

'I know you keep newspaper cuttings, Mr Dolland. Do you have any of that case?'

'Oh, it's only theatre things he cuts out,' said Mrs Harlow. 'This play and that . . . and what actor and actress. That's right, ain't it, Mr Dolland?'

'Yes,' replied Mr Dolland. 'That's what I keep. What did you want to know about the case, Miss Rosetta?'

'Oh . . . I just wondered if you kept cuttings, that's all. I knew you had albums . . . you see, it was just before I went away . . .' I trailed off.

Glances passed between them.

'Oh, I reckon that's all done with now,' said Mrs Harlow, as though soothing a child.

'The police never close a case,' added Mr Dolland. 'Not till they've found the murderer and it's settled and done with. They keep it on their files, as they say. One of these days they'll catch up with him. He'll make a false step. Perhaps only one is needed, and then hey presto . . . they've got him.'

'They do say,' said Mrs Harlow, 'that murderers can never resist coming back to the scene of the crime. That's what this Simon whatever-his-name-is will do one of these days. You can bet your life on it.'

Would he ever come back? I wondered.

What could I do? I had only this wild dream that I should prove his innocence and then he could come back without fear. He would know freedom again and we should be together.

* * *

Several weeks had passed. After living in perpetual fear and apprehension, the predictably peaceful days seemed to go on interminably.

Aunt Maud tried to interest me in household matters – all the things which it was good for a girl to know. She believed firmly that it was her duty to do what my parents had failed to: prepare me for my marriage. I must learn how to deal with servants. My manner towards them left much to be desired. It was necessary, of course, to maintain a certain friendliness but it should be aloof. I was too familiar and it encouraged them to be so with me. One could not blame *them*. What I needed was a mixture of indiscernible condescension, amiability without familiarity, so that, however friendly one felt towards them, the line between up- and downstairs was never allowed to slip. She did not blame me. *Others* were responsible. But there was no reason why I should continue in this unsatisfactory strain. I must first of all learn how to deal with servants. I should listen to her, Aunt Maud, ordering the meals; I might be present on one or two occasions when she paid her daily visit to the kitchen. I must try to improve my needlework and practise more on the pianoforte. She hinted at music lessons. Soon, she told me she would launch her scheme, for bringing people to the house.

I wrote to Felicity.

'Please, Felicity, I want to get away. If you could invite me . . . soon.'

There was an immediate reply. 'Come when you can. Oxford and the Graftons await you.'

'I am going to stay awhile with Felicity,' I told Aunt Maud.

She smiled smugly. With Felicity I should meet young men . . . the right sort of young men. It did not matter from which spot the scheme was launched. Operation Marriage could begin just as well in Oxford as in Bloomsbury.

* * *

To arrive in Oxford was an exciting experience. I had always loved what little I had seen of it . . . that most romantic of cities standing where the Cherwell and the Thames – Isis here – meet, its towers and spires reaching to the sky, its air of indifference to the workaday world. I loved the city, but what was most pleasant was to be with Felicity.

The Graftons had a house near Broad Street close to Balliol, Trinity and Exeter Colleges, not far from the spot where the martyrs Ridley and Latimer were burned to death for their religious opinions. The past was all around one and I found peace from Aunt Maud's efficiency and the far from subtle care which everyone in the house seemed determined to bestow upon me.

With Felicity it was different. She understood me better than the others. She knew that there were secrets which I could not bring myself to discuss. Perhaps she thought I should one day. In any case she was perceptive enough to know that she must wait for me to do so and make no attempt to prise them from me.

James was tactful and charming and the children provided a great diversion. Jamie chattered quite a lot; he showed me his picture-books and proudly pointed out a pussycat and a train. Flora regarded me suspiciously for a while, but eventually decided that I was harmless and condescended to sit on my lap.

The day after I arrived Felicity said: 'When I knew you were coming I wrote to Lucas Lorimer. I said how delighted we should be if he came for a visit and I guessed you and he might have something to talk about.'

'Has he accepted?' I asked.

'Not yet. When I saw him before, he clearly did not want to talk of his adventures. It may be that he will be afraid it will bring it all back too painfully.'

'I should like to see him.'

'I know. That's why I asked him.'

All that day I thought of his being taken ashore to board the corsairs' galley and that moment on the island when they had seemed to hesitate whether to take him or not. I had seen very little of him after that.

What had happened to him? How had he got away when Simon and I had been sold into slavery? Yet he . . . maimed as he was . . . had eluded his captors as we had been unable to.

There was so much I wanted to ask him.

The next day we were at breakfast when the mail was brought in. Felicity seized on a letter, opened it, read it, smiled and looked up waving it.

'It's from Lucas,' she said. 'He's coming tomorrow. I'm so glad. I thought he would want to see you. Aren't you pleased, Rosetta?'

'Yes. I am delighted.'

She looked at me anxiously. 'I dare say it will be a little upsetting, perhaps . . .'

'I don't know. We're both safe now.'

'Yes, but what an experience! Yet I am sure it is better for you both to meet and talk openly. It doesn't do to bottle these things up.'

'I shall look forward so much to seeing him.'

Felicity sent the carriage to the station to meet him. James went with it. We had debated whether we should both go too, but we finally decided it would be better for us to wait at the house.

My first sight of him shocked me deeply. I had, of course, seen him in worse condition; on the island, for instance, and when we had dragged him into the lifeboat, but I was contrasting him with the man whom I had first met. There were shadows under his eyes and that certain cynical sparkle was replaced by a look of hopelessness. The flesh had fallen away from his features, which gave him a gaunt look. The tolerant amusement with which he had appeared to look out on the world had disappeared. He looked weary and disillusioned.

Our meeting was an emotional one. His expression changed when he saw me. He smiled and came towards me, leaning on his stick. He held out his free hand and took mine. He held it for some time, looking intently at me.

'Rosetta,' he said, and his lips twitched a little. The obvious emotion he felt made him look different again . . . defenceless in a way. I had never seen him look like that before. I knew he was remembering, as I was – the island where Simon and I had left him to watch while we had gone off together, the arrival of the corsairs, those days we had spent in the open boat.

'Oh, Lucas,' I said. 'It is good to see you here . . . safe.'

There was a short silence while we continued to gaze at each other, almost as though we could not believe that we were real.

Felicity said softly: 'I know you two will have lots to say to each other. First . . . let's show Lucas his room, shall we?'

* * *

She was right. There was a great deal to talk about. The first evening was something of a strain. James and Felicity were the perfect host and hostess, full of understanding, skating over awkward pauses with skill and ease.

Felicity was the soul of tact. She knew that there would be things of which we would want to talk to no one but each other – and only then when we were ready, and the following day James went off to his college, and she told us that she had an engagement which she must fulfil.

'Do forgive me,' she said. 'I'll have to leave you two to entertain each other this afternoon.'

There was a pleasant part of the garden, walled in with mellow red bricks with a pond in the centre – the Tudor-type of intimate small garden within a garden. The roses were in bloom and I suggested that I show them to Lucas.

It was a mild afternoon, pleasantly warm without being too hot and we made our necessarily rather slow progress there. There was a stillness in the air and within the walls of that garden we might have stepped back two or three centuries in time.

'Let's sit here,' I said. 'The pond is so pretty and it is so peaceful.'

There was silence and I went on: 'We'd better talk about it, Lucas. We both want to, don't we?'

'Yes,' he agreed. 'It's uppermost in our minds.'

'Does it seem to you like a dream?' I asked.

'No,' he said sharply. 'Stark reality. I have a perpetual reminder. Here I am now . . . like this.'

'I'm sorry. We didn't know how to set it . . . and we had nothing that would help us.'

'My dear girl,' he said almost angrily. 'I'm not blaming you . . . only life . . . fate . . . or whatever you like to call it. Don't you see? I have to spend the rest of my life . . . like this.'

'But at least you are here . . . at least you are alive.'

He shrugged his shoulders. 'Do you think that is a matter for great rejoicing?'

'For some at any rate. Your friends . . . your family. You are lame and I know there is pain now and then . . . but so much worse might have happened to you.'

'You are right to chide me. I am selfish, disgruntled and ungrateful.'

'Oh no, no. Do you think . . . it is possible . . . that something may be done?'

'What?'

'Well, they are very clever nowadays. There have been all sorts of medical discoveries . . .'

'My bone was broken. It was not set. It is too late to do anything about it now.'

'Oh, Lucas, I'm so sorry. If only we could have done something . . . how different it would have been.'

'You did a great deal and I'm a selfish creature thinking of my own misfortunes. I just cannot bear to contemplate what happened to you.'

'But I escaped. My fears were only in the mind.'

He wanted to know in detail what had happened, so I told him of my friendship with Nicole and how she had given me the drug and saved me from the Pasha's attentions, and how the drug had been supplied by the Chief Eunuch who was a great friend of hers. He listened intently.

'Thank God,' he said. 'That could have scarred you as deeply as I have been . . . perhaps more so. And what happened to that man . . . John Player?'

It seemed as though the silence went on for a long time. I heard the buzz of a bee, and the high-pitched note of a grasshopper. Be careful, I was telling myself. You could so easily betray him. Remember it is not only your secret. It is yours and Simon's.

I heard myself say: 'He . . . he was sold to the same Pasha.'

'Poor devil. I can guess what his fate would be. He was a strange man. I always had an odd feeling about him.'

'What sort of feeling?' I asked apprehensively.

'I felt that things were not all they seemed. Now and then I had a fancy that I had seen him before somewhere. Then sometimes he seemed as though he were hiding something.'

'What do you mean? What could he have been hiding?'

'Anything. I've no idea. That was just the impression he gave. He wasn't the sort of man you'd expect to find swabbing the decks, was he? He was very resourceful, I must say.'

'I think we could both say that we owed our lives to him.'

'And you are right. I wish I knew what had happened to him.'

'A great many men were employed in the gardens. He was big and strong . . .'

'He would have fetched a fair price, I dare say.'

There was silence again. I was afraid to speak lest I should betray something. He went on musingly: 'How strange that we were all on that island together . . . never knowing whether we should be found before we died of starvation.'

'How did you manage to get home, Lucas?'

'Well, I'm a wily old bird, you know.' He smiled, and when he did so he was the man I had known when I first met him. 'I seized my opportunities. I had a smattering of their language, I found. It helped a lot. I had picked up a few words when I was travelling round the world some years ago. It is amazing how being able to communicate helps. I offered them money . . . for the three of us. I said that in my own country I was a very rich man. They believed me because they knew I had travelled a good deal. They wouldn't consider releasing you or Player. You were too valuable. I was not. Being crippled, I was useless.'

'You see, there is some advantage in everything.'

'There have been times when I wished they had thrown me overboard.'

'You must not say that. It is accepting defeat – no, welcoming it. That is not the way to live.'

'You are right, of course. Oh, it is good to be with you, Rosetta. I remember how resourceful you were when we were on the island. I owe a lot to you.'

'But most to . . .'

'To that man Player. Well, he was a sort of leader, wasn't he? He was cut out for the part . . . and it fell to him. He played it well, I'll admit. And I was the impediment. I was the one who slowed down the progress.'

'You did nothing of the sort. How could you have done on the island? Tell me the rest.'

'When I saw that I could not save you and nothing would make those men part with you and Player, I concentrated on my own case. They were more amenable in that direction. What price could they get for me? A man in my state? Nothing. I told them that if they would let me go, I would send them a valuable jewel. If they tried to sell me they would get nothing, for who would want a man who can't even walk without a stick? If they threw me overboard that would be equally unproductive. But if they took my offer of the jewel, then they would at least have something for their pains.'

'So . . . they agreed to let you go for the promise of a jewel?'

'It was simple logic really. They had two alternatives. Throw me overboard or despatch me in some other way and lose everything, or take a chance that I would keep my word and send the jewel. It would occur to them – as it would to any – that I might not keep my side of the bargain. And if I did not, well, they might just as well throw me overboard. The wise thing, of course, would be to take a chance, for at least if they did there could be a hope of getting something. So . . . I was dropped at Athens . . . a street or so away from the British Embassy. The rest was simple. My family were informed and I was on the way home.'

'And the jewel?'

'I kept my word. It was a ring which belonged to my mother . . . really one of the family jewels, you might say. They were divided between my brother and myself. It had been my mother's engagement ring and my father's mother's before her. If I had become engaged it would have been my fiancée's.'

'Of course, you need not have sent it.'

'No. But those people have long memories. I did not want to spend the rest of my life wondering if fate would throw me in their way again. Moreover, suppose some other poor devil was caught by them and tried my tactics? Once deceived, they might not have given the chance again. Then again, the ring would probably have lain idle for a very long time. It is not likely that anyone would want to marry me . . . in my condition.'

'Did you take it yourself and where to?'

'They had arranged where it should be taken. There was an old inn on the Italian coast. I was warned not to swerve from the instructions. It was to be taken to this inn – I think it was one frequented by smugglers, and there it would be collected. I did not go myself. I was scarcely in a fit state and they recognized that. I told them who would bring it. It was Dick Duvane. He was my batman during my spell in the Army. When I came out, so did he, and we have been together ever since. He's a valet . . . confidant . . . and frequently fellow-traveller. He's not just a servant. He's one of the best friends I ever had. I don't know what I'd do without him. I trust him absolutely.'

'I'm glad you got away, Lucas.'

'I suppose I am myself . . . only . . .'

'I know. I do understand.'

We fell into silence. We were still in the garden when Felicity came out to find us.

* * *

That visit to Oxford was of considerable help to me. Lucas's logical outlook on life – bitter though it was – brought me down to Earth. What could I do? How could I prove Simon's innocence? I was not even on the spot. I knew nothing of the family at Perrivale Court except what I had gathered from Simon and had read in the newspapers at the time of the murder. If only I could find some means of meeting them, of going to Perrivale Court! What hope was there? I thought of Lucas. What if I asked his help? He was resourceful. The manner in which he had extricated himself from a dangerous situation showed that. He was not very far from Perrivale Court; he was not on terms of friendship or even casual acquaintance with the family, although he had once, long ago, visited the place with his father. I wished I could have discussed Simon with him, perhaps enlisted his help. Dare I? I wondered. But I could not be sure what his reaction would be.

I felt as helpless as ever but that visit did cheer me a little.

He left Oxford the day before I did. When he said goodbye he looked forlorn and rather vulnerable and I felt a great desire to comfort him. I thought at one stage that he was going to make a suggestion for a further meeting, but he did not.

Felicity and I went with him to the station. He seemed reluctant to leave us and stood at the carriage window watching us on the platform as the train steamed away, taking him back to the West Country.

'It is so sad,' said Felicity. 'There is a changed man.'

The next day I went home.

* * *

Aunt Maud wanted to know whom I had met in Oxford.

I told her there had not been a great deal of entertaining because Felicity had thought I needed a restful time. When I was at dinner with her and my father it slipped out that Lucas Lorimer had been staying in Oxford while I was there.

My father was immediately interested. 'Oh yes . . . the young man who was with us on the *Atlantic Star*.' He turned to Aunt Maud. 'It was most extraordinary. He discovered a stone in his garden in Cornwall. Ancient Egyptian. How it got there is a mystery. But it was quite an exciting discovery. Yes, he was with us on the *Atlantic Star*.'

'He was one of the survivors,' I told Aunt Maud.

I followed her line of thought. I *had* met a man in Oxford, then? Who was he? Was he of good family? Was he in a position to support a wife?

I said shortly: 'He is crippled. He was hurt in the wreck.'

Aunt Maud looked disappointed, then resigned. I could imagine her mustering her ideas to bring eligible young men to the dinner table; and how I missed Felicity and the peace of Oxford.

Aunt Maud relentlessly pursued her policy. There followed several dinner parties to which men whom she considered suitable were asked. She harried my father into bringing some of his associates home to dine; to my amusement and her chagrin, most of them were middle-aged, so fanatically devoted to their work that they had no plans for putting any impediment to it in the form of a wife, or else cosily married with erudite and energetic wives and a family of prodigies.

The weeks passed into months. I was restive and I did not see any escape.

Felicity paid us a flying visit. It was difficult to leave the children for long. The nanny was good and she enjoyed the responsibility of being in sole charge of the nursery, but Felicity hated to leave them. I was sure she came only because she was worried about me.

I was able to tell her how I missed the old days in our pleasantly disorganized household. I knew I should be grateful to the indefatigable Aunt Maud, but there was more to life than polished furniture and meals on time. Aunt Maud was such an overpowering person that she subdued us all, and her influence was particularly felt in the kitchen where I had spent so many happy hours.

Felicity said: 'Rosetta, have you something on your mind?' I hesitated and she went on: 'Wouldn't you like to talk about it? You know I'd understand. But I won't press you. I know that, terrifying as an ordeal can be while you live it, at times what can happen afterwards can be equally important. It's happened, Rosetta. It's over. Don't think I don't understand what it was like in that harem. It must have been quite terrible. But you escaped. It was a wonderful piece of luck. It's left its mark, though. I worry about you . . . and about Lucas, too. I always liked him. He used to be so amusing. He's travelled so much and talked so easily about it. He was always so light-hearted in a blasé sort of way. And now I think he's shutting himself in with his bitterness. It is all wrong. It's agonizing for him, of course. He was always so active. I'm going to be rather bold. James is going to Truro again to lecture at that college. I shall go with him and I shall suggest that, as we are in Cornwall, we call on him. It would be nice if you came with us. What do you think?'

I could not hide my enthusiasm for the plan. To go there, to be not far from Perrivale Court . . . well, however far it was, I should be comparatively near. What I should do when I got there I was not sure. There was one thought uppermost in my mind: I must not betray Simon.

'I can see the idea appeals to you,' said Felicity.

When the matter was broached Aunt Maud seemed mildly pleased. Her own attempts to bring me into contact with marriageable young men had not been very successful. She was always hoping that something would be more productive.

The Graftons moved in the right circles. James Grafton was 'something at Oxford'. Aunt Maud was not well informed about such details. People were either suitable or unsuitable and the Graftons – in spite of the fact that Felicity had been a governess – were eminently suitable. Aunt Maud was in favour of the idea. So was my father when he was told by her that it would be good for my future.

So it was arranged that I should accompany James and Felicity to Truro.

At the instigation of Felicity, James had written to Lucas to tell him that we should be in Cornwall and he thought it might be an opportunity for us to call and see them while we were in the Duchy.

There was a prompt reply that we must certainly do so. We must stay a few days at least. Trecorn Manor was too far from Truro for us to come for a day.

The change in me was obvious.

Mrs Harlow said: 'You always did get on with that Felicity. I remember the day she came and we was expecting some stuck-up madam. From the moment she stepped out of that cab I took to her . . . and so did you, I'd say.'

'Yes,' I said. 'She is a wonderful friend. How lucky we were that she came to us.'

'I'd say you'd got the right bull by the horns there.'

Oh yes, indeed, I owed a great deal to Felicity.

* * *

Trecorn Manor was a pleasant Queen Anne mansion built in an age noted for its elegance. It was set in well-kept grounds. I was thinking how interesting it would be to see Lucas against the background of his own home.

We were warmly welcomed by him.

'It is so good of you to come,' he said; and I felt he meant it.

We were introduced to his brother Carleton and Carleton's wife Theresa. Carleton looked a little like Lucas, but they were of very different temperaments, I soon discovered. Carleton was bluff, easygoing, completely immersed in the running of the estate – in fact the typical squire – and Theresa was entirely suited to be his wife. She was absorbed in her family, carrying out her duties on the estate with charm, tolerance and total efficiency – clearly the excellent wife and mother.

There were two children, twins, a girl and a boy, Henry and Jennifer, aged four years. I knew that Carleton and his wife would be admired and respected throughout the estate, that she would work indefatigably in the affairs of the church and the general community. She was the sort of woman who would do her duty unstintingly and make a pleasure of it.

I could not quite see Lucas fitting into this environment.

When we were alone, Felicity said: 'Lucas couldn't have a better home to come back to.'

I wondered. This display of well-being might be galling to a man in his position. It was something I felt he would never have wanted before the shipwreck. Indeed he had, by his frequent absences, shown that he could not tolerate it. It was sad that such virtues as those of Carleton and his wife and Aunt Maud, so admirable in themselves, create a less than perfect atmosphere for those around them.

We planned to stay in Cornwall for about a week, which was all the time James could spare, and I knew that Felicity did not want to leave the children for longer than that.

We were given rooms on the first floor overlooking moorland. James and Felicity's room was next to mine.

Theresa took us up.

'I hope you'll be comfortable,' she said. 'It's a pity you can only stay a week. We love having visitors. Unfortunately, we don't often. I'm so glad you came. Lucas is pleased you are here . . .' She trailed off.

'We hesitated about suggesting coming,' said Felicity. 'It was rather forward of us.'

'We should have been most put out if you had come all this way without seeing us. Carleton worries about Lucas . . . so do I. He is so changed.'

'Well, it was a terrible ordeal,' said Felicity.

Theresa laid her hand on my arm. 'And for you, too. I heard about it. Lucas doesn't talk much. Carleton says it is like getting blood out of a stone to get information out of him. He was so active. And this has hit him hard. But he did cheer up quite a lot when he heard you were coming.'

'He likes to talk to Rosetta,' said Felicity. 'After all, they were together. I always think it helps people to talk.'

'It is wonderful that you both came through. We had been so worried about Lucas. And when we knew he was coming home . . . it was wonderful. And then . . . he was so different. And Lucas being the man he is . . . it was never easy for him to be the younger brother.' She shrugged her shoulders and looked faintly embarrassed, as though she thought she was saying too much.

I knew that she was right. Before the accident Lucas had been constantly preoccupied by the fact that his elder brother was head of the household when their father died. He was a man who liked to lead and it could never have been easy for him to take second place. So he had travelled widely after he left the Army and of course while he was in it. He had tried archæology. He had written a book, inspired by his discovery, and had been on the point of lecturing about it when disaster had struck. It must have seemed then that he was making a life away from Trecorn Manor, which was what he had wanted; and then he was brought back . . . as he was now. I could understand that he was disillusioned with life. I looked forward to more talks with him. Perhaps I could try to make him see the future differently. Perhaps I could inspire him with a little hope. I did not think there was a very good chance of this, but I could try.

He could still ride, which was a blessing. True, he needed a little assistance in mounting and dismounting, but when he was on his horse, he was all that he had been before. He had always been an excellent horseman and I noticed at once that there was a strong relationship between him and his mount, Charger, who seemed to understand that his master had changed and that he needed to be looked after.

Theresa said: 'We never worry about Lucas when he goes off for long spells. If he's on Charger we know he will be brought home when he wants to come.'

The first night at dinner he wanted to know if I rode.

'There was little opportunity at home,' I told him. 'But when I was at school we had riding lessons. So I cannot call myself quite a novice but . . . somewhat inexperienced.'

'You ought to get in a bit of practice while you're here,' suggested Carleton.

'Yes,' agreed Lucas. 'I'll undertake to be your tutor.'

'It will be a little boring perhaps for such a practised rider,' I said.

'I know it will be a pleasure,' he replied.

Theresa beamed on us. She was such a kindly woman and I realized how happy she was that I was here because she thought it would be pleasant for Lucas, and that we were good for each other.

It had been arranged that after two days at Trecorn Manor James should go back to Truro to do his work while Felicity and I remained behind to wait for him. He would return to the Manor when his work was done and after a day or so we should all leave together.

I soon settled into a routine. Lucas and I rode together and talked a good deal, often about our adventure. We often went over the same ground, but I am sure it did us both good. As far as I was concerned, it made me all the more eager to find out something about Perrivale Court.

I found myself drawn into life in the nursery. Jennifer seemed to have taken a liking to me. I had had little to do with children and was unsure how to deal with them, but Jennifer solved that. She informed me that her name was Jennifer Lorimer and that she lived at Trecorn Manor. She was four years old. All this was told as if in great confidence and it was almost as though we shared a special confidence. Although the girl in the twinship, she was the leader. She was vivacious and chattered a good deal. Henry was much quieter, a serious little boy; he always followed Jennifer and as she had decided that she liked me, he must do so too.

Moreover, there was Nanny Crockett – another ally. I think it must have been because I got on well with the twins that she accepted me. She was by no means young, but a power in the nursery. Ellen, the fourteen-year-old nursery maid, behaved towards her as though she were the Queen. I gathered she was in her late fifties. She had iron grey hair which was plaited and worn round her head in a rather severe manner; her grey eyes were alert and she had a way of pursing her lips if she disapproved of anything and then she could be indomitable. She was a woman of definite opinions and once they became hers she determined to stick to them.

'We were lucky to get her,' said Theresa. 'She's a very experienced nanny. She's not young, of course, but that's all to the good. She's as active as a young woman and there's the experience as well.'

Nanny Crockett liked to have a little chat now and then and when the children had their afternoon nap, if I were not with Lucas, I would be with her.

Felicity and Theresa had interests in common – the running of a home and the care of a husband and children. They were ideal companions. I imagined when they were together they discussed Lucas and me. They thought we were 'good for each other' and we were certainly thrown together on every possible occasion. Not that their efforts were necessary, for Lucas showed clearly that he preferred my society to that of anyone else. It was a fact, I believed, that since we had arrived, he had become a little more like the man he used to be. He laughed occasionally now and then and sometimes would deliver a witty quip, but alas, very often with a hint of that bitterness which seemed to have become a feature of his conversation.

I knew this routine must soon be interrupted by the return of James. I was enjoying my stay, but ever present was the need to find out the truth about Simon and there were times when I felt a deep frustration and despair.

It was maddening to be so near to his old home, but how could I get to it without arousing suspicion? I was afraid to make outright enquiries. The very fact that Lucas had met him at some time implied that it would be very easy to make a false step and reveal to him who John Player really was. And if he discovered, how did I know what action he would take? True, John Player had saved our lives, but if Lucas believed him to be a murderer, a fugitive from justice, what would he feel he ought to do about it?

It would have been such a relief to talk to him about Simon, but I dared not do it. Sometimes I thought of telling Felicity. I was indeed often on the verge of doing so, but I always drew back in time.

But I was getting desperate and that day at luncheon I had to speak. I said tentatively: 'Wasn't there a murder somewhere about here . . . ?'

Theresa wrinkled her brows. Then she said: 'You must mean that affair at Perrivale Court.'

'Yes,' I cried, hoping I did not show the emotion I always

felt when the subject was raised. 'I . . . I think that was where it was.'

'It was the adopted son,' said Lucas.

'He'd been cared for all his life,' Carleton added, 'and he showed his gratitude by murdering one of the sons of the house.'

'I think we mentioned it before,' I said to Lucas. 'Didn't you say you'd met him?'

'Oh yes . . . years ago . . . and briefly.'

'How far is the place from here?'

Theresa looked at Carleton, who pondered for a few moments. 'As the crow flies, I'd say seven or eight miles, but if you are not a crow it could be a little longer.'

'Is it near some place . . . some town . . . or village?'

Carleton said: 'It could be near . . . where would you say, Lucas? Perhaps Upbridge is the nearest town.'

'It's a mile or two from there,' said Lucas. 'The nearest village would be Tretarrant.'

'Well, that is little more than a hamlet.'

'Yes. Upbridge is the nearest big town.'

'If you can call it big,' added Lucas. 'It's hardly a teeming metropolis.'

'Oh, it's a pleasant little place,' said Theresa. 'Not that I've been there much.'

'I dare say it seemed more important . . . after the death of that man.'

'Well, of course the *Upbridge Times* was in great demand,' said Lucas. 'They had inside information. They knew the family well. I see you have a morbid interest in the place, Rosetta. I tell you what we'll do. Tomorrow we'll ride out there and you can see the notorious town of Upbridge for yourself.'

'I should like that,' I said, my heart beating with triumph.

It was progress.

* * *

The next day Lucas and I set out. When he was in the saddle, I could almost believe that he had not changed since our first meeting.

'It's all of eight miles from here, you know,' he said. 'Do you feel up to it? Eight miles there and eight back? I'll tell you what we'll do. We'll have a meal there. Perhaps in good old Upbridge. Now I come to think of it, I believe there's quite a good place this side of Tretarrant. Do you feel you can do that?'

'Of course. It's a challenge.'

It was, in more ways than one.

Then I was admonishing myself. What good would it do just to look at the place? Still . . . who knew what might come out of it?

Lucas went on: 'The inn I'm thinking of is called the King's Head, I believe. Original, you'll think? The King in question is William IV – not the most popular of monarchs except in the matter of inn signs. I am always hoping to find one with Charles I. The Severed Head instead of merely the King's Head. But, brewers being the most tactful of men, he has never appeared.'

I found myself laughing with him. He could forget bitterness for a while; but there was often something on hand to remind him.

We passed some blackberry bushes.

'There'll be a good crop this year,' he said. 'Do you remember how thrilled we were when we found some on the island?'

'We were thrilled to find anything edible.'

'Sometimes I marvel . . .'

'Yes, so do I.'

'I wonder what would have happened to us if the pirates had not come along?'

'Heaven knows.'

'But it proved to be out of the frying-pan into the fire.'

'At least we escaped the fire.'

'You and I did. I wonder about Player.'

'Yes, I do, too.'

I was silent. I felt that before long I would be telling him, in spite of my determination not to. The temptation was great.

'I expect he'd be all right. He looked like one of nature's survivors to me.'

'He would need to be,' I said. 'By the way, how far are we?'

'Getting tired?'

'Oh . . . no.'

'I'll tell you something. You'll be a champion rider one day.'

'I only want to be a reasonably good one now.'

'Then you are almost there.'

'Coming from you, that's a great compliment.'

'Tell me the truth. Am I what is called an old curmudgeon?'

'Coming towards it. You could become entitled to it before I become a champion rider.'

He laughed. 'That's right,' he said. 'Be frank. Don't cushion me. I'm tired of being protected. Carleton and Theresa . . . I can *hear* them thinking, "Now what shall we say, not to upset the poor devil?"'

'Well, I shall say what I think.'

'It's good to be with you, Rosetta. I hope you won't leave Trecorn for a long time.'

'Well, I shall go back with James and Felicity. Felicity hates to leave her children.'

He sighed. 'We must make the most of the days you are here. What an excellent idea it was coming out like this. I only hope it won't be too long for you.'

'Didn't you say I'd be a champion rider one day? Well, that day may not be far off.'

'Good. We'll go across this field. I think it might be a short cut.'

When we had crossed the field, he pulled up.

'There's a view for you. Pleasant bit of coast, isn't it?'

'Pleasant! It's spectacular and very rugged. I'd hardly say pleasant. That doesn't fit somehow.'

'You're right. Along that coast the wreckers used to ply their evil trade . . . enticing ships in rough seas on to the rocks out there so that they could steal their cargoes. I'll bet you anything the locals hear the cries of shipwrecked sailors on rough nights. Winds can make strange noises and if they fall on susceptible ears, there are your ghosts!'

'Were you born a cynic?'

'I expect so. We couldn't have had two saints in the family.'

'You're referring to Carleton as a saint. Why are people always slightly patronizing about saints?'

'There's an easy answer to that. Because we find it so difficult to follow in their footsteps. We sinners have to feel we are slightly superior because we're having a better time.'

'Do sinners have a better time than saints?'

'Oh yes. At the same time they feel it is unfair that they should do so. That is why they have to take up that patronizing attitude towards sainthood. Carleton is a good sort. He always did the right thing. Learned the management of the estate, married the right girl, produced Henry the heir and the charming Jennifer; he is adored by the tenants, the estate is more prosperous under him than it has ever been. Oh yes, he has all the virtues. Well, you can't have too many good people around. They'd overcrowd the market and would lose much of their glory. So you see, sinners have their uses.'

'It is a great advantage that Carleton is such a good squire.'

'Everything about Carleton is good.'

'You have your points . . . just as he has.'

'Oh, but he has two sound legs to go with his.'

The bitterness was there, always ready to come to the

surface. I was sorry that I had allowed the conversation to get to this point.

'Everything goes right for Carleton,' he said. 'It always has done. Oh, don't mistake me. I know it comes right because of his nature.'

'Lucas,' I said soberly, 'you've had bad luck. But it's done with. Nothing can change it now. There is still a lot left.'

'You're right. I often think of Player and wonder what happened to him. It shows my evil nature that I can get a modicum of comfort out of it. At least I'm free.'

'Yes,' I said. 'You're free.'

'Oh look. You can see the house over there.'

'The house?'

'Perrivale Court. Look straight ahead and turn a little to the right. That's it.'

At last I had seen it. It looked grand and imposing, built on a slight incline facing the sea.

'It's quite impressive,' I said.

'Very ancient. Trecorn is modern in comparison.'

'Could we take a closer look?'

'We could.'

'Let's go, then.'

'You'll sacrifice Upbridge if you do, by the way.'

'I'd prefer it.'

'Getting a little tired, I believe.'

'Perhaps,' I admitted. And all the time I was thinking: This was Simon's home since he was brought here at the age of five.

We rode on. I could see the house clearly now. It was almost like a castle – grey stone with a tower and castellations.

'It looks medieval,' I said.

'Part of it undoubtedly is . . . but these old places are restored down the ages and sometimes you get something of a mixture.'

'You went there once, didn't you?'

'Yes, but I don't remember much of it. It had completely slipped my memory until the murder. That brought it back, of course.'

I was hoping that someone would emerge. Perhaps the brother who had survived or the beautiful woman who might have been the cause of it all. I should like to have had a glimpse of her.

Lucas said suddenly: 'I am sure the King's Head is not far off.' And as the winding road took a turn away from the coast he cried: 'Ah, there it is. Only it's not the King's Head. The right place but the wrong name. It's The Sailor King. Same monarch but with a different soubriquet. Come on. We're going to leave the horses in the stables. They can do with a rest, I dare say. And while they're refreshing themselves we'll do the same. If there is time after . . . though I doubt it . . . we'll look in on Upbridge. But you mustn't be disappointed if we don't.'

I assured him that I was having a thoroughly enjoyable day and should not be in the least disappointed.

I helped him dismount as unobtrusively as I could, and after seeing that the horses were in good hands we went into the parlour. There was no one else there and it was pleasant to have the room to ourselves.

The host came bustling in. 'Now what shall it be, sir . . . my lady. It's only cold, I'm afraid. But I can promise you some prime beef and ham. And there's hot lentil soup.'

We said that sounded just what we needed and cider in pewter mugs was brought to us. Then we settled down to the meal.

A maid brought the food, which was excellent, and while we were eating, the host's wife came over to see that we had all we needed.

She was clearly a garrulous woman who enjoyed chattering to her customers.

She wanted to know how far we had come.

We told her we came from Trecorn Manor.

'Oh, I know it well. A fine old place . . . not so old as Perrivale, of course.'

'Oh, Perrivale Court,' I said eagerly. 'We passed that. Is it occupied now?'

'Why, bless you, yes. The Perrivales have been there since time was. Come over with the Conqueror, so they boast, and they liked it so much they've stayed ever since.'

'There are a lot like that,' said Lucas. 'They are pleased they got in at the start.'

'Oh, there's been Perrivales round here forever. There's only Sir Tristan now, Mr Cosmo having been . . .'

'Didn't I read something in the papers about that?' I said. 'Oh, it was some time ago.'

'That's right, you did. And at the time people could talk of nothing else. They forget quick, like. People be fickle. You ask 'em about the Perrivale murder now and some of these young 'uns . . . they don't seem to know anything. I say, it's history, that's what it is and people should know it.'

'Some might think you have a morbid mind to absorb and retain such knowledge,' said Lucas.

She looked at him as though she thought he was a little mad and I could see the mischief rising in him so that he wanted to convince her that he was entirely so.

'Well,' she said defensively, 'when it did happen the place was swarming with people . . . reporters . . . detectives and such like. Two of them stayed . . . right under this roof. Making their investigations, they did say. So you do see, we be right on the spot.'

'Very conveniently placed,' put in Lucas.

'Well, I must go and see to things. Mustn't stop chattering.'

She went away and I said: 'It was getting interesting. I wanted to hear more.'

'Lookers on often get a distorted vision.'

'At least they are close to the scene.'

Trifle was brought by the maid. It was delicious and well laced with sherry. I was glad that the hostess found it difficult to resist further gossip and while we were finishing the trifle she came up for a little more.

'People don't come here much,' she confided. 'Well, we get the locals, like . . . but visitors like yourselves . . . they don't come this way much. It was different at the time . . . you know what happened at Perrivale.'

'Murder is good for business,' said Lucas.

She looked at him warily and I prompted: 'You must have known a good deal about the family.'

'Well . . . being here all my life, could hardly help it, could I then? I was born in this inn. My father had it . . . and then when I married William he took over. My son – another William – he'll do the same one day, I shouldn't wonder.'

'A dynasty of innkeepers,' murmured Lucas.

I said quickly: 'It's very good to keep it in the family. It gives you a certain pride, doesn't it?'

She beamed on me. I could see that she was thinking I was nice and normal enough to enjoy a bit of gossip in spite of my companion.

'Do you see much of the Perrivales?' I asked.

'Oh yes, they be always in and out. I can go back years. I remember when that Simon was brought here. That's the one . . . you know.'

'Yes,' I said. 'I know.'

'It must have been all of twenty years ago when he came. Me and William was just married. There was a bit of a scene, I can tell 'ee, when Sir Edward brought him into the house and said he'd be staying there. Well, it stands to reason there'd be fireworks. What woman's going to stand for that, I ask you?'

'I quite agree,' I said.

'Now why does a man like that bring a strange child into his home? Everyone said her ladyship was a saint to put up with it. And she wasn't the sort either. A bit of a tartar by all accounts. But Sir Edward was the sort of man who didn't say much . . . but he'd have his own way. He said the boy would stay and stay he did.'

'That was Simon,' I said.

'Well, what can you expect? Can't make a silk purse out of a sow's ear, they tell you. Nor can you.'

'You mean . . .'

'Well, where did he come from, I ask you? Some back street somewhere, I shouldn't wonder.'

'Why should Sir Edward let him live in a back street and then decide to bring him to Perrivale Court?'

'Well, people get things on their consciences, don't they? Anyways, he came. Treated like one of them, he was. Time came they had a tutor . . . that was before they went away to school. A nice fellow, he was. He used to tell some tales about the life up there. Then he faded out and it was school for them. Simon, he went too . . . just like Cosmo and Tristan. And how did he repay them? He murders Mr Cosmo. There's gratitude for you.'

'But can you be sure that he was the one who committed the murder?'

'Plain as the nose on your face. Why else did he run away?'

'It certainly seems conclusive,' said Lucas.

'There could be other reasons,' I protested.

'Oh, a definite sign of guilt,' commented Lucas.

'Yes, he was guilty all right. Jealous, he was. Of course there was that widow woman, Mirabel . . . She was Mrs Blanchard then. Now, of course, it's Lady Perrivale. She came down here with her father . . . the Major . . . and a nicer gentleman you could not wish to meet. Her father and that young Kate. There's a piece of mischief for you, Mrs Blanchard she was then. Oh, she was a beauty . . . one of them red-haired ones. You couldn't help looking twice at her. She set her cap at Mr Cosmo and we all knew that it wouldn't be long before she was mistress of Perrivale. Cosmo was mad about her. Tristan liked her too, to say nothing of Simon. There they were, the three of them, all in love, they said, with the same widow woman. And what does Simon do? He lures Cosmo to that old farmhouse – Bindon Boys they call it – and he just shot him. Through the head, they said. Might have got away with it too, if Mr Tristan – Sir Tristan now – hadn't come in and caught him red-handed.'

'Where is the farmhouse?'

'Oh . . . just along the coast. It's still there. A bit of an old ruin. They were going to put it right when this happened. After that they just let it slide. Nobody would want to live in a house where there'd been a murder. Well, I'm talking too much. William says I always do.'

'It's been very interesting.'

'Well,' she said proudly, 'it's not every place that's had a murder committed on its doorstep, you might say. Mind you, it's not everybody as wants to hear about it. When it happened people didn't want to talk about anything else.'

My feelings were mixed as we came out of the inn. I was a little depressed by the opinion she had expressed of Simon. Apart from that, I had been excited to talk to someone who had actually lived near him at the time all that happened. I suspected that she had no doubt of his guilt. I was afraid that would be the general verdict. He had damned his case by running away.

As we rode off, Lucas said: 'You seemed to enjoy our garrulous hostess. Did you find it so absorbing to gather a little local colour?'

'I did find it interesting.'

'Murder fascinates most people. It is the mystery of this one. Though is it so mysterious?'

'Why? What do you think is the truth?'

'It's clear enough, isn't it? He ran away.'

There was nothing I dared say. I wanted to shout out: He's innocent. I know he's innocent. It was hard to stop myself.

I was tired when we reached Trecorn Manor. I had so looked forward to seeing Perrivale Court, but I had discovered nothing and it had been brought home to me what a strong feeling there was against Simon. Of course I had heard only one person's opinion. But always against him would be the fact that he had run away.

* * *

I was having one of my cosy sessions with Nanny Crockett. The twins were having their afternoon nap which, said Nanny Crockett, was good for them. It was Ellen's free afternoon and she had gone to visit her parents in a nearby village.

I was learning a little about Nanny Crockett's background. She had come from London to take up her first post in Cornwall.

'It was a bit of a wrench at first,' she said. 'Couldn't get used to it. Missed all the life. Then you get your little ones and they starts to mean something to you. I got quite caught up with the place, too . . . the moors and the sea and all that. You want to have a look at the place while you're here. It's worth looking at.'

I was telling her I enjoyed my ride. 'We went a long way. Near to a place called Upbridge. Do you know it?'

'Know it!' cried Nanny Crockett. 'I'd say I know Upbridge. I lived in the place at one time. I was close to it before that.'

'Did you know Perrivale Court?'

She was silent for a moment. There was a strange expression on her face which I did not understand. Then she said: 'I should think I do. I lived there for nigh on eight years.'

'You mean . . . in the house!'

'I do mean in Perrivale Court, Miss.'

'You really lived there!'

'Well, I was nanny to the boys, wasn't I?'

'You mean Cosmo . . . Tristan . . . Simon . . . ?'

'I do. I was there in the nursery when little Simon was brought in. I remember that day. Never to be forgotten. There he was, handed over to me. Sir Edward said, "This is Simon. He's to be treated like the others." And there he was . . . a little scrap of a thing. I could see he was frightened . . . bewildered like, so I took him by the hand and said, "Don't you fret, lovey. You're with Nanny Crockett and everything's all right." Sir Edward was pleased with me and that was something rare, I can tell you. He said, "Thank you, Nanny. Look after the boy. He'll feel a little strange at first." We took to each other . . . Simon and me . . . from that moment.'

I could scarcely suppress my excitement. 'What a strange thing to do . . . to bring a child into the house like that. Was there any explanation?'

'Oh, Sir Edward wouldn't give explanations. He was the one who said what was what and that was the end of it. If he said the boy was to be in the nursery, that was where he would be.'

'Tell me about the boy. What was he like?'

'A nice little fellow . . . sharp as they come. Pining he was for someone he called Angel. I could only think it was his mother. I got little scraps from him . . . but you know how it is with children. They don't always see things the way we do. He talked about Angel and there was an Aunt Ada who struck terror into his little heart. It seemed they'd buried Angel and he had been brought to Perrivale then. He couldn't abide to hear the church bells toll as they did for a funeral. I found him once hiding under the bed . . . hands over his ears, to shut out the noise. He'd thought this Ada was going to take him away . . . and then Sir Edward had brought him to Perrivale.'

I listened. I was back there on the island and it was Simon's voice I heard telling me how he had hidden under the table when Aunt Ada came.

'Well, there he was and there was a regular lot of gossip about that, I can tell you. Who was the boy? Why should he be brought in? Sir Edward's, they all said, and I reckon they were right. But it was strange, because he wasn't the sort of man to go chasing women. All very proper he was . . . stern and upright.'

'Sometimes such people have a secret life.'

'You can say that again. But somehow you just couldn't picture Sir Edward up to that sort of lark. It's difficult to make you see him. Wanted everything run like clockwork. Meals on the dot . . . quite a to-do if anyone was late. You know the sort. There was a footman who'd been in the Army. He said it reminded him of a military camp. So you see, Sir Edward was not the sort who'd go chasing girls. Not like some I've heard of, where no young woman in the house was safe. They were safe enough in Perrivale Court . . . even the prettiest.'

'Was he kind to the boy?'

'Not kind . . . not unkind. He just brought him in and said he was to be treated like the other two. Then he seemed to forget him. The servants didn't like it. You know what servants are . . . afraid someone's going to get above themselves. They didn't think young Simon had a right to be there in the nursery with the other boys . . . and I reckon they showed it.'

'Did he mind?'

'Who's to know what goes on in their little minds? But he was a sharp one. I reckon he knew all about it.'

'But you loved him.'

She smiled reminiscently and tenderly. 'Of all the children I ever had, he was my special boy. As for him . . . I reckon I took the place of this Angel. I was the one he'd run to if there was any trouble – and there was bound to be that.

Mind you, he was older than the other two . . . just a year or two, that was all. But when they were little, it was an advantage. But they soon got to know the difference. They were the sons of the house and he was the outsider. You know what children are? Cosmo . . . he was the eldest . . . gave himself airs, he did. He thought he was *Sir* already, and Tristan could be a little tartar. I've often found that with younger sons. You know what I mean? Ah . . . but Simon . . . he was my special one. Of all my children, he was the one. I don't know what it was . . . perhaps being brought in like that . . . missing his mother . . . and then to think that he got himself into that mess . . .'

'You knew them so well,' I said earnestly. 'What do you think happened?'

'What I think is . . . no, what I *know* is . . . he didn't do that. He wasn't the sort. He couldn't have.'

'He ran away,' I said.

'Oh, that's what they all say. Well, so he did, but he'd have his reasons. He could look after himself. He was always like that. He'd find a way out of anything. That's what I remind myself . . . because I worry a bit. I wake up in the night and think: Where is he? Then I tell myself, wherever he is, he'll know how to look after himself. I feel better then. He'll manage. When the two boys played tricks on him, he'd always get the better of them. He was clever, you see, and being in the position he was in . . . well, it made him able to look out for himself. He'd do what was best for himself at the time . . . and I reckon he'd be the one to know what was best.'

'I was in the inn . . . The Sailor King. Mr Lucas and I had something to eat there. The woman there seemed to think he was guilty.'

'That would be Sarah Marks. What does she know? The old gossip. Thinks just because she's the wife of the landlord she knows everything. It's all for a bit of gossip with her. She'd tear anyone's reputation to bits if it gave her something to talk about. I know her . . . and I know Simon. I'm ready to stake my life in his innocence.'

'Oh, Nanny, where do you think he is?'

'Well, there's no knowing, is there? He got away all right. He'll be biding his time.'

'You mean he'll come back when he's found some light to throw on the affair?'

'I think that could be.'

'Would he write to you . . . do you think?'

'He might. He'd know it would be safe enough with me. On the other hand, he wouldn't want me to be involved. Isn't there something in the law about that?'

'I believe it's called being an accessory.'

'That would be it. Though *I* wouldn't mind. I'd give a hundred pounds – if I had it – just to have a word from him.'

I warmed towards her. She was an ally. I had lured her to talk. And after that I was often in the nursery when the children were asleep, so that I could chat with Nanny Crockett.

* * *

My friendship with the twins was growing. Jennifer had marked me as hers and had assumed a proprietorial attitude towards me, which gave me a great deal of pleasure. I was treated to confidential details about her dolls. I learned of their foibles, of the good ones and the bad ones. There was Reggie the bear who would not take his medicine, and one-eyed Mabel – she had lost an eye in some mysterious accident – who was afraid of the dark and had to be taken into Jennifer's bed at night. I invented adventures for them to which both children listened entranced.

The time was passing too quickly and I was not looking forward to going away; but of course we should have to leave before long. Felicity was getting restive, but she did feel that our being there was good for me . . . and for Lucas, and being the unselfish creature she was, she curbed her own wishes and rejoiced for us.

Even she could not guess how much good it did me to be near Simon's home and especially to discover Nanny Crockett's involvement. Felicity was just happy to see me with Lucas and my enjoyment of the nursery.

Then one day events took a dramatic turn.

The day began ordinarily enough.

At breakfast the talk was about the heavy rainfall during the night and it turned to old Mrs Gregory, the mother of one of the farmers.

'I owe her a visit,' said Theresa. 'It's nearly a month since I was there. She will be thinking I have deserted her.'

I gathered that Mrs Gregory was bedridden and her great treat was to have a visitor who would chat with her. Theresa, with her knowledge of neighbourhood affairs, was especially welcome. She told me that she visited the old lady as regularly as she could, taking some little gift of cakes or sweets or a bottle of wine – anything she felt might please her. But the great thing was to stay for an hour or so and chat.

'Then,' put in Carleton, 'there's that little matter of the Masons' roof. If you get an opportunity, you might drop in and tell them that Tom Allen will be along this week.'

'I'll go over in the trap this morning,' said Theresa.

It was a pleasant morning, blandly mild . . . not too hot, ideal for riding. Lucas seemed more light-hearted than usual, and we took the road towards Upbridge.

He looked at me and smiled. 'Your favourite ride,' he said. 'I believe old Snowdrop goes there automatically without waiting for instructions. I think you have a morbid mind and are fascinated by that murder.'

'It's a pleasant road,' I said.

That day I really did feel that I was making progress. We were a few miles from Upbridge and had decided we would turn back or we should be late for lunch. We could go on and have something at The Sailor King, but as we had not mentioned that we should not be back, we thought we had better return.

We were passing along a narrow winding road when we turned a bend and saw right ahead of us a shepherd with a flock of sheep blocking the road. We pulled up and watched and as we did so a rider came up behind us. It was a young woman of remarkable good looks. Her black riding hat was set jauntily on her red hair and her long green eyes, heavily black-lashed, regarded us with the amused look people usually wear when confronted by such an obstruction.

'The hazards of country life,' she said.

'Which we must accept,' replied Lucas.

'Have you come far?'

'From Trecorn Manor.'

'Oh . . . you must be Mr Lorimer who was shipwrecked.'

'The very same. And this is Miss Cranleigh who was shipwrecked at the same time.'

'How interesting! I'm Mirabel Perrivale.'

'How nice to meet you, Lady Perrivale.'

I was so overcome that I could only marvel. She was decidedly beautiful. I could imagine how impressed they must all have been when she came among them.

'Thank the sheep,' she said. 'Oh hello . . . they're nearly off the road.'

We moved forward. At the end of the lane the road branched in two directions. She took the one to the left; we turned right.

'Good day,' we said and she had gone.

'What a beautiful woman,' I said. 'So she is Mirabel . . . the *femme fatale*.'

'And looks the part, you must admit.'

'I do. Indeed, I could do nothing else. How strange to meet her like that.'

'Not really. She lives close by.'

'And when you mentioned Trecorn she knew who you were.'

'Well, I'm as notorious in my way as she is in hers. The survival of a shipwreck is worthy of a little notice . . . it's not like being concerned in a murder case, it's true, but still it is something.'

When we reached Trecorn Manor one of the grooms came running out.

'There's been an accident,' he said.

'Accident?' cried Lucas. 'Who?'

'It's Mrs Lorimer. The trap . . . they've just brought her back.'

* * *

It was a house of mourning.

Early that day Theresa had been full of life, now she was dead. We were all too stunned to take in this tragic truth.

Apparently she had paid her visit to Mrs Gregory and delivered her gifts; she had chatted with her for an hour and then left. On her way to Mason's farm she had taken the hilly path. It was a road she had taken many times and had not been considered dangerous. But there had been heavy rain and there was a sudden fall of earth from the hillside. It must have fallen right in front of the horse, which took fright and bolted, taking the trap down the slope into the valley below. And thus . . . Theresa had been killed and Trecorn Manor had become a tragic household.

Felicity said to me: 'I'm glad we're here. Not that we can do anything to comfort Carleton. They were so happy together . . . so suited . . . and what on Earth will he do now?'

'Poor, poor Carleton. He is too shocked to realize fully what has happened. Do you think we should stay awhile?'

'Well, I suppose we must wait a bit. We couldn't discuss anything with them at the moment. Perhaps after the funeral . . . let's wait and see how things go.'

When the opportunity came I asked Lucas if he thought we should go.

'Oh, not yet, please,' he said. 'My poor brother is in a state of numbed misery. I don't think he can accept what's happened just yet. We have to think of him first of all. He relied on her more than even he realized. They were quite devoted to each other. I'm afraid we all took Theresa too much for granted . . . her good nature . . . her unselfishness . . . her way of playing down all the good she did to us all. We now see what a wonderful person she was. Carleton has been lucky . . . but that means it is going to be so much worse for him to face up to what he has lost. He'll miss her every minute of the day. We shall all miss her terribly . . . please don't go yet, Rosetta.'

'James will have to go back to his work.'

'Yes . . . and he'll be coming here soon to collect you.'

I nodded.

'But that doesn't mean *you* have to go.'

'But of course I shall have to go with them. I shall have to leave when they do.'

'I can't see why. *You* haven't work to get back to.'

'I . . . I don't think I should be wanted here . . . at a time like this.'

'That's nonsense. I know your presence will help.'

I told Felicity what he had said.

'He's right,' was her verdict. 'You've made a difference to him. I think you've been able to talk to him about that terrible time.'

'But I couldn't stay here without you.'

She wrinkled her brows. 'I dare say your Aunt Maud would think you ought to go home. But, after all, I don't see why you shouldn't stay on a little. James will have to go back, of course, and I shall go with him.'

It was left at that and very soon after James arrived. His shock was great and by this time we were all learning something of the enormity of the tragedy which had overtaken this house.

Nanny Crockett said: 'The place will never be the same again. Mrs Lorimer was the one who saw it all went like clockwork. This is going to make a very big difference. But it's the children I'm most worried about. They're going to miss their mother. Oh, they've got me and they've got you now, but by golly, they are going to miss her. She was always in and out of the nursery. They used to wait for her visits. I don't know what this is going to do to them.'

It was such a sad time. I was so desperately sorry for Carleton. He walked about like a man in a bewildered dream. Lucas said it was impossible to discuss anything. He could only talk about Theresa.

Lucas himself was deeply affected. 'This is the worst thing that could have happened to Carleton,' he said. 'I've been a selfish brute moaning about my own troubles . . . telling myself he was the lucky one . . . everything fell to him and so on . . . and now there he is . . . there's no comforting him.'

I was dreading the funeral. People came to the church from all over the neighbourhood. This was genuine mourning. Theresa had been loved and respected by so many.

Nanny Crockett kept the children in the nursery. I wondered what they were thinking as I listened to the dismal tolling of the bell. I thought of Simon who, years before, had heard a similar bell. To him it had meant the sound of doom, the loss of Angel and the plummeting into the unknown.

When everybody had left and the house was quiet, I went up to the nursery. Nanny Crockett was dressed in deep black. She shook her head sadly.

'They keep asking questions,' she said. 'What do you tell such little ones? They don't understand. "She's gone to Heaven," I say. "When will she be back?" they ask. "Well," I say, "when people go to Heaven they stay a little while."

Jennifer said, "It would be bad manners to go away too soon, wouldn't it?" I nearly broke down. Then she said, "She's having tea with God, I think, and the angels will be there." It breaks your heart.'

The children had heard us and came running out.

They stood still, looking at me, their faces solemn. They sensed that something terrible was happening and everyone was very sad about it.

Jennifer looked at me and her face suddenly crumpled.

'I want my mummy,' she said.

I held out my arms and she ran to me. Henry followed her. I held them tightly.

That decided me. I could not leave immediately. I must stay for a while.

* * *

I was glad I stayed. I felt I was doing something useful and that I brought a modicum of comfort to that stricken household.

I spent a great deal of time in the nursery with the children at that hour when it had been their mother's custom to be with them; and between us Nanny Crockett and I managed to get them over the first tragic days of heartbreak. They were too young to understand fully what had happened and we smoothed away some of that uneasiness which they would inevitably feel; there were times when they would be absorbed in something and forget; but sometimes one of them would wake in the night and cry for Mummy. The other would wake and share the terrible loss. But usually either Nanny Crockett or I was there to offer comfort.

Carleton continued to be dazed. The blow was all the sharper for being unexpected. Fortunately there was a good deal of work to be done on the estate; that kept him busy and he was met with sympathy and understanding wherever he went. I knew he would never be the same again. He was particularly shattered because life had followed an even stream of contentment and he had expected it to go on doing so. I knew at times he found it hard to believe that this had really happened to him and he seemed unable to grasp that Theresa was no longer there and never would be again.

Lucas had grown philosophical. *He* did not expect life to flow peacefully. Tragedy had already struck him and he was not surprised that it had come again. Perhaps that was why he was able to face it more realistically.

He said to me: 'You have done a great deal for us. It was fortunate for us that you were here when it happened.'

'I wish I could do more,' I told him.

'You and Nanny Crockett have been wonderful with the children. As for Carleton . . . only time will help him.'

We took short rides together and the days began to pass.

The Governess

I could not stay at Trecorn Manor indefinitely and I was not by any means looking forward to returning to London. I had come to Trecorn Manor with the hope of discovering something which would help me unravel the mystery; now I was seeing how ridiculously optimistic I had been.

Theresa's death had temporarily forced that other tragedy into the background of my mind, but my obsession was returning. I sometimes felt that if I could get into Perrivale Court, really become acquainted with some of the main actors in the drama, I might make some progress. I had been foolish to hope that just because I was staying near the house I might accomplish this. I felt inadequate and alone. There were times when I was on the verge of taking Lucas into my confidence. He was clever, subtle. He might have ideas. On the other hand, he could dismiss my belief in Simon as romantic folly. In his realist way he would say, 'The man was found with the gun in his hand and he ran away and would not face investigation. That speaks for itself. Simply because he happened to show a certain resourcefulness and helped save our lives does not make him innocent.'

No, I could not entirely trust Lucas, but how I longed to confide in someone . . . someone who would work with me, join in the search . . . someone who believed in Simon's innocence.

There was no help for it. I should have to go home. I had already stayed on two weeks after Felicity had left with James; and in the first place I had only intended to stay one.

When I thought of returning to Bloomsbury and the domination of Aunt Maud I was distinctly depressed. I could not face that. Moreover, I had to consider my future. My fantastic adventure had put a bridge between my childhood and my adult life.

I felt lost and lonely. If only, I kept saying to myself . . . if only I could prove Simon's innocence. If only he could return and we could be together.

We had forged a bond between us which it seemed could never be broken. Lucas had shared that adventure with us but he was not involved as we were. Close as he had been to us during those days, he had never shared the secret and that set him apart. He was very perceptive. I often wondered whether he had guessed anything.

How many times a day I was on the point of pouring out my feelings to him . . . telling him everything!

He might have helped a great deal in solving the mystery. But dared I tell him?

And so I pondered and as each day drew to a close I knew that I could not go on in this way. I should have to make some decision sooner or later. Should I give up this quest which seemed hopeless? Should I return to Bloomsbury and let myself fall into Aunt Maud's capable hands?

One of my greatest comforts was talking to Nanny Crockett. She was my strongest link with Simon. She loved him as, I admitted now, I did; and that was a great bond between us.

She was a compulsive talker and the murder at Bindon Boys was as absorbing a topic to her as it was to me. As a matter of fact, she would return to the subject without my prompting her and gradually certain facts began to emerge which were of vital importance to me.

She even knew something about the Perrivale household at that time.

She said: 'I used to go over now and then. That was just

before it all blew up. You see, when the boys went to school I took a post in Upbridge . . . quite close really. A dear little thing she was . . . named Grace. I got very fond of her. She helped to make up a bit for the loss of my boy. Not that that was a dead loss. Simon wasn't the sort to let that happen. He used to come over to see me and sometimes I'd go over to Perrivale and have a cup of tea with the housekeeper there, Mrs Ford . . . she was a friend of mine. We'd always got on. She ran things over there . . . still does. Even got the butler under her thumb. She's that sort of woman . . . good-hearted though . . . but knows how to keep things in order. Well, that's what a housekeeper should do, I reckon. Not that I'd have had her interfering in the nursery. She never tried that on me . . . and we were the best of friends always . . . or almost always . . . and I'd be over there for a cup of tea and it was nice to catch up with the news.'

'So it was only when you came here that you didn't see them.'

'Oh, I still go over now and then. If Jack Carter's taking a load of something over Upbridge way he'll come and pick me up. He'll drop me at the house and when he's done his business come for me and bring me home. It makes a nice little outing and it keeps me in touch with them over at Perrivale.'

'So you still go over to Perrivale Court!'

'Well, it's a month or two since I was last there. And when all this was on I didn't go at all. It wouldn't have seemed right somehow . . . and there was the police and everyone prying . . . if you know what I mean.'

'When was the last time you went?'

'It would be three months ago, I reckon. It don't seem the same now. Never has . . . since Simon went.'

'That's some time ago.'

'Yes . . . some time. When there's a murder in a place it seems to change everything.'

'Tell me about the household. I'd like to hear.'

'You're like everyone else, Miss. You can't resist a murder.'

'Well, this is a mysterious one, isn't it? And you don't believe Simon did it.'

'That I don't. And I'd give a lot to prove it.'

'Perhaps the answer is somewhere in the house.'

'Now what do you mean by that?'

'Someone must have killed Cosmo and perhaps someone in the house knows who did.'

'Someone somewhere knows the truth, that's for sure.'

'Tell me about the house.'

'Well, there was Sir Edward, wasn't there?'

'He's dead now.'

'Yes. Died about the time of the murder, didn't he? He was very ill before it happened . . . not expected to live.'

'And old Lady Perrivale?'

'She was a bit of a tartar. One of them Northerners . . . different from us. She'd been used to having her own way and Sir Edward . . . he let her . . . except when it was something like bringing the boy into the house. She didn't want that . . . natural like, but he said it was to be and be it was. Well, there she was, never forgetting that it was *her* money that saved Perrivale. Mrs Ford said the woodworm and death watch beetle would have done for the place – and pretty quick – if she hadn't come into the family in time. And she had her boys – Cosmo and Tristan. She was proud of them. And then Simon comes. It might have been better for the poor little mite if there'd been open ructions, I used to think sometimes, rather than all that snide picking on him. It wasn't only her ladyship. There were the servants and others. I wouldn't have had that in my nursery . . . but I've told you all this before.'

'I like to hear it and a bit more comes out every time.'

'Well, as I was saying, up at Perrivale it wasn't a very happy house. Things wasn't quite right between Sir Edward and her ladyship. You can always tell. Mind you, he was always very proper . . . always treated her like the lady of the house . . . but you could tell. Her ladyship was one of those women who'd have had her own way with any other man. But Sir Edward, he was a funny one. He was the master but it was her money that had saved the place. She didn't want anyone to forget that. And Sir Edward, he was that strict. If the girls got up to a bit of malarkey with the men, it would be wedding bells for them before there was the first sign of a bundle of trouble. It was prayers in the hall every morning and everybody in the house had to attend.'

We were silent for a while. She sat there, smiling into the distance, seeing the past, I knew.

'Then came the day when the boys went away to school and they didn't want Nanny Crockett any more. But I got this job in Upbridge . . . a stone's throw away, you might say, so I didn't feel quite cut off. A nice little thing, Grace was. Her parents were the Burrows . . . highly respected in Upbridge. Dr Burrows was her father. She was the only one. I was with her right till the time they sent her to school. She used to say to me: "You'll be nanny to my babies, won't you, Nanny Crockett . . . when I get some." And I used to tell her that nannies get old like everyone else and there comes a time when they have to give a little thought to their own comfort, as they once did to that of their little ones. It's sad, saying goodbye to them. You get attached. They're your children while you've got them. That's how it is.'

'Yes, I know. The wrench is very sad.'

'I've been lucky with mine. Simon used to come over to see me, and now and then I'd walk over and have a cup of tea with Mrs Ford.'

'And after Grace Burrows, you came here?'

She nodded. 'It was in my last year at the Burrows' that it happened.'

'So,' I said, hearing the note of excitement in my own voice as I spoke, 'you were close when it happened?'

'I saw her once or twice.'

'Saw whom?'

'The widow.'

'What did you think of her?'

She was silent. Then she said: 'With a woman like that around, things happen. There's something dangerous about them. Some said she was a witch. They go in for that sort of thing round here. They like to think of people riding out on broomsticks and cooking up mischief. Well, there was mischief at Perrivale after she appeared on the scene.'

'So you think she was involved in it?'

'Most seem to think so. We hadn't seen many of her sort down here. She looked different even. All that red hair and them green eyes that didn't go with the hair somehow. All of a sudden there was this widow among us with a child . . . and she was almost as strange as her mother. Now her father, he was different. Oh, everybody liked the Major. He was jolly with everybody. Always passed the time of day. A very nice gentleman. Quite different from her.'

'Tell me about the child. You know a great deal about children. What did you think of her?'

'It's my own I know . . . all their little ways and habits . . . I can read them like a book. But that one . . . well, I never had much to do with her . . . nor should I want to. I reckon she'll be another like her mother. Kate, her name is, I think. A nice, ordinary sort of name. Different from her mother's. Mirabel. What sort of name is that?'

'Hers apparently. And mine is Rosetta. You probably think that's odd.'

'Oh no. That's pretty. It's Rose really and what's nicer than a nice rose?'

'Tell me what you found out about Mirabel and Kate?'

'Only that they were a peculiar pair. They came with her father and took Seashell Cottage and it was clear that the widow woman was looking for a nice rich husband. So she settled on the Perrivales. They said she could have had any of them and she settled on Cosmo. He was the eldest. He'd get the estates and the title . . . so it had to be Cosmo.'

'Did the family approve of this woman coming from nowhere? I should have thought Sir Edward, with his conventional tastes, might have objected.'

'Oh, Sir Edward was too far gone. As for Lady Perrivale, she was as taken with Mirabel as any of them. Story was that the Major was an old friend of hers. He'd married her old schoolfriend and Mirabel was the result of that marriage. She had wanted them to come and settle in Cornwall in the first place. I don't know how true that is but that's how the story goes. The Major was always up at Perrivale. Oh, she was very taken with him. He's the sort who'd get on with anyone. Oh yes, Lady Perrivale was all for the marriage.'

'And then . . . it happened.'

'They all thought Simon, like the others, was smitten by her. That was where the motive came in.'

'He didn't do it, Nanny,' I said earnestly. 'Why should he have done? I don't believe he was in love with that woman.'

'No,' she said. 'He'd have too much sense. Besides, it didn't mean that because Cosmo was dead she would turn to him. No . . . that was not the answer. How I wish I knew what was.'

'You believe in Simon's innocence, don't you, Nanny? I mean, you believe absolutely?'

'I do. And I know that boy better than any.'

'Do any of us really know other people?'

'I know my *children*,' she said staunchly.

'If you could help him, would you, Nanny?'

'With all my heart.'

And then I told her. I went through the whole story, beginning with our encounter on deck, to the time when we parted company outside the Embassy in Constantinople.

She was astounded.

'And you've been here all this time and not told me before?'

'I couldn't be entirely sure of you. I had to protect Simon. You understand?'

She nodded slowly. Then she turned to me and gripped my hand.

'Nanny,' I said solemnly. 'More than anything, I want to solve this. I want to find the truth.'

'That's what I want,' she said.

'You know a great deal about them. You have access to the house.'

She nodded.

I said with a sudden upward surging of hope: 'Nanny, you and I will work together. We're going to prove Simon's innocence.'

Her eyes were shining. I felt happier than I had for a long time.

'We'll do it,' I said, 'together.'

* * *

What a difference it made to share my secret with Nanny Crockett. We talked continuously, going over the same ground again and again; but it was surprising how ideas occurred to us as we did so. We had convinced ourselves that someone in that house knew who had killed Cosmo Perrivale, and we shared the burning desire to find out the truth and prove Simon's innocence.

A few days after I had taken Nanny Crockett into my confidence, Jack Carter left a message at the house to say he was taking a load over Upbridge way and if Nanny Crockett would like a lift he'd be more than happy with the company and do her a good turn at the same time, for he knew how she liked the little trip.

It seemed like an answer to our prayers. Nanny Crockett

said that if I would look after the children, she would go; and she set off in a state of great excitement.

It seemed a long day. I did not see Lucas, as I spent the whole time with the children. I played with them, read to them and told them stories. They were quite content, but I was counting the minutes till Nanny's return.

I do not know what I expected she would find out in that short time.

She came back in a mood of suppressed excitement, but she would tell me nothing until the children had had their supper of milk and bread and butter and were safely tucked up in bed.

Then we settled down to our chat.

'Well,' she said. 'It was a blessing that I went. It seems that Madam up there is in a bit of a state.'

'You mean Lady Perrivale?'

'I mean *young* Lady Perrivale.'

She folded her hands on her lap and surveyed me with great satisfaction, and, like some people who have exciting news to impart, she seemed to derive a certain pleasure in holding it back for a while, savouring the pleasure she was going to give me.

'Yes, yes, Nanny,' I prompted impatiently.

'Well, it's nothing unusual to them up there. It happens regular, but they are getting desperate. It's Madam Kate.'

'Do tell me what she's done, Nanny, and what has it to do with us?'

She pulled herself back in her chair and smiled at me knowingly, which was irritating to me being so very much in the dark.

'Well,' she went on, 'it's like this. The governess up there has walked out again. It's a regular way with governesses up there. None of them can stand young Kate for more than a week or so. But it throws the household in a turmoil. Really, this Kate must be a bit of a demon if you ask me. Well, there's Mrs Ford telling me that they're all praying to get a governess who gives Kate the education she ought to have . . . and keeps her out of the way of the grown-ups, I wouldn't mind reckoning. And how they can't, how they're all in despair and young Kate is laughing her head off because the last thing she wants in the house is a governess. There's been goodness knows how many . . . and not one stayed. Mrs Ford reckons that soon it will get round and they wouldn't even give it a trial. She's a little imp, that Kate. Wants her own way. Mrs Ford said if they don't get someone to control her sometime, governesses won't be the only ones who are leaving. Well, that's how it was up at Perrivale.' She paused and looked at me steadily.

'I said to Mrs Ford, "I wonder . . ." and she looked at me sharply and said, "What do you wonder, Nanny?" I said, "Now I don't know whether I'm speaking out of turn . . . but an idea has just come to me."'

'Yes, Nanny,' I said, a little breathlessly.

'I said to her, "Well, I don't know . . . I may be speaking out of turn . . . so don't bank on it," I said. "But there's a young lady staying at the house . . . a well-educated young lady. Best schools and all that. Well, she was saying the other day she thought she'd like to do something. Not that she needs to, mind. But she was just feeling a bit restless, like. Well, she's very good with my two . . . likes teaching them things. Well . . . I don't know, I'm sure. It's just a thought that came into my head." You should have seen Mrs Ford's face. I reckon it would be a feather in her cap if she could find them a governess.'

'Nanny, what *are* you suggesting?'

'Well, we always said if you could get into the house . . . we reckoned the secret was tucked away in there somewhere. And there's no way of finding out when you're outside it.'

As the possibility swept over me I felt enormously excited. 'Do you think they would take me?'

'They'd jump at you. You should have seen Mrs Ford's

face. She kept saying, "Will you ask her? Do you think she would?" I played it very cautious. I wanted to make them think you might need a bit of persuading. "I can only just mention it," I told her. "I can't vouch for anything . . . I don't know, I'm sure." But she wouldn't leave it alone. She was on it like a ton of bricks.'

'I've had no experience. How do I know if I could do it?'

'Look how you are with the twins.'

'They're not difficult nine-year-olds.'

'That's true enough. But when Mrs Ford told me, I thought it sounded like manna from Heaven, as they say.'

'It does look rather like that. I've longed and longed for an opportunity.'

'Well, now here it is.'

'What else did Mrs Ford say?'

'She did wonder how long you'd stay . . . if you came. She didn't understand how anybody – particularly someone who didn't have to work – would want to be governess to Miss Kate. I couldn't tell her that there was rather a special reason. Then she stopped talking like that, being afraid I might put you off. She said, "Well, perhaps Miss Cranleigh might be able to manage her . . . perhaps it's because the others haven't been much good," going on like that. Ever so anxious she was to get me to ask you. She'd be in high favour with her ladyship if she was the one to find a governess who stayed. I told her not to hope for too much but I'd have a word with you.'

I had been so astounded by the suggestion that it was difficult for me to take in its implications at first. I was trying to be calm. I should go into a strange household as a sort of higher servant. What would my father think? Or Aunt Maud? They would never allow it. Moreover, what would my position be with a child who had a reputation for making life intolerable for past holders of the post?

And yet . . . only a few hours before I had been praying for a chance. I had seen clearly that unless I could get a footing in that house, unless I could learn something about its inhabitants, I should never discover the truth behind the murder of Cosmo Perrivale.

Even while I hesitated I knew I had to seize this God-given opportunity with both hands.

Nanny Crockett was watching me intently; a slow smile spread across her face.

She knew that I would go to Perrivale Court.

* * *

It was soon quite clear that I should be very welcome at Perrivale Court. Lady Perrivale must have despaired of ever getting a governess for her daughter and the suggestion that I might take the post was received with enthusiasm.

Lady Perrivale sent the carriage over to Trecorn Manor to take me to Perrivale Court so that we could discuss the matter without delay.

I was relieved that Lucas was not there when I left, my trepidation overcome by the elation I felt at the prospect of making headway in my self-appointed task.

I had sworn Nanny Crockett to secrecy about the project, for I was anxious that Lucas should not know anything about it until it was definitely settled. I knew he would be astonished and would ask awkward questions and of course attempt to dissuade me, for, not knowing my reasons, he would naturally find it difficult to understand why I should take on such a post.

I had ceased to marvel at the amazing turn of fate which had brought me this opportunity. So many strange things had happened to me in the recent past that I was prepared for anything. I suppose that when one steps out of the conventional life one must be prepared for the unexpected and unusual. And there I was, speeding along the road in a splendid carriage drawn by two noble horses, one black, one white, and driven by a coachman in the smart Perrivale livery.

We arrived at Perrivale Court. In the distance I could see the sea. It was a light blue today, in a gentle mood, smooth and benign. Whenever I came face to face with the sea – whatever its mood – I would visualize that raging angry torrent which had played such havoc with my life and that of many others. I would never trust the sea again. And if I lived at Perrivale I should see it every day. I should be reminded.

If I lived at Perrivale? I must. I was becoming more and more certain how imperative it was that I should secure this post.

There was an air of timelessness about the place. The grey stone walls, battered by the winds of centuries, gave it the impression of a fortress, and the machicolations the look of a castle. Lucas had said it had been restored so often that it had lost its original identity. That might be so, and I found it difficult to analyse my feelings as I passed under the gatehouse into a courtyard where the carriage drew up.

A door was immediately opened and a woman appeared. She was middle-aged, verging on the elderly, and instinct told me that this was Mrs Ford.

She had come to welcome her protégée personally and she showed clearly that she was very pleased that I had come.

'Come along in, Miss Cranleigh,' she said. 'I am Mrs Ford. Lady Perrivale would like to see you at once. I am so glad you could come.'

It was an effusive greeting, hardly the sort that a governess would expect; but when I reminded myself of the reason for it I was less euphoric.

'Nanny Crockett has told me *all* about you,' said Mrs Ford.

Not all, I thought. I could imagine Nanny Crockett's glowing terms, and I was sure she credited me with qualities I did not possess.

'I'll take you to her ladyship right away,' she said. 'Will you follow me?'

We were in a hall – long and lofty, the walls of which were adorned with weapons and there was a huge fireplace with inglenooks and seats on either side; the floor was tiled and our footsteps rang out as we walked across to the stairs. It was typical of many such halls except for the stained glass windows at one end with their beautiful shades of ruby red and sapphire blue which were reflected on the tiled floor. Placed strategically at the side of the staircase like a sentinel was a suit of armour. It seemed lifelike and I could not help glancing uneasily at it as I followed Mrs Ford up the stairs.

We went along the corridor until we came to a door at which Mrs Ford knocked.

'Come in,' said a voice.

Mrs Ford threw open the door and stood aside for me to go in.

She called: 'Miss Cranleigh, my lady.'

And there she was, seated in a rather throne-like chair which was covered in dark velvet. She wore a gown of emerald green which was very becoming to her red-haired beauty. I noticed a gold necklace in the form of a snake about her neck. Her glorious hair was piled on top of her head and her green eyes glittered with pleasure.

'Miss Cranleigh,' she cried. 'Do come in. Thank you, Mrs Ford. Sit here, Miss Cranleigh, and we can have our little talk.'

She was immensely affable. Clearly she was very eager that I should accept the post. She must be desperate, I thought, and I shuddered to think what the child might be like.

'Mrs Ford tells me that you want to come here to teach my daughter.'

'It was suggested to me that you were in need of a governess,' I replied.

'Kate's last governess had to leave in rather a hurry and naturally I do not want her studies to be interrupted too long.'

'No, of course not. I must tell you that I have never taught before.'

'Well, we all have to start somewhere.'

'Your daughter is eight years old, I believe . . . or is it nine?'

'She is just nine.'

'She will be in need of advanced education soon. Do you propose to send her to school in the near future?'

I saw a look of dismay in the green eyes. Was she imagining this daughter of hers being expelled from school after school?

'We had no plans for a school yet.'

We? That would be Tristan, the girl's stepfather. Images flashed into my mind. I saw him, coming into the farmhouse . . . finding his brother dead and Simon standing there with the gun in his hand. I must stop my mind from wandering on. This house would be full of such reminders. But this was what I had wanted. Those people who had been nothing but names to me were now going to take on flesh and blood, and I had to assess their part in the drama if I were to find out the truth.

She was saying: 'Mrs Ford tells me you are very good with children.'

'She would be referring to the two at Trecorn Manor. They are only four years old.'

'Oh yes . . . Trecorn Manor. You are visiting there. We met, didn't we? Those sheep. What a terrible time Mr Lorimer had. That ghastly shipwreck.'

'Yes,' I said. 'I was shipwrecked too.'

'What a dreadful experience! I heard about it from Mrs Ford. But you have emerged, fortunately, in better shape than poor Mr Lorimer.'

'Yes, indeed I was more fortunate.'

She was silent for a few seconds denoting sympathy. Then she said brightly: 'We should be so happy if you came. It would be good for Kate to have a . . . lady . . . to teach her. Mrs Ford tells me that you have had an excellent education.'

'There was nothing outstanding about it.'

This was becoming a most unusual interview. I seemed all the time to be stressing why she should not employ me and she seemed determined at all cost that she should.

'We have rather pleasant nursery quarters here. You know, the family's children have been brought up there over the years. That makes a difference . . . somehow.'

I was trying to shut out of my mind images of that frightened little boy being brought into the nursery by a determined Sir Edward and by good fortune falling into the hands of loving Nanny Crockett.

It was obvious that my next words unnerved her.

'Perhaps I could meet your daughter.'

It was the last thing she wanted. There was apprehension in the green eyes. She was clearly thinking that one look at the little monster would be enough to make me decline. I felt almost sorry for her. She was so anxious to find a governess – any governess, I imagined – for her daughter.

Never could a prospective governess have been in such a position. I was amused at the feeling of power which came over me. It would be entirely my decision. I knew I was not going to enjoy my work, but at least I should not have to cringe before my employer. I knew I was coming to this house for Simon's sake and I was certain that I should discover some of its secrets which, with luck, might lead me to the truth.

'She may not, of course, be in her room,' she said.

'I think we should meet before we make the decision,' I said firmly, and I somehow managed to convey that this was an ultimatum.

Reluctantly she went to the bellrope and in a few moments a maid appeared.

'Would you bring Miss Kate to me?' she said.

'Yes, my lady.'

Lady Perrivale looked so nervous that I wondered what I was going to discover. If she is quite impossible, I thought, I shall at least have a chance to look around and if it is really bad I can always follow the example of the other governesses and leave.

When she came, I was surprised rather agreeably, but that was perhaps because I was expecting something worse.

She was very like her mother. Her hair was a little less bright, her eyes a little less green. There was a hint of blue in them but that might have been because she was wearing a blue dress; her lashes and brows were inclined to be sandy and her mother owed a great deal to her dark brows and luxuriant lashes for her arresting good looks. But it was obvious at once that she was her mother's daughter.

'Kate, my dear,' said Lady Perrivale. 'This is Miss Cranleigh. If you are lucky she may be your new governess.'

The girl looked at me appraisingly. 'I don't like governesses,' she said. 'I want to go away to school.'

'That's not very polite, is it?' asked Lady Perrivale mildly.

'No,' said her daughter.

'And shouldn't we be?'

'Perhaps you should, Mama. I don't want to be.'

I laughed and said boldly: 'I can see you have a great deal to learn.'

'I never learn unless I want to.'

'That's not very clever, is it?'

'Why not?'

'Because you will remain ignorant.'

'If I want to be ignorant, I'll be ignorant.'

'It is your choice, of course,' I replied mildly, 'but I never heard of any wise person wanting to be ignorant.'

I looked at Lady Perrivale and I could see her fear that I would reject her daughter was growing.

'Really, Kate,' she said. 'Miss Cranleigh has come all the way from Trecorn Manor to see you.'

'I know. And it's not "all the way". It's not really very far.'

'You must assure her that you will try to be a good pupil or she may decide not to come.'

Kate shrugged her shoulders.

I was surprised to find myself feeling almost sorry for Lady Perrivale. I wondered why she, who looked as though she might be the sort of woman to have her own way, could allow a child to behave so.

I fancied Kate felt a certain antagonism to her mother and at the root of her behaviour might be a wish to discountenance her. I wondered why.

I said: 'If I am coming to teach Kate, I think we should get to know each other. Perhaps she could show me the schoolroom.'

Kate turned to face me. I could see she was finding me very different from the governesses to whom she was accustomed. I imagined those poor needy women desperately eager for the post and fearing to do anything that might mean losing it.

I felt more alive than I had for a long time. I was actually in Simon's old home and these were the people who had figured in the drama. Moreover, I was a little stimulated at the prospect of battles to come with this child.

'If you think . . .' began Lady Perrivale uneasily.

'Yes,' said Kate. 'I'll show you the schoolroom.'

'That's good,' I said.

Lady Perrivale rose as if to accompany us.

I turned to her. 'Shall Kate and I get to know each other . . . alone?' I suggested. 'We shall know better then whether we can get along.'

I was not sure which was greater – her relief or her

apprehension. She was glad to end this interview but she was afraid of what would ensue when I was alone with Kate.

The girl led me up the stairs, taking two at a time.

'It's a long way up,' she said over her shoulder.

'Schoolrooms usually are.'

'Miss Evans used to puff and pant coming up the stairs.'

'Miss Evans being the unfortunate lady who tried to teach you before?' I asked.

She gave a little giggle. Poor Miss Evans! I thought. At the mercy of such a creature.

'It's not very nice up there,' she went on. 'It's haunted, you know. Are you afraid of ghosts?'

'Never having made the acquaintance of any, it is difficult to say.'

Again she giggled. 'You wait,' she said. 'They're very frightening. There are always ghosts in old houses like this. They come out in the night when you are asleep . . . particularly if they don't like you, and they never like strangers.'

'Oh, don't they? I should have thought it was members of the family whom they would come back to see.'

'You don't know anything about ghosts.'

'Do you?'

'Of course. I know they do horrid things . . . like clanging chains and frightening people in the night.'

'Perhaps you have been listening to gossip.'

'You wait,' she said ominously and with plans in her eyes. 'If you come here, you'll be frightened out of your wits. I promise you.'

'Thanks for the promise. So this is it?'

'It's right at the top of the house. You can look right down into the well . . . because the stairs go round and round. Someone hanged herself once from these banisters. She was a governess.'

'Perhaps she had a pupil rather like you.'

That made her laugh and she looked at me with some appreciation.

'Moreover,' I went on, 'it would have been rather a difficult operation and she must have been very skilful. So this is the schoolroom. What books have you?'

'A lot of boring old things.'

'You mean they bore you. That's probably because you don't understand them.'

'How do you know what I understand?'

'Well, I gathered from you that you never learn anything unless you want to, and I surmise that very often you don't want to, which would account for your ignorance.'

'You're a funny sort of governess.'

'How do you know? I haven't been a governess yet.'

'I'll give you a piece of advice,' she said conspiratorially.

'That's good of you. What is it?'

'Don't come here. I'm not very nice, you know.'

'Oh yes. I had already discovered that.'

'Why . . . ? How . . . ?'

'You've told me yourself and in any case it's rather obvious, isn't it?'

'I'm not so bad really. Only I don't like to be told what to do.'

'That's not very unusual, you know. You're just going along with the common herd. But there are people who want to learn and they do. They are the people who have rewarding lives.'

She stared at me with a puzzled look.

I said: 'I have seen the schoolroom. Now I will go back to your mother.'

'You're going to tell her how awful I am and that you don't like me and you won't come here.'

'Is that what you want me to tell her?' She did not answer, which mildly surprised and pleased me. I went on: 'Do you often tell people what they are going to do?'

'Well, of course you're not coming. You're not poor like

Miss Evans. You don't *have* to. Nobody would come here unless they had to.'

'If you would like to take me to your mother, I should be pleased. If not, I dare say I can find my own way.'

We surveyed each other like two generals on a battlefield. I could see that in spite of herself she was mildly interested in me. I had not behaved like the ordinary governesses; and she had certainly not acted like a prospective pupil. But I sensed that she had – as I admitted to myself that I had – enjoyed our little bout of sparring. I thought her a spoilt child, but there was another reason – as there usually is – why she behaved as she did. I could not grasp what her attitude towards her mother was, but I felt a growing curiosity and I wanted to find out.

Oddly enough, this difficult child, who had driven governesses away in despair, attracted me in an odd way. I wanted to know more of her. I knew I was coming to the house in any case, but, having met Lady Perrivale and her daughter, I was finding myself intrigued by their personalities.

Kate pushed past me and started to go downstairs: 'This is the way,' she said.

I followed her back to the room where we had left Lady Perrivale. She looked up anxiously as though she were ready to accept defeat.

I said: 'Kate has shown me the schoolroom. It is very light and airy and in such a pleasant spot . . . at the top of the house.'

I paused, savouring my power with a certain complacency, then I went on: 'I have decided that, providing we can agree on the usual details, I should like to come on trial . . . on both sides . . . for say a month and if at the end of that time we feel the arrangement is satisfactory we can plan from there.'

Her smile was dazzling. She had made up her mind that a short time with Kate would have decided me. She was ready to promise anything and the salary she offered I was sure was beyond what was normally paid to a governess.

'When . . . ?' she asked eagerly.

'What about Monday . . . the start of the week? You see, I have not far to come.'

'That would be admirable.'

Kate was looking at me in astonishment. I said coolly: 'If the carriage could take me back to Trecorn Manor . . .'

'But of course,' said Lady Perrivale. 'We shall look forward to seeing you on Monday.'

I felt triumphant as I was driven back. I was going to succeed, I knew. I was going to find Cosmo's murderer. And then I should have to find Simon. How, I did not know. But I'd think of that when the time came.

I kept thinking how lucky it was that I had confided in Nanny Crockett, for that had certainly taken me along a few steps further. I was certain that I was on the only possible road to discovery.

* * *

Nanny Crockett was waiting for me and she could hardly restrain her impatience. I did not keep her long in suspense.

'I'm starting on Monday,' I said.

She flew at me and hugged me. 'I knew you would. I knew it.'

'Lady Perrivale was determined. No applicant for a post can ever have had such an extraordinary interview. You would have thought she was the one who wanted the job.'

'Well, Mrs Ford told me how it would be.' She looked at me anxiously. 'Did you see . . . the girl?'

I nodded. 'She's a challenge,' I said. 'And if it is possible to find the truth I have to.'

'For Simon's sake. Poor lamb . . . out there in the wilds somewhere. If only he could come home to us.'

'We're going to succeed, Nanny. We are on the way.'

Now that I had come so far, I had to face the difficulties.

I should have to tell my father that I was taking a post as governess. That would bewilder him. And I did not forget Aunt Maud. I was sure she would be most disapproving because becoming a governess would not enhance my chances of what she would call a good marriage. But by the time they heard, I should be installed in Perrivale Court.

I should have to write to Felicity. I wondered what her reaction would be. If she knew the truth behind it, of course, she would understand, for she did realize how restless I was. She herself had been a governess, but I had been a very different child from Kate, and Felicity and I had had good times together from the beginning.

I was unprepared for Lucas's reaction.

I did not see him until dinner that evening. It had become a dismal meal since Theresa's death. We were all conscious of the place where she used to sit at one end of the table opposite Carleton. Now that place was empty and every now and then one of us would gaze furtively towards it. Conversation was laborious and there would be certain gaps when Lucas and I sought for something to say. In the past we had lingered over meals; now they were occasions which everyone wished to be over as soon as possible.

Lucas said: 'I haven't seen you all day. I looked for you this afternoon.'

'No,' I said. 'I went to Perrivale Court.'

'Perrivale Court!' he echoed disbelievingly.

'Yes . . . as a matter of fact I'm going to work there.'

'What?'

'As a governess. Lady Perrivale has a daughter . . . Kate. I am going to act as her governess.'

'Whatever for?'

'Well, it's something to do and . . .'

'It's a ridiculous idea!' He looked at Carleton, who was staring gloomily at his plate. 'Did you hear that?' he said. 'Rosetta plans to go to Perrivale Court as governess to the girl there.'

'Yes, I heard,' said Carleton.

'Well, don't you think it's crazy?'

Carleton coughed slightly.

I said: 'I shall be starting on Monday. I have to do something, and I thought this would be a start.'

Lucas was speechless.

Carleton said: 'It was good of you to stay with us so long. The children are so fond of you. We knew of course that you would only be here temporarily until they had recovered a little from . . .'

Then we all fell into silence.

As soon as dinner was over, Lucas hustled me into the drawing-room.

'I'd like to talk,' he said.

'Yes?'

'It's about this nonsense . . .'

'It's not nonsense. It's perfectly reasonable. I want to do something.'

'There are lots of things you could do. If you're so eager to look after children, what's wrong with the two here?'

'It's not the same, Lucas.'

'What do you mean – not the same? Do you realize what you are letting yourself in for?'

'If I find it intolerable I shall just leave.'

'That place! There's something about it. You there! I just can't imagine it.'

'Lots of young women take posts as governesses.'

'You're not qualified.'

'How many of them are? I have had a fair education. I could teach some things.'

'It's absurd. Tell me, Rosetta, why are you doing this? There must be a reason.'

I was silent for a few seconds. I longed to tell him. On impulse I had told Nanny Crockett, but then I had seen that she was emotionally involved and it was obvious that I had then taken a step in the right direction. I wavered.

But I was uncertain of Lucas. He should feel grateful to the man who had saved his life, but Lucas was a calm realist, and I was unsure of what action he would take.

He answered for me. 'After going through all that . . . well, it's natural that you should feel unsettled. Life at home seems dull . . . well, predictable. You are reaching out for change. I can only think that it was that which made you take this ridiculous action.'

'I don't see it as ridiculous, Lucas.'

'You get on so well with the twins and you and Nanny Crockett seem to be in some conspiracy or other. You're always together.'

I caught my breath. Conspiracy? It was almost as though he guessed.

He said sharply: 'How did you know that they wanted a governess at Perrivale? Through Nanny Crockett, I suppose. I've heard she is still friendly with someone up there.'

'Well, yes . . .'

'I thought so. And you concocted this between you. I tell you, it's madness. That place! There's something unsavoury about it since the murder. It's not the sort of place you should go to. All that trouble . . . and that woman being engaged to the victim and then promptly marrying the other . . .'

'That has nothing to do with the governess.'

'Governess!' he said contemptuously. '*You* a governess!'

'Why not?'

'You're not the type.'

'What types are governesses? There are all sorts, I do assure you.'

'Well, you don't fit into any of the categories. You'd better marry me.'

I stared at him. '*What* did you say?'

'You're restless. Since you've been back, everything

seems dull after such hair-raising adventures as you have experienced. You want something to happen. Very well. Marry me.'

I burst out laughing. 'Really, Lucas, who is being absurd now?'

'Still you. I'm as calm and sensible as ever. The more I think of the idea the more I like it.'

'You don't care for me.'

'But I do. Next to myself I love you best in the world.'

That made me laugh again and I was glad of the light relief.

'I am not taking you seriously, of course,' I said, 'but this must be the most unusual proposal anyone has ever received.'

'It's honest, anyway.'

'Yes, I grant that.'

'And it is not so unusual either. It's just that people don't tell all the truth. Most people love themselves passionately and when they declare their love for someone it is always for their own comfort and pleasure. So you see, I am just the same as most other people – except that I am more honest.'

'Oh, Lucas, it is good of you, but . . .'

'It's not good at all and *but* . . . I knew there would be a but.'

'I really can't take you seriously.'

'Why not? The more I think of it the better solution it seems. You are in the doldrums . . . which ever way you turn. Everything has changed for you. Your forthright aunt has entered your old home and changed it. You have recently come through an almost incredible adventure. Nothing like it will ever happen to you again, so therefore life seems a little flat. You are not sure which way to turn. But turn you will . . . anything . . . anywhere to take you out of the slough into which you have fallen. If governessing in a house of somewhat shady reputation is considered, why not marriage with a curmudgeon who is a poor thing, but at least cares for you and understands?'

'You don't put it very romantically.'

'We are not discussing romance but reality.'

I couldn't help laughing again and he joined in with me.

'Oh come, Rosetta,' he said. 'Give up this mad idea . . . and at least consider the other proposition. It has certain advantages. We are good friends, aren't we? We've faced death together. I understand you as few people ever will. And do you want to go back to Aunt Maud and her plans for you?'

'I certainly don't want to do that,' I replied. 'You are right in a way. You do understand me . . . to some degree.'

'Then abandon this idea. I'll send Dick Duvane over to Perrivale to tell them to look for a new governess. Think about what I suggested. Stay here for a while. Let's enlarge our acquaintance. You don't need to leap into this. Let's make plans.'

'You are so good to me, Lucas.'

I placed my hand in his and he put it to his lips.

'It's true, you know, Rosetta,' he said earnestly. 'I am fond of you.'

'I really am second with you?'

He laughed and held me against him for a moment.

'But . . .' I went on.

'Yes, I know about that "but". You're going to Perrivale, aren't you?'

'I must, Lucas. There's a reason.'

Warnings of danger flashed into my mind. Once again I was on the point of telling him why I must go to Perrivale. He would understand then.

He saw that I was really determined.

He said: 'Well, I shall be close. We'll meet at The Sailor King. And when you find it quite unbearable, you only have to walk out and come to Trecorn.'

'That is a great comfort to me,' I told him. 'And, Lucas . . . thank you for asking me. It means a great deal to me.'

'It's not the last time I shall ask. There'll be others. I don't give in as easily as that.'

'It was a great surprise to me. I think it was to you.'

'Oh, it has been smouldering in my mind for a long time . . . even on the island perhaps . . .'

'Do you think often of that time now?'

'It's always there . . . in the background. I am constantly ready to be reminded. I often think of John Player, too. It would be interesting to know what happened to him.'

I was silent, apprehensive as I always was when he referred to Simon.

'I wonder if he is still in the seraglio. Poor devil. He came out the worst of the three of us . . . though none emerged unscathed.'

His face had hardened. The grudge against fate for making a cripple of a healthy man was never far away.

'I'd give a good deal to know what became of him,' he went on.

'We must remember we should not be here if it were not for him,' I said. 'Perhaps one day we shall hear something.'

'I doubt it. When that sort of thing happens people disappear from your life.'

'We didn't disappear, Lucas.'

'It is rather miraculous that we are here like this.'

'Perhaps he will come back, too.'

'If he escaped . . . which seems impossible.'

'I did, Lucas.'

'That's quite a story, but who is going to let him out? No, we shall never see him again. Yes . . . while we were there . . . that island . . . the three of us . . . we became very close to each other. But that is over now. We've got to grow away from it. And let me tell you, you'll do that far better as Mrs Lucas Lorimer than as governess to some hateful little brat in a household which was once the centre of a murder case.'

'We shall have to see, Lucas,' I said.

* * *

My first days at Perrivale Court were so crowded with impressions and suppressed emotions that they left me quite bewildered. The house itself was fascinating. It was full of unexpected features. It seemed vast, like a medieval castle in some places, a Tudor manor in others, and in some rooms a note of modernity had crept in.

Lady Perrivale had greeted me warmly but briefly and had handed me over to Mrs Ford, who from the first showed herself to be my ally. I was her protégée; she had won the gratitude of Lady Perrivale for producing me and she was going to take me under her wing and do her utmost to keep me in the house.

She took me to my room. 'If there's anything you want, Miss Cranleigh, let me know. I'll see you're as comfortable as I can make you. Nanny Crockett said I was to take care of you, and I promise you, I will.'

My room was next to the nursery, and Kate's was next to mine. It was a pleasant room with a window that looked down on to a courtyard. Across the courtyard other windows faced me. I immediately had the impression that I was being watched and I was glad of the heavy drapes.

From the first I felt as though I had slipped into a dream. I was overwhelmed by the knowledge that I was actually living in the house where Simon had spent the greater part of his boyhood, and my determination to prove his innocence intensified.

It soon became clear that Kate felt an interest in me. She was certainly determined to find out all she could about me.

No sooner had Mrs Ford left me to unpack than she

came into my room. She did not knock, feeling, I was sure, that there was no need to stand on ceremony with a mere governess.

'You came, then,' she said. 'I didn't think you would, and then I did . . . because you wouldn't have said you'd come if you didn't mean to, would you?'

'Of course not.'

'A lot of people say they'll do things and don't.'

'I'm not one of those.'

She sat on the bed.

'Horrible old room, isn't it?'

'I think it's pleasant.'

'I suppose as a governess you haven't been used to much.'

'In my home in London I have a very pleasant room.'

'Why didn't you stay in it, then?'

'You are not very well-mannered, are you?'

'Oh no. Actually, I'm very ill-mannered.'

'Well, at least you are aware of it . . . which is a point in your favour. But as you appear to take a pride in it, that's one against you.'

She laughed. 'You are funny,' she said. 'I do and say what I like.'

'I had gathered that.'

'And nobody's going to change me.'

'Then you'll have to do the job yourself, won't you?'

She looked at me curiously and I went on: 'And would you mind getting off my bed? I want to sort out my things.'

To my surprise she moved and stood watching me.

'Is that all you've got?'

'Yes.'

'It's not much, is it? I suppose you think you're going to marry the master of the house, like Jane Eyre. Well, you can't, because he's married already . . . to my mother.'

I raised my eyebrows.

'Don't look so surprised,' she said. 'It's what a lot of governesses think.'

'I was expressing surprise at your erudition.'

'What's that?'

'In your case, a certain knowledge of literature.'

'Did you think I didn't know anything?'

'I gathered you had difficulties with your governesses.'

'I like reading books about people. I like it when awful things happen to them.'

'I'm not surprised at that.'

She laughed. 'What do you think you're going to teach me?'

'We shall do some history, English literature ... grammar, too, and of course mathematics.'

She grimaced. 'I shan't do what I don't like.'

'We'll have to see about that.'

'You *are* like a governess sometimes.'

'I'm glad you recognize that.'

'I like the way you talk. It makes me laugh.'

'I think you must be rather easily amused.'

'You're not like Miss Evans. She was ever so silly. Right from the first she was just frightened all the time.'

'By you?'

'Of course.'

'And you took advantage of your position.'

'What do you mean?'

'She was trying to do her work and you did all you could to prevent her. You made her so miserable that she had to leave.'

'I didn't want her here. She was a bore. I don't think you're going to be a bore. I wonder how long you'll stay.'

'As long as it suits me, I imagine.'

She smiled secretly. Clearly she was planning her campaign.

Oddly enough, I found her stimulating and I was quite enjoying our verbal battles. She went with me to the schoolroom and I inspected the books that were in the cupboard. It was well stocked. There was a blackboard, several exercise books, slates and pencils.

'I shall have to ask you to show me some of your previous work,' I said.

She grimaced.

'When?' she asked.

'There is no time like the present.'

She hesitated and seemed poised for flight. I wondered what I should do if she refused to stay with me. I knew she was quite capable of that and deeply I pitied my predecessors whose ability to earn a living rested on the whims of this creature.

I wanted to stay for as long as it was necessary, but at least my living did not depend upon it.

At the moment, however, she was mildly intrigued by me and she decided to cooperate; we had an interesting half an hour when I discovered that she was not as ignorant as I had feared she might be; in fact she was exceptionally bright. She had read a great deal which was a help. In that, at least, we had something in common.

During the first day I learned a little about the household. There were three estate managers, Mrs Ford told me. 'Because ever since . . . you know what, Miss Cranleigh, we don't talk about . . . You see, Mr Cosmo had gone and so had Mr Simon. There'd been three of them and now there was only Sir Tristan left. Well, it was too much for him. There'd always been one agent, even . . . before . . . and afterwards, there were two more. Perrivale's a big estate . . . the biggest round here. Of course, it's all different since . . . *that* happened . . . and Sir Edward being gone . . .'

During that first day I had a glimpse of Tristan and from the moment I saw him I began to suspect that he knew something of what had really happened in the old farmhouse.

He looked the part of the stage villain. He was very dark: his hair was smooth and shiny, so sleek that it looked like a black cap, particularly as it came to a point in the middle of his forehead, which gave him a rather mysterious and sinister appearance.

Our meeting was brief. Kate had taken me out to show me the gardens and I met him coming with Lady Perrivale from the stables. She looked beautiful in a dark blue riding habit, with top hat in the same colour. Her hair looked brilliant under the darkish hat.

She said: 'Oh, Tristan, this is Miss Cranleigh, the new governess.'

He took off his hat and bowed in a very courtly manner.

'She and Kate are getting along so well together,' said Lady Perrivale, with more optimism than proof.

'I've shown her the schoolroom,' said Kate. 'And now I'm showing her the gardens.'

'That's very good,' said Lady Perrivale.

'Welcome to Perrivale,' put in Sir Tristan. 'I hope your stay with us will be a long and happy one.'

I saw Kate smirk and I wondered what she was planning for my discomfort.

And there and then I, illogically, assigned to Tristan the role of murderer, telling myself that I might not have any evidence against him, but my conclusions were due to my sixth sense.

I was very thoughtful as I examined the gardens. Kate had noticed this. I was beginning to realize that there was little she missed.

'You didn't like Stepper,' she said.

'Who?'

'My stepfather. I call him Stepper. He doesn't like it much. Nor does my mother.'

'I suppose that is why you do it.'

Again that hunching of the shoulders, the grimace, as she laughed. 'I always give people names,' she said. 'You're Cranny.'

'I'm not sure that I approve of that.'

‘You don’t have to approve. People have no choice when it comes to names. They have to have what’s given them. Look at me, Kate. Who wants to be Kate? I should have liked to be Angelica.’

‘That would make people think of angels,’ I reminded her. ‘Hardly apt in your case.’

She was laughing again. There was quite a lot of laughter that morning.

I said to her: ‘We’ll start lessons tomorrow morning at nine-thirty and we shall finish at twelve noon.’

‘Miss Evans started at ten.’

‘We shall start at nine-thirty.’

Again that grimace, but it was still good-tempered.

I really thought we were getting on much better than I had thought we should. She seemed interested in me. I wondered whether I should be able to get her to work at her lessons.

I was soon to have a rude awakening.

* * *

It was understandable that on my first night at Perrivale Court I should find that sleep evaded me. The events of the day kept crowding into my head. Here I was at last, in Simon’s home, almost at the scene of the crime, one might say; and I was dedicated to the monumental task of proving his innocence. I felt greatly comforted by the thought of Lucas to whom I could turn at any time. I was touched that he had offered to marry me. I had been truly amazed. I had never thought of him in such connection, or only vaguely when Aunt Maud had had that speculative look in her eyes when she knew I had met him at Felicity’s home.

I was turning over in my mind how I should begin my research. This was what would be called a wild goose chase and it was only because of the fantastic adventures through which I had passed that I could contemplate embarking on it.

In the meantime I had to cope with Kate. Quite a task in itself. The beginning had been easier than I had thought it would be, but that was merely because I had managed to make her mildly interested in me. I could visualize her quickly becoming bored and then the campaign against me would begin. I hoped she would not make my life intolerable before I had made some progress in my search.

I must learn something about Cosmo, who had been engaged to marry the fascinating Mirabel who had become a definite personality to me. I was getting my cast together. Simon, I knew well; I had glimpsed Tristan. How enamoured had Simon been of Mirabel? Having seen her I could imagine how attractive she would be to most men.

I must have dozed, for I was awakened suddenly by a sound outside my door. I opened my eyes and saw the door handle slowly turning. The door was silently pushed open and a figure glided into the room. It was covered with a sheet and I knew at once who was under that sheet.

She stood by the door and said in a sibilant whisper: 'Go away. Go away . . . while there is still time. No good can come to you here.'

I pretended to sleep on. She came closer to the bed. My eyes were half closed and when she came near enough, I caught the sheet and pulled it off.

'Hello, ghost,' I said.

She looked deflated.

'It was a poor impersonation,' I added. 'And a sheet . . . obviously a sheet. Couldn't you have done better than that?'

'You were pretending to be asleep. It wasn't fair.'

'You were pretending to be a ghost and all's fair in love and war, and war is what this is, isn't it . . . since it certainly isn't love.'

'You were scared.'

'I wasn't.'

'Just for a minute?' she said almost pleadingly.

'Not for a second. You could have done better than that.

In the first place, if you planned to stage a haunting, it wasn't very clever to talk so much about ghosts when we first met. You see, you put me on my guard. I said, "This girl fancies herself as a governess-baiter."'

'A *what*?' she cried.

'You see, you have such a limited vocabulary. I'm not surprised, as you won't learn. You like taunting governesses because in comparison with them you feel ignorant. You think that for a moment they are in a weak position and you are in a strong one. That's rather cowardly, of course, but people who are unsure of themselves do things like that.'

'I frightened Miss Evans.'

'I've no doubt you did. You don't care about other people at all, do you?'

She looked surprised.

'Didn't it occur to you that Miss Evans was trying to earn her living and the only reason she would want to teach an unpleasant child like you was because she had to.'

'Am I unpleasant?'

'Very. But if you gave a little thought to others besides yourself, you might be less so.'

'I don't like you.'

'I don't greatly care for you.'

'So you will go away, will you?'

'Probably. You don't think anyone would want to stay to teach you, do you?'

'Why not?'

'Because you have stated so clearly that you do not want to learn.'

'What of that?'

'It shows you have no respect for learning and only stupid people feel like that.'

'So I am stupid?'

'It would seem so. Of course, you could change. I tell you what. Why don't we make a truce?'

'What's a truce?'

'It's a sort of agreement. You make terms.'

'What terms?'

'We could see if you like the way I teach and if you are prepared to learn. If you don't, I'll go and you can have another governess. It will save you racking your brains for methods to make me uncomfortable. Let's go about it in a civilized way without all these childish tricks to make me go.'

'All right,' she said. 'Let's have a truce.'

'Then go back to bed now. Good night.'

She paused at the door. 'There are ghosts in the house, though,' she said. 'There was a murder here . . . not long ago.'

'Not in this house,' I said.

'No, but it was Stepper's brother. One was killed and the other ran away. They were all in love with my mother before she married Stepper.'

She was very observant. She had noticed the change in me. She came back and sat on the bed.

'What do you know about it?' I asked. 'You weren't in the house at the time.'

'No, I came here when my mother married Stepper. Before that we were at Gramps's house.'

'Whose?'

'My grandfather's. He's in the Dower House now. He went there when my mother got married. He had to have a better house then because he was the father of the lady of the manor. Gramps didn't like living in a little cottage anyway. He's really a very grand gentleman. He's Major Durrell and majors are very important. They win battles. We used to live in London but that was years and years ago. Then we came here and everything changed.'

'You must have known them all . . . the one who was killed and the one who went away.'

'I knew them . . . in a way. They were all in love with

my mother. Gramps used to laugh about it. He was ever so pleased, because when she married Stepper we moved out of the cottage. But first there was all that fuss. And then Cosmo was killed and Simon ran away because he didn't want to be hanged.'

I was silent and she went on: 'They do hang them, you know. They put a rope round their necks and they . . . swing. It hurts a lot . . . but then they're dead. That was what he was afraid of. Well, who wouldn't be?'

I could not speak. I kept seeing Simon stealthily leaving the house . . . making his way to Tilbury . . . meeting the sailor, John Player.

She was watching me closely.

'Ghosts come back when people are murdered. They haunt people. Sometimes they want to know what really happened.'

'Do you think something happened . . . which people don't know about?'

She looked at me slyly. I was unsure of her. She could be teasing me. I had betrayed my interest and she had noticed. She would already have guessed that I was extraordinarily interested in the murder.

'I was there, wasn't I?' she said. 'I remember. I was with Gramps . . . my mother was upstairs. Someone – one of the grooms from Perrivale – came to the door and said: "Mr Cosmo's been found shot. He's dead." Gramps said: "Oh my God." You're not supposed to say Oh my God. It's taking the Lord's name in vain. It says something in the Bible about it. And Gramps went upstairs to my mother and he wouldn't let me go up with him.'

I tried to think of something appropriate to say but nothing came.

'Do you ride, Cranny?' she asked, seemingly irrelevantly.

I nodded.

'I tell you what. I'll take you to Bindon Boys . . . the scene of the crime. You'd like that, wouldn't you?'

I said: 'You're obsessed by the crime. It's all over now. Perhaps one day we'll ride out to that place.'

'All right,' she said. 'It's a pact.'

'And now,' I said, 'good night.'

She gave me a grin and, picking up the sheet, left me.

I lay for a long time, wide awake. I had come to teach Kate, but there might be a good deal she could teach me.

* * *

Kate had long decided that the lives of governesses should be made so uncomfortable that they found it impossible to stay, so they left, which gave her a period of freedom before the next one came, and she had to start her eliminating tactics once more.

I was different from the others, mainly because she sensed that it was not imperative for me to keep the job as a means of livelihood. That took a little of the spice out of the baiting and gave me the advantage. I tried to tell myself that all children had a streak of cruelty in them because they lack experience of life and therefore an ability to imagine the extent of the suffering they cause.

Apart from the fact that I was becoming sure that she could be of use to me in my quest, I wanted to take up the case of other governesses who had suffered before me and in particular those who would suffer after me. I wanted to teach Kate a little humanity. Oddly enough, I did not despair of her. I believed something must have happened to make her the callous little creature she had become; and I had a feeling that it must be possible to change her.

The next morning, rather to my surprise, she was in the schoolroom at the appointed time.

I told her I had worked out a timetable. We would start with English, perhaps for an hour or so; we would see how that worked. I should want to test her reading ability, her spelling, her grammar. We should read books together.

I had found a collection in the cupboard. I picked up *The*

Count of Monte Cristo and when I opened it I saw 'Simon Perrivale' written on the flyleaf in a childish hand. I felt my own hands tremble a little.

I managed to hide my emotion from her alert eyes. I said: 'Have you ever read this book?'

She shook her head.

'We'll read it one day and, oh, here's another. *Treasure Island*. That's about pirates.'

Her interest was aroused. There was a picture on the frontispiece of Long John Silver with his parrot on his shoulder.

She said: 'In that other book . . . that was his name . . . you know, the murderer.'

'We don't know that he was,' I said, and stopped myself abruptly, for she was looking at me in surprise. I should have to go carefully. 'We shall then do history, geography and arithmetic.'

She was scowling.

'We'll see how they fit in,' I said firmly.

The morning passed tolerably well. I discovered that she could read fairly fluently and I was pleased to discover that she had a definite taste for literature. The personalities of history interested her but she shut her mind to dates. There was a revolving globe in the cupboard and we had an interesting time discovering places on it. I showed her where I had been shipwrecked. The story intrigued her, and we finished off the morning by reading a chapter of *Treasure Island*; she was absorbed by the book from the first page.

I was amazed at my success.

I had decided that we should work until midday. Then she could follow her own pursuits if she wished until three o'clock when we might walk in the gardens or in the surrounding country and learn something about plant life, or take a walk. We could resume lessons at four and work until five. That was our scholastic day.

In the afternoon she showed no wish to be on her own

and offered to show me the surrounding country. I was rather pleased that she sought my company and seemed to retain her interest in me.

She talked about *Treasure Island* and told me what she thought would happen. She wanted to hear about my shipwreck. I began to think that it was this which had made her ready to accept me . . . perhaps briefly . . . as had not been the case with the other governesses.

She took me to the top of the cliffs and we sat there for a while, watching the sea.

'We have rough seas here,' she said. 'There used to be wreckers along these coasts. They had lights and they lured the ships on to the rocks, pretending that it was the harbour. Then they stole the cargo. I'd like to have been a wrecker.'

'Why do you want to be evil?'

'Being good is dull.'

'It's better in the long run.'

'I like short runs.'

I laughed at her and she laughed with me.

She said suddenly: 'Look at those rocks down there. A man was drowned down there not very long ago.'

'Did you know him?'

She was silent for a moment. Then she said: 'He was a stranger here. He came from London. He's buried in St Morwenna's churchyard. I'll show you his grave. Would you like to see it?'

'Well, I suppose it is hardly one of the local beauty spots.'

She laughed again.

'He was drunk,' she said. 'He fell over the cliffs and right down on to the rocks.'

'He must have been very drunk.'

'Oh, he was. There was a fuss about it. They didn't know who he was for a long time.'

'How you love the morbid!'

'What's that?'

'Unpleasant . . . gruesome.'

'I like gruesome things.'

'It's not the wisest of preoccupations.'

She looked at me and laughed again. 'You are funny,' she said.

Looking back over that day when I retired to my room that night, I could say it had been unexpectedly satisfactory. I had some hope – however flimsy – of coming to an understanding with Kate.

* * *

A few days passed. To my secret delight, I was discovering that my somewhat unorthodox methods of teaching were more successful with a pupil like Kate than more conventional ones might have been. We were reading together a great deal. In fact, I held those reading sessions as a sort of bribe for good conduct during the less attractive projects. She could have read by herself but she preferred that we do it together.

She liked to share her enjoyment, which was a sign in her favour, I thought; moreover, she liked to talk about what we had read afterwards; then sometimes she might be held up because she did not know the meaning of a word. She was avid for knowledge, in spite of the fact that she had expressed her contempt for it; and she was completely intrigued by *Treasure Island*.

It was too much to expect a complete change in the child merely because our relationship had progressed more favourably than I had dared hope. I think it was on my fourth morning that she did not put in an appearance in the schoolroom.

I went to her room. She was looking out of the window, obviously expecting me, and I could see she was preparing to enjoy a battle.

I said: 'Why are you not in the schoolroom?'

'I don't feel like lessons today,' she replied jauntily.

'It doesn't matter how you feel. This is lesson-time.'

'You can't make me.'

'I certainly would not attempt to take you there by force. I shall go to your mother and tell her that you have made up your mind not to learn and there is no point in my being here.'

It was a bold step. I could not bear the thought of leaving now. Yet I knew I could get nowhere unless I had some authority over her.

She looked at me defiantly. My heart sank but I hoped I hid my feelings. I had gone too far to turn back.

'You really mean you'd go?' I saw the fear in her eyes mingling with disbelief. I sensed that she was as uneasy as I was.

I said firmly: 'If you will not come to the schoolroom I have no alternative.'

She hesitated for a moment. 'All right,' she said. 'Go, if you want to.'

I walked to the door. I must not show my despair. If this was to be the end, what good had I done? But there was no turning back now. I went out. She did not move. I started down the stairs. Then I heard her. 'Come back, Cranny.'

I paused and turned to look back at her.

'All right,' I said. 'I'll come.'

I felt flushed with victory as we made our way to the schoolroom.

She was in a difficult mood all day. I wondered why. Perhaps she felt she had been good too long and it was not in her nature to be so.

I found a dead shrew mouse in my bed that night. I carefully wrapped it up in tissue paper and went along to her room.

'I think this poor little thing belongs to you,' I said.

She looked aghast. 'Where did you find it?'

'Where you put it. In my bed.'

'I bet you screamed when you found it.'

'I did not think it frightening or funny. It's just a rather silly cliché really.'

I could see her pondering on the word cliché. She loved discovering new words; but she was not in the mood to ask me what it meant.

I went on: 'I wonder how many times some mischievous child has put a shrew mouse in someone's bed. It's really rather silly. You do the expected thing, Kate.'

She was a little downcast. Then she said: 'Well . . . you brought it back, didn't you? You were going to put it in my bed.'

'I should have done no such thing. I merely wanted you to know that your silly trick had not had the effect you thought it would. Now, if we are going to have a truce, we should put an end to these childish tricks. It would be more interesting to get on well together. There are many exciting things we could do. We don't want to waste time having tantrums and playing silly tricks. We can talk . . .'

'What about?'

'About life . . . people . . .'

'Murder?' she put in.

I thought: Yes, about one. I said: 'What we can do is finish *Treasure Island*.'

'"Fifteen men on the dead man's chest,"' she sang, '"Yo, ho, ho, and a bottle of rum."'

I smiled. 'There are lots of books we can read. You haven't read *The Count of Monte Cristo* yet. I saw it in the cupboard. It's about a man who was wrongfully imprisoned and escapes to have his revenge.'

Her eyes were round with interest.

'Well,' I went on, 'if we don't waste our time in silly ways, we might tackle that. And there are many more.'

She did not answer, but I felt I had won another battle.

I said: 'What shall we do with this poor little mouse?'

'I'll bury it,' she said.

'That's right. And all your silly prejudices against

governesses with it. Then perhaps we can start to enjoy our lessons.'

On that note, I left her. I was victorious and triumphant.

* * *

My handling of Kate was the wonder of the household. At last someone had been found who could turn the *enfant terrible* into a normal child – or at least who had found a way to control her.

Mrs Ford fêted me. She was delighted. She mentioned my name in an awed whisper, as though I were a battle hero covered in military glory. I was quite an important figure in the household.

It was about a week after my arrival when Lady Perrivale asked me to come to her in the drawing-room.

She was very gracious.

'You and Kate seem to be getting along very well,' she began. 'That is very good. I knew all would be well if only we could get the right person.'

'I am quite inexperienced in governessing,' I reminded her.

'Well, that is just the point. These old women have too many rules. They are too set in their ways to understand the modern child.'

'Kate is rather unusual.'

'Well, of course. But clearly you understand her. Are you completely satisfied with everything? Is there anything . . . ?'

'I am satisfied, thank you very much,' I replied.

Sir Tristan came into the room as though on a cue. It amused me to think he had been called in to add his praise to that of his wife. Kate must have plagued them a good deal.

The thought crossed my mind that it was odd that a man who could murder his brother should be nonplussed by a wayward child. I pulled myself up sharply. It was nonsensical to have settled on Sir Tristan as the murderer, just because of his saturnine looks. Though, of course, he had inherited the title, the estates . . . and Mirabel.

His shrewd dark eyes were assessing me. I felt guilty. I wondered what he would say if he could read my thoughts.

'I hear you are managing Kate,' he said, and added, with a little laugh, 'Quite a feat. It's very clever of you, Miss Cranleigh, to do what your predecessors so lamentably failed to.'

'She's not an easy child,' I said.

'We are well aware of that, aren't we?' he replied, looking at his wife.

She nodded ruefully.

'I think she needs a great deal of understanding,' I told them. I was wondering what Kate's relationship was with these two. She had not given me an inkling. What of her father? What had happened to him? How did she feel about her mother's engagement to Cosmo, and then, very soon after his death, the marriage to Tristan? These were matters I should like to know about. I believed they might help me solve the mystery.

'And you seem to be able to supply that.'

'As I have explained, I have never been a governess before.'

'You are too young, of course,' he said, smiling at me warmly. 'And too modest . . . is she not, my dear?'

'Far too modest,' added Lady Perrivale. 'Miss Cranleigh, I hope you will not be bored here.' She looked at her husband. 'We were going to say that perhaps . . . now and then . . . when we have a dinner party . . . you might care to join us. As a matter of fact, your friends are quite close neighbours of ours.'

'You mean the Lorimers?'

'Yes. So sad about the accident. I dare say they would not be in the mood for visiting just yet. But perhaps later we might ask them . . . and then, of course, you must be among the guests.'

'That would be very pleasant.'

'We don't want you to feel . . . isolated.'

I was thinking: This is what happens to some governesses when they are short of a guest and want to make up numbers, and if the governess is fairly presentable she is called in to fill the gap. On the other hand, they were clearly very anxious to keep me. How strange it was that I was the only one who had found a way to make this recalcitrant child less objectionable.

I said: 'You are very kind. There is one thing . . .'

They were eager to know what.

'If I could occasionally have a free afternoon. I should like to visit the Lorimers. You see, there are children there. I was with them at the time of the accident. I stayed on a while after the friends with whom I was travelling left.'

I was amused to see the light of alarm in Lady Perrivale's eyes. Children? Might they be needing a governess? Really, I thought, I shall get a very high opinion of myself . . . and all because I had for a time found a way of making Kate behave mildly reasonably.

'Of course,' said Sir Tristan quickly. 'Certainly you must take the time to visit your friends. How will you travel? It is quite a few miles to Trecorn Manor, is it not? You are a rider, are you?'

'Oh yes.'

'Well, that's settled. Ask Mason down at the stables to find a suitable mount for you.'

'You are most kind. Kate has mentioned riding and I think she would like us to do it together.'

'Excellent. I believe she is quite good on a horse.'

'I am sure she is. I look forward to outings with her.'

It was a most satisfactory interview.

* * *

The next day Kate and I went for a ride. She had a small white horse of whom she was very fond. It pleased me to see the care she lavished on him – an indication that there was some capacity for affection in her nature.

The head groom, Mason, had found a chestnut mare for me. Her name was Goldie, he told me. 'She's a good little thing. Treat her right and she'll treat you right. Good-tempered . . . easygoing . . . make a bit of fuss of her . . . and she likes a lump of sugar after the ride. Give her that and she'll be your slave.'

Kate was a good little horsewoman, inclined to show off at first, but when I told her I knew she was aware of how to manage a horse, and in any case she would not have been allowed to go without a groom if she did not, she stopped doing so.

I was wondering how I could pose tactful questions about her home life, for I knew I had to be very careful. She was extremely observant; and she was watching me as closely as I was watching her.

She announced that she was going to take me to Bindon Boys.

'You know,' she said, 'the old farmhouse where the murder took place.'

'I remember.'

'You'll like that, Cranny. You know how you love anything about that old murder.'

I felt uneasy. I had betrayed my interest and she had noticed.

'It's an awful old place. People won't go there after dark . . . I mean they won't even go near it. I reckon quite a lot would want to go in daylight . . . but never alone.'

'Bricks and mortar can't hurt anyone.'

'No. It's what's inside. Once it was a real farmhouse. I can remember it before . . . before that happened . . .'

'Can you?'

'Well, of course I can. I wasn't all that much of a baby.'

'And you lived near . . . when you came from London.'

'That's right. The cottage we lived in was close to Bindon Boys. It was the nearest cottage to it. And the sea was just down the slope. I'll show you when we get there.'

'Is it far?'

'No, about a mile.'

'That's easy.'

'Come on. I'll race you.'

We galloped across a meadow and when we emerged we were very close to the sea. I took deep breaths of the invigorating air. Kate came up close to me.

'There,' she said. 'You can see it just down there. That's the old farmhouse and there, not very far off . . . Seashell Cottage. Seashell . . . what a silly name! Someone had done the name on the soil outside the door in seashells. Seashell Cottage . . . all in shells. I used to pull them up. I took off the Seas and made it Hell Cottage.'

I laughed. 'Just what I would expect of you.'

'Gramps thought it was funny. I tell you what. After you've seen the farmhouse I might take you to see Gramps. He'd like to meet you. He likes meeting people.'

'I shall find it all most interesting, I am sure.'

'Come on. The farmhouse first.'

We rode down the slight incline, and there it was. It was in a state of dilapidation. The roof looked as though it were falling in. The heavy door was slightly ajar. The bolt had evidently gone.

'It looks as if it is on the point of collapse,' I said.

'Coming in? Or are you scared?'

'Of course I want to go in.'

'We'll leave our horses here.'

We dismounted near an old mounting-block and tethered the horses. We pushed open the door and stepped straight into what I presumed was a living-room. It was large with two windows, the panes of which were cracked. Several floorboards were missing. Threadbare curtains hung at the windows and dusty cobwebs hung from the ceiling.

'They didn't touch it . . . after the murder,' said Kate. 'This is where it was . . . in this room. It's haunted, isn't it? Can you feel it?'

I said: 'It's eerie.'

'Well, that's because it's haunted. You'd better keep close to me.'

I smiled. She was eager not to be too far away from me in this place.

I was seeing it all clearly: Simon, tying up his horse at probably the same spot where we had tied ours . . . unsuspecting . . . coming in and finding Cosmo lying on the floor, the gun beside him. I saw Simon picking up the gun and just at that moment Tristan bursting in. It was too neat.

'You look funny,' said Kate.

'I was thinking about it.'

She nodded.

'I reckon Simon was waiting for him. And as soon as he came in . . . bang, bang. It was a good thing Stepper came in, though . . . and caught him red-handed. He ran away.' She came close to me. 'What do you think Simon is doing now?'

'I wish I knew.'

'Perhaps the ghost is haunting him. Can ghosts travel? I reckon they can go a little way. I wonder where he is. I'd love to know. What's the matter with you, Cranny?'

'Nothing.'

'Ever since you came in here, you've had a funny look in your eyes.'

'Nonsense.'

Then suddenly I thought I heard a movement overhead.

'The fact is you're scared, Cranny.' She stopped suddenly. Her eyes widened as they turned towards the stairs. She had heard too. She came closer to me and as I gripped her hand, I heard the creak of a floorboard.

Kate was dragging on my arm, but I did not move.

'It's the ghost,' whispered Kate, and there was real fear in her face.

I said: 'I'm going to look.'

She shook her head and drew back in alarm.

For a second or two she stood very still. Then she came to me and I started up the stairs with her following close behind.

We were on a landing. I could hear deep breathing. So could she. She gripped my hand tightly.

There were three doors on the landing and all of them were closed. I stood listening. Then again I heard the sound of breathing. I stood very still, listening. Behind the door nearest to me I knew someone was waiting.

I went to the door and turned the handle. I pushed open the door and stepped into the room.

A man was standing there – unwashed, unkempt, and there was a pile of rags on the floor with a paper bag beside it. I noticed crumbs on the floor and relief swept over me. This man was human anyway. I did not know what I had expected. Perhaps, like Kate, I feared the ghost of Cosmo. And this was just an old tramp.

'I be doing no 'arm,' he said.

Kate was beside me. 'It's Harry Tench,' she said.

Harry Tench. The name was familiar. I had heard it mentioned in connection with the murder.

'Who be you?' he demanded. 'I know who that one be.' He pointed at Kate. 'And what do 'ee want 'ere? I bain't doing no 'arm.'

'No,' I said. 'No. We just came to look at the farmhouse. We heard a noise and came up.'

'Nobody comes prying round 'ere. What 'arm be I doing?'

'None, none. I'm sorry we disturbed you.'

'It was just a place to sleep. Drove out, I was. There's no 'arm done. Don't 'ee get no ideas about having me put out.'

'We haven't any ideas about doing that,' said Kate, who

was fast recovering from her fright and was almost herself. 'We thought you were a ghost.'

His lips were drawn back in a grin showing yellow teeth.

'Don't worry,' I said. 'Come on, Kate.'

I took her hand and we went out of the room. I shut the door on Harry Tench and we went downstairs.

'Come on,' I said. 'Let's get out of here.'

As we rode away, Kate said: 'You were really scared, Cranny.'

'Not half as much as you were. You were going to run, remember.'

She was silent for a while and then went on: 'He's rather brave . . . sleeping there, in a place where a murder happened. You wouldn't want to, would you, Cranny?'

'I would like to be more comfortable than that poor man obviously was.'

We rode on and after a few moments she said: 'Look, there's Seashell Cottage. That's where we all used to live.'

It was a neat little place with a well-kept garden and clean lace curtains at the windows. We rode close enough for me to see that the Seas had been replaced in the shells so that it was now respectable Seashell Cottage. It was difficult to imagine Lady Perrivale living in such a place; and her daughter and father had been with her too.

I wondered about Kate's father. Could I ask her? Perhaps at the appropriate moment I could put a few carefully chosen questions. I must remember how shrewd Kate was and be very careful.

'Come on,' she said. 'Let's go and see if Gramps is at home.'

The Dower House was very different from Seashell Cottage. I had seen it in the distance, for it was not very far from Perrivale Court. There was a copse between the two and we rode through this.

It was a charming residence. I imagined it had been built during Elizabeth's reign, for it was definitely of Tudor architecture – red brick with latticed windows. Virginia creeper grew on some of the walls and there was a neat lawn before it bordered by flowerbeds.

We slipped off our horses, tethered them and walked through the gate. The house seemed quiet.

'I bet you he's in the garden,' said Kate.

She led the way round the side of the house, past a small orchard, to a walled garden reminiscent of the period, with plants climbing over the red brick wall and beds of what I guessed to be aromatic herbs surrounding a pond, in the centre of which was a small fountain. What struck me most was the aura of absolute peace. A man was sitting on a carved wooden seat close to the pond.

'Gramps,' cried Kate.

I was amazed that he looked so young. I realized later that he must have been in his mid-fifties, but he looked ten years younger than that. He was straight-backed, very upright and undoubtedly handsome. I noticed the resemblance to Lady Perrivale and Kate. His hair was similar in colour to theirs but had a little white at the temples – and there was a hint of green in his eyes. But, like Kate, he lacked those dark brows and lashes which made Lady Perrivale such a startling beauty. *His* brows were so light as to be almost invisible, which gave him a look of youthful surprise.

When he saw us he came striding towards us. Kate flew at him. He picked her up in his arms and swung her round. She laughed gleefully, and I thought with pleasure: Here is someone she really cares about. I was glad to see she was capable of affection.

'Hey, young Kate,' he said. 'You're forgetting your manners. What about an introduction? Don't tell me. I know, of course . . .'

'It's Cranny,' cried Kate.

'Rosetta Cranleigh,' I said.

'Miss Cranleigh. What a delight to meet you. Your fame

has spread to the Dower House. My daughter, Lady Perrivale, has already told me of what wonderful work you are doing with our miscreant here.'

'What's a miscreant?' demanded Kate.

'It's better for you not to know, don't you agree, Miss Cranleigh? I am so pleased that you have come to visit me.'

'This,' said Kate, 'is *Major* Durrell. Majors are very important, aren't they, Gramps?'

'If you say so, my dear,' he said, raising one of those pale eyebrows in a conspiratorial manner in my direction. 'Now, come and sit down. Refreshments?'

'Oh yes, please,' said Kate.

'A little wine, eh?'

'And some of those wine biscuits,' she said.

'But of course. Look, my dear. You go and tell Mrs Carne that you're here and tell her what's required.'

'All right,' said Kate.

As she ran off he turned to me.

'Mrs Carne comes in every weekday morning to look after me. She also comes two afternoons a week as a special favour. Fortunately this is one of the afternoons. Apart from that, I look after myself. You learn in the Army. I'm quite a handyman . . . which saves a lot of trouble. Come and sit down, Miss Cranleigh. Don't you think this is a delightful spot?'

'Oh, I do indeed. It is so peaceful.'

'That's what I feel, and peace is a very desirable acquisition when one reaches my age. You can believe that, I'm sure.'

'I think it is desirable at any age.'

'Ah, the young prefer adventure. They want any excitement, no matter what they have to pay for it. I have had my share and now . . . thank Heaven . . . I can appreciate peace. I am so pleased you have come to teach my granddaughter and are making such a success of it.'

'It is too early to say. I have only been with her a short time.'

'But they are all delighted. There have been so many trials. Poor child, it has not been easy for her. She's a good little thing . . . underneath it all, you know. The trouble is you have to find a way to that goodness. She needs understanding.'

I felt drawn to him. He was clearly fond of her and he was confirming what I had thought of Kate.

'Yes,' I said. 'I do agree. One has to find the way to understand her.'

'You know what I mean . . . uprooted . . . stepfather. A child has to adjust herself and with one of Kate's nature that's not easy.'

There was something so frank about him. He was so much easier to talk to than either Kate's mother or her stepfather could possibly be.

He went on: 'If there are any difficulties at any time . . . you know, with Kate . . . I hope you will not hesitate to come to me.'

'That is good of you,' I said. 'It is a great comfort to me.'

He made me feel that we were allies, and it was remarkable that he could have done this in so short a time.

Kate came out. Mrs Carne would be bringing out the wine and biscuits soon, she said.

'Now come and sit comfortably by the pond. There are some new goldfish, Kate. Can you see them?'

'Oh yes. They're lovely.'

'Your gardens are well kept,' I commented.

'I'm a keen gardener myself. There's peace in a garden, I always think.'

How he harped on peace! Well, why not? It was a good state to be in.

Mrs Carne came out with the refreshment. She was just as I had imagined her – plumpish, rosy-cheeked, middle-aged and clearly had an affection for her employer, which did not surprise me. She was protective, admiring and authoritative towards him.

'There we are, Major, and the biscuits were baked this morning.'

'Mrs Carne, you are an angel.'

She bridled. 'Well, it's a pleasure, I'm sure.'

He went on: 'This is Miss Cranleigh.'

There seemed to be no need to explain my reason for being with Kate. I expected Mrs Carne was well aware of all that went on at Perrivale Court.

She nodded in my direction, and was gone.

'She's a good sort,' said the Major. 'Treats me like a babe in arms sometimes, but I confess I like to be spoiled. So you like my garden? I do a lot of it myself . . . the designing and planting and all. There's a man who comes in every morning and does the mundane jobs.'

'Have you been here long?'

'Since my daughter married. The house was a sort of wedding present. Unusual, you are thinking, for the father of the bride to be so pampered, but Mirabel couldn't have her old father living in a little cottage. She made it as though coming to live here was a favour to her.'

'We saw Seashell Cottage only this afternoon.'

'It's quite charming in a way. Not much garden, of course. Not to be compared with the Dower House.'

'I told Cranny how I took the Seas out of Seashell and made it Hell Cottage.'

'There you see, Miss Cranleigh, what I have to contend with.'

'You thought it was funny, you know you did, Gramps.'

'Well, perhaps I did. What was I saying? Oh, a great improvement on the cottage, and I am very happy to be here.'

'How comforting it must be to be so contented.'

'Yes – particularly after a rather chequered career. Army life is no bed of roses, believe me. And then I come to this . . . My daughter happily settled . . . and my granddaughter now firmly placed on the strait and narrow path with her most excellent governess.'

He raised an eyebrow at me and I could see the gesture was a habit with him.

'Gramps has been all over the world,' Kate informed me. 'He's been just everywhere.'

'A mild exaggeration, you will understand, Miss Cranleigh.'

I smiled.

'Majors are the most important people in the Army,' went on Kate.

'My dear granddaughter brushes aside all those generals, field marshals, colonels and the rest who are under the impression that they are the ones.'

'Well, *you* were,' she said.

'Who can be so churlish as to contradict such a loyal supporter? It is true that I have done a bit of travelling. India, Egypt, wherever my duty lay.'

'Tell us, Gramps,' pleaded Kate.

Over the wine he talked a great deal. He spoke of his life in India as a young officer. 'Those were the days . . . but the climate . . . uncertainty too. I was too young for the Mutiny . . . but the feeling was always there.'

As he talked, Kate kept glancing at me to make sure that I was duly impressed. It was clear that he was a hero to her. He talked of Egypt, the Sudan and India. At length he said: 'But I'm talking too much. It's Kate's fault. She always lures me to talk, don't you, granddaughter?'

'I like it,' said Kate. 'So do you, don't you, Cranny?'

'It is quite fascinating,' I said.

'I'm glad you find it so. I hope it will tempt you to come and visit me again.'

'I wish I'd been there,' said Kate.

'Ah. Sometimes things are better to talk about than to live through.'

'You must miss all this adventure,' I said.

'I was telling you how much I appreciate the peaceful life. I've had enough adventuring. What I want now is to settle down and enjoy the visits of my family . . . and to know that they are well and happy.'

'It seems a very noble ambition,' I said. 'And how the time has flown. We must be on our way back, Kate.'

'Promise you'll come again.'

I thanked him and Kate leaped up and flung her arms about his neck. I was astonished by her conduct. She was like a different child. And I was delighted to see this affection between her and her grandfather.

As we rode home, she said: 'Isn't Gramps wonderful?'

'He has certainly had a very interesting life.'

'It's the most interesting life anyone ever had. Of course, you were shipwrecked . . . that counts for something. You ought to have told him about it.'

'Oh, his adventures were far more interesting, I am sure.'

'Oh yes. But yours are not bad. You can tell him next time.'

And of course there would be a next time. I was glad of that.

When I was in bed that night I kept going over that afternoon's adventure. It had been quite eventful. First Harry Tench and then the Major. Both of those men would have been here at the time of the murder.

I imagined the Major living in Seashell Cottage with his daughter and granddaughter. I might learn quite a lot from him. A man like that would know what was going on and probably had his own theories.

I must cultivate the acquaintance of the Major.

I believed it had been a profitable afternoon.

The Sailor's Grave

The visit to the Major appeared to have been a great success in more ways than one. Kate became more friendly. I had liked the Major and she had made up her mind that the Major liked me; and as he was a hero in her eyes, I rose considerably in her estimation.

She talked of him freely, telling me of the wonderful adventures he had had, how he had fought battles single-handed and was solely responsible for the success of the British Empire. Kate could never do or think anything half-heartedly.

But I was delighted by the growing friendship between us.

Lessons had become quite painless. It had been a wise stroke to introduce her to books with a good strong narrative. We had almost finished *Treasure Island* and *The Count of Monte Cristo* was lying in wait for us.

I used the books blatantly as a sort of unconscious bribe.

'Well, I know these sums are a little difficult, but when we get them right, we'll see what's going to happen to Ben Gunn.'

My success with her amazed me as much as everyone else. I was beginning to see that Kate was more than a rebellious girl bent on making trouble. I supposed there were reasons behind everything. And I was determined to discover more about her.

Through all this I did not forget for one moment the reason why I was here. I wished I could see the Major alone. It would be difficult to ask leading questions in Kate's presence. She was already a little suspicious because of my intense interest in the murder. I could not call on the Major, of course. Perhaps, I told myself, the opportunity would come and when it did I must be ready to seize it.

I had always known that Kate had an interest in the morbid, so I was not particularly surprised when I discovered what a fascination the graveyard seemed to have for her.

The church was an ancient one, famed for its Norman architecture. It was not far from Perrivale Court and we often passed it.

'Just imagine,' I said as we rode up to it. 'It was built all those years ago . . . about eight hundred years.'

We were, as Kate said, 'doing' William the Conqueror, and she was getting quite an interest in him since learning of the particular manner in which he had wooed his wife Matilda by beating her in the streets. Such incidents delighted Kate and I found myself stressing them whenever I found them, to stimulate her interest.

'He built a lot of places here,' she said. 'Castles and churches and things. And all those people in the graveyard . . . some of them must have been there for hundreds of years.'

'Trust you to think of that instead of the beautiful Norman arches and towers. The church is really interesting.'

'Let's go in,' she said.

We tied up the horses and did so. The hushed atmosphere subdued her a little. We studied the list of vicars which dated back a long way.

'There's a wonderful feeling of antiquity,' I said. 'I don't think you get that anywhere as much as you do in a church.'

'Perrivale's very old.'

'Yes, but there are people there. Modernity creeps in.'

'Let's go into the graveyard.'

We came out and were immediately among the tottering gravestones.

'I'll show you the Perrivale vault if you like.'

'Yes. I'd like to see it.'

We stood before it. It was ornate and imposing.

'I wonder how many are buried there,' said Kate.

'Quite a number, I suppose.'

'Cosmo will be there. I wonder if he comes out at night. I'll bet he does.'

'How your mind dwells on the macabre.'

'What's macabre?'

I explained.

'Well,' she said. 'That's what makes graveyards interesting. If they weren't full of dead people it would be just like anywhere else. It's the dead who are ghosts. You can't be one until you are dead. Come on. I want to show you something.'

'Another grave?'

She ran ahead and I followed her. She had come to a standstill before one of the graves. There was nothing ornate about this one – no engraved stone, no ornamental angels or cherubs, no fond message. Just a plain stone with the words 'Thomas Parry' and the date. A rough kerb had been put round it to separate it from the others and on it was a jam-jar containing a few sprigs of meadowsweet which looked as though they had been picked from the hedges.

'Who was he?' I asked. 'And why are you so interested in this grave?'

She said: 'He was the one who fell over the cliff and was drowned.'

'Oh . . . I remember. You did mention him.'

'They said he was drunk.'

'Well, I suppose he was. I wonder who put those flowers there. Someone must have thought of him. Someone must remember him.'

She did not speak.

'Who was he?' I asked. 'Did you ever know?'

'He didn't live here. He just came here and went over the cliff.'

'How foolish of him to get so drunk that he did such a thing.'

'Perhaps someone pushed him over.'

'But you say he was drunk . . .'

'Well, someone could. I reckon he walks by night. He gets out of his grave and walks about the graveyard talking about murder.'

I laughed at her. She turned to me and her face was serious.

Then she shrugged her shoulders and started to walk away. I followed her, turning once to look at the pathetic grave, uncared for but for a jam-jar filled with meadowsweet.

* * *

Dick Duvane rode over from Trecorn Manor. He had brought letters for me together with a note from Lucas.

He said he would wait for a reply.

The letters were from London – one from my father and the other from Aunt Maud.

I opened Lucas's note.

> Dear Rosetta,
>
> How are you getting on in the governess role? Aren't you tired of it yet? Say so and I will come over and fetch you. In any case, I must see you. Could we meet tomorrow afternoon? We could see each other at The Sailor King. Should we meet there or would it be all right for me to come to the house? I could bring a horse for you. I want to talk.
>
> Always devoted to your interests,
>
> Lucas

I remembered my interview with Lady Perrivale who had said I might be free to take time off when I wanted to. So I wrote a hasty note telling Lucas that I would meet him at The Sailor King the following afternoon at half past two.

Then I took the letters to my room to read them. They were both as I expected. My father's was rather stilted. He could not understand why I had thought it necessary to take a post. If I had wanted some work he could have found something congenial for me, perhaps at the Museum. He hoped that I would soon be home and we could talk about what I wanted to do.

I could not imagine myself explaining to my father. I was sorry for him. I guessed Aunt Maud had urged him to write in a disapproving manner.

There was no doubt of her feelings.

> My dear Rosetta,
>
> How could you? A governess! What are you thinking of? I know some poor females are *forced* into such a position but such is not the case with you. If you take my advice you will give up this nonsense without more ado. Do so quickly. People need never know . . . or if it came out it would be called a mad prank. Of course, the ideal thing would be a London season for you, but you know that is out of the question. But you are the daughter of a professor, a highly respected man in academic circles. You would have had your chances . . . but a governess! . . .

It went on in this strain for several pages through which I lightly skimmed. The reaction was so much what I had expected that it left me unmoved.

I was far more interested in my coming meeting with Lucas.

I told Kate the following afternoon that I was meeting a friend.

'Can I come?'

'Oh no.'

'Why not?'

'Because you are not invited.'

'What shall I do while you are gone?'

'You'll amuse yourself.'

'But I want to come.'

'Not this time?'

'Next time?'

'The future's not ours to see.'

'You are the most maddening governess.'

'Then I match my pupil.'

She laughed. We had indeed come a long way in the short time I had been here. There was a rapport between us which I would not have dreamed was possible.

She was resigned though disgruntled. She referred once to my desertion.

'I've shown you things,' she grumbled. 'I showed you Gramps and the grave.'

'Both suggested by you. I did not ask. Besides, people have a private side to their lives.'

'And this one you're meeting is in your private life?'

'As you have never met him . . . yes.'

'I will,' she said threateningly.

'You may . . . perhaps . . . one day.'

She would have liked to make a scene but she dared not. I knew that her life had changed since I had come and it was due to me. She looked upon me, in a way, as her protégée. She enjoyed being with me, which was why she was making such a fuss because I was leaving for a few hours; but there was a real fear, which I had managed to instil in her, that I might leave altogether; and that restrained her.

In my room that night I looked over the last days and thought how far I had come, though not, alas, in my main project. That had remained more or less static – but in my new life as governess to Kate Blanchard I had progressed amazingly. True, I had met people who had been close to the scene of the murder, and that gave me hopes of coming on some discovery. I needed time to talk to them, to get to know them, and I must do this in a natural manner . . . so that they did not guess my real motive.

I wished I could find out something about Mirabel's first husband, Mr Blanchard. What could he have been like? When had he died? How long was it after that when she came down to Cornwall with her father and her daughter? They could not have been very well off, for the cottage was quite a humble dwelling . . . at least in comparison with Perrivale Court and the Dower House.

Idle curiosity, perhaps. But not entirely. Mirabel was one of the chief actors in the drama, and it would be advantageous to know as much of her as possible.

Then I was thinking of Lucas, remembering with a certain tenderness his proposal. I felt a great longing to tell him why I was at Perrivale and I knew that when I was with him that longing would be intensified.

I sat at my window looking at those across the courtyard. I was trying to persuade myself that Lucas would be a help to me. What a relief it would be to share this with him. He cared for me . . . next to himself. I smiled, remembering his words.

If I made him swear not to betray Simon . . . was it possible?

I must not yet, I told myself. It was not my secret. Simon had told me because it had seemed possible that we might never get off the island and he had felt it necessary to confide in someone. Besides, there was a special relationship between us. I had been aware of that – as he had.

Suddenly my eyes were caught by a light in one of the windows opposite. It was faint . . . from a candle, I imagined. It flickered and then was gone.

I was startled. I was remembering a conversation I had had with Kate some days ago. We had been standing at my window and we had looked out across the courtyard.

'Whose rooms are those over there?' I had asked.

'The one next to the top floor, do you mean? Do you see something special there?'

'No. Should I?'

'I wondered if you'd seen Stepper's father's ghost.'

'Your preoccupation with ghosts is becoming quite a mania.'

'It's like that in big houses, especially when there's been a murder. That's Stepper's father's bedroom over there. Nobody goes in there much now.'

'Why not?'

'Well, because he died there. My mother says you have to show respect.'

'Respect?'

'Well, he died there.'

'Someone must go in to clean it.'

'I expect so. Anyway, no one goes there . . . except Stepper's mother's up there with Maria. They stay there most of the time.'

'Maria?'

'Her maid. I reckon it's haunted. Sir Edward died there.'

I thought it was just another instance of Kate's preoccupation and forgot about it. Yet when I saw the light a faint shiver ran down my spine.

I laughed at myself. Kate was affecting me with her obsession.

As she would have said, it was because there had been a murder connected with the house.

She was right. It was because of that murder that I was here.

* * *

Lucas was in The Sailor King waiting for me, and I felt extraordinarily happy to see him.

He stood up and took both my hands in his. We looked searchingly at each other for a few seconds, then he kissed my cheek.

'Governessing suits you,' he said. 'Well, sit down. How is it going? I've ordered cider. It's too early for tea, don't you think?'

I agreed.

'So they allow you a horse to ride, do they?'

I nodded. 'They are most gracious.'

'And the pupil?'

'I'm getting her tamed.'

'You do look proud of yourself.'

'Lucas, how are they at the Manor? The children . . . ?'

'Very hurt by your desertion.'

'Oh, not really.'

'Yes, really. They ask for you twenty times a day. When is she coming back? I'm going to ask the same question.'

'Not just yet, Lucas.'

'What satisfaction do you get out of it?'

'I can't explain, Lucas. I wish I could.'

I could feel confession trembling on my lips. But it is not your secret, I kept reminding myself.

'A governess! It's the last thing . . .'

'I have had letters from home.'

'Aunt Maud?'

I nodded. 'And my father.'

'Good old Aunt Maud!'

'Lucas . . . please understand.'

'I'm trying to.'

The cider was brought and for a few seconds we were silent. Then he said: 'You and I went through an extraordinary experience, Rosetta. It was bound to do something to us. Look at us. It has made you into a governess and me into a cripple.'

'Dear Lucas,' I said and, stretching my hand across the table, touched his. He held mine and smiled at me.

'It does me good to see you,' he said. 'If ever governessing becomes intolerable and you don't want to go back to Aunt

Maud . . . well, there is a haven waiting for you, as you know.'

'I don't forget it. It's a comfort. I am so fond of you, Lucas . . .'

'I am now waiting for the "but".'

'I wish . . .' I began.

'I wish too. But don't let's be maudlin about it. Tell me of this place. There seems to be something of a mystery hanging about it.'

'Well, of course. It is because of what happened.'

'There is something about an unsolved murder. It's so very unsatisfactory. There's always a question-mark. For all you know, you could be living in the same house as a killer.'

'That could be so.'

'You speak with some conviction. No. It was all so obvious. Didn't the man run away?'

'He might have had other reasons for doing so.'

'Well, it's not our affair. It is just that you are in this house. I don't like your being there. It's not only because of the murder. Do you see much of them?'

'I'm mostly with Kate.'

'The little horror.'

'Well . . . I'm finding her interesting. We're just finishing *Treasure Island*.'

'What bliss!'

I laughed. 'And we're going to start on *The Count of Monte Cristo*.'

'I cannot express my wonder.'

'Don't mock. If you knew Kate you'd realize what tremendous strides I've made. The child actually likes me, I believe.'

'What's so extraordinary about that? Others like you.'

'But they are not Kate. It's fascinating, Lucas. The whole place is fascinating. There seems to be something behind it all.'

'I believe you are harking back to the murder.'

'Well, there was a murder. I suppose when something violent happens it does something to people ... to places ...'

'Now I see what interests you. Tell me, what have you discovered?'

'Nothing ... or very little.'

'Do you see much of the fascinating Mirabel?'

'Occasionally.'

'And is she so fascinating?'

'She is very beautiful. We saw her, you remember, when the sheep held us up. You must admit that she is outstanding.'

'H'm.'

'I only see her in my capacity as governess. She has made it clear that she is very pleased with me. Apparently I am the only governess who has been able to make her daughter behave with some resemblance to a normal girl. It was quite easy really. From the first she knew that I did not *have* to come and I threatened to go if things became too difficult. It is amazing what strength there is in indifference.'

'I've always known that. That's why I pretend to be indifferent to circumstances.'

I leaned my elbows on the table and studied him.

'Yes, you have done that, Lucas. And all the time you are not as indifferent as you seem.'

'Hardly ever. For one thing, I'm not indifferent about this governessing. I feel very strongly about it. That's something I can't pretend about. Tell me more of them. They've behaved well to you, have they?'

'Impeccably. I can have time off when I want and, you see, a horse to ride. A special one has been chosen for me – a chestnut mare. Her name is Goldie.' I laughed. I felt so happy that he had asked me to meet him.

'Sounds cosy,' he said.

'It is. She wants me to know that they don't regard me as an ordinary governess. Professor's daughter and all that. It reminds me of when Felicity came to our house. It's very like that.'

'Only she had an easier ride.'

'Dear Felicity. We were friends from the start.'

'Have you told her of your foolish exploits?'

'Not yet. I've been there such a short time really. I'm going to write to her. I wanted to work myself in first. I was telling you about Mirabel, young Lady Perrivale. There is an older one, you know. I'm inclined to think of her as Mirabel because that was what they called her in the papers. She is gracious and so is Sir Tristan.'

'So you have made his acquaintance?'

'Only briefly, but it was he who suggested the mount for me. And I may be invited to join the occasional dinner party.'

'A perquisite for a good governess . . . when it is a not very important occasion and someone is wanted to make up the numbers?'

'I think there might be one important occasion. They are thinking of asking you and Carleton. They have put it off because of Theresa's death.'

I saw the interest in his eyes. 'So you and I will be fellow guests?'

'You will come when they ask, won't you, Lucas?'

'I most certainly shall.'

'Is Carleton any better?'

He lifted his shoulders. 'I don't think he'll ever get over it. We're a faithful lot, we Lorimers.'

'Poor Carleton. I grieve for him.'

'I feel guilty. I used to envy him, even saying to myself: Why should everything go right for him? Why should this happen to me while he sails happily through? And now he is in a worse condition than I. I've got a useless leg and he has lost the one who was more important to him than anyone else. I wish I could do something for him, but I don't know what.'

'Perhaps he'll marry again.'

'It would be the best thing for him. He needs a wife. He's lost without Theresa. But of course that would be in the future . . . far in the future. Trecorn is not a very happy household at the moment. If you came back it would relieve the gloom.'

I said: 'The children . . . they are happy?'

'They are too young to grieve for long. I think they still ask for their mother and cry for her . . . and then they forget. Good old Nanny Crockett is wonderful with them, but I don't forgive her for bringing all this about. Whatever possessed her to set it in motion?'

He was looking at me closely and I felt myself flushing. 'There must be a reason,' he went on.

I was telling myself: Explain, you owe it to him.

But I could not. It was not my secret to divulge.

After a while he said: 'I think I understand. We shall never be as we were before, shall we? Sometimes I look back to the first time we met. How different we were then . . . both of us. Can you remember me as I was?'

'Yes, perfectly.'

'And was I very different?'

'Yes,' I said.

'You were different, too. You were at school . . . very young . . . eager . . . innocent. And then on the ship together . . . how we used to sit on the deck and talk. Remember Madeira? We were so unaware of the monstrous thing that was about to happen to us.'

As he was talking I was living it all again.

He said: 'I'm sorry. I shouldn't have reminded you. If we had any sense we'd do our best to forget.'

'We can't forget, Lucas. We can't ever forget.'

'We could . . . if we made up our minds. We could start

a new life together. Do you remember when we talked of our initials? I said it was significant that Life had brought us together, little knowing then what we were to endure. How close we have become since then. I said my initials spelt HELL . . . Hadrian Edward Lucas Lorimer, and as RC you could bring me back to the path of righteousness. Do you remember?'

'Yes, I do, very well.'

'Well, it's true. You could save me. You see, it has come to pass. I was speaking prophetically. You and I . . . we could face everything together . . . we could make life better than it was before . . .'

'Oh, Lucas . . . I wish . . .'

'We could go right away from here. Anywhere we fancied . . .'

'You couldn't leave Trecorn, Lucas. Carleton needs you there.'

'Well, would it matter where we were? We could help him together.'

'Oh, Lucas . . . I am so sorry. I truly wish . . .'

He smiled at me ruefully. 'I understand,' he said. 'Well, let's make the best of what is. Whatever happens, what we went through together will always make us special friends. I often think of that man Player. I wonder what happened to him. I should like to know, wouldn't you?'

I nodded, afraid to speak.

He went on: 'I understand why you did this, Rosetta. It's because you want to move away from all that went before. You're right in a way. So you have gone to that place. It's entirely new . . . new surroundings, new work . . . a challenge. Particularly the girl. You have changed, Rosetta. I have to say I think she is helping you.'

'Yes, I am sure she is.'

'It's brave of you to have done this. I think I'm something of a coward.'

'Oh no, no. You suffered more than I did. And you brought about your own freedom.'

'Only because I was a useless hulk.'

'You're not useless. I love you very much. I admire you, and I am so grateful because you are my friend.'

He took my hand and held it firmly. 'Will you always remember that?'

'Always,' I said. 'I'm so glad to have seen you. I feel so safe . . . to know that you are nearby.'

'I shall always be there,' he said. 'And perhaps one day you will call me in. Now . . . let's get out of this place. Come. Show me your Goldie. Let's ride out to the sea and gallop along the beach. Let's tell ourselves that our good angels are smiling on us and all our wishes will be granted. There is a nice sentimental speech for an old cynic, is it not?'

'Yes, and I like to hear it.'

'After all, who knows what will be waiting for us?'

'One can never tell.'

And we went out to the horses.

* * *

Mrs Ford caught me as I was going to the schoolroom for the morning lessons.

'Nanny Crockett is coming over this afternoon,' she said. 'Jack Carter is taking a load to Turner's Farm, so he'll be bringing her over for a couple of hours. She'll want to see you, so do come up to my room for a cup of tea.'

I said I should be delighted to do so.

As we were talking, there was a commotion in the hall. I heard the voice of the head gardener; he was saying something about roses.

Mrs Ford raised her eyebrows. 'That man,' she said. 'You'd think the whole world depended on his flowers. He's making such a noise down there. I'd better go and see what it's all about.'

Out of curiosity, I followed her.

Several of the servants were in the hall. Littleton, the head gardener, was clearly very angry.

Mrs Ford said in a commanding voice: 'Now what is all this about?'

'You may well ask, Mrs Ford,' said Littleton. 'Four of my best roses . . . in their prime . . . someone has stolen them . . . right from under my nose.'

'Well, who's done it?'

'That's what I'd like to know. If I could get my hands on them.'

'Her ladyship may have fancied them.'

'Her ladyship never touches the flowers. I've looked after those roses. I've been waiting all this time to see them in bloom. Beautiful, they was. A sort of pinky blue . . . a rare colour for a rose. Never seen anything like them before. They was special, they was . . . and I've been waiting all this time for the flowers. Took a bit of rearing they did . . . and then someone comes and picks them . . . without a by your leave.'

'Well, Mr Littleton,' said Mrs Ford, 'I'm sorry, but I've not touched your roses . . . and if you can find who has that's up to you, but I can't have you disturbing my servants. They've got work to do.'

Littleton turned his agonized face to Mrs Ford. 'They were my special roses,' he said piteously.

I left them and went up to the schoolroom.

It was difficult to settle to lessons that morning. Kate wanted to hear about my meeting with Lucas on the previous day.

'I was staying with his family, you know,' I told her. 'So he thought he'd come over to see me.'

'Did he ask you to leave here?'

I hesitated.

'He did,' she said. 'And you told him you would.'

'I did not. I told him we were reading *Treasure Island*

and that you and I get along moderately well. That's right, isn't it?'

She nodded.

'Well, now let's see if we can master these sums and if we can we'll have an extra fifteen minutes' reading. Then I believe we could finish the book today.'

'All right,' she said.

'Get out the slate and we'll start right away.'

Simon was very much in my thoughts that morning. The meeting with Lucas had been unsettling, and the prospect of seeing Nanny Crockett had brought back memories more vividly than usual.

When I reached Mrs Ford's room Nanny Crockett had not yet arrived but she had a visitor. It was the rector, the Reverend Arthur James. Mrs Ford was evidently a great church worker and he had come to consult her about the flower decoration for the church.

She introduced me.

'Welcome to Perrivale, Miss Cranleigh,' he said. 'I have been hearing from Mrs Ford how well you are managing with Kate.'

'Mrs Ford has been very kind to me,' I said.

'Mrs Ford is kind to everyone. We have good reason to know that. My wife and I often ask each other what we would do without her. It is the decorations, you know. We rely so much on Perrivale for so many things. The big house, you see . . . garden fêtes and so on. It has been the same through generations. Sir Edward took a great interest in the church.'

'Oh yes, he was a real churchman,' said Mrs Ford. 'He'd be at church twice every Sunday . . . and so were the rest of the family too. Then we had prayers every day in the hall. Yes, he was a real one for the church, was Sir Edward.'

'Sadly missed,' added the rector. 'We don't have many like him nowadays. The younger generation haven't the same commitment. I hope to see you there with your charge, Miss Cranleigh.'

'Yes,' I said. 'Of course.'

'Miss Kate is a bit of a handful,' said Mrs Ford, 'but Miss Cranleigh is working wonders. Her ladyship is very pleased. It was my idea that she should come, Rector. Nanny Crockett and I worked it out between us. Her ladyship can't thank me enough.'

'Very gratifying.'

'This is the list,' said Mrs Ford. 'Mrs Terris always likes to do the altar. So I've put her there. And the windowsills I thought could go to Miss Cherry and her sister . . . on one side of the church, that is, and on the other, Miss Jenkins and Mrs Purvis. I thought if I added the flowers they're to use there'd be no squabbling.'

He had taken out his spectacles and was studying the list.

'Excellent . . . excellent . . . I knew I could trust you, Mrs Ford, to make the arrangements amicably.'

They exchanged mischievous glances which implied that trouble could ensue, but for Mrs Ford's skilful handling of the affair.

In due course the rector rose to go. He shook hands and repeated his hope that he would see Kate and me in church on Sunday, and departed.

Not long after he had left Nanny Crockett arrived. She was delighted to see me and Mrs Ford looked on benignly while we greeted each other.

'My word,' said Nanny Crockett, 'you do look well. And what's this I hear about you and Miss Kate getting on like a house on fire?'

'The change in Miss Kate is really remarkable,' said Mrs Ford. 'Sir Tristan and my lady are very pleased.'

'Miss Cranleigh has a way with children,' said Nanny Crockett. 'Some of us have it, some of us don't. I saw it right from the start with my two.'

'How are the twins?' I asked.

'Poor little mites. To lose a mother . . . well, that's not something it's easy to get over. Though they're young . . . I'm thankful for that. If they'd have been a year or two older they'd have understood more what was going on. Now they think she's gone to Heaven and that to them might be like going off to Plymouth. They think she's coming back. They keep asking when. It breaks your heart. They ask after you, too. You must come over and see them some time. They'd like that. Of course, there'd be tears when you left, most likely. Well, I do what I can.'

'And how is Mr Carleton, Nanny?'

She shook her head. 'Sometimes I think he'll never get over it. Poor man. He goes about in a sort of dream. Mr Lucas . . . well, you never know with him. He broods a lot, I think. It's a sad household. I try to make it as merry as I can in the nursery.'

She was looking at me intently, hoping of course to get a word with me so that I could report progress. What progress? I wondered. When I considered it I had not come very far, and apart from the fact that I was being moderately successful with Kate, my little exercise was really quite fruitless.

We chattered about things in general . . . the weather, the state of the crops, little bits of gossip about the neighbourhood.

Mrs Ford did leave us together for about half an hour. She said she had to go to the kitchen. Something she had to attend to regarding the evening meal. She wanted a word with Cook and it really couldn't wait.

'You two can look after each other while I'm gone,' she said.

As soon as we were alone Nanny Crockett burst out: 'Have you found anything?'

I shook my head. 'Sometimes I wonder whether I ever shall. I don't know where the key to the mystery lies.'

'Something will turn up. I feel it in my bones. If it doesn't, my poor boy will spend the rest of his life abroad . . . wandering about. That can't be.'

'But Nanny . . . even if we discovered the truth and he was cleared, we shouldn't be able to get in touch with him easily.'

'It would be in the papers, wouldn't it?'

'But if he's abroad . . . he wouldn't see them.'

'We'd find a way. First we've got to prove him innocent.'

'I often wonder where to begin.'

'I think *she* had something to do with it.'

'Do you mean Lady Perrivale?'

She nodded.

'Why should she?'

'That's what you've got to find out. And him too . . . he came into everything, didn't he? That would be the motive. You have to have a motive.'

'We've gone into all that before.'

'You're not giving up, are you?'

'No . . . no. But I do wish I could make some progress.'

'Well, you're in the best place to do it. If there's anything I can do . . . at any time . . .'

'You are a good ally, Nanny.'

'Well, we're not far apart. I expect you'll be coming over to Trecorn sometimes and I can get Jack Carter to bring me here now and then. So we're in touch. I can't tell you what I'd give to see my boy again.'

'I know.'

Mrs Ford came back.

'I do believe this place would go to rack and ruin without me. If I've told Cook once I've told her twenty times that her ladyship can't abide garlic. She wanted to put some in the stew. She was with a French family for a few months and it's given her ideas. You have to keep your eye on them. I stopped her just in time. You two had a nice cosy chat?'

'I was saying that if I can get Jack Carter to bring me I'll come over again soon.'

'Any time. You're welcome. You know that. Oh look, Rector's left his spectacles behind. That man would forget his head if it wasn't fixed on his shoulders. He'll be lost without them. I'll have to get them over to him.'

'I'll take them,' I said. 'I'd like a little walk.'

'Oh, will you? I wonder if he's missed them yet. If he hasn't, he soon will.'

I took the spectacles and Nanny Crockett said she must be going. Jack Carter would be here at any minute and he didn't like to be kept waiting.

'Then you'd better go down,' said Mrs Ford. 'Well, goodbye, Nanny, and don't forget, any time . . . and there'll be a cup of my best Darjeeling for you.'

I went with Nanny Crockett to the gate and we had not been there more than a few minutes when Jack Carter drove up. Nanny Crockett climbed up beside him and I waved as the cart trundled off.

Then I made my way to the church. The Reverend Arthur James was delighted to receive his spectacles, and I made the acquaintance of his wife, who said with mock severity that he was always losing them and this would be a lesson to him.

I was invited in but I said I had to get back as Kate would be waiting for me. I came out of the rectory and found myself walking through the churchyard. It is strange the fascination such places have. I could not resist pausing to read some of the inscriptions on the gravestones. They were of people who had lived a hundred years ago. I wondered about their lives. There was the Perrivale vault. Cosmo was buried there. If only he could speak and tell us what really happened.

My eye was caught by the sight of a jam-jar, for in it were four exquisite roses – pink roses with a blueish tinge about them.

I could not believe my eyes. I went close to look. There was the cheap headstone, inconspicuous among the splendour of the other graves; and I knew that those were the very roses the loss of which Littleton the gardener had been mourning this very day.

For some moments I stood staring at them.

Who had put them there? I thought of the meadowsweet, obviously picked from the hedges. But these roses . . .

Who had taken the roses from the Perrivale garden to put in a jam-jar on the grave of an unknown man?

Why had Kate shown me the grave?

I walked thoughtfully back to Perrivale Court. The more I thought of it, the more likely it seemed that Kate was the one who had taken the roses and put them on the grave.

She was waiting for me when I returned and I had not been in my room for more than a few minutes when she came in.

She sat on the bed and looked at me accusingly. 'You've been out again,' she said. 'Yesterday you went to see that man and today you were with Mrs Ford and when I went up there you'd gone again.'

'The rector left his glasses behind and I took them back to him.'

'Silly old man. He's always losing something.'

'Some people are a little absent-minded. They often have more important things to think about. Did you hear all the commotion this morning about the roses?'

'What roses?' She was alert and I knew instinctively that I was on the right track.

'There were some special ones. Littleton had taken great care with them and was very proud of them. Someone took them. He was furious. Well, I know where they are.'

She looked at me cautiously.

I went on: 'They are in the graveyard on the grave of the man who was drowned. Do you remember? You showed me his grave. There was some meadowsweet in the jam-jar then. Now there are Littleton's prize roses.'

'I could see you thought the meadowsweet was awful.'

'What do you mean?'

'Well, wild flowers. People usually put roses and lilies and that sort of thing on people's graves.'

'Kate,' I said, 'you took the roses. You put them on that grave.'

She was silent. Why? I wondered.

'Didn't you?' I persisted.

'All the others have things on them . . . statues and things. What are a few flowers?'

'Why did you do it, Kate?'

She wriggled. 'Let's read,' she said.

'I couldn't settle down to reading with this hanging over us,' I said.

'Hanging over us! What do you mean?' She was bellicose, a sign of being on the defensive with her.

'Tell me truthfully why you put the flowers on that grave, Kate.'

'Because he didn't have any. What are a few old roses? Besides, they're not Littleton's. They're Stepper's or my mother's. *They* didn't say anything. They wouldn't know whether they were in the garden or on the grave.'

'Why did you feel this about this man?'

'He hadn't got anything.'

'It's the first time I've realized you have a soft heart. It's not like you, Kate.'

'Well,' she said, tossing her head, 'I wanted to.'

'So you cut the flowers and took them to the grave?'

'Yes. I threw the wild flowers away and got some fresh water from the pump . . .'

'I understand all that. But why did you do it for this man? Did you . . . know him?'

She nodded and suddenly looked rather frightened and forlorn – quite unlike herself. I sensed that she was bewildered and in need of comfort. I went to her and put my arm round her and, rather to my surprise, she did not resist.

'You know we are good friends, don't you, Kate?' I said. 'You could tell me.'

'I haven't told anybody. I don't think they'd want me to.'

'Who? Your mother?'

'And Gramps.'

'Who was this man, Kate?'

'I thought he might be . . . my father.'

I was astounded and for the moment speechless. The drunken sailor . . . her father!

'I see,' I said at length. 'That makes a difference.'

'People put flowers on their fathers' graves,' she said. 'Nobody else did. So . . . I did.'

'It was a nice thought. No one could blame you for that. Tell me about your father.'

'I didn't like him,' she said. 'I didn't see much of him. We lived in a house in a horrid street near a horrid market. We were frightened of him. We were upstairs. There were people living downstairs. There were three rooms with a wooden staircase down the back into the garden. It wasn't like this. It wasn't even like Seashell Cottage. It was . . . horrible.'

'And you were there with your mother and your father?'

I was trying to picture the glorious Mirabel in the sort of place Kate's brief description had conjured up. It was not easy.

'He didn't come home much. He went to sea. When he came back . . . it was awful. He was always drunk . . . and we used to hate it. He'd stay for a while . . . then he'd go back to sea.'

'And did you leave that place then?'

She nodded. 'Gramps came and we went away . . . with him. That's when we came to Seashell Cottage . . . and everything was different then.'

'But the man in the grave is Tom Parry. You are Kate Blanchard.'

'I don't know about names. All I know is that he was my father. He was a sailor and he used to come home with a white bag on his shoulder . . . and my mother hated him. And when Gramps came it was all different. The sailor . . . my father . . . wasn't there any more. He was only there for little whiles anyway. He was always going away. Then we got on a train with Gramps and he took us to Seashell Cottage.'

'How old were you then, Kate?'

'I don't remember . . . about three or four perhaps. It's a long time ago. I only remember little bits. Sitting in the train . . . sitting on Gramps's knee while he showed me cows and sheep in the fields. I was very happy then. I knew that Gramps was taking us away and we wouldn't have to see my father any more.'

'And yet you put flowers on his grave.'

'It was because I thought he was my father.'

'You're not sure.'

'I am . . . and then I'm not. I don't know. But he might have been my father. I hated him and he was dead . . . but if he was my father I ought to put flowers on his grave.'

'And so he came back here?'

She was silent for a moment. Then she said: 'I saw him. I was frightened.'

'Where did you see him.'

'I saw him in Upbridge. Sometimes I used to play with Lily Drake and she'd come over to Seashell Cottage and play with me. Gramps used to think of lovely things for us to do. Lily liked coming to us and I liked going to her. Mrs Drake used to take us into the town when she went shopping . . . and that was when I saw him.'

'How could you be sure?'

She looked at me scornfully. 'I knew him, didn't I? He

walked in a funny way. It was as though he were drunk . . . though he wasn't always. I suppose he was drunk so much that he forgot how to walk straight. I was there with Mrs Drake and Lily by the stall. It was full of shiny red apples and pears. And I saw him. He didn't see me. I hid behind Mrs Drake. She's very big, with a lot of petticoats. I could hide myself right in them. I heard him speak too. He went up to one of the stall-holders and asked if she knew a red-haired woman with a little girl. Her name was Mrs Parry. I heard the man at the stall say he knew of no such person. And I thought it was all right because my mother was not Mrs Parry; she was Mrs Blanchard. But I thought he was my father . . .'

'Did you tell your mother what you'd seen?'

She shook her head. 'I told Gramps, though.'

'What did he say?'

'He said I couldn't have. My father was dead. He'd been drowned at sea. The man I had seen was someone who looked like him.'

'Did you believe him?'

'Yes, of course.'

'But you said you thought this man was your father.'

'Not all the time I don't. Sometimes I do . . . sometimes I don't. Then I thought if he was my father he ought to have flowers.'

I held her very close to me and she seemed glad that I did.

'Oh Kate,' I said. 'I'm glad you told me.'

'So am I,' she said. 'We had a truce, didn't we?'

'Yes,' I said. 'But the truce is over. We don't need it now. We're friends. Tell me what happened.'

'Well . . . then the man I'd seen was drowned. He fell over the cliff when he was drunk. That was the sort of thing my father . . . he . . . would have done . . . so this man was very like him. It was very easy to make a mistake.'

'His name was Parry. What was your name when you were living in that place . . . before your grandfather came?'

'I don't remember. Oh, yes, I do . . . it was Blanchard . . . I think.'

'Do you think it might have been something else?'

She shook her head vigorously. 'No. Gramps said I was always Kate Blanchard and that was my father's name and it wasn't my father I had seen in Upbridge. It was another man who looked like him. He was a sailor too. Sailors look alike. All those sailors in *Treasure Island* looked different, didn't they? But they were special ones. Oh, Cranny, I shouldn't have told you really.'

'It was good to tell me. Now we understand so much about each other. We've found out that we are real friends. We're going to help each other all we can. Tell me what happened when the man was found on the rocks.'

'Well, he was just found. They said he was a sailor and he didn't live here. He came from London. He'd been asking for someone . . . some relation. That was what they said in the papers.'

'And you'd told your grandfather that you thought he was your father.'

'Gramps said it wasn't my father and I had to stop thinking he was. My father was dead and I didn't belong to that place where we used to live any more. My home was with him and my mother in our nice Seashell Cottage by the sea.'

'There was quite a fuss when the man's body was found, wasn't there? Where did they find it?'

'On the rocks at the bottom of the cliff. The tide might have carried him out to sea, they said, but it didn't.'

'What will you do now, Kate? Shall you go on putting flowers on his grave?'

I saw a stubborn look on her face.

'Yes,' she said. 'I don't care about Littleton's old roses.'

She laughed and for a moment was her mischievous self. 'I'll take some more if I want to. They're not his. They're old Stepper's really . . . and my mother's because she married Stepper and what is his is hers.'

I thought: In her heart she believes the man in that grave is her father; and I was becoming more and more sure that I had made an important discovery.

Some Discoveries

My thoughts were preoccupied with what I had learned from Kate and I had a conviction that it must have some bearing on the mystery I was trying to solve.

I had made up my mind that the drunken sailor was Mirabel's first husband and since she had been contemplating becoming the mistress of Perrivale Court, it was imperative to her that he should not find her.

A husband would ruin all her chances. And then he had conveniently been found at the bottom of a cliff. She would be the one who wanted to be rid of him. What if she had wanted to be rid of Cosmo as well? Why? She was to have married him. But she married Tristan immediately afterwards.

Of course, the man who had died might have nothing to do with Mirabel. There was only Kate's evidence to suggest this. I knew how imaginative she could be. She had been very young when she had last seen her father and this man who looked like him. She mentioned the way he walked as one of the reasons why she recognized him. Many sailors had that rolling gait. It was acquired through constantly adjusting their balance on an unsteady ship.

It was all very vague and I did not know what to believe, but on the other hand I felt I had taken a little step forward, if only a short one.

The very next day Lady Perrivale sent for me. She was very affable. She looked so feminine that it was impossible to imagine her luring her first husband to the cliff edge and pushing him over. That was too wild a conjecture. I felt sure that the man was a stranger. Thomas Parry. How could he be the husband of Mirabel Blanchard? It was possible that she could have changed her name. And so ran my muddled thoughts.

'I believe you met your friend Mr Lorimer the other day,' she said.

'Oh yes.'

'Kate told me. She missed you very much.' She smiled at me benignly. 'There is no need for you to have to meet in The Sailor King, you know. He would be very welcome to come here to see you. I don't want you to feel you can't have visitors.'

'That is most kind of you.'

'As a matter of fact, I was thinking of asking him and his brother over to dine soon.'

'I think his brother is too shocked at the moment to want to pay visits. It has been such a terrible blow to him.'

'Oh yes, indeed. However, I shall invite them both and perhaps Mr Lucas Lorimer will accept.'

'I feel sure he will be happy to do so.'

'You will join us, of course. There won't be many guests. It will be just an informal occasion.'

'It sounds very pleasant.'

'I am sending a note over to Trecorn Manor today. I do hope they will accept.'

I had an idea that she was arranging the party to show me that, although I was the governess, she did not regard me as such. I remembered so well, when Felicity came to us, that my parents had been anxious that she should not be treated like a servant because she had come to us through the recommendation of a man who could have been one of my father's colleagues—but then ours was not a conventional household.

I was pleased that Lady Perrivale should have been so sensitive of my feelings; but all the time she was talking to me I was seeing her in three sordid little rooms, escaping from them when Thomas Parry went to sea. I imagined his coming back and finding her and his little daughter flown from the nest . . . and setting out to look for them.

I wanted so much to talk to Lucas. How I wished that I could tell him all I knew. Perhaps I should. If Thomas Parry had been murdered by someone who was living in the neighbourhood today, why should that person not have treated Cosmo in the same way? And what could Simon have to do with Thomas Parry? I needed advice. I needed help. And Lucas was near.

I longed to see him and I was so anxious that he should accept this invitation to dinner that when I saw the messenger leave with the note for Trecorn Manor I hung about waiting for his return. I managed to be in the courtyard when he came back.

'Oh hello, Morris,' I said. 'Have you been over to Trecorn Manor?'

'Yes, Miss. No luck, though. They were out – both Mr Carleton and Mr Lucas Lorimer.'

'So you couldn't deliver your note to them?'

'No. I had to leave it. Someone will bring the answer over later. A pity. Makes two journeys instead of one.'

It was the next day when the answer came. I went down because I thought Dick Duvane would bring it, but it was not Dick. It was one of the Trecorn stable men.

'Oh,' I said. 'I thought Dick Duvane would come. He usually does these things for Mr Lucas.'

'Oh, Dick's not there now, Miss.'

'Not there?'

'He's gone abroad.'

'Without Mr Lucas!'

'Seemingly. Mr Lucas, he be at the Manor and Dick Duvane, he be gone. I did hear to foreign parts.'

'Mr Lucas will miss him.'

'Aye, that he will.'

'Shall I take the note to Lady Perrivale?'

'If you'd be so good, Miss.'

I took it to her.

She said: 'Mr Carleton declines. He doesn't feel up to it. Poor man. But Mr Lucas accepts with pleasure.'

That was what I wanted to know. I was puzzled about Dick Duvane though, for I knew that he and Lucas had been together for so long. However, I suppose they parted company sometimes. For instance, Dick hadn't been on the ship with Lucas.

The dinner party was to take place at the end of that week. I was glad there was not long to wait before I saw Lucas again.

Kate had been a little withdrawn after her confession. I think she must have been wondering whether she had told me too much. We got through our lessons with moderate ease, but even *The Count of Monte Cristo* did not entirely hold her attention.

She was not very interested in the dinner party because she was not to attend. If I were doing something she liked to share in it. She may have regretted her confession, but in a way it had made ours a more intimate relationship.

The evening of the dinner party arrived. I dressed carefully in a gown of lapis lazuli blue which had streaks of gold in it so that it really did resemble the stone. It was one of the dresses I had brought with me when I had visited Felicity. Aunt Maud had said there would certainly be dinner parties and I should have something becoming to wear.

I dressed my yellow hair high on my head and I noticed with pleasure that the colour of my dress made my eyes look more blue. I think I could say I was looking my best.

Kate came in to see me before I went down.

'You look quite pretty,' she said.

'Thank you for the compliment.'

'It's true. Is that a compliment if it's true?'

'Yes, it is. It's flattery that can be false.'

'You sound just like a governess.'

'Well, I am a governess.'

She sat on the bed and laughed at me.

'It will be a boring old party,' she said. 'I don't know why you think it's going to be such fun. Is it because that old Lucas is going to be there?'

'He's not exactly old.'

'Oh, he is. He's ever so old. You're old and he's older than you.'

'You think that because you are young. It is a matter of comparisons.'

'Well, he's old and he can't walk straight either.'

'How do you know?'

'One of the maids told me. He was nearly drowned and it almost killed him.'

'Yes, she's right. I was nearly drowned too.'

'But you're all right. He's not.' I was silent and she went on: 'The old Rev is going to be there with his awful wife . . . and the doctor . . . all the most boring people you can think of.'

'They may be boring to you but not to me. I'm looking forward to it.'

'That's why your eyes sparkle and look bluer. Tell me about it after.'

'I will.'

'Promise . . . everything.'

'I'll tell you all I think you should know.'

'I want to know *everything*.'

'All that is good for you.'

She put out her tongue at me. 'Governess,' she said.

'Not the most pleasant part of your anatomy,' I said.

'What's that?'

'Work it out for yourself. Now I'm going down.'

She grimaced. 'All right. Don't let that Lucas persuade you to go back.'

'I won't.'

'Promise.'

'I promise that.'

She smiled. 'I'll tell you something. Gramps will be there, so it won't be so boring after all.'

The guests were already assembling. I went down and very soon we went in to dinner. I found myself sitting next to Lucas.

'What a pleasure!' he said.

'I am so glad you came.'

'I told you I would.'

'What happened to Dick Duvane? I hear he has gone away.'

'It's not permanent. He's just gone away for a spell.'

'I'm surprised. I thought he was your good and faithful servant.'

'I've never looked upon him as an ordinary servant, nor has he regarded himself as such, I believe.'

'That's why I'm so surprised he's gone.'

'Dick and I used to travel a lot together. We had an adventurous time. Now I'm stuck at home . . . can't get about as I used to. Poor Dick, he gets restive. He's gone off on his own . . . just for a spell.'

'I thought he was so devoted to you.'

'He is . . . and I to him. But because I'm afflicted and restricted, there's no reason why he should be. How are you getting along here . . . really? I suppose we can't discuss it here . . . right in the middle of the family. You must be getting to know them well.'

'Not all. It is the first time I've seen the Dowager Lady Perrivale.'

He looked along the table to where she sat. She looked rather formidable. It was indeed the first time I had seen her. She had had to be helped downstairs and I gathered that she spent most of her time in her own room. The Major was sitting beside her, carrying on an animated conversation with her which she seemed to enjoy. Tristan at the other end of the table was talking to the doctor's wife.

Lucas was right: we could not speak of the family at their dinner table.

Conversation was general, embracing the Queen and her advancing years, the merits of Gladstone and Salisbury and such-like.

I was not paying a great deal of attention. I so much wanted to be alone with Lucas. There was a great deal to say. I was longing to ask him what he thought about the drunken sailor.

I really believed then that, had it been possible to talk intimately with Lucas, I would have told him everything at that point.

With the ladies I left the men over the port and went into the drawing-room. To my surprise I found myself seated next to the Dowager Lady Perrivale. I thought perhaps it might have been arranged and she wanted to inspect Kate's governess.

She was one of those women who must have been formidable in her prime. I could see from her face that she was accustomed to having her own way. I remembered what I had heard of her; how she had restored Perrivale Court when she brought her money into the family, and I imagined she had a certain fondness for the place.

'I'm glad to have the opportunity of a chat, Miss Cranleigh,' she said. 'My daughter-in-law tells me that you are doing very well with Kate. My goodness, that is an achievement. The governesses that child has had! And not one to stay more than a month or two.'

'I haven't completed a month yet, Lady Perrivale.'

'I do hope you will . . . and many months. My daughter-in-law is so happy with the outcome. She said Kate is a different child.'

'Kate needs to be understood.'

'I suppose we all do, Miss Cranleigh.'

'Some of us are less predictable than others.'

'I expect you are very predictable, Miss Cranleigh. I am most unpredictable. This is what they call one of my good days. I shouldn't be down here if it were not. You look to me as if you have a very orderly mind.'

'I try to have.'

'Then if you try, you will. I have given up trying. Though I used to be the same. I could never endure mess and muddle. One grows old, Miss Cranleigh. Things change. How do you like Perrivale Court?'

'I think it is one of the most interesting houses I have ever been in.'

'Then we agree. I was fascinated by it from the moment I saw it. I am so pleased Tristan is married and settled. I hope there will be grandchildren . . . soon enough for me to see them before I go. I should like several.'

'I hope your wishes will be granted.'

'I want this place to pass to my grandchildren . . . children of the Arkwright blood mingling with the Perrivale . . . you know what I mean. Arkwright money made it what it is today . . . so it is only right. It would be just the right mixture, you see . . .'

I thought this was an odd conversation. I noticed that her eyes were slightly glazed and I wondered whether she had forgotten to whom she was talking. I saw Mirabel cast an anxious look in her direction.

The Dowager Lady Perrivale noticed Mirabel's glance. She waved her hand and smiled.

'Don't you think she is delightful, Miss Cranleigh? My daughter-in-law, I mean. Did you ever see anyone so beautiful?'

'No,' I said. 'I don't think I have.'

'I knew her mother and her father . . . the dear Major. It is so nice to have him as a neighbour. Her mother was my best friend. We went to school together. That was why the Major came down here after her death . . . when he left the Army, of course. I said, "Come and settle in Cornwall." I'm thankful that he did. It brought dear Mirabel into the family.'

'She lost her first husband,' I said tentatively.

'Poor Mirabel. It's sad to be left a widow with a child to care for. Of course she had her wonderful, wonderful father . . . and he came out of the Army just at the right time. He has been a tower of strength to us all. Such a delightful man. Have you met him . . . I mean apart from tonight?'

'Yes. Kate took me to see him at the Dower House.'

'She would. She adores him. He's so good with children. Well . . . he's good with anyone. He's devoted to Mirabel. He was delighted with the marriage . . . so was I. It was just what I wanted. And it means the Major is here with us . . . a charming neighbour . . . and a member of the family really.'

'He has a lovely home there at the Dower House.'

'He seems to like it. I'd like to go along and see him there . . . but I can't get out now . . .'

'What a pity.'

'Yes . . . indeed. But I have a good woman. She has been my maid for years. She's my constant companion. I'm in the rooms next to those used by my husband when he was alive. It's almost a separate part of the house. My husband was a man who liked to be alone. He was very religious, you know. I always said he should have gone into the Church. Well, it has been nice to chat. You must come along and see me. Maria – that's my maid – will be pleased to see you. In fact she keeps me informed.'

'I don't think I've met Maria.'

'No, you wouldn't. She's mostly in my part of the house.'

'I think my room must be opposite yours.'

'You're up in the nursery. Yes, that would be about it . . . across the courtyard. Oh look, the men are coming back. They'll split us up now. I have enjoyed getting to know you. And thank you for what you're doing with Kate. That child did know how to make a nuisance of herself. My daughter-in-law tells me she is greatly relieved.'

'I really don't deserve all these compliments.'

Mirabel was coming towards us. She smiled at me. 'Miss Cranleigh must come and talk to her friend,' she said to the old lady.

Then she drew me to one side. 'I hope my mother-in-law didn't confuse you. She rambles on a bit. Since the tragedy she's been a little strange. It's rarely that she comes to things like this. But she seemed a great deal better and wanted to meet you. She's not always lucid . . . and talks wildly quite often.'

'No, no,' I said. 'She talked normally.'

'Oh, I'm glad. Oh, here's Mr Lorimer.'

Lucas was coming towards us. There was someone with him and the evening was almost over before I found myself alone with him.

'Oh, it's such a shame. I did want to say so much to you.'

'You're making me very curious.'

'But not here, Lucas.'

'Well then, we'd better meet. What about tomorrow at The Sailor King?'

'I'll manage to get there.'

'Two-thirty as before?'

'That's a good time.'

'I'll look forward to it,' said Lucas.

The evening was over. Kate came to my room as I was getting undressed.

'What was it like?' she asked.

'Interesting. I had a long chat with the Dowager Lady Perrivale.'

'You mean Stepper's mother. She's an old witch.'

'Really, Kate!'

'Well, a bit mad anyway. She stays in those rooms where Sir Edward died. She and that old Maria are up there all the time. She's with the ghost up there. I don't like her much.'

'She seemed concerned about you.'

'Oh, she doesn't like me. She likes my mother and Gramps, though. Did you talk to Gramps?'

'Not really . . . just greetings. It is amazing how little one can talk to people.'

'What about old Lucas?'

'Why is everyone old to you?'

'Because they are.'

'Well, they are certainly not ten years old. Go away now, will you? I want to go to bed.'

'I want to hear all about it in the morning.'

'There's really nothing to tell.'

'I suppose you think you are going to parties here to find a rich husband.'

'Most of the men seem to have wives already,' I said with a smile.

'All you have to do is . . .'

'What?' I asked.

'Murder them,' she said. 'Good night, Cranny. See you in the morning.'

And she was gone.

I was disturbed. What was actually in the child's mind? I wondered. What did she know? And how much did she make up when she did not know? I kept thinking about the sailor. I had almost made up my mind to tell Lucas.

* * *

When I met Lucas the following day, I was still wavering. But the first thing he said when we were seated was: 'Now, out with it. What's on your mind? Why don't you tell me? You've wanted to for a long time . . . and in any case that's why you've brought me here today.'

'There *is* something,' I said. 'Lucas, if you promise . . . promise you won't *do* anything that I ask you not to . . .'

He looked at me in puzzlement. 'Is it something that happened on the island?'

'Well, yes . . . in a way.'

'John Player?'

'Yes. But he isn't John Player, Lucas.'

'That doesn't surprise me. I knew there was some mystery.'

'Promise me, Lucas. I must have your promise before I tell you.'

'How can I promise when I don't know what I'm promising?'

'How can I tell you if I don't know you will?'

He smiled wryly. 'All right, I promise.'

I said, 'He's Simon Perrivale.'

'What?'

'Yes, he left England on the ship . . . taking the place of one of the deck hands.'

Lucas was staring at me.

'Lucas,' I said earnestly. 'I want to prove his innocence . . . so that he can come back.'

'This explains . . . everything.'

'I thought it would. And I was afraid that you might think it your duty to tell the authorities . . . or someone.'

'Don't worry about that. I've promised, haven't I? Tell me more. I suppose he confessed this to you on the island when I was lying there, unable to move.'

'Yes, it was like that. There is something else you must know. He was in the seraglio . . . or rather just outside it, working in the gardens. I told you how I became friendly with Nicole and she was the friend of the Chief Eunuch. Well, he – Simon – managed to ingratiate himself with the Eunuch and I think because of it and because of Nicole . . . he helped us both. Simon escaped with me.'

Lucas was speechless with incredulity.

'We were taken away together and left close to the British Embassy. I went in . . . and in time came home. Simon dared not be sent home. He left me there. He was going to try to get to Australia.'

'And you have heard nothing of him since?'

I shook my head.

'I understand now,' he said, 'why you have this crazy idea of proving his innocence.'

'It's not crazy. I know he's innocent.'

'Because he told you?'

'It's more than that. I got to know Simon very well . . .'

He paused for a few seconds before he said: 'Wouldn't it be better for him to come home and face things? If he is innocent . . .'

'He *is* innocent. But how could he prove it? They have all decided that he is guilty.'

'And you think you are going to make them change their minds?'

'Lucas, I know there is some way of doing this. There must be. I'm certain of it. If only I could find the answer.'

'This is the most important thing in the world to you, is it?'

'I want it more than anything.'

'I see. Well, what good is it playing governess to that child?'

'I'm here. I'm close to the people who were involved in it. It's a way . . .'

'Listen, Rosetta. You're not being logical. You're letting your emotions get in the way of your common sense. You've had some fantastic adventures; you were plunged into a world so different from the one you knew that you are not thinking clearly. What happened to you was melodramatic . . . beyond what you could have imagined before. Miraculously, you came through. It was a chance in a thousand . . . but because it happened you expect life to go on like that. You were in that seraglio . . . a prisoner . . . everything was so different there. Wild things could happen. You're in another sort of seraglio now . . . one of your own making. You're a prisoner of your imagination. You think you are going to solve this murder, when it is clear what has happened. The innocent rarely run away. You should remember that. He couldn't have said, "I'm guilty" more clearly. You're not being logical, Rosetta. You're living in a world of dreams.'

'Nanny Crockett believes in him.'

'Nanny Crockett! What has she to do with it?'

'She was his nurse. She knew him better than anyone. She says he is incapable of such a thing. She knows.'

'That explains this friendship. I suppose she put you up to this governessing.'

'We worked it out together. We didn't think of my being a governess until the possibility arose. Then we saw that it was a way of getting me into the house.'

I was looking at him appealingly.

'Do you want my opinion?' he said.

I nodded. 'Please, Lucas.'

'Drop it. Give up this farce. Come back to Trecorn. Marry me and make the best of a bad job.'

'What do you mean, a bad job . . . ?'

'Say goodbye to Simon Perrivale. Put him out of your thoughts. Look at it like this. He ran away when he was about to be arrested. That is too significant to be ignored. If he returned he'd be tried for murder and hanged. Let him lead a new life in Australia . . . or wherever he lands up. As you're so certain of his innocence, give him a chance to start a new life.'

'I want to prove that he was wrongly accused.'

'You want him to come back.' He looked at me sadly. 'I understand absolutely,' he said. He shrugged his shoulders and looked grave, as though communing with himself. Then he said: 'What discoveries have you made so far?'

'There was a drunken sailor.'

'Who?'

'His name was Thomas Parry. He fell over a cliff and was drowned.'

'Wait a minute. I remember something about that. There was quite a stir about it at the time. It was some while ago. Didn't he come down here . . . from London, I think. Got drunk and fell over the cliff. It's coming back to me.'

'Yes,' I said. 'That's the one. Well, he's buried in the graveyard here. I discovered Kate putting flowers on his grave. When I asked her why she said he was her father.'

'What! Married to the glorious Mirabel?'

'One can't be sure with Kate. She romances. She said that she saw him in the market in Upbridge and he was asking if anyone knew a woman named Parry with a little girl. She was frightened and hid herself behind the woman she was with . . . the mother of a little girl she had gone to play with. She was frightened of him. Apparently she remembered something of a father who was a brute.'

'And he was found at the bottom of the cliff.'

'You see, it seemed so fortuitous. If Mirabel was hoping to marry one of the Perrivales and a husband from the past who is supposed to be dead turns up, it could be awkward.'

'And as far as the glorious Mirabel was concerned, he was more useful at the bottom of the cliff than making trouble for her. It makes sense.'

'Not completely. You see, I have only Kate's word for it. I asked her if she had told her mother she had seen him. She said no. But she had told Gramps. Gramps is her name for her grandfather, Major Durrell. He said she had made a mistake and she shouldn't mention it because it would upset her mother and her father anyway was dead. He'd been drowned at sea.'

'Why should the child think it was her father?'

'She's a strange child . . . given to fantasy. It occurred to me that she might miss a father and was inventing one.'

'She has Sir Tristan as a stepfather.'

'He doesn't take much notice of her. She calls him Stepper in a rather contemptuous way . . . but then she is contemptuous of most of us. It occurred to me that she had seen people putting flowers on graves and thought she would like to do it and so invented a father. The sailor had no relations so she put flowers on his grave and adopted him.'

'It seems plausible . . . but how is all this going to solve Simon Perrivale's troubles?'

'I don't know. But just suppose someone now in the house did the murder . . . well, people who commit one might not hesitate at another. It might be part of the whole picture.'

He looked at me in some exasperation.

I said: 'I knew you'd take it like this. I thought you might help me.'

'I'll help,' he said. 'But I don't think it is going to get anywhere. Simon, it seems, was jealous of the other two. He killed one in a rage, and was caught by the other. That's it. As for the sailor, I think you may be right. The child wanted a father so she took up with the dead man who had no relations around.'

'She cut the head gardener's prize roses to put on his grave.'

'There you are. That bears it out.'

'All the same . . .'

'All the same . . .' he repeated, smiling at me quizzically. 'If we are going to investigate, we have to pick up the most likely point and there is a faint possibility that something might be lurking behind the untimely death of the sailor. At least that is something we could start with.'

'How?'

'Find out something about him. Who was he? Who was his wife? Then if she should happen to be the present Lady Perrivale it might begin to look as though we were on to something. And if someone actually got rid of the sailor because he was making a nuisance of himself . . . well, there is a possibility that that person, having successfully accomplished one crime, might try another.'

'I knew you'd help me, Lucas.'

'So we begin to unravel the skein,' he said dramatically.

'How?'

'Go to London. Look up records. What a pity Dick Duvane isn't here. He would throw himself into this with enthusiasm.'

'Oh Lucas . . . I'm so grateful.'

'I'm grateful, too,' he said. 'It relieves the monotony of the days.'

I went back to Perrivale Court in a state of euphoria.

I knew I was right to have taken Lucas into my confidence.

* * *

Lucas was away for three weeks. Each day I looked for a message from him. Kate and I had settled into a routine. She still had her difficult moments, but she made no attempts to play truant. We read together, discussed what we read, and I made no reference to the sailor's grave which she continued to visit. She did not take any more flowers from the garden but contented herself with wild ones.

A few days after Lucas had left for London, Maria, the Dowager Lady Perrivale's maid, sought me out and said that her mistress would like to have a chat with me.

Maria was one of those servants who, having been in the service of a master or mistress for a long time, feel themselves to be especially privileged. Moreover, they are usually too useful to their employers to be denied what they expect. They look upon themselves as 'one of the family', and I could see that, as far as Maria was concerned, this might be to my advantage.

It was the first time I had been in that part of the house

which, when I looked from my own window, I could see across the courtyard.

Maria greeted me, putting her finger to her lips.

'She's fast asleep,' she said. 'That's just like her. She'll ask someone to come and see her and when they come she's dead to the world.'

She beckoned me and opened a door. There, sitting in a big armchair, was Lady Perrivale. Her head had fallen to one side and she was fast asleep.

'We won't disturb her for a bit. She had a bad night. Gets them sometimes. Having nightmares about that Sir Edward. He was a bit of a tartar. Eee . . . but you know naught about that. She's up and down. Quite her old self sometimes. Then her mind goes wandering.'

'Shall I come back later?'

She shook her head. 'Sit you down here for a bit. When she wakes she'll ring or bang her stick. Oh dear me, she's not what she was.'

'I suppose that happens to us all in time.'

'Reckon. But she went down when Sir Edward passed away.'

'Well, I suppose they'd been married for a long time.'

She nodded. 'I was with her when she came south. Sorry to leave Yorkshire, I was. Ever been, Miss Cranleigh?'

'No, I'm afraid not.'

'The dales have to be seen to be believed . . . and the moors. 'Tis a gradeley place, Yorkshire.'

'I am sure it is.'

'Here? Well . . . I don't know. I could never get used to these folks. Full of fancies. Now that's something you couldn't accuse us of.'

She looked at me in a somewhat bellicose manner which I thought was undeserved as I had no intention of accusing her of being fanciful.

'A spade's a spade up there, Miss Cranleigh. None of this fancy stuff. Airy-fairy . . . people walked out of their graves . . . little men in the mines . . . and goblins and things sinking the boats. I don't know. Seems a funny way of going on to me.'

'It certainly does,' I agreed.

'Mind you, in a house like this, some people might get the creeps.'

'But not a Yorkshire woman.'

She grinned at me. I could see she was regarding me as . . . well, not quite as a kindred spirit . . . but, coming from London, at least I was not one of the fanciful Cornish.

'So you came here with Lady Perrivale when she married,' I said.

'Well, I was with her before that. And what a to-do it was. Marrying a title. He had the brass, old Arkwright did . . . rolling in it. But brass ain't everything. And when she became "my lady", she was on clouds of glory. This house . . . what she did to it. It was in a right old mess. This house . . . and her ladyship too, if you please. Of course, she had to take Sir Edward with it.'

'Was that such an ordeal?'

'He was a strange sort, he was. You never got to know him. She was used to having her own way. Old Arkwright adored her. Good-looking, she was, and all that brass of course. Only child . . . heiress. You could see what Sir Edward was after.'

'How was he such a strange one?'

'He didn't say much. He was always so very proper. My goodness, he was strict.'

'I've heard that.'

'At church every Sunday . . . morning and evening. Everyone had to go . . . even the tenants . . . or it was a black mark against them. He was making sure of his place in Heaven . . . and then that boy . . .'

'Yes?' I said eagerly, for she had paused.

'Bringing him in like that. If it was anyone else's you would have said . . . you know what I mean . . . men being what they are. But you wouldn't believe it with Sir Edward. I often wondered who that boy was. Her ladyship hated the sight of him. Well, you could understand it. Old Nanny Crockett used to stick up for him. I wondered her ladyship didn't get rid of her . . . but Sir Edward wouldn't have had that. He'd have put his foot down hard about that . . . though mostly he didn't interfere about the house . . . as long as they all went to church and attended the prayer meetings every morning in the hall. I've heard her ladyship storm and rage, say she wouldn't have the little bastard in the house . . . yes, she went as far as that. Well, you could understand it. I heard everything, me being her personal maid and all that, having been with her when we was in Yorkshire. She wanted her own maid and she settled on me. There's not much I haven't seen. Here, why am I talking to you like this? Well, I look on her as my child, really. It's like talking about myself. And you're here . . . one of the family, you know. You must have seen a bit of life with that Miss Kate . . .'

She pressed her lips together and I had the impression that she was reproaching herself for having talked of such intimate matters to me, almost a stranger.

'You must have seen a great many changes here,' I said.

She nodded. 'I was always one for a bit of gossip,' she said, still excusing herself. 'And I don't get much chance of that up here all day. It gets a bit lonely. You've got one of them sympathetic natures, Miss Cranleigh, I can see that. You're an understanding sort.'

'I hope so. I find it very interesting here . . . the house and the people.'

'That's so. As you was saying, I've seen some changes. People don't come to this part of the house much. You know what they're like round here, as we were saying . . . Sir Edward died here. They think he'll come back and haunt the place. There's talk about it. They've seen lights. They say it's Sir Edward looking for something because he can't rest.'

'I saw a light once,' I said. 'I thought it was a candle. It flickered . . . and then I didn't see it any more.'

She nudged me. 'I can tell you what that was. That was her.' She jerked her head towards Lady Perrivale's room. 'She does that sometimes. Gets up in the night. She'll light a candle. I've told her many times. I said, "You'll set the place alight one day . . . your own nightdress perhaps." She said, "I have to look. I have to find it." "Find what?" I say. Then she gets a funny look in her eyes and shuts her mouth and won't say a thing.'

'Do you think she is really looking for something?'

'People get notions when they get old. No . . . there's nothing. She's just got this notion in her head. Time after time I've told her, "If there's something you've mislaid, tell me what. I'll find it for you." But no . . . it's just some fancy that comes to her in the night. I have to watch out, though. She could start a fire and there's a lot of wood in a place like this. What I do is hide the matches. But that don't stop her. I've heard her groping about in the dark.'

'In her room?'

'No, in his room . . . Sir Edward's. They had separate rooms, you know. I always think there's something amiss with separate rooms.'

'You must be kept busy here, looking after Lady Perrivale.'

'Oh yes. I do everything. Keep the place clean . . . cook her food. It's not often she goes down to parties like she did the other night. But she'd been better for the last week or so. They lead their own lives and she's very content with the present Lady Perrivale. She wanted her to marry one of the boys.'

'Yes, I heard that she knew her mother.'

'Yes, school friend, she was. She wanted the Major to come here; she found Seashell Cottage for them and before long Miss Mirabel was engaged to Mr Cosmo.'

'He died though . . . didn't he?'

'Murdered. I can tell you, that was a time. It was that boy Simon. They'd always been against each other.'

'He went away, didn't he?'

'Oh yes. Ran off. He was a sharp little fellow when he was little, even. It was the only thing he could do . . . or hang by the neck. I reckon he'll fall on his feet. He was that sort.'

'What do you think happened?'

'It's plain as the nose on your face. Simon had had enough. He had his eyes on Mirabel. Not that he had a chance.' She lowered her voice. 'Perhaps I'm speaking out of turn, but I always thought she had her eyes on the title, so she took Cosmo. I think Simon shot him in a temper.'

'But why should he have the gun handy like that?'

'Now you're asking me. Looks like he took it there for a purpose, don't it? Eee. You never know. There's nowt so queer as folk, as we say in Yorkshire. And by gum, we're right. Well, everyone seems to have made up their minds it was jealousy . . . and jealousy's a terrible thing. It can lead anywhere.'

'So then Lady Perrivale married Tristan.'

'Yes. Well, they always had a fancy for each other, those two. I've got a pair of eyes in my head. I've seen things. And I'll tell you this: I said to myself, more than once, "Ho, ho, there'll be trouble when she marries Cosmo because Tristan's the one she wants." I've seen a thing or two.'

She stopped abruptly and put her fingers to her mouth. 'I'm talking out of turn again. It's so nice to have a chat with someone who's interested.'

'I am certainly interested,' I assured her.

'Well, you're one of the family now, I suppose. And, after all, it happened some time ago. It's all over and done with now.'

I could see that she would need but little prompting to overcome her qualms of conscience, and I continued to prompt her.

'Yes, of course,' I said. 'And I dare say everyone was discussing it all at one time.'

'My goodness yes. That's a fact.'

'You were saying you'd seen a thing or two.'

'Oh . . . I don't know. It was just that I noticed one or two things . . . so it didn't surprise me at all when she turned to Tristan. People said it was on the rebound . . . and poor things they comforted each other. Well, you know what people say . . .'

She was frowning slightly. She was, I think, trying to remember how much she had said.

'Her ladyship and me . . . we used to have some fun together. She'd tell me everything . . . two girls together, that's what we were like . . . and then of course she's changed since Cosmo's death. You wouldn't believe how it's aged her. It's a long time since I've had a chat like this. Well . . . I'd better take a look at her. Catnaps, that's what she takes. Then she'll wake up suddenly and want to know what's going on.'

She rose and went to the door. I was hoping that Lady Perrivale would not have woken up, for the conversation with Maria had been very interesting and illuminating. I had always been aware that servants knew as much as anyone did of the family's secrets – perhaps even more.

I heard a peevish voice: 'Maria . . . what's happened? Wasn't someone coming?'

'Yes, you wanted to have a chat with the governess. She's been waiting here for you to wake up.'

'I am awake.'

'Now you are. Well, here she is. Miss Cranleigh . . .'

Lady Perrivale smiled at me.

'Bring a chair, Maria, so that she can sit down.'

The chair was brought.

'Close to me,' said Lady Perrivale, and Maria complied.

We talked for a while but I could see that her mind wandered. She was not nearly as lucid as she had been on the night of the party, and was not sure which of the governesses I was; and then suddenly she remembered I was the successful one.

She talked about the house and told me what a state it had been in when she came and how she had repaired it and given it a new lease of life.

After a short while I saw her head nodding and she fell into a doze.

Quietly I rose and looked for Maria.

She said: 'It's not one of her good days. She had a bad night. I'll bet she was wandering about in the dark . . . looking for something which isn't there.'

'Well, I must go now, and I did enjoy talking to you.'

'I hope I didn't say too much. Got carried away by having someone to talk to for a bit. You must come again. I've always enjoyed a bit of a gossip.'

'I will,' I promised.

I went back to my room. It had not been a wasted afternoon.

* * *

A message from Lucas was sent to the house.

He was back and wanted to see me as soon as possible. I could not wait for the meeting and soon after I received the message was in the parlour at The Sailor King with him.

'Well,' he said. 'I've made some discoveries. I think Miss Kate must be romancing.'

'Oh, I'm glad of that. I should have hated to think Lady Perrivale had murdered her first husband.'

'It seems that this Thomas Parry was a sailor.'

'That's the one.'

'He married a Mabel Tallon. She was a chorus girl.'

'Lady Perrivale, a chorus girl!'

'Might have been . . . before she acquired her airs and graces. But listen . . . isn't her father down here?'

'Yes, Major Durrell. Mirabel Durrell doesn't sound much like Mabel Tallon.'

'A Mabel might call herself Mirabel.'

'Yes, but it is the surname which is important.'

'She could have changed that.'

'But there is her father.'

'Listen. There is a child. I looked that up. She was Katharine.'

'Kate! Well, that could be.'

'It's a fairly common name.'

'But it's the only thing that might fit.'

'And you want to hitch on to that?'

'No, I don't. I think Kate imagined the whole thing. She's lonely really. I know by the way she so quickly became friendly with me. There's something pathetic about her. She wants a father. That's why she has adopted this sailor.'

'You would have thought she would have looked for someone more worthy.'

'She had to take what there was. He was there in the grave . . . unknown . . . and don't forget she had seen him in the market-place.'

'Had she, do you think? Or did she imagine that?'

'I think she must have, because he was there and he was seeking information about his wife and child.'

'We have proved that he had one and she happened to be named Katharine.'

'Well, there are other diminutives for the name . . . Cathy, for instance.'

'Yes, that's so. But I suppose Kate is the more usual. But that alone is too flimsy to hitch on to. And Mirabel's father gives a touch of respectability. Major Durrell. She could hardly have involved him. No. Let's close the books on that one and look for another strand to unravel.'

'I must tell you that I have made a little discovery while you've been away. I've spoken to Lady Perrivale's maid Maria . . . that is, the Dowager Lady Perrivale.'

'Ah. And what has she revealed?'

'Not a great deal that I didn't know already. But she was very garrulous.'

'Just what we need.'

'She remembered Simon's being brought to the house and the fuss and consternation because no one could figure out how he came to exist. With some it would seem obvious that there had been a misdemeanour on the part of the master of the house . . . but not Sir Edward. He was not the type to indulge in that sort of thing. He was God-fearing, a pillar of the church, eager that high principles be upheld.'

'By others, but perhaps he was a little more lenient where he himself was concerned. Some people are like that.'

'Yes, of course. But not Sir Edward. And this misdemeanour must have occurred before his marriage.'

'Well, they do now and then.'

'To people like Sir Edward?'

'Maybe. But he came to repentance after it happened because he brought the boy into his house . . . but do you think there could have been some other reason why Simon was brought to the house?'

'Perhaps that is one of the things we have to find out.'

'He might have been sorry for the child left alone with that aunt.'

'Do you think the mother might have been some poor relation?'

'What was to prevent his saying so? As far as I can see, he just brought the child into the house and let people draw their own conclusions. No, it just doesn't make sense. It must have been a lapse. Even the most virtuous have been known to stumble.'

'But he was so insistent on morality.'

'Repentant sinners are often like that.'

'I can't believe it of him. There is something behind it.'

'Listen to me, Rosetta . . . you're chasing shadows. You're believing something because you want to. You're dabbling in dangerous waters. Just suppose you are right. Just suppose there is a murderer in that house and suppose he – or she – discovered you are meddling? I don't like the idea. If this person murdered once, why shouldn't he – or she – do it again?'

'So you believe there is a murderer in the house?'

'I did not say so. I think the police version is the most likely one, and Simon the most plausible suspect. Running away seems to make it fit.'

'I don't accept it.'

'I know you don't . . . because you don't want to. You knew the man we were with all that time. That was different. We were all fighting for our lives. He was heroic and resourceful. We both owe our lives to him, but that does not mean that in different circumstances he might not be a murderer.'

'Oh, Lucas, you can't believe that!'

'I did not know him as well as you did,' he said ruefully.

'You were with him all the time. He dragged you out of the sea. He was most concerned for you.'

'I know. But people are complex. When his passions of jealousy were aroused he could have been a different person.'

'You won't help me because you don't believe in him.'

'I will help you, Rosetta, because I believe in you.'

'I don't know what that means, Lucas.'

'It means that I'll help you all I can, but I think you have set yourself a hopeless task and one which could be dangerous.'

'If you think it could be dangerous you must believe in Simon's innocence. Otherwise the people in that house would have nothing to hide.'

'Yes, that may be so. But I do want you to be careful. In your enthusiasm you might betray your thirst for knowledge and just suppose you were right . . . then it could be dangerous. Please be careful, Rosetta.'

'I will. By the way, something came out of my talk with Maria. Apparently while Mirabel was engaged to Cosmo she was having some sort of flirtation with Tristan.'

'Oh?'

'Well, according to Maria it was Tristan Mirabel preferred all along.'

'That's interesting.'

'I thought it might be a motive.'

'She could have transferred her hand to the brother without murder.'

'And lose the title and everything that went with it?'

'I am sure that would have been important to her, but would she have murdered for it?'

'They might have . . . Tristan and she between them. There was something to gain.'

'Well, it's the best you've come up with so far. But I wouldn't rely too much on servants' gossip. By the way, I may be going back to London in a few days' time.'

'Oh . . . so soon after . . . Shall you be away long?'

'I'm not sure. As a matter of fact, I'm going to have an operation. I've been thinking about it for some time.'

'You didn't mention it.'

'Oh, I didn't want to bother you with such a thing.'

'How can you say that! You know I am enormously concerned. Tell me about it.'

'It's this fellow in London. Something very new, of course. It may work . . . it may not. He's quite frank about that.'

'Lucas! And you just mention it casually like this!'

'I don't feel exactly casual about it. I saw this man when I went up on my sleuthing operation concerning the drunken sailor. I killed two birds with one stone, you might say.'

'And you've only just told me!'

'I thought I'd better explain my absence. You might have been expecting some messages. "Come at once. Murderer discovered" or something like that.'

'Don't be flippant, please, Lucas.'

'All right. The fact is my leg is in pretty bad shape. It's getting worse. Well, this extremely clever bone man has introduced certain methods. He can't give me a new leg, alas, but he may be able to do something. If it's successful . . . I'd always walk with a limp . . . but it could be an improvement. And the fact is, I'm ready to take a chance.'

'Lucas, is it dangerous?'

He hesitated just a second too long. 'Oh no. I couldn't be made more of a cripple than I already am, but . . .'

'Tell me the truth.'

'To tell the truth, I'm a bit in the dark myself. But there is a hope . . . a faint one perhaps . . . but I want to take it.'

'Why didn't you tell me before?' I demanded.

'I wasn't sure that I was going to do it. And then I thought: Why not? It can't be much worse if it goes wrong and it could be a lot better.'

'And I'm going on about all this when you've got this on your mind!'

'Your concern touches me deeply, Rosetta,' he said seriously.

'Of course I'm concerned. I care very much about you.'

'I know. Well, I shall be leaving in a few days' time.'

'How long will it take?'

'I'm not sure. If it's successful perhaps a month. I'm going into this man's clinic. It's just off Harley Street.'

'I shall hate to think you are not here.'

'Promise me you'll be careful.'

'About probing. Of course I will.'

'Don't make it too blatant and don't take too much notice of servants' chatter.'

'I promise you, Lucas. Will you give me the address of this clinic?'

He took a piece of paper from his wallet and wrote it down.

'I shall come to see you,' I said.

'That will be pleasant for me.'

'I shall keep in touch with Carleton. What is he going to feel about your going away like this?'

'I don't think my being here makes much difference. It doesn't bring Theresa back. He'll be all right. He throws himself into his work and that's the best thing for him.'

The news had cast a gloom over the day for me. It was typical of Lucas that he should make light of a serious matter. What was this operation? Was it dangerous in any way? If it were, I knew he would not tell me.

I felt very uneasy.

We left The Sailor King and went out to the stables.

'I'll escort you back to Perrivale,' he said.

We rode on in silence and all too soon the house came into view.

'Oh, Lucas,' I said. 'I wish you weren't going. I shall miss you very much.'

'I'll remember that,' he replied. 'It won't be long. You'll see me galloping up to The Sailor King . . . a changed man.'

I looked at him sadly.

Then he said seriously: 'But I *am* concerned about you, Rosetta. Take care. Give up the search until I return. That's the best plan.'

'I promise to be very careful, Lucas.'

He took my hand and kissed it.

'*Au revoir*, Rosetta,' he said.

* * *

I felt depressed. These meetings with Lucas had meant a great deal to me, and to be deprived of them made me wretched. Moreover, I was worried about him. What was the operation? I wondered. Had he been a little secretive about it?

When I went riding with Kate I suggested we call in at Trecorn Manor one day.

'It's rather a long way. We couldn't do it in an afternoon.

But why shouldn't we have a day's holiday? I will ask your mother if it would be permitted.'

Kate was excited by the prospect and, as I had been sure, there was no difficulty in getting the required permission.

My riding had improved since my arrival and I could manage a long ride easily now, and Kate was quite capable of it.

I was delighted to see her so pleased at the prospect of our little outing.

'It's quite grand,' she commented, when she saw the house. 'Not so grand as Perrivale, of course . . . but it's all right.'

'I am sure the Lorimers would be pleased by your approval.'

'Are we going to see that old Lucas?'

'No. He's not there.'

'Where is he?'

'In a clinic.'

'What's a clinic?'

'A sort of hospital.'

'What's he doing there?'

'You know he hurt his leg.'

'Yes, in the shipwreck. He can't walk very well.'

'They are going to see if they can do something about it.'

She was thoughtful. 'Who shall we see, then?'

'His brother, I hope, and the twins and Nanny Crockett.'

We left our horses in the stables and went to the house. Mr Lorimer was on the estate but Nanny Crockett should be informed that we were here.

She came hurrying down.

'Oh, Miss Cranleigh. How nice to see you! And Miss Kate! Well!'

'Where are the twins?' asked Kate.

'Oh, they'll want to see you. They remember you, Miss Cranleigh.'

'I hope I shall be able to see Mr Lorimer before I leave.'

'Oh, he's gone to London.'

'I mean Mr Carleton.'

'I was thinking you'd come to see Mr Lucas. They're going to do something about his leg.' She shook her head. 'They're *supposed* to be very clever nowadays. I don't know.'

'I knew he was going. I wanted to talk to Mr Carleton about it.'

'He'll be back before long, I reckon. Come up to the nursery and see the twins.'

Jennifer recognized me at once and ran to me. Henry was unsure, I could see, but he followed his sister.

'Now tell me how you've been getting on,' I said. 'This is Kate, who is my pupil now.'

Kate was looking at the children with slightly scornful interest.

I asked Jennifer how one-eyed Mabel was and also Reggie the bear. She laughed and said they were as naughty as ever.

I talked with the children for a while and Nanny Crockett said why didn't they show Kate the dolls' house.

The twins jumped with glee. I looked anxiously at Kate, who might well state her lack of interest in such childish toys.

I think my glance must have been appealing for she said: 'All right.'

The dolls' house was in a corner of the nursery. The children went over to it and Nanny Crockett signed to me to sit down.

'Is there any news?' she asked in a whisper.

I shook my head.

'It's difficult. I can't find out anything. Sometimes I think it's an impossible task.'

'I know you'll find something. I know there's something to be found . . . and it's in that house. That's where the secret lies. I wish I could get there.'

'I get little bits of information but they don't lead anywhere.'

'Well, you go on trying. Have you tried talking to Mrs Ford? She knows most of what's going on.'

'Perhaps you could talk to her. You are on friendly terms.'

'I've tried but I don't get very far.'

'Perhaps she doesn't know anything . . . or if she did, thinks she shouldn't talk about the family.'

'She might talk to someone in the house while she wouldn't to someone outside it. And you're there now. You're one of them. I'm out of it now.'

I could see that Kate was listening to what we were saying and I flashed a sign to Nanny Crockett. She understood at once and we talked of the children and how they would soon be needing a governess.

Kate called: 'You won't come back here, will you, Cranny?'

So I knew she was taking note of what we were saying.

'Not while you continue to be a good pupil,' I replied.

Kate grimaced. But it was clear that there could be no intimate conversation with Nanny Crockett.

In due course one of the maids came to say that Mr Lorimer had returned.

I left Kate in the nursery and went down to see him. He looked very sad but he was pleased to see me.

I said: 'I'm worried about Lucas. What do you know about this operation?'

'Very little. He went up to London recently to see this man and to have a thorough examination. Well, this is the result.'

'What do they think they'll be able to do?'

'It's a little vague. They say they have made a lot of advances in that field. It is an attempt to put right what went wrong when his leg was left to set itself.'

'I constantly regret that we did not know what to do. We could have prevented all this.'

'It's no use blaming yourself, Rosetta . . . nor the man who was with you. You did the best you could. You saved his life between you. You couldn't have done more. Believe me, he is eternally grateful to you. I know he talks lightly of these things, but he does feel more deeply than you would think.'

'Yes, I know.'

'He knows best what he should do, Rosetta. You see, this is a chance. He's ready to take it. It may be that if it fails he'll be worse than he was before, but if it succeeds he'll be a great deal better.'

'It's rather a risk, I gather.'

'I gathered that, too.'

'They will let you know the result of the operation as soon as they see how it is going, I suppose?'

'Yes, I'm sure of that.'

'Carleton, when you hear, would you send a message to me?'

'Of course I will.'

We were silent for a moment. Then Carleton said: 'It was a great tragedy to him. He always hated it when anything went wrong with his health. And that sort of deformity . . . it hit him hard.'

'I know.'

'I wish . . . he could marry. I think that would mean a lot to him.'

'Providing of course that it was a happy marriage.'

'A happy marriage is the perfect state.'

'Yes . . . if it's perfect. Otherwise it has to be a compromise.'

I could see that Carleton was thinking of his own marriage.

'And then,' he said sadly, 'it can all end . . . suddenly . . . and you wonder whether it wouldn't have been better never to have known it.'

'Carleton, I understand perfectly, but I think you should rejoice in what you have had.'

'Yes, you're right. Here I am, revelling in my misery. What do you think of the twins?'

'They're all right. Nanny Crockett is wonderful. They've grown, haven't they?'

'We'll have to be thinking of a governess for them.' He looked at me speculatively.

'I'm not really a governess, you know.'

'I hear you've done well with that girl.'

'How my fame travels!' I said lightly.

'You must have some luncheon before you go back.'

'Well, thanks. I suppose we should need something. It's a good ride to Perrivale from here. I'll call Kate.'

'Yes. They'll be ready to serve it in a few minutes.'

Kate was delighted to have lunch in the Trecorn dining-room. Carleton was quite attentive to her and treated her like an adult, which she enjoyed. She did justice to the food and talked quite animatedly about Perrivale, which amused Carleton and seemed to lighten his spirits a little. So it was a successful visit.

He came out to the stables with us.

'Thank you for coming,' he said to Kate as well as to me. 'I hope you'll come again.'

'Oh, we will,' Kate told him, which I found gratifying, and so did he.

On the way back Kate said: 'The lunch was nice. But those silly twins with their old dolls' house were a bore, though.'

'Didn't you think it was rather a lovely dolls' house?'

'Cranny, I am not a child. I don't play with toys. He wants you to go back, doesn't he?'

'Who?'

'That old Carleton.'

'I feel that your vocabulary must be very limited. You use the same adjective to describe almost everyone.'

'Which adjective?'

'Old.'

'Well, he is old. He does want you to go back and teach those silly twins, doesn't he?'

'At least they are not old. Why should you think that?'

'Because Nanny Crockett wants you to go back.'

'Not *old* Nanny Crockett?'

'Well, she's so old you don't have to say it. She said she'd keep in touch and so did Carleton.'

'He meant about his brother. He's going to let me know about his operation.'

'Perhaps they'll cut off his leg.'

'Of course they won't and trust you to think of such a thing. They're going to make it better. He's a great friend of mine and naturally I want to know how he gets on. So . . . his brother and Nanny Crockett will keep me informed if they hear of his progress.'

'Oh,' she said and laughed.

Suddenly she burst into song.

'"Fifteen men on the dead man's chest,
Yo, ho, ho and a bottle of rum.
Drink and the Devil had done for the rest . . ."'

I thought: I believe she really cares for me.

* * *

During the next days I felt very depressed. I was realizing how important it was to me to know that Lucas was close at hand. I grew more and more worried about the operation. Carleton knew no more than I did, and it was typical of Lucas to be reticent about such a thing.

It was brought home to me how futile were my investigations. Lucas thought they were absurd and he was right.

If only he were at hand and I could send a message over to Trecorn and arrange a meeting.

I wondered what this operation would do to him, and I greatly feared the result.

Kate sensed my melancholy and tried to cheer me up. When we were reading my attention would stray and this puzzled her. It was during this time that I began to be sure that she had some affection for me. That would have been very comforting at any other time but now I could think only of Lucas.

She would try to cajole me to talk and I found myself talking to her about the past. I told her of the house in Bloomsbury, of my parents and their preoccupation with the British Museum. She was amused that I had been named after the Rosetta Stone.

She said: 'It is like that with me. I haven't got a father . . . but my mother has always had other things . . . not the British Museum but . . . other things . . .'

At any other time I should have questioned her about her feelings but I was so obsessed by Lucas that I let the opportunity pass.

She wanted to hear a great deal about Mr Dolland. I told her about his 'turns' and she was particularly interested in *The Bells*.

'I wish we had them here,' she said. 'Wouldn't it be fun?'

I admitted that it would and it had been fun in the old days.

She put her arm through mine and squeezed with a rare show of affection.

'It didn't matter about them only caring for the old British Museum, did it? It doesn't matter . . . if you have other things . . .'

I was touched. She was telling me that my presence made up for her mother's neglect.

When I told her of Felicity's arrival she squealed with delight. I saw why. It was the similarity with my coming to Perrivale.

'You thought some awful governess was coming,' she said.

'Old, of course,' I added, and we laughed.

'Well, they are all old,' she said. 'Did you think of how you were going to make her go?'

'No, I didn't. I wasn't such a monster as you are.'

She rocked back and forth in merriment.

'You wouldn't go now, would you, Cranny?' she said.

'If I felt you wanted me to stay . . .'

'I do.'

'I thought you hated all governesses.'

'All of them except you.'

'I'm flattered and honoured.'

She smiled at me rather shyly and said: 'I'm not going to call you Cranny any more. You're going to be Rosetta. I think it's ever so funny, being named after that thing.'

'Well, it was a rather special stone.'

'An old stone!'

'The adjective fits this time.'

'All those squiggly things on it . . . like worms.'

'Hieroglyphics are not in the least like worms.'

'All right. You're Rosetta.'

I think because I had told her about my childhood she wanted to tell me about hers. And that, of course, was just what I wanted to hear.

'We must have been a long way from the British Museum,' she said. 'I never heard of it till now. We were always waiting for him to come home.'

'Your . . . father?' I prompted.

She nodded. 'It was awful. My mother was afraid . . . not so much as I was when I used to be there . . . all by myself. It was dark . . .'

'At night was this?'

She looked puzzled. 'I can't remember. It was a horrid room. I had a bed on the floor in the corner . . . my mother was in the other bed. I used to look at her hair in the morning. It was like red gold all spread out over the pillow. I used to wake up in the morning . . . I didn't know what to do. Then she'd be there . . . and she'd be gone again. There was someone from downstairs. She used to look in to see if I was all right.'

'And you were all alone there for a lot of the time.'

'I think so.'

'What was your mother doing?'

'I don't know.'

I thought: A chorus girl . . . Tom Parry married a chorus girl.

'You had Mr Dolland and Mrs Harlow . . .'

'Tell me, Kate . . . tell me all you can remember.'

'No, no,' she cried. 'I don't want to. I don't want to remember. I don't want to remember.' She turned to me suddenly and flung herself against me. I stroked her hair.

I said: 'All right. Let's forget it. It's all over now. You've got me now . . . we'll have some fun together. We'll ride . . . we'll read . . . we'll talk . . .'

I was learning so much . . . not about what I came to learn, but about Kate. She was a lonely child; she behaved as she did because she had been starved of love and attention. She was trying to attract it in the only way she knew. I felt resentful against Mirabel who had failed to give her the love she needed. She had had to work perhaps . . . but not now.

Kate disengaged herself abruptly, as though ashamed of her emotion.

She said: 'It was all right when Gramps came.'

'Yes,' I said. 'Your grandfather. He loves you very much, doesn't he?'

A smile illuminated her face.

'He came and took us away. He brought us here . . . and then it was all right. He tells lovely stories . . . all about battles.'

'It must have been wonderful when he took you away.'

She nodded.

'I remember . . . it was in the room . . . he sat on the bed. He said something about a contact . . .'

'A contact?'

'A contact in Cornwall.'

'Oh, he meant a friend, I suppose.'

She nodded. Her mood had changed. She was smiling. 'We went in a train. It was lovely. I sat on Gramps's knee . . . and then we came to Seashell Cottage. I loved it . . . because Gramps was there. He was there all the time. He was there when it was dark. I liked the sea too. I loved to hear it banging against the cliffs. I could hear it ever so loud in my bedroom at Seashell Cottage.'

'And then,' I said, 'there was Perrivale. You soon became friendly with them, didn't you?'

'Oh yes. Gramps knew them and they liked him a lot. Well, everybody likes Gramps. They liked my mother too because she's so beautiful. Then she was going to marry Cosmo and we were going to leave Seashell Cottage and live in the big house. She was ever so pleased. So was Gramps . . . though he wasn't going to live there, but he was pleased all the same. Then Cosmo died while we were still at the cottage. He died in Bindon Boys and the murderer ran away, so everyone knew who'd done it.'

'And what happened after that?'

She wrinkled her brows. 'My mother went away.'

'Went away? I thought she married Tristan.'

'She did . . . but at first she went away.'

'Where did she go?'

'I don't know. She was ill.'

'Ill? Then why did she go away?'

'She was very sick. I used to hear her. She looked very white. Once when she was ill and she didn't know I was there, she looked in the glass at herself and said, "Oh God, what now?" I was little then. I thought God might say and I'd know what was the matter. Now I know people only say "Oh God" when they're frightened or angry. She was frightened because she was ill. Then Gramps said, "Your mother is going away for a while." I said, "Why?" Gramps said because it would be good for her. And she went. Gramps went with her to the station. He was going with her just at first. I was to stay with Mrs Drake for two days. Then Gramps came back and I went back to Seashell Cottage with him. I said, "Where's my mother?" He said, "She's visiting friends." I said I didn't know we had any. Then he said, "You've got me, my darling. I'm your friend." And he hugged me and I felt all right. It was great fun in Seashell Cottage with Gramps. He used to do the cooking and I helped him and we laughed a lot.'

She began to laugh at the memory.

'What happened after?' I asked.

'My mother came back and she was better then. Her friends had done her good. Then she was engaged to Stepper and they were married and we went to Perrivale Court. I wished Gramps could come with us. But he went to the Dower House. He said it wasn't far away and I'd know where he was.'

'And you never met the friends your mother went to?'

'Nobody ever talked of them. I know they lived in London.'

'Did your mother or Gramps tell you that?'

'No. But it was the London train they went on. It always is at that time. I know they got on that one because Mrs Drake took us to see it off. Gramps had taken me to her the night before. I said I wanted to see them off so Mrs Drake took me to the station and I saw them get on the train.'

'They might have got off somewhere along the way.'

'No. I heard them talking about going to London.'

'And Gramps came back and left your mother there.'

'He was only away one night. But she was gone what seemed like ages. It might have been about three weeks. I don't remember much about time. But I know how ill she was when she went . . . she didn't smile at all.'

'She must have been very ill.'

She nodded and started to tell me about the shells she and Gramps had found on the beach.

* * *

I had been up to see the Dowager Lady Perrivale on two or three occasions. Our chats were not very rewarding. I had hoped to discover something as she rambled on about the past and the days of opulence in her native Yorkshire.

I was always hoping for an opportunity to talk to Maria, and as Maria hoped for it too, it was inevitable that one day it should come about.

One day when I went up, I was greeted by Maria who put her fingers to her lips and said with a wink: 'Her ladyship is fast in the land of nod. But come in, Miss Cranleigh, and we'll wait for her to wake up. I never like to rouse her. Another bad night, you see. I always know by the look of her. Roaming about, I expect . . . looking for something that's not there. In any case she can't get at the matches. I see to that.'

We sat opposite each other.

'My word,' she went on. 'You and Miss Kate are getting on better than ever. Thick as thieves, you two are.'

'I think we understand each other. She's not a bad child.'

'Eee. I wouldn't go as far as that, but she's better since you've been here. That's for certain sure.'

'And how has Lady Perrivale been?'

'Up and down. One day she's clear enough . . . all there, you might say . . . and the next she's a ha'porth missing. Well, she's getting on in years . . . can't last much longer, I shouldn't wonder. When I think of her in the old days. Mistress of the house, she was. And then, hey presto! . . . overnight, she's like a different person.'

'Perhaps she was very fond of Sir Edward and the shock of his death was too much for her.'

'Quite the reverse, I should have said. They weren't exactly what you'd call a Darby and Joan. Oh dear me, no. There was differences between them . . . right up to the end, I can tell you. I heard them arguing something shocking. She was in tears. He was laying down the law. I couldn't quite catch . . .'

I thought that was a pity, and so clearly did Maria.

'He died about the time of that shocking affair, didn't he? I mean the killing in the farmhouse.'

'Oh yes . . . the murder. He was on his deathbed then. I don't think he knew much about that, though. He was too far gone. Well, you wouldn't go to a man on his deathbed and say, "Your son's been murdered and by the boy you brought into the house." I mean to say, nobody would tell him that. He didn't know anything about it. Passed away soon after.'

'It's a very strange case, don't you think, Maria?'

'Well, murder's murder whichever way you look at it.'

'I mean it was a very mysterious affair.'

'Jealousy, that's what it was. He was jealous of Cosmo. Some said he was sweet on the present ladyship. Well, you've got to admit she's a handsome body.'

'Very handsome. You told me that Sir Tristan was fond of her before his brother died.'

She winked and nodded. 'A funny business. But then love is a funny thing. She seemed all right with Cosmo. Well, she would be, wouldn't she? But I reckoned it was all pretence. I could see there was something between her and Tristan. You feel it, you know. That's if you know anything about such things.'

'I heard someone say she was very ill and went away for a few weeks and when she came back she was her old self.'

'I think that was just before the murder . . . just before. I noticed she was beginning to look a bit . . . well, if she'd been married, I would have said she might have been expecting . . .'

'And when she came back . . . ?'

'Well, then it happened. It must have been a week or so after, as far as my memory takes me.'

'And then she married Tristan.'

'Well, it was some months after. They couldn't rush into it quite as fast as that. It was fast enough, though.'

'Do you think she was relieved because she could have Tristan and the title and everything?'

Maria frowned. I thought: I'm going too far. I must be careful. Lucas warned me of this.

'Oh, I couldn't say that. Mind you, I believe there was something between her and Tristan, so I suppose she'd rather have had him. Cosmo was one for throwing his weight about. He was the great Cosmo. He'd be Sir Cosmo one day . . . only he didn't live long enough for that. The tenant farmers didn't like him much. They liked Tristan better . . . so she wasn't the only one. It was a quiet wedding. It had to be, didn't it? Her ladyship was chuffed when they married, though. She thought such a lot of Mirabel. She'd wanted her for a daughter-in-law. You should have seen her and the Major together. Well, she'd always had a soft spot for him, hadn't she?'

'Yes, I believe you said she had.'

'I knew that. Her ladyship's mother was supposed to be her best friend . . . but there was a bit of jealousy there. It was over the Major . . . only he wasn't a major then. I didn't hear what he was . . . but he was always a bit of a charmer. Her ladyship was Jessie Arkwright then. She used to talk to me while I brushed her hair. She was sweet on him . . . just like her friend was.'

'You mean the schoolfriend who married him?'

Maria nodded. 'There was a time when I thought it would be Jessie who married him. But old Arkwright put his foot down, thought the charming young man was after

Jessie's fortune. I thought it was the schoolfriend he really wanted, but of course, like a lot of them, he had his eyes on old Arkwright's money. Well, Jessie had had a lot of her own way, but where his money was concerned, old Arkwright had his own ideas. Jessie was not going to throw herself away on an adventurer who was after his money, he said. If she did marry him, there'd be no money. Poor Jessie was heartbroken, but she married Sir Edward, became Lady Perrivale and came down here. And the Major married the schoolfriend. That's how it was. And then all those years later, when his wife was dead and he had a daughter – herself married with a little girl, and he wrote renewing his friendship with her ladyship. She was over the moon with joy and wanted him to come down here. Seashell Cottage was found for them . . . and ever since, she's looked on Mirabel as her daughter.'

'She wasn't jealous because the Major had married her friend?'

'She'd got over that. The friend was dead and the Major was here. She's pleased to have Mirabel now as her daughter-in-law . . . and the Major's always in and out.'

'And young Lady Perrivale's fond of her?'

'Oh yes . . . well, it's nice for the old lady. I remember how upset she was when Mirabel went away . . . that was before the marriage. She was really worried. I remember seeing a letter from young Lady Perrivale to her. "Darling Aunt Jessie . . ." She had called her Aunt Jessie when she first came down and it never changed. I can see that letter now. She was staying at a place called . . . what was it? . . . Oh, I remember. Malton House in a place called Bayswater in London. I remembered Malton because I was born close by. It's near York. That's why it stuck in my mind. When she came back, her ladyship made such a fuss of her. And then soon after that there was the murder . . .'

'It must have been a terrible shock for Lady Perrivale to lose her son like that.'

'Oh, it was . . . and Sir Edward dying at the same time. It was enough to finish her off. We were all surprised that she came through as well as she did. But it did something to her . . . her mind started wandering then, and there was all that prowling about at night.'

She went on to talk about the difficulties she had with Lady Perrivale and gave examples of her strange conduct, to stress the change in her after the tragedy.

While we were talking the Major arrived.

'Oh, hello, Major,' said Maria. 'Her ladyship's fast asleep. Been prowling in the night again, I'm afraid.'

'Oh dear, dear. Nice to see you, Miss Cranleigh. You haven't been over to see me lately. I must speak to Kate about that. I've told her to bring you any time you're passing. You're almost certain to find me in the garden.'

'Thank you, Major. I should like that.'

'Maria takes such good care of Lady Perrivale. What we should do without Maria, I do not know.'

'I don't know what I'd do without her ladyship,' said Maria. 'We've been together so many years.'

I said that I would go as I guessed that when Lady Perrivale awoke she would be delighted to see the Major and would not want another guest to spoil her tête-à-tête with him.

He said politely that he was sure she would be most disappointed to miss me.

'Oh, I can easily look in tomorrow.'

He took my hand and said: 'Now, don't forget. I shall expect to see you soon.'

When I went downstairs it was to find a message awaiting me.

It was from Carleton. It told me briefly that Lucas's operation was to take place on the following Wednesday. It was then Friday.

A Visit to London

I had made up my mind that I was going to London. I wanted to be there when Lucas had his operation. I wanted to see him before it took place, so that I could assure him that I should be thinking of him all the time; and that I was praying that the operation would be successful.

I could stay with my father, where I should not be very far from the clinic. I must be close at hand and I wanted Lucas to know that I was there.

I approached young Lady Perrivale.

I said: 'I am very sorry, but I have to go to London. A very dear friend of mine is having an operation and I want to be there. Moreover, it is time I saw my father. I haven't seen him since I left with my friends Professor and Mrs Grafton for Cornwall, and I really owe it to my family to explain a few things.'

'Oh dear,' she said. 'I'm afraid Kate will be most upset. You two have got along so well together.'

'Yes, but I have to go. I'll talk to her. I'll see that she understands.'

I did talk to her.

'Why can't I come?' she said.

'Because I have to go alone.'

'I don't see why.'

'I do.'

'What about me while you're away?'

'You managed before I came.'

'That was different.'

'I'll tell you what I'll do. I'll find some books for you to read and you can tell me all about them when I get back. I'll set you some lessons, too.'

'What's the good of that?'

'It'll pass the time.'

'I don't want the time to pass. I don't want you to go unless I go with you.'

'Alas. That is another lesson you have to learn. Things don't always turn out the way we want them to. Listen, Kate. This is something I have to do.'

'You might not come back.'

'I will. I swear it.'

She brought a Bible and made me take an oath on it. She seemed a little more satisfied after that.

I was deeply moved to see that I meant so much to her.

* * *

My father was pleased to see me. Aunt Maud was cool and disapproving – as I had expected her to be.

My father said: 'This was a strange decision for you to take, Rosetta.'

'I wanted to do something.'

'There were so many more suitable things you could have done,' said Aunt Maud.

'I could have found you something at the Museum,' added my father.

'That would have been far better,' said Aunt Maud. 'But a governess . . . and in the wilds of Cornwall.'

'It is a very important family. They are neighbours of the Lorimers.'

'I am so glad you are near them,' said my father. 'What are you teaching?'

'Everything,' I told him. 'It's not difficult.'

He looked amazed.

'In any case,' said Aunt Maud. 'No matter what you teach and to whom, I think it is a very foolish thing to have done. A governess indeed!'

'Felicity was one, remember.'

'You are not Felicity.'

'No, I'm myself. I was just saying that she managed very well and was not the least bit ashamed of having been once a governess.'

'It was with friends . . . and to oblige.'

'Well, I'm obliging. They're very glad to have me.'

Aunt Maud made an impatient gesture.

I had a very good welcome in the kitchen. Mr Dolland looked a little older. There was a little more white at his temples. Mrs Harlow seemed larger than I remembered her and the girls were the same.

'So you're a governess now, are you?' said Mrs Harlow with a faint sniff.

'Yes, Mrs Harlow.'

'And you the master's daughter!'

'I enjoy it. I have a very bright and unusual pupil. She was quite unmanageable until I came.'

'I wouldn't have believed it . . . nor would Mr Dolland . . . would you, Mr Dolland?'

Mr Dolland agreed that he never would.

'It used to be such fun down here,' I said. 'Do you still do *The Bells*, Mr Dolland?'

'Now and then, Miss Rosetta.'

'It used to frighten me so. I used to dream about the Polish Jew. I've told Kate – she's my pupil – about you. I'd love to bring her up to meet you all.'

'We miss not having a young 'un in the house,' said Mrs Harlow reminiscently.

I went to her and put my arms round her. She hugged me tightly for a few moments.

'There,' she said, wiping her eyes, 'we often talk about the old days. You were an old-fashioned little thing.'

'I must hear *The Bells* before I go back.'

'I heard Mr Lorimer is in London.'

'Yes. I shall go to see him while I'm here.'

I intercepted a knowing look which passed between Mrs Harlow and Mr Dolland. So they were pairing me off with Lucas.

The next day I went to the clinic. Lucas was delighted to see me.

'I'm so touched that you came,' he said.

'Of course I came. I wanted to be here while it was done, and I want you to know that I'll be thinking of you all the time. I shall come round tomorrow afternoon with my father or Aunt Maud and find out how it went.'

'That might be too early.'

'Nevertheless, I shall come.'

His room was small with a single bed and a small table beside it. He was in a dressing-gown. He said that he had been advised to rest for the last two days and was spending the time mainly reading. They had to prepare him apparently and this was what they were doing.

'I'm so glad you came, Rosetta,' he said. 'There's something I wanted you to know. Sit down there, by the window, so that I can see you.'

'Does the sound of the traffic disturb you?' I asked.

'No. I like it. It makes me feel there's a lot going on outside.'

'What do you want to tell me, Lucas?'

'I took some action. It was a little while ago, before you confessed to me that John Player was Simon Perrivale.'

'Action, Lucas? What action?'

'I sent Dick Duvane off to look for him.'

'You . . . what?'

'I didn't have much to go on. Dick went off to Constantinople. I thought Simon might still be working for the Pasha and there might be a possibility of bribing someone to get him back. I know how these people work. It was just the sort of thing Dick would do well. If anyone could bring it off, he would.'

'Why did you do it, Lucas?'

'Because I knew that he was the one you wanted. I used to tell myself that there was a sort of bond between the three of us. We'd been through so much together. That does something to people. But I was in a way the outsider. On the island I felt that.'

'It was because you weren't able to walk. We had to go off together to see what we could find to eat. You were never the outsider, Lucas.'

'Oh yes, I was. It was to you he confessed his secret and here you are, intent above everything on proving his innocence.'

I was silent.

'There have been times when I thought you and I . . . well, it was what I wanted. Life has been different for me since you came to Cornwall. I've felt a certain optimism . . . just a thought that miracles can happen.'

'We saw one miracle . . . more than one. It really seemed as if Providence . . . fate . . . or whatever you call it, was looking after us. Look how we survived in those seas . . . and then on the island, and how fortunate I was in the seraglio. I did at times feel my good angel was looking after me. You too, Lucas. The way in which you came home was certainly . . . miraculous.'

'Like this . . .' he said, looking down at his leg.

'I don't think any of us have escaped unscathed. But, Lucas, you did this for me. You were trying to find him to bring him back to me.'

'I admit that at times I thought I was a fool. Let him go, I said to myself. Let him stay away for ever. Then you and I could make something of our lives . . . together. That's the way I used to think. Then I thought: She'll always hanker. She'll always think of him. So I came to the conclusion that I'd try to find him and bring him back . . . if that were possible.'

'I shall never forget that you did this for me. You once told me that you loved me next best to yourself, and that all people loved themselves best and when they said they loved someone else it was because of the comfort and pleasure that person brought *them*. Do you remember? I don't think you have shown that is true . . . of you.'

He laughed. 'Don't make a hero of me. You'll be horribly disappointed if you do.'

'Oh, Lucas . . .'

'All right, all right. No more. Don't let's get sentimental. I thought you ought to know, that's all. When you told me who he was and that he had said he would try to get to Australia, I wrote to Dick and he'll be on his way there now. It's a sparsely populated place. It might be a fraction easier to find him there. But even if we did . . . he can't come back, can he?'

'Until we prove him innocent.'

He looked at me sadly.

'You think I am never going to prove it, don't you?' I said.

'I think you have set yourself a very difficult task.'

'But you are going to help me, Lucas.'

'Rather a broken reed, you know.'

'But you are going to be much better after . . . you know you are. You're sure of it.'

'Well, that's the whole purpose, isn't it?'

'I can't wait for tomorrow to be over.'

'Thank you, Rosetta.'

'It's got to be a success. It's got to be.'

He nodded. I kissed him on the forehead and left him. I was unable to hide my emotion and I did not want him to see how fearful I was.

After I had left him I asked if I might have a word with the surgeon and I was finally conducted to him. I said that I should be grateful if he would tell me if there was any danger of Lucas's not coming through the operation.

When he hesitated for a few seconds I felt numb with terror.

‘I believe you are his fiancée,’ he said. I did not deny it. I thought in that role he would be more frank with me. He went on: ‘It is a long and delicate operation. If it is successful, he will be able to walk with much more ease and painlessly . . . although there will always be a slight limp. Because it is long and complicated, it could be a strain on the heart, and that is where the danger lies. Mr Lorimer is strong and healthy. He is in moderately good condition. There is a good chance that he will come successfully through the operation. It is just that we should not forget the strain on the heart.’

‘Thank you,’ I said.

He laid a hand on my shoulder.

‘I am sure it will be all right,’ he said.

I came out of the clinic feeling very disturbed. I wanted to go back to Lucas and tell him how much I cared for him, and at this time the most important thing in the world to me was that the operation would be a success.

* * *

The next day seemed as though it would never pass. In the late afternoon my father, Aunt Maud and I went to the clinic. We saw the doctor whom I had seen on the previous day.

‘He has come safely through,’ he said. ‘It is too soon yet to see how successful the operation is. But Mr Lorimer is doing well. You might look in and see him, but don’t stay more than a few minutes. Just Miss Cranleigh, of course.’

I saw Lucas. He was lying in his bed, his leg under a frame. He looked very different from how I had ever seen him before . . . defenceless, vulnerable.

‘Hello, Lucas.’

‘Rosetta . . .’

‘They say you’ve done well.’

He nodded and looked at the chair beside his bed. I sat down.

'Good to see you.'

'Don't talk. They've told me I mustn't stay more than a few minutes.'

He smiled faintly.

'I just want you to know that I'm thinking of you all the time. I'll come again as soon as they let me.'

He smiled.

'And you'll be out of here soon.'

A nurse looked in and I rose.

'Don't forget. I'm thinking of you,' I said, and kissed him.

Then we went back to Bloomsbury.

* * *

Lucas was progressing 'as well as could be expected'. He was in bed and I gathered that the success of the operation was not yet known and would not be until he was able to put his feet to the ground. Visits had to be brief. It made the days seem long, and one day I decided to go and look at the place where Mirabel had stayed when she had come to London with her mysterious illness.

I could not forget that Maria had said: 'If she had been married I should have thought she was expecting.' She must have been wrong. There was no child. I wondered if there was some evidence hidden in the fact that she had come to London in that way.

Malton House was in Bayswater. That was all I knew, but it might not be impossible to find the place.

Lucas had occupied my mind exclusively during the last week, and because I was unable to see him except very briefly, I needed something to occupy me and to take my mind from the fearful feeling of uncertainty that all might not have gone right with him after all.

I would take a cab one afternoon and go and see if I could find Malton House. I reminded myself that I must 'leave no stone unturned'. Who knew, important evidence might be found in the least expected places.

It was true that the need to prove Simon innocent had taken second place to my anxiety about Lucas lately, but I had gone too far in my search to slacken now. The need to prove Simon's innocence was as strong as ever.

I knew the name of the house and the name of the district. I would hail a cab and ask to be taken to Bayswater. Cab-drivers were very knowledgeable about London. They had to be. It was essential to their jobs.

It was early afternoon. My father was at work in his study. Aunt Maud was taking a nap. I came out of the house and hailed a cab.

The cab-driver looked a little dismayed when I told him I wanted to go to Malton House in Bayswater.

'Malton House? Where's that?'

'In Bayswater.'

'That all the address you've got?'

I told him it was.

'Well, we'll get to Bayswater. That's easy enough. Here . . . wait a minute, I know of a Malton Square.'

'I think it would very likely be there.'

'All right then, Miss. We'll go and see.'

When we arrived at Malton Square he slowed down and studied the houses as we went along.

We saw a woman with a shopping-bag. She was walking briskly along.

The cab-driver slowed up and touched his hat with his whip.

'Excuse me, lady. You know Malton House round here?'

'Why, yes,' she said. 'The one on the corner.'

'Thank 'ee, M'am.'

The cab stopped before a house.

I said: 'Will you wait for me? I shall not be long.'

'I'll just wait round the corner, into the next street,' he said. 'Can't very well stay here right on the corner.'

'That will suit me beautifully.'

And it did, for it occurred to me that he might think it odd that I had made the journey just to look at the place.

The house lay back from the road. Steps led to the door, and among the few rather dingy bushes in the front garden there was a board on which was printed 'Malton House. Maternity Nursing Home.' And in the corner, 'Mrs B. A. Campden' with several letters after her name, the significance of which I was unsure of.

I stood staring at the board for some moments and as I did so a woman came up to me. I recognized her at once as the one whom the cab-driver had asked about the house.

'Can I help you?' she asked pleasantly.

'Oh . . . er . . . no, thank you,' I said.

'I am Mrs Campden,' she said. 'I saw you alight from the cab.'

This was becoming awkward. She must know that I had meant to come here as the cabby had asked her the way. How could I tell her that I just wanted to look at the place?

She said: 'Why don't you come in? It's easier to talk inside.'

'I . . . er . . . I only wanted . . .'

She smiled at me. 'I understand.' Her eyes swept over me. I found myself following her up the steps. The door was open and we stepped into a hall in which was a reception area.

'Come along in,' she said.

I began to protest. 'I only . . .' How could I tell her that I wanted to see what sort of place this was? She seemed to have drawn her own conclusions about me.

'Really I shouldn't waste your time . . .' I began.

She took my arm and drew me into a room.

'Now, let's be comfortable,' she said. She pushed me into a chair. 'You mustn't be embarrassed. So many girls are. I understand that. We're here to help.'

I felt I was getting deeper and deeper into a ridiculous situation, from which I must extricate myself as quickly as possible. What could I say? How to explain? She knew that I had purposely come to the place. It was most unfortunate that the cab-driver should have spoken to her. I tried to think of some reason why I should be here.

'I have to ask a few questions, of course,' she was saying, while I was desperately racking my brains for some plausible excuse for being here. 'Now don't be nervous. I'm used to this sort of thing. We'll put everything right. Have you any idea when conception took place?'

I was horrified now. I wanted to get out of this place as quickly as I could. 'You're making a mistake,' I said. 'I . . . I just came to enquire about a friend of mine.'

'A friend? What friend?'

'I believe she came here. It was some time ago . . . I have lost touch with her and I wondered if you could help me. She was Mrs Blanchard . . .'

'Mrs Blanchard?' She stared at me blankly.

I thought she would surely remember. Anyone would remember Mirabel. Her unusual beauty would make that inevitable.

A sudden thought came to me. On the spur of the moment I said: 'Or perhaps she came as Mrs Parry . . .'

As soon as I had spoken, I wondered what I was thinking of. It was just that the thought had flashed into my mind that her visit here would be of a secret nature and she might not have used the name of Blanchard. There had always been a faint suspicion in my mind that she was in fact the wife of the sailor whose grave Kate visited . . . that she was in truth at that time Mrs Parry.

I was losing my head. I just wanted to get away.

I said: 'I thought if you could give me her address.'

'I must tell you right away that we never divulge the addresses of our patients.'

'Well, I thought you might not. Thank you very much. I'm sorry to have taken up your time.'

'What is your name?'

'Oh, that's not important. I was just passing and I thought . . .'

Just passing! In a cab which brought me here specially! I was making a mess of this.

'You are not the Press, are you?' she asked rather threateningly.

'No . . . no, no, I assure you. I was just thinking about my friend and wondering whether you could help me find her. I am so sorry to have bothered you. I shouldn't have come in if . . .'

'If I hadn't come along just at that moment. Are you sure you are not in need of our services?'

'I'm quite sure. If you'll excuse me. I'm so sorry to have troubled you . . . Goodbye, and thank you.'

I made for the door while she watched me through narrowed eyes.

I was trembling. There was something about the woman, about the place, which made me very apprehensive.

It was with great relief that I came out into the street. What a disaster! How was I to know I should encounter the proprietress! What bad luck that she should have come along at that precise moment. And I had been quite unprepared. I was hopeless in the role I had set for myself. Because I had managed rather well as a governess, I fancied myself as a detective. I felt humiliated and shaken; and my desire was to get away as quickly as possible.

It was a lesson to me. My methods of investigation were both crude and amateur.

I ran round the corner to where the cab was waiting.

'That was quick,' said the cab-driver.

'Oh yes.'

'Everything all right?'

'Oh, yes . . . yes.'

I knew he was thinking: A girl in trouble going to one of those places. Maternity Home, yes – but not averse to helping a girl in trouble.

I sat back, thinking of it all, going over every excruciating minute. Why had I mentioned Mrs Parry! It had just come into my head that she might have gone there under that name. How foolish of me! One thing I did know, and that was that Mirabel must have been pregnant when she went there and not so when she came out. What could it mean? Whose child was it? Cosmo's? She was going to marry Cosmo at that time. Or Tristan's?

Was this an important piece of evidence?

It seemed to me that the chain of events was becoming more complicated and I was no nearer to the solution.

When I reached our house I was still shaken from the encounter.

* * *

The next day I went to see Lucas. When I knocked at his door it was opened by him. He stood standing there.

'Lucas!' I cried.

'Look at me.' He took a few steps and I could see the difference.

'It's worked!' I cried.

He nodded, smiling triumphantly.

'Oh, Lucas . . . it's wonderful.'

I threw myself at him and he held me close.

'You've helped a lot,' he said.

'I?'

'Coming every day. Caring.'

'Of course I came. Of course I cared. Tell me all about it.'

'Well, I'm still something of a poor thing.'

'You don't look it.'

'This business has worked, they tell me. I've got to do exercises and such like. But I'm better. I feel better. I feel lighter. Less like an old hulk.'

'Wonderful! It was all worthwhile.'

'I have to be here for another week or two, while they

put me through my paces. I have to learn to walk again . . . like a baby.'

I could only smile at him. I felt near to tears. I was so happy because the operation had been a success.

'You'll be here for a while?'

'Yes. I shall come and see you every day and watch for improvements.'

'There are quite a few needed.'

'But it's better, Lucas.'

'I shall still be a bit of a cripple. There are things they can't put right. But they have done a great deal. This man is something of a genius. I think I was a bit of a guinea-pig; but he's pleased with me . . . though not half as pleased as he is with himself.'

'Don't let's grudge him his glory, Lucas. I'm so happy . . .'

'I haven't felt like this for a long time.'

'I'm glad . . . so glad.'

On the way out I was waylaid by the surgeon. His delight was obvious.

'Mr Lorimer was such a good patient,' he said. 'He was determined and that is a great help.'

'We don't know how to thank you enough.'

'My reward is the success of the operation.'

When I went home and told them, my father said how gratifying it was that modern medical science had advanced so far; Aunt Maud showed her pleasure in a manner which told me she was speculating on the possibility of a match between Lucas and me; but it was in the kitchen that I was able to celebrate with abandon.

Mr Dolland, wise as ever, leaned his elbows on the table and talked about the wonders of medicine today with far more enthusiasm than my father had done; and Mrs Harlow sighed romantically, so I knew her thoughts were on the same lines as those of Aunt Maud, but it did not irritate me as Aunt Maud's speculation had done.

Then Mrs Harlow told of her cousin's operation for appendicitis and how she had come near to death under the surgeon's knife. Mr Dolland remembered a play in which a man was supposed to be a cripple unable to move from his chair when all the time he could walk with ease and was the murderer.

It was like old times and I was happier than I had been for a long time.

It was not until a day or so later that I told Lucas about my unpleasant experience at the Maternity Home.

'But at least,' I said, 'I did find out that Mirabel was going to have a baby before Cosmo was killed and evidently she went to that place for an abortion.'

'What an extraordinary turn of events! What bearing do you think this has on the murder?'

'I can't think.'

'If it were Cosmo's child they could let it be thought that it was a premature birth . . . unless it was too late for that.'

'Sir Edward wouldn't have approved, of course.'

'But he was on his deathbed.'

'It could have been Tristan's and when she thought she was going to marry Cosmo she had to do something about it.'

'That seems likely. It's all very complicated. There is a possibility that you didn't go to the right place. After all, you only had the address . . . and verbally at that . . . from Maria.'

'Well, I'm afraid it hasn't got us very far. There was something rather sinister about the place and this Mrs Campden was really very put out when she thought I was making enquiries.'

'Well, I suppose she would be. She thought she had a client.'

'She looked a little alarmed when she thought I might be from the Press.'

'Which suggests she might be in fear of them, as what

she is doing is illegal. Listen to me, Rosetta. I suggest you drop this sleuthing.'

'I must find out, Lucas.'

'You don't know what you're getting into.'

'But what of Simon?'

'Simon should come home and work out his own problems.'

'How could he? He'd be arrested.'

'I have a feeling that this is becoming more than a little unpleasant for you.'

'I don't mind a bit if it's unpleasant.'

'Moreover, you could be dealing with dangerous people. After all, it is a murder you are investigating, and if you believe Simon wasn't the murderer, then someone here probably is. How do you think the guilty person would feel about your probing?'

'That person would not know I am doing it.'

'What about that woman? She didn't seem to be very pleased. And if she is dealing in abortions . . . at a good price, I imagine . . . she could be in trouble.'

'She had a board outside. It was a maternity home. That is legal.'

'It might be a cover. I have a feeling that you ought to stop it . . . keep out of it.'

'I have to clear Simon.'

He shrugged his shoulders. 'All right,' he said. 'But keep me informed.'

'I will do that, Lucas.'

* * *

The next day Felicity arrived in London. I was overjoyed to see her.

'I had to come up to see Lucas,' she said. 'And I guessed that you might be here, too. How is he?'

'Coming along very well. The operation was a success. He'll be delighted to see you, as I am.'

'I came straight from the station,' she went on. 'I thought I'd get the news of Lucas and see you at the same time.'

Aunt Maud came in and greeted Felicity warmly.

'I'll see that a room is made ready for you right away,' she said.

Felicity replied that she had been thinking of staying at an hotel.

'Nonsense,' said Aunt Maud. 'You must stay here. And if you'll excuse me, I'll go and see about it right away.'

Felicity smiled at me. 'Still the efficient Aunt Maud.'

'Oh yes. Mrs Harlow says the household runs like clockwork.'

'And what is all this about becoming a governess . . . following in my footsteps?'

'You could say that.'

She looked puzzled. 'We have such a lot to talk about.'

'Let's get you settled in first.'

We went up. Meg was putting the final touches to the room. Felicity exchanged a few pleasantries with her and then we were alone. I sat on the bed while she put the few things she had brought with her into drawers and cupboards.

'Tell me honestly. Is Lucas really improved?'

'Oh yes. There's no doubt of that.'

'I'm glad you came up from Cornwall.'

'I just had to.'

She nodded. 'Tell me all about this idea of being a governess.'

'Well, there was this girl. No one could manage her. It was a sort of challenge.'

She looked at me disbelievingly. And then suddenly it dawned on me that I might have confided in Felicity long ago. I could trust her completely; she was resourceful. Nanny Crockett and Lucas already knew; and I could not keep it from Felicity any longer.

So, having extracted a promise of absolute secrecy, I told her everything.

She listened incredulously. 'I thought your stay in the seraglio was fantastic,' she said. 'And now, this . . .'

'People have been sold into harems before,' I said. 'It happened to Nicole. It's just that it is more rare than it used to be . . .'

'But this Simon . . . he really is Simon Perrivale?'

'Do you remember the case?'

'Vaguely. It raised quite a storm at the time, didn't it, and then it dropped out of the news. And you are convinced of his innocence.'

'Yes, I am. You would be, Felicity . . . if you could have known him.'

'And you were alone on this island . . .'

'Lucas was with us . . . but he couldn't walk. He just lay in the boat and kept a lookout for a sail.'

'It sounds like Robinson Crusoe.'

'Well, all those who are shipwrecked and cast up on an island are like that.'

'Are you . . . in love with this . . . Simon?'

'There was a very strong . . . bond between us.'

'Did you discuss your feelings for each other?'

I shook my head. 'No . . . not really. It was just there. We were all so intent on survival. When we were on the island we thought we were doomed. There wasn't enough to eat or drink . . . and then we were picked up and there was no opportunity.'

'He left you at the Embassy and then you came home and he stayed behind.'

'He would have been arrested if he had come back.'

'Yes, of course. And Lucas shared in all this . . . to a certain extent.'

I nodded.

'I've always been fond of Lucas,' she mused. 'It was very distressing to see him when he came back. He had always been so full of vitality. James is fond of him, too. James said he had a flair for living. I think Lucas loves you, Rosetta.'

'Yes.'

'Has he asked you to marry him?'

'Yes . . . but not very seriously . . . really . . . rather flippantly.'

'I think he might be inclined to flippancy where his feelings are most concerned. You could do a lot for him and, I think, he for you. Oh, I know you think you don't need him . . . as he needs you . . . but you do, Rosetta. All that you went through . . . well, my dear, you couldn't really endure all that and remain as you were before.'

'No, I couldn't.'

'Lucas was there part of the time. There is so much he would understand.'

I was silent and she went on: 'You're thinking Simon was there, too. And there was this special bond between you and him.'

'It started before . . . when he was cleaning the decks.'

'I know. You told me. And now you are dedicated to proving his innocence.'

'I must, Felicity.'

'If he came back . . . if you saw him with Lucas . . . you might decide. Lucas is really a wonderful person.'

'I know, Felicity. I've learned that. This operation . . . when there was just a slight fear that he might not come through . . . I realized how important his friendship was to me. I have confessed to him what I am trying to do, Felicity, and he is helping me. He has sent Dick Duvane out to see if he can find Simon. He was going to bring him back if he could . . . he thought they might take a ransom for him as they did for Lucas himself. That was before he knew that Simon couldn't come back.'

'And you will never be completely content if you don't see him again. He will haunt you for ever. You would always remember . . . and perhaps build up something which was never there.'

'He can't come back until his innocence is proved.'

'How can he hope to prove it from afar?'

'But how could he do it if he were in prison awaiting death?'

'So . . . it is for you to find the solution.'

'I want to do it. I shall never stop trying.'

'I know. I remember your stubborn nature of old.' She laughed. 'Some would call it determination.'

We went on talking about it. I dare say I went over the same ground again and again, but she said she wanted the complete picture. It was typical of Felicity to throw herself wholeheartedly into my affairs.

She said: 'It would be interesting to know why Sir Edward brought him into the household.'

'The obvious conclusion is that he was Sir Edward's son.'

'It certainly seems likely.'

'But the mystery is that Sir Edward was so morally conventional . . . a strict disciplinarian.'

'But that sort can have their lapses.'

'That's what Lucas says. But from what I've heard Sir Edward was particularly censorious with those who erred in that respect.'

'Well, as I say, that often happens, but it is just possible that the key to the mystery may be in the secret of Simon's birth. And when one is studying a case of this nature it is as well to know everything possible about the characters in the drama. See if you can remember more of what you have heard about Simon's beginnings.'

'I've told you about Angel. You see, he doesn't even say she was his mother. She was just Angel.'

'That's explainable. I expect she called him her angel, as

mothers do. It was probably the first thing he remembered. Then he transferred the name to her. I've known that sort of thing happen with children. I know with mine. Was she his mother? Or was she someone who had adopted him as a baby? That's a possibility.'

'What difference would it make?'

'Possibly none. But we don't know, do we? And every detail can be important. What else about his beginnings?'

'There was a wicked aunt. Aunt Ada was her name. He was scared of her and that when Angel died she was going to take him with her. Sir Edward seemed to sense his fear and stepped in. At least that is the impression he gave.'

'Do you remember anything about the aunt? You haven't got a surname . . . just Ada.'

'Just that. He thought she was a witch and he and Angel went to visit her. It was a place called Witches' Home, and as it was her home they were going to that was significant.'

'Did he say anything about the place?'

'He said there was water at the bottom of the garden, I think. Yes, he did. It could have been a river.'

'Is that all?'

'Yes. He must have been under five years old, because he was five when he came to Perrivale.'

'Well,' said Felicity, 'we've got Witches' Home and presumably a river and Ada.'

'What are you suggesting?'

'I was thinking that we might try and find Ada. A little talk with her might be rewarding.'

'Felicity, you mean that you . . .'

'I have an idea. Why don't you come back with me and we'll spend a few days together before you go back to Cornwall. James and the children would love to see you.'

'I do have my work. I've been away longer than I should.'

'The *enfant terrible*. Oh yes. By the way, how is she getting on without you?'

'Well, I hope. But I must get back. I can't take too much time, although they are very amenable.'

'A few more days won't make much difference. In any case, they won't dismiss you. They'll be so pleased to have you back.'

'Kate might revert to her old habits from which, I believe, I am weaning her.'

'That will only make them appreciate you all the more. I have a plan. We'll find out if there is a place called Witches' Home . . . or something like it. It could be on a river . . . or some sort of water. That could be useful.'

'It might have been a pond at the end of the garden. All we really have is Ada and Witches' Home. It will be rather like Thomas à Becket's mother coming to England, her only knowledge of the English language being London and Gilbert and going through the streets of the capital calling Gilbert's name.'

'I'm glad you remember the history I taught you.'

'Well, London is rather different from Witches' Home and a great deal larger.'

'I imagine Witches' Home is a small village where everyone will know everyone's business.'

'And where are we going to find this Witches' Home.'

'We'll consult maps.'

'Little villages are not marked on maps.'

She was downcast but only for a few moments. Then her eyes sparkled. 'I have it,' she said. 'Professor Hapgood. That's the answer.'

'Who's Professor Hapgood?'

'My dear Rosetta, I don't live in Oxford for nothing. Professor Hapgood is the greatest authority on the villages of England. It's his passion . . . his life's work. He can go right back to the Domesday Book and beyond. If there is a place called Witches' Home in England, he will tell us in the winking of an eye. Ah, I can see your scepticism fast disappearing. But trust me, Rosetta, and Professor Hapgood.'

How glad I was that Felicity knew. I was reproaching myself for not having told her before.

* * *

Felicity and I went to the clinic. Lucas was improving and was now walking with great ease. He said he was no longer in pain with every step; all at the clinic were very pleased with his progress. He still had to rest a good deal and would be going home in about a week.

I told him that I had taken Felicity into my confidence and we had plans for trying to locate Aunt Ada. He was amused at the prospect; he said the information we had to go on was very flimsy; however, he was impressed at the mention of Professor Hapgood, of whose reputation he was aware.

I said that as Oxford was on the way I could go straight to Cornwall from there. I could not delay my return much longer and I should be at Perrivale perhaps a few days before Lucas returned to Trecorn Manor.

'I shouldn't hope for too much success in this new venture,' he warned me. 'Even if you do find the place – and you might with Professor Hapgood's help – you've still got the search for Aunt Ada.'

'We know,' I told him. 'But we're going to try.'

'Good luck,' he said.

The next day Felicity and I left for Oxford where I was greeted in a most friendly fashion by James and the children. Felicity explained that she and I were taking a little trip and she would accompany me on part of the journey back to Cornwall, but only be away for a night or two.

James was always understanding about the close friendship between myself and Felicity and he never raised objections to our taking a little time to be together. So that was easily settled and our first task was to get into touch with Professor Hapgood, who was delighted to help.

He took us to his study which was lined with massive tomes; and it was clear that the prospect of a search delighted him.

He could find no Witches' Home, which we rather expected.

'You said a child under five mentioned the name. Well, it must be something that sounded similar. Witches' Home. Let me see. There's Witching Hill. Willinham . . . Willin-under-Lime. Wodenham. And what about Witchenholme. That might sound to a five-year-old like Witches' Home. More than the others, I think. There's Willenhelme . . . well, those two would be the most likely.'

'Holme sounds more like home than helme,' I said.

'Yes,' agreed the professor. 'Let me see. Witchenholme is on the River Witchen . . . it's hardly a river . . . a tributary of, let me see . . .'

'A tributary sounds just right,' said Felicity. 'The boy said there was water at the bottom of the garden.'

'Let me look at Willenhelme. No, there is no river there. It's in the north of England.'

'That can't be the one. Where is Witchenholme?'

'Not far from Bath.'

I looked at Felicity with delight. 'In the west,' I said. 'Much more likely.'

'We'll try Witchenholme,' said Felicity. 'And if it isn't the one, we shall probably be troubling you again, Professor.'

'It's a great pleasure,' he said. 'I pride myself I can produce the smallest hamlet that existed in England since the days of the Norman Conquest, and I like to have a chance to prove it. Now, let me see. Your nearest town would be Rippleston.'

'Is there a railway?'

'Yes, there's a Rippleston station. Witchenholme would be no more than a mile or so out.'

'We're extremely grateful.'

'Good luck in the search. And if it's not the one, don't hesitate to come back to me and we'll try again.'

As we left him I felt amazingly optimistic.

'Now,' said Felicity. 'We shall have to go through Witchenholme as Mrs Becket did through London, only we shall not be calling Gilbert but Ada.'

* * *

We booked a room for the night at Rippleston, which proved to be a small market town.

'We may have difficulty in locating Ada and may need two days to do it,' said Felicity.

It was good to have her with me. I remembered how she had always thrown herself wholeheartedly into any project. It was one of those characteristics which had made her such a stimulating companion.

All the way down in the train we chatted about how we would set about finding Ada, and what we should say to her when we found her. We had both made up our minds that we were going to find her, which was perhaps a little naïve of us, but we were very happy to be together, and somehow seemed to slip back into the old days when most things were so exciting.

When we arrived in Rippleston, we booked into our hotel and asked about transport. There was a trap and a man at the hotel who would drive guests where they wished to go. So that was settled quickly.

We decided to waste no time and were soon rattling along the road on our way to Witchenholme.

A hundred yards or so from the village was an inn called the Witchenholme Arms. Here we decided to stop and perhaps ask a few questions in the hope that someone might know of a Miss Ada Something who lived nearby. We arranged for the driver to wait with the trap at the inn.

There was a middle-aged woman at the counter serving

ale and cider and we asked if she knew of anyone in the village named Ada. She looked at us as though she thought we were a little odd – as well she might, and said: 'Ada . . . Ada who?'

'That's what we're not sure of,' said Felicity. 'We knew her long ago and we can't remember her surname . . . all we can think of is Ada.'

The woman shook her head.

'Come in here much, does she?'

'We don't know,' I answered.

'Ada . . .' She shook her head. 'It's mostly men who come in regular.'

'I was afraid so,' said Felicity. 'Well, thanks.'

We came out of the inn and started to walk into the village.

'Well, you'd hardly expect Aunt Ada to frequent the Witchenholme Arms, would you?' said Felicity.

The village was, as the Professor had told us, very small. And there was a river, yes – and houses backing on to it.

I felt sure this was the place.

A man on a bicycle rode by. We were on the point of stopping him but I realized, as did Felicity, that he would think we were crazy if we stopped to ask if he knew someone called Ada. If only we had her surname, how much more plausible it would all have sounded.

Felicity said suddenly: 'Oh look, there's the village store. Now if anyone would know, they might in there. Everyone would go in there at some time or other surely . . .'

We went into the shop. One had to step down and a bell overhead tinkled as the door was opened. There was a pungent smell of paraffin oil and the shop was crowded with goods of all descriptions – fruit, cakes, biscuits, bread, sweets in glass bottles, vegetables, hams and poultry, note-paper, envelopes, fly-papers and much more.

'Yes?' said a voice.

Our hearts sank. It was a girl of about fourteen and her

face was only just visible above the glass bottles of sweets on the counter.

'We've come,' said Felicity, 'to ask you if you know someone named Ada.'

The girl stared at us in amazement.

'We're trying to find an old friend,' went on Felicity, 'and all we can remember is that her name is Ada. We just wondered whether she lived around here . . . she might come into the shop as most people would, I suppose?'

'What . . . ?' she stammered.

'Do you know any of the people round here?'

'No. I don't live here . . . always. I've just come for a bit . . . I'm helping my aunt.'

'Perhaps we could see her?'

'Aunt . . .' she called. 'Aunt Ada.'

Felicity and I exchanged glances of wonder.

'Aunt Ada . . .' whispered Felicity.

'There's people here wants to see you,' shouted the girl.

'Half a tick,' said a voice. 'I'm coming.'

Was it possible? Could our search be ended? As soon as we saw the woman we knew this was not so. No one could mistake her for a witch. Never could this one have been Simon's Aunt Ada. She was very plump, shaped like a cottage loaf, with a rosy, good-humoured face, untidy greying hair and very alert blue eyes.

'Now what can I do for you ladies?' she said, beaming on us.

'It's a very strange request,' said Felicity. 'We are looking for someone who, we believe, lives here, and we can't recall her surname. All that we know is that her Christian name is Ada.'

'Well, she's not me. I'm Ada. Ada MacGee, that's me.'

'Our Ada had a sister called Alice.'

'Alice . . . Alice who?'

'Well, we don't know her name either. But she died. We

just wondered if among the people here . . . and you must know most of them . . . there was an Ada.'

I guessed she was the sort of woman who loved a gossip. She was naturally interested in two strangers who had come into her shop, not for apples or pears or a pint of paraffin oil, but because they were looking for an Ada.

'You must know almost everyone in Witchenholme,' I said, almost pleadingly.

'Well, most of them come in at some time or other. It's a bit far to go into Rippleston to shop.'

'Yes, I should imagine so.'

'Ada,' she said. 'Well, there's Ada Parker down at Greengates . . . she's not Parker any more now . . . she married again. It's her third. We always call her Ada Parker . . . though not to her face. But Jim Parker was her first husband. Names stick here.'

'Perhaps we'll call on her. Are there any others?'

'Well, there's Miss Ferrers. I've heard she was an Ada. I remember the Adas . . . seeing as I'm one of them. I've never heard her called Ada, mind . . . but I've got a notion that's her name.'

'Yes, I can see why you remember the name. I think we were lucky we came to you.'

'Well, I would if I could help you find this friend of yours, of course. Ada . . . yes, I'm sure Miss Ferrers is an Ada. I've heard it somewhere. Keeps herself to herself. A cut above the rest of us. I'm sure that's what she thinks, anyway.'

'Did she have a sister, do you remember?

'Couldn't rightly say. She's been in that cottage for years. I don't recall a sister. It's a pretty little place and she keeps it like a picture. Rowan Cottage, it's called, on account of the tree outside.'

'You've been so helpful to us,' said Felicity. 'Thank you very much.'

'Well, I hope you find what you're looking for.'

'Good day,' we said, and came out. The bell rang as we opened the door and stepped into the street.

'Perhaps we ought to have bought something,' I said. 'She was most obliging.'

'She didn't expect that. She enjoyed talking to us. I think we'll dispense with the much-married Mrs Parker and go to her if the lady at Rowan Cottage fails us. I somehow feel that our Aunt Ada wouldn't have had three husbands.'

'Look,' I said. 'The houses back on to the river.'

We had walked through the street which seemed to be the whole of Witchenholme without finding Rowan Cottage. We stood blankly staring about us. Then we saw a house some short distance from the rest and to our delight the rowan tree.

'Well, she would be apart from the others,' said Felicity. 'Remember, she thinks herself "a cut above". I imagine she will be formidable.'

'Simon thought so.'

'Come on, let's beard the lioness in her den.'

'What on earth are we going to say? "Are you Aunt Ada? Simon's Aunt Ada?" How does one open a conversation like that?'

'We managed with the shop lady.'

'I believe this one will be different.'

Boldly I took the brass knocker and brought it down with an authoritative rat-tat. The sound reverberated through the house. There was a pause and then the door was opened.

She stood before us – tall and thin with greying hair severely drawn back from her face into a knot at the back of her neck; her eyes behind thick glasses were shrewd and alert; her crisply white blouse came right up to her chin, held there by bone supports. A gold chain hung about her neck with what I presumed was a watch tucked in at her waist band.

'Please forgive the intrusion,' I said. 'Mrs MacGee at the shop told us we should find you here.'

'Yes?' she said, coolly enquiring.

Felicity took over. 'We are trying to find a lady called Ada, but unfortunately we don't know her surname. Mrs MacGee told us you were Miss Ada Ferrers and we wondered if you were the lady we sought.'

'I'm afraid I don't know you.'

'No, you wouldn't. But did you by any chance have a sister named Alice who had a son called Simon?'

I saw her flinch behind her glasses; her colour changed a little and I knew then that we had found Aunt Ada.

She was suspicious immediately; 'Are you from the Press?' she asked. 'They've found him, have they? Oh . . . is it all going to start again?'

'Miss Ferrers, we are not from the Press. May we come in and explain? We are trying to prove Simon's innocence.'

She hesitated. Then she stepped back uncertainly, holding the door open for us to pass into the house.

The hall was small and very neat, with a hatstand on which hung a tweed coat and a felt hat – hers obviously – and on a small table there was a brass bowl and a vase of flowers.

She threw open a door and we went into a sitting-room which smelt of furniture polish.

'Sit down,' she said, and we did so. She sat facing us.

'Where is he?' she asked.

'We don't know,' I said. 'I must tell you that he was on a ship. I was also on that ship. We were shipwrecked and I survived with him. He saved my life and that of another man. We were taken to Turkey and there I lost sight of him. But during the time we were together, he told me everything. I am convinced of his innocence and I am trying to prove it. I want to see everybody who can tell me anything about him . . . anything that might be useful . . .'

'How can you prove he didn't do this terrible thing?'

'I don't know, but I'm trying to.'

'Well, what do you want of me? You're sure you're not from the newspapers?'

'I assure you we are not. My name is Rosetta Cranleigh. You may have read about my survival. There was something in the papers about it when I came home.'

'Wasn't there a man who was crippled or something?'

'Yes, he was with us, too.'

She frowned, still disbelieving.

'I don't know,' she said. 'It sounds a bit odd to me. And I've had enough of it. I don't want to hear another word. I knew it would go wrong right from the beginning.'

'You mean . . . when he was a boy?'

She nodded. 'He ought to have come to me. I would have taken him in. Not that I wanted a child . . . I've never had anything to do with children . . . but someone would have had to have him and she was my sister. There were only the two of us. How could she have got caught up in that sort of thing?'

'It's that which we think might help us,' I said tentatively. 'If we could go back right to the beginning . . .'

'How's that going to prove he didn't do it?'

'We're hoping it might help. We feel we can't ignore anything . . . I got to know him very well. We were together in most extraordinary circumstances. We escaped in a boat and drifted on to an island . . . an uninhabited one. We had this tremendous adventure together. We got to know each other very well, and I'm convinced he couldn't have killed anyone.'

'He was caught red-handed.'

'I believe that could have been arranged.'

'Who'd arrange a thing like that?'

'It's what we have to find out. I want your help. Please, Miss Ferrers, he's your nephew. You want to help him, don't you?'

'I don't see how *I* can. I hadn't set eyes on him since he was taken away.'

'By Sir Edward Perrivale?'

She nodded.

'Why did Sir Edward take him?'

She was silent. Then she said: 'All right. I'll tell right from the beginning. Alice was beautiful. Everyone said so. It was a curse in a way. If she hadn't been, this wouldn't have happened to her. She was a fool . . . soft as they come. Gentle, loving and all that . . . but she had no sense at all. Our father owned a nice little inn on the other side of Bath. It was a profitable place. Alice and I used to help with the guests. Then one night Edward Perrivale came. He saw Alice . . . and kept coming. I warned her. I said, "He'll be no good to you." She could have had John Hurrell who had a sizeable farm, and he wanted to marry her. But no, it had to be this Edward . . .'

I looked at Felicity. The story was working out as we had expected. The good man had had his lapse and fallen into temptation, and as was the general way, repentance came afterwards.

'I used to say to her time and time again, "He's no good to you. He'll take what he wants, and then it will be goodbye. That's how his sort go on. He's not for you. His class don't marry innkeepers' daughters." You could see what he was. A real gentleman and we didn't get many of his sort at the inn. He'd just come in by chance one night, horse had gone lame or something. Otherwise he would never have come to a place like ours. But then he kept coming . . . because of Alice.

'She would say, "He's different. He's going to marry me." "Not him," I said. "He's got you on a bit of string. That's where he's got you." She wouldn't believe me . . . and it turned out she was right in a way. They were married. I can testify to that. It was in the church . . . a simple affair, though. He wouldn't have it any other way. But married they were. I was there . . . so I know.'

'Married,' I said. 'But . . .'

'Yes, they were married. We'd been brought up strictly. Alice wouldn't have gone with him in any other way. Nor would he with her. He was very religious. He made Alice turn to it. Oh, we had to go to church every Sunday. Father always insisted on that – but it was more than that with this Edward.'

'So they were really married!'

'Really and truly married. He set her up in a nice little house and then he'd go away and come back. He paid regular visits. I said, "Where does he go to, then?" And Alice said, "Oh, he's explained all that. He's got a big house in Cornwall. It's been in the family for years. He said I wouldn't like it . . . and he wouldn't want me to be there. I'm better off here." Alice was a girl who didn't ask questions. She liked everything to be peaceful. That's all she asked. Any trouble and she didn't want to know. So that's how it was. He would come to see her and then they'd be like any other married couple. Then he'd go away for a spell. Then the boy came.'

'I see,' I said. 'And when he was five years old . . . Alice died.'

She nodded. 'There was the question of where Simon would go. I guessed I'd have to have him, she being my sister. I didn't know what I'd do with the boy. Father had died a year or so before. He'd never liked that marriage . . . though he'd been to the church and seen that it was all properly done and this Edward never stinted her with anything. She was better off than any of us and there was no doubt he thought the world of her. When Father died, I was left comfortably off. Everything was for me. Father had said that Alice was well taken care of. I got this cottage. Alice came here once, bringing the boy.'

'Yes,' I said. 'He mentioned the place to me. That is how I found you.'

'Well, it came out that the one who was murdered was Sir Edward's son. It was the first time I knew he was *Sir*

Edward. At first I thought that he had deceived our Alice and that when he'd gone to the church with her he was married already. But then it came out when there was a lot about the family in the papers that he'd married a Miss Jessica Arkwright and when . . . and that was *after* he'd married our Alice. The one who was murdered, his eldest son, was a year or more younger than Simon. It was all a bit fishy, I thought . . . but it was clear as daylight. Alice was his wife and this other woman had no right to the title. Our Alice was the real Lady Perrivale. So the two boys he'd had after were the illegitimate ones . . . not Simon. It's all a bit of a mystery . . . I was well out of it then, and I did not want to hear another word about it. You don't believe me, do you?'

'Oh yes, I do.'

'Well, I can prove it. I've got the marriage lines. I said to Alice, "That's something you want to keep by you always." She was careless about that sort of thing. But I thought there was something odd even at the start. Husbands don't usually go off like that and leave their wives . . . not unless they're trying to get away from them. So I made her be sure to keep her marriage lines. Not that he wanted to get away from her. He was really sad when she died. Then I made sure that I kept the lines. I'll show them to you.'

'Will you?' I said.

'Of course I will. She was married and no one's going to say she wasn't. I've got them upstairs. I'll go now and get them.'

When we were left alone, Felicity said to me: 'We didn't expect this.'

'No.'

'It seems incredible. That strong pillar of the church to commit bigamy.'

'If this is a genuine certificate of marriage . . .'

'It must be. And she was there at the ceremony. She's not the sort to say so if she wasn't.'

'Might she have some idea about protecting her sister's honour?'

Miss Ferrers came back into the room, proudly waving the document.

We looked at it. There could be little doubt of its authenticity.

'I think,' I said, 'it may be that someone knew about this, and that Simon was the true heir to his father's estates and title. It makes a motive.'

'But they didn't kill him.'

'No . . . but he was implicated.'

'You mean someone arranged to be rid of both the elder brother and Simon at the same time.'

'It could be. It would be useful if we could have this proof of the marriage.'

I could see at once that Miss Ferrers in no circumstances would allow the certificate to pass out of her hands. 'You can see it in the church records,' she said. 'It's St Botolph's in Headingly, near Bath. You really do believe in his innocence, don't you?'

'Yes,' I said firmly.

'It would have broken Alice's heart,' she said. 'I was glad she died before she could know that. But then if she'd been alive he would never have gone to that place. Alice would never have let him go. She loved him so much.'

'You have helped us a great deal,' I said. 'I can't tell you how grateful I am.'

'If you can clear his name . . .'

'I'm going to try. I'm going to do everything in my power . . .'

She insisted on making us a cup of tea. She talked to us while we drank it, going over everything she had already told us; but we did get an impression of the affection she had had for Alice, which was none the less genuine because it was faintly contemptuous. Alice had been soft . . . too trusting . . . loving unwisely . . . believing all that was told her. But Alice had been her dear sister, closer to her than anyone had been before or after.

I was glad we had convinced her of our sincerity.

And so we left Rowan Cottage with the knowledge that Sir Edward Perrivale had married Alice Ferrers and the date on the certificate showed clearly that the marriage had taken place before the ceremony he had undergone with the present Dowager Lady Perrivale.

Encounter in a Copse

That night Felicity and I talked continuously of our discovery. It was beyond our wildest hopes.

'I still can't believe it!' I said. 'How could Sir Edward, with his strong moral stance, enter into a bigamous marriage, have two sons whom he accepted as his own, while his legitimate son, though brought up in the house, was treated as an outsider?'

'We have to remember that he wanted the boy to be given every chance.'

'Poor Simon!'

'Well, he had your Nanny Crockett.'

'It would have been sad for him if he hadn't.'

'Oh, there are always compensations. But why did Sir Edward not only break the law but go against his strong religious principles?'

'I think I can guess. You see, there is a great tradition in the Perrivale family. The old house is at the root of it. The place was falling down and Sir Edward was in financial difficulties. He had never brought Alice to Perrivale. Much as he loved her, he did not think she would be a suitable chatelaine. You see how strong the family tradition was. I daresay he had been brought up to believe that the great family of Perrivale was all-important. It had been kept going all through the centuries by its members doing their duty. It was his, therefore, to save Perrivale. Along comes the ironmaster or coal owner, whatever he was, from Yorkshire. He will supply the money required to save the house. Sir Edward's financial problems can be solved . . . but at a cost, of course. The price is marriage to the rich man's daughter.'

'But Sir Edward couldn't accept those terms. He had already married little Alice.'

'But who knew? Only those people in the country. Alice was quiet and docile. She would accept everything he told her. She would not make trouble, even if she knew what was happening . . . but she didn't. He thought he could pull it off, and he did. I dare say it troubled him a great deal. There was no other way of saving Perrivale. He had always been brought up to believe that his first duty was to tradition . . . to the family name. You can see how he was torn. He had to save his house; the family must go on living in the style to which it was accustomed. Alice could not rise to what would be demanded of her. He had loved Alice . . . he had been led into the temptation of marrying her. But she was not suitable to be a Perrivale wife. I can see how it happened.'

'You certainly make it sound plausible.'

'I think Sir Edward could not die with this secret on his conscience. I think he may have confessed when he was near the end. And to whom would he confess but to the one whom it concerned most . . . the woman who thought she was his wife? Imagine it: "I cannot go like this. I must tell the truth now. My heir is Simon, the boy I brought into this house. I married his mother and that means I am not truly married to you." That was how it must have happened. Maria said that she heard them quarrelling violently and that Lady Perrivale went very strange at the time of his death. It must have been because of this.'

'Are you suggesting that she was involved in the murder? You can't think she killed her own son just to get Simon accused.'

'Of course not. What she did was tell her son. She would, wouldn't she? Or perhaps Sir Edward told them. Yes, of course, it would concern them most . . . next to Lady Perrivale, of course.'

'But it was Cosmo who was murdered.'

'I always had a notion that Tristan was the murderer. I used to think he killed Cosmo because he wanted the title and estates . . . and Mirabel. Just imagine what he would feel to be in second place and miss all the prizes.'

'Lucas is in a similar position.'

'Well, before his accident he didn't want to stay at home.'

'And he had his army career for a while.'

'Yes, and he gave that up and travelled a great deal and was rather restless. I begin to see it more clearly. I always thought Tristan was involved somehow. He had everything to gain. And there was Mirabel. She married him very soon after Cosmo was killed.'

'And what of the child she seems to have got rid of?'

'I don't understand that. It's too complicated, but at least if Tristan was aware that Simon was really his father's heir . . . he would want to get him out of the way. So he kills Cosmo and arranges that Simon is blamed for it. So both encumbrances are removed. Sir Edward dies . . . there is nothing to say that Tristan is not the rightful heir.'

'It's taking shape,' said Felicity. 'But how are you going to prove all this?'

'I don't know . . . yet. But we've taken a great step forward . . . thanks to you, Felicity. I think I shall know what to do when the time is right.'

'And in the meantime . . . ?'

'I shall tell Lucas, when I see him, what we have discovered. He is very astute. He will suggest what action we take next. Something has occurred to me. Lady Perrivale – the Dowager Lady Perrivale – is searching for something in Sir Edward's room. She lights candles at night – or she did before Maria hid them for fear she burned the house down – and went prowling round looking. What was she looking for, do you think?'

'Simple logic would point to a will.'

'Exactly. The last will of Sir Edward Perrivale in which he states that Simon is his legitimate son and heir. He cannot go to his grave with that secret on his conscience.'

'So to purge his own soul he plunges those who for years have believed themselves to be his only family into turmoil.'

I nodded. 'He knows that if someone gets his – or her – hands on the will while he is too ill to know what is happening, it will be destroyed. So he hides it, meaning to produce it to the solicitor or someone whom he can trust when he gets the opportunity to do so. Now Lady Perrivale knows that this will exists. She must find it and destroy it for the sake of her sons, if for nothing else. She is not very clear in her mind . . . but she hangs on to the fact that it exists. That is why she wanders about at night looking for it.'

'H'm. Sounds likely.'

'I often visit Lady Perrivale. There might be an opportunity . . .'

'You'd better be careful.'

'That's what Lucas says.'

'If this is true and Tristan killed once, he might not hesitate to do so again, and people who know too much might be in danger.'

'I'll be watchful.'

'I'm really serious, Rosetta. I'm worried about you.'

'Don't be. I'll be careful. They don't suspect anything. I'm just the governess.'

'But no ordinary governess.'

'Oh yes, I am really. It just happens that I have found a way of getting on with Kate better than most could.'

'Well, don't be rash.'

'I promise.'

'Now we'd better get some sleep, I suppose.'

'Felicity, I can't tell you how grateful I am for your help.'

'Oh really . . . it was fun. I like a mystery as well as anyone.'

'One of the nicest things that ever happened to me was when you came to teach me.'

'Well, on that happy note, we'll say good night.'

* * *

When I arrived in Cornwall, Kate greeted me sullenly.

'You've been away a long time,' she said.

'It wasn't really so long. I met a friend who used to be my governess.'

I told her about Felicity's coming to the house and how I had been imagining she would be an ogre, how they had all liked her in the kitchen and she used to join us for meals.

Her mood changed. She was really very pleased to see me back.

'Did Mr Dolland do *The Bells*?'

'Yes.'

'I wish you'd take me up there.'

'I might . . . one day.'

'One day, one day,' she mocked. 'I don't want one day. I want now. You ought to have taken me with you.'

I was glad when I was able to retire to my room. I wanted to brood on all that had happened. I was sure we were right in our theories. I could picture it all so clearly. Sir Edward, on the point of death, had made his startling revelations. If Tristan could kill Cosmo and have Simon hanged for murder, no one need ever know of the previous marriage. It would be between Tristan and his mother. He would certainly trust her to keep quiet. She would not want it to be known that, though she had lived with Sir Edward and borne him two sons, she had not been his wife.

How could the truth be brought out? How could Simon be exonerated? There was the marriage certificate in the hands of Miss Ada Ferrers. There would be the records in

St Botolph's Church. But even though Simon was proved to be the true heir to the Perrivale estate, that would not clear him of the charge. Even if the will – if there was one – were found, that would not be enough.

I felt we had come to an impasse. We had uncovered dark secrets, reasons for murder . . . but we had not found the identity of the murderer.

Still, if I could find that document . . .

Sir Edward could move only with difficulty, I imagined. It would be in his room. Where would he be likely to hide a document?

I was becoming more and more certain that it was a will for which Lady Perrivale was searching, and I was going to try to find it. That would be my next venture. There could be an opportunity of slipping into that room . . . perhaps if Lady Perrivale were asleep . . . and Maria did not happen to be there. If I could produce the will I could at least prove a motive.

The next afternoon I went up to see Lady Perrivale. She was asleep but Maria was there.

'It's nice to see you back,' she said. 'Her ladyship's been sleeping most of the day. That's how it is nowadays. The Major came in to see her pretty often while you were away. She cheers up for his visits.' She gave me a wink. 'Well, she always had a soft spot for him.'

'Even though he married her best friend.'

'Ah yes. She might have had him herself but old Joe Arkwright was a hard man when it came to the brass. She was heartbroken when her father put an end to it. Then of course she married Sir Edward. It was what Joe Arkwright wanted. Stands to reason . . . *Sir* Edward and the title and Jessie brought the brass. What people will do for brass!'

I went away with those words ringing in my ears.

It was indeed revealing . . . what people would do for money!

It was two days later when my opportunity came. I went

up to see Lady Perrivale. Maria was not there and Lady Perrivale was in her chair snoring slightly.

My heart was beating fast as I slipped out of the room and into that which I knew to have been Sir Edward's.

I saw the big four-poster bed with a table beside it on which lay a very large Bible with leather covers and brass clasps.

I looked round the room. Where would he be likely to put something he wanted to hide? Why should it be necessary to hide it? Because he did not trust the woman who for years had thought she was his wife.

There was a cupboard near the window. I went to and opened it. There were some clothes in it and a tin box. I picked up the box. It was locked.

I wondered what was in it, but it was impossible for me to open it; and in any case whoever was searching for a will would immediately look in such a place. I could be sure someone had opened that box and inspected the contents since Sir Edward's death.

For a moment I paused by the window and glanced across to my own room, and just at that moment the Major came into the courtyard. He looked up and immediately I dodged back. I was not sure whether he had seen me. I did not think he had. But it was a warning. I must get out of this room. He would clearly be coming to pay one of his frequent visits to Lady Perrivale.

When I emerged, Maria was still not there and Lady Perrivale remained asleep. I hurried downstairs and was in the hall when Major Durrell came in.

'Good afternoon, Miss Cranleigh,' he said. 'And what a pleasant afternoon it is.'

I agreed.

'I trust you had a good trip to London.'

'Oh yes, thank you. It seemed a long time since I had seen my family.'

'And I hear Mr Lorimer is progressing favourably.'

'Yes, that's so.'

'Then all's well with the world.'

He smiled benignly on me as he started up the stairs.

* * *

It was the next day. Kate and I had been at lessons all morning, which had passed pleasantly enough. I was still brooding on my discoveries and felt frustrated because I did not know which way to go next. I had attached great importance to discovering the will but if I did, what would that tell us which we did not know already?

I wanted to be alone to think. As soon as possible I must see Lucas. He would be home very soon. I expected he would be rather exhausted immediately after his return, but I was very eager to tell him what Felicity and I had found out.

However, the need to get away was imperative. I wanted to be by myself to think. I took an opportunity of slipping out of the house, unseen by Kate, who would have wanted to come with me, and I walked briskly away from the house. I was near the Dower House when I saw the Major.

'Oh hello, Miss Cranleigh,' he called. 'How nice to see you. You're looking well.'

'Thank you.'

'The trip to London was obviously a great success.'

'Yes, I think it was.'

'How's Kate getting on now?'

'Very well.'

'I get rather worried about that girl. I've been wanting a little chat with you about her for a long time.'

'What is worrying you?'

'Look, why don't you come in? It's not easy to talk out here.'

He led me up the path to the front door, which was ajar. I said the garden was looking beautiful.

'I take a great pride in it. I have to have something to occupy me now I'm free of the Army.'

'It must be difficult to adjust to a civilian's life. But it is some time since you retired now, isn't it?'

'Yes, but one never really gets used to it.'

'I can well imagine that.'

The drawing-room was quite large with oak beams, latticed windows and a big fireplace.

'It's a lovely house,' I said.

'Yes, the Tudors may not have been so elegant as their successors, but they did seem to create a certain atmosphere. Do sit down.'

I sat on the settle near the window.

'Are you comfortable there?' he asked solicitously.

I told him that I was very comfortable.

'What worried you about Kate?' I asked.

'I'm going to give you a glass of wine first. It's always more cosy to talk over a drink.'

'Thank you . . . but I'd rather not . . .'

'Oh come, I insist. I want you to try this. It's very good. I only serve it on special occasions.'

'Oh . . . is this one?'

'Yes, because for so long I've wanted to talk to you and to thank you for what you are doing for Kate.'

'You're very fond of her, I know, as she is of you.'

He nodded. 'Now, just a small glass, eh?'

'Well, thanks . . . just a small one.'

He brought it to me and then went and poured one out for himself.

'To you, Miss Cranleigh. With my heartfelt thanks.'

'Oh really, you make too much of it. It's only a matter of getting to know her . . . understanding her.'

'There have been so many . . . and you took the trouble. That's what I'm grateful for. Mirabel, my daughter, Lady Perrivale . . . said to me the other day, "The change in Kate since Miss Cranleigh came is really remarkable."'

'Then why are you worried?'

'That's what I want to talk to you about. What do you think of the wine?'

I took another sip. 'It's very pleasant.'

'Well, drink up. And have another. I told you it is very special.'

Just at that moment there was a sound of footsteps coming round the house. The Major looked startled.

'It's me, Gramps,' said a well-known voice. 'Rosetta's here, I know. I saw her come in.'

I put my glass down on a small table near the settle as Kate entered.

'What are you doing here?' she cried. 'I watched you leave. I followed you. You didn't see me, did you? I kept behind. I stalked you. Then I saw you speak to Gramps and come in here. You're drinking wine.'

'Yes,' said the Major, and although he smiled at his granddaughter, I fancied I saw a flicker of annoyance cross his face. It was understandable. He had wanted to talk to me confidentially and about her. That would be impossible in her presence.

'Well, come and sit by Miss Cranleigh.'

He took her by the arm and brought her towards the settle. I was not sure what happened because I was looking at Kate who was so pleased with herself at having caught up with me. But as she sat down the glass toppled over and the wine went trickling all over the carpet.

'Damnation,' muttered the Major.

'Oh,' cried Kate. 'You swore!'

'Forgivable,' he said. 'That was my very special wine. I wanted Miss Cranleigh's opinion.'

'It wouldn't have been of much significance,' I told him. 'I'm no connoisseur.'

'And you shouldn't swear, Gramps. Your guardian angel will be writing it all down in a little book and you'll have to answer for it one day.'

'If that is all I have to answer for, I am not particularly worried, and in any case I am sure you would intercede for me.'

Kate laughed and I looked down at the shattered glass. I stooped, but he said quickly: 'Don't touch it. Broken glass can be dangerous. It's those horrible little splinters. Leave it. I'll get it cleared away. I'll give you a fresh glass.'

We moved away from the mess on the floor to the windowseat. Kate begged to have a glass of wine.

'Not suitable for little girls,' said the Major.

'Oh, Gramps, don't be so mean.'

'All right. Just a taste, eh? You see how she wheedles me, Miss Cranleigh.'

'You can't resist me, can you, Gramps?'

'We are putty in the hands of our enchantress,' he said.

I could see Kate was enjoying this.

About half an hour later we left and went back to Perrivale Court. I was yawning.

'What's the matter with you?' said Kate. 'You look half asleep.'

'It's due to the hard work I have to put in to keep you in order.'

'No, it's not. It's the wine. You always say it makes you sleepy in the day.'

'You're right. It does and it is.'

'Then why do you drink it?'

'Your grandfather was rather insistent.'

'I know,' she said, laughing.

* * *

It was late morning. We had finished lessons and Kate and I were going into the gardens. As we came down into the hall the Major was just arriving.

'Good morning, my dears,' he said. 'How nice to see you. Just on the point of going out, I see.'

'Have you come to see old Lady Perrivale, Gramps?' asked Kate.

'That's so, and it is a great pleasure to see you as well. I did enjoy your visit. But it was too short. You must come again.'

'We will,' Kate assured him.

'And Miss Cranleigh will, too?' he said, looking at me.

'Thanks. Of course,' I said.

Just at that moment one of the grooms from Trecorn came to the door.

'Oh, Miss Cranleigh,' he said. 'I've got a message for you. Mr Lucas is back. He wants to know if you could meet him this afternoon. Two-thirty at The Sailor King.'

'Yes, yes. I'll be there. Is he all right . . . ?'

'Getting on a treat, Miss.'

'Oh, I'm glad.'

He left us and Kate said: 'You're going off again this afternoon. You're always going to The Sailor King.'

'Only in my own time, Kate.'

'What a little slave-driver she is,' said the Major. 'You mustn't make a prisoner of Miss Cranleigh, Kate. You wouldn't like anyone to do that to you, would you? And if you do, she might fly away and leave us. Well, I shall see you soon, I hope. *Au revoir.*'

He went up the stairs.

'But you are always going to that inn,' said Kate.

'I have to meet my friends now and then.'

'Why can't I come?'

'Because you're not invited.'

'That's no reason.'

'It's the very best reason possible.' She was a little sulky during our walk. But I could only think of meeting Lucas.

* * *

I left just before two o'clock. It did not take more than fifteen or twenty minutes to reach the inn. I could have walked, but I did like to exercise Goldie and I enjoyed the ride. Moreover, it meant that I could stay a little later if I rode and Lucas could ride back with me.

It was a lovely afternoon. There was only the slightest breeze to ruffle the trees. There was no one about. There rarely was at this hour. I took the coast road and turned inland. I had to go through a small copse. It could hardly be called a wood, but the trees grew closely together and I always enjoyed wending my way along the narrow path among them.

I was in good time. I should be there ten minutes before two-thirty.

I don't know whether it was a premonition of danger, but as soon as I entered the copse I was aware of a certain uneasiness. I had the feeling that there was something strange about it on this day, that I was being watched. It was uncanny. Usually I went through without giving the solitude a thought.

I was aware of a sudden cracking of a branch . . . a movement in the undergrowth. Some small animal, I supposed – the sort of thing I must have heard a hundred times before and scarcely noticed. I was in a strange mood today.

I knew what it was. Felicity had said: What you are doing is dangerous. Lucas had said it, too. What if Tristan knew what I was doing? What if he had been watching me . . . as I had been watching him?

Guilty people must be ever on the alert.

'Come on, Goldie,' I said. 'Let's get on.'

Then I realized that someone was in the wood . . . very close to me. I heard the sound of horse's hoofs behind me and my impulse was to urge Goldie into a gallop, but that would have been impossible in the copse where she had to pick her steps carefully.

'Hello,' said a voice. 'If it isn't Miss Cranleigh.'

It was the Major. He was right behind me.

'What a bit of luck. Just the one I wanted to see.'

'Oh, hello, Major,' I said with relief. 'I was wondering who was in the copse today. One doesn't usually meet anyone at this time.'

'All taking their afternoon nap . . . or siesta perhaps they call it.'

'I expect so.'

'You're just the one I wanted to see. I did want to have a word with you.'

'About Kate.'

'Yes. She interrupted us when I thought I was going to have the opportunity I wanted.'

'Something is worrying you, isn't it?'

'Yes.'

'What? I think she's getting on very well.'

'It's difficult to shout. Could we dismount and sit down on that tree-trunk over there?'

'I haven't much time . . .'

'I know. I heard you make your appointment this morning. But this won't take more than five minutes.

I dismounted and he did the same.

He came close to me, and taking my arm led me to the fallen tree-trunk.

'What is worrying you?' I said.

His face was close to mine. 'You,' he said.

'What do you mean?'

'Why did you go and see Mrs Campden?'

'Mrs Campden?'

'Of Malton House, Bayswater.'

I felt suddenly cold with fear. I did not answer.

'You don't deny you went. You have very beautiful hair, Miss Cranleigh. Unusual colour. It's very noticeable. I knew who it was right away. And what are you doing at Perrivale? You're not a governess. You are an inquisitive young woman.'

He turned my face to a tree. He held me there with one hand while with the other he produced a tie from his pocket.

For a moment I wondered why and then the awful truth dawned on me.

I had looked for my murderer and here he was. I had found him, but in doing so I was going to become another of his victims.

I thought of the sailor . . . of Cosmo . . . of Simon . . . and now I was the one.

'You've none but yourself to blame,' he said. 'I don't want to do this. I hate doing it to you. Kate will grieve . . . Why couldn't you let sleeping dogs lie?'

A wild hope came to me. If he were going to kill me why didn't he do it? Why did he talk like this? It was almost as though he were putting it off. He was speaking the truth when he said he didn't want to do it. He was doing it because he thought he must . . . it was necessary because he was already caught up in a maze of murder.

I said: 'You are planning to do to me what you did to the sailor . . . you'll kill me and throw me over the cliff. Kate told me . . . about the sailor . . . I understand now.'

'You understand . . . you understand too much. I know what's happened. It was Harry Tench, wasn't it? He's talked. Oh, Miss Cranleigh, why did you have to meddle?'

I was suddenly aware that Goldie was walking away. I felt desperately frightened. He seemed to realize that he was wasting time. He might be thinking of Lucas who could come to the inn and wait in vain.

With a deft movement he released his hand. He needed them both to strangle me with the tie. I attempted to dodge away . . . but he was watchful of me.

Any minute now . . .

It must not be. I had found the murderer. I had succeeded. I would not die and let the secret die with me. I must make a super-human effort to break away . . . to get to Lucas.

I was praying silently to Lucas . . . to Simon . . . to God.

I had to tell them. I had to save Simon . . . and Lucas was waiting for me.

He had the tie round my throat. Somehow I managed to get my two thumbs under it which relieved the pressure. I lifted my leg and kicked backwards.

Luck was with me. He was not expecting that. He let out a cry of pain; the tie fell from his hands. I had a second or two in which to act; and I did. I broke away. I was agile and I was fighting for my life.

I had to get out of the copse before he caught me. Instinctively I knew he would not dare attack me in the open country. Someone could easily come into view.

Through the trees I dashed. He was after me, fully aware of the necessity to catch me before I emerged into the open.

I could hear him close on my heels. The branches caught at me, but somehow I managed to keep a step or two ahead of him, just out of his reach. If only Goldie were here . . . if only I could mount her.

The trees were thinning. There was not far to go. I was going to make it.

I could hear him close behind me, breathing heavily. He was not a young man, I thought exultantly. I had the advantage of youth.

I was thinking: Lucas! How right you were. I should have been more careful. I had had a warning with the wine. Of course, he was going to drug me . . . and then throw me over the cliff . . . just as he must have done in the case of the sailor, Mirabel's husband. I had had a warning and I had been too blind to see. But . . . I had found my murderer. Success had been thrust upon me and it had nearly cost me my life.

I was out in the open. I dare not stop. I went on running as fast as I could. Cautiously I glanced over my shoulder.

He was no longer there. I had escaped. And suddenly I saw Lucas galloping towards me.

'Lucas!' I panted. 'Lucas!'

He leaped from his horse. He took me in his arms and held me tightly.

'Rosetta . . . my love . . . what happened?'

'I've found him, Lucas . . . I've found him. He was going to kill me.'

'Rosetta . . . what . . . ?'

'He followed me into the copse. He was going to strangle me . . . and then he would have thrown me over the cliff . . . as he did the sailor.'

'You'd better tell me all about it. I thought you'd had an accident when Goldie arrived at the inn without you.'

'Goldie . . . yes, she wandered off.'

'I was looking out for you when I saw her trotting along. She came straight to the stables.'

'Oh . . . good old Goldie . . .'

'I'd better take you home with me.'

'No . . . no, I must tell you. There isn't much time . . . or there may not be . . .'

'You're distraught . . . I want to know everything that happened. Who . . . ?'

'Let's go into the inn. Tell them I took a toss. I can't let them know what really happened yet.'

'Who was it, Rosetta?'

'It was Major Durrell.'

'What?'

I put my hand to my throat. 'He had a tie . . . he was going to strangle me. It was round my throat. I thought I couldn't stop him. But I . . . managed . . . somehow . . . and I got away. He couldn't catch me. I ran faster than he did.'

He stared at my throat.

'There are bruises,' he said. 'Rosetta . . . what in God's name is this all about?'

'I want to talk to you, Lucas. I've got the answer . . . I think. It hasn't been in vain.'

I got up behind him and we rode back to the inn. My thoughts were in such a jumble that I did not know where to begin. I was deeply shocked, trembling violently, but I knew that something had to be done . . . quickly. And I had to get Lucas's help.

'Don't talk till we get to the inn,' he said. 'A good strong brandy would be the thing for you. You are shaking, Rosetta.'

'I don't get nearly murdered every day,' I said with an attempt at humour.

The innkeeper's wife came running out, followed by her husband.

'My patience me!' she cried. 'When I saw that horse coming without you . . . well, I was in a shocking state really!'

'Thank you,' I said. 'I wasn't badly hurt.'

'Let's get Miss Cranleigh inside,' said Lucas. 'And I think some brandy, please. That's the best for her.'

'Right away, sir,' said the host.

'I'm glad to see you in one piece, Miss,' said his wife. 'I shouldn't have thought that Goldie would have played tricks like that . . . and then to come walking back, meek as you like.'

'I'm glad she came here,' said Lucas.

'A real bit of luck.'

I was in the inn parlour, the brandy was brought, and at last I was alone with Lucas.

'I'll begin at the beginning. I've been careless. I ought to have guessed something . . .'

I told him about the wine.

'You see, he intended to drug me and throw me over the cliff, as he did in the case of the sailor who was without doubt Mirabel's husband and had come back to spoil her chances at Perrivale. But Kate came and foiled his plan and at Perrivale this morning when your groom came over he heard me make arrangements to come here this afternoon. So he waylaid me.'

'That was a daring thing to do.'

'Yes, it would have been so much easier with the wine,

but I think he thought he had to act quickly. He was annoyed, I realize now, when Kate spoiled that plan which would have been so much easier to carry out.'

I told him about our visit to Ada Ferrers and what we had discovered through her.

'But,' I said, 'it was the visit to the nursing home which betrayed me. You see, I mentioned Mrs Parry . . .'

Lucas caught his breath.

'I knew it was foolish, as soon as I said it. But I was caught up . . . and so embarrassed. I had only meant to look at the place. I made such a mess of it. But he must have known her fairly well and that was why he sent Mirabel there . . . and she described me and then he knew that I was on the track and he planned to get rid of me . . . just as he had the sailor.'

'So you think he killed Cosmo?'

'Yes.'

'I thought you'd selected Tristan for that.'

'I don't know whether he was concerned in it, too. Oh . . . by the way, he said something about Harry Tench. He said I'd been talking to him . . . or something like that. He was the one who came under suspicion in the beginning and was quickly dismissed by the police. He's the farm hand who lost his cottage because of Cosmo and hated him for it. He could of course have witnessed the murder.'

'How . . . ?'

'Because it took place in Bindon Boys and that is where Harry Tench sleeps. He made the derelict farm his home . . . since he had no other. Lucas . . . that's what we have to do quickly . . . we have to talk to Harry Tench. We have to do it now.'

'I'm going to take you back to Trecorn. You can't go back to Perrivale after this. That's the first thing.'

'No, Lucas. I couldn't rest. I've got to see Harry Tench, and I want you to come with me.'

'When?'

'Now . . . without a moment's delay. Who knows? We may have delayed too long already.'

'My dear Rosetta. You have just been nearly murdered. You're deeply shocked.'

'I can think about that afterwards. I *know* this is important. I've got to see him. I've got to talk to him without delay.'

'Do you think you'll be all right . . . ?'

'I wouldn't be all right if I didn't go. I should be tortured by what might be happening. Already the Major may have gone to him.'

'Look . . . I'll go alone.'

'No, Lucas. This is my affair. I started it and I want to be in at the end. I hope this is the end.'

He could see that I was determined and at length he agreed that we should go to Bindon Boys together.

* * *

I mounted Goldie. I was feeling shaken but somehow buoyed up by the thought of further revelations.

The farmhouse looked more desolate than ever. We dismounted. The front door was open. It was a long time since the lock had disappeared. The place sent a shiver down my spine. I kept thinking of Cosmo's coming here and facing death. I had very recently been made aware of how that could feel. I had faced it before, but it was not the same when one was being threatened by the elements. To be fighting for one's life against a murderer is a different experience.

A streak of sunshine shone through the dirty window. It accentuated the cobwebs and the accumulation of dirt and dust on the floor.

'Are you there?' called Lucas. His voice echoed through the house and there was no answer.

I pointed to the stairs and Lucas nodded.

We were on the landing and the three doors faced us.

We opened one. The room was empty; but when we tried the next we found him there, lying on a pile of old clothes. He put his hand up to his face as though to shield himself.

'Hello, Harry,' said Lucas. 'Don't be afraid. We've just come to talk.'

He lifted his head and leaned on his elbow. He was dirty, unkempt and very thin. I felt a surge of pity for him.

'What you want?' he muttered.

'Just a word or two,' said Lucas.

He looked bewildered.

Lucas went on: 'It's about the day Mr Cosmo Perrivale was killed.'

Harry was really frightened now. 'I don't know nothing. I weren't here. I didn't do it. I told 'em I didn't.'

'We know you didn't do it, Harry,' I said. 'We know it was the Major.'

He stared at me.

'Yes,' said Lucas. 'So it doesn't matter about keeping quiet any more.'

'What do you know about it, Harry?' I asked gently.

'He robbed me of my 'ome, didn't he? What 'arm was I doing? The place stood empty for three months after . . . my little 'ome . . .'

'It was cruel,' I said soothingly. 'And then you came here.'

'There was nowhere else. It was a roof. And then they was going to do it up . . . I stayed here . . . I wasn't going till I 'ad to.'

'Of course not. And you were here on that day.'

He didn't answer.

I said: 'It's all right now. You can talk. The Major has told me now . . . so it doesn't matter.'

'He were good to me, he were. I wouldn't have been able to get by but for 'im.'

'Payment for your silence?' asked Lucas.

'He said not to tell. He said I'd be all right then. He said he'd kill me if I told . . . in a jokey sort of way . . . like he always had.' He shook his head, smiling. I could see that the Major had charmed him, too.

'Tell us what happened on that day, Harry,' I said.

'You sure . . . ?'

'Yes,' I replied. 'The Major knows I know. So it's all right for you to talk.'

'You sure . . . ?' he said again.

'Oh yes . . . quite sure.'

'I want to be left alone.'

'You will be . . . when you've told us.'

'I didn't do it.'

'I know you didn't and nobody said you did.'

'They asked questions.'

'And they released you. They knew you didn't do it.'

'I didn't tell them what I see.'

'No. But you're going to tell us.'

Harry scratched his head. 'I mind that day . . . never forget it. Dream about it sometimes. It was being 'ere when it happened. Can't get it out of me 'ead.'

'Yes, of course.'

'I was 'ere. I didn't know when they was coming in to measure an' all that. But there was always time when I heard 'em come in to slip down the back staircase to the back door and out.'

'And you heard Mr Cosmo come in.'

'No, it weren't Mr Cosmo who come first. It was the Major. That's why I didn't get right away. I thought it was one of them coming to measure up. I didn't expect to see the Major.'

'What did he do?'

'Well . . . he came in and went over to the door what leads down to the basement. He opened it and went in. I wondered what 'e were doing in the basement. But he didn't go down . . . couldn't have. He was just waiting behind the door. Then Mr Cosmo came in. There wasn't a word spoke.

I saw the basement door open. The Major stood there. He lifted the gun and shot Mr Cosmo.'

'Then what happened?'

'Mr Cosmo fell to the floor and the Major came out and he put the gun right down by Mr Cosmo. I was on the landing, wondering what to do . . . when Mr Simon come in. The Major had gone then . . . and Mr Simon picks up the gun just as Mr Tristan comes in and finds 'im standing there with the gun in his hand. Mr Tristan was very upset . . . so was Mr Simon. Mr Tristan starts shouting and says Mr Simon's killed his brother . . . and Simon says Mr Cosmo was dead when he come in . . . and I thought it was time I got out. So I went out . . . down the back staircase.'

'So you were a witness of the murder,' said Lucas.

'And the Major . . . how did he know that you'd seen it all?' I asked.

''Cos he'd caught a look at me up there on the landing. He didn't give a sign he'd seen me . . . not then . . . only after. I wasn't at Bindon then. I was over at Chivers. Old Chivers said he didn't mind me sleeping in one of his barns. The Major gave me money and said he'd kill me if I told the police I'd seen him. Old Chivers were good to me. I knew I'd have to find some place when they started on Bindon . . . but they never did after all that.'

'Harry,' said Lucas, 'will you tell this to the police?'

He shrank from us.

'I don't want none of that.'

'But you will. You'll have to.'

He shook his head.

'You should,' I said. 'It's your duty.'

His face crumpled.

'It'll do you no harm,' said Lucas. 'Look, Harry, you come along and talk to the police, and I tell you what I'll do. I'll ask my brother if he can find a little place for you on Trecorn estate. Perhaps you could give a hand now and then on some of the farms. I'm sure there'd be work for you to do somewhere and you'd have your own little cottage.'

He stared at Lucas unbelievingly.

'I don't want you to think it has anything to do with this. I'm sorry that you had the bad luck to be turned out of your home. I'll speak to my brother in any case, but please . . . please come along and tell the police this.'

'And if I don't, you won't get this place for me?'

Lucas said: 'I didn't say anything of the sort. I'm going to try and get this place for you whatever you do. I'll ask my brother and I am sure when he hears how helpful you've been he'll want to do all he can. I'll do it in any case. I promise you. But you should talk to the police.'

'We shall have to tell them what you've told us, Harry,' I explained. 'It's our duty to. You see, an innocent man has been blamed for what he didn't do. So we have to. The police will question you. You have to tell them the truth this time. It's a criminal offence not to.'

'I ain't no criminal. I didn't do nothing. It were the Major. He were the one who fired the shot.'

'Yes, I know. And you are going to tell the truth when they ask you.'

'When?' asked Harry.

'I think,' said Lucas, 'now.'

'I can't.'

'Yes, you can,' said Lucas. 'You're going to ride on the back of my horse, and we are going to take you there . . . now.'

How right he was. We must get there before the Major had time to get to Harry. I wondered what he would do now that his attempt to murder me had failed.

'All right,' said Harry.

The Return

The months which followed were some of the most wretched I have ever known. I witnessed much of the unhappiness at Perrivale Court, and I knew that, although I had acted as I had to bring justice to an innocent man, I was to a large extent responsible for this misery.

On the very day when the Major had attempted to take my life he had gone back to the Dower House and taken his own.

He had realized that when I had escaped from him, I had taken from him his only chance of surviving in the manner which was important to him. When I had run out of the wood I had destroyed all that he had spent his life trying to achieve. He had been ready to murder to keep it. When I looked back and had all the pieces of the puzzle in their place, I could see how much more sophisticated had been his plan to drug me and throw me over the cliff, as had been his first intention. It was ironic that the granddaughter who so dearly loved him and whom he loved should have been the one to defeat him. His plan had failed on a flimsy coincidence. She had happened to see me leave the house and followed me. If she had not, my death would have been just another mystery.

The second method was not so clever. But of course he had had to plan hastily. He dared not let me live. He was afraid of what information I might pass on to Lucas. I had betrayed myself so utterly when I had visited the nursing home run by one of his friends. He must have been in a panic. He had to dispose of me before I reached The Sailor

King. He was convinced, I think, that Harry Tench had betrayed him.

I often wondered what he would have done if he had succeeded. Hidden my body in the copse . . . perhaps let my horse wander away? Perhaps throw her over the cliff with me, so that it would appear to be an accident. Fate worked against him when Goldie escaped and went to the inn to which she had been so many times.

A great deal was revealed about him and that was very distressing for the family at Perrivale, for there was no doubt that he had been greatly loved by his daughter as well as by Kate. He had been popular everywhere, which was an indication of how complex human nature can be when one considered that he was a cold-blooded murderer as well as a caring family man. His whole life was based on fantasy. He had never been a major as he had led everyone to believe, but he had served in one of the Army's catering corps as a sergeant-major. He had been cashiered from the Army because of certain nefarious deals regarding stores in which he had been involved. He had narrowly escaped prison. He was an extraordinary man, a man of great charisma who should have been successful. He had been a devoted husband and the welfare of his daughter was very important to him, so much so that he was ready to murder for it.

A certain amount of this information came out through the Press, but there was a good deal I learned later. He had left a note at the Dower House before he shot himself. He was anxious that his daughter and her family should not be involved in any way. He only was to blame.

He had known that Cosmo would be at Bindon Boys that day and had waylaid him. Cosmo had had to go because he had discovered that Mirabel had been unfaithful to him with his own brother Tristan and he was threatening to make trouble and destroy everything that had been so carefully planned. Lady Perrivale, who had considered the

Major to be her greatest friend, had confided to him that Sir Edward had confessed to a previous marriage. Thus, when Simon had been accused of Cosmo's murder, it had seemed like a heaven-sent opportunity to remove him from the scene when he would cease to be a threat to Mirabel's future.

It was Mirabel herself who made me understand a great deal of this, for I became very close to her during the months that followed. The death of the Major had affected the Dowager Lady Perrivale so greatly that she had had a stroke and a few days later had died. Maria had then gone back to Yorkshire, so the household had changed considerably. Lady Perrivale had not been the only one deeply affected by the Major's death. Kate was in such a state of depression, brought about by the death of her grandfather, that I was the only one who could rouse her from it. I found myself drawn into the family circle, and when the revelations about her father were made known by the Press, Mirabel seemed to find some comfort in talking to me.

There was no longer any pretence. She was quite humble. It was all her fault, she said. She had made such a mess of her life. Her father had wanted so much for her. He had done everything for her.

She had been barely seventeen when she had married Steve Tallon. That was before her father had been turned out of the Army. Feeling it to be a respectable way of life, he had apprenticed her to a milliner. She had hated the life.

'Cooped up in rooms with three other girls all learning the trade,' she said. 'Long hours at the workbench . . . no freedom. How I hated the sight of hats! I met Steve when I was out making a delivery. Not that we had much opportunity of meeting people. I used to creep out at night to be with him. The girls used to help me. It was a relief from the tedium. I was headstrong and so foolish. I thought I'd be free if I married him. He was only about a year older than I was. My father was bitterly disappointed – and how right he was. Poor Steve. He tried. He had a job in a foundry. We had very little money. I soon found out I'd made a terrible mistake. We had been married just over a year when Steve was killed. There was a terrible accident at the foundry. I must have been very callous, because the first thing I thought was that I was free.

'And then . . . I got a job with a dance troupe. We toured the London music halls. Sometimes there was work . . . sometimes not. I dreamed of meeting someone . . . a rich man who would carry me away to luxury. It became an obsession. There was one . . . I believed him. He promised to marry me, but when I became pregnant with Kate, he went off and I never saw him again. I had made a mess of everything. And when Tom Parry came along he was very keen to marry me and because of the child I took that way out. I seemed then to have a talent for landing in desperate situations. I had gone from bad to worse. I grew to hate him.'

She closed her eyes as though she were trying to shut out memories. 'Rosetta, it was terrible. Those awful rooms. I used to dread those times when he came home from sea. He drank a great deal. After Kate was born I went back to the troupe. I had the idea that if I could keep myself we'd get away. I used to have to leave Kate alone. I didn't get back until late. Then my father came out of the Army . . . disgraced. But it was better when he was there. He had some money which he had saved. I felt a lot happier then. But there was Tom coming home. I was thankful that his leaves were not frequent. Kate was growing up and there came a time when I could endure it no more. We would have to find a better way of life for her if not for ourselves, my father said . . .

'He had the idea that we would go to Cornwall. He remembered Jessica Arkwright who had become Lady

Perrivale. She had been a friend of my mother and according to what I had heard Jessica had at one time been very fond of my father.

'We'd get right away, he said. But we had to plan carefully. We had to make sure that Tom Parry would not find us. I would change my name. I'd be Mrs Blanchard. That did not bother me. I'd had three different names already. Instead of Mabel Parry I'd be Mirabel Blanchard. So . . . that was how we came here.

'Everything was different. Lady Perrivale was very friendly. She made a great fuss of me and both the brothers liked me. My father was eager for me to marry Cosmo. It was like a fantastic dream to him. I would become the lady of the manor. I should have a title when Sir Edward died . . . It was all wonderful. There was, of course, Tom Parry. My father said we must forget all about him. It must be as though he had never existed.'

'And you could agree to that?'

She nodded. 'I was desperate. I would have done anything in order to get away from him . . . Then he came down here looking for me. I did believe that he fell to his death. He always drank too much, so it seemed reasonable, I would never have believed . . . my father . . . could have done that. He was always so kind and gentle. Everybody said so.'

'I know,' I said.

'Even then, I spoiled things. You see, it was always Tristan I loved. He was the only one. There had been Steve Tallon, Tom Parry and Cosmo. It had to be right next time. He felt the same about me. We couldn't help it. We loved each other. Then I became pregnant and I went to that dreadful nursing home. My father arranged it – he knew the woman who ran it. But Cosmo found out about Tristan and me. He had a violent temper, he was arrogant and vindictive. He could not bear to think that we had deceived him. He threatened to ruin us. He would get Tristan cut off without anything. We could marry if we wanted to and get out. I told my father. Then . . . it happened . . .'

I was sorry for her. She had suffered enough. I hoped she would be happy with Tristan.

'I cannot believe my father did all those wicked things,' she said. 'He stole . . . he cheated . . . I understood that in a way. But that he should commit murder . . . All I know is that he was the kindest of fathers to me. He started with nothing. He spent all his life trying to get what he called a place in the sun. He said he didn't want to be out in the cold all his life. That was what he was doing . . . finding a place in the sun . . . for me . . . for Kate . . . and himself. And when he thought he had found it . . . when it was about to be snatched away from him . . . You see, don't you? You see how it happened?'

I said: 'Yes. I see.'

Our friendship grew. We talked a good deal about Kate. I said that Kate had been lonely. She had behaved badly in order to call attention to herself. She was asking to be noticed . . . to be loved.

'Yes,' replied Mirabel. 'I was so involved with my own affairs, I neglected her.'

'She admired you. But, you see, she was alone in that room when she was a child. Frightened at night . . . thinking nobody wanted her.'

'It is difficult to explain to a child.'

'She must have been terrified when Tom Parry came home. She needed comfort . . . assurance.'

'My father gave her that.'

I agreed that that was so.

'And now she has lost him,' I said. 'We must remember that. We must be very gentle with her.'

'Thank you for what you have done,' she said with real feeling.

What had I done? I had uncovered the truth, and my actions were responsible for the present situation.

Kate did not mention her grandfather to me. I wondered how much she understood of what was going on. We continued our lessons. We read a great deal. The mischief had gone out of her. She was subdued – a sad little girl.

The will was read. It was found in the Bible which Sir Edward kept by his bed. I wondered why no one had thought of looking there before. It was as we had thought. He had written a letter telling of his previous marriage and naming Simon as his heir. Tristan was left comfortably off but the title and the house would go to Simon.

Lucas and I met often in the inn parlour of The Sailor King. I wondered how I could have lived through those melancholy months without him.

There was a certain tension between us. These were the waiting months. We knew something had to happen before too long and we were waiting for it.

Dick Duvane was in Australia and on the trail. But now the lawyers had taken over. They wanted to find Simon Perrivale and bring him back to England so that the estate might be settled. They advertised in papers all over Australia; no place, however remote, was left out; no possibility was forgotten.

I began to wonder whether he would ever come home. He might not have reached Australia. Something might have happened to him. Nanny Crockett was sure he would come back. She prayed every night that he would do so . . . soon.

And then . . . it was six months after I had almost lost my life in the copse . . . there was news. Dick Duvane had written home. He had found Simon living on a property just outside Melbourne. Simon was coming home.

There was a letter to me.

Dear Rosetta,

Dick has told me all you have done. I shall never forget it. Lucas too, Dick says. Both of you have done so much for me. I have often thought of you and now I am coming home. Soon I shall be with you.

Simon.

* * *

Tristan and Mirabel went to the station to meet his train. Mirabel had suggested that I might accompany them, but I did not want our first encounter to take place in public. I guessed there would be several people at the station to give him a welcome, for it was well known that he was coming home.

I went to my room and waited. I knew that he would come to me soon, and, like me, he would want our meeting to take place in private.

He stood in the doorway. He had changed. He seemed to have grown taller; he was bronzed with the antipodean sun; his eyes seemed a brighter blue.

He held out his hands.

'Rosetta,' he murmured. He looked searchingly into my face. 'Thank you for what you did.'

'I had to do it, Simon.'

'I thought of you all the time.'

There was silence. It was as though there was a restraint between us. So much had happened to him . . . and to me . . . I supposed we had both changed.

'You . . . you are well?' I asked. It sounded banal. Here he was, standing before me, glowing with health. We had both passed through some horrific adventures and I asked him if he were well!

'Yes,' he said. 'You . . . too?'

There was another pause.

Then he said: 'So much has happened. I must tell you about it.'

'Now that you are home . . . everything will be so different for you.'

'Just at first it doesn't seem quite real.'

'But it is, Simon. You're free now.'

And, I thought, I am free, too. Once I was a prisoner within the walls of the seraglio and when I escaped I built a wall about myself . . . a seraglio of my own making. My jailer this time was not the great Pasha but my own obsession. I did not see what was clear about me because I could only see one thing – a dream which I had built up, forming it to fit my fantasy . . . blind to the truth.

He was saying: 'And it was you who did it, Rosetta.'

'I was helped by Nanny Crockett . . . by Lucas . . . by Felicity. They did a great deal . . . particularly Lucas.'

'But it was you . . . you were the one. I'll never forget.'

'It's wonderful to know it is over . . . it worked. And now you are here . . . free.'

It *was* wonderful, I assured myself. It was my dream come true. I had waited a long time for this meeting . . . dreamed of it . . . lived for it . . . and now it was here, why must it be tinged by sadness? I was over-excited, over-emotional, of course. It was only natural.

Simon said: 'We'll talk . . . later. There's so much to say.'

'Yes,' I said. 'We'll talk about it . . . later. Just now . . . it seems too much. And people will be waiting to see you. *They*'ll want to talk to you.'

He understood.

* * *

It was true there were many people waiting to see him. His vindication had been much publicized. He was the hero of the day. Although it was some time since his innocence had been made known, his return to England revived interest in the case. So many people wanted to talk to him, to congratulate him, to commiserate with him on all his sufferings. I was glad that he was so occupied. He was different, of course. Sir Simon Perrivale now, no longer humble deck hand, castaway, man on the run.

The first night I dined with the family.

'We thought you'd want to be quiet,' said Tristan to Simon. 'Just the family. Later, I dare say you'll be inundated with invitations and it might be difficult to refuse some. We shall have to invite people here . . .'

'It will pass,' said Simon. 'And quickly. I shall be a nine days' wonder.'

The talk at dinner was mainly about Australia. Simon was enthusiastic. I could see that. He had acquired a small property. 'Land goes cheap out there,' he said. 'I got quite excited about it.'

I saw him there, working, making plans for a new life . . . thinking he would never come home. But even then I supposed he would have been on the alert, never sure when his past was going to catch up on him. Now he was free. It was small wonder that he felt a little strange – just as I did. It must be a deeply emotional experience for him to come back to the house to which he had been brought up as a frightened little boy . . . the place where he had experienced the horror of being accused of murder.

Lucas came over the next day. He, too, had changed. He reminded me very much of the man I had first met at the house of Felicity and James. There was, of course, the limp, but even that was scarcely perceptible. He seemed to have regained that nonchalance . . . that rather cynical attitude to life.

Simon said: 'I have to thank you for what you did for me, Lucas.'

'Small payment for a life, and I should have said goodbye to mine if you hadn't hauled me into the boat and looked after me when I was a burden to you. In any case, what I did was under Rosetta's orders.'

'It wasn't like that, Lucas,' I protested. 'You were eager to do everything you could.'

'Thank you, Lucas,' said Simon.

'You're embarrassing me,' replied Lucas. 'So let's forget it. Too much gratitude embarrasses the one who gives it and the one who takes it.'

'Nevertheless it's there, Lucas,' I put in.

He did not stay long.

'Good old Lucas!' said Simon. 'He doesn't really change much.'

'No,' I said, trying to smile brightly.

I kept thinking of Lucas. In fact, I could not stop myself thinking of him. He had truly loved me. He had helped bring back Simon . . . he had given Simon to me. That was true love, I supposed.

* * *

A few days passed. There was much coming and going at the house. Kate was subdued. She did not ask questions, but I could see she was watching Simon and me closely.

Since the death of her grandfather, she had changed a great deal; she had loved him so deeply; she had admired him so much, looked up to him, the Major of the Guards who, she had once told me, had been the bravest man in the Army, the hero of every battle. It must have been a terrible shock to her. I knew that she would have learned a great deal about him, though she never spoke of him. She relied on me more than ever, I believed; and she was looking anxiously into the future.

Simon talked to me more freely now. We seemed to have recovered from that first restraint.

'Tristan is just made for this place,' he said. 'He and Cosmo, they were brought up to believe it would be theirs. I never felt like that. I think poor old Tristan would be broken-hearted if he had to go away from here.'

'Couldn't he stay? There's plenty to do.'

'But he thought the place was his. He had complete control. It's a difficult situation. Do you know, I think I might go back to Australia. I could get a big property out there . . . I could have people working for me. I wonder . . . what you'd think of the place?'

I thought: It's coming. At last he is going to ask me. That thought was immediately followed by another: Australia? I should never see Lucas again.

He saw the look in my eyes. He said: 'It was a dream of mine . . . all that time. I'd make a go of it and somehow I'd get a message to you. I'd ask you to come out and join me. We forget . . . people change. We're apt to think they go on just the same . . . I always thought of you as you were on the island . . . and when I left you outside the Embassy . . . You're different . . .'

I said: 'You're different too, Simon. Life changes people. So much happened to me . . . after. So much happened to you.'

'You couldn't leave England,' he said. 'You couldn't *now*. Perhaps if we had gone together then, it might have been different. What you want is here. You will have to do what is best for yourself. We mustn't either of us blind ourselves to our romantic and adventurous past. Perhaps we both dreamed of a future . . . forgetting that life was going on . . . changing us . . . changing everything around us. We are not the same people who said goodbye to each other outside the Embassy.'

'You wanted to come back to England more than anything then.'

He nodded. 'You see,' he said rather sadly, 'we have to face the truth.'

'You've explained it,' I told him. 'We're different.'

'We've come through dangerous times, Rosetta. We must make sure we are on the right course now. You will always be a very special person to me. I shall never forget you.'

'Nor I you, Simon.'

* * *

I felt as though a great weight had been lifted from me.

I rode over to Trecorn Manor. Lucas heard me and came out of the house.

'I wanted to talk to you, Lucas,' I said. 'Simon and I have discussed things. We understand each other perfectly.'

'Yes, of course,' said Lucas.

'Simon wants to go back to Australia.'

'Oh yes,' he said. 'I thought he might. And you are going with him.'

'No, Lucas, of course I couldn't go. How could I leave you?'

He turned to me and I had never seen him look like that before.

'Are you sure?' he said.

'I am absolutely sure that it is the one thing I shall never do.'

* * *